This book may be kept

old

14   **SEVEN DAYS**   14

A fine will be charged for each day the book is kept overtime.

APR 4 1974		
APR 13 1974		
APR 2 5 1974		
APR 30 1974		
MAY 1 4 1974		
MAY 2 8 1974		
MAY 2 9 1974 A1		
JUN 1 1 1974		
AUG 28 1974		
SEP 6 1974		
SEP 1 6 1974		
OCT 8 '74		
OCT 2 1974		
OCT 2 5 1974		
OCT 3 0 1974		
DEC 1 1 1974		
JAN 7 1975		
GAYLORD 72		PRINTED IN U.S.A.

BIJOU

BIJOU

A NOVEL

BY DAVID MADDEN

☆

☆

☆

☆

☆

CROWN PUBLISHERS, INC.

New York

59533

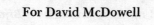
For David McDowell

I wish to thank the Rockefeller Foundation for providing me with a grant that enabled me to begin work on *Bijou*.

CONTENTS

BIJOU

I

The Shadow Stage

THE SCORCHING sun drying, prickling his scalp, wet from swimming in Crazy Creek, Lucius reached out both hands, a sudden fear of snakes chilling him, to part thickly hanging vines that hung over the narrow path he never walked alone without fear, but he thirsted for the jungle shade, reeling off images of Sam Gulliver waking up in a secret cave, his neck across the boots of a half-breed Indian, staring into the eyes of a black panther.

"Hey, there, little boy!"

Arm, foot in the jungle, Lucius paused, glanced back to see *what* "little boy." A girl in a plaid shirt, red ribbon in her hair, leaned out an attic window under a peaked red roof in the white house at the end of the alley, waving, beckoning to Lucius. To see her, he had to look into the sun, shading his eyes. Disoriented at first, he recognized the rear of a house he approached daily by the front.

Looking up, he walked back between the rusty trash barrels and the coal house, through the victory garden's corn patch, their odors stronger now. A girl in a lighthouse, she kept waving him up, one finger at her lips. In a hammock slung between a mimosa and a sycamore, a soldier was sleeping. Lucius climbed the steep yard toward the house, that in the back looked, with basement and attic, four storeys high. He'd often watched the girl in the window flip through movie magazines on the rack in the drugstore on his paper corner. Glancing from the basement door back down the yard at the soldier, seeing a bright trickle of spit at the corner of his mouth as he breathed, Lucius saw his Uncle Luke, lying in Salerno, one arm flung back over his head, one hand resting gently on his cods, blood on his jaw.

Looking straight up, he saw that the girl's small breasts touched the sill as she leaned out and whispered, "Come on up, Lucius."

Thrilled she knew his name, he stepped into the dark cellar that smelled of the jungle. A coal furnace squatted in a dark corner. From the open kitchen door at the top of the steps, light fell, showing preserves in blue Mason jars, cobwebbed on warped shelves.

Crossing the kitchen seemed strange—the same look of waiting emptiness his own had when he came home from school and Momma and Mammy were at the cafe. He felt like a burglar. Knowing the girl waited for him in the attic made his knees go weak, his pecker tingle. She'd be lying naked on a pile of old dresses in a mote-swarming beam of hot sunlight.

In the bathroom washbowl, bursting suds and panties, stained red. He found stairs in the living room where voices on the radio, turned low, rumbled over the carpet: "Holy Cow, Ma, do you really think so?" "Well, it's happened before, child," said Ma Perkins.

Rising to the second floor landing, Lucius saw the yellow soles of two slender feet on a bed, the big toes spread inward toward each other, away from the rest. Looking along the bare legs, seeing a dark mat of hair under the dress, he blushed, as a gray-haired head rose suddenly, a folded washcloth dropping from her forehead. "What are you doing in this house?" Her eyes startled bright.

"She told me to."

"Aren't you our paper boy? Who told you to what?"

"Lucius, hush, you'll wake Momma up," the girl hissed, from the attic.

"He's *give* me the fright of my life!"

"I'm sorry, ma'am."

"Beverly, what in this god's world are you *up* to?"

"I'm about to give him the treasures of my girlhood, Momma! Take your nap!"

"Shut that door," Mrs. Taylor said.

Lucius shut it, and looked up a ladder that had been pulled down out of the ceiling. Beverly, in a boy's plaid shirt, blue jeans, bobby socks, and saddle oxfords, stood at the top, a weak light burning behind her, looking straight down as Lucius climbed straight up. He hoped she wouldn't smell sweat and creek water in his armpits. Reaching the steps just below, he smelled *her*. Panties in the sink. Thinking that this girl who resembled Hedy Lamarr had the rag on, he felt ashamed of desecrating one of his favorite stars.

Under the peaked roof, the piney rafters, the dome of weak light, in the pulsing heat, thousands of glossy movie pictures lay sprawled in a clearing—fan magazines packed in Lucky Strike, Stokely's Peas, and Corn

Flakes boxes all around. "I been pickin' 'em over to see what ones I still yet want. I thought maybe you'd love to take the rest."

Unable to breathe in the pulsing heat, Lucius almost puked up the RC and Moon Pie he'd wolfed down after he'd climbed out of Crazy Creek. "Yes, *ma'am*. I sure would. I sure 'preciate it."

"This is *my* stack," she said, picking up a puny pile of photographs and magazines, hugging them to her breasts, starched cotton shirt, tail out, dark under her arms.

"And that's *all?*"

"Honey, I *am* twenty-two years old, and gettin' married Sunday, so I reckon I ought to *act* grown up, whether I *feel* it or not. How old are *you?*"

"Thirteen last month."

"Look more like tin to me. . . . I see you hauntin' that magazine rack at the drugstore, way *I* did since I was nine. And I was on the verge of tossing this junk out the window and burning it in the alley—Momma can't wait to see it all go up in smoke—when, wait now, here comes that little lightnin' blond, and I said to myself, wouldn't he be tickled to death to haul away my old pictures and magazines?"

Taking slurred stacks of pictures from Beverly's arms into his own, Lucius saw Spencer Tracy in priest's garb put his arm around Mickey Rooney in *Boys Town*, Humphrey Bogart emerge from a tank squinting at the Sahara sun, Errol Flynn kneel to be knighted by Queen Elizabeth in *The Sea Hawk*.

"I would have become a movie star, but I'm getting married to a public accountant instead."

"How come you to *have* all this stuff?"

"See that GI Joe laying in that hammock, don't you?"

Standing at her side, Lucius looked straight down at the soldier as a covey of birds flew out of the sycamore, and they watched him lick his lips in half-sleep, stroke his cods. "Used to usher at the Tivoli when we was going together in high schoo'. Give me any picture I craved—calls 'em *stills*—and lots of 'em I wrote off for. But I bought these magazines myself with my lunch money." Beads of sweat pearled her temples at the roots of her black hair. "Ever' *Screen Romances* and *Silver Screen* and *Photoplay* from 1933 to 1946."

"I've done got more'n forty myself."

"Stopped it this summer when I started Lonas Business Schoo'."

"I'm *never* gonna give *these* away."

"I just didn't have the heart to burn 'em, Lucius."

"I know how you feel, Beverly."

His heart pumping pure joy, his arms loaded with stills, his satchel sawing into his shoulder, so full of stills the strained, weak seams finally tore a little, Lucius huffed and puffed up the hill past the tile factory, knowing Dusty's Buick, hauling bundles of Cherokee *Messengers,* had gone on to the curb at the next stop by now, putting Lucius one notch higher on his boss's shit list. Waiting for a freight train to pass, he looked at Conrad Veidt, on top of the stack, stare down at Joan Crawford as she leaned back against Melvyn Douglas, their faces starkly shadowed, in *A Woman's Face.*

"Looks like you got a load," said a sweat-drenched mailman.

Gravel in his shoes, Lucius limped. People in a passing streetcar stared.

Unable to run, galloping down Prater Hill into the hollow that was coal black when he walked home after the last show at the Hiawassee Theatre, Lucius stumbled and skidded on his belly. The satchel strap broke and all the stills spewed out, a pool of glossy light on the hot tarred rocks.

Carrying the satchel in his arms, loose stills on top, Lucius crept up the hill out of the hollow, the pain in his side making him feel each step.

"Hey, Bucky!" Nobody answered, but Bucky had left the back door open again. Out roaming Cherokee with that lummox Emmett. Still holding his treasure, Lucius hooked his little finger in the screen handle and jerked, shoved it wide open with his foot, staggered inside, dumped the stills on his and Bucky's bed in Uncle Luke's room: Greer Garson and Walter Pidgeon hugged their little boy and girl in the bomb shelter in *Mrs. Miniver.* Claudette Colbert, afraid, held onto Henry Fonda's arm in *Drums Along the Mohawk,* and Lucius saw him running from Indians through the woods, miles and miles to the fort, and felt a pang of fear, a chase he remembered often since he first saw it at the Tivoli, and when someone chased him, he felt as he had watching Henry Fonda. Pinocchio, long-nosed, jackass-eared, stone-weighted, sinks to the bottom of the sea, and Lucius saw Monstro the Whale and remembered Fartso the Whale that Earl said lived with his seven gremlin helpers in Crazy Creek and wouldn't swallow you when you passed over the bridge if you threw him flowers and a nickel, or, coming back in the dark, popcorn blossoms.

Taking a leak, Lucius stared at a still showing Alan Ladd in a leather jacket hugging Loretta Young in a trench coat, a posed shot for *China* that Lucius saw at the Tivoli and four times more at the Hiawassee and tracked down again at the Imperial. He decided to see Alan Ladd in *The Blue Dahlia* again tomorrow, held over at the Bijou.

He put the *China* still in the bed of Bucky's wobbly red wagon and went out the front way through the high hedges past Uncle Luke's green

Dodge parked by the fireplug. Pulling the wagon so fast and hard it bucked and leaped over the rough macadam, Lucius ran up and rode down all the hills to Beverly's house.

Lucius loaded the rest of the magazines and stills into Bucky's wagon and very carefully, slowly pulled it, overflowing, creaking, away, waving good-bye to Beverly Taylor, fresh now out of a bath, wearing a dotted Swiss white and blue dress, sitting in a swing beside her lame duck, ex-usher fiancé, who seemed mystified by Lucius.

The wagon backward in front of him, the tongue pressed down to hold the slithering stills, Lucius backed down hills, looking at the exposed pictures: Alan Ladd in *China* always on top, Erich von Stroheim, whom Earl loved to imitate, in a studio pose as Rommel in *Five Graves to Cairo*. Fred Astaire and Rita Hayworth, dancing, their shadows on a wall.

Hot, he felt grimy and bone weary, his scalp itched from creek silt, his skin ached from sunburn and the abrasive struggle with the wagon. As he strained up the hills, the twisted tongue handle cut into his palm, but the pictures were so alive with his memories of the movies, they squirmed in the bed of Bucky's wagon. They had the raw, bright look of Sunday papers, wrapped in colored funnies. The sun flashing off them cast wavering light like water reflections on branches of trees that hung over Crazy Creek, flashed against windows of houses, the metal of cars as the stills glided by.

Fatigue made him bleary-eyed and muscle-sore, but as he turned onto Holston Street and saw Uncle Luke's little green 1938 Dodge parked beside the yellow fireplug, a sudden giggling thrill rushed through him, making him say, "This is the most wonderful day of my life!" To show Jesus he wasn't ashamed to praise him, he got down on his knees on the scorching macadam. But when he caught Mrs. Ford, clothespins clenched between her teeth, staring at him, he pretended to find a dime he'd dropped, and rose guiltily.

Lucius imagined the smell of the prickly seat of the Dodge where he often sat, sunlight pouring through the windshield. "Momma, leave my chariot parked out front—the tank's full—cause when you hear the horn blast some night, it's me, ready to take you for that ride to the Smokies I always promised." During the war, Momma couldn't beg or bitch hard enough to get the keys, and even though Uncle Luke had been reported missing, Mammy wouldn't turn them over to Daddy when he returned from the European Theatre of Operations.

In front of Uncle Luke's Dodge on the gravel outside the high, ragged hedges, a blue Buick was parked, looking familiar, but strange. The driver's door flung open just as Lucius reached the break in the hedge, and Dusty Harper, tall, stooped, thin, his slouch hat cocked, the wide brim curved nattily, a cigar cold in the side of his rubber-band mouth under the precise moustache, stepped out.

"Ut—Where the hell you been, Lightnin'? What's all *that* shit?" Dusty backed into the car behind the wheel that had a pearl knob.

"Stills—from good shows. I had to get 'em now or she'd a-burned 'em up."

"I'm burning your ass, boy. But you under bond, by god, so you better deliver your bill at noon tomorrow and train another carrier."

"You firing my ass?"

"Lucius, I told you and I told you till I'm purple."

"Yes, sir."

"Now, ain't I?"

"Yes, sir." Lucius stared down at Brian Donlevy, who stared back up at him, a scar on his face, a cigarette in his mouth, a foreign legion officer's cap on his head in *Beau Geste.*

"Pickin' up late is *one* thing, but *missin'* is a hell of a lot worse."

"I know it, Dusty, but I tell you—" Lucius tautened his throat muscles to keep from crying.

"Tell me, shit! You always got some wild-ass excuse."

"Aw, come on, Zorro, don't I get another chance't?" Lucius suddenly realized that a still of Reed Hadley as Zorro must be somewhere in the wagon bed.

"After three comes freeze-ass zero." Dusty never understood why Lucius called him Zorro, but he sat up straighter when he did, and looked just like Reed Hadley. "I ain't even counting the fact I fired you before."

"How many I miss yesterday?" Dusty handed Lucius four pink slips. "Aw—four?"

"Jesus, Lucius, don't give me that hurt, surprised look, like it's somebody's trying to do you dirty."

"Well, I don't see how I done it."

"Lucius, they's people all up and down Clayboe Ridge over yonder *looking* for you. Now, do *I* have to carry and collect tonight—or you going to do right?"

Lucius pulled Bucky's wagon around to the back door, emptied the stills and magazines on the bed that had been Uncle Luke's, propped Alan Ladd in his leather jacket against the oval mirror of the dresser, dug into the dirty clothes basket, took a big safety pin out of Bucky's overalls and repaired his satchel strap, then went out and got in the blue Buick beside Dusty.

On the corner of Grant Street where his route started, Dusty let Lucius out. He rolled 22 NAZIS PROTEST INNOCENCE AT NUREMBERG TRIAL tightly and, wishing he had time to see what was playing at Cherokee's twenty-eight theatres, threw it on Mrs. Acuff's porch, where it hit the rusty glider, broke open, and woke her cat.

Two rotting papers lay on Beverly Taylor's roof. The front door was shut. Throwing her paper, Lucius noticed Mrs. Taylor's Gold Star Mother flag in the window next to the iceman's card. Mammy refused to hang a flag, proclaiming Uncle Luke dead, in *her* window.

His sunburnt flesh steaming inside his abrasive shorts and striped polo, his face gritty from flakes of dried sand, his mouth dry, his feet feeling each rock in the macadam, Lucius was eager to deliver the last paper and finish collecting and go back home to the stills. He commanded himself to walk fast and not daydream. Paths and alternate paths, muddy and gravelly roads sprawled over Clayboe Ridge, and he had to cut through dense jungles into brief clearings and weave among houses that from the streets below he couldn't see for the pines and oaks. He remembered the still of James Stewart pushing against Marlene Dietrich's forehead with one hand, grabbing one of her ankles with the other when she tried to kick him in the midst of her fight with another woman in the saloon in *Destry Rides Again.* When he heard Warner Brothers' background music for *To Have and Have Not,* one scene after another came to him, and crossing the L & N tracks, he hoped he had a still of Lauren Bacall in the part where she said, "If you need anything, just whistle."

He always felt as if the ridge were set up, in isolation and solitude, for sudden confrontations. Suddenly, he might come onto a boy, a dog, a girl, a snake, an old man, a Negro. He expected rattlesnakes every moment. Saw only turtles, frogs, spiders, birds, swarms of flies and wasps and mud daubers. But at night, people loved to tell him, wildcats and polecats and a lonesome bear off Black Mountain prowled. In sunlight, he felt their sleeping presence. Always an aura of expectation: that he would glimpse a woman pulling on or off her "bloomers," a woman washing her pussy, a girl taking a pee in an outhouse, the door ajar, two people "doing it" in the jungle, where he sometimes found rubbers, soiled handkerchiefs, and frequently stepped over piles of dog and human squat on the paths. At the end of the route each day, he felt he'd just missed at least twenty well-staged scenes.

The smell of coming rain in the thick shade of the jungle gave him a hard-on. Cupping his hands around his mouth, he threw back his head and let a Tarzan call rip, and beat his chest, giving the yell a lusty trill.

The jungle path broke out into a muddy road. Coming onto most of the houses suddenly gave him a feeling of moving in a tree-congested Casbah. Lucius waved to the old Negro couple sitting on their front porch, the Smokies stretching blue, far in the distance, before them. "Comin' lil' late, ain't you, Lightnin'?"

At the city limits, where the Oak Ridge Highway cut through Clayboe Ridge, Lucius read aloud for the thousandth time: WELCOME TO CHEROKEE, GATEWAY TO THE SMOKIES. The names of things and places had magical properties that he liked to feel on his tongue. He hated to miss his regular Friday night wrestling matches at the old Pioneer Theatre, but the stills on Luke's bed drew him toward the last street on his route at the bottom of the ridge.

"My Love for Laura," Lucius intoned, then imitated the rumbling sound of Warner Brothers' background music. With a musical inflection, in the tone of voice he heard with previews, Lucius said aloud, over and over, the titles of his stories, the names of his characters, that, like the names of movies and stars, put him in a trance. " 'While the Sea Remains' by David H. Scott, starring Alan Ladd as Sam Gulliver and Vivien Leigh as Marina Crockett, with Robert Taylor as Jason Gulliver, alias Wyatt Thorp, and Laurence Olivier as Colonel Corrigan, Hedy Lamarr as Sandra Laskin, and Claude Rains as Mauridune." Lucius took up the story from where he'd imagined it yesterday, missing four houses.

Lying on a very expensive couch in Jason Crockett's library, Sam Gulliver hears a moan that drifts softly about the room. A woman is crying somewhere in the enormous mansion. Thinking it's his imagination, he tries to sleep again. Later, the same moaning, a little louder, wakes him. The room is dark, then suddenly bright, then dark. It's raining, lightning. Sam goes into the hallway, thinks the cry may have come from outside, opens the front door, goes out onto the wide porch. Straining to see through the rain, Sam discovers that the house stands on a cliff above the ocean. The moaning is fainter, so he returns to the library, hears it again, whirls around, leaps up the wide, curving stairway.

Sam comes to a door, opens it. A flight of stairs. Climbs to the top, opens a door. A dimly lighted, damp room. In a corner, a girl about twenty, chained to the decaying wall, kneels on a blanket, only a silk shawl, fringed, around her shoulders. In front of her, his back to Sam, sits a man dressed in seaman's duds, his chair resting on two legs, the back braced against the wall, a rifle in his lap. Barefoot, Sam creeps across the room to where the man sleeps, sticks his foot behind a back leg of the chair, jerks hard, and both man and chair land on their backs. Before the man can get up, Sam clips him on the jaw.

The girl looks at Sam, perplexed. Trying to resist looking at her nakedness, Sam kneels at her side. He starts to speak, but she breaks him off. "Why did you do that? Why didn't you leave me alone? I didn't need your help." "I can't sleep to the music of a woman's crying voice. Who chained you here, anyway? And who are you that you need to be chained and seem to know it?" "That's no concern of yours, stranger. Now leave me alone." She bursts into tears. Sam leaves the room.

Off the ridge now, up ahead, in the last block on the route, was LaRue Harrington's house. When he tossed her paper on the porch, he hoped to catch a glimpse of her, but knowing what time he came along, she'd probably hidden in the back. At Clinch View Grammar School, he used to make his gang chase her down and hold her so he could kiss her, and she kicked his shins. As beautiful as Scarlett O'Hara, and as spirited. To let her know he was passing her window and to tease her, he always sang "Sweet Rosie O'Grady," his song about her that he'd picked up three years ago from Betty Grable.

Lucius came out of Peck's sipping a Grapette, holding a Moon Pie, and sat on the green iron bench against the sooty stucco wall where an empty streetcar, its electric motor purring, its doors flung open, was parked, its skinny conductor snoozing, his bill cap over his eyes. Lucius wished he were at Mammy's Cafe, a plateful of pinto beans, mashed 'taters, and country-fried steak and sliced 'maters and cucumbers on the counter before him, the wrestling match at the Pioneer coming up.

He unrolled his extra and turned to the movie ads. Bijou: Alan Ladd and Veronica Lake in *The Blue Dahlia*. "Every guy dreams of meeting a girl like you," said Lucius, imitating Alan Ladd. "The trick is to find you."

Bugs Bunny Club. He'd heard it was going to start tomorrow. Every Saturday. Local talent. Kids. Singing and tap dancing, and prizes. He was eager to see what it would be like. "Racing with the moon," he sang, imitating Vaughn Monroe. Tivoli: *The Postman Always Rings Twice*, with John Garfield and Lana Turner. Previews looked good when he saw *The Blue Dahlia* there Monday. Plus Donald Duck cartoon.

All those movies, some double features, showing at twenty-eight theatres, excited Lucius. Even though he'd seen most of them, not being able to see them all again tonight made him feel sad.

Seeing LaRue's yellow bike parked on the sidewalk in front of Mrs. Lester's house, Lucius was thrilled at the possibility she and Judy might answer his knock. But Mrs. Lester answered.

"C'lect f' *Messenger*," said Lucius, working backward on his route.

As Lucius went back down the steps, flipping the quarter, dropping it, Judy swooped around the house on her big brother's bike, the seat jacked up, and LaRue ran behind her, holding onto the raccoon tail, giggling, like some silly girl. When she saw Lucius, she straddled her own parked bike and gazed up into the pines.

"Least you can do is speak," said Lucius. "We been married four years now."

LaRue turned her large blue eyes straight on Lucius. He was used to her freezing stare.

"Okay, if *I* talk to him?" asked Judy. Lucius knew she liked him. She answered all his questions about LaRue.

"If you don't mind talking to trash that's got a brother in the reform school and ought to be there himself."

Lucius walked on to the next house, ashamed she'd rejected him for four years, ever since the third grade. But one day he'd be famous, she'd come to him, ask him to forgive her, tell him she loved him, and he'd say, "Frankly, my dear, I don't give a damn."

Worried this might be almost his last day on the route, Lucius felt nostalgic for the times he used to daydream, on his first route, of becoming like Captain Marvel, Jr., and on his second route, wearing a tight white sweat shirt like Kid Eternity in a funny book series he didn't see anymore, dreaming of having adventures all over the world as the Tennessee Kid in that shirt.

Passing the Hiawassee, he gazed at the stills for *Badman's Territory,* with Randolph Scott and wanted to see Linda Stirling in chapter 4 of *The Tiger Woman,* but he went into the outer lobby and bought a striped sack of popcorn and ate it on the walk home.

On the hill above the dark hollow on Prater Street, surrounded on both sides by black jungle, Lucius invoked the protection of his friend Frankenstein's monster against the Wolf Man and other creatures of the shuddering dark.

Tensing himself against whoever or whatever might be crouching behind the hedge to spring upon him, Lucius stroked the hood of Uncle Luke's ghostly Dodge and stepped onto the flagstone walk leading up to the small front porch of "good ol' 702 Holston."

Through the open front door and the screen, theme music swelled, and an announcer said, "And now, ladies and gentlemen, here's Phil Baker." Must be nine thirty, "Everybody Wins" on WXOL.

The living room was littered—the carpet, the davenport, the chairs, and Mammy's, Momma's, and Bucky's laps—with the stills Beverly Taylor had bestowed upon him. He'd looked forward to watching their excitement, but for a moment Lucius resented people who felt less intensely about them than he did pawing over the finest things he had ever owned.

"Lordy, *mer*-cy, Lucius," said Mammy, mock crying in her voice and face. "Where in this world did you *get* these pictures?"

"They call 'em stills."

"Why, they're just the most wonderful . . ."

"We been goin' over 'em ever since we hit the front door," said Momma. She and Mammy still wore hats. "Bucky had 'em all spread out."

"Who said you could touch my stills?"

"They just nas'y ol' pictures," said Bucky.

"Then don't drool over 'em."

"Irene, I wish you'd look," said Mammy, holding up Orson Welles as Rochester, bearded, blind, about to kiss Joan Fontaine as Jane Eyre.

"Ain't this from?—" Momma looked closely at a still. "Oh, what was the name of— Momma, *you* remember, where Errol Flynn was in World War I, flyin' . . . a air ace after some German pilot."

"Not *Dawn Patrol*, Momma." Lucius looked over her shoulder at Errol Flynn in a leather flier's jacket. "That's *Dive Bomber*, no, *Desperate Journey*, *Desperate Journey*. Uncle Luke took me to see *Dawn Patrol* at the Bijou when I was little."

Momma frowned and gritted her teeth, flashing her eyes at Lucius, then toward Mammy, a look that always made him feel guilty for Uncle Luke's being missing. Since he was only missing, Mammy believed he'd honk the horn of his Dodge and leap up to the screen door before long. Claudette Colbert's husband finally showed up in *Since You Went Away*. But Momma never doubted Uncle Luke was killed in the invasion at Salerno.

"Seems like what I remember 'bout him is the funny things," Mammy said.

"What's *this* 'un from, Lucius?" asked Bucky.

"*Jesse James*." Tyrone Power stood on a chair to remove a painting from the wall.

"Oh, yeah, where he got his foot caught in the railroad track?"

"No, that was Zorro in the chapter play. Saw *Jesse James* at the Smoky again last week." John Carradine shoots Jesse with his own gun through a window.

"Oh, Lucius," said Momma, "I wish you'd stay out of that Smoky."

"Get rat bit," said Mammy, in an I-told-you-so voice.

"People that go there ain't had a bath since the deluge."

"Irene, I want you to look!" said Mammy, her voice gay, her smile embracing all Lucius's memory.

"Momma, Mammy wants to show you."

Momma looked up from *her* stack, and Lucius leaned over Mammy's shoulder, thrilled to see Clark Gable kissing Vivien Leigh, leaving Scarlett outside Atlanta on the road to Tara. "Ain't it 'bout time for 'em to bring it back?"

"Let's see—it's been . . . Law . . . ," said Momma.

"Daddy took me to see it at the Hiawassee just 'fore he went in the army."

"I'm gonna shoot your daddy like Scarlett plugged that Yankee if he don't get hisself home," said Momma. "I'll be lucky if I see two cents out of that paycheck."

"Ain't that lil' ol' Judy Garland?" Mammy leaned sideways, held the still under the floor-lamp shade.

Doing a straw hat and cane routine in the living room with Margaret O'Brien. "*Meet Me in St. Louis,*" said Lucius, knowing it reminded Mammy and Momma of the few good years they lived there.

"She ain't done no good since *The Wizard of Oz,*" said Mammy. "Never will forget that wicked ol' witch. You youn'uns remember when your Mammy used to dress up like the witch of Oz and go cackling across Mr. Stookesbury's cornfield while you'uns was roastin' marshmellers?"

"I can't wait till Hallowe'en," said Bucky.

"Can't do it no more, honey. Your big wiseacre brother Earl got suspicious few years back and snuck in on me when I's just settin' my peaked black hat on my head."

"Here's good ol' Gary Cooper in *Sergeant York,*" said Momma. "York was a Tennes*see* boy, children."

"Played Lou Gehrig, too, in *Pride of the Yankees.*"

"Oh, and when he was about to die and he give that speech on the ball diamond," said Mammy, "I thought I'd *never* stop cryin'."

"Never give a sucker an even break," Lucius imitated W. C. Fields. Wearing a top hat, holding a bottle of whiskey, looking calmly into the eyes of a gorilla.

"*Swiss Family Robinson,*" said Momma. "Remember that one?"

"You and Daddy took us to see it at the Imperial when we lived over on Park Street."

"You was still in sunsuits, Bucky," said Mammy, "and long curls."

Lucius gathered a stack for himself and sat on the davenport beside Momma. "*The Man in the Iron Mask.*" Lucius had seen it with Earl at the Bijou, and Earl climbed over the brass rail and sat in one of the gilded box seats, red velvet curtains and darkness behind him, Lucius trembling, afraid he'd get arrested and thrown into a dungeon, because you weren't allowed. And when they removed the iron mask, Louis Hayward looked like Earl.

"Oh, Bette Davis in *The Letter,*" said Mammy. "Never forget her shooting her lover *as long as I live!*"

"Mammy, you ever see Spencer Tracy, Clark Gable, and Hedy Lamarr, and . . . oh, who else?" asked Momma.

"Claudette Colbert," said Lucius. "*Boom Town.*"

"I remember this one." Mammy picked up the still Momma put

down, showing Clark Gable and Spencer Tracy fighting in the mud in an oil town.

"Mammy, that's the very one we 'uz *talking* about," said Momma, rolling her eyes, exasperated.

"Oh, well, I'm so deep in *my* pile. . . . Lot of these is after my time. Give me John Gilbert and Gloria Swanson."

"Give *me* Johnny Mack Brown," said Bucky.

"Give you a loose tooth," said Lucius.

"Yeah, and I'll mooooow you down," said Bucky, imitating Charlie McCarthy exactly.

"Law, that bullfight picture, with Tyrone Power and Rita Hayworth," said Momma. "She was kinda new then. Says *Blood and Sand* on the back."

"Hey, *The Sea Hawk!* Tun tuh duh!" said Bucky, scrambling the background music.

"Oh, you was too *little* to remember that one," said Lucius.

"Shoot, I 'member 'at colorin' book of *The Sea Hawk,* and you told me the story of it one time. Remember?"

"*The Great Dictator,* ol' Charlie Chaplin on his back, spinning the world with his feet," said Mammy. "Lord have mercy on us."

"Heil Hitler!"

"Shut up, Bucky."

"Don't you fuss at that youn'un, Lucius," said Momma. "He's behaving himself."

"Irene. Here she *is. Together Again,* with Charles Boyer and Irene Dunne."

"Did you name Momma after Irene Dunne?" asked Lucius.

"Why, no."

"*I* was named after Buck Jones," said Bucky.

"Lana Turner in *Honky Tonk.*" Momma looked at one of the large stills, turned sepia tone by overexposure to sunlight. "Lord, lord."

"Stop pickin' your blamed nose," said Lucius. Bucky did a Harpo Marx smile.

"*High Sierra,* with Humphrey Bogart," said Mammy. Lucius imagined Mad Dog Earl getting caught, holding up a small-town drugstore.

"Oh, I can't stand that man!" said Momma.

"That's who Earl got his nickname from—Mad Dog Earl," said Lucius.

Mammy gave Lucius a warning look, shaking her head, lips pursed, glancing at Momma to see how she took it. "First *I* heard of it," said Momma, not looking up. Nobody in the family knew where Earl was, and they hoped the police didn't either.

"Big Chief Chew-Tabacca's what they called him over on Avondale," said Bucky.

"Aw, you was too little."

"Well, it was you told me."

"Reckon I must a *missed* this one," said Mammy.

"Let's see," said Lucius. "Oh, that's Dana Andrews in *Swamp Water*."

"Let *me* see it," said Bucky.

"Some day, children," said Mammy, "after me and the Chief is married, we're *going* to Florida—fishing, and see the Everglades."

"Bring me back a baby alligator!"

"Oh, Bucky, you kill me," said Mammy, laughing.

"Remember *Kings Row?*" asked Momma. "Saw it at the Venice the night before Fred set the coal house on fire. Daddy was still alive then."

Pitifullest sight ever I saw when little ol' Ronald Reagan woke up and found out he didn't have no legs."

"Lucius, here's your hero," said Bucky.

"Let me have that." Alan Ladd trying to cure Loretta Young of deafness in *And Now Tomorrow*. Lucius set it aside.

"*My Sister Eileen*," said Mammy. "I like a good comedy."

Lucius loved the tone of Mammy's voice, differently when coal burned in the heater and she and Momma put their feet up on the fenders.

"*The Jungle Book*, Bucky," said Momma. "Remember Sabu riding that python in the river."

"Pass it over."

"That Sabu is *so* cute," said Momma.

"Looks like a nigger to me," said Mammy.

"Oh, Mammy," said Lucius.

"Well, he *does*. Like he come right off Clayboe Ridge."

"Bucky, here's *Bambi*," said Momma.

"Aw, Momma, he's getting too old for Bambi," said Lucius. They were in St. Thomas' Episcopalian orphanage while Momma was in the hospital, and all the kids went in a fleet of police cars, a special event.

"I just hope Lassie comes back to the Hiawassee sometime," said Bucky.

"Who cares?"

"Hey, Lucius, reckon how Tiger Woman's gonna get out of that fix in the temple?"

"Wait and see. Don't spoil it."

"I wanna know *now*, now, Lucius."

"Lucius, look, look. It's Straight Hair and Fatsi," said Mammy. Stan Laurel, wearing floppy socks, his feet turned inward, reading to Oliver Hardy, who's asleep, a bedtime story in *Saps at Sea*.

"*Madame Curie*," said Momma. "I just love Greer Garson and Walter Pidgeon, but I thought I'd fall asleep 'fore it was over."

"Hey, ain't *Saratoga Trunk* playing at the Imperial now?" asked Lucius, looking at Gregory Peck, standing over Ingrid Bergman with a razor in his hand as she sleeps in *Spellbound*.

"That *Oxbow Incident*," said Momma, "was *the* slowest Western I ever saw."

"I thought it was great," said Lucius. "*There* you go, Bucky." He passed a shot of the monster in *The House of Frankenstein*. "Picture of your ol' buddy, Emmett."

"Lucius, don't you tease that child," said Mammy.

"You can *have* your damn ol' pictures." Bucky went over to the corner and crawled between the legs of the console radio, and folded his arms and legs, glared at Lucius out of the dark.

"*See Here, Private Hargrove*," said Mammy. "That was *so* cute."

"I want to see *Laura* again," said Momma, holding a still out in front of her.

"Oh, yeah, that was really great!" said Lucius. "Let me know if you come across *Leave Her to Heaven*. Gene Tierney was sort of like she was in *Laura*."

"Lucius," said Momma, her tone introducing something special. She held up Joan Fontaine holding a tray of fruit, her leg jacked up on a chair, giving Nigel Bruce a saucy look, while Basil Rathbone looked on in *Frenchman's Creek*. It had inspired the first story he ever wrote down, "Blue Waters."

"Where *is* that little story you wrote, honey?"

"I let Marion Cassiday, this girl at Clinch View, take it to read and she never gave it back."

"*Lady in the Dark*. Looks good," said Mammy. "Lordy, I have so little time for movies."

"Here's *Thirty Seconds Over Tokyo*," said Lucius, holding up Irene Dunne and Spencer Tracy.

"Spencer ought to stick with Katharine Hepburn," said Momma. "If you come across *Woman of the Year*, yell."

"*Wilson*," said Lucius. "Most boresome movie I ever saw."

"I saw it held over at the Bijou," said Momma. "I was a little girl in St. Louis when Wilson was president. Remember, Mammy?"

"Bucky, quit that sulking under the radio," said Mammy.

"I'm listening to my program."

"That's a blamed quiz show!" said Momma.

"I don't care."

"*The Picture of Dorian Gray*," said Lucius, looking at Hurd Hatfield horrified by his decayed portrait.

"*Mildred Pierce,*" said Mammy. "Did *I* see that?"

"The story of my life," said Momma.

"Be nice if you got the Academy Award for it," said Mammy.

"Mammy, don't you think Momma looks like Joan Crawford?"

"Why, Lucius," said Momma, "don't be silly."

"She looked better 'fore she got that feather bob."

"*Tobacco Road,*" said Momma. "Why they'd make a movie about a bunch of trash like that is beyond me."

"I hope it comes back sometime," said Lucius. "I ain't never seen it."

"You stay away from that filthy thing."

"Here's *Dillinger,*" said Lucius.

"Dillinger come *through* Cherokee one time," said Mammy. "Somebody caught him coming out of the Smoky Theatre on Market Street."

Hunched under the radio, Bucky made the sound of a machine gun.

"*The Lost Weekend,*" said Lucius, looking at Ray Milland sitting in a chair, terrified of the shadows of bats on the ceiling.

"Starring Fred Hutchfield," said Momma.

"Irene! That poor boy's come through a war."

"Momma—the war's over."

"Well, nobody knows what he had to go through. . . ."

"*The Bells of St. Mary's* Bing Crosby, Momma. 'When the blue of the night' . . . ," sang Lucius. "*A Tree Grows in Brooklyn.*"

"It don't neither," said Bucky.

"Pass that over here," said Momma. "We's living on Beech Street and I remember—"

"Shhhhht," said Mammy.

"Wasn't Joan Blondell—"

"Irene, will you hersh?"

"*What?*"

Mammy listened. "Thought I heard somebody on the walk."

"Lucius, look and see," said Momma, hopeful. "I bet it's Earl sneaking up to surprise us."

Bucky scooted on his butt out from under the radio. "Eooow! You all scare me." He pulled up the shade.

"You tear that shade, Bucky," said Mammy, "and I'll bust your little ass."

"Nothing but moonlight out there," said Lucius.

"Lord, ever' little sound just tears me all to pieces," said Mammy. "Could be Earl or Fred or . . ."

"Or Uncle Luke," everybody was thinking. Mammy made Lucius believe it might be.

"*Hitler's Children,*" said Bucky, sitting next to Momma on the davenport. "Reckon they're all dead by now."

"I'm looking for *National Velvet* myself," said Lucius. He'd seen Elizabeth Taylor first in *Lassie Come Home* in 1943 when his love of LaRue was most intense, and she looked both like a younger Vivien Leigh and LaRue. And after *National Velvet,* Elizabeth Taylor was his unreachable ideal of a pure and beautiful girl. But now he was ashamed to think of her in relation to LaRue because he'd heard recently that Elizabeth Taylor had played with her titties to make them bigger so she could get the part of the girl who became a jockey and fell off her horse and the doctor opened her shirt.

"Well, I'm looking in *my* pile for a picture of you-know-who Hutch-field," said Mammy.

"Who?" they all asked.

"Little lightnin'-haired hellion to play in *The Yearling.*"

"Momma!"

"Lord have mercy, I've done it now." Lucius expected some awful revelation. "I'm sorry, Lucius. It was a surprise. Me and your momma sent in your picture to be the child star of this new movie they're a-making called *The Yearling.* Don't cry, Bucky. You got to be thirteen."

"Me? You sent in my picture? Gosh bum!" Lucius remembered the announcement of the contest last fall, a talent search almost as big in scale, the fan magazines said, as the one for Scarlett O'Hara.

"I hope it ain't bad luck to tell it."

Lucius wasn't sure, but he thought he'd seen an ad for the movie, already. Some freckled-faced kid, hugging a doe.

"Mammy, did you see *A Song to Remember,* with that new actor, Cornel Wilde?" asked Momma.

Lucius leaped across the room to the davenport and looked at Cornel Wilde playing the piano as Chopin, while Merle Oberon, dressed like a man, watched.

"She turns my stomach dressed like that," said Momma. "And smokes cigars in it."

Lucius' hand trembled as he held the glossy Technicolor still from the movie that inspired him to write his second story. He'd used his own name as author of "Blue Waters," but inspired by *The Adventures of Mark Twain*—Fredric March striking out his own name with a pen and writing in Mark Twain—he had put Cidney Cornel Chesterfield on "Chopin."

"*I* used to write stories," said Mammy.

"You did?" asked Lucius, surprised, impressed, dubious.

"Sent one to the picture show people in Hollywood way back yonder and they did it up into a movie."

"Aw, really?"

"Sure as the world. But the blamed crooks didn't never send me no money for it."

"She was on the train bound for California when Gran'paw Burnett jerked her off. Fifteen years old."

"I was gonna take it out of their asses."

"Momma!"

"Well, I was!"

Sitting in her favorite chair across from the front door, looking like Wallace Beery, Mammy reminded Lucius of the summer nights during the war when they sat in the open doorway in the blackouts and scanned the sky for German planes, telling stories by the bomber's moon. About Gran'paw Charlie's momma and the wildcat, how it was so hungry it got up on the roof of the cabin in the mountains and tried to come down the chimney, and she boiled some water, and it fell into the black iron kettle she washed clothes and made soap in, and she cooked it down to skin and bones, and that made Lucius tell Bucky about little Black Sambo and the tiger and the pancakes.

"Mammy, tell 'bout the time Gran'paw Charlie beat up the principal."

"He didn't beat him up, honey."

"Tell it, tell it," said Bucky, sitting on the magic carpet in front of Mammy.

"Well, children, the way it was, the principal sent little Luke home one day with this note to Gran'paw Charlie, sayin', 'Mr. Foster, it has been brought to my attention that your son has poured library paste all over Mrs. Rankin's erasers. I must insist that you accompany your child to school in the morning. Bring a switch with you, as I want you to be present when I give Luke a whipping.' " Mammy bent her head and rubbed her nose to recall the scene. "Boys, I tell you, when Gran'paw Charlie read that note, he hit the ceiling." Bucky looked up at the ceiling, Lucius looked up. "He stormed and he raged from room to room of this little ol' house, yelling, 'That g. d.—' "

"He may a been just a little feller," said Momma, "no taller'n you, Lucius, but he had a bullhorn voice. Used to go out and stand in the backyard and holler for Luke to come on in for supper and Luke, curb-hopping at Howell's Drug Store, would hear him all the way through the woods, across Crazy Creek to Grand Boulevard and Luke'd come running lickety-split."

"Irene, I'm telling this."

"Well, pardon me for living."

"So, next morning, Charlie says to Luke, 'Son, go cut me two switches!' 'Two?' 'Don't wrangle with me. I said, "Two," now git 'em.' So little ol' Luke drags hisself over to the hedge outsyonder and breaks off two switches—I was watching from the kitchen winder, wondering what Charlie was up to myself—when all of a sudden, Luke threw them switches down, and broke off a littler one and a bigger one, and come back in the house just a-smiling to beat the band. Looked like he'd figured something out, but I didn't know what it was till Luke come home that afternoon and told me."

Knowing what was coming increased Lucius's fascination, anticipating the way Mammy transformed each part with her voice, her gestures, her embellishments. He was conscious of listening to Mammy, while another self stood off to the side, observing the behavior of the teller and her listeners. He felt the rhythm of response in the room, noticed Mammy's ways of capturing, holding, playing with their interests, even Momma's, despite her hostility at being told to hush.

"Way it turned out, was this. Gran'paw Charlie marched hisself up to Clinch View Elementary, little Luke trottin' behind—and he was almost by then as tall as his daddy—but Charlie was just like a buzz saw when he got wound up. So he sashays into the principal's office, and this old man looks across his desk at this sawed-off little feller. 'Wait outside, sir, until I'm ready to see you,' says the principal.

"Well, he ort'n a done that. Should a kept his mouth shut and let Charlie talk. Charlie raises up on his toes—wore a size six shoe that's even too small for *you* now, Lucius—and in that deep, cocky voice of his, says, 'Mr. Turner, you will see me *now,* for I have come just like your note says, and I have brung two switches.' 'Two switches?' asked Mr. Turner . . . and a hatefuller man you never met. Wore *out* a switch on Earl the second year *he* went. Dead now, ain't he, Irene?"

"I don't know *nothin'*."

"So, anyway, Charlie says, 'Yes, sir. One for you to use on my boy, and when you g'done, I'm a-gonna use t'other on *you!*"

"Then did he whup him, Mammy?" asked Bucky.

"Don't know, honey. That's the end of the story."

As they basked in the luminous silence, Lucius wished they all loved him as much as they loved Uncle Luke. He would earn it someday.

"Tell me some more stuff," said Bucky. "Like the kids at St. Thomas's orphanage pestering Lucius to 'tell another one, tell another one.'"

"One more, and I must hush."

"Tell about Uncle Luke riding his motorsickle through Howell's Drug Store after they fired him," said Bucky.

"Did I miss 'The Lone Ranger'?"

Lucius squinted beyond the lamp light, saw Daddy behind the screen.

"Mammy's telling us a story, Daddy," said Bucky, jumping up to open the screen door.

"Missed 'The Lone Ranger' all across Europe, and here I am missing him again. What time is it?"

"Time for all drunks to fall all over the living room, I reckon," said Momma.

"Now, Irene, I'll do the bossing in my house."

"It's my daddy's house, too," Momma said.

"Gran'paw Charlie's momma built it herself, children," said Mammy, "forty years ago. One-room cabin, like the one she left behind in the mountains, when she brought her fatherless son to Cherokee. Fields and jungles all around, and only one or two houses."

"Tell 'bout the time Uncle Luke come in drunk and peed on all the lampshades," said Bucky, sitting on the davenport. "Listen, Daddy."

Daddy sat beside Bucky.

"Watch out, Daddy, it's my stills."

Daddy stared at Lucius. "Your what?"

"Stills."

"You makin' fun of me?"

"Pictures."

"You got some pictures of a still? Where at?"

Bucky and Mammy got to laughing, Momma tight-lipped, as Lucius eased the stack from under Daddy.

"Listen, son," said Daddy, tugging at Lucius's polo shirt. "I *had* to blow that bridge. Patton was counting on me."

"I know, Daddy."

"What bridge?" asked Bucky.

"Don't get him started on *that*," said Momma.

"One night, Gran'paw Charlie was coming home from a dance," said Mammy, her storytelling tone hushing everybody, "after he'd took me home, so he thought he'd take a shortcut through this field, and, well, sir, he's going along, a few drinks under his belt, when all of a sudden—"

"I know what's going to happen," said Daddy, shaking his finger, grinning, his hat riding low on his Clark Gable ears.

"—something big and black rared up and made a racket in the high grass, and Charlie—whupped out his gun and shot five times at it. . . . Well, sir, next morning, he heard they had the law out looking for somebody that shot Mr. Sproul's cow."

Lucius smelled Gran'paw Charlie's empty holster that he and Earl used to play Gang Busters with. Lucius had sworn that when he grew up, he'd put a gun in it and track down the man who shot his gran'paw. He always saw Victor Jory's face as Injun Joe in *Tom Sawyer.* Last summer, he'd gone looking for it.

"What happened on 'The Lone Ranger,' son?"

"Nothing," said Lucius, smelling stale bread and cinnamon from the Hutchfield Bakery where his daddy made the rolls.

"I *had* to blow that bridge."

"Well, children," said Mammy, "I've gone as far as I can go. Bucky, turn off the radio, honey. You all hit the hay now. Big day at Jane's Cafe tomorrow. Be a bunch of old country hoojers drifting in. Chief's day off."

"You going Bugs Bunny Club, Lucius?" asked Bucky, swaying sleepily.

"Maybe," Lucius yawned.

"Grown women poring over those silly movie pictures," said Momma. "Lucius, you get this junk picked up now, honey. Where you gonna *put* it all?"

"I'll find a place," said Lucius, gathering the stacks.

"He's got it all in his head," Mammy told Momma, as Lucius tucked the last stack under his raised chin. "Don't know what he needs pictures fer. He ort to charge admission."

In the back room that Gran'paw Charlie built on when he and Mammy moved in, in Luke's bed, Bucky, sticking his feet straight up under the sheet, asked, "Tell me a story, Lucius?"

The room's only window was open, the honeysuckle-laden air came through the screen door, latched against burglars, niggers, Jews, and Catholics. Mist over the grass in the backyard and the victory garden and in the hedge-berry tree where the chickens roosted, dew on the roof of the coal house that was once a circus wagon.

"Once upon a time . . . there was a mouse! And his name—was—Mighty Mouse!" Lucius announced dramatically, and paused, as Bucky, thrilled, kicked his feet rapidly, his body shuddering with delight. "The end."

Bucky whined. "Telllll it, Lucius."

"One morning, Straight Hair and Fatsi woke up. . . . The end."

Bucky whimpered. "Looooo-shus!"

Somebody in Mammy's room pounded on the wall. "Lucius, you all shut up in yonder!"

"Mammy, make Lucius tell me a story!"

"You all pipe down now, or I'll come in there with Gran'paw Charlie's belt."

"Momma!" yelled Bucky. "What's you and Daddy whispering about?"

"We'll put in a milk bottle and give it to you in the morning."

"In the old days of the West," whispered Lucius, "lived a Mexican prince, and when it got dark, he turned into . . . Zor-ro! . . . The end."

Bucky growled and kicked. Lucius saw again the still of Tyrone

Power, thrusting with a long, graceful stretch, a rapier into Basil Rathbone, the mark of Zorro on the wall beside him.

"Okay, Bucky, I'm going to *tell* this one. The moon was shining
bright on the prairie and coyotes were howling on one of the buttes
above Tombstone, when a lone rider appeared on top of another butte,
like a shadow, against the big, big moon. And reckon who it was?"

"Zorro?"

"No."

"The Durango Kid?"

"No. It was—Buck Jones!"

"Oh, boy!"

Anticipating Bucky's reaction made Lucius giggle. "The end."

Bucky let out a loud, body-wracking, throbbing cry-whine.

"I said, You'uns hersh!" yelled Mammy. "I got your momma squab-
bling with Fred in the living room and you all raising a ruckus in
yonder."

"Get under the sheet," Bucky whispered in Lucius's ear, his breath
smelling of stale blow gum.

Pulling the sheet over their heads, Lucius remembered the two
weeks in the juvenile detention home, the six weeks at St. Thomas's
orphanage when, after lights out, twenty kids gathered under his cot
and under his quilts, to hear a story about Huck and Jim, continued
each night, risking Mr. Morgan's bolo paddle. All twenty of them, one
night, bare-assed, in Mr. Morgan's room, exposed to sudden electric
light that made them blink their eyes until they shot open when the
paddle smacked their flesh.

" 'While the Sea Remains,' " Lucius announced, and whispered
some background music. "The Adventures of Sam Gulliver."

"Oh, boy, you gonna tell the rest of it?"

"Remember somebody shot him in the belly."

"And he woke up in a dungeon on this ship."

"Yeah, and for weeks the only person he sees is this doctor. Well,
the doctor wouldn't answer any of his questions about Jonathan
Crockett or the little man or the Indian in the cave, and he got so he
was madder'n hell, so when his belly got healed, he got hungry for the
smell of the ocean, being a sailor, so he called in one of the guards that
stood outside his door. And all of a sudden the door jars open and
this great big monster steps in, his eyes bloodshot with hate, a dagger
in his hand ready to make sliced baloney out of Sam's neck. Sam sees a
chain and grabs it and slams it into the big guy's chest and a swift
kick in the jaw finished it."

"Then what did the *other* guy do?"

"He come charging in wearing these brass knucks, and Sam threw him over his shoulder. He locked the door, then strolled down the deck just like he was one of the crew."

"And then he dived off and swum back home."

"No, too far out, so he decided to take his chances when they docked, if he lived till then. So he goes into the mess hall and starts talking to this little French cook. 'Say, where we bound?' 'Africa.' Then the cook turns around and his mouth falls open. 'You a sailor on board. ain't cha?' 'Yeah, why?' 'What cha got that bandage on for? You're Wyatt Thorp. Get the hell out of here, you son of a bitch, or I keel you!' "

"Shhhhh," said Bucky.

Lucius listened with Bucky under the sheet, then peeled it down to hear more clearly the yelling in the kitchen. Something crashed against the wall.

"Irene, that better not be one of *my* dishes!" yelled Mammy, from the bedroom.

"I have dishes, too, Mother! *Some* things in this house are mine, you know."

"*Too* many things! I wish you'd take what's yours and move it out of my sight!"

"Don't worry. I'd do it tonight if I had even a cardboard box to move *into*."

"Till then, you'uns hush that racket. I got to open that cafe at the crack of dawn. Thanks to Fred and poor little Luke," she began to cry, "they's peace in all Europe and Asia, too, but not two minutes at a whirl at 702 Holston Street."

Bucky started whining. An ache in his throat, Lucius said, "Stop that bellering, and listen," and pulled the sheet over their heads and patted Bucky's shoulder.

"So, Sam just stood there, wondering who the hell Wyatt Thorp was, and why the cook called him that. The little French cook must of thought he was dangerous because he came at him with a butcher knife. But ol' Sam grabbed his wrist and slid his arm around his neck and twisted his arm behind his back. 'Say, what gives, Buster?' Sam asks.

"It seems like ever' time he asks a question, he gets clipped from behind. Which is what happened, and when he opened his eyes, it was a filthy sight. He was in the ship's dungeon again. . . . Tune in tomorrow night for the next episode of the thrilling adventures of Sam Gulliver in 'While the Sea Remains.' This is WXOL signing off. 'Oh, say can you see. . . .' " Lucius stood up in bed and saluted, and Bucky smothered his giggles with a pillow over his face.

Settled for sleep, Bucky said, "Lucius, I really am named after Bucky Jones, ain't I?"

"I reckon," said Lucius.

"Lucius, is they really such of a thing as the sandman?"

"Why, of course. Just like Santa Claus and Fartso the Whale, only the sandman don't bring you nothing but sleep."

"Have they stopped fussing?"

"Yeah. Go to sleep."

Tomorrow, he would count up his stills and his magazines and find a good place to keep them. Robert Taylor as Billy the Kid dressed in black with silver buckles, wearing a short black leather vest. Lucius became aware of the dark, so pitch black he thought of the dark that hung over the big clothes box Gran'paw Charlie's momma built and that Lucius had slept in, on top of old clothes and quilts, when they visited Mammy that night Gran'paw, night watchman at Peerless Glass Company, was found murdered. Laurence Olivier about to embrace Joan Fontaine in *Rebecca*. "Last night I dreamed I went to Manderley. . . ." Alan Ladd as Sam Gulliver, asking the French cook, "Say, where we bound?"

Every night, Lucius reviewed his life serial-fashion until he felt his mind drifting into sleep, recalling not just in images but in flashes of feeling, and when he came up to the present, he'd replay his life over again. Trying to remember where he'd left off last night, Lucius eased into the first part of his night ritual. St. Thomas's Orphanage? No. Coming back to Clinch View Elementary in the middle of the year, saying his name was Lucian? No. All through the time they had lived at Mammy's up to the morning Daddy returned from France? Yeah, up to that morning. He focused the images, deliberately resurrecting, re-creating the past, within two weeks of the present: Voices from Mammy's bedroom. A man talking. A deep, mellow voice. Slipping up to the door, now half ajar, expecting to see Luke, sitting on the edge of the bed, come back, as Mammy vowed he would. Duffle bag upright, but leaning, in the middle of the floor. Daddy's voice, after three years. Running into the bedroom where the shades are down on the west side of the house. Daddy sitting up in bed, the red glow of his cigarette, pulsing, showing his olive-drab undershirt. "Hey. . . ." Daddy laughing, nervous, shy, any time people show affection. Lucius leaping over Momma, who, naked from the waist up, jerks the covers to her chin. Hugging Daddy, feeling his whiskers against his sunburned cheek. Inhaling the odor of nicotine and fresh cigarette and match smoke. Lucius smells again another strange odor.

"How you doing, Bub?"

"Okay. I carry the Cherokee *Messenger* up on Clayboe Ridge now."

"Yeah, you momma's tellin' me, son."

Lucius seeing through his tears his daddy bow his head, hiding tears himself.

"Lucius, you got your knees in my belly," says Momma, pushing at his hip.

Suddenly, Bucky, yelling, leaping into bed, too, hugging Daddy, then Momma, then crawling under the sheet between them, putting his arms around both of them, grinning, like posing for a picture. Lucius getting under the sheet too, on the edge, next to Daddy, feeling shy.

"Ain't that a picture!" says Mammy, in her ripped housecoat, in the doorway, holding the morning paper, the *Herald*.

"Daddy," says Bucky, "read us the funnies like you used to."

Lucius raising the shade behind the sewing machine to make the room a soft shell. "Better help your Mammy get breakfast started," said Momma, a tinge of jealousy in her voice, like when they lived on Avondale and she screamed at them all day long and took a switch to them and they said, "I'm gonna tell Daddy," and he came home at dark, drunk, and they hugged his legs and jumped into his arms, and Momma said, "Good god, I slave here the livelong day and he stays out drunk, and soon's he hits the door, it's like the return of the King of England. Makes me sick!" No, he'd been over that part several months ago, and Momma screaming at Daddy over Barbara, a younger woman who worked in the bakery with Daddy and whose husband was in Petros Penitentiary, and Momma saying she hoped he'd break out and catch them. Lucius waited some nights for a convict to break in and murder them all in their beds.

Daddy that morning back from war reading Dick Tracy aloud, Bucky tucked under his arm, looking on, hanging on every word, slightly buck-toothed mouth open, Lucius listening to the sweet, rich voice out of a time when he was young as Bucky, staring at the bent, leaning, stuffed duffle bag, its mouth gaping.

Maybe in the morning, Uncle Luke's voice will wake him.

"Tomorrow, Alan Ladd in *The Blue Dahlia!*" Lucius whispered aloud.

A shadowy man at the screen door, rattling the hook, a blue nimbus of misty moonlight around his body. Lucius's heart pounded fiercely and he began to tremble. "Lucius. . . . Lucius. . . ." Luke's ghost. "Let me in, Bub."

"Luke?"

"It's your Daddy, son. Unlock it."

Lucius got up and eased up the hook. Smelling of sour dough and white lightnin', Daddy staggered into the little room and crawled into bed, still wearing his vest, shirt, and pants, in his sock feet.

"She kicked me out the front door," he said. "Your own Momma."

Lucius locked the screen again and got in bed beside Daddy, Bucky asleep against the wall. I made it happen by remembering that morning, being in bed with him, and he came in here because I was imagining it again. And now he's back at good ol' 702 Holston Street, lighting a cigarette. The fumes lulled Lucius.

Lucius started the second part of his nightly ritual. "Everybody seems so strange to me," he said to God.

Momma's vicious whisper startled him: "Fred, you want to burn us all up!" Momma stood over the bed, reaching across Lucius for the cigarette. Fred surrendered it to her. "Wasn't burning up the coal house enough for you? . . . Are the kids asleep?"

"Kids? You asleep?" Lucius kept quiet. "They said, Yeah."

"Smart aleck. . . . Listen, Fred, honey, I just came in to say, you and me've got to *try*. We got to move out of this house and have our own family life. Will you promise to try, Fred? I still love you, honey. Fred? Fred? Are you *asleep*? . . . You son of a bitch!"

Lucius heard Daddy's cigarette hiss as Momma, passing the bathroom, tossed it into the toilet.

"Everybody seems so strange to me, even people I know, even my own momma and daddy—even Mammy." Lucius drifted off to sleep as he'd done every night for six years, since they'd lived on Avondale, having a friendly talk with God.

Stepping up to the tail end of the line to the ticket booth, a raised cage, wanting to hear Alan Ladd say to Veronica Lake, "Every guy's dreamed of meeting a girl like you. The trick is to find you," Lucius gazed up at the enormous poster perched on iron legs atop the marquee. Impressionistic blue contrasting with black gave the lettering and the illustration impact: a swath of blue linked Veronica Lake, looking scared, with Alan Ladd slugging a man who dropped a gun, with William Bendix in the background in a leather jacket, aiming an automatic. Stills in precise frames, gold dust glittery, surrounded smaller but large posters out front in the gilt facade under the bright red, solid marquee.

As a streetcar entered the carbarn through a narrow alley between the Bijou and the Algonquin Tavern, a little boy mimicked the cocky, cross-ankled pose of the freshly painted cutout poster of Bugs Bunny, taller than Lucius himself. The girl in the ticket booth, whom he often glimpsed as he walked past or rode on the streetcar, gave everybody a cold, haughty look, her face averted to conceal a splash of red across one cheek, but when Lucius reached up and put his nine pennies on the marble ledge, she looked straight down at him, her small mouth puckered, her square, stained jaw set. "How old are you?"

"Twelve."

"When will you be thirteen?"

"On my birthday."

"Don't get smart."

"I *came* to get a ticket to see Alan Ladd."

With a steady stare of contempt, she tapped the keys with her slender fingers and a red ticket spat at him from her copper-plated lap, and the Bijou became the last of Cherokee's twenty-eight theatres to believe what people often told Lucius: "You look young for your age."

Following the other kids, as though they were guides, across the cracked mosaic tile of the outside lobby, Lucius felt an amorphous fear, going into a theatre he did not know well, among kids who came from the five hills of Cherokee, kids from four to fifteen, none of whom he knew. Since he'd seen only a few movies at the Bijou, it seemed foreign, beyond his life, as if he were entering a special Bijou experience prematurely. The Bijou was somehow for other people, people who were superior to him because they'd had Bijou experiences he hadn't had.

Through rough-textured gold doors, he entered the outer lobby, walked on white and black tiles, a pattern different from the outside lobby, between two ornate marble benches and two elaborate still boxes showing scenes from *The Postman Always Rings Twice,* still at the Tivoli, Lana Turner and John Garfield huge on the poster, shadowy, he gray and tired-looking, she electric with platinum hair and a fat long, stark white cigarette in her puckered, glistening mouth, he offering his lighter, as if it were some secret potion. Up a few marble steps, between brass rails, shined to a luster, finger-smudged this morning, to gold doors, flung wide. A tall, handsome woman in a uniform, a soft blue coat that her breasts bulged out, iron gray hair cut short like Mary Astor, and a lingering smile, welcoming each kid, even Lucius.

In the grand lobby, Lucius stopped cold—behind the candy counter, too busy to notice him, Thelma—what was her last name?—Matlock!— waited on a cluster of kids, three deep. She'd lived in the half of the house on Beech Street that Momma rented out during the war when Lucius was nine, after Daddy went into the army. Despite her crossed eyes and dyed black hair, Thelma, in some ways, resembled Momma. Her body was plump, fleshy, fat at the hips, like Momma's. Round breasts under the blue uniform jacket, and bee-stung lips of the twenties that Lucius saw in old movie magazines. She had a pretty, lithe daughter a few years older than Lucius, Carolyn, whose eyes were only slightly crossed, whose breasts Lucius had watched fill out. Junior, her husband, a drunkard with acne scars, wore clothes just the other side of teen-

ager style. Thelma Matlock! Head down, Lucius worked into the moil
before the candy altar.

"What for you? Lucius! Well, I'll be! My, ain't you grown! You
getting to look more like your momma than you do your daddy. How is
she?"

"Okay."

"Your grandmother still have that cafe next to the Morning Bird
Coffee factory?"

"No, ma'am, she got her another one crost from the firehall."

"What *for* you, honey?" Same old high, baby voice that always
made him feel awkward.

"Oh, popcorn, I reckon." All the candy wrappers blurred in his
pleasant embarrassment. "And give me a Milky Way, please."

"Say, we startin' Bugs Bunny Club today."

"Yeah, I know. Boy! Well, see you after while."

"Okay, honey, have a good time."

Lucius remembered hating to hear her voice come through the
walls when she talked to sassy Carolyn or sullen, wordless Junior, or to
. . . . In the dark of the inner lobby, feeling the deep soft red carpet, aware
of the roar of voices and laughter and banging of seats and the glow
of the still boxes in the middle and at each end of the wide-flung,
narrow lobby, Lucius felt a stab of fear and guilt, remembering the
way he'd tormented Thelma's senile mother as she tried to iron clothes
for Lucius, Earl, and Bucky on Beach Street on hot summer days. He
always thought that if there is a hell, it exists to punish such motiveless
evil, especially in a kid who knew what he was doing. The guilt that
made him a fervent Christian at nine included, in prominence, that
incident. Standing in the middle of the aisle, surveying the turmoil of
squirming, aisle-galloping kids, Lucius had a hard knot in his throat
that hurt.

Walking down to the front where the red curtains, yellow-fringed,
were closed, Lucius turned and looked back up, aware that girls would
notice his pompadour, pushed forward to resemble Alan Ladd's, hoping
no tough guys would take his turned-up shirt collar as a challenge to fight.
The balcony that had seemed so mysterious and scary when he and
Luke watched *The Dawn Patrol* was a swarm of color, packed with
kids. The second balcony was too dark to see anything but the soles
of Negro kids' shoes on the rail. Seeing no one he knew down here,
Lucius went up to the first balcony.

In the last of three rows in front of the projection booth sat two
boys from Bonny Kate Junior High, glaring at Lucius. Maybe this year
he'd finally have to fight them. Way over at the other end of the cross
aisle, the light from the red-carpeted staircase and golden wall cast a

glow upward, creating a little stage where an usher stood, wearing a light blue waist jacket, a bow tie, dark blue trousers.

"Step back out of the aisle," said another usher, behind Lucius. The command made him angry, embarrassed, as when a safety patrol boy told him to step back up on the curb. But ushers were so privileged, able to see a movie ten times over, that Lucius could hardly comprehend them as real people. Even though he knew that Luke had gone to the aisles of the Hollywood Theatre out of the same bed from which he'd risen himself this morning, ushers seemed servants of the gods, transported each day from movie studios.

As Lucius walked, self-consciously, in front of the projection booth, below its dark windows and slots, toward the other side, drawn by the glowing light, one of the Bonny Kate boys said, "Hi, fart blossom!"

Lucius turned and struck an Alan Ladd stance. "I'll see *you* at Bonny Kate."

"Want us to throw your ass *off* this balcony, Shorty?"

"Where's your army?"

"Hey, Frank," said the other boy, "let's don't get throwed out. Just *got* here."

Sneering, Lucius walked on, waved to a girl he knew who sat with four boys, all wearing white socks, feet stuck up on the seat backs in front of them. Two girls came up the stairs into the light on the cross aisle, following their shadows. LaRue and Judy. Seeing Lucius startled LaRue, then she seemed afraid and stepped back closer to the usher, who said, "Step back out of the aisle, please."

As LaRue and Judy walked toward the other side of the balcony, the two smart-asses said something to her that made her ignore them as she passed, and he felt the urge to go over and knock them into next week. LaRue sat on the back row of the first tier, the cross aisle level with her shoulders. Lucius tried to stand and gaze around casually like Alan Ladd in a nightclub. "I said, Step back out of the aisle," the usher said.

Music: "Sioux City, Sue."

The curtain parted. The Bugs Bunny cutout poster now stood to the left of the forestage, and Terry Turner, WXOL announcer—the first time Lucius had seen him in the flesh—stood at the mike and introduced Mrs. Potter, a fat, sharp-faced woman whose short black hair made her head look too small for her body. She taught the audience how to sing the Bugs Bunny Club song to the tune of "Sioux City Sue," and then, in a first-grade teacher's voice, said, "And now, boys and girls, give a rousing welcome to our very first contestant, Loraine Clayboe."

The cheering and whistling and stomping made Lucius snarl. Among kids, he hated acting in unison, especially on cue from some grown-up. But he didn't like the booing from some smart alecks—he imagined how that would make this Loraine Clayboe feel. If she wasn't good, he'd stand still. If she deserved it, he'd clap.

A straw-mellow spot followed Loraine Clayboe, long naturally curly but peroxide blond hair, wearing a yellow, starched cotton sleeveless dress, a red rose pinned to her waist, black ballerina slippers, to the piano. She played and sang "Heartaches," and Lucius knew that he would love her the rest of his life. The clapping this time was for the quality of her singing, and Lucius's augmented the applause she bowed to. Glancing over the audience to observe the various reactions, Lucius caught LaRue staring at him.

Although Loraine Clayboe left the stage amid the applause, Lucius went downstairs, to be closer to her. By virtue of his intense response to her, he had a stronger claim on Loraine Clayboe than whoever may have brought her to the Bijou. He felt possessive about any kind of experience, very quickly, especially encounters with girls. Sometimes he walked straight toward such a girl, then veered away at the last moment.

Lucius sat in the back, aware of the handsome usher across the aisle, standing at his post, turned half toward the stage, arms folded, a flashlight in one hand, watching. The footlights reflected in his eyes, a smile like Errol Flynn's on his face, he seemed in control of himself.

Lucius enjoyed this new experience—kids with talent, singing, playing the piano, dancing on the stage of a special theatre. He hated school talent shows.

"And now, boys and girls," said Mrs. Potter, sounding worse than the woman on the "Let's Pretend" radio show he was missing by being at the Bijou, "give a warm welcome to—"

"Where's that shit-hook Tiller?"

Lucius turned and watched the Errol Flynn usher talk to the one from the balcony, who did his eyebrows like Sonny Tufts.

"Damned if *I* know. Elmo saw him uptown last night, drunker'n forty-'leven hells."

"Beat his ass. . . . How we goin' to lunch, by God?"

"I rubbed airplane glue on the inside of his dickey, 'i God." Lucius wondered what a dickey was.

"No shit?"

"Jerks it off—no chest hair."

Lucius heard fans whining, but packed bodies in constant commotion kept the theatre humid. Finished with his candy, he got up to get a drink. The fountain burped lukewarm dribbles. Kids still milled around in the lobby and hung on the candy counter.

Directly across the lobby from the ladies' room door, where the fountain sat, the door to an office stood open. An usher, taller than the others, wearing a slightly different uniform, a long blue jacket with dark blue trimming like the women's instead of waist-length, stripes down his trousers' legs, stood in the doorway, his back to Lucius. Behind the desk, facing out, a flabby man, thin blond hair and blushed skin, talked on the phone, fingertips stroking his forehead. Brightly lit, the scene looked very serious, an official office action, a hot view of the nerve center behind the Bijou luster. Jealous, Lucius felt he should be part of the scene.

From the fountain, Lucius aimed himself straight across the lobby at the office. Just as he started to veer left, the tall usher did a smart about-face, colliding with Lucius. "Sorry, partner." The usher joined Errol Flynn and Sonny Tufts in the inner lobby on the main aisle.

Lucius paused outside the office. The blond man sat behind his glass-topped desk, his head in his hands, a look of disgust on his face that turned quizzical when he saw Lucius.

"Don't need any ushers, do you?" asked Lucius, high on impulse, knowing it was unlikely, that he was being brazen.

The man stood up—the desk had concealed his paunch—and took up the blue coat draped over the back of his tan leather swivel chair. "How old are you?" Putting on his coat had some connection with putting the question. Lucius sensed that the man liked the audacity of a little kid asking for a big job.

"Fourteen in July," said Lucius, nervous, feeling ten.

"You have to be at least fifteen. You *look twelve*."

"People all the time tell me that."

"I don't think we can even outfit you. Elmo!" Lucius turned, watched the tall usher lope from the inner lobby to the office door, brace his hands on the gold gilt stucco outside and lean in over Lucius's shoulder. "We got anything back there to fit this boy?"

Elmo turned Lucius around, stepped back with a flourish, mugged *no*.

"My momma could make it fit. . . . Listen, I sure would like to work here, sir. Always wanted to be a theatre manager myself when I grow up."

"Have to wait for me to retire, then Elmo. . . . Ever work before?"

"Yes, sir. Picked pole beans when I was eight."

"Yeah?" said Elmo. "I never did pick pole beans myself. Maybe I ort to. I bet that builds character."

"I only did it for four days. But I've mowed enough lawns to stretch to Chattanooga, and I've had three paper routes since I was nine."

"Elmo, shut that door. Those screaming kids bring on my migraine." Elmo stepped out and shut the door behind him, and Lucius, imagining the manager looked nervous and slightly frightened most of the time, felt enclosed with him in the cramped office. "Your momma allow you to work after school? Can you show up at four o'clock?"

"Yes, sir. I get out at three and I can hop right on the streetcar."

Behind the man, to the left, the ceiling slanted, and to his right another door opened, and Lucius glimpsed a pretty Negro girl perched on a high stool, heard her say, "Mr. Hood, I needs a pack of quatuhs."

Hood opened the safe behind his desk under the staircase slant and handed a pack through the door and elbowed it shut. Lucius imagined the toy entrance on the side of the Bijou, with its own ticket booth, still racks and popcorn, candy counter, and pretty Negro girls climbing, climbing, to the peanut gallery, sitting high, snug, up under the gilded dome. Only three black theatres in Cherokee. Bijou, only theatre where whites and Negroes watched the same movie, together, because, he now realized, only the Bijou had two balconies.

Hood got up, opened the lobby door, leaned out, whisper-shouted, "Elmo. . . . Take this boy back and see if you can't outfit him. If you can, put him on the floor, if you can't"—Hood turned to Lucius—"come back in a year or two. What's your name, before I forget?"

"Lucius Hutchfield."

"Sounds like an alias," said Elmo.

"Sir, I have to carry papers at three o'clock—but I'll be through with it after Sunday."

"Then take off at two thirty. Pay's twenty-five cents an hour."

"Don't think I don't appreciate it, sir."

Following Elmo past the Errol Flynn usher, Lucius realized he'd miss turning in his bill at the *Messenger* office at one. Could they put him in the reform school? Turning left at the rounded corner of the inner lobby, Lucius looked at another still stand: COMING. CHARLES COBURN, DEAN STOCKWELL, and TOM DRAKE in THE GREEN YEARS. As the aisle sloped sharply past the exit doors, Lucius smelled the long brass handles and drifted toward dark velvet curtains with Alan Ladd's gait.

Holding a flashlight slightly behind him, Elmo lit the way for Lucius, down the slanting floor along the wall, then suddenly, his feet hit flat the level aisle that went through heavy velvet curtains, and then through a break in more drapes, he saw the chairs in the box seats, the fat brass rail, and light from the screen showed the faces of the audience, a perspective he'd never had on a theatre before. Seeing an usher go backstage had always made him jealous. Music he recognized as the opening of a Paramount movie filled the theatre out there, muffled back here. "This is the captain of the ushers' dressing room where *I* hang out," said Elmo. "Kind of a storeroom, too." Lucius tripped on some steps. "Watch your step, partner." Elmo's voice was deep, friendly, but a little intimidatingly all-knowing. "You'll learn to see in the dark." Backstage was a dark, shadowy place—dim pools of light, sacks piled up, sandbags hanging high over Lucius's head. *This belongs to me.*

Bright sunlight burst onto the backstage. "Shut that door!" Elmo whisper-shouted, running up the ramp as Loraine Clayboe came in, sideways. Then only a dim yellow light beside the door lit the ramp. It seemed strange—spotlighted on a stage awhile ago, then by the bright sun behind her golden hair, then almost a meager shadow in the yellow light, whispering, "I forgot my stuff." She took a package from a chair near one of the three black curtains that hung from long rods high up. Darkness soared among vague shapes and ladders and bags and ropes and walkways, the Phantom of the Opera gazing down through his gold mask upon Loraine Clayboe. Hugging her prize, she ran out again in a blaze of light.

Behind the screen an enormous black object, an exotic shape, mounted on a sort of truck, with a network of supporting arms, that must be the loudspeaker for the movie, jutted through a part in the longest drape. He followed Elmo behind the drape, along a bare brick wall. He glimpsed many doors, some small, some like enormous arches. Elmo slid back a heavy, thick steel door set on rollers. A narrow corridor, mellow yellow, lighted by yellow bulbs in the ceiling that was flaking. About three doors to the right, then they passed narrow stairs, then more doors. About six dressing rooms. Elmo opened a door onto a room full of uniforms hanging.

Elmo watching him undress, hang his shirt and pants on a hook, embarrassed Lucius. Forcing the brass buttons, he helped Lucius try on four stiff white celluloid collars that felt damp and sticky on his neck in the humid, windowless room. He kept seeing Loraine come through the stage door in a burst of light. A dickey turned out to be the stiff bib that stuck out from his chest as in a hundred comic movies about people in evening clothes. A black bow tie on an elastic band went with it. He felt silly. Stan Laurel, getting into a tux. Scratchy and clammy, the blue uniforms smelled of underarm sweat. The fourth one fit better than the others, but the sleeves were too long and the cuffs too bulky wide. Manipulating the suspenders, Elmo pulled up the trousers. The pants were too bunchy in the waist, the cuffs so flappy Lucius trod on them in back as he followed Elmo, who'd been popping wisecracks all along in a likable way, Lucius laughing nervously, back through the thick door, which he slid shut behind them, like a stone tablet over a secret passage in a jungle movie.

Flickering light from the screen revealed at moments a scary bank of electrical switches bigger than any Lucius had ever seen. As he passed behind the speaker, Alan Ladd's voice, muffled slightly by the thick dusty drape, said, "I'm going to find out who killed my wife."

"Okay, Lightnin', you're *on the spot*," said Elmo, pointing to the post where the handsome usher stood. "Let's go," Elmo said to Errol Flynn. Standing at the main aisle, On the Spot, Lucius watched them go backstage. Alan Ladd in Howard Da Silva's nightclub was about to say it to Veronica Lake. Waiting for it, Lucius became aware of the audience and watched and listened with them, thinking, I was sitting out there with *them* awhile ago. Alan Ladd looks at Veronica Lake: "Every guy's dreamed of meeting a girl like you. The trick is to find you."

Four kids at once came at Lucius, asking where the bathroom was, and when he stepped out into the main lobby to show them, Thelma, sacking popcorn, bugged her eyes and said, "The Lord have mercy, Lucius, where did you *get* that rig?"

"They hired me."

"That's wonderful, honey, but that outfit's miles too big for you."

Elmo and the handsome usher came out into the lobby in street clothes, looking like anybody else. The handsome usher still walked with the grace and controlled style of Errol Flynn, while Elmo loped along, stoop-shouldered and gangly. Lucius remembered selling extras around the Market House about Errol Flynn's trial for raping a girl.

On the Spot again, Lucius watched Alan Ladd open his eyes. He is lying on the floor, tied up. The hood with glasses sits near the lamp, soaking his feet, hurt in the fight Alan Ladd started when they first brought him to the remote shack. The pug-nosed hood has gone off somewhere. Loud crickets made the shack seem more isolated. The hood's misery seems to be subsiding, a look of relief on his face now, not the face of a hoodlum, but of a high school principal. Alan Ladd pushes the table over on the hood's toe, and the hood screams, and the audience roars with admiration. Lucius shook his head, awed by Alan Ladd's cleverness.

From his post, Lucius enjoyed watching Mrs. Atchley, her back toward him, reach for tickets as people came in. She was very statuesque, perfect posture, with an aristocratic poise and dignity, and listening to her voice was very soothing. He wondered what she would look like with long hair, like Greer Garson's.

Lucius imagined the Negroes up in the second balcony more keenly, conscious that together, without seeing each other, they were watching the same Alan Ladd, hearing him speak.

When *The Blue Dahlia* ended and the house lights came on, the kids ran out as if fleeing a fire. Lucius stood in the main lobby, looking for Loraine Clayboe, but missed her. He was glad the sight of himself in uniform surprised LaRue, coming down from the balcony with Judy. Bucky, chocolate smeared across his mouth, came down in the crowd, and Lucius ducked back into the inner lobby and patrolled the aisle, remembering Bucky on his hands and knees under the seats of the Hiawassee, scavenging for spilled popcorn.

The house lights faded out again, the Paramount News came on: JEWISH IMMIGRANTS TO PALESTINE INTERNED ON CYPRUS. A ship packed with Jews from concentration camps turned away from Palestine. Feeling sorry for the homeless Jews, his back turned to Paramount News, Lucius heard the announcer describe scenes in the Jewish war for independence in Palestine. The voice he'd heard all during his childhood evoked images of D-Day and the invasion of Normandy, and the crash of an airplane into the Empire State Building the same month the bomb blew Hiroshima to Kingdom Come, and King Kong on top of the Empire State Building, grabbing biplanes, crushing them in his paws. Lucius sensed that someone was walking up behind him. Pale blond hair and a pink face with white eyebrows startled him.

"You read about Father Divine marrying that girl named Edna Rose?"

"Huh?" Lucius saw that he wore an usher's uniform, and his hands, too, were pink. "No. I mean, yeah, I—"

"Be not afraid. 'Tis only I. Hood sent me up to scare the niggers so they wouldn't act up, and to keep me from scarin' the kids down here. I bet you think it's fun livin' in a boathouse. Do like this." He stretched the skin over his forehead above his nose with thumb and forefinger. "Now do like I do."

Touching the stretched skin, Lucius said, "Eoooowwww. Feels like a corpse," remembering his little brother, Ronald Dennis, and Gran'paw Charlie.

"That's the point. . . . I'd rather work at the Bijou than Randall's Funeral Home." Embalming fluid must smell like the Listerine on the albino's breath.

"Did you hear on the radio that Tito apologized for shooting down five of our pilots over Yugoslavia?"

"No, I didn't catch that."

"I hate to read. It hurts my weak eyes so bad." He wandered vaguely away.

The Paramount cameraman swiveled around and aimed his lens at the sparse audience, making Lucius feel part of the world that impressive ending evoked.

"Say, how long's that albino been ushering here?" Lucius asked Thelma.

"He's new, too. Hired last week. There's just a terrible shortage of men until all the boys get back from the services. That's how come Mr. Hood hired you, too, I reckon. Albinos don't live long."

As *The Blue Dahlia* started again, a young couple came in holding hands and popcorn, staring at Alan Ladd. Lucius straightened his tie. "How far down, please?"

The young man said to his girl, shyly, "Where you want to set, honey?"

"Oh! anywhere," she said, shyly.

Lucius expected them to follow him down the aisle. At a row containing two empty seats, he shined his light. They were still up the aisle, staring at the screen. When Lucius reached them, they were feeling for a seat, blinded by the sunlight they'd come out of and the different light on the screen. He shined his flash to help them see the seats. "Pardon me," said the boy, shyly. "Pardon me," said the girl, shyly. They were backing away from the only seat in the row. They walked ahead of Lucius, who skipped by them and, backing down the aisle, shined the flashlight at their feet. "We'll try the other aisle," said the girl, smiling. Lucius skipped ahead of them, lighting them back up to the Spot. Sweat stuck the dickey to his naked chest. No wonder they called it "the Spot" —the busiest spot in the theatre.

Slowly, Lucius picked up a sense of his duties: Keep the aisle clear in case of fire. Keep the people's feet off the seats. Maintain perfect quiet at all times. And enforce the no smoking regulation. Keeping an eye on the screen wasn't one of his duties. "Face front, Lucius, always face front," said Mr. Hood, shoving his lank blond hair up off his forehead, "so you can greet the patrons. And don't slouch."

But when weird, discordant music cued William Bendix's confession for killing Alan Ladd's wife, Lucius turned and watched. "She kept picking at that flower."

Stepping over the sill into the coal house, a stack of stills in his arms, Lucius saw Gran'paw Charlie astride a mule, pulling the red circus wagon down the alley, years before Lucius was born. Now it was full of coal and the kind of stuff other people stored in attics. Lucius reached behind the coal-dust-streaked cream-yellow baby bed. Mammy had hidden Gran'paw's holster in the back of the radio that had burned out before he was murdered, and Bucky had found it again. "You all'll wear it out, or lose it, playing," Mammy'd said. Lucius lifted the cool German helmet Daddy had sent from Belgium, remembered the feel of the soft leather when he'd thrust his hand into the holster and raised it to his nose to sniff, remembered that last summer Earl'd found it under the helmet where Lucius had hidden it, and sold it.

Before daybreak, lusting to handle and look carefully at each still, Lucius had raced down the steep hill and over the dangerous narrow bridge where many cars had wrecked and zoomed past the sawdust pile where one of Uncle Luke's childhood friends had suffocated, and he'd known he would never forget that last time on the route. "I quit," Lucius had told Dusty yesterday afternoon when he handed him six pink slips for missing. A favorite exit line in his family, on both sides. The great moment all jobs existed for. "Well, the sonofabitch fired me" was another classic line. Played with as much vigor from the victim's as from the victor's point of view. Either way, it provided an emotionally charged evening. Lucius had reenacted it at Mammy's cafe, where Momma had often replayed the scene so well herself. "They made me an usher at the Bijou."

As he'd passed the dim Hiawassee Theatre in the blue mist of morning, the sight made him feel sleepy, and the shadowy ticket booth where pretty girls had sat vaguely aroused prickles of sex. Pee Wee wore overalls and went barefoot as Lucius showed him the route. His nose runny, he never said a word, except "I'm scared a niggers," and looked glassy-eyed as Lucius tried to tell him about Sam Gulliver's adventures.

Coming back up the alley, bumping over the rocks and ruts on his Western Flyer, no empty satchel wadded in the wire basket, looking over five backyards to Mammy's victory garden where she moved in the early light among the hollyhocks and cornstalks, Lucius had felt more sad than relieved. The end of Clayboe Ridge, and the fresh ink and paper smell and the bright colors of Li'l Abner on the outside starting off the tone and feeling of Sundays, and the sweet, dewy moment of flipping fast to the Sunday magazine section and the photographs and ads of movies to come. He wished he hadn't sold the satchel to Pee Wee, so he could hang it on a nail on the charred wall of the circus-wagon coal house. He'd squirmed through Sunday school at the Clinch View First Baptist Church, Uncle Luke's church, where he'd married Hazel.

Hearing the soft, rhythmic clucks of the chickens outside the coal house made Lucius see the speckled hens, settled snugly in the soft loam, and imagine them in the hedge tree where they roosted at night. He liked to be in under the ceiling of leaves and hedge berries, or perched on the long low limbs like rafters, where the strong smell—chicken squat, rotten sour mash, and the slop Mammy tossed over the fence, and a cavey smell he imagined came from the old outhouse and the coal house, made a zone of secrecy. He had grown up afraid he'd step accidentally on the sinkhole where the outhouse had stood and fall to China.

Up at the house, Mammy and Momma were fussing at each other, screaming sporadically at Bucky. Daddy sat on the long grey wooden bench under the leaves of the oak tree that was stuffed with plaster where the trunk had rotted, a rose trellis in full burst between him and the house.

Lucius often crawled over and under things and squatted in cluttered corners of the circus-wagon coal house, looking out, the door framing the long yard and garden that two rows of hedges, higher than his head, enclosed. Before the fire, it was only a storage place, but now chunks of coal, tossed through the high window in the back lay under his bare feet. Hanging from hooks in the cobwebbed ceiling and nails on the wall all kinds of junk: Grandpaw's night watchman lantern, hedge clippers, hand sickles, rusty buckets full of rusty nails and screws, Luke's combat boots left behind the time he went AWOL, white porcelain doorknobs, bedsprings, broken chairs, Mason jar lids, old milk bottles, chicken feed troughs, bottomless coal buckets, a shovel with a broken handle that pinched, the yellow, wooden-slatted baby bed Lucius used to confuse with the casket Gran'paw lay in. Lucius put on and buckled Uncle Luke's mildewed combat boots.

Bucky was afraid to go into the circus wagon alone, but when they all three played, afraid any minute it would burst into flames again, it was spooky fun. Lucius and Bucky were playing with little cars in soft dirt at the edge of the garden under the shade of cornstalk blades when they heard boots in the coal grit on the sill of the circus wagon and looked up at Earl, wearing the German helmet, Uncle Luke's combat boots, a coal-dust stain under his nose, his black hair combed down over his forehead, the spitting image of Adolf Hitler, barking, "Heil Hitler!" Watching Erich von Stroheim in *Five Graves to Cairo* at the Hiawassee the summer Earl ran away, Lucius had thought of him.

Salesman at the Smoky Lumber Company next to the baseball fields where the tents had gone up, Gran'paw had paid five dollars for the wagon, left behind with a broken axle, repaired it, and pulled it home with an old plow horse he borrowed from a farmer near the factory. The procession across town, Uncle Luke riding on top, sloppy drunk, attracted as much attention going down Grand Boulevard as the circus parade down Sevier Street had. When Uncle Luke and Gran'paw waved at Mammy passing in a streetcar, she pretended not to know them. As they came up the alley, she yelled from the back porch, "You ain't bringing that contraption into *my* yard!" Without a word, Gran'paw parked it, the front door facing the back of the house, next to the old outhouse sinkhole and the chicken coop.

The walls were charred black now. When Lucius was one and they were living in the little shotgun house on Park Street, on the sloping floor of which he'd learned to walk, they were visiting Mammy, and Daddy went off with Uncle Luke and came back drunk alone, and Gran'paw Charlie made Daddy go sit in the coal house in the December cold to sober up. He stumbled, so the story goes, over the bent cornstalks and withered pole-bean vines and sat in the red and white wagon, watching the snow come down to make a white Christmas, and smoked one cigarette too many. He came back up to the house, grinning, and said to Gran'paw, "Charlie, I'm sober as a judge." From the window by the stove that made the kitchen suffocatingly hot in the summer, Mammy screamed, "Lord God, he's set my circus wagon afire!"

The wheels were yard ornaments now, the tongue a fence post, and the wagon was jacked up on blocks of marble from the quarry in Marble Station. And the family photographs that they'd stored in the circus wagon were now in the bottom drawer of Mammy's chiffonier, burnt around the edges, water-mottled, brown from fire, smoke, and age.

The picture that made Lucius love Gran'paw Charlie more than anything else did came to mind again. In glowing sunlight, he sat cocked back in a chair, braced against the wall, wearing a light hat, a dark vest, grey striped trousers with that wide brown belt and the gun and holster, and Lucius saw the tops of the shoes he'd worn himself last year because he had his feet resting on the rungs of the chair: little chubby man with a soft face, a gentle, sad mouth, misty eyes that looked out of the picture at you as though he was wondering why in the world you'd want to take a picture of him. Clearest in the picture now were the big bottle of sweet milk he held in one hand, a coconutted marshmallow cookie in the other. Snapped right in the glass factory watchman's shed where his old enemy murdered him a few weeks later, during the Depression. Wearing the holster secretly, crouching in the coal house, Lucius had sworn to find the killer and shoot him. Everybody always said Lucius took more after his Gran'paw than even Luke did. Why hadn't *Luke* stalked the killer? Maybe he had.

He opened the cedar chest built before Lucius was born. When he'd slept in it on top of old quilts at the foot of Mammy's bed, staying all night, he was always afraid the lid would slam, shutting him in, smothering him. Full now of his and Bucky's and Earl's baby clothes. And since spring, it hid all his writings and his movie magazines. He flipped through the notebook that held "The Face of a Chinaman," enjoying the diminishing bulk of it against his thumb, the longest story he'd ever written, unfinished on page 63.

Taking out all his magazines and setting them on top of a junked icebox, Lucius noticed Uncle Luke's portfolio of cartoons. "When I come home, I'm gonna go to art school and become the greatest cartoonist in the world." Lucius looked through the cartoons, ashamed to feel that he could draw better than Uncle Luke now. He was delighted to find again Luke's old diary, in the back of the portfolio. He'd found it last summer in the back of a drawer in Uncle Luke's bedroom. "Today I met Hazel. She's for me." "Ted got drafted, poor guy." "Red says some big lummox is after my ass for running off with his girl at the Inferno." Broke off in March 1942 when he joined the infantry. The pages bore only the date, leaving the day and the year to be written in. So Lucius had started it up again with his own entries on April 1, 1945.

Lucius backed into an old rockerless wicker rocking chair, conscious that his childhood was "gone with the wind."

April 1, Dear Dialry, I went to the show. April 2, Pud and I built a fire behind Larue's on the railroad. It was pretty cold today. April 3, I walked home with Marion Cassidy and let her have "Blue Waters" for her mother to read. April 4, Walked home with Marion. In school Larue and I had a fuss and I sung "And her tears flowed like wine" to her when she cried. I went to her house to apolise to her. April 5, I wrote one chapter of "Across the Snow." April 6, After sunday school me and Pud made a hide out. April 7, I was sick at my stomach and stayed home from school. P. S. Daddy sent us home Greman hats and things. April 8, I wore my new shoes to the show and saw The Postman Didn't Ring with Richard Travis and Brenda Joyce. April 9, I payed no attion to Larue. We had a show at school. I walked home with Marion and Pud and we went up to his house and wrote our show— The Three Stoogers Go West—and cleaned up his mothers house. April 10, I went to the show. The Adventures of Mark Twain with Fredrick March was on. He fell in love with this girl's picture. Then he had a whole bunch of adventures out West, dreaming of her—O'Livia—as his perfect woman. Her daddy didn't think he was good enough to marry her. He got famous just telling stories—even in India. A good ol' show. April 11, Changed seats with mary. I had to stay in for Mrs. Coatsworth. April 12, I asked Dusty for a job. He gave me Clayboe Ridge. April 13, I stayed home all day and bought a movie book and a funny book. April 14, I beat up Walter Ford. April 15. We start frist aid today. Pud and Warren and we went to the woods and played commandos and build a fire. And played in the tile factory. April 16, Walked home with Betty Lou. Dear Dialry you will hear a lot about Betty Lou from no on. Oh that doll. April 17, Got up early and went to join the YMCA. Went to see Here Comes the Waves Betty Hutton, Bing Crosby, Sonny Tufts was in it. April 18, Marion got mad at Betty Lou and she is jelous of me and Betty Lou. Went to Puds. Betty Lou likes me alot.

Eager to count his new movie stills and magazines, Lucius skipped ahead.

August 20, Dusty woke me up early it was still dark outside to sell extras. Truman dropped the adam bomb on the Japs. . . . August 30, I got sick in the Hiawassee and the Chief had to come and get me. Crime school was on. Humphrey Bogart and the Dead End kids.

Severe gutache had seized him and he'd sweat and felt he was going to die, and with his belt unbuckled, his pants unbuttoned, he'd climbed the aisle, bent over like an old man, passing LaRue who was just coming in with her Momma and Daddy and big sister, and he'd called Mammy's cafe and the Chief had come in his Chevrolet, and Momma'd given him an enema. He was always constipated that year, got fierce bellyaches.

His entries stopped August 31, 1945. In the September 1 slot, Lucius wrote Sunday, 1946: "My destiny began yesterday." He counted the stills. Like skin. The magazines. A different skin texture. The effluvium of old magazines evoked the aroma of girls' hair, and the starched blouses of the Woodbury-soaped girls was like the new movie magazines on the racks in the drugstore where he often knelt, waiting for Dusty to dump the *Messengers*. "This girl Beverly on my paper route gave me 587 stills (photographs) and 114 movie magazines to go with my 33." He went back through the diary and counted the movies he'd seen in 1945. One hundred and twenty in five months.

He sought and found the still from *Frenchman's Creek* and ached to know exactly when he first saw the movie. He loved the sound of the man's voice in the preview: "Daphne du Maurier's best-selling novel of adventure on the high seas, *Frenchman's Creek*." Sometime in the fall of 1944, after Luke was reported missing. When school started Tuesday, he'd look for Marion Cassidy in the halls. The possibility that she'd lost "Blue Waters" nauseated him.

Lucius skimmed back through the diary to June 1945. June 11. At the Hiawassee, he'd first laid eyes on Cornel Wilde, a new actor, incredibly beautiful creature, who seemed to come straight out of the past. Playing Frederic Chopin. The names alone were almost enough to make the impact. Even the Technicolor seemed more luminous, vivid, precise. Disorienting, though, to see Paul Muni, whom Lucius often remembered as Scarface, doing an old man, Chopin's teacher. Merle Oberon, incredibly beautiful, resembling LaRue even more in some ways than Vivien Leigh did. George Sand was something new in Lucius's life. A soul mate, looming over the life of the artist, a figure who had, he sensed, stood dimly in the wings of his own dreams long before. Like Alexis Smith as Fredric March's wife in *Mark Twain* the year before. But George Sand heightened Chopin-Wilde's romantic aura. What Cornel Wilde mainly bodied forth for him in his sensitive face and voice as he moved through Chopin's life was the artist. Mark Twain was simply a storyteller. Revolution. A bizarre romance. Exertions of willpower, lunges of audacity. Sudden bursts of creativity. Postures of anguish and romantic turmoil. Immediately after seeing *A Song to Remember*, Lucius started his second literary effort, a biography of Chopin that ran to twenty pages, and last winter he'd rewritten it, and again this spring, and decorated the cover with a drawing of Chopin he made from a photo in a reference book. Too caught up in the momentum of outpouring stories, he'd written no more than one version of anything since. Lucius found stills from *A Song to Remember* and *Leave Her to Heaven*.

Last fall, *Leave Her to Heaven* exposed Lucius to Maine. When Bar Harbor burned that year in the newsreels and on the radio, Lucius imagined nature expressing outwardly the inward turmoil of people on the screen. Gene Tierney tosses herself down the stairs in their cottage to abort her child by Cornel Wilde. Cornel Wilde became almost as thrilling as Alan Ladd, though in a poetic, soulful way, and Maine took on the lingering romantic aura of Chopin and became Lucius's paradise on earth, even though he knew that when Mammy finally took him to the Smoky Mountains, Maine might pale. Though he'd seen neither the Smokies nor Maine, he was in awe of the information that a trail started in the Smokies and went straight on up into Maine.

A Song to Remember and *Leave Her to Heaven* were not total discoveries, but accidental catalysts, culminating expressions of the notions, attitudes, inclinations he'd always had. But they were turning points. They were not stories he could retell at recess on rainy days, backed up against the blackboard, where kids watched the stories he narrated like movie scenarios. He couldn't leap from Buck Jones and Zorro and Laurel and Hardy to Chopin and George Sand and to Gene Tierney aborting her baby. He sensed now that his awareness that he couldn't tell *A Song to Remember* and *Leave Her to Heaven,* not even *Frenchman's Creek,* compelled him into the habit of writing that replaced his compulsive storytelling. Having ceased to tell them, lacking an appropriate situation or audience, feeling too old, he'd shut his mouth and pushed his pencil until his right thumb became soft, and a hump rose on his second finger, getting long, epic-scoped, years-spanning, cast-of-twenty scenarios down.

Someone shifted gears on Prater, the next street over behind the circus wagon. Lucius listened, hearing Luke's motor. He imagined a glimpse of the '38 Dodge through Mr. Stookebury's bean poles. Just in from Oak Ridge firehall, the Chief was giving Luke's "chariot" its weekly spin around the block, "to work up her circulation." Ever since Bucky, imitating Earl in Gran'paw Charlie's Packard, disengaged the handbrake and pushed in the clutch and the Dodge rolled a hundred feet until the open door caught on the telephone pole, the Chief kept it locked, the keys stayed in his pocket.

When tractors came to Anderson County to clear the land to build Oak Ridge, as during the Depression the TVA had cleared land nearby for Norris Dam, Chief Buckner and his fleet of fire trucks had been on the scene. As the prefab town grew, he'd stayed on, a federal employee, knownig all along no more about what they were making than Lucius did, reading about it, along with the rest of Cherokee and the world, in the extras Lucius sold that morning last August. Maybe after they visited Cades Cove in the Smokies where Mammy was born, the Chief would show him Oak Ridge, too. But the thought of the Chief taking Gran'paw Charlie's place made Lucius feel sad.

Uncle Luke's motor faded off toward Crazy Creek bridge. "Running on the same tank of gas Luke put in her the day he left," the Chief liked to say, each Sunday after he parked it.

Lucius closed Luke's diary, and set it aside, vowing to write in it each night until Uncle Luke returned or it ran out.

But as Lucius packed away his magazines, stills, and writings and drawings in the old clothes box, Uncle Luke stayed on his mind. They are all out in the front yard, inside the enclosure of hedges, lying on quilts on the grass, looking up at the clouds, listening to "The Green Hornet" through the open window, and Lucius hears somebody walking on rocks and raises up and sees Uncle Luke coming down the alley across Holston Street, wearing blue denim fatigues. "It's Luke!"

"Where?" screams Mammy, as they all raise up and Luke, grinning, lifts his round blue fatigue hat. " 'Fore the Lord God, the youn'un's gone AWOL."

Earl jumps the hedge, his long legs in knickers, and Uncle Luke sails his hat into the air and Earl chases it down.

Lucius's last glimpse of Uncle Luke was against a patch of blue sky when one flap of the cardboard box he sat in, cramped, on the sidewalk beside Peck's store, where a streetcar was turning, opens, and Uncle Luke, wearing his rich brown cunt cap, looks down at him. "What you doing in that box, boy?" He smiles that crooked, cocky but sweet way. His black curly hair, his lucid blue eyes, his dark skin. "You get on home before dark, you hear? I got to head back for camp after supper." Uncle Luke closes the lid, and in the soft dark, Lucius says aloud, "See you tonight, Uncle Luke." And he sees "camp" as a bunch of men, all vaguely resembling Uncle Luke, sitting around fires in the woods among tents, even though he'd seen the real thing—James Cagney in *The Fighting Sixty-Ninth*. A few minutes later, Uncle Luke's hand pokes a pair of red paraffin lips, full of cherry juice, through the flaps and it drops into his lap. "Luke's mad at *you*, boy, for not seeing him off," they all tell him when he runs into the house, having forgotten until midway through the third showing of *The Mark of Zorro*, when it occurred to him Uncle Luke looked like Tyrone Power. They are all listening to the Judy Canova show, their eyes red from crying.

Lucius wanted to make them love him as much as they loved Uncle Luke. Then he felt guilty for being envious of Uncle Luke and guilty for failing to do anything to prevent his being missing at Salerno or being buried among thousands of graves identically the same, no memorial in Cherokee except the red star service flag in the window beside the red star card telling the iceman how many pounds to chip off. For a while, he'd been determined to become the rich and famous cartoonist Uncle Luke had dreamed of being, but now maybe he would atone by becoming a writer and making them all rich and proud.

When the sun went in and the light grew dim, Uncle Lucius looked around the circus wagon at all the shapes, surfaces, textures. As if memorizing. And with the musty clothes and coal and rust, he inhaled the smell of rain about to start.

Two years ago, when everybody was gone, he'd started writing at the kitchen table. Last summer, after writing partway into "Glory in a Sanctuary," he'd seen a resemblance between the burnt-out cathedral, in which his hero had taken refuge from the Chilean police, and the circus-wagon coal house—the Foster-Hutchfield attic, since the shack Gran'maw Foster built had neither attic nor basement. It became Lucius's sanctuary.

As grey as the wall itself, like an insect with protective coloration, Luke's old sled clung to the charred wall, hung by a cord from a big nail beside the door, one rung warped by the impact when Luke's pal, famous for having made an enormous, beautiful flag for their secret club, zipped down Breedin Hill into the back of a lumber truck and ran a two-by-four into his head. Lucius took it down off the wall and sat on the cedar chest and opened his fourth notebook, fat with new wide-lined, side-ruled Blue Horse notebook paper, and, with sunlight coming througn the one window, over which Gran'paw Charlie had nailed the grate of a broken stove, falling on the page and his knees and the grey, worn sled, began the first chapter of "The Sea and the Sand" or "While the Sea Remains," by Luke Scott, using a new pen name, feeling as if it made Mammy's belief she'd hear Luke blow the Dodge's horn late one night more real. Dedicating it to LaRue. The first time he'd ever let one of the characters tell the story himself, hearing Alan Ladd's voice.

I lay there smoking, waiting for the man. He came and I layed him out. I went down stairs and two seamen went up. I walked outside and saw the row boat glide out from under the dock. I had shanghied my brother for five-thou.

I had hated my brother and visa-versa. I had owed a debt to Jonathan Crockett, whom I've never seen, and was told to pay at a certain time. I didn't have the money so I made arangements for a kidnapping of my rich brother. This was suggested by a slimey little stooge of Crockett's. Now it was done.

And the stooge was waiting for me. He presented me with a black piece of satin.

"Blindfold yourself with this, then follow me. By the way, it's against the rules for you to strike me."

"You seem to know all the rules, Buster."

"I've played this game many times before. And the name is not Buster."

We walked quiet a distance before I relized that we had been walking in circles. I guess he had done it to make me think that we had gone ferther than the place to where he was taking me really was. Finely, we came to some steps. When at the bottom of the stairway, he warned me to watch my head. When my skull glazed a two-by-four I relized what he had meant by the warning.

Then my feet came upon what I belived to be a board walk. Under the boardwalk and all around it I could smell the ocean and hear it splash against the bank. I then knew that I was under the dock. I heard a trap door squeak open. The little man was breathing down my neck now. I could smell his bath powder. He nudged me with the gun giving me the sign to walk down the steps.

I had not gone more than four yards when someone planted a black-jack in the back of my head. It was as if I were a light bulb and someone had cut the switch off.

The next thing I knew I was on the floor of a cave, my seamans coat was dusty with rich dirt. The back of my head felt like a maternity ward full of crying babies. I was lying on my chest my face buried in the dirt. I looked up moving my head and glanced about the cave.

Off to one corner the little man who as I so vaguly remembered, was setting with his back against the wall of the cave, cleaning his nails. Katty corner was a cot and on it, sleeping soundly, was a man of the sea; his hair was bushy and one of his ears was red where he had slept on it too long.

I managed to lift my neck another joint to find out who sat at the table in front of me. He was a tall man with an indian face. His long black boots expanded a great distance from under the table and his heels were buried in the dirt not far from my face. Then to my startled surprise my eyes fell upon a shocking sight. Lying under the table with his neck across the foot of the indians boots, was a huge black panther, his glassy eyes starring right at me.

The rain on the tin roof made Lucius feel melancholy. He put the notebook in the cedar chest on top of the stills and magazines and, still wearing Uncle Luke's AWOL combat boots, went outside and sat under the hedge tree among the chickens. Through the leaves and hedge berries and cornstalks, he watched Mammy in the Chief's black raincoat tie a chicken's legs to the clothesline, near the prop pole, saw its neck off with a butcher knife, step back, suddenly, as though she had seen a black widow spider, and, still as a statue, bent a little, rain glistening on her back, watch the chicken thrash and bleed.

When the sun came out, glittering among the hedge leaves, Lucius went up to the house. The only entrance from the back was to Luke's room, so Mammy handed food out the window to Lucius, and Momma and Mammy spread Sunday dinner out on an old wooden table Gran'maw Foster had brought down out of the Cumberland Mountains and they all sat under the mimosa tree and ate fried chicken and green beans with shellies and whole new potatoes and candied yams and lemonade and corn bread and peach pie, almost everything out of the garden at the back, and the flies did too.

"Well, I wouldn't be surprised if Luke or Earl was to come walking right up that alley," said Mammy, in her high-pitched, mock-crying voice.

"Why?" Lucius, Bucky, Daddy, and the Chief followed Momma's gaze up the alley.

"*Had* bread," said Mammy, "and *took* bread."

After dinner, Lucius listened to Sammy Kaye's orchestra with Don Cornell singing "It Isn't Fair" on the radio in the living room and drew pictures of the characters in "While the Sea Remains," casting Alan Ladd as Sam Gulliver. When he lived on Avondale, his hand was a magnet on the Webb Park playground. Even grown-ups and the art director, a tall blonde, who said she was his sweetheart, watched him draw Dick Tracy, Flash Gordon, Captain Marvel, the Green Hornet, and his old hero Roy Rogers.

Bucky kept begging Lucius to draw a picture of him. "I'm gonna hunt your movie pictures and hide 'em from you, if you don't."

"Yeah, and I'll be hunting your ass, too."

Bucky's threat made Lucius so nervous he couldn't concentrate. He kept going to the kitchen window to look down the yard through the cornstalks at the circus wagon. The fifth time, he saw Bucky go in. Lucius ran outside, down the garden path, the hedge flicking against his shoulder, and grabbed Bucky by the back of his shorts.

"This ain't *your* coal house!" Bucky yelled.

Lucius pulled him backward to the doorway but he held on to the narrow frame. As Lucius pulled and slapped at his arms, Bucky screamed and cried and whined.

"You all hersh that squallin'," Mammy yelled. "Irene, you gonna keep them hellions quiet? It's Sunday everywheres else but here!"

"Bucky," yelled Momma, "you better not let me hear another squawk out of you today!"

"Lucius's beatin' on me!"

"Lucius, honey, jump on your bike and whiz over to Howell's for me some Stanback Headache Powder!"

"Okay, but make Bucky get away from my stuff."

"Come up to this house, Bucky, this second!"

When Lucius returned from Howell's, Momma said, "I need a double dose now." Bucky'd whined around the house until he'd made her so nervous she'd slapped him, and he'd shot out the front door and up Holston Street toward Beech where Emmett King lived. "Hop on your bike and bring him back home."

"Momma, I got more to do in life than run after Bucky ever' breath I take."

"You ain't gonna be *able* to breathe if you don't hit the road."

Almost crying, Lucius viciously mounted his bike, and it became the Western Flyer in action. Joe Campbell on Beech Street told him he'd seen Bucky and Emmett get on a streetcar. Lucius hid his bike behind First Baptist Church, confident no one would steal from a church, and caught the next streetcar.

When Lucius was in the fifth and sixth at Clinch View Elementary, Bucky, whose grade let out earlier, would slip into the back row of Lucius's last class and wait, because Momma was at work and Lucius had to take care of him. Bucky wanted to go wherever Lucius went, but sometimes, sick of Bucky tagging along, he and his buddies would sneak away from him. Bucky wandered up and down the streets and alleys of the neighborhood, alone, looking for buried treasure in trash cans. He loved to watch racks at filling stations go up and shooosh down, and press the button on the air hose. He'd sneak into car junkyards and play all day, trying out the driver's seats, turning the moldy keys, and looking through shattered windshields at imaginary six-lane highways. The single seat up front across from the streetcar conductor was his favorite.

After the Hutchfields moved to Mammy's, the Kings moved to Beech Street, three doors down from Lucius's old house. Emmett became not only a buddy but a link with the old neighborhood Bucky and Lucius had both missed, where the whole family had last been together. Emmett lived in a toy house with two short brothers, a short daddy, square as the railroad ties he laid, and a tall sister and a tall mother. Emmett's stoop must have been shaped by the low ceilings.

Lucius often glimpsed Bucky and Emmett, Mutt and Jeff, Laurel and Hardy, George and Lenny in *Of Mice and Men* that Lucius and Bucky had seen at the Hiawassee years ago, walking at a distance, Emmett slouching, Bucky slapping along skinnily, down a street, up a hill, through somebody's yard, along Crazy Creek where Fartso the Whale lived and where Lucius was afraid Bucky would drown.

Lucius chased them through the tile factory, or into the woods, or up on Clayboe Ridge, and usually they eluded him, but sometimes Lucius'd be on his paper route, and he'd see them in some alley, rooting in the trash cans, and he'd streak between the houses on his Western Flyer, chase them down the alley, gain on clomping Emmett, leap on him like Zorro from his horse, and ride him down and beat him up, taking out on Emmett his guilt for deserting Bucky. "Goddam your ass, I better not ever catch you with my little brother again or I'll kill your soul!" Even though Bucky seemed to be the brains of the outfit, it made Lucius sick and angry and frustrated to imagine Emmett maybe doing nasty things to Bucky, and he tried not to, but when he lit into them, those images were behind his fists, in the slapping palms of his hands, and the toes of his shoes. If he caught Bucky, who was frail and skinny but fast as a jackrabbit, Lucius would spank him or take a switch to him and send him off toward Holston Street or put him on a streetcar on Sevier, and watch Emmett fade into one vista and Bucky into another. Seeing them again an hour later one time, Lucius suspected that they must've reconnoitered every time he split them up. Lucius always felt tough beating up such a big and older boy, but after a while he felt ashamed and depressed. Emmett wasn't an idiot, just vigorously backward, and Lucius wondered why it never seemed to enter his numb skull that if he exerted a little of his bull-like muscular system, he could break Lucius like a bird.

Bucky failed the first and second grades, and when Bucky was finally in the third, the principal called Momma more often. The truant officer, a stern-faced, grey-haired lady, who Lucius later discovered was a kindly woman, said Bucky would have to be committed to Ephraim Lee Institute for wayward children if parental supervision was not possible. Even with Daddy home again and back in Hutchfield Bakery, Momma *had* to work, because now Mammy said they had to move. Earl might come home anytime, and Mammy was sick of not having privacy with Chief Buckner. So Momma whipped Bucky when he layed out and threatened him with Ephraim Lee, and she tried, but failed, to get the police to restrain Emmett, who was exempt from school. But between Bucky and Emmett was a bond that nobody in the family nor any specter of authority could weaken. Bucky himself seemed unable to link yesterday with today and today with tomorrow—to see that he was drawing nearer and nearer the home for wayward children.

"Symphony, symphony of love . . ." Lucius sang, his cheek against the grill over the open streetcar window. Next Saturday, in uniform, On the Spot, Loraine Clayboe would see him standing at the back under the balcony and sing "Heartaches" right to him, over rows of heads. "Sam, where are you going?" "To kill your husband," said Lucius, sending the voices of Marina Crockett and Sam Gulliver out into the humid air.

As the streetcar approached the main intersection of Grand and Sevier, two men from the workhouse were trimming the grass around the black iron fence that kept kids like Bucky from trampling the grass on the Cherokee Indian mound, where a neon sign lit up the action of a woman lifting a Coca-Cola to her lips. As the streetcar curved between the mound and the courthouse that stood on a bluff above the River Street slums and the Tennessee River, Lucius remembered the time before the war when Daddy on the workhouse gang looked up from cutting the grass into Lucius's eyes as he watched from the streetcar window and put his finger to his lips, grinning shyly.

Lucius rode past the giant carbarn door and got off in front of the Pioneer. A four-storey, ancient, formerly legitimate theatre where Mammy had seen Mrs. Fisk perform and where Friday night wrestling matches now drew the kind of people who hung around Market Square, the Pioneer, green paint scaling, sat directly across from the Bijou, three times as wide, its seven glass doors throwing a wash of variable light across the front of the Bijou. Watching wrestling matches each Friday night, Lucius always imagined John Wilkes Booth shooting Lincoln in there.

Lucius crossed over to the Bijou, thrilling to the sight of JOHN GAR-FIELD AND LANA TURNER IN THE POSTMAN ALWAYS RINGS TWICE on the marquee, BIJOU in fat white letters. An old theatre, but well kept up, not even on the verge of being run-down, the Bijou was not like the Pioneer —its elegance not soot-crusted, spit-slimed, not glutted inside with tobacco smoke. Mammy had told him of the Bijou's own glorious past in the legitimate theatre, but he'd sensed even the time Uncle Luke took him to see *Dawn Patrol,* confusing it for years with *Wings,* a silent film, and *Hell's Angels* that Mammy and Momma had only told him about, that the Bijou was a special theatre. Since *The Blue Dahlia* had been held over from the Tivoli where he'd seen it first, he knew that the Bijou was in the third rank of importance, for the Venice, showing first-run B movies, was second to the Tivoli, Queen of the Palaces. He would get to see *The Postman* tomorrow twice. And again twice Wednesday, after his first day in the eighth grade. He wondered if movie stars ever visited the important theatres, like the Tivoli. Closed for Sunday, the Bijou facade looked like a still photograph.

Lucius went around the corner to look at the Negro entrance under the fire escapes. Earlier in the summer, now that the war was over, the Bijou building had been painted rust red. Then it occurred to him that the prisoners working around the Indian mound might have attracted Bucky and Emmett.

Somebody's bare legs and feet hung down from the hat of the statue for the soldiers who fought and died in Cuba. Leaves obscured the face of the boy perched on the soldier's broad hat, but Lucius knew that out of all the kids in Cherokee, it must be Bucky Hutchfield, and—crouched behind the thick, rough-stone base of the spikelike monument to John Sevier—Emmett King. But no, Emmett was coming up the steps from the sidewalk, holding two ice cream cones. "Bucky! It's *him!*" Emmett started running past the new, white board, broad as the side of a house, that listed Cherokee's World War II dead—except for Luke because Mammy insisted that a *missing* man could be found. Momma didn't know that Lucius had scratched off Luke's name, so when she took her friend Gay to see it, she called the police to report vandals. Bucky swung down, hanging from the statue's pointed rifle and dropped to the ground and lit out after Emmett. Lucius chased them down the side of the courthouse, past the Stonewall Jackson Hotel, the River Bridge Book Store, onto Sevier Street Bridge.

A little way out on the bridge, Lucius passed between a motorcycle parked at the curb and a man in a leather jacket standing at the rail. Emmett's ice cream cones were leaving a trail of chocolate spots. On the other side of the bridge in South Cherokee, Bucky and Emmett climbed the red clay bluffs and kicked dirt down on Lucius as he tried to get a footing in the flaky, sun-baked earth between outcroppings of jagged rock. Chocolate dripped from Emmett's hands as he held on to the empty cones. When Lucius reached the crest of the bluff, he couldn't see them. Hot, tired, disgusted, crying mad, he sat on a piece of cardboard and skidded back down the bluff.

Lucius liked walking alone across the Sevier Street Bridge at dusk, even though he was always afraid somebody might sneak up behind him and toss him off, as in his nightmares. He liked to look back uptown at the buildings against the sky, the marquees of the Bijou, the Tivoli, the Venice, the Hollywood. Down along Fort Loudon Lake, the Tennessee River came out of the hills, and a private plane rose out of the trees from a small airport on an island. Cows bawled in the Smoky Mountain Packing House. The Hutchfield Bakery sat on a hill, owned by his daddy's uncles, the rich Hutchfields, including the one Lucius was named after, against Momma's objections. Lucius walked slowly, looking now toward North Cherokee. The roofs and lights of the River Street slums, the houseboats, where Bruce the albino usher lived, and the fires of the fishermen on the spit excited, frightened him. Somebody had set up a huge tent out on the spit, and cars were parked all along the opposite side of the railroad tracks. Mammy and Momma warned him never to mention River Street in the presence of the Chief, who, born and raised by Crazy Creek under the bluff, was a preeminently self-made man with a third-grade education who had risen from that swamp of rot and sin.

Lucius reveled in the mystery of the things he saw in this panoramic view. But he wanted to belong to and still somehow remain ignorant of all these places, people, the river, the kudzu vines that covered the bluff, the cars and streetcars at his back. He felt inferior among people who were at ease in low-down, sinister, dangerous, disease-ridden, sinful places like the Smoky Theatre, the Pioneer, and the River Street slums. They didn't belong to him, he was outside, but sadly thrilled, as if someday, in some way, if he looked and listened and smelled it often enough, he'd absorb it all. Before he came here, none of this really existed. He felt that. Everything looked, smelled, made noise this way only recently, and now that he had discovered it, the life of it all throbbed for the first time. Still, he was now and would always be a stranger to these smells, these voices rising from the river, the animal cries of dogs, of cats, of horses in a fenced place under the bridge, the sounds of speedboats, the smell of houseboats, of outdoor privies, the parade of rubbers floating in the water below, the soot from Cherokee coal stoves and factories drifting down, and flowers, weeds, grass, trees, macadam, cooling after the hot sun all day, contracting, gritty, like his scalp and body after swimming in Crazy Creek that emptied into this river.

A crowd lined the railing of the bridge where the rider had stood. His black motorcycle, one of a few in Cherokee, used only by police and drugstore delivery boys, idled, leaning, behind the crowd at the curb. Lucius crossed in front of a streetcar and, kneeling behind a tall thin man, looked between his legs through the green, iron lattice of the rail, and saw the lights of boats playing on a motorcycle cap.

"Muddafuggah did the prettiest swan dive you ever seen, outside the Olympics."

As men dragged the river, Lucius remembered Rudy McElroy, big brother of the first girl he ever "did it" to. Killed delivering paregoric on his motorcycle last summer. Lucius could have read about it himself in the newspaper he delivered, but he liked the way Mammy told it that Sunday morning in the backyard, sitting on the long wooden bench under the oak tree, the bottom whitewashed, snapping pole beans.

Sadly, Lucius crossed back to the other side. Scared of the water now, remembering tales of boys caught on the railroad trestle, unable to make it across or back, or who dove daredevil into the river and drowned, and the time the conductor announced, "Cherokee," while the train was still over the river, stopped a moment before backing into the L & N station, and two drunk corset salesmen stepped off the train into the Tennessee River, Lucius walked faster, until he saw rooftops below. In a little black tarpaper shack, light from a kerosene lamp came through a window and lit the sloping yard where a man and his kids flattened and stacked cardboard boxes. Lucius had often seen them roaming the streets and alleys uptown, picking up cardboard boxes behind the stores, pulling them home in carts with bicycle wheels. The porch and yard were full of junk, and twenty hound dogs lived in little hutches among the trees and vines on three terraced levels of the steep slope.

He'd looked down on these houses and houseboats from the bridge many times, wanting to go down there, go inside each, sit with the people, be part of their lives for a while. Pretending he was the rider of the motorcycle, who had not drowned but parked and crossed the street, Lucius descended an iron stairway that led down to River Street directly across from the River Bridge Book Store. Maybe he'd see the motorcyclist down there, dripping wet, alive, laughing with a Falstaff in his hand.

People sat outside on the porches and passed each other on the sidewalks. He hoped he wouldn't see any kids his age. They were mean and tough around here and "would just as soon kill you as look at you," as Mammy would say. He wanted to yell out, "Don't plan on robbing me, cause I only got two car checks to my name."

Momma and Mammy and the movies and Earl and the kids he ran with and the Sunday school and grammar school teachers had created for him a world of terrors, had so prepared him that some element of fear was connected with everything, but the dramatic way of scaring him also made him expectant, so that the tension he felt, as he thought about venturing or did venture into the world beyond the yard or neighborhood, was between the fear that had been instilled in him and the fascination and anticipation of whatever could so impress those people that they would need to warn him: Don't eat fish with corn bread or you'll choke to death on the little bones. Walk on the left side of the street or you'll get run over. Stay out of the woods unless you want poison ivy. Stay off Clayboe Ridge or you'll get bit by a rattlesnake. When you see a nigger woman coming, cross over to the other side of the street because they carry razors. Stay out of that old pile of lumber or you'll step on a rusty nail and get lockjaw. Take the Lord's name in vain and you'll burn forever in hell. Stay out of Crazy Creek if you don't want to get drowned. Don't mess with strange girls or you'll get syphilis. You can't swim in the municipal pool this summer 'cause they's a lot of polio going around. Don't pet strange dogs or you'll die of rabies—and there's no cure for it. If you "do it" to a girl and the law catches you, you'll go to the electric chair. They's German spies crawling all over Cherokee trying to get to Oak Ridge—so be on the lookout. If the Japs win the war, they'll rape all the women, kill all the old people, and send you to Siberia. Watch out for Jews, they'll gyp you every time. The Catholics will kidnap you and dunk you in scalding water. If they catch you stealing, they'll ship you to Nashville and put you in solitary confinement on bread and water and whip you over a barrel with a strap. Don't touch the radio or the light switch when it's thundering and lightning or else you'll get electrocuted. Don't ride your bicycle on Grand 'cause the cars go lickety-split. When you see that big man in the overalls rolling that rubber tire, run. If I catch you saying a bad word, I'll worsh your mouth out with P & G soap. Don't leave the vent shut on the stove or you'll blow us all up. Watch out with that sickle—you want to cut a finger off? Keep away from the bat or you'll get hit in the head. If you see Sonny Hawn coming, you better run. Don't point a gun even if it's not loaded, for it's the unloaded gun that kills. Stay away from the back of parked cars and horses. Keep your hands off the sewing machine or you'll run a needle in your finger. Every time you do something bad, God writes it down in his big book. And stay away from River Street unless you want your throat cut.

He wondered where the gospel singing was coming from. Even though they reeked of pee-stained mattresses, stale beer, turnip greens, fried river fish, dirty clothes, dog squat, slop, he was drawn to the old houses. On the edge of a railingless second-storey porch three turds squatted precisely in a row. From the porch, a pure drop down the cliff into the river. Behind one of the dirty windows at the end of a row of six houses, a little Negro girl with braces on her legs perched up on the back of a couch, looking out. Down here along the river, Negroes and whites lived more thoroughly mixed than anywhere else in Cherokee.

This was real life down here in the shadow of the bridge, streetcars passing above, cattle bawling across the river at the packinghouse. In the high weeds, Lucius took a leak, a little scared of the shadows inside the deserted Cherokee Tavern, built long before the bridge. Hearing a noise inside, Lucius, afraid Emmett might jump him with a knife, ran through the high weeds, cutting his arms on blackberry briars.

River Street extended right and left, three blocks both ways of nothing but slums and slummy stores and old factory buildings about to collapse.

Between a Negro house and the ruins of a fire, Lucius found a path to the river, where the gospel singing seemed to come from. Dead hollyhocks, high grass, horse chestnut trees bent over the path, and from the Negro's window came the voice of an announcer, saying, "This is WXOL, Cherokee, Tennessee, Gateway to the Smokies. Correct Eastern standard time now is eight o'clock. Stay tuned for 'Sam Spade.'" It seemed very strange that when he sat on Sunday listening to Fred Allen at good ol' 702 Holston, these people sat inside this house, the railroad tracks and the river behind them, listening to the same voices.

A complex network of paths, big rocks, trees, little and scrawny, kudzu vines, made the bluffs behind the houses rugged. Lucius stood on the railroad tracks. Along the shore, bottles, broken glass, old tires, shoes, tin cans, dead fish, a car seat, logs. "When I was thirteen," Chief Buckner once told him, "I used to jump in the river and pull in logs floating down and sell 'em and I couldn't swim a lick, and still can't." He looked back toward the houses. The backyards were full of garbage, trash, crude rabbit hutches, beehives, chicken coops, and a few pigpens. The houses looked as if they had been there since the beginning of Cherokee. Maybe these people years ago had dug those caves under the streets uptown that the Chief had told him about, and that most people had forgotten and nobody could find anymore. The stretch of houses seemed all one place, a close community set apart from Cherokee, having its own way of life. Lucius wished he could live here. Maybe someday when he grew up, he would rent a room in one of the big old houses by the river and draw and write his stories, and LaRue could work at the Tivoli, and he could live among these strange, raw, real people. He finished pissing into the bright streak of moonlight on the railroad tracks toward the spit, where weak bulbs burned naked in the tent he'd seen from the bridge.

He wanted to look closely at each object that had washed ashore, maybe find something valuable, but mainly he just wanted to know what had been flung down or washed up on the bank, but the tent drew him on. In the mud along the bank were many footprints, from shoes, bare feet, the prints of dog, cat, and maybe rat paws. About twenty houseboats lined the bank and the spit on this side, about thirty on the opposite bank, some half-sunk in the water and mud. White, red, green, yellow, blue, some with red tarpaper roofs. He was resentfully envious of the albino. Washing hung on the porch rail that ran around one of them, made him wonder, Did they wash them in the water where Crazy Creek emptied into the river, full of toilet flushings and rubbers? Moving toward the tent over the spit, feet had trampled the wilted grass of August. Cars and pickup trucks, parked running board to running board along the bank of Crazy Creek, had brought folks from other parts of Cherokee.

As the singing from the tent became clearer, one voice, a girl's, soared above the rest, keen, forlorn, with the mournful overtone of Kitty Wells singing "Honky-Tonk Angel," and an elusive undertone of raucous delight and self-satisfaction. Lucius had not intended to go in. He'd been saved in a revival tent on sawdust-littered grass the summer night he saw *King Kong* at the Hiawassee, but during the few years since, tents had come to put him in mind of Smoky burlesque and Pioneer wrestling. But the girl's voice drew him toward the entrance where the tent flaps were drawn back. The moon over the river was full. Familiar currents of feeling had moved through strange terrain in the past few days, and strange regions of experience had suddenly become like fulfilled prophecies. He felt both controlled by forces beyond him and in control of forces that had always awaited his readiness. He shivered at the premonition of some great moment in his life. Stepping over the trampled grass toward the yellow light that fell through the tent flaps, he gave himself up to the feeling that he'd walked toward something momentous in the same way before, and as he stepped over the sawdust threshold, he felt something give itself up to him.

So many people had abandoned the benches in the rear to surge toward the girl on the platform that Lucius could hear only her voice, lucid above the amens, the crying, and the singing of the others. Standing on a bench in the back, he saw her just as she was climbing onto a chair. Her long bleached hair shimmered in the light of yellow bulbs, her green eyes were aglow, a misty quality that always drew him to a girl, and her body leaned back, lithe in a green dress, showing the shadow of her navel, and he was ashamed to notice the faint impression of her nipples, because she was Loraine Clayboe from the Bugs Bunny Club, and she was pure and beautiful and he knew he would love her forever. God had destined them to meet again, and he thanked Him.

When he moved closer, she loomed above him, raised up on the two-foot-high platform, now loaded with people, elevated farther on a peeling red, round-backed kitchen chair that wobbled from abuse. In the shoving and swaying of the people against her, she kept her balance doing a little dance.

> "Tell me the story of Jesus,
> Write on my heart every word;
> Tell me the story most precious,
> Sweetest that ever was heard."

Around her stood three girls who seemed to be her close friends, a tall, skinny redhead who instantly resembled the Bijou ticket girl, and a tall, dark-eyed, olive-skinned, wide-hipped, foreign-looking girl, and a slender, shorter girl with light brown, curly hair and sharp hipbones, her face ashine with pimples, but a look of authority and self-containment about her. Looking around at the congregation as they sang, the girls conveyed a sense of having full lives elsewhere in Cherokee.

"Tell me a sto-reee!" yelled the preacher, a country man in clothes of the twenties, his rough hands pushing his black hair back.

A heavy, lopsided old woman with brown hair and no teeth, held a snotty baby who kept unbuttoning her blouse, making the girls giggle and elbow each other. Still, Lucius sensed that Loraine was different from the others—her misty eyes, her beauty, and the voice that soared over them created an aura, a halo of echoes. The preacher's deep voice rose and fell, "Tell me the storeee of your suffering!" as he looked each person in the eye.

People lay on the sawdust before the platform, some were falling on the platform itself, in the aisles, the preacher moving among them as they reached up their arms, their hips rolling, their dresses hiking, solicitous older women on the watch, veiling them with frayed, thin bandanas. The preacher moved suddenly, quickly through packed bodies to a woman standing, shaking, her eyes closed. "Has the devil poisoned your body, sister?" The woman nodded yes, murmuring. The preacher placed one hand behind her head, the other on her forehead, and pressed, then he pulled his hand away, raised it high, called on Jesus's healing power, slapped the woman's forehead hard and let her fall back on the sawdust among the others.

Even when he saw tears in Loraine's eyes as she sang, tears in the eyes of her friends, the pimply-faced one on the verge, Lucius held back. Feeling transported to old Palestine, to some rocky field in Galilee by the Jordan River near the Sphinx, Lucius wanted to respond to the preacher's call. The Clinch View First Baptist church, despite Preacher Hobart's yelling, was sedate and dignified, but he'd come close the past three Sundays to going up to the railing. These river people seemed to conjure up Jesus, flesh and blood. And he knew that Mammy, if not Momma, who was raised in St. Louis when Gran'paw Charlie went up there to work in the twenties, had come from people like this, even though Mammy, on occasions that called for control or indignation, could turn on an aristocratic hauteur.

Lucius wanted to give himself up to Jesus tonight—he *was* a sinner, liable to lose heaven and in danger of hell, and he did love Jesus, and God *knew* from their night talks before he fell asleep and when he walked Cherokee that he wanted to be a Christian and serve Jesus only and always, forever, and his heart overflowed. Why couldn't he just get down off the bench in the back and go up front?

"Tell me the story of Jesus,
Write on my heart every word."

That he was in a tent was a small matter, that he was among strangers did not deter him strongly enough, but he didn't want— As soon as he admitted that he didn't want to look silly in front of Loraine and her girl friends, a scorch of shame for his betrayal of Jesus made him go immediately to the platform behind an old woman, her hair tied back in a knot, who walked side to side like a drunk on a sidewalk.

"Tell me the story most precious,
Sweetest that ever was heard."

As the preacher asked the old woman what ailed her and she replied in a voice Lucius couldn't understand, Lucius felt upon him the tearful eyes of Loraine and the other three girls and the few boys he'd spotted. In the midst of the congregation, Lucius caught the reek of poverty, of raging and ebbing sicknesses. He didn't mind if they knew that from the time he was five up until he was saved at eleven, he was guilty of stealing, and, caught with Earl and Sonny Hawn and Hike Joplin, was taken to the police station and almost sent to the reform school, where Hike was now—Earl having escaped last spring, unseen since. They wouldn't suspect Lucius's guilt in teasing Thelma's old mother the day she died of rat poison, nor the guilt he felt that Uncle Luke had not come home. But he was certain they saw the hairs that flourished above his pecker because he'd "done it" to girls since he was five, beat his pud since he was six, and cornholed boys three summers at Boy's Club camp up on Lone Mountain.

"What ails you, son?"

"Nothing, sir, just sin."

"Sin? What kind a sin?"

"All kinds a sin—except I ain't murdered nobody yet."

"I was callin' folks that needed some sickness cured by the Holy Physician, boy. And you don't have nothing wrong with your body?"

Mortified he'd answered the wrong call, Lucius hoped God wouldn't whisper to the preacher about the hairs. "No, sir. But I wanted to be saved."

"You ain't yet a Christian?"

"No, sir, not washed in the blood."

"Then may Jesus have mercy on you, boy, and he'p you to do right."

"Thank you, sir, I will."

Knowing he'd spoiled something, Lucius got up off his knees and sidled over to a vacant chair at the front, on the side opposite the girls, sawdust flaking off his trousers. Ashamed he'd gone to the front with no sores or blindness, he understood now that the preacher was a faith healer. Had everybody else here been cured of some sickness? Loraine and her three girl friends? Was the tall, skinny, string-haired redhead who limped with a touch of polio worse before the preacher laid hands on her? Would they start handling snakes d'reckly? Watching the preacher try to regain control, Lucius felt sorry for him, and liked him, wanted to be a part of his performance.

Despite the embarrassment—women on each side of Lucius shrank away from him as though he had leprosy—he felt closer to Jesus tonight because these people seemed so close to each other.

Just as Lucius noticed that Loraine was sweating under her arms, too delicately hairy to shave yet, and in the moist curves under her neck and on her blushing chest, she lost her balance on the wobbling red chair, and leaned a moment, as if defying gravity, above the thrown-back heads, open mouths, and lidded eyes, before she fell, sideways, backwards, with a gust of laughter, no arms catching her, though Lucius, too far away, rose, stretching out his own. The shoulders of men and women and her three friends broke her fall, but she seemed to stagger and reel with the hope of bowling them all over, and the feeling was contagious to the three girls, who fell backwards giggling and whooping, deliberately pulling, as only Lucius seemed aware, Loraine with them. Seeing a flash of the pimply-faced girl's panties and Loraine's tan legs, her peroxide hair sparkling in the light, Lucius turned away to preserve her purity.

When emotions had dwindled and people seemed ready to quit, Lucius left the tent, feeling the eyes of Loraine and her three friends on him, as he led the exodus across the spit toward the clump of horse chestnut trees at the railroad.

> Sunday, September 1, 1946. Arranged stills & mags. Started Sea Remains. Chased after Bucky and Emmett. A man jumped off the bridge—left his motorsickle at twilit. Saw Loraine at revival tent. Thanks you God. Tomorrow, Bijou, and The Postman always Rings Twice, with John Garfield and Lana Turner.

Lucius was ten minutes early, a good start. But sourpuss, ready to spit tickets—to no one at that hour—seemed unaware. She glared at him, perched up in her glass booth under a long banner telling that *A Walk in the Sun* with Dana Andrews and Richard Conte was the Next Attraction. Had she discovered that he lied up and down about his age? Out front, John Garfield in black trunks carried Lana Turner in a white bathing suit. "Their love was a flame that destroyed." A picture of James M. Cain's book, "that blazed to Best-Seller Fame." When he entered the first inside lobby, he heard her booth door click open.

"Just where do you think *you're* going?"

"I'm an usher."

"Don't get smart. You trying to slip *in*."

"Call Mr. Hood."

"Don't you move a muscle, you little smart aleck."

"*Smart* aleck?"

She held the door open with one foot and twisted in her chair to dial, giving Lucius a view up her leg. "What's your name?"

"Lucius Hutchfield."

"You're lying. . . . Mr. Hood, sorry to bother you, there's a little kid out here acting smart—says you hired him. . . . Oh. . . . You did?"

Hearing that, Lucius walked on up the steps, past Miss Atchley the ticket taker, and into the main lobby, where Thelma, smiling, said, "*There* he is. Ready to go to work, Lucius?"

"Yeah, if that ticket girl'll let me." The manager's gold door was shut. "Tried to throw me out."

"Better steer clear of her, honey. She can't forget she was here before any of *us*. When Mr. Hood ain't here, Minetta's in charge."

"What about Elmo?"

"Next in command. Then Miss Atchley, *then* me."

Gale Booth, the Errol Flynn usher, leaned in from the dark inner lobby, then gracefully walked on in, up to the candy case.

"Say, Gale, did you meet Lucius yet?"

Gale spun around on his heels and, reeling, stuck out his hand. "Nope." Lucius shook his hand. "You supposed to relieve me?"

"I reckon."

"Well, the other," he whispered, "asshole quit, so I guess you get to take his place, Remember how to find your uniform?"

"Yeah, but I hope I can find it without a flashlight."

"Take mine."

Hot, sweaty, from being in Gale's hand, it smelled brassy. As Lucius walked down the side aisle, looking at Lana Turner in a white dress and John Garfield in a dark suit, walk down the open road of California in bright sunlight, she saw a girl sitting almost alone in the theatre, on a side aisle seat, near the heavy velvet curtains that Lucius parted before him, remembering Lana stopping, too tired to go, hearing her, as he passed the wings, say, "Can't you understand, Frank. I want to *be* somebody."

In the small dressing room alone, at the end of dark labyrinthine corridors, he was afraid a rat might suddenly appear in the doorway. But the familiar background music made him feel secure. In the uniform pants that fit even more sloppily than on Saturday, he felt disoriented, being *here* at this time of day, instead of delivering papers on Clayboe Ridge.

Passing the electric switches on the light board, Lucius felt a tingle of fear. Walking behind the curtain that slightly muffled the huge black loudspeaker, he heard Nick singing, "I got a woman crazy 'bout me, She's funny that way." Going up the aisle, he saw the girl's face in the light from Lana Turner's white dress and platinum hair as she lies on a plaid couch, sullenly polishing her white shoes, while Cecil Kellaway, her fat, old husband, Nick, sits in the foreground in shadows, playing the guitar, singing. The girl's hair was coal black, and she was very pretty.

Gale stood at semiattention On the Spot. "You can hold onto the flashlight till Elmo assigns you one. Say, Lucius, how about doing me a flavor?"

"Sure, Gale."

"See the orchestra pit down front? They's a big steel door in the middle with curtains over it that's open a crack. If Hood starts waddling backstage before I come back up, go down front, lean over the balustrade, and shine this light through that crack. Okay?"

"Sure, but how come?"

"Same way I *always* do." His crooked grin spread across his face as his hand went out to touch Lucius's. "I'll do something for *you* sometime. See you in a few d'recklies."

Gale walked down the side aisle, stooping beside the girl's seat as if to pick up a piece of paper stuck tenaciously to the carpet, while she kept watching Lana sneak into Garfield's room. "Frank, what are we going to do?"

On the Spot, in uniform, Lucius was aware of the sloping floor of the auditorium behind him, the thick velvet curtains, the tiers of box seats on each side in which he was not to allow anyone to sit, the wide stage, the screen no larger than the Hiawassee's, and the woman coming in out of the sun, adjusting her eyes to darkness, in which Lucius saw clearly now, and she could not imagine, as Lucius could, how it looked backstage. He was aware of the places of dark and light, the modulations between. In the main lobby, Hood's office was the brightest, then the glow from the still stands in the inner lobby, then the yellow light over the stage door, the brighter lights around the mirrors in the dressing rooms where great actors—Sarah Bernhardt among them—once applied makeup to their faces. Two women leaving made Lucius imagine the feeling emerging out of the Bijou's darkness into the bright sunlight that the Pioneer Theatre's long row of glass doors across the street reflected.

His hair combed into a pompadour like Alan Ladd's, a long blond wave, Lucius felt cute. Girls coming in would think he was a doll. And he didn't take no crap off nobody, by God. Caught the virus listening to Momma dramatize, act out a hundred scenes with her bosses or customers, telling them off, or Uncle Luke, what he said to some guy in a saloon, how he was going to stomp his ass into the sawdust. At the least thing, Lucius was ready to fight (like, they often told, Gran'paw Charlie, cocky little guy from LaFollette).

Thelma looked in at Lucius and motioned for him. She showed him how to use a little brass-handled sweeper on the carpet. As he pushed it back and forth, it squeaked. Lucius kept watch over Hood's gold door. What did he do in there all shut up alone? Write letters to David O. Selznick, Frank Capra, Cecil B. De Mille, Preston Sturges, Alfred Hitchcock, John Ford, and Mark Hellinger about their next pictures? Was Elmo, too, in there, conferring, planning what movies to show?

Sweeping in the inner lobby at the rounded corner where the side aisle to backstage started, Lucius saw the curtains at the foot of the aisle waver, part a little, and a vague motion of flesh. The black-haired girl left her seat, and, without looking around, walked through the curtains, her shoulders slightly hunched. The inside of Lucius's jacket got hot, the celluloid collar clammy.

Standing On the Spot again, flashlight in hand, Lucius imagined Gale back there somewhere, underneath the stage—Lana Turner in white and Garfield in black swimming in the loud surf and music—"doing it" to the girl who'd looked so lovely, so innocent, and pure in the light from the screen. She should be *his* girl. He would take good care of her, tell her about Jesus, keep her a virgin, and "do it" to other girls. The rare girls he loved and the stars on the screen were as pure and beautiful as Jesus' mother and as remote from a grasp of sex as the stars in the sky. He knew that between scenes, Cora and Frank made love, but he didn't want to experience it imaginatively with Lana and John. What made the impact was this idyllic scene in the ocean, John vowing eternal love, proving he's not going to kill her in revenge for the way she double-crossed him, taking her back to the beach, now. But she'll be killed in a car wreck as they're going home. In a dark room in the basement among posters, stills, large sacks of raw popcorn, what were Gale and the girl doing right this instant? Where, exactly, were they? Heat vapor pulsed inside his jacket, his skin itched.

An old woman came in. "This way, please," and he led her down front so he could try to get a glimpse through the curtain over the door that led beneath the stage out of the orchestra pit, but the old woman had stopped at the back and was stumbling, her eyes not yet adjusted to the dark, over two men. Through the curtains, he saw only a slit of black. He wished Hood would start backstage so he could flash the light and maybe catch the girl naked in the beam.

On the Spot, his back to the screen, Lucius tried to keep from getting a hard-on, but the heavy, loose material of his trousers kept scraping against the head of his pecker. The pants had no pockets. To shift his prong around in his jock shorts so it didn't poke straight out where patrons coming in could see it but lay straight up against his belly, he had to go between the doors that backed the candy case and the curtains that hung above the middle section of the half-wall and push his hand down the front of his pants at the waist.

The head of his pecker was hot against his navel as he smiled at the middle-aged lady, her hair freshly done up, her arms full of crackling packages from department stores. "How far down, please?" and led her to her seat. Coming back up the aisle, he saw Hood leaning over the balustrade. "Take your feet down, please," Lucius said, to a man who had his feet propped on the seat back in front of him. Lucius nodded to Hood, who nodded back. Ready to warn Gale if Hood started backstage, he felt his heart beat hard and fast.

"Straighten your tie."

Lucius did, then Hood went back into his office. His pecker had gone soft.

"Thelma, okay if I go back to the bathroom?"

"Have to wait till Bruce comes on, honey. 'Bout five o'clock."

Lucius wished he could hop up to the first landing to the balcony and take a leak in the tiny men's room, but the trousers had no fly and he didn't want a patron to catch him with his pants down.

"Monday's usually a very light night," said Thelma, "but it being Labor Day, they'll be laying in the aisles like Saturday." Lucius saw literally what she said. In his imagination, events measured up instantly to the language people used to describe them.

A short man in flappy-legged trousers and a hat too large for him and an Eisenhower jacket walked swiftly past Miss Atchley, who pretended not to see him, cut sharply right and ducked under the rope with its wooden sign, SORRY! BALCONY CLOSED!, and trotted up the carpeted stairs.

"Did you see that?"

"No," Thelma whispered, "and you didn't neither."

"What's going on?"

"If it was me, I'd fire him so quick it'd make your head swim, but I reckon it *is* hard to get a good projectionist these days. Still yet, letting a bootlegger walk brazenly into the theatre the way we let the po-lice, it ain't right."

"And he just waltzes on in like that and takes the guy some white lightnin'?"

"Ain't it awful?"

Scared, excited, Lucius felt the presence of evil up in the first balcony, shut in the tight little booth with a projectionist he'd not even glimpsed yet.

"But when a poor feller's spent three years in a German prison camp. . . ."

As Lucius returned to the Spot, an atom bomb lit up the theatre. The Paramount News of the Day (always three days late) was that they were testing on Bikini Island. When he was little, the news, except for the funny part at the end and some of the war scenes—though they, too, were often tedious—was boring as church. His eyes began to sting and ache, his feet went to sleep, and he had to pee. The events of the day were a fuzzy background to the action on the screen. The News of the Day montage seemed to take forever, and the RKO Pathé rooster was monotonous, but when the cameraman swung around and dollied in on the audience at the end of the Paramount News, Lucius always felt a little thrill. Hans Frank at Nuremberg confessed his guilt.

All during the war, Lucius strained hard when the news showed the fighting, to see if he could catch a glimpse of Uncle Luke and Daddy. And when the invasion of Europe was shown over and over, in documentaries, he tried to catch Uncle Luke getting shot. Paul Mantz sits in the cockpit of his plane, after winning the Bendix Trophy air race, flying from California to Cleveland at an average speed of 435.604 mph.

Ships anchored in New York harbor, the announcer saying a strike is threatened, reminded Lucius of looking up from Smilin' Jack in the Sunday funnies, aware of somebody at the front door screen, looking in. Sunburst around the dark figure's hunched shoulders and head, crowned with a merchant seaman's cap, blinded him at first, then he yelled, "Earl!" and Earl put his finger to his lips and said, "Shhhhhh. Let me surprise Momma."

Sir Shafaat Ahmad Khan, Indian Moslem, is stabbed by two un-identified assailants, five hours after accepting a post in the new Indian government.

As the human interest segment came on, Lucius noticed that some-one stood in the middle of the other aisle, where no usher was on duty. When it appeared the patron wasn't going to take a seat, Lucius walked over there. "Step back out of the aisle, please."

Bruce, turning, said, "I never miss the news."

Lucius had seen only one or two albinos in his life, and wondered whether he'd seen Bruce when he was younger.

"Well, Old Goering poisoned himself just a few hours before they could hang him," said Bruce, as if it reflected well upon himself.

Bruce remained standing there, as if he were already in uniform.

"What time does the next feature start?" a woman asked. Lucius shined his light on a little framed, glass-covered schedule: Trailers, Cartoon, News, Short Subjects, Feature. " 'Bout ten minutes, ma'am." Lucius showed her to a seat near the front and checked the curtain in the orchestra pit. During the short subject, he tried not to think of Gale and the girl.

The roaring of the oval-framed MGM lion made Lucius eager to see the little parts of *The Postman Always Rings Twice* that he'd missed between the stretches he'd already glimpsed, and to listen more carefully to what Frank and Cora said to each other. Until Saturday, he'd never watched a movie in fits and starts. Somehow it made *The Postman Always Rings Twice*, although he'd first seen it at the Tivoli without interruption, strangely interesting, special.

"Face the front," said Mr. Hood. "Gale gone already?"

"Think so, sir."

"I'm going up to the Tivoli for a while."

"Yes, sir." Lucius wondered why he was telling *him*. And why was Hood going? To see *A Walk in the Sun?* He could wait until it was held over here.

As the golden doors in the lobby stopped swinging after Hood's exit, Lucius heard Lana's lipstick hit the floor and roll, and turned to watch John Garfield bend over to pick it up, seeing open-toed, high-heeled white shoes at the foot of some steps, and long, already darkly tanned legs, with sexy knees, then stark white very short shorts, bare midriff, a white short-sleeved blouse, the shoulders padded, and Lana Turner's beautiful face, moist large eyes, a pouty, glistening mouth. She wears a white turban, holds a compact, and John Garfield bites his lip slowly as he hands her the lipstick. His and our first sight of her.

But thinking of Gale and the girl, down there so long, Lucius was unable to concentrate on *The Postman Always Rings Twice*. Facing front, he got deeper and deeper into "While the Sea Remains," until he sensed one of his favorite scenes coming. He looked out over the ten or fifteen heads in the theatre at John Garfield entering the dark kitchen of the restaurant where Lana stood in a black robe with a butcher knife, her platinum hair illuminating the kitchen, but not the theatre, saying, "It's for me, Frank," and Lucius saw Gale's girl sitting in the same seat. Then the scene shifted to the next night, a lighted room, and Lucius saw that the figure was Gale, and the red velvet curtains moved slightly, and in a few moments, the girl came out and walked up the aisle and behind the balustrade toward Lucius. She wore a blue dress and white and brown oxfords and carried a red wallet. Her hair was mussed a little.

"What time do you have?" she asked. Her breath had an odd, smothery, musty smell that he had encountered only once or twice before and that simultaneously turned his stomach and excited him.

"Sorry, I ain't got a watch." As she went on into the lobby, Lucius watched her walk, expecting a bowlegged limp, but she looked natural. He waited for Gale to come up, but he must be watching the scene.

Startled, Lucius turned around. Nick was kneeling over in the front seat beside Lana, struck by Frank with the wine bottle from which he'd gotten drunk, the echo of his voice sounding in the canyon near Malibu, ". . . well. . . . well. . . ." Watching the scene, he noticed Gale out of the corner of his eyes, rise and climb the steep side aisle, Frank behind him setting the car up for a fake accident. It slips and carries him over the cliff, and Lana claws her way up the cliff screaming, and there, in the lights from his own car, is the D.A., who has been observing Frank and Cora, while seeming very affable, and Gale came toward Lucius, a mock serious look on his face, scuffing his feet on the carpet, and reached out his finger as if to poke him in the eye, but touched Lucius's cheek, and a spark startled him, and he almost peed in his pants. Then Gale stuck his finger out again. "Oh, no," said Lucius, laughing.

"No, sniff."

Lucius sniffed. The smell of pussy, blended with brass from the flashlight he held and the sweeper handle, was strange, exotic, smothery.

"Don't say I never *give* you nothing," said Gale, with his Errol Flynn grin, and he went out into the lemony lobby and through the shimmering doors.

Lucius hurt so bad to go to the toilet, he was about to cry. Like the gods, ushers were not supposed to need to pee. And his feet hurt worse than when he had finished delivering Clayboe Ridge at about this time of day.

"You can take off for supper, now, Lucius." Bruce stood behind him, in uniform.

"Oh. Thanks."

"Say, how old are you, anyway?"

"Old enough to forget more than you can remember," said Lucius, smiling.

"That's a hot one."

Out of uniform, eager to eat supper at Mammy's cafe, Lucius turned on impulse to the narrow wooden stairwell, and by the light of a weak yellow bulb, descended into the basement. Wandering, he saw giant fans under the stage and switches and a cooling system of sprinklers and water troughs, and on a level below the basement, the furnace room, full of coal. Imagining where Gale and the black-haired, musty-breathed girl had lain, Lucius heard a sweeping noise and someone whistling "Shoofly Pie and Apple Pandowdy."

Sweeping out a brightly lighted room with a push broom, Brady, the Sonny Tufts usher, raised dust that settled on bins of stills and giant posters. Lucius felt as if he were in a shrine, a sacred place.

"This your special job?"

"Hi, Lucifer. Yeah. All mine. Good deal. Hood lets me off the floor to do it. Keep the stills in order, sweep out the shit 'n' corruption."

Standing in the brightest room he'd ever seen, Lucius looked at the glossy, perfectly clean, sharp-edged stills for features to come, aware of the plyboard walls, the two-by-four ribs showing raw, the used-lumber shelves, hairy with splinters, little cribs for sorting the stills and tables for handling, cutting, pasting posters. Why should Brady get to handle the glossy stills, when Lucius knew even the minor players, if not by name, their faces and bodies were as familiar as the faces on Cherokee streets, as Brady's, even Gale's? And Brady didn't seem at all impressed to have this privileged task.

Anticipating the eighth grade, Lucius wondered what shadowy bullies from various parts of Clinch View neighborhood might step forth to join the others, who at any moment, like Sonny Hawn, last year, might slug him on the shoulder every time he passed him in the hall. Freshly bathed in water heated on the kitchen cookstove and lugged, splashing the floor, into the bathroom, he dug into the corner closet Mammy rigged up years ago for the green box his Phantom outfit came in four Christmases back. He pulled out a batch of photographs of Charles Atlas, demonstrating exercises that built up muscles by tension and stress. Having placed them in two rows of ten across the cluttered dresser top and stripped to his jock shorts, he watched himself in the oval, beveled, cherrywood—framed mirror as he flexed his muscles.

All last year, he'd done the exercises. His shoulders were unusually broad anyway, as the Bonny Kate coach and many others often said, but he had no interest in football, although in all's-up-goes-down on the playground, he could throw ten guys before anybody got him down. Atlas's exercise had brought God-given muscles to the surface, but when he woke up screaming one night, his bowels feeling locked together like one snake gorging on another, and Mammy had bound him tightly in sheets, he'd given in to Momma's and Mammy's urging and stopped, $19.99 of his paper route money shot. But now he put his right fist into his left palm and pressed against the resistance in his biceps. In the mirror, his face showed a frown, bulging blue eyes, gritted teeth, and taut neck muscles, reddening as his bones began to creak and crack.

Monday (Labor Day), September 2, 1946. Second day as an usher. Postman Always Rings Twice. Dreamed last night I was walking down Sevier Street naked. I didn't cuss today. God bless us all.

Lacing his shoes, Lucius glanced at Bucky, who lay sprawled on his back, wearing only an undershirt, an uncircumcised piss hard-on, sheet jerked loose, scab on his knee, mouth open, spit stain where he'd drooled. His body tan from running half-naked all over Cherokee, his filthy feet had soiled the sheet. In sleep, smacking his dry lips to wet them, he had a look both cherubic, as in the pink-toned pictures of him when he was three, wearing curls, and moronic because of his running with

Emmett. On his forehead, over his left eye, dewy with night humidty, was the scar from the wound Earl inflicted when they were playing base-ball with a bat but no ball in the living room on a rainy day, Lucius pitching, Bucky catching, Earl at bat. Shooing a fly that lit on Bucky's left eyelid, Lucius wanted to wake him, tell him he was sorry for smack-ing him so often last summer when he'd had to look after him at the Hiawassee Theatre.

Sore from the Atlas exercises, Lucius stepped up from the back room into the kitchen, inhaling the smell of Bucky's freshly ironed clothes, stale coffee, and smoldering coal in the cookstove. Momma and Mammy already putting mugs of hot black coffee before firemen and railroaders, Daddy cutting pastry. A blue jay sat on top of the fence post, shitting white. Something glowed in the morning light that came through the window straight ahead and fell on the oilcloth on the round table. A long black case set open on the table that was usually loaded with bread, jam, white margarine, dishes, and coffee cups. What glowed in the case was a golden clarinet.

Under the rooster-shaped saltshaker was Momma's morning note that he always dreaded reading:

Dear Lucius,
Surprise, honey! It's from Luke. He sent the money, little by little, until he was *killed*, so you could learn to play music. Benny Good-man better watch his step. Stop by the cafe after you get out of school and tell us how you like it. I picked it out, Mammy swears Luke would have wanted you to play the silver one with the scrawly designs on it, but I know you like gold! ! ! We wanted to see the look on your face, but your daddy hid it in the coal house last week and forgot where he put it until this morning. Listen, now you get an early start so you can take Bucky by the hand and deposit him in Miss Carr's hands, otherwise Emmett is certain to intercept him on the way. I got up at five o'clock this morning to iron Bucky's new outfit, so tell him he better not get spot *one* on it, and to keep his shoelaces tied so he won't tromp on them. Eggs and bacon in the icebox—*don't* forget to empty the icebox pan or Mammy will murder us all.

Momma
P.S. Don't forget to unplug the iron and turn off the radio before you leave.

Trembling with excitement and gratitude to Luke and fear of failing to learn how to play, Lucius shut the black case and hid the clarinet behind the stove and reached up on top of the warmer above and turned on the radio, and got the tail end of Freddie Martin's theme song.

"Bucky! Bucky!"

"What?"

"Get your little ass out of that bed!"

"Go fly a fu— Go fug a flying donert!"

Lucius remembered he'd been saved. "Forgive me, Bucky. But get up, buddy, we got to start school this morning."

Bucky didn't say anything.

Bucky's whining, stomping, and screaming persuaded Lucius to let him ride in the basket of his Western Flyer to Clinch View Elementary, where he turned him over to Miss Carr, the health and art teacher. It was good, after a long summer, to be inside his old school the first day of the new year.

"You still writing those love letters to LaRue?" Miss Carr was the biggest woman he'd ever known and tough as a bull.

"No, ma'am, I ain't—"

"I'm *not*—"

"—in any of her classes. Wasn't. Last year."

"Well, I've kept all those love letters I confiscated from you."

"You *did*?" She seemed to have forgotten telling him that last year.

"I *cer*tainly have."

Grinning, glad she still kept them, Lucius went back outside, jumped from the parapet beside the steps down onto his bicycle seat like Roy Rogers, his hero before Alan Ladd showed up in *This Gun for Hire*, and raced down the sidewalk past the flagpole, jumping four steps on the bicycle, and rode back toward the house to pick up his clarinet.

He let a Hutchfield Bakery truck pass and pull in behind the school, knowing that a large poster of the Lone Ranger riding Silver covered the other side. The bakery sponsored the Lone Ranger on WLUX. He liked seeing his name moving across the Cherokee landscape and among the houses and the buildings uptown, but the trucks made him feel inferior to the rich Hutchfields. Momma always said that if Daddy weren't such a drunkard, he could've worked his way up to be manager or even vice-president, and they'd all be living in a mansion.

Lucius was grateful to Miss Carr for letting his talent for drawing grow unhindered, unlike the first- and second-grade teachers at Leon Hooker Elementary, where the principal made him stand in a small, pitch-dark cloakroom, the door locked, for drawing hanging cowboys. Then last year when he went to pick up Bucky, who got sick in the middle of the day, Miss Carr had told him that his old love letters to LaRue had showed a great maturity and literary gift for a boy his age, and Lucius had got to wondering whether his writing was something more than fun. He'd always planned to be an artist when he grew up and she'd encouraged him, knowing that her old student Luke expected that of him, too, but he was almost sad to realize that writing stories was more thrilling. Still, when kids and grown-ups leaned over his shoulder, he loved to hear somebody crowded out of the circle say, "Let *me* see. Let *me* see!"

As he took the black case from behind the Home Comfort cookstove, Lucius wondered why Luke, on the march across Italy, had sponsored this new direction for him. Nobody in the family could play an instrument except Momma, who tinkled old favorites and hit tunes from movies on the piano with great gusto and verve, and Mammy could pick out a few hymns. To Lucius the clarinet suggested serious music, but Luke knew nothing of his love of Chopin. With the black case bouncing in his basket, Lucius sped down Holston. No students stood under the mimosa outside Bonny Kate. Scared, he pumped the pedals as hard and fast as he could.

"Being late on the first day of the new school year entitles you to double demerits, Lucius Hutchfield." Last year, Miss Kuntz had torn up more of his stories than any other teacher. "I hope you will make up your mind *this* year to walk the straight and narrow." Not knowing where they came from nor what they referred to, Lucius hated such glib phrases, but the hostile tone was clear. He wanted to tell her she was talking to a boy who'd gotten saved last Sunday night, but he knew she would curl her lip at the tent and sawdust, and would cling to the conviction that even if his soul had been washed whiter than snow, his heart remained black as Cherokee's soot fall.

Miss Kuntz's long silver hair was shaped like a young girl's, but her black moustache, emblem of a sinister private life, made him think of a nun, a Catholic spy, in disguise. Maybe she was a witch. But she had the softest voice in Cherokee, and when Lucius heard the words, purveying the mean rainfall in foreign lands and other raw geographical data, it sometimes sounded beautiful. Without raising it a decibel, though, she'd hiss viciously, dig her long fingernails into Lucius's arm. A weird, in the instant of pain almost sexual, sensation, it ignited in Lucius a blinding, soaring rage.

They'd signed up for classes last spring. What musical instrument interests you most? Lucius had answered piano, thinking intensely of Cornel Wilde as Chopin, but forgetting his mother's interest and his own desire to be different. Confronted with tangible, black-cased evidence of a good reason, Miss Kuntz allowed Lucius to drop drama as an elective and substitute band.

Not seeing LaRue's face among the students in homeroom depressed

Lucius. While Miss Kuntz read off some instructions by Principal Bronson about matters pertaining to the coming year, Lucius wrote a poem, intending to pass it to LaRue in the halls or in a class, if they were put together.

As he walked the jammed hall toward his first class, "straight and narrow" rang in his ears, marking his mouth with a sneer. Down the straight and narrow, he dragged a load of unnameable sins the warning conjured up.

As Prissy Cobb, a feisty young teacher new last year, passed him, Lucius turned to watch her tight little ass, and somebody behind him said, "Shake it but don't break it." Seeing the different fanny of Della Snow, Lucius walked faster, let the back of his hand bump her butt. She looked at him over her shoulder. "I *knew* it was you. I just *knew* it." Tiny little spit bubbles fizzed at the sharp corners of her mouth.

"And you know something?"

"What?"

"You was right."

Red stringy hair—Loraine's tall girl friend startled him, passing, slightly limping. He almost waved, but realized he didn't really know her. Joe Campbell, his buddy from the sixth grade, was getting a drink, and Lucius goosed him as he passed. Harry Marcum, a boy from Tapp Elementary who befriended Lucius when he lived awhile at St. Thomas's Orphanage, waved as he went into shop class, and somebody hit Lucius's shoulder hard. Sonny Hawn, bully of the Beech Street years, looked back, grinning, bouncing his eyebrows up and down, tauntingly.

Sore, Lucius was burning with anger when he entered art class and saw a beautiful, tall young woman at the desk. "My name is Kay Kilgore." She had long black hair and resembled a flat-chested Jane Russell. Because *The Outlaw* had been banned for four years, Lucius had seen only photographs and double-page, movie-magazine ads of Jane Russell. While Kay Kilgore explained the color wheel, Lucius drew pictures of the characters in "While the Sea Remains," glancing up to soak in her beauty, making her the model for Marina Crockett. "You must stop looking at funny books—your faces are too crude," said his seventh-grade art teacher, whom Kay Kilgore had replaced, but he'd sensed she wasn't just another grown-up warning him off funny books.

Miss Redding, another new teacher, wrote her name on the clean blackboard. She had a soft, delicate prettiness, a figure like a student, and seemed to be the shyest teacher he'd ever seen.

It was odd to eat again in the cafeteria, as if no summer had gone by. Seeing LaRue in line, Lucius was thrilled to know that she had lunch same period. As she passed his table, carrying her tray, he took the poem from his shirt pocket and stuck it under her ice-cream brick. She sighed disgustedly, said, "Tsk!" He watched her sit and read it, holding it over the vapor from her tomato soup. He turned back to his peas and carrots, and a few moments later, the poem dropped beside his tray. Turning, he saw Judy walking away from him.

LaRue had written at the bottom, "You're no poet, Don't you Know it? I am a Christian. I never liked you, and I never, never will. So stop it!"

On the playground, remembering Alan Ladd in *The Glass Key*, telling off Veronica Lake, Lucius told LaRue, "You think you're too good for me. Well, sister, it so happens I think I'm too good for you."

The notes on the page scared the hell out of him, but band was going to be exciting. The director, Mr. Sproul, looked like Dusty Harper with t.b. Behind the director, in the stone clubhouse indoor chimney, was a large open fireplace.

Lucius had seen Mrs. Dakins, his health teacher, in the hall many times. She wasn't a screeching witch but a murmuring mortician who'd killed with kindness and then embalmed her students five days a week for more than a quarter of a century. In her class, he thought up a great title for a story. "Destroy the Flame by Luke Scott," he wrote on the first page of a clean pack of Blue Horse. Later, he would dream up a story to go with it.

All summer, and all day, he'd dreaded American history. Last year, Miss Cline was his homeroom teacher. Every morning, she looked as if she'd just stepped out of a severe beauty parlor with a permanent, her hair short, tightly curled. Cherokee's ugliest woman, she spoke through bucked teeth and squinted behind horn-rims. Wiry arms like a ditch-digger's jutted out of her short-sleeved old maid's uniform. Miss Kuntz and Miss Cline were often seen whispering together under the double. rows of mimosa trees, arms folded, their heads, long silver and tight-curled hair, shaking "no," "awful," "disgusting." Himself, Lucius imagined, the cause.

When Lucius walked into the room, the familiar smell struck him, and Miss Cline looked up with a vigorous snap, her spine straight as a rod. "Mr. Hutchfield, do you realize you are the *last* pupil to arrive?"

"Am I late?"

"Don't sass me, young man. I've got your number." Another occult phrase that said more than Lucius could grasp. Like Vip's cartoons, Lucius always saw vivid images literally for every cliché people used so glibly, and the inappropriateness startled him.

The class was a blur of faces until Lucius caught a few expectant expressions up front. "What do I do *now?*"

"Stop that stupid snickering," rapid-fire, Miss Cline staring at a few kids—they *all* ducked their heads. "Sit right over there, *Mister* Hutchfield." There was always an instant when Lucius thought she was cueing him in a comic act only *she* had rehearsed.

"Thank you, ma'am." Lucius sat over there. "I just love this seat. I'm glad you give me this seat, Miss Cline. Thanks a whole bunch. Gosh bum!"

Glacing over the laughing faces, Lucius saw the Bijou–Gospel Singer, three seats behind him in the next row. The drama with Cline and the blinding thrill of seeing Loraine forced his heart to pump faster, harder. She wore a white cotton blouse, with short puffed sleeves, and a tiny blue ribbon woven in the cuffs and the neckline, and a wide blue band in her hair, and a dark starched, blue skirt with straps which hung loosely against the puff of her sleeve, as if it would fall down over her arm if the puffs weren't there.

"Everyone deserves three chances, Mr. Hutchfield. You've just used up yours for the entire year." Miss Cline enjoyed the laugh she got for that one, even from Lucius.

Beside Lucius sat Lard Fogel, the Opal Boulevard Cherokee *Messenger* carrier. They nodded to each other.

"The first day, pupils, is no different from any other day. In *my* class, from the first day to the very last day—you, what? *Work*. Book monitors to the front."

In the commotion, Lard Fogel asked Lucius, "Who you think's the prettiest girl in the room?"

"Miss Cline when she's curled," said Lucius, resenting the question from such a fatso with Loraine in the same room.

Lard laughed so hard, Miss Cline sent him out to stand in the hall.

Lucius stared at Loraine, who resembled Veronica Lake before she did her hair over her eye. When she caught him staring, he turned around, and a kid in the first row read aloud from the history text, "In 1492 . . ."

Lucius wrote:

> Your hair tingles about your well-shaped head,
> Like a mass of morning glories, sweet
> And made for me to admire.
> Your cheeks are bright and soft with the rouge
> Of youth and flowery fragrance,
> Your pink velvety lips are untouched by the gory
> Lips of vulgar passions.
> And made for me to praise.
> Your eyes have viewed with pleasure only
> The goodness in life,
> For you are in the essence of life

And must appear as the uncomparable
Creature you are.
And made for me to worship.
LH

As the voices droned on about the discovery of America, a dropped book startled Lucius. It lay beside Loraine's desk and she couldn't reach over the armrest to get it. Lucius got up and walked around the back of the row and picked it up. The smile she gave him, looking up, made him slack in the knees.

"*What* did I *tell* you, Lucius Hutchfield?"

"I'uz just pickin' up her 'mercan hist'ry."

"You put that book right back where you found it."

The splat when he let it drop echoed like a pistol shot down the empty hallway. Returning to his seat, Lucius did a Groucho dip at the turn.

"You're treading on quicksand, young man. . . . Now, young lady, what's *your* name?" Miss Cline scanned her seating chart. "Yes. Loraine Clayboe. Odd last name. Clayboe Ridge? Did you drop that book on purpose, Loraine?"

"No, ma'am."

"Then I believe you. You look like a very well-reared girl."

Only Miss Cline and Lucius didn't laugh. But Loraine herself got so tickled, Miss Cline sent her out in the hall to stand on the other side of the door from Lard Fogel.

Under "Destroy the Flame," Lucius crossed out LaRue and wrote "For Loraine, My Earthly Angel."

Tuesday, September 3, 1946. First day of 8th grade. She's in my history class. I love her. Day off from Bijou.

Having reached the present in his nightly ritual, Lucius returned to the beginning of his life for the third time since the ritual began. . . . His small hand dipping into a pickle jar, eating with the baby next door a whole economy-sized jar of dill pickles. . . . In the autumn, in the kitchen on Coker Street, Momma cooking dinner while Otto's Momma watches, drinking coffee, and Otto says, Momma? What, Otto? Whyfor's Ducious got a bigger dodopeepeesoso than me do? . . . Summer. Blossoms. Warm sunlight. Along Coker walks a dirty, humped Negro woman, a sack over her sharp, thin shoulders. The whiplike stem of the lilac bush cracks in Lucius's hands, and he smells the stem's raw insides. The Negro woman crosses the street, Lucius stands in the next-door-lady's front yard, frightened. "You burn in hell fer tearin' up 'at 'er flower bush." Yellow snaggled teeth, black eyes staring. The kitchen smells good, like the inside of the stem. Momma is making a lemon pie. Lucius tells her about the mean ol' lady and his fear of hell. Momma laughs. Lucius sees the old woman several times. He is afraid of her. He pities her. . . . Momma ties a rope to the gallusses of Lucius's overalls and the other end to the clothesline to keep him from wandering out of the yard while she does the washing in a tub with a washboard in the kitchen. He climbs out of his overalls. It's autumn, he's cold. A big boy finds him sitting on a railroad track and takes his hand. "I found him down on Thompson Street, ma'am.". . . The girl across the street has short, golden hair. Her name is Clarice Simms. She has a nice momma and daddy. She is older than Lucius, but they are sweethearts. . . . They are in a photograph, holding hands, smiling, under cherry blossoms. Lucius wears a sunsuit, staring at the camera very seriously. . . . It's summer and on the high back steps, tied with pretty ribbons, packages are piled. Lucius sits in the middle of the table in a sunsuit, his legs around the cake, three candles stuck in it. Around him are presents he's opened. It is a photograph. But outside the photograph, he cries because some of the presents belong to Earl whose birthday comes when it's too cold to throw a party.

> Wens. September 4, 1946. Postman Always Rings Twice. Tomorrow is A Walk in the Sun. Loraine smiled at me in American history. Wish I had give her the poem. We are going to move. Writing While the Sea Remains. Feels funny not to be delivering papers on the ridge no more.

> Thurs. September 5, 1946. Day off. Me and daddy went looking for a house. Got stranded near the insane asylum. He was drinking white lightnin'. We sat on a pile of lumber on the edge of a hole they dug for a basement for a new house and he told me about the invasion and the Cathedral at Metz, and we p—— in the hole. We had to walk home —five miles—because we missed the last streetcar and I told him the story of "Glory in a Sanctuary" and he cried. Momma said she found a house. I am writing this the next morning before school.

On the Spot, half asleep in the humid air, Lucius bent slightly, repeatedly, at the knees, easing his legs, his feet hurting. After the Bugs Bunny Club crowd had seen the first showing of A Walk in the Sun, Lucius had felt the dead lull, only a few people in the theatre.

Hood loped in, slapping the carpet flat-footedly, leaned forward before, it seemed, he was close enough, rested his arms on top of the balustrade, panned the theatre, slowly, left and right, as if he were the high priest of silence. Lucius was surprised to learn from the albino that Hood had been a major during the war. It seemed long, long ago. Hood spent a great deal of time with his arms draped over the wooden railing, glancing over the audience and at the movie. Sometimes, he felt as though Hood glanced over at him the way some guys did in the Greyhound Bus Terminal toilet or the Pioneer Theatre during wrestling matches.

Lucius watched Hood cross the lobby and speak to Elmo by the water fountain, then push through the raw gold doors to go outside, up to the Tivoli, probably, to meet his wife for lunch. Lucius wondered what she looked like. All he knew was that she was manager of the Tivoli, had a cute shape and was tough, and had probably got her husband his job at the Bijou.

Imitating Gale's feigned nonchalance, holding his flashlight as Gale was, Lucius watched Richard Conte walk down a hot, dusty road in *A Walk in the Sun,* and Lucius did an Errol Flynn smile, a Clark Gable brow-wrinkle, thinking of Loraine, who'd sat two rows down with her three girl friends during the Bugs Bunny Club that morning, and he'd caught her three times, glancing back at him. He almost wished she wouldn't come to the Bijou, afraid she might fall eternally in love with Gale instead. Listening to machine-gun fire behind his back, Lucius resolved to write Loraine a note in history and ask her to go with him to see Olivia de Havilland and this new guy named John Lund in *To Each His Own* at the Tivoli.

Loyalty to his image of LaRue was weakening. LaRue was a pretty, animated picture, but, like Luise Rainer, too pretty to be real. Loraine's arrogant, aggressive, boisterous girl friends created a volatile ambience around her that made her seem vital and electric. Lucius saw himself years later, a famous writer living in Paris, attending a dinner in his honor, like Mark Twain in the movie, Loraine in evening dress walking beside him, Alan Ladd and Veronica Lake accompanying them, the photograph appearing in the Sunday Cherokee *Messenger,* LaRue seeing it, jealous of Loraine, envious of the *life* she could have had.

Aware of Gale gliding across the carpet toward him, Lucius realized too late to duck, that Gale's hand was aimed at his cheek, and he felt the shock of the spark Gale's scraping feet had generated on the carpet.

"Let's knock off for dinner, blue eyes."

"Okay, Curly."

Elmo swooped past them, Brady, down from the balcony, following. As Bruce Tillotson stepped up to the Spot, Lucius followed the others backstage to change, glad he could go to lunch with the Bijou Boys. He'd not had a chance to go beyond the walls of the Bijou with "Gale and them." Their working schedules conflicted—Lucius was either Gale's or Brady's relief—or they ran into the night together. While he was in school, Lucius imagined Gale and them working. High school dropouts, they talked of joining the army, the navy, or the marines. He was jealous to learn from Elmo that Gale and Brady were cousins. Their life among the woolen-mill workers and gravel-barge laborers in Pottertown in South

Cherokee across the river where Daddy was born and raised and now worked in the bakery seemed foreign to Lucius.

What their uniforms did to them stayed with them, Lucius noticed, awhile after they took them off. In his short-sleeved green shirt in bright sunlight, even Brady shot his cuffs, then snapped the twist band on his wristwatch. Gale steered, Elmo acted as if he were the one who steered, Captain of the Ushers, but Brady and Lucius followed Gale, laughed at Elmo, his Adam's apple jogging along above them. When Elmo suddenly looped his leg over a parking meter, then bared his teeth, grinning, Lucius sensed it was routine and kept looking ahead, as Gale did, smiling faintly, because although the leg-loop was nothing to praise, it wasn't to be discouraged. Having admired and imitated the way Gale stood at his post, Lucius now took up his walk, which seemed natural to Gale. Brady didn't seem aware of the way *he* walked, but Elmo made Lucius think of Ray Bolger in *The Wizard of Oz*. Imitating Gale's grin, his playful, put-on frown, his mellow tone of voice, Lucius walked with them up the gentle slope of the Bijou side of Sevier Street toward the Tivoli's marquee.

Lucius was surprised to see Harry Marcum coming toward them, walking with the Tivoli ushers.

"How you and Loraine doing, Lucius?" asked Harry, his grin almost as calculated and controlled as Gale's.

"You know her?"

"Used to live down the damn street from her on River Street. She's up at the Tivoli now with Peggy and them."

"Peggy's got hot pants for Harry," said one of the Tivoli Boys.

"You work at the Bijou now?"

"Yeah. *You* up at the Tivoli?"

"Hell, yeah, started last week. Take it easy, greasy."

"We'll see you."

Lucius caught up with "Gale and them," a little jealous that Harry was ushering at the Tivoli, but Harry was a year older, looked older than that, tall, lithe, black hair raked back elaborately, showing the track of a wide-toothed comb, like a boy from the country trying to look fancy. Lucius didn't like the looks of the Tivoli ushers. He felt better walking up Sevier with the Bijou Boys. Passing Ryder's window, Lucius noticed a Keystone movie projector he'd been hoping to buy since last spring.

Gale's lithe body inclined toward the curb and they started across on the yellow light toward the Tivoli. The marble floor of the main lobby sloped long as a football field to the sour-faced woman who took tickets, facing the bright sun and the street that flashed at her from streetcar windows passing. A miniature Taj Mahal, gold domed, wide, swooping marble stairs, oriental and Renaissance tapestries and suits of armor. But the Tivoli was too enormous, cold, forbidding. Among marble statues of goddesses, velvet drapes, and crystal chandeliers, he felt inferior.

The Bijou Boys walked through the outer lobby of the Crockett Hotel and downstairs, past the poolroom, where Luke used to lean over the green to break a setup, then, seeing Lucius, poke "hello" toward the ceiling with his cue stick. The Bijou Boys spread out at the gleaming urinals. Each shift, they averaged three pisses an hour, chances to stretch their legs backstage, lie on mounds of raw popcorn in tow sacks. While the rest dribbled, Elmo freckled his cuffs, but beamed, knowing the sound came from him. "Don't splatter," said Brady, scooting backward, zipping up. They stood around Lucius, watching him wash his hands. "Pee on 'em?" asked Gale.

"Scroungy bunch of assholes," said Elmo pleasantly, looking at the group in the four touching mirrors. The Negro restroom attendant was as grim-faced as Minetta Samins.

Gracefully, they glided in and out of the S & S Cafeteria and Toots' Grill, and past the Venice, which lacked magnificence—it didn't even have a balcony—but it was very clean and showed the first-run movies the Tivoli couldn't fit into its schedule, along with a few high-grade B pictures, and most of the epics. And in and out of Athena Gardens and the Gold Sun Cafe, and past the Hollywood, that belonged to the Rat House Chain. Across the street from the Greyhound Bus Terminal, the Hollywood was full of country folks on Saturdays and showed all the cheap movies and the chapter plays first.

Lucius enjoyed passing through the ancient, three-storey, block-long, brick Market House, its arched ceiling looming over them, a line of rough little tables running down the spine of the building where country women sold butter, eggs, shelled walnuts, jams, and honey. Permanent butcher and flower and fruit stalls and restaurants and lunch counters on each side. They walked along the sidewalks flanking the Market House where produce and flower trucks, mostly canvas-covered Ford pickups of the thirties, were parked, backed up to the curbs, their overladen tailgates hanging heavy, the country folks standing by, ready to sack up some pole beans or okra. The police loved to park at each end of the Market House, where the ornate fountains attached to the sooty brick walls were dry.

The Bijou Boys walked past the Jewel, a hole in the wall so tiny it seemed almost a play house, the symphonic background music, the shooting and the galloping reaching out to them over a loudspeaker above the sidewalk, and a few skid row stores down, past another hole in the wall that sold tobacco, practical jokes, and Trojan rubbers, the Ritz, the Jewel's twin, owned by two Italian brothers, where they heard only the sound of spurs clinking on a broadwalk and Charles Starrett as

The Durango Kid was featured on a poster. Passing them, Lucius always felt guilty of some nameless sin. When he wasn't roaming all over the United States with carnivals, Earl took the farm girls or the River Street girls he picked up in the Market House to the Jewel, the Ritz, or the Smoky. His natural element, his domain. The girls had big bellies, mail order titties, hairy legs, and wore red socks and pumps, had stringy, peroxide hair, cross eyes, bad teeth, and wore flaming red lipstick, round red rouge spots on each cheek, heavy blond powder, and glassy jewelry at earlobes and wrists. He bought them rings at Kress's and gave them stolen red wallets and loaded them with popcorn and fingered them in the back rows.

On Vine, they stopped in front of the Smoky, Queen of the Rat Houses, the whole front a solid bank—an eyewash—of stills, glossy, rich as eating a whole twenty-five-cent pecan log, for Gene Autry in *South of the Border, They Died with Their Boots On,* Hopalong Cassidy in *Three on a Trail,* and episode 11 of *Batman,* the side panels showing the burlesque girls. Live strippers to a live band continuous from ten A.M. till midnight. It seemed immoral that the Smoky showed triple features. The aroma of relentlessly exploding popcorn, mingled with the smell of farmers' feet, piss, and sweat came out to them in gentle waves. The Smoky reeked of the forbidden. Momma and decent people in Cherokee regarded it as a hellhole of germs and flesh. "See they got a new picture of your mother, Lucius," said Gale. Lucius acted shy, as if Gale's teasing favored him over the others.

He liked the feeling of pushing through the door of Dozier's Cafe, people looking up as Gale, then Elmo, then Brady, then Lucius came in. The Bijou Boys passed the one empty booth out front and went straight to one in the back in the corner that seated six. As if rehearsed, they let Lucius in first, then with one smooth swipe, slid in on him from both sides, squashing him in the middle. He felt like a little kid and like Alan Ladd simultaneously. Two waitresses seemed to be arguing over who *didn't* have to serve them. The one who lost came over and stood like a target, and they took turns sniping at her. Some of the wisecracks were funny, but she shifted her feet, sighing through the long fits of cackles. When Lucius took a stab at her, they all turned up their collars and turtled their heads into their shoulders.

Stuffed with lunch, Lucius watched them shoot pool in the YMCA. Every Saturday morning before his paper route, Lucius had brought Bucky to the YMCA. In a hot little room that smelled of chlorine drying on flesh and hair, he and Bucky watched dumb-ass movies about the daily life and habits of rabbits or robins that put Lucius to sleep.

Showering, they soaped up. Using only their hands, they startled Lucius when they sudsed between the cheeks of their asses. It looked odd, raunchy, but logical if you wanted to get absolutely clean, so he soaped between his, somewhat more ostentatiously, and they jeered at him, as if it disgusted them, and he couldn't figure out what they'd been doing if not the same thing. When they kidded him, he had the feeling they thought he was a cute kid trying to do and say the right things, and he knew he was half trying to live up to that image, but after such an incident, he felt uneasy.

Swimming nude in the indoor pool, Lucius felt strange to be with the Bijou Boys where he'd often been with the kids of the old neighborhoods. Watching a muscular boy rise out of the water and trot heavily to the diving board, his huge peter flopping, Lucius imagined the titties of forty girls jouncing, glistening under the lights as they ran toward the diving board. "Be great to watch the girls at the YWCA swimming naked," said Lucius softly.

"Yeah," said Elmo, "love to have me a piece of ass out on the end of that diving board."

Thinking "piece of ass" referred to cornholing boys, Lucius edged away from Elmo. When Gale said, "Girl with a spring in her ass?" Lucius realized he was learning a new expresion.

After their swim, Lucius parted with the Bijou Boys in front of the Hollywood. He stopped in Stokes's Jewelers and put five dollars of his pay down on a thirty-dollar gold-plated Elgin wristwatch with green dials that glowed in the dark. "Radium," the man said. Seeing Alan Ladd in *China,* he put a leather jacket on layaway at Penney's, hoping to get the jacket within a few weeks.

Stepping out of the bright sun under the marquee, aware of the gigantic billboard mounted on top, the fringed banners skirting the rim, the long poster boards hanging at each side, the pattern of light bulbs in the ceiling of the marquee, onto the tiles of the outside foyer where the ticket booth sat between four brass-handled doors, then into the inner foyer, a marble bench with a poster and stills above it on each side, then up the carpeted stairs, into the main lobby, where Miss Atchley took tickets and Thelma sold candy, on into the inner lobby where ushers stood at the two main aisles and posters and stills were lit up in ornate stands the shape of jukeboxes, Lucius felt as if he'd always been entering the Bijou.

> Sat., September 7, 1946. A Walk in the Sun was on. Peggy Stansberry called and asked me do I like Loraine Clayboe. I said yes. Then Loraine called me up. Backslid. Cussed all day.

Desperate—homecoming troops worsened the already bad housing short-age—Momma took an apartment on the corner of Rader and Trescott, four blocks from Mammy's, three blocks from Beech Street, where Lucius had lived the most memorable two years of his childhood and where Emmett lived now. Only two rooms, and they had to share the bath with the young couple who owned the house. Momma had found a Negro from Clayboe Ridge who owned a truck and promised to get the stuff moved in before people started going to church. Lucius got up before daylight, as he had last Sunday to carry papers for the last time, to help Mr. Washington and his three sons and daughter. Daddy hadn't come home last night.

As they carried stuff into the house through the back door, Mrs. Easterly washed her three-year-old boy in a tub on the back porch. "How many times I have to tell you to keep your hands *off* that thing?" she kept saying, but the little boy kept flipping his pecker with his thumb. Mrs. Easterly was pregnant and wore her black hair cut short, old-fashioned style, but she was pretty, and Lucius imagined *her* playing with *his* pecker.

Lucius was glad to have a different bed, even if he had to share the fold-up cot with Bucky. Through a window over the bed, he saw a street-car go by and cross the railroad tracks that curved into the trees between an empty field and the fenced-in coal company yard.

He saw the church he attended when he lived on Beech. Maybe he'd start up there again and be near LaRue. One Sunday afternoon the minister's little granddaughter sat on a tricycle in the backyard in her new yellow Easter outfit and a bullet struck her in the head. One of the Trotter boys had fired a rifle into the air up on Clayboe Ridge. Lucius had never seen the child, but he imagined her sitting on his own green trike, hair as curly and radiantly blond as Bucky's had been at that age, the sun bright on her yellow Easter dress. Last autumn, Lucius had attended a funeral service for the Trotter boy who'd fired the shot five years before. His family had had his body shipped home from Palermo. In Lucius's imagination, the soldier was buried in the same cemetery with the preacher's granddaughter.

From the front porch, he saw, on the opposite side of the kudzu-vine-congested bank, the W. W. Drummond furniture mill, a rambling, shambling two-storey sprawl of buildings covered with silver, corrugated tin. A water tower rose above the roofs and a whistle blew at noon all over Clinch View. In back of W. W. Drummond was a narrow projection of land, on a rise—Stein's Auto Salvage yard. Lucius used to climb the fence with Sonny and Jim Bob Hawn and steal keys turned green out of the ignitions of old cars and trucks. A steep red clay bank rose from the tracks to a street that intersected with Beech. Between the baked clay and horse chestnut trees and the steaming metal of the junkyard, Lucius and the boys used to hop freights to Luttrell Farms or start the long trek on foot. Suddenly, several things that had seemed very impressive to him when he was a child converged, where he now lived on a hillock in a white house under a red tar-paper roof.

Entering the long, low chicken house for the first time, carrying a box of old clothes Momma had stored in Mammy's circus-wagon coal house, Lucius was awed to be where LaRue had *not* tried to fit the nozzle of an Orange Crush bottle into her— He rejected Norman Tate's lie. Still the ghostly smell of chicken shit as the morning sun hit the tin roof. To Lucius, coincidence was the elixir of daily life. Norman claimed that it was here he caught LaRue and Geneva Likins, who lived in the house then, trying to shove Orange Crush bottles up their— When Norman, three years ago, told him that in Sunday school class, Lucius twisted his arm behind his back and made him confess it was a lie. "Can't you do nothing but fight?" LaRue had asked Lucius, disgusted, ignorant of the reason. But the image stuck and when he passed the shack, walking or on the streetcar, Lucius had always turned his head, but had seen it clearly. Except for that, he kept his image of LaRue unblemished. She was his Scarlett O'Hara, but his imagination gifted her also with Melanie's saintly purity, just as he was a composite of Rhett Butler and Ashley Wilkes.

Momma's piano took up much of hers and Daddy's bedroom-living room. When they lived on Cold Springs Road, Lucius used to watch her walk up the street, her sheet music of popular songs under her arm, to a fine house on a hill where a widow she'd met in Howell's Drug Store allowed her to play her idle piano. Age had palsied the lady's hands and she liked to hear live music in the house. Momma had not told Daddy that she'd bought the new piano with the check he received as a winner of the Bronze Star for volunteering to dash across a plain into the mountains under fire, his medic truck turning over several times, to bring wounded back out of the hills. Lucius knew he wouldn't give a damn, but Momma thrived on secrecy, even though in her own mind she was convinced she deserved the piano for all the suffering that being married to Fred Hutchfield had inflicted upon her fun-loving nature.

The cramped living space—Momma's and Daddy's bed in the front room with the piano, Lucius's and Bucky's cot in the kitchen with the stove—wasn't so bad. What depressed him was the overflow into the two rooms and the hall of the junk Momma had carried like a nomad from house to house, from one end of Cherokee to another numerous times within his memory, out of the past into the future. Even after they'd packed the shed, half-full already with coal and kindling, she stacked barrels and boxes full of stuff too precious to her to risk roof leaks and prowlers, in corners of the two rooms, scraps of cloth draped over them, and along the wall in the hall, despite Mrs. Easterly's disgust.

Peeking into one of the boxes, Lucius asked, "Momma, you ain't gonna save these old sugar ration books, are you?"

"You just hush. You never know."

Once each spring, summer, and fall, Momma sorted through her junk, some of it accumulated before his birth—stored in a garage, a coal house, an attic, a hallway, a basement, sometimes half of it stored at Mammy's—to shake out the mice crap and dead bugs, cluck her tongue over evidence of moths, and rearrange, repack, restack it. He hated the days when she lit into the barrels and boxes, screaming, crying, cursing as he did everything wrong. After the stuff had been repacked, and the boxes, barrels stacked again, she threw away or gave to the Salvation Army very little. These worn, rain-streaked, soot-stained, mildewed boxes and barrels seemed mute testimony of the travail she'd endured raising three kids alone, losing one baby.

And ever since he could remember, Lucius had awakened late at night, bright light in his eyes, discovering his mother bent over dresser drawers, sorting—scratch, rattle, clink. She kept everything: Christmas ribbons, bows, cards, price tags, colored paper bags, candy boxes, bills, receipts, picture negatives. When Lucius or Bucky happened to find a corner of a bargain towel sticking out of a hideaway drawer, she'd scream, "That's my good towel!" Wanting to save it for the time when they'd have a "decent" home. Or she'd be bending over the foot of the mattress he slept on, picking bedbugs out of the seams and batting, fingernails cracking, clicking as she mashed them, and the light, really not so bright, since she couldn't afford more than 40 watts, seemed part of the movements, the sounds, the smell of bug blood.

And when Lucius begged her to throw some of it away or bring it more into the mainstream of their lives, she, irritated, reminded him that these pitiful rags were all she had to her name, and, more practically, someday they might really need them—don't forget how sudden the Depression came—and be glad she'd saved them. The outgrown baby and kid clothes, including every stitch that had been his dead baby brother's, things Lucius wore and was expected later to grow into, were kept because she could bear neither to look upon them, except when she had to "clean out her things," nor part with them. Lucius was more fascinated than repelled by Momma's epic struggles with her stuff, more impressed by the action than by the objects themselves.

Evicted by circumstances from Mammy's circus wagon, Lucius sat on the front steps that evening and looked through his own boxes.

"I'll pay you," said Momma, through the dirty screen in her room, the landlady's swing obscuring her face, "if you'll throw that junk in the trash and give us a little more room to breathe."

"I'll take a million dollars as a down payment." She slammed the window, trapping herself in the hot air of the room.

Digging through his writings, he found a letter he'd written Momma from Boys' Club Camp at Lone Mountain State Park when he was nine. Nostalgic for his childhood, he thumbed through the large black portfolio with CLINCH VALLEY BANK in silver letters on the front and a black ribbon to tie it shut, where he kept his drawings of movie stars done from portraits in magazines, of faces and scenes from his stories, comic strips of cowboy stories he'd made up, done on notebook paper, manila drawing paper issued in class, paper sacks. Often, he drew faces of his characters when he'd made up only their names and the titles of their stories.

In the backs of some *National Geographic*s he and Bucky had found in trash cans in alleys, Lucius hid the fuck pictures he'd drawn, some out of his head, some using photographs from newspapers, *Life, See, Look, True Detective,* but never from his movie magazines. Except in the few crudely drawn fuck books he'd encountered, he saw naked women only in *National Geographic*s. Sometimes, he sneaked into the jungle with one and, looking at the naked titties and shiny asses of African women who scared him but for whom he felt an odd affection, jacked off.

Lucius gathered all his writings into one stack on the top step and measured it. He laughed. With six inches, he was well hung.

There was no place for a sanctuary here—the chicken house was more tightly packed than the circus wagon had been—and there was no glory outside a sanctuary. For a while, he'd kept his writings and drawing material, his modeling clay and other stuff in one small drawer of the little desk Momma bought for Lucius, Earl, and Bucky one Christmas on Beech Street, but it had to be stored in the chicken house. Such sharing at Christmas was unusual, but he remembered with a slight bitterness that until Earl began to wander, when he was eleven and Lucius was eight, Lucius's birthday parties in August were still a shared celebration of Earl's and Bucky's birthdays because theirs fell in December and January when it was too cold and nasty to have a party outside and too cramped inside. So in August, the loot was evenly divided, with squalling contention, among the three evenly divided boys. Bucky always pilfered Lucius's drawer, so even before they moved to Mammy's and he began to use the circus wagon as a sanctuary, he'd dreamed of a private hideout.

Lucius put his stills and magazines and drawings and letters and Luke's diary back into the banana boxes he'd found behind the A & P and shoved the boxes under the cot in the kitchen. Then he went into Momma's and Daddy's room and talked her into giving him the bottom drawer of her dresser for his writings.

Before laying his writings away in the drawer, he spread them out on the sidewalk at the foot of the front steps and arranged them in the sequence in which he'd written them. Most of the stories broke off abruptly where his teachers, Miss Kuntz the most vigilant, had swooped down on him, ripped the page on which he was writing from the rings, and with a flourish wadded it up and slammed it into the wastebasket. "Where it belongs!" Remembering those encounters, he burned with rage. He'd never finished a story anyway, but he wrote hundreds of titles and lists of characters, casting movie stars in the parts, and five or six page starts of stories and novels. Something about the light on the side of a house at sunset or a fresh pack of three-ring, narrow-lined, side-ruled paper inspired him to start a new story or pick up an old one and try to climax it. He first liked the rough texture of Tarzan tablets, but then the slick finish of Blue Horse seemed more like a writer.

At the end of the previous school year, he'd written brief synopses of the best of the stories he'd started. Sticking his head in a banana box, so the neighbors wouldn't hear him and make fun, he tried to mimic the voices of the guys who announce the preview of forthcoming movies, reading off the titles and some of the summaries.

" 'Blue Waters' by Lucius Hutchfield. 'Great Moments in Music' by Cidney Cornel Chesterfield. 'Across the Snow' by Cidney C. Chesterfield." Clark Gable and Loretta Young and Jack Okie with Buck the St. Bernard moving across the snow to Dawson in *Call of the Wild*. " 'My Love for Laura' by Sidney Chesterfield. A gangster and a playboy match wits to see which can win the beautiful girl of their affection. Murder is involved, a sudden strength blooms in the playboy. A modern duel takes place and adventure and suspense runs high. 'The Adventure of Cider Flynn' by Lucian Chesterfield. 'Heading for the Stars' by Lucian Chesterfield." Paul Henreid and Maureen O'Hara in *The Spanish Main* wasn't as good as *Frenchman's Creek* but it inspired him to start another sea story. " 'Dangerous Waters' by Jordan Rogers. 'Adventure Beneath the Sun' by Jordan L. Rogers." After seeing *Gone With the Wind* for the third time two years ago, he'd mowed lawns so he could take LaRue, but her mother, she said, wouldn't let her. " 'The Ring' by Lamont Loy. Two old antique collectors meet and converse with each other. Richard Lombard has a ring in his possession which has an amazing history. This story tells of how the ring was involved with the lives of three adventure-seeking men and their loved ones. 'Madison Guy, FBI' by Lamont Loy. 'Racial Conflict' by Lamont Rogers. During heavy fighting, the Germans' only chance is to supply the best men with American uniforms acquired when a whole detachment of men had been killed before they'd moved up. Eric and his pal volunteer. They attack once across the American lines and Eric is hurt. He wakes with

a case of amnesia and wanders to an American camp. 'Reap the Poor'
by Tyrone L. Birchfield. 'The Face of a Chinaman' by Tyrone L. Birchfield. A convict escapes from Alcatraz, and realizing the danger of being
caught, he orders a surgeon to change his face. The surgeon tricks the
convict by giving him a Chinaman's face. The convict goes to China
and many things follow. 'Guardian Angel' by Tyrone Birchfield. 'My
Love for Madeline' by T. L. Birchfield. 'Hellbound' by Sidney Cornel
Birchfield. Brother against brother in this gripping story of the lawless
nineties. Guns ablaze and men die while the women wait and pray. One
brother is a detective, the other a criminal. Both fighting for the same
girl whose hands aren't any too clean. 'The Highwayman' by T. L.
Birchfield. 'Lady of France' by T. L. Birchfield. 'Half-Breed' by Tennessee Hutchfield. A drama of the lawless west is this novel of two
brothers who hate each other like a snake. This story of a town in which
only men lived is indeed a novel of hate and gunplay which make up
a great drama. 'Of Blood and Glory' by Tennessee Hutchfield. 'The
Roaming Texan' by Tennessee Hutchfield. 'On the Trail' by Tennessee
Hutchfield. A boy leaves his home in Kentucky to wander over the states
in search of Adventure. During his travels, he meets a girl who changes
his ideas and ambitions. They run off together and adventure begins.
'Buckskin Territory' by Tennessee Hutchfield. 'Safari Assignment' by
Ladd Hutchfield. The story takes place in Africa where the Safari
savages are on the warpath, the British on the alert, and ready for war,
with brave hearts. This is a story of a woman's jealousy and a man's
hatred. All this combined forms a great story of the wildest Africa.
'Angel Face, the Notorious' by Ladd Hutchfield. 'Blood on the Sand'
by Ladd Hutchfield. An Arabian fights for his country and at the same
time fights for the love of two women of whom he knows not which he
loves most of all. An American ambassador, a news reporter, and an
actress fit into this breathtaking novel of Arabian war and love. 'Mul-
titude of Condemned Souls' or 'Desert Romance' by David Scott Hamilton. 'While the Sea Remains' by Luke Scott."

Lucius wondered whether he ought to go back and strike out Cidney
Chesterfield, Jordan L. Rogers, Lamont Loy, Tennessee Hutchfield, Ladd
Hutchfield, and T. L. Birchfield now that he'd settled on Luke Scott.
How many names did Samuel Langhorne Clemens run through before
he struck Mark Twain ("Safe Water")? In the movie, only Mark Twain
was mentioned. He wondered whether any writer ever used his whole
real name? Lucius disliked his own. People made fun. And he didn't want
his writing to be associated with all the contempt talk in the old neighborhoods against Earl and Bucky and Daddy. His life as Luke Scott was his
own. Feeling that to strike out the other names would be a betrayal of
his other selves in the fifth, sixth, and seventh grades, Lucius left them.

Stacking the stories in order, Lucius set the scenario for "Glory in a Sanctuary" aside, and put the other stories in the bottom drawer of Momma's dresser. Back outside on the front porch, Lucius read "Glory in a Sanctuary," remembering that he'd shifted the locale from Chile to France, inspired by the movie of *Les Misérables* with Frederic March and Charles Laughton that he'd seen last year at the Smoky.

(Summary of)

Glory in a Sanctuary

by Ladd Hutchfield   Dedicated to LaRue

Characters

Rondógay Lavichichi	Cornel Wilde
Captain Valjean La Sauve	Charles Laughton
Kerel Bonnay	Vivien Leigh

Rondogay escapes from the French police to find refuse in an old sanctuary. Rondogay stays, under guard, in the sanctuary for a few days. His frist food and water he acquired when a village girl, Kerel, slipped into see him.

An old piano is his only past time although he cannot play. Soon the gril came again and with her, at Rondogay's request, she brought him paper, a bible and books.

Soon he learned to play the piano and when he did a huge crowd gathered to listen but was soon discounted when Capt. Sauve ordered them to leave. Capt. Sauve passed an order that death was the penality for helping the criminal. But somehow food and paper continued to get to Rondogay, he must be getting food else how could he live. Sauve could not understand it.

Before long the music and books Rondogay wrote began to curculate. Capt. Sauve relized this when he was invited to a grand supper meeting in France. They played a song he had heard Rondogay play not long ago. He asked the conductor who the composer was. He was known well all over France as "The Unknown Pinist."

Capt. Sauve returned determined to bring distruction to Rondogay. One day he goes to Rondogay for a confrence as he had many times before. Was he to surrender as he had been asked before? No that was all over. Capt. Sauve would not have to ask for surrender, he had a plan.

All intrances were sealed. All except one. Kerel came to Rondogay through the only intrance. By that time they are in love. Kerel's father who is a policeman finds red paint, subject of Sauves trap, on her dress. To save his daughter he sends her away to a grils school in Paris.

Rondogay misses her and thinks of her as dead. His music ceases and the publishers of his books go mad. What has happened to "the Unknown Pinist?" Food does not come and Rondogay becomes sick. From the sanctuary there comes no more music and the village grieves and goes to the steps of the sanctuary to pray for Rondogay. From the shadows Rondogay watches the ceremony.

Sauve investagates while keeping his distance. But this time he is alone for he thinks Rondogay dead. Rondogay jumps him and with a rope chokes him and takes his gun. At the door he appears with Sauve beaten and scared in front of him. Sauve has pride and refuses to order his men to lay down thier arms he also says that death would come to anyone who did. Rondogay shoots him in the side. But Sauve resists.

Kerel's father revolts and leads the peasents in the rebellion. He tells Rondogay to go to a grils boarding school in Paris, there he will find Kerel. Across mountain turraine he traveles and at last Paris is attained.

There he sees where his music is to be played in the fore most theatres of Paris. It warms his heart.

He goes to the school and is told that Kerel has ran off.

Kerel returns to the village only to be siezed by Sauves successor as a collaborator with a murderer. The village is wrecked. And already twenty people has been taken prisoner and are to hang. Kerel's paint dress was found before her return. Her father was executed.

From an excaped villager Rondogay learns of conditions in the village and realizes that it is his fault. He stops his constant walking of the streets looking for Kerel and returns.

Before giving him self up, he wishes to play one more time his last and best composition. Through out the whole up roar of the village the music drifts and the shouting threats of the villagers outside the court house ceases and fades into silence and stern listening. Down in the dungeon the music drifts and Kerel hears it.

For the last time the usal crowd assembles in front of the sanctuary. Presently Rondogay appears at the door to meet the new Capt. He's ready if all the villagers are to go free. The Capt. agrees but Kerel must die with him. Rondogay had not expected that Kerel was as notorious as the Capt. discribed her. But there was nothing he could do now for he was already under guard.

At dawn the next morning Kerel and Rondogay stood against the breeze with a noose before them. The court yard was empty but low mortal singing could be heard. In front of the sanctuary the towns people sung & prayed and when the huge clock in the square struck eight, the people knew that glory was just being born.

The End

Moved even more deeply by reading the story than telling it to Daddy on that long midnight trek home four days ago, Lucius went in and got his notebook and a number two pencil. Coming out onto the front porch, a sense of new life starting in this new house made him want to change his name again. Sitting where grass grew raggedly, against the soot-streaked trunk of the cedar tree, Lucius began chapter one of *"Glory in a Sanctuary"* by. . . . . Will Cosgrove.

France, in the village of youthful Naples, was very beautiful in the spring of 1863 and the flowers were nearly all in bloom and boasting with thier colors. The afternoons had been hot and sticky. The hills and ridges surrounding the village were covered with green leafted trees, spralled out vines and wild flowers and berries all these things the heat was attached to and they were affected as were the marketers in the middle section of the village. They scampered about from one bargain wagon to another. Purses were dug into and money accepted.

Thus was the atmosphere of May 5th, France, 1863. On this day Glory was to begin but would not be recognized until years into the furture.

The hub-bub of the crowds and the clatter of horses and oxen on the cobble-stoned streets was slowly halted when police whistles were blown in command to halt. People wondered and looked about in serch of the desporado in escape from the evil police of the un-fortunate village of Naples. Then to crowds by crowds in area and area he appeared and was emedidately recognized and feared. Then they were glad that thier evil police force were on the job.

He was Rondogay Lavichichi from the Netherlands, notorious, handsome, admired and hunted. By "The Dutchman" he was better known.

He ran in fashion of a grey hound his life was at steak. He fell and rose to run again leaving far behind his opponents in uniform. Far to a distance a symbol of hope attracted his attention. Towering high above the other two & three story buildings of the village there loomed into the upper atmosphere a sanctuary ruined by a recent war. There he would receive safety. And so his fast feet carried him there at its door in short time.

Far behind the police chief watched the thief inter and rage against an odivious fact formed inside his abdomen. At the fore head of the church he signaled his men to a halt then peered inside for signs of Rondogay.

From a window above he appeared and spoke, thus causing everyone to raise their head.

"Sorry, Sauve, that again you have failed to hang my rogueish body from the neck. And again and again I feel sory for you because of your future failures."

Captain Sauves lip trembled with hates affect and he bellered out in gesture. "There will be no more, "Dutchman." Next time I intend to demolish you, if not then demolish myself I will."

Rondogay laughed aloud and the intire village heard him but Captain Sauve stalked away in direction of his quarters.

Rondogay turned after Captain Sauve had faded away through an alley and examined his new home—darkness and solutude were his surroundings, the very atmosphere of eternal lonelyness. Within these walls of shaken stone and stained broken glass he—

The sound of steel taps on the sidewalk made Lucius look up. A tall, skinny boy, wearing a leather jacket, came down the walk, clipping along at a cocky rate, deliberately scraping steel taps on his shoes to make sparks. Long hair with a beautiful blond pompadour set off his bony, box-jawed face. As he walked along unobserved, glancing right and left, snapping his fingers, his head slightly lowered, as if he were performing for a reluctant audience that needed a little bullying, he began to seem familiar. When he saw Lucius up on the bank, he stopped dead, reared back, kicked out one foot, grabbed his cods in one hand, flung the other hand wide and high, snapped his fingers, and grinning, brought his thumb down, pointing at his prick. "Gobble a goot, boy! Gobble a goot! Gobble a goot!" But as he started walking again, half dancing, grinning, raking up a mock-fiendish laugh, a virile version of Peter Lorre's killer giggle in *The Maltese Falcon,* his eyes twinkling, Lucius sensed this was the guy's tough sort of friendly greeting.

"Ain't I seen you before?" Lucius looked down at the guy from the slope, shored up along the sidewalk by a concrete wall.

"Shit, yeah, boy, we was in Boys' Club camp together 'bout four years ago. Lone Mountain! I remember you had hair on your dick when I was bare as a baby's ass. You talking to Duke Rogers, boy!"

"Hell, yeah, how you doin', Duke?" Lucius remembered him as a sissified, shy little kid who cringed when anybody approached him.

"Gettin' more pussy than I can stir with a stick."

"Yeah? How 'bout lettin' me in on a little?"

"Shit, man, I can get you any pussy that walks Clinch View and half a Cherokee."

"No shit."

"I wouldn't bird you, boy. This place is *full* a good pussy."

"Where 'bouts you live?"

"I just *had* me some, and I'm on my way to tear off some more, by God. . . . You ever fuck a girl?"

"Yeah. But not in four years."

"What?"

Lucius told him about the girls he'd "done it" to since he was five, but Duke didn't believe him.

"You live around here?"

"Hell, I feel like stompin' the livin' shit out of somebody." Duke's fidgety movements were so abstract, Lucius felt only mildly threatened. "Let's go pile some bastard's ass."

"Well, right now, I'm—"

"What you doin' there?"

"Uh— I'm—Well, you know—" Oh, hell, "writing."

"Huh?"

"Writing a story."

"Writing a story?" He looked at Lucius as if he were an albino usher. "Fuck story?"

"No, it's—"

"Hell, man, write a story about *me*. You ought to get you some taps for those shoes. Hell, I come home at midnight, climb that fuckin' hill, shit, wake the mudduh fuggers *up*."

"Where bouts you live?"

"Clayboe Ridge. Way up on Natchez."

"Hey, you know Elmo Hatcher? *He* lives on Nat—"

"You move in here? My old man started to *buy* this fucking house."

"Yeah? Why didn't he?"

"Shit, man, my cock hurts. That woman loves to fuck."

"What kinda work your daddy do?"

"Let's barrel ass, man. Scrounge us up some pussy."

"Thought you just *had* some."

"My old man's the traffic cop front of the Tivoli Theatre." Duke exaggerated all the standard traffic hand signals rapidly, making a whistling sound. Then he spit through his teeth and hiked his cods. "The sonofabitch. Blow his head off."

Lucius had seen that traffic cop all his life, a flurry of white-gloved hands at the heart of Cherokee.

"Wish I had me a good pistol, man. Damn thirty-five automatic. You see *The Last Crooked Mile* at the Hollywood?"

"Missed it. But I'm ushering at the Bijou now."

"Hell, how'd you like to drive a car like that lightnin' ass fucker, the Green Hornet? Come on, som'bitch, le's go."

Lucius resisted an impulse to reach out his foot to kick Duke in the face for calling him a son of a bitch, but he sensed that he used such names in a friendly way. Duke's manner of talking and scampering about in a small space suggested a world of his own making out of which he came and into which he was going at great speed, making it up as he went along.

Lucius got up and put his notebook in the bottom drawer of Momma's dresser and yanked on Luke's combat boots that he'd stolen from Mammy's circus-wagon coal house, and got in step beside Duke Rogers. All the pussy in Clinch View and half of Cherokee seemed on the verge of being his. It eluded him that day, but the search was exhilarating, though finally exhausting.

> Sunday, September 8, 1946. Bijou Dark. We moved. Straightened out
> my stuff. Met tough guy named Duke, used to be named Donald when
> he was little.

NIGHT RITUAL: Zachary Street is only one long block, a steep hill. The house is two storeys. It is winter, the rooms upstairs are ice cold, full of boxes. It's summer. Feet black on the bottom from walking up there. Earl crawls out of a window onto the tar-paper roof, and Bucky is so scared he screams and pees on the sooty floor. Where the limbs of the big tree reach is high. Lucius is afraid to go out on the roof. Then he follows Earl out onto the roof and holds onto a tree limb. A big one, a middle-sized one, and a little one. . . Standing shivering on a corner in crisp night air, waiting for the last streetcar, Bucky in Momma's arms, Lucius and Earl trying to yell like Tarzan in *Tarzan and the Apes* that they'd just seen at the Avalon, Daddy laughing, Momma embarrassed, Lucius aware of the gigantic swarm of electric wires looming above and behind him in towers across the railroad tracks, next to the red-brick Cherokee Knitting Mill, and a vast pond across the street, infested with lily pads, cattails, weeds, and deep green water, showing through a vine-crawly fence. Once a municipal swimming pool. The scariness of the dark, the creepiness of the jungle. . . . Lucius, Earl, and Bucky lie on the dusty-choky rug by the radio, the yellow waxy dial glowing mellow, and looking up in the dim light see Gran'paw Charlie, rocking in the wicker chair, his small feet not touching the figured rug, holding the buckle of his brown leather belt in one hand, a White Owl in the other, while Major Bowes' deep voice on "The Amateur Hour" that makes Lucius sleepy throbs out of the radio, and he hears the wicker chair creak suddenly, and knows they have talked too loud and that Gran'paw's leather belt is zipping through the loops. . . . . Lucius sits in the thick heat of the back seat of Gran'paw Charlie's car, parked in the alley, watching Gran'paw walk down the backyard in the bright glare of the sun, lugging a freezer full of homemade banana ice cream that he has churned hard as jawbreakers. . . . . Gran'paw Charlie beats his own serving of banana ice cream with a spoon until it gets soupy and eats it with cold corn bread and Momma and Mammy and Hazel have to turn their heads, and Uncle Luke laughs at them. . . . . The sun is a crooked square of soft yellow on the faded wallpaper. Hazel lifts Lucius into her arms, and he looks down at Gran'paw Charlie, lying in the barred bed Lucius and Earl and Bucky had slept in and Baboo would sleep in. He is dressed up in black, his hands on his chest as if he is smoothing down his lapels, and his face white as pie dough. . . . . Lucius sleeps in the clothes box that smells of mothballs and musty cotton in the bedroom where Gran'paw and Mammy used to sleep together. It is the coal-blackest place he has ever been, and he keeps worrying, afraid the heavy wooden lid will come crashing down over him. But he is afraid to cry loud because it still seems he will wake Gran'paw, who lies in the living room by the radio.

The smell of hot fudge woke him. In the dim light of the forty-watt bulb that hung on a cord from the cracked ceiling, Momma sat at the kitchen table she'd painted yellow and green while he slept—the fumes made his eyes sting—her hair up in curlers, wearing her night-gown and the quilted housecoat, her feet propped on a box, a book with a cellophane cover that glowed in her lap—probably *The Foxes of Harrow* that she'd borrowed from Ringgold's Department Store rental library—a plate of fudge cooling at her elbow, the dangling light casting a yellow sheen over it. The kitchen clock on top of the Home Comfort cookstove said 1:00. He wondered if Daddy, two days missing, had come in yet. Sometimes the smell woke both of them, Earl, too, years back, and they went to the kitchen door in the other houses. "We smell candy." Surprised, she'd tell them to get back in bed, they could have some in the morning. They took it in their lunch to school. But sometimes she sat there until two o'clock, undetected, and in the morning, only a film of butter gleaming on the plate.

Sam knows that somewhere Crockett's men are ready to jump him. Sam seizes Crockett around the throat from behind and jabs the revolver in his back, and shouts as if he wants all Frisco to know that he has the great Crockett at last.

"All right, you damn sonofabitches, I've got a gun in his back and I got the girl hid. The first hack I see, I'll plug him between the eyes. I ain't going to the girl, so don't follow."

Sam kicks the cabin door open and pushes—

"You have the loveliest blue eyes."

Lucius thought the voice came to him from *The Green Years* on the screen behind him. But Charles Coburn, bushy-faced, big red nose, wearing suspenders, sits on the edge of his bed, paring a corn with a big razor. Looking right, Lucius saw a girl sitting in the back row on the aisle, staring into his eyes. He remembered her sitting there through *A Walk in the Sun* last Friday.

"How can you tell in the dark?" Lucius tried to control the quaver in his voice.

"They glow even in the dark." Her voice, deep, rich.

"With my back to you?"

"I wanted you to turn toward the screen. That's when your eyes look most beautiful."

She'd often seemed to be looking more at him than at the screen, but she'd seemed so distant, untouchable. About his own age, she dressed very properly in a warm, rich brown coat with darker shiny brown velvet trim and a round little brown hat with a brown ribbon of velvet, on her dark brown, short, curly hair. She seemed very well bred, well mannered, poised, inwardly quiet, her face and her legs very pretty, but he couldn't see her eyes. He imagined brown.

Even though others had praised his eyes before, "You have the loveliest blue eyes" was the most impressive one-liner any girl had ever delivered to him. He wished LaRue or Loraine had said that.

Lucius wanted to tell her the climax of "While the Sea Remains."

"Go feed your germs, Lightnin'," said Gale, coming up behind, touching his neck, sparking him.

Getting into his street clothes to go eat supper at Jane's Cafe, Lucius decided he wouldn't try to sit beside the girl because that might spoil the mood. And even though he hadn't taken Loraine out yet, he'd sworn to himself to love her forever, and all other girls would have to suffer, unless they just wanted to "do it."

Scruffing his feet on the carpet Lucius tried to work up some static electricity, but when he touched Gale's cheek from behind, no spark flew.

Gale gave him an odd look. "Touch, but don't kiss."

The girl in brown was gone.

A one-storey, shotgun construction at the top of ten wooden steps with a rusty, wobbly iron railing, Jane's Cafe hugged up against the Avon Arms that had once been the YMCA and resembled a castle, painted cheaply, white and orange. It sat across the street from Cherokee's main firehall. No bigger under the mulberry tree than a good place to play marbles, Mammy's place was not much wider inside than Chief Buckner's arm spread. A long counter with stools, booths against the opposite wall. Lucius loved the smell from the Morning Bird coffee factory nearby, where she and Momma worked before Gran'paw Charlie's murderer put some insurance money in Mammy's hands.

Momma was pouring coffee for two firemen. The smells of turnip greens, salt pork, corn bread, pinto beans, onions, 'arsh potatoes, hot lard grease, pork chops, liver, dirty dishwater, clogged drains were all one aromatic swim that made the cafe pulse with possibilities.

"Lord, that little booger did the cutest thing few months ago," said Mammy, who sat in the booth with the firemen. "Come home and found the kitchen flooded with water and Rinso suds foaming up around the table legs where that poor youn'ern had tried to clean up his Mammy's house for her."

Then why had she screamed for an hour and fussed with Momma two more, and why had both of them ganged up on Bucky, slapping him winding and taking a switch from the hedge to his bare legs, and why should Lucius clean up the house every day, as he had since he was six, and many different houses before Mammy's, if they were going to tell with such epic affection of Bucky's one disastrous attempt to imitate Lucius? Bucky was present in the glowing eyes of the firemen who often gave him a penny for the jawbreaker machine or stuffed him with lemon meringue pie.

Walking back to the Bijou, Lucius remembered Luke coming for him and Bucky and Earl when Momma used Gene Autry, Buck Jones, Roy Rogers, Johnny Mack Brown, and Wild Bill Elliott as babysitters all day in the summer in the Hollywood Theatre, a nickel bag of popcorn to share for breakfast. After they'd seen the movie twice, Luke, off duty as an usher, swung Bucky up on his shoulders and Lucius held onto his thumb and Earl to his pocket as they walked five blocks to Mammy's little cafe. Barefoot, wearing shorts, sometimes no shirts— the Hollywood was not air-cooled—perched on wobbly stools, they wolfed hot roast beef sandwiches and mashed 'taters.

Stuffed with Mammy's cooking, his feet aching, Lucius stood On the Spot, a good view of Miss Atchley's short hair and full but trim butt, and her smile in profile when she handed customers their stubs as they stepped through the golden doorway, the doors hooked open now. He loved listening to her voice, deep and resonant.

Lucius held the flashlight that smelled of sweat and brass behind him, leaned slightly against it, braced against the post, as if it were a metal rod, clamped to the wall, soldered to a statue's back to make it stand up. The underarm smell of the uniform was strong, and he wondered how often it was sent out to be cleaned.

Between customers, Lucius turned his gaze inward, the screen at his back.

Sam kicks the cabin door open and pushes Crockett into the room. He falls on the floor and rolls over in agony, and Sam sees his face for the first time.

Marina is lying on the bed. She jumps when she sees the man: "Mr. See."

"What do ya mean, Mr. See? He's that damn husband of yours, ain't he?"

"Hell, no, that's Jonathan's lawyer."

Sam walks toward Mr. See, his teeth clenched, blood in his eyes, a look of fear comes over Mr. See's face, and he grabs him by his collar and jerks him to his feet. "Well, well, so your name's See, huh?"

"Yes, sir."

"You're not so tough now, are you?" Frightened, Mr. See hesitates. "Answer me!"

"No, sir."

"No, sir, what?"

"I'm not tough anymore."

"You bet you ain't. Now go over there in the corner and sit, sit and shut up."

Sweating, Mr. See squats in the corner and lets his head drop between his raised knees. Sam checks his gun and starts for the door.

"Sam, where are you going?"

"To kill your husband."

Sam slams the door and runs out onto the dock. Marina follows him, screaming. Sam is about to climb aboard when she says, frantically, "Sam, if you kill Jonathan, you'll live to regret it."

Sam yanks the rope loose—

"Hutchfield, better get those smoochers."

Lucius went down the aisle as Charles Coburn said, "Could you be letting me have half a crown?"

Coming back up the aisle, the Irish daylight from the screen on their faces, Lucius caught the couple in the act.

"Sorry, no kissing allowed in the theatre."

Grown-ups obeying his orders gave Lucius an odd feeling of imbalance. Hood was nodding his head, pushing his thin blond hair away from his eyes.

On the Spot again, Lucius started to return to the mood of the climax, but a small, slender blond woman of about twenty-six came in alone, wearing a flowered dress like a young girl's. She looked very familiar, but he couldn't remember where he'd seen her. She had a sad look, and walked hesitantly through the main lobby, as if expecting some one to walk up to her. "How far down, please?"

Lucius lighted her walk down the aisle.

Coburn was telling little Dean Stockwell about the time he fought in the Zulu wars. She stopped halfway and sat one seat in from the aisle, as if she knew exactly the one she wanted.

People he'd known and who had drifted away from him or he'd just seen often on the streets entered the Bijou, as if onto a stage, carrying a warm bag of popcorn. On the Spot, Lucius enjoyed the fact that all Cherokee might come through that lobby in the coming year.

Sam yanks the rope loose and the yacht slides out onto the surf.

He steps onto the concrete porch. The house is dark and desolate. Not a sound. Sam searches the entire house but finds nothing except a huge dog sleeping beside the fireplace. No signs of servants. Maybe Crockett has set the stage for a showdown.

"Hutchfield, look alive," said Hood, walking away. Gale stood at the office door.

Lucius led a woman down the aisle, seating her halfway down, re-membering Lana applying lipstick to her luscious lips. She and Garfield had been swimming in the ocean at night, vowing their love again after tormenting each other for weeks. As he returned to his post, Lucius heard brakes squeal, a loud truck horn, a crash, and saw a close-up in memory of Lana's hand as the lipstick rolled out of it onto the floor of the car.

Taking up his rigid position again, Lucius saw Bucky floating down the Tennessee River on a houseboat, Emmett waving down to him from high up on the Sevier Street Bridge as it floats under. Saw Earl spoon-feeding the fat, armless, legless man in the midway. Daddy reeling drunk down the steep streets of Cherokee (sensed some customers pass him by, to find seats on their own in the dark). Momma and Mammy joking with the firemen and railroaders.

The kids in the village make fun of Coburn's big red nose, and he chases after them with his cane.

Lucius had to squeeze to keep from going in his pants. It hurt to hold it, but it seemed to stimulate more vivid and langorously exciting images of the past, of what had happened in school that day, of what he imagined in the future, and scenes in his stories.

Coburn's wife makes Dean Stockwell sleep with her. He's not al-lowed to sleep with the old man anymore because of the bad influence of his wild stories. She undresses in front of the kid, telling him she'll make a God-fearing man of him.

Sam goes to the attic. He opens the door, the gun in his hand. In the dark corner across the room someone sobs. The same corner where Sam found Marina that stormy night, chained to the wall. At last he had Crockett cornered, the man who has caused him so much torture. A voice bursts forth, echoes along the wall of the attic, startling Sam: "Why don't you shoot, Sam?"

It sounds like the voice of Sam's brother.

Mon., September 9, 1946. This girl said, "You have the loveliest blue eyes." Al Jolson contest coming Wensday. Mrs. Hood came down to the Bijou from the Tivoli. She's real cute. Looks like Lili Palmer in Screen Romances story of Cloak and Dagger. Me & Gale ate some pie and talked about Mary, Betty, Janie, and etc., and he forgot to pull the curtain when The Green Years ended. Dragonwick coming to the Tivoli.

Duke's piercing whistle made Lucius drop his fork in his lap. Wiping egg off his fly, he raised the window over the cot. "Better go on, Duke. Have to take my little brother up to Clinch View first."

"Walk up there with you. Need to kill me a few teachers."

Lucius started to push his bicycle off the back porch, but he felt childish riding a bike in front of Duke. When he saw they were going to have to walk it, Bucky started whining and jumping up and down.

"I'm gonna store it in the damn chicken house," said Lucius. "Getting too old to ride a bicycle."

"Let me have it."

"Your feet won't touch the pedals."

While Duke stayed outside on the long sidewalk, sneering, spitting through his teeth, Lucius escorted Bucky to the door of Miss Carr's room. "And don't run off, by God." Last Wednesday, Bucky, playing at recess, had seen Emmett crouching in the jungle at the far edge of the playground and slipped away with him. The truant officer had started seeking Momma out at Jane's Cafe, and the severe-looking elderly woman made the firemen nervous.

Walking to Bonny Kate, Lucius tried to fascinate Duke with the story of the Raven, inspired by his memory last night of Alan Ladd as Raven in *This Gun for Hire,* but Duke's attention was fitful. He seemed to have no ability to listen carefully enough to a single sentence to see how it linked up with another. Duke's bragging leapt rapidly from one exploit to another, interrupting Lucius at every crucial point. He seemed to have a wild imagination, but was insensitive to anybody else's.

Lucius missed good old Joe Campbell who used to walk to Clinch View with him from Beech Street. Lucius's working hours cut down opportunities for running around with Joe, who'd taken up with a Clinch View group of kids who were more or less momma's boys, yard-bound. One time, he started telling Joe a story as they walked to school.

continued it at recess, at lunch, during noon recess, during change of classes, the afternoon fire drill, walking back home, and ended it sitting on the front porch steps, eating a peanut butter and jelly sandwich, half-watching some utility men pound a new telephone pole in the ground where lightning had cut one down. Lucius's efforts to tell Duke a story made him dizzy, left him with a headache. But he felt challenged to win his attention. He'd work on him again in the morning.

At the end of the alley of mimosa trees, Peggy, Joy, and Cora leaned against the trunks that were whitewashed four feet up. Lucius wondered where Loraine could be.

As he passed them, his legs felt weak. They giggled, obviously pretending to be unaware of him.

"Hey, you dropped something," said Cora Samins. Lucius glanced over his shoulder and smiled to show her he wasn't going to fall for that one. "No shit," said Cora.

Joy and Peggy yelled, "Cora!," turned, bent over giggling, and waltzed around among the mimosa trees, hugging the trunks, pretending to hide their faces in girlish mortification.

Lucius saw a note lying on the ground. He beat Duke to it, put it in his pocket. Glancing back, he saw Loraine standing behind a fatter trunk, her books in her arms, observing the scene.

Going down the hall, he saw Joe Campbell at his locker.

"Hey, Lucius, ain't you going out for football?"

"Naw, I don't care nothing about it."

"Wish *I* had shoulders like that."

"I didn't have nothing to do with it. It was God."

"Who needs shoulders?" said Duke as they went on. "Give me a damn .38."

In Miss Kuntz's homeroom, Lucius looked at the note, folded intricately, a skill he'd never learned himself. On the outside, Loraine had written "To the cutest boy in the world." Lucius unfolded the note.

B.K.J.H.S.

Hello, Handsome,

I just love your blue shirt, the one with the dark stitches on the pockets. I like that poem or ever what it was you wrote about me. I thought I would write you this because you wrote that poem to me. I'm writing it on stationary paper because I want you to keep it. I dreamed about you all night. Peggy and Joy and Cora stayed all night for my slumber party and Joy said I talked in my sleep but was too sleepy to listen. Cora said she stayed up all night and heard every word but she won't tell. She's hateful sometimes. We had a good time last night but we could of had a better time if you

were there. Harry kissed Peggy and I thought they were going to fall over the banisters he had her bent over so far. I run out there 3 times telling her to hurry. I can't find a book for Miss Cline's class. Did you? You know where you put "and made for me to worship?" You thrilled the fool out of me when you wrote that. I like you and I know you like me, don't you? I may be conceited but I like to be that way. I can't think of nothing else to say. Oh yes, did Della Snow give you another note in the library? You can answer this if you want to. Don't let anybody read this. Your friend, Loraine Clayboe.
P.S. This note don't make sence to me. & I doubt if it does to you, but wrote, Just to have something to do. Doubt if you can read it.

In Miss Redding's English class, Lucius wrote a note to Loraine. He liked her name, but when he felt an impulse to call her Raine, the emotion was almost like what he felt when he created and named the loved one in his stories.

Dearest Raine,
I adore you in a way that no one has yet discribed in words, one can discribe it only in taking part in that feeling. The beauty of words have no beauty when they attempt to say to you the things so tender in my heart. You know if all the love I have for you was devided among all the females on earth and in heaven, they would have enought to satisfie them for until the end of eternity. God took his time when he created you. I love you trully, Lucius.

Lucius gave it to Cora Samins as she came limping arrogantly off the playground from gym period.
"Hey, my sister works at the Bijou, too. Minetta Samins."
"Oh," said Lucius.
Miss Cline started off reading the first paragraph of the history text aloud, then the girl sitting in the first seat in the first row picked up where she left off, and each took a turn, until everybody was half-asleep.
Behind propped up books, one kid was reading a Phantom funny book and Lucius, well aware at first that his ass would be mud if Miss Cline caught him, but now too immersed to care, began

Manuscript for
"A Killer for Hire"
by Will Cosgrove

The Raven was a professional killer. He was neither handsome nor homely. He was a monster who helt high favor from the devil, and most people in those days belived seriously that he was the son of satan. Naturally that was merely a blind belief—yet one can never tell. His hair gave him his name for it was pure black like the slick feathers of the bird raven. And he walked with softness of a feather and swiftness of an attacking vulcher. In synopsis the person of the Raven was said to be that of an inhuman creation. Perhaps in the event of his birth there should have been a mother in the form of a reptile beside him, but actually it was a pure, God-fearing, spanish—

"Lucius Hutchfield!"
"Ma'am?"
"Are you in or out of this world at the moment?"
Finding the place, Lucius, a remedial reader, read aloud: "The con-federa-tion of New England was com-posed of colon-ial settlements that joined together to protect each other. It was organized in 1643 and was pro- pro- claimed as a 'firm and per-per—"
"Perpetual. . . ."
"Perpetual league of friendship. We re-vere it as the first attempt at a con-fed-eracy of colonies in North America. . . ."

—woman who gave this man birth.
Everyone who resided anywhere near the west, over which this man spread his black cape of terrow during the period that knew the saga of the great spanish-american war, knew distintly the character of the Raven, for even though many people never saw him, his evil stood out like the historic events in the war of that decade.

Aware that Loraine was looking at him, wondering what he was writing, maybe thinking it was another love letter, Lucius tried to look like Cornel Wilde writing "the Polanaise," with George Sand, hovering near, smoking her thin cigar. Under the title, he wrote "To Raine."

He was not talked about in the manner a man's perssonage is discussed. In the controary the Raven was talked of as a—

Pausing to conjure, Lucius made his fingers ripple like Paul Muni as *Scarface* when he made a silver dollar travel the back of his hand.

—a menacing beast, a new specie added to the catagory of other wild animals which roamed the great plains.
Any lawless man with gold could be the employer of the Raven.

Hearing Loraine's voice, Lucius looked up and listened: "In time, Maryland had sixty manors, each of about two thousand acres. They were managed by nobles. Commoners performed the labor. There was a wide gap between the two classes."

After school, Lucius rode on the back of Lard's bicycle down to the old paper corner and Dusty Harper gave him back his five dollars for the bond he'd put up. He went ahead of Pee Wee on the route and collected almost all of the nine dollars his old customers still owed him.

Making another payment on his watch at Stokes's Jewelers, he said, "Sure wish I could wear it now."

"You're Jane's grandson, aren't you?"

"Yes, sir."

"Well, if she'll sign for it, I can let you have it on credit."

Lucius went to the cafe and got Mammy to sign.

When he walked into Penney's, he was wearing the gold-plated, radium-dialed watch.

The saleslady wouldn't let Lucius charge the leather jacket he had put on layaway. Looking at one just like it on a rack, imagining how good he would look to Raine, Lucius counted his money. Including what he'd paid down and what was left from last Saturday's pay, he had eleven dollars more than he needed.

Passing the window of Ryder's Photo Shop, admiring the way his new leather jacket fit, Lucius paused to gaze at the movie projectors. Most of them were much too expensive, but a little grey Keystone 8 mm was only $11.99, about what his Western Flyer bicycle cost him three years ago. His desire for the projector was so intense, he went in to put it on layaway.

"I'd buy it now, but I only got eleven dollars."

"We don't handle layaways, son. But I tell you what, you take it on, and pay me the difference next payday. New usher at the Bijou, aren't you?"

A free Tim McCoy movie came with it, but the man also let him have a Charlie Chaplin that got broken in three places one time when he was demonstrating the machine.

Lucius walked fast to the Bijou, hot inside the leather jacket that he knew he wouldn't really need for a month. He remembered an even smaller, red projector that Momma and Daddy had given him, Earl, and Bucky to share one Christmas when they lived on Cold Springs Road. They showed cowboy movies on a pillowcase stuck to the wall with adhesive tape. Lucius last saw the projector in the alley. Bucky had broken it. But for a year, long coils of film were entangled among their toys until only a frame or two showed among the Chinese checker marbles, the yo-yos, and lead soldiers in the dirt on the bottoms of their toy boxes. Lucius had never forgotten the little red projector and the sadness he felt when he saw it on the trash pile. Now that the war was over, projectors were in store windows again, and at least once every day he'd thought of buying the one he carried now in his hand, a feeling of power thrusting him along toward the Bijou marquee on his day off.

An old man in overalls and a baseball cap stood on top of the marquee holding a bucket while another old man in the coveralls of a railroad worker used a long brush to push up, unrolling, a large poster showing the heads of the Marx Brothers, eyes bugged at the torso of a woman in a harem costume, her long legs stretched out under their chins. "A NIGHT IN CASABLANCA. Groucho, the Look, Harpo, the Ogle, Chico, the Leer. WHAT A TREASURE THEY'RE AFTER. Their 1946 Howl-raiser." What the two old men were doing was a serious adult job but they looked like cartoon figures.

As Lucius turned in off the bright sidewalk, the sight of Hood sitting in the ticket booth broke his stride. Like Minetta, he paid no attention to Lucius's entrance, as if, off duty, he didn't exist.

Walking the dark narrow aisle behind the box seats, sensing darkness like a thick curtain at his back, he always shivered.

Lucius looked for the best dressing room to try out the projector. On the ledges under the light-bordered mirrors all kinds of magazines were strewn, except movie magazines: *Captain Marvel, Wonder Woman, True Detective, Superman, Human Torch, Batman, The Green Lantern, Argosy, The Spectre, Hawkman.* Lucius had stopped collecting and trading funny books long ago, on Avondale. It depressed him to look upon this evidence, by absence, of lack of interest in movies. To the other boys, ushering at the Bijou seemed to be just a job. The only movies that really interested the Bijou Boys were a few from the past that they mentioned in comas of nostalgia as they lay on the sacks of raw popcorn or leaned back in the round-backed black and brown chairs in the big dressing room upstairs: *One Million B.C., King Kong, Tom Sawyer, Frankenstein, Hurricane, Double Indemnity, Curse of the Cat People.*

Lucius tried showing Tim McCoy on the wall, but it was too grimy. Then he propped his uniform dickey against a mirror and the picture was clearer but bowed.

Lucius was so deeply absorbed in the strangeness of a silent movie image—a stagecoach racing over a western landscape with no thundering hoofs, no symphonic brass and drums, and the mute cloud of dust when Tim McCoy leaped from his horse, dragged the villain off *his* horse, and they rolled down a sandy hillside, looked as if it should have made a sound of some kind, looked odd, as if it were a dream from his childhood—Elmo's voice startled him, saying, "Wha'fuck's'at?"

"Didn't you ever see a movie before?"

"Wise ass."

Then Gale came in wearing his uniform and sat in a chair blocking the propped-up dickey and let the images flicker on his own, delighted, giggling as if it tickled. Brady came in, in uniform. "Thought you'd fell in," he said, and stayed in the doorway watching. Lucius felt the way he did at recess at Clinch View on rainy days when he'd backed up against the blackboard and told stories, holding each student and the teacher with his voice.

"Lucius," said Thelma, as he came into the main lobby, "you mind running up to the Blue Circle for some coffee and a Bar-B-Q for Clancy?"

In the outer lobby, Hood held the ticket booth door open, and Lucius saw Sabra's smooth olive-skinned legs, with high Carmen Miranda heels, the muscles flexing, as she swiveled on the leather-cushioned chair toward a customer outside, and then he saw her lovely buttocks. During the day and on Tuesday afternoons when Minetta was off, it was Sabra who perched out there in that raised cage. She was shorter than Lucius. It was a different effect from having tall Minetta look down on him from the booth, the red birthmark splashed across her cheek. Sabra's long jet-black hair was probably dyed, but real in Lucius's eyes. Her face was heavily made up, vivid red lipstick, and her body was tiny, with firm, full breasts. Going up the hill wearing his creaky new leather jacket, Lucius was glad the air had turned cooler.

Taking the food up the carpeted steps to the first balcony, he was excited to be going inside the projection booth for the first time. He'd never even laid eyes on a veteran of a German prison camp. Gale had told him that Clancy lived in the Jasper Hotel that had a narrow entrance on the corner next to the Bijou. Clancy was always screwing girls in the booth on an army cot. One time, a boy got his girl hot, went for popcorn, and by the time he got back Clancy had already fucked her. Speedy Gonzales. Gale said Clancy was a tall, skinny, hollow-eyed man because he spent most of the war in a German prison camp, but he had thick curly black hair. Lucius knocked on the tin-encased door.

The sight of a tall, thin, specterlike man in a bright doorway looking down on him, wearing only his undershorts and undershirt, his feet bare, his toenails large and yellow, startled Lucius.

"Dash in here, buddirow, 'fore the women jump us."

The booth was very bright and hot. Clancy was dripping sweat. A small fan waved on a stool above a high table that had large reels of film hooked onto wheels with crank handles. The sight of the gigantic projectors overwhelmed Lucius. Clancy sat at a little school chair–desk combination with an armrest like the kind at Bonny Kate, *True Detective* open under his elbow, and dug into the white bag and started wolfing down the Bar-B-Q, licking the rusty-looking juice that dripped onto his fingers. Lucius noticed that he had a pencil-thin moustache, like Zachary Scott. He didn't seem embarrassed to be in his underwear in front of a strange kid. Lucius wondered if Foster Bagwell, who called himself a Christian, worked in his underwear, too.

He looked through the apertures at the screen. Tom Drake kissing Ann Tyler on the bridge in the village again. It looked exactly the same but gave him an entirely different feeling. Lucius imagined the projectionists up here watching Hedy Lamarr, Greer Garson, Barbara Stanwyck, Ida Lupino, Rita Hayworth, Betty Grable, the room at their backs strewn with *Esquires* and *Popular Mechanics* and *Field and Streams*. He imagined the balcony full on Saturday night, bodies radiating heat, people wandering along the aisles and coming up the carpeted steps, Lucius posted at the top, stepping aside, the projectionist in here in his underwear and all those people out there, unaware. Being almost naked and isolated, did they jack off? Lucius blushed and turned from the window, no bigger than his head. Inside his leather jacket, his blue shirt was sweat-drenched.

Wanting to see Maria Montez in *Tangier* at the Venice, Lucius asked Mr. Hood for a pass.

"Hutchfield," he said, shoving his hair away from his eyes, "you are a glutton for punishment. Look at movies half your waking life ushering, then rush out in your free time and plant yourself in front of a screen."

The pass was pink, like the "miss" slips Dusty Harper used to hand him every day.

On the streetcar that night, Lucius anticipated the thrill of magnifying the McCoy and Chaplin movies on a bedsheet.

He found a neatly pressed sheet in Momma's dresser drawer and tacked it up on the door in the living room–bedroom and backed toward the window until the image was as big as the sheet. He imagined his mother almost crying with nostalgia to see a projector like the old one when her kids were little and a movie of Charlie Chaplin who she and Mammy said was so wonderful in the years when Momma was growing up.

Though dull and indistinct, the image made him feel more like being in a big theatre. Suddenly, the sheet began to wobble and he saw Momma's high-heeled shoes beneath it, and she was fighting it as it clung to her face. She stepped to the side and turned her head to see Charlie Chaplin doing his funny little waddle, twirling his cane jauntily into the sunset.

"Lucius! That's one of my brand-new sheets!" She walked briskly across the room, lighted only by the projector, Charlie wobbling across her brown coat, and slapped Lucius's face. He was shocked and humiliated, as if he'd done something childish and stupid, like one of Bucky's antics.

Somebody fought the sheet again and Mrs. Easterly's face was full of flickering numbers as she exploded a terrific bodily scream for them to shut up: "You just woke up my baby!"

> Tues., September 10, 1946. The Green Years ended today. Al Jolson talent show tomorrow. Bought watch, leather jacket, and projector. Saw Mammy uptown in front of Kresses. I'm always dreaming that I'm suddenly naked in front of people, and sometimes they notice and sometimes it's just me, and I feel very bad. And I dream of flying, and it's easy. When I get in fights in my dreams, I can't hit hard. Raine called said she liked me very much. Clancy let me have the pieces of film on the projection booth floor that he cuts out of the real—mostly prevues. It looks good on my projector.

NIGHT RITUAL: Floyd is as old as Lucius. In his kitchen, Floyd drinks a whole glass of water in one swallow, then says, "Awwwwwww. . . ." The fat boy across the street, Floyd, and Earl, and the Jackson boys sit on Momma's front steps and talk. It is turning cool and getting dark. Lucius tells stories about Buck Jones. He doesn't know why they laugh. He gets cold. Momma calls him to come in to bed. Bucky is already asleep. He looks like a little girl. . . . Lucius goes into the little bathroom just off the back porch and takes a crap and flushes and runs outside to the front of the house where Bucky and Earl stand beside the sewer drain, sunken, busted, exposed, and watch the turd float by. A mysterious, awesome sight. . . . Lucius and Earl sit at Mammy's feet, Bucky in her lap, as she tells about the old man who spent on tombstones the money his wife saved up all year to buy the children some play-pretties. . . . The long street to Howell's Drug Store, the long walk on over to Mammy's. On the way home Momma and Daddy fuss. It is very cold. . . . In a field of sage in the heat of summer, the black-haired fat boy across the street says, "Cock back your leg, see, and it makes a pussy behind your knee. It's fun, boy. I'll show you." Lucius, wearing a pink sunsuit, scrambles his pecker out and tries to do as the fat boy is doing. They try it on each other, but he is so fat Lucius can't get his worm to fit.

The curtain opened, Uncle Chester skipped out from the wings and up to the microphone that stood in the middle of the stage. Behind him, a man stopped playing the piano. Sequined letters pinned to the black backdrop that covered the screen spelled out THE AL JOLSON TALENT SHOW, a publicity stunt to whip up interest in *The Jolson Story* that was to be released a few months later.

"Good evening, ladies and gentlemen, and Cousin Zeke." Laughter from the audience that spilled into the lobby and clogged the aisles. His voice sounded different, not imitating a smart-aleck old country uncle, but younger, deeper, more resonant, with a faint twang and that slightly superior country tone that suggested he had already gotten a joke started that would have everybody laughing at *you* if he decided to drop his friendliness and let you have it. Lucius detected under his ridiculous antics and postures as Uncle Chester a strong, controlled personality that was superior to the character he'd created and to the people it appealed to. He was a little in awe of him and felt as if he were being made fun of. As Uncle Chester, the mayor of Chicken Gap, on the Midday Harvest program, he used jokes right out of the cheap paperback booklet of skits Earl once bought at the novelty store down by WLUX and the L & N viaduct.

"Morning Bird Coffee brings you the mid day Harvest." Laughter. "Now *that* don't sound right. . . . It ain't Middey." Laughter. "Out here on this big o' Bye-Joe stage, without my Uncle outfit on, I feel so . . . . so *naked.*" Laughter. "You know, I can't walk out on a stage without wanting to cut loose and sing." Cheering, the audience urged him with foot-stomping demands that exhilarated Lucius. He loved to listen to Uncle Chester sing a few crazy songs with vulgar sounds like wet farts bursting through, then shift to a hymn, his beautiful baritone harmonizing with all the rest. "Naw, I don't want to bore you tonight with a lot of talent." Laughter. "All seriousness aside, neighbors, I do want to inform you that this *is* the Al Jolson Talent Contest, sponsored by the managements of the Tivoli and the Bye-Joe Theatre and Ott's poolroom." Laughter. Suddenly, he turned, pointed at the piano player, *"That's* a cue, nephew," making the man jump, strike a chord.

"Now we gonna have a whole raft of people," he said, lapsing into his Uncle Chester voice, "come out in front of you and try to sing like Al Jolson, and you supposed to scream and holler which one you think does him the best. Since even Al Jolson hangs his head in shame when *I* sing 'Mammy,' I disqualify myself to give my neighbors from Chicken Gap a chance. Now each contestant is supposed to do a little routine of his own that is not a copy of Al Jolson—to prove that he's got talent and not just a little phonograph up his nose." Laughter. "Now, you that come here tonight expecting to see some *girls* on this stage, you either never heard of Al Jolson or you're *confused* about him." Raucous laughter. "Neighbors, I want you to welcome our first contestant—Bill McDougal of 1458 Cold Springs Pike, or so it says on this matchbook, doing his best to imitate Al Jolson, singing 'California, Here I Come.'"

Clapping, igniting sparks of applause in the audience, Chester backed from the microphone halfway to the curtain as Bill McDougal strolled shyly onstage from the left, then Chester turned and skipped to the wings, doing a burlesque-girl backward kick at the last instant.

Lucius, still in uniform, watched Brady go backstage early and get out of uniform and come up with the stills and change the displays. Lucius was jealous. That ought to be *his* job.

Between wrestling bouts with the overflow audience—"Step back out of the aisle, please"—keeping his eye on the fire marshal, who stood backed up against the wall, Lucius listened to the singers imitate Al Jolson, then do a brief skit of their own, and watched Chester, with the greatest ease in the world, lead the audience away from one contestant, focus a moment on himself, then turn the magnet over to the next contestant.

"And now, neighbors, I give you Luke Foster of 1206 Avondale Street, with his imitation of Al Jolson, singing 'Mammy.' " As Chester backed away from the microphone, Lucius's knees gave, and he almost screamed out of joy that his uncle had returned just as Mammy always said he would, and a familiar young man of about twenty came out, wearing a blue, double-breasted suit too baggy for him, but he looked cocky like Humphrey Bogart, and when the spotlight hit him full at the mike, he turned into Earl Hutchfield.

It seemed as if Earl was on the stage, spreading his arms, as a result of a conspiracy with Uncle Chester. Lucius's heart beat fast as he looked at Earl's face, but it was Jolson's voice he was listening to. He didn't seem real up there on the stage. Maybe he was really Al Jolson in disguise.

When Wade Bayliss the big ex-football-hero cop who kept an eye on the Bijou, stepped up to the balustrade in uniform, Lucius remembered clearly, what he had vaguely been aware of, caught in the performance, that the man on the stage was not twenty but sixteen, and that he'd escaped from State Training School in Nashville last spring and had been wandering ever since. Lucius had not seen him since last Christmas. He imagined Bayliss stomping up to the stage, arresting Earl. Because now, as Earl went into his own routine, the drunk-who-gets-tangled-up-in-a-piece-of-chewing-gum-picked-up-on-the-sole-of-his-shoe pantomime that Earl had seen at the old Charles Street Burlesque Theatre in Boston and mimicked in Mammy's living room many times, Lucius knew the whole world could see very clearly that the man, boy, on the stage was "Big Chief Chew Tabacca," sometimes known as "Maddog Earl" Hutchfield. Even at age ten, Earl's face had looked like a man's —the skin dark, the grey eyes objective, the hair black, full, thick lips crimped into a sardonic smile, and he'd look straight at you, nodding his head—an ambivalent look—as if he saw you very distinctly, but only physically. Lucius waited for Wade Bayliss to push him aside now, and charge down the aisle, but he merely stood there, laughing, expectant, as if hoping Earl would follow up with his "Fairy at the Ball Park" routine.

Earl finally got the chewing gum off the sole of his shoe, but his hands became entangled in it. His facial expressions and body gestures were clearly Earl's, as distinctive as the voice he kept mute. Lucius stood in awe of such audacity—a fugitive from the law returning to his hometown, stepping off a bus or out of a truck or a boxcar onto the Bijou stage before he even contacted his folks. Hell, Lucius was jealous. *He* hadn't performed on the Bijou stage, but he'd claimed the world of entertainment as *his* territory, even though Earl had traveled with carnivals and circuses, companion once to an armless, legless fat man in the sideshow. But Earl radiated a cocky confidence up there that Lucius lacked. As brazen as Uncle Chester, who, Lucius imagined, stood in the wings, admiring the act, leaping to the conclusion that the audience would pick Earl the winner of the $25 prize. Finished, Earl threw kisses to the audience, backing off the stage as Chester had done, as none of the *other* contestants had.

Two contestants later, Chester called all the performers out, and they stood in a ragged line while the stomping, whistling audience cheered Earl the winner.

"Well, Luke," said Chester—Lucius feeling odd, hearing his uncle's name from the stage—"what you going to *do* with all that loot?"

"Buy me a Uncle Chester outfit." Laughter.

Uncle Chester feigned alarm. "Buy you a who done *what?*"

"An Uncle Chester outfit."

Uncle Chester did a double take. Laughter. "Neighbor, what you want with a Uncle Chester outfit?" Uncle Chester looked around, as if for help.

"Well, I tell you," said Earl, imitating Uncle Chester's voice, "I plan on runnin' for the mayor of Chicken Gap, Tennessee."

"Oh, yeah? Then you better start runnin' right now." With exaggerated gyrations, Chester, mingling a mock locomotive with a country hick high-stepping racer, quit the stage, while Earl, as the curtain closed, tried to detach chewing gum from his shoe so he could chase down Uncle Chester.

Starting to dash backstage, Lucius ran into Wade Bayliss, a brick wall, who muttered, "Dangerous usher!" and heard Hood call, "Lucius, come here!"

"Sir, could I go backstage just a second?" Lucius was afraid that when he stepped out onto the sidewalk, Earl would be arrested and taken by night train back to Nashville before he could talk with him.

"Open the front doors! Quick!" said Hood.

"Okay!" said Lucius, curtly, remembering Hood had told him to do that just before Earl came on. He ran, breaking through the departing crowd, to the front, pushed open the gilt doors, struggled to make

the stoppers brace them back, then wove back through the people flooding out, and bulldozed down the aisle and asked for Earl backstage,
then remembered he'd used Uncle Luke's name. But Spit, the stagehand,
said he saw the winner go out with Chester. Looking out the stage door,
up and down the street, where cold rain fell, Lucius saw no trace of
his brother.

Sweeping crud into the dustpan with the long brass handle, Lucius
watched Hood escort Minetta, carrying a tray of money, into the first
lobby, climb the three steps to the main lobby, imagining what they did
locked up together in the office, and the difference in age made it sinister. The red splash on her cheek, the severe acne problem that an inch
of makeup only accented, she was repulsive, but perversely sexy, too.

"Luscious, how 'bout dousing the lights backstage?" said Elmo,
coming in from the marquee with a stack of letters.

He transferred them to Lucius's arms. He put them in the still room
in the basement, turned out the light, felt along the wall in the dark
up the stairway, having forgotten his flashlight. Suddenly, he felt something skitter up his pants leg and he shook it violently, feeling the fur
and tail of a rat against his ankle.

"What was all that screaming?" asked Elmo, clomping to the head
of the stairs.

"Run into a Varga girl down there," said Lucius, still trembling,
leaning against the wall, halfway up the stairs, "and showed her my
dick."

"Prob'ly thought it was a roach."

On the last streetcar home, Lucius stared out the window, watching the few people left on Sevier Street. The cold rain had stopped, the
wet streets glistened under the lights. The streetcar motor throbbed
under the green seat. Dust on the seats and window made him sad, and
he saw Earl, returning, wearing a seaman's uniform, only thirteen years
old. When he appeared at the screen door that summer noon in 1943,
he returned from a world composed of images out of the movies they'd
seen together at the Hollywood and the Hiawassee in the years before.
Lucius sometimes daydreamed now of the time when he'd sail out of
New Orleans into the Gulf of Mexico.

Lucius remembered the time on Beech Street when he had to go
with Earl to pick up a Thanksgiving basket, distributed at the Market
House. He wondered whether Earl's solemn look masked a deep resolve
—which he'd never have confided with Lucius—not to lead a life of
handouts. Instead, he'd either stolen what he wanted in Cherokee, or
cheated people out of it in carnivals that moved all over the South.
And now he was running from the police. Two years ago, Earl's example persuaded Lucius to stop stealing. But to Bucky, stealing was a

glamorous adventure that made him feel grown-up and, like Earl, in control.

One time over on Avondale, the brown and yellow police car pulled up to the house, and the cops took Earl away because he and some other boys had stolen stuff out of L. T. Dobbs's boarded-up grocery store. "The Depression did it," said Momma. She and Mammy and them often referred to the Depression, "It's the Depression, it's because of the Depression," as if it were something before Lucius, but he sometimes realized that he'd been there, remembering the picture in the paper in about 1938: Roosevelt speaking at the L & N railroad depot in Cherokee.

The streetcar stopped and people came up the steps and dropped car tokens in the box. Earl, wearing the blue double-breasted suit, walked toward the rear of the car with that I-don't-give-a-damn-for-anybody-but-Earl-Hutchfield walk. Lucius looked at him as if from a distance—the sleepy eyes, the broad forehead, the thick mouth that could take any shape, the rounded shoulders. Lucius smiled and waved and Earl came on back, not smiling, and sat heavily beside him. Lucius thought, Here we are, two brothers, sitting on a green dusty seat inside a yellow streetcar, motor throbbing, the Tennessee night outside.

> Wens. September 11, 1946. Al Jolson talent night and Earl was the winner! He's here in the house right now, sitting on the edge of Momma's and Daddy's bed, talking to them. Next is A Night in Casablanca, Marx Bros. That's us, me and Earl and Bucky. I was almost late to work again today. Had to stay in for Miss Cline.

Bucky slept with Momma and Daddy, and Earl slept on the cot in the kitchen with Lucius.

"Nobody knows me anymore," Earl said. "All my buddies are in the reform school." Lucius had never thought of Earl as having "buddies." Accomplices, but not buddies. "I'm a stranger in my own hometown. I don't feel like I belong to anything, not even to you all. I've seen and done everything, Lucius, and now I wanted to come home and just be like anybody else my age." Lucius heard him sobbing. "But I can't quit it. . . . I'm the last of the Mohicans. . . . I reckon I got the call of the wild goose in me." Lucius patted Earl's naked shoulder. "Boo hoo," said Earl, and Lucius took his hand away as if Gale had sparked carpet-electricity into it. "Boooooo-hoo! Fell for it, didn't you? They all do."

Lucius was angry, but didn't say anything. After he'd reviewed his life awhile, and talked with God, he heard Earl sobbing again, very softly, and couldn't decide whether he was acting or not.

Somebody pulling on his wrist woke Lucius. Frost crystals made the window beside the low-slung cot opaque silver. When Lucius turned his head in the grey light, Earl was trying to slip Lucius's brand-new, gold-plated, radium-dialed Elgin watch off his wrist.

"Earl, what in the hell you trying to do?"

Lucius jumped straight up in the bed, staggered back and forth to keep his balance on the saggy springs.

"Just wanted to borrow it, Lucius, wear it while I look for a job."

"Job, hell. The cops are looking for you, by God, and you tryin' to steal my—"

"You accusin' your own brother of—?" Earl's imitation of an indignant person would have looked good on the stage of the Bijou, but up close it was straight out of jerky, old-timey movies. Standing in the middle of the kitchen linoleum, the water he had combed into his black hair glittering, Earl wore Lucius's new leather jacket that made him feel like Alan Ladd in *China*.

"Gimme my new jacket, Earl!"

"Let me wear it today," said Earl, using the Yankee accent he'd picked up in his wanderings, backing slowly toward the kitchen door, "and you can have it back tomorrow."

"You come back here with my fuckin' jacket, Earl! Momma!"

"She's done gone to the cafe."

Jumping down off the cot, Lucius reached for his jacket, but Earl dodged and ran down the hall. Lucius caught him at the front door,

"You're gonna tear it, Lucius," said Earl, as if talking to a kid.

"I'm gonna tear your arm off, if you don't shuck off my jacket."

Earl pushed Lucius against the wall and tried to unlock the nightlock. "Won't even take your own brother's word!"

"Don't try to snow *me* with that brother act!" said Lucius, feeling guilty. He wished he *could* trust Earl, but if he didn't work fast, he'd never see his jacket again—only his brother, again and again. He pulled at his arm until Earl turned loose of the nightlock and grabbed Lucius's arm and whirled him around with sudden, awesome force and slung him against the wall.

"Bucky, help me!"

"He snuck off with Emmett King!" yelled Earl, running back down the hall.

"Earl, don't do me this way!" Lucius tried to beat Earl to the back exit. He tackled him at the kitchen door. Wrestling with him on the filthy hall linoleum, grimed with coal dust and grease, Lucius thought of Dynamite Farrell wrestling the Red Roach at the Pioneer. As they broke holds and made new ones, got halfway up, then pulled down again, they giggled and cursed the way they did during the war on

Avondale and Beech, when Earl seemed more like Billy in *Crime School* than Bogart in *High Sierra*.

They struggled into the kitchen, cursing, spitting, biting, slapping, trying to keep away from the hot cookstove. When they broke, Earl started for the door, but Lucius jumped in front of him, a poker cocked over his shoulder.

"Would you hit your own brother with that thing, Lucius?" Earl backed toward the bed, Lucius following closely. Then Earl broke his rigid crouch, straightened up, relaxed between the cot and Lucius. "Ah, hell, all right. . . ."

Smiling, Lucius tossed the poker into the coal bucket and saw the ceiling, then the frost window coming at him and landed on his back on the sidewalk outside, in a garland of glass, still frosted, Raine, Peggy, Joy, Cora looking down at him, a streetcar passing at their backs.

"We come to walk to school with you," said Cora, laughing with Raine and Peggy and Joy. Over Raine's shoulder, he saw a black hole in the window, jagged white edges. The girls helped him up, laughing, Lucius embarrassed to be wearing only his jock shorts, and he saw the folding doors of the streetcar clap over the tail of his leather jacket. Lucius was uncut, unbruised, but stunned into three o'clock. The watch had slipped off his wrist into Earl's hand as he flipped Lucius over his head and through the window glass.

Thurs. September 12, 1946. Earl stold my watch and jacket. Threw me thru window. Raine and them was standing there. Found out Raine lives up on Clayboe Ridge, but not the part where my old paperroute went. Della Snow called. Betty M. called. Then Betty R. called. I like Betty R. the best. Raine called several times. Landlady got mad because I used her phone too much. My day off. Can't wait to see Harpo tomorrow in A Night in Casablanca. After school, Joe and Teddy came up to the house and said they could draw better than me.

Morning sunlight coming through the door at the end of the hall turned Raine and Peggy into nimbused silhouettes. Lucius saw Peggy's black arm rise to her mouth and reach across the iridescence to Raine's. Blowing her a kiss?

While the rest of Miss Redding's class was diagramming sentences for the regular Friday quiz, Lucius wrote: "Career Gril, A Story of the Shadow Stage by Will Cosgrove, for Raine." Looking over the movie magazines Beverly Taylor had bestowed upon him, he'd been impressed with *Photoplay*'s 1933 subtitle, "The Shadow Stage," not knowing what it meant. He drew a picture of Chris Booth standing under a floodlight, wearing a dress like Scarlett O'Hara's.

Chapter I

Chris Booth sat motionless watching Pearl White and John Barrymore make love on the screen of the Bijou Theater in a little town in Louisiana, when a message suddenly flared out on the screen. The message read: Christine Booth wanted at Box Office. Then the message was gone. And Chris once again regained intrest in the feature. Suddenly Chris realized that the message was for her.

She jumped up from her seat and squandered up the alise to where an usher waring a gray and Blue uniform stood leaserly with flashlight in hand. "What—"

"Lucius," said Miss Redding, suddenly at his side. "Do you need any help with your diagrams?"

"No, ma'am."

"May I see what you're writing?"

"Do I have to?"

"No." She smiled and walked back up the row toward the exercises on the board, her long, wavy brown hair bouncing on her shoulders the way he liked.

Imitating Vaughn Monroe singing "Racing with the Moon," Lucius, coming up behind her, startled Della Snow in the lunch line.

"I thought you was really him." Despite the pimples on her cheeks, her smile was lovely. "Hey, want to take a test?"

"What kind of test?" he asked, leering, doing his eyebrows like Groucho Marx.

"Here, just answer these questions on a separate sheet of paper and skip a line between each one."

"You sound like Miss Cline," said Lucius, taking the questions.

In study hall, on a separate sheet of paper, Lucius answered the dumb-ass questions, and passed them across the auditorium. They reached Della just before the study hall supervisor, Mrs. Waller, who taught Home Ec, looked up and shot her gaze like a prison searchlight across the auditorium. Della wrote on the sheet and passed it back to Lucius. She had written different questions on the lines he'd left blank between his answers, so that he ended up answering: "Did she kiss you? Yes. How many times? 13. What did you say? Makes my ass crave cold buttermilk. Where did it happen? Girls shower room. Have you ever done anything you were ashamed off? Yes. With whom? LaRue Harrington. Where at? In bed. How long did it last? 7 hours. What was the results? Girls. Would you do it again? Yes. Why? It tastes good."

Lucius got Della's attention, picked his nose with one finger and pretended to lick it, having switched to another. Della stuck out her tongue as if she were gagging, then smiled, pushed one finger in and out of a ring she made with her other hand, then sucked the finger. Lucius gagged, remembering that Earl said it tasted like pork and beans.

The more Lucius gazed at Raine in Miss Cline's American history, the more she looked like Veronica Lake. He mingled the pure body of Raine with the pure body of Veronica. His memory unconsciously and his willful vision deliberately superimposed the faces, but never the bodies, of goddesses upon the girls he worshipped. The goddesses and the girls he loved were pure, and his vile fantasies never desecrated them. But when he thought of screwing Della Snow, he sometimes saw the bodies of Claire Trevor in *Dead End,* who had syphilis, or Adele Jergens or Dolores Moran or Evelyn Ankers or Jean Parker or Marie Windsor, for the girls in the low-grade movies were less sacrosanct. He associated the starlets and stars of these movies with the cheap theatres where he saw them and where he hoped to pick up tough girls. The cheap costumes and sets and the bad acting made the girls seem more real and so more vulnerable to his sexual hunger.

After Miss Kuntz released her homeroom at three o'clock, Lucius saw Raine, Harry Marcum, Peggy, Joy, and Cora standing together in the hall. He wished he'd tracked down Earl and gotten his leather jacket back, but he was wearing the dark blue shirt with the decorative stitches around the collar that Raine liked and Luke's combat boots for the first time in school, so he approached them with a steady gait. Raine seemed to be pretending she didn't notice he was coming toward her. She whispered to the others, turned aside, then glanced at him, turned away again, blushing, putting one hand over her mouth, bent at the waist, holding to Joy's arm with the other. The mouths and eyes of the other girls self-consciously awaited the effect on Raine as they saw Lucius coming straight at them.

"Hey, Lucius, how you doing, fella?" asked Harry, showing the long-toothed grin that was the most immediate thing about him.

"Aw, just going to work," said Lucius, using Alan Ladd's cool voice.

"Hell, me, too, fella. Walk on up the hill with us. Catch the Clinch View streetcar with me at Peck's. Only takes ten minutes longer than taking the Grand."

"Okay."

They started walking out toward the daylight at the end of the clean-dungeon corridor. Raine kept looking at him shyly and he smiled at her, and the other girls gave each other looks, and Harry's hand rode Peggy's shoulder as they strolled.

Lucius had seen Harry several times in the johns and on the streets uptown and on the floor at the Tivoli, and he'd learned that he and Peggy were going steady and walked to school almost every morning.

Lucius's working hours conflicted severely with Harry's so he couldn't run as often as he wanted to with him, nor with Raine and "the Clayboe Ridge Gang," as he called them.

Harry had an easy cocky walk and stance, as calculated as Lucius's, and Lucius liked the casual way he held his head, slightly to the side, a narrow face, with a long skull that curved sharply in toward his neck at the nape. He'd frequently told the story about the time in the third grade at Tapp Elementary when Harry scrubbed Kyle Tetter's scalp with his knuckles and the teacher called him down and he said, "Kyle said I been eating beans," and Lucius had smelled it, and everybody and the teachers laughed, but he still had to write the Pledge of Allegiance fifty times because she said he wasn't a good citizen to make smells and assault his own classmate.

Other afternoons, Lucius had watched them climb the steep hill, slowly, moving oddly, seen from a distance, weaving side to side, almost sideways climbing. Other kids covered the hill, but the four girls and Harry stuck out, Raine's red dress with the white trim standing out several days ago. On the other side were a few flat blocks, then the streets climbed again halfway up Clayboe Ridge, becoming rocky, then dirt, then paths.

Cora did a sudden Groucho dip and everybody laughed. "You 'member when that lady said, 'I'm Mrs. Hotsitah, I stop at the hotel,' and ol' Groucho said, 'I'm Roland Hitchbottom, I stop at nothing'?" Cora asked Lucius, coming up out of the dip.

"I ain't seen it yet. It's on now, though."

"'At's a good ol' shoooow. Hey, look at them nutty birds."

They watched a covey go over the treetops.

"I loved the part where that old nasty Nazi's trying to pack his shirts and stuff and Harpo and them keep sneaking it all back into the closet," said Joy.

"'Member the part where they was in the cockpit of the plane," said Raine, "and Harpo kept twiddling the dials and punching the buttons like it was just an old play-pretty? Cora, will you stop plucking at my hair?"

"Loraine, you ever see *Gone With the Wind?*" asked Lucius.

"My brothers took me to see it when I was nine years old—at the Hiawassee."

"I saw it there, too!"

"Hey, we might of even *set* next to each other and didn't even know it!" That delighted Raine, and Lucius loved her.

"Next one sits in that swing's gonna bust his unmentionable," said Joy. Lucius glanced at the rotten ropes of a tire swing hanging in front of a house. He enjoyed the easy way they all wove into the steady stream of jokes, teasing antics, wisecracks, the trivial things they saw or did as they walked.

Peggy started singing "A Hubba, Hubba, Hubba," and they all laughed and Raine said, "You all hush." They seemed to be teasing her, bumping their shoulders up against hers, all the girls singing to her, Harry grinning.

Joy started a snatch of a song from The Hit Parade and the others picked it up and improvised a medley of others: "Let It Snow, Let It Snow, Let It Snow," "On the Atchison, Topeka, and the Santa Fe," "Give Me Five Minutes More," and they got into country songs: "Cool Water," "Dear John," and "Night Train to Memphis."

Lucius wanted to hear them tell more about the things they'd done together. "You should a been there, Lucius," said Cora, "more fuuuuuuunnnnn, more people killlllled!" And about the crazy antics of the little kids in their families, and about their mommas and daddies and big sisters and brothers and cousins, and the food they ate, the dresses they bought or made, mended, altered, wore. Lucius sensed they came straight from country people, factory workers, and probably lived in slummy houses on Clayboe Ridge, but their clothes were neat and clean, though not as nice as most of the girls at Bonny Kate. Even as they trudged slowly up the steep hill in the sun, they seemed electrically alive and Lucius's memory of the visual image of them as he'd watched them from under the mimosa trees was a physical thing that he felt, blended with his own act now of climbing with them.

"Reckon could you go to church with us this Sunday?" asked Raine, suddenly close to him, her voice quiet.

"*Us,* hell," said Cora, "she wants you to go with *her.* She can't talk about nothin' but Lucius Cornfield."

"Who told you to shoot off *your* mouth, Cora?"

"I don't need to get *your* permission."

"Then give me back my chewing gum."

They stopped arguing to catch what Harry was telling Peggy. "Then Mrs. Slocum slaps her hand on the door of the shower room and yells in her deep man's voice, 'Shut your eyes, boys, I'm coming through.' "

Cackling, Harry dropped gracefully to the pavement and rolled on his back, kicking his feet into the air, not in an abandon of merriment, but in a cockily controlled way. He had an odd thrill-giggle that endeared him to people who knew him, but it could unnerve others, make a person feel ridiculed. Excited, delighted, surprised, he laughed the same way, and Lucius's pulse quickened, as if the laugh came out of a rich context and promised possibilities of which Lucius could be a part.

"They ort to get a man gym teacher for the boys," said Peggy.

"Don't worry, Peggy," said Cora, "Harry could hide *his* behind a soap bubble."

When they finished laughing, Raine said, "That's nothing, you all shoulda heard what Miss Cline said to Lucius today. Said, 'I'm leaving the room for one second. Dolores, will you be responsible for taking the names of any poor citizen who talks or otherwise misbehaves?' 'Yes, ma'am.' " Lucius loved the way she imitated the voices. " 'You needn't waste time. Put Lucius Hutchfield's name at the top of the list.' And Lucius said, 'Want *me* to take names, Miss Cline?' And that old hag said, 'You'll get your turn the day St. Peter takes names up yonder.' "

"She needs a Saint Peter herself," said Cora, and Raine blushed and walked half a block ahead, and Lucius wished she wouldn't say such stuff in front of Raine.

"My turn for the Juicy Fruit," said Joy.

"Shoot a monkey, girl, I just got it from Loraine while ago," said Cora.

Waving good-bye to the girls from the rear of the streetcar as it pulled away from Peck's store, Lucius saw Cora take the chewing gum from her mouth and pop it into Joy's. He figured out that the same piece of gum went from Peggy's to Raine's to Cora's mouth all day long, like Tom and Huck cutting their arms for a blood-brother bond. The ritual, totally new to him, made him nauseous. But then he envied them their intimacy.

Riding the streetcar uptown to the Tivoli and the Bijou with Lucius, Harry said, "You know what I dream about more than anything? A red Ford pussy wagon like my big brother's got. Have to fight 'em off the hood."

Commissioner Truckston offers Lew Fogarty ten thousand dollars to fly through the storm to San Francisco and stop Chandler's execution at Alcatraz. "I'll take it. But I ain't forgetting you took away my private dick license, Truck. So give me an opportunity, and I'll take sweet revenge, too."

At the airfield, they have much trouble getting the plane ready for takeoff. Truckston and his men did Lew good luck, but he spits in his face. Up in the air, Lew is being guided by all the airports on his route of flight. He smashes up in a cornfield. And he and a farmer use a broken-down Ford to get to the docks. Lew pulls a gun on a fisherman to force him to take him to the Rock—Alcatraz.

In a cell, Chandler waits thirty minutes. A fine meal is cold before him and a minister talks to him. He cries and pleads to God. He tells the priest about his life and the job for Kinkaid. Then he is taken by three men through the last mile. Lew is admitted at the gates and gets to the execution room in time to prevent the electrician from pulling the switch. Chandler is so relieved he has a heart attack. The reporters run to phone the press, but remember the wires are down.

Holding it in too long gave Lucius a severe stomachache. And his feet hurt. His body seemed to make fun of him.

"Usher, I think you'd better patrol the aisle," said an old lady in a fur-collared coat.

"What you mean, ma'am?"

"You'll see. And when you do, you'd better call the police."

Lucius followed the lady over to the other aisle and walked down, looking the backs of heads over. Coming back up, he got the light from *A Night in Casablanca* on the faces. Seeing nothing, but allowing the old lady had seen something, he sneaked, his heart beating hard, slowly down the seldom-used left side aisle against the rough-textured stucco and watched for any deviation from the spectator trance.

Two little girls about nine and eleven were glancing over at a man who sat four empty seats away from them. Looking closely, Lucius saw the man flop his dong and the little girls turn their heads and giggle into their chubby little fingers, drawing their legs up against their chests, showing their panties, making Lucius feel ashamed to be looking, as if he were a pervert himself.

Groucho watches the beautiful woman walk out of the room, her ass rolling like Prissy Cobb's. As he knocked on Hood's door, he heard Groucho say, "That reminds me, I must get my watch fixed."

Behind his ornate desk, in his shirt sleeves, Hood was typing a letter, his cigarette smoldering in a black holder in his green ashtray. "Sir?" Hood looked up quizzically, wiping his straight blond hair off his forehead. "We gonna have to kick somebody's ass out."

Hood saw that Lucius was fuming mad. "Oh, now wait a minute." He stood up and put on his coat (Why are you doing *that?*) and loped along behind as Lucius, distracted by outrage, snapped on the flashlight and shot the beam behind at Hood's feet as if he were a patron.

More quickly than Lucius had, Hood saw, and crossed the inner lobby to go down the side aisle. Lucius watched him lean over and speak to the man as Groucho says, "Waiter, bring this lady a cheese sandwich and charge it to *her*." In the dark, the man resembled Hood. He rose and went out like a doctor called to the telephone. A blur, he passed through the brightly lighted main lobby, descending into the first lobby as the golden doors went whopwhop whop.

Then Hood went to the wooden partition next to the Spot where Lucius stood, sprawled over the balustrade and surveyed the backs of heads and profiles, to make sure he'd gotten them all. Was that what Hood had been on the eagle eye for?

That old phony showing his doo-lolly to little girls made Lucius mad. A little ashamed, too, remembering standing in the WPA ditch house on Avondale, showing Sally and Louella, girls his own age, how a boy pees, as they watched above, peeking through the honeysuckle-laden wire fence at the back of the yard.

When Bruce Tillotson came on duty, Hood told Lucius to go out and fix the banner that had blown loose from the marquee. "I couldn't find Elmo and them."

Getting out of uniform to go to supper at Mammy's cafe, Lucius heard loud talking upstairs.

In street clothes, he climbed the narrow stairway and walked along the corridor past smaller dressing rooms to the large one at the back.

"Looks like a little Schmoo to me," said Brady.

"Yeah, and that damn Minetta looks like Lena the Hyena," said Gale.

Gale and Brady were sitting in the dressing room, eating apple pie, using the Blue Circle to-go bags to catch the juice and crumbs.

Laughing, they looked up at Lucius who stood in the doorway. "*Who* does?"

"*We* does. Don't *you?*"

They were drinking Blue Circle coffee and their mood seemed receptive to him, but Lucius wanted to be in control, so he told them about the man who showed his hobby to the two little girls.

"Would you fuck a little girl?" asked Gale.

"Few years ago, that's all I craved," said Lucius, kidding along.

"I mean now that you ain't such a little boy no more?"

"He fuck anything that moves," said Brady.

"Any warm hole will do?" asked Gale.

Sometimes Lucius felt jealous of Brady. Then he'd remember that he was Gale's cousin, and Brady was very likable, shy, quiet, with that Sonny Tufts smile. Still, they often worked a story around, even Lucius's own, until he was a target and they were sharpshooters. Lucius felt older in his thinking, and in the way he saw some things, than they were, but kidding and ridicule cut ages and intellect down. Though in the hot-faced moment their jokes seemed malicious, Lucius usually decided later they weren't.

"How 'bout Minetta?" Gale asked Brady, in a tone that implied they'd been over that before, and Brady blushed.

"I wouldn't fuck that bitch with *your* dick."

"Ain't what you told Elmo when you first come to the Bijou. Elmo claims she'll put out, if you want it, Brady. Says *Hood* gets a little."

"Who wants to come in behind where Hood's been?"

"Not me."

"Everybody seems scared of her," said Lucius.

"Everybody but you?"

"Hell, me, too!"

"Speaking of pinup girls, how about Thelma, Lucius?"

Off guard, Lucius was embarrassed. Jerking off, he often thought of her as much as of her daughter Carolyn, and dreamed of her, and felt her more keenly in fantasy and dreams than most girls.

"Give me her daughter any day," said Brady, "ten times a day."

Carolyn had genuine black hair and a lovely slender figure, but was worried about a mild acne problem. Her skin always had a shine. She came into the Bijou now and then, sometimes with her daddy, a grim-faced but sweet man, and the Bijou Boys always found a little job to do, or several, to necessitate trips to the lobby to look at her. Lucius's mother had a picture of Carolyn in shorts, standing tall between Bucky, wearing a cape and shorts, saluting, and nothing but grass on his feet, and Lucius on the other side, in shiny blue swimming trunks, sheeny grey in the black and white picture, and vivid nipples, his belly sucked in to thrust out his chest—in front of Mammy's house, the original wood, unpainted, showing a texture he liked.

Gale offered Lucius a third cup of coffee that they'd brought for Elmo, but Hood had sent him on an errand. The star's dressing room was a good place to hide out from Hood—a secluded, private place where they could laugh and horse around and play the radio without the patrons out front hearing them. Leaning on the sill, sipping coffee from the Blue Circle cups, they looked out the wide, open window over the curved, tar-paper roof of the streetcar barn, at the clock tower of the courthouse, and west on a hill at the college's tower that Lucius once thought was a church's steeple, and over the river's three bridges, and the ridges of South Cherokee, and the blue haze of the Smoky Mountains, and heard the cattle being slaughtered at the packinghouse by the river. Lucius spat on the roof of a streetcar entering the back of the carbarn through the alley between the Algonquin Tavern and the Bijou. In the dressing room below, he sometimes put his ear to the wall and felt the vibrations in his cheek as a streetcar passed. Lucius couldn't remember whether he'd ever told Thelma what he'd done to her mother. He wanted to go out and tell her now.

"Damn, that bakery smells good!" said Brady. "Good ol' fresh bread!"

"You trying to say you like it?" asked Gale.

"My uncle that I was named after owns it."

"Like shit."

"Hutchfield."

"You ain't kin to them!"

"My daddy's rolling rolls over there right now. Call 'em up."

"Yeah, and I reckon that's your daddy 'neath that mask in them posters of the Lone Ranger that goes out on them trucks all over."

"Looks like him, but it's really *me*."

"Them trucks go into four states, boy. You'd be rich enough to *own* the Bijou."

"I wish we did. But my gran'paw on my daddy's side died drunk, so we all got left out." Even when they talked about himself, he felt he was as much a spectator as a member of the group.

Lucius asked them what their daddies did for a living. Brady's drove a Huber and Huber truck, Gale's was killed at Corregidor and his Momma worked at Smoky Mountain Knitting Mill. They said Elmo's father worked on the railroad. As they talked about their families, Lucius learned that Brady had four brothers and two sisters and Elmo was an only child. Gale had three big sisters, but he ignored Lucius's questions about them.

"Hey, Lucius, you 'posed to be On the Spot." Bruce Tillotson stood in the doorway shining his flashlight in Lucius's eyes. "What you all been talking about?"

"Pounding our pork," said Gale.

Dangling in the doorway, Tillotson threw in a contribution. "I got this little Santa Claus made of plaster that we always put under the tree. But my baby sister broke it a few years ago. When they all asleep, I pull out this board in the side of the houseboat by my bed and reach in between the walls and take out this Santa Claus and stick it over my doololly so when I come it don't make no mess. Then I fit his head back on and put her back."

The silence made Lucius gag on the coffee at the back of his tongue. Cocked back against the wall, Gale let his chair slam down.

"Reckon I better get back in uniform," said Lucius.

"You all hear about President Truman putting off the third Bikini atomic bomb test?"

"No," said Brady, "but I heard Chief Ballard's arresting everybody caught with a broken Santa Claus in their houseboat." Even after they'd ribbed him for a month about it, Bruce continued to broadcast the news, seeming now to do it in response to the teasing.

When Lucius went On the Spot, Harpo is leaning against the wall of a little house again, a suspicious-looking character. A policeman comes up and snarls, "Say, what you think you're doing, holding up the building?" Harpo nods sweetly, shyly. The cop jerks him away and the building collapses.

Stepping out of the inside dark. illuminated by the silver screen, into the outside dark, dominated by the green and red neon across the top and around the windows of Max's Restaurant across the street, Lucius felt a dramatic change in his physical response to his surroundings.

The facade of the Greek's restaurant, with its slightly foreign aura, dominated the activity of the Bijou block. Black and yellow patterned tile surrounded two large windows. A sooty white curtain stretched along the lower part of the windows and the fronds of ferns curved up several inches above the curtain rod. Lucius saw people go in and come out, frequently, but it was always a little stunning to walk into the activity: all the tables and booths and counters full, coats and hats loading the racks and hooks, the waitresses dashing in and out of the kitchen, yelling, Max himself sitting on a high stool behind the cash register, wearing a suit, a dirty towel around his neck, casting out over the gigantic room an aura of foreignness.

Scared and expectant, Lucius always paused at the door to get his bearings, to strike a pose of nonchalance, to declare visually that he wasn't just a kid coming into a room full of grown-ups. Some night a fight would break out, or someone would walk up to a table and shoot someone. Maybe while Lucius was there. The place created possibilities that might become inevitabilities.

Max's was full of people who'd just come out of the wrestling matches at the Pioneer next door. Short Dynamite Farrell came out of the men's room, smoothing his curly hair back with both enormous hands. His face was sad whether he won or lost. Maybe even Earl's favorite, the Red Roach, his mask off, sat in the crowd, smiling to himself that none of his enemies knew who he was.

When Lucius came back out to Sevier Street, Hood's coffee-to-go in his hand, he had to hunch against a light rain. Pausing on the brink of a puddle in the wavy sidewalk, he watched two streetcars pass each other in front of the Bijou, their trolley arms flashing blue at the wires above. Momma rode up front on the single seat across from the conductor.

The last showing of *A Night in Casablanca* had just ended, and a crowd had gathered under the marquee, waiting for the rain to let up. The faces seemed strange, like people only pretending to be standing there, waiting for a streetcar where none stopped.

He recognized Wade Bayliss in the crowd at the curb, out of uniform, off duty, holding a woman's arm in his own. The woman was almost as big and stocky as Bayliss, her face heavily rouged, and she wore a fancy red dress and a fur coat, too hot for this weather, open at the front, and her very high heels and a hat like one Hedda Hopper wore made her as tall as Bayliss who wore only a white short-sleeved shirt, open at the neck, and ordinary trousers. Lucius had seen him only at the back of the inner lobby, looking over the heads of the audience and into the faces of the gods and goddesses on the "shadow stage." Something was wrong with the picture he made with the woman. The way he held her arm looked odd, and the people waiting for the rain to stop were giving them sidelong glances. Water plunged full in the gutter, pushing debris along to the corner into the rain drain.

As he crossed, Lucius got a glimpse of Sevier Street north, toward Clinch View, up the hill, where neon lights, the Tivoli's marquee standing out, were beautiful in the rain-cleansed, slightly misty atmosphere, and the black pavement and silvery double streetcar tracks glistened as he stepped up onto the curb beside the cop and the woman. Pain twisted her face as she yelled, "Ohhhh! Goddam it! You're hurting my fuckin' arm!" Bayliss was pressing down on her wrist, the way Dynamite had probably done the Red Roach in the Pioneer.

Men and women were trying to sidle closer to the curb to get a better look, smiling, whispering, obviously afraid to speak out against or even to encourage Bayliss as he manhandled the woman. From what he could pick up from voices behind him, Lucius began to get a sharper focus on the tableau. The woman had been raising hell in the Algonquin Tavern next door to the Bijou when Bayliss came in for a beer, and he'd dragged her to the door, shoved her outside, and she'd cursed him, hit him with her purse, he'd called the Black Maria, and was waiting for it now, his grip on her. Lucius wondered whether she was a whore from the Jasper Hotel next to the Bijou on the corner.

"Please, please, Wade, don't hurt me, please let go of me, I promise I won't try to get away again, please, Wade, I promise," and then she cut loose and cussed him, through gritted teeth. "Goddam it, I said I was sorry, now you turn loose of me!" Standing slightly behind Wade, Lucius saw a muscle in his bare arm ripple a little. "Oh, oh, you fat sonofabitch!" she cried, biting her lip. Then Wade jerked suddenly, and she rose up on her toes, showing a fringe of her pink slip, pinned up with a tiny gold safety pin, and the soles of her high-heeled shoes, a hole in one of them. "You pigfucker!" Then she screamed blue murder. And Wade stood solid, just his arm moving, a separate mechanism, without looking at her, gazing straight ahead like Duty, out from under the marquee, the fringed banner of *A Night in Casablanca,* over the gurgling water in the gutter, into the light rain, at the dark glass panes in the seven-door facade of the Pioneer Theatre.

Outraged, Lucius wanted to jump on Wade's back, the way he'd jumped the Red Roach the time he left Dynamite lying in a pool of blood in the ring and the spectators on the stage, ringside, surged around him. Lucius wanted to choke Wade from behind, make him turn her loose, let the woman make a run for it. She gritted her teeth, bit her lip, then opened her mouth wide, wailing. Wade bent her wrist, making her jump up on her toes and bounce to relieve the pressure, and Lucius felt ashamed to notice her large breasts jiggle when she was in such pain.

Having rehearsed what he was going to say, Lucius was on the verge of looking up at Wade and telling him that Jesus told him to tell him to stop hurting her, when the Black Maria pulled up to the marquee, splashing Wade, the woman, Lucius, and a row of other people who stepped back too late, too little. Wade shoved her in to the back and shut the door softly and walked back into the Algonquin Tavern with a light step—to finish his Miller High Life, Lucius imagined—as a streetcar marked CARBARN turned between the tavern and the Bijou.

> Fri. September 13, 1946. Walked with Raine and them. Thought up some more about Lew Fogarty in "Black Dust." Me and Harry rode to work together. Bought me a wide, black leather belt like Alan Ladd in China. Groucho reminds me of Earl. It's a funny show. Mammy called and told me two boys from Beech St. jumped on Bucky. Wait till I catch them out.

> Sat., September 14, 1946. Raine, Peggy, Joy, and Cora came to Buggs Bunny Club, but Raine didn't sing. The Everly Brothers were pretty good. Betty and Betty and Mary and JT came to B.B.C. Momma locked daddy out last night and we all stayed at Mammy's. I slept on the floor and dreamed that Earl raped Raine. This dream went all night long, keeping me awake. I started to ask in the middle of the night if Earl was home. Moon-empty yard. Writing this Sunday night.
> Sun. September 15, 1946. Ate at Mammy's. Didn't cuss all day. Thank you, Jesus. Chief Buckner came in from Oak Ridge to see Mammy. Saw Emmett sneaking down the alley. Chased him all the way to Grand Boulevard but he excaped.

Eager to finish, so he could catch the best parts of *To Each His Own*, Lucius moved into the main lobby, flicking tiny bits of dirt and trash into the brown receptacle of the brass-handled dustpan that left a lingering smell on his sweaty palms. It was worn out, warped, always clogged up, and the creak, creak, creak made him nervous, afraid he might distract the patrons from the sad love scenes.

A large woman turned toward him from the fountain on the opposite side, water glistening on her vivid red lips. She wore a lime suit, with deeper green, large glassy buttons, a green band in her jet-black hair, high heels. Not fat but stout, she stood with her legs spread a little too wide for a lady, letting the water drip from her lips down the front of her blouse like a kid. Fleshy hips, a high, thick chest, but small breasts. Her mouth was fleshy and she had the most beautifully shaped lips he'd ever seen, and blue eyes, and her soft hair, black as LaRue's, was wavy, coming down around her shoulders. She smiled at Lucius as if she'd known him a long time. He was too startled to respond before she turned and walked back into the auditorium.

Sweeping quickly over toward the fountain, he passed the doors, saw her standing at Gale's post, the way Hood stood beside the Spot, pressed up against the half-wall, arms spread out, bent, on the rounded top of the balustrade, her chin on her stacked fists. Olivia de Havilland as Jody Norris back in 1916 hears an airplane pass over her father's drugstore where she works the fountain in a fluffy dress, sweet as Melanie in *Gone With the Wind*. Hearing the squeak of the sweeper, the woman pivoted her head on her fist, looked at Lucius. He smiled back, boldly, then ducked his head and continued, crisply graceful, to sweep.

As he'd crossed the lobby, Thelma had seemed busy at the popcorn machine, but he sensed now that she had her eyes on him and was sizing the situation up. He didn't look at her directly, but realized faintly that her body resembled the woman's. "You all better watch out."

"What?"

"She's been parading up and down the lobby out *here* and in *there* all day, slurping enough water to float a battleship, and Gale's been strutting around in front of her like a rooster and gabbing with her. If you all don't watch out, Mr. Hood's gonna catch on and raise sand."

Lucius saw a cloud of sand whirl in the lobby. "I haven't said a word *to* her."

"Good idea. Keep your trap shut, your mind above your belt, and stand up straight, Lucius. You wanna end up stoop-shouldered like your daddy?"

She was always telling him to stand and walk straight, that he was stooped and round-shouldered like his daddy, but "Freddy" or "your daddy" always sounded, even in a negative statement, soft and tender. Lucius loved his daddy's stoop-shoulderedness, his easy stride. "They ain't nothing wrong with the way he stands." When he visited the bakery out on the Smoky Mountain Highway and followed his daddy through the plant where the ladies worked fast at the machines and the men carried heavy stuff on their shoulders, Lucius deliberately imitated Fred Hutchfield's walk, knowing that the women were saying, "I wish you'd look at the way that boy of Fred's walks. Just like his daddy."

To keep from getting mad at Thelma, Lucius worked back toward the Spot, set the sweeper in its corner behind the hooked-back golden door, and stepped over to, turned, and stood On the Spot. The woman stood over at Gale's post. She looked about twenty-five. Lucius wanted to start talking to her before Gale got back from his break, but if he stood over there, Hood would tell him to get back On the Spot.

Lucius listened again to hear the name "Captain Bart Cosgrove" spoken at his back. His body facing front, he turned his head. John Lund, a new actor, takes Olivia up in his airplane. He just wants to "do it" to her, but he's handing her an elaborate line of bull. The theme music is very beautiful and Lucius remembers in quick flashes all the agony Jody will go through after she lets Corin—that sickening Mary Anderson—have her illegitimate baby. She'll grow old, getting rich in the cosmetics business in New York and London and make Corin give her back her boy, and he'll cry for his momma, and Olivia will give him up again, and years later when she's a bitter woman, she'll be reunited with her son in London and he's played by John Lund again, who, as the father, was killed in WWI, and now the son will be in uniform to go to WWII, and he'll say, "Holy Canarsie" when Olivia gets him extra leave to be with his girl a little longer, and Lucius, anticipating the last scene, was about to cry when he sensed that the woman was coming toward him, voluptuous lime undulating across the electric carpet, taking the orange lights of the still-stand as she passed behind the doors that backed the popcorn machine. He noticed that, oddly, she carried no pocketbook.

"I love this movie," she said, standing in the middle of the aisle, her feet apart, arms akimbo, squared off at him. "Maria Montez is who *I* want to be," said the woman in lime. "You see *Tangier?* You be here tomorrow? What's your name? Mine's Shirley."

"Lucius." Suddenly, he realized that this woman was not just frank and loud and gay. And perhaps not as old as he'd thought.

"When's Gale get back?"

" 'Bout six."

"I'm gonna sit by *you*." She sat where Gloria Fletcher, the girl in the rich brown outfit, always sat. He waited for her to tell him he had lovely eyes, but by the light of Olivia's skin, he saw that Shirley's own blue eyes were big and watery and fringed with long, black lashes. He began to think of her along with Maria Montez, remembering the previews at the Venice, and got very nervous and excited, and his palms moistened, and he began to smell the brass of the flashlight, and he got hot inside his pants and under his arms where the jacket was too tight, though the sleeves were too long and hid his knuckles.

He'd not done it to a girl in four years, since he was nine on Beech Street and used to do it to the Brummett sisters, Diana, Alice, and Judy (the same ages as Earl, Lucius, and Bucky) all the time. He's going to the store, passing the Brummetts' house. Alice, Diana, and Judy are sitting on the fender of their uncle's Model T Ford and Lucius asks them if they want to go in the weeds and they all want to and go into the field behind the houses where all kinds of candy bars and chewing gum that Lucius and Earl and the Hawn boys swiped in raids on drugstores and the A & P are stashed in the blackberry bushes and anytime they want one they can go and get it, but the sun is melting them down and rain has made the paper stick and they're gobbling them down each day before they spoil. And the girls lie in the dead grass of September and pull their panties down around their ankles and their dresses up under their chins, and the wind is blowing in the trees over them, and they all walk away sore.

The four years since then were filled with fantasies and meat-beating sessions with kids in the neighborhood and cornholing at camp on Lone Mountain and endless jerking, even before he could jack off. Sonny and Lucius used to go over by W. W. Drummond furniture factory on Sunday along the railway between the silver walls of the factory and the red clay bank, covered with honeysuckle that smelled like come and the high wire fence of Stein's auto graveyard, and cornhole in boxcars, or under a low trestle while trains passed over. The great thrill at the first threads of come, drawn out like a rubber band or a stretched string of bubble gum.

Now he was in love with "the one and only girl," Raine, LaRue fading out, slowly eclipsed, and he could never allow himself for a moment to think of *her* that way—nor wanted to—he wouldn't touch her breasts because he would dirty her. Sex means Jesus hates your guts if you do it, and God, checking out the demerits in his big book, rejects you, and the devil, stoking up the fire, claims you. Sex was dirty more because of guilt over beating his meat than doing it to a girl. Girl-sex now was only fantastic daydreams and wet dreams, once desecrating Hedy Lamarr, pure like all the stars, even though he'd heard about Hedy's nude swim in *Ecstasy* and seen her as a dark-skinned native in *White Cargo*. Lucius didn't know whether to think of this woman—Shirley— as a piece of ass or somebody he might fall in love with.

Olivia walks where she can look upon her growing son from afar.

A spark on his neck made him drop his flashlight and chase it down the aisle. When he returned to the Spot, Shirley-lime was gone. Gale stood at his own post, grinning like Errol Flynn. Shirley sat across the aisle from him.

Now and then, Gale came over to Lucius and whispered, "Smell," and Lucius said, "I don't smell nothing," and Gale said, "Just warming it up." Lucius went over and whispered in his ear, "She already let me have some while you was eatin' supper," and Gale said, "And what was *you* eatin'?" And when Lucius sneaked up behind him with electricity in his soles and sparked Gale, Shirley giggled, saying, "Oh, law!"

Wade Bayliss in uniform strolled in and looked around and Lucius kept his eye on his every move, wishing Wade would break a Bijou rule, plant himself in the aisle so Lucius, also in uniform, could command him to "step back out of the aisle! It's a city ord'nance."

Near closing time, as Lucius stood, sore-footed, weary, immersed in images of Raine, conjuring images of Lew Fogarty, private detective, in "Black Dust," listening to the final scene of *To Each His Own*, on the verge of tears, Hood at his side, he felt a spark sting his cheek and started to pretend to hit Gale with his flashlight, but it was Shirley, saying, "You the cutest little dickens," going on out into the main lobby. Hood, engrossed in the ending of *To Each His Own*, didn't seem to notice the spark go off, the woman in lime go by.

Mon., September, 16, 1946. To Each His Own is on. Walked to school with Duke. Tried to tell him about The Raven again. LaRue saw me walking down the hall with Raine and Peggy. Met this woman in Bijou.

Tuesday, September 17, 1946. Raine and the Clayboe Ridge gang came by to walk to school with me. Glad Duke laid out. My day off, but took Gale's place because his mother died. To Each His Own. Writing "Black Dust."

Wens. September 18, 1946. Gloria Fletcher, the girls name that said I had beautiful eyes, had a fuss with me. I told her that if she was Gale's girl I had no bisness takening her to the show. She tried to explain but I wouldn't listen. Then she got mad. To Each His Own. Hood called a staff meeting. Had to fix a lot of things around the Bijou. Brady got off the floor to help Elmo clean up basement. Tangier starts tomorrow.

NIGHT RITUAL: Wilda's short blond hair hangs straight down and bounces. She's always pushing it out of her dirty face with her fingers. A tooth is missing in front. Lucius sees a yellow spot on the middle of her panties under her dress. . . . Some ladies in Woolworth's look down at Bucky. "What a beautiful baby." Momma smiles and strokes Bucky's long golden curls. . . . In the back of the orange and white bread truck, the Lone Ranger on the sides, Lucius and Bucky and Earl bounce when the truck hits a bump, and roll all over the back like loaves of bread, laughing, giggling, scared to death by Momma's predictions more than by the speed and curves. Momma keeps screaming at Daddy, "Fred, you're driving too damned fast! We're going right off that cliff into the Tennessee River!" Lucius sees dark on the round little windows in the two back doors. . . . In the white garage, the ground is black and a black bucket of tar sits in one corner, a cat and new kittens in another. Wilda pulls her panties down around her ankles and Lucius keeps poking it in. . . . Lucius, Earl, and Bucky are walking down the sidewalk on Zachary Street. Fay Nell, Jesse's sister, is carrying groceries. She breaks into a little trot. Lucius and them can't keep up. "I'll race you," Fay Nell yells in the dark. She beats them to the kitchen table as the sack breaks and the groceries spill all over the table and cans and apples roll off onto the floor, and she keeps running right on out the back door into the backyard, Lucius running after her, giggling so hard his side hurts, and she flips up her flowered dress as she squats over the fresh cut grass and wild onions, pearled by moonlight, near the lawn mower, pisses from dangling fuzz like a sparkler, long and hard, her back to the three of them, who stand like Tom, Dick, and Harry on the buckled back porch, her slender white ass gleaming. The sight gives Lucius a funny feeling in his belly. Sinful, sinful. He's never seen anything so exciting and beautiful, and never stopped thanking and loving her. . . . In the ice cream are tiny pieces of paper with a number on each. Lucius finds the right number and gets an extra cone of strawberry—the only thing he ever won.

> Thurs. September 19, 1946. Started and finished "No Love Like Ours." I didn't take Betty to the show. Gale sat with Mary. Saw Scarlet Street with Joan Benett, Dan Duryea and Edward G. Robinson at the Imperial. Tangier. Bought Screen Romances—Notorious and Night and Day in it, both of them Cary Grant.

> Fri. September 20, 1946. Didn't go on the floor, had to go up to colored gallery because the ticket girl vomited on the steps. Duke walked to school with me. Raine gazed at me across the playground while me and Duke and Harry played blackjack under the little tree near the street.

Saturday night, as Lucius stood at the foot of the ladder and took TANGIER from Elmo's hands, Duke came ambling toward the marquee. Stopping melodramatically, he went into a menacing crouch, snapped his fingers, pointed at his pecker. In those dancing, prolonged moments of greeting, he looked like a moron imitating a hotshot. "What the fuck you doin', boy?"

"Taking *Tangier* down and putting *Dragonwyck* up. What *you* doing out this late?"

"Hell, nobody tell *me* how late to be out. I'll kill the mudduh-fugguhs." Lucius wondered how his innocent question had put such a fierce look on Duke's face.

"Where you headed?"

"*Hell*, if I don't *do* better."

"Hey, don't you live up around Clinch View?" asked Elmo, looking down, taking a big D from Lucius.

"I see you before," said Duke, nodding, as if that took care of Elmo.

Duke gyrated around the lobbies until Lucius got off work. Suggested they have a cup of coffee before they started home. Duke entered Max's as if he were Scarface and Lucius were George Raft, his bodyguard. By the time Duke had exhausted his impressive repertoire of sneers, sudden head gestures, hunches, hand flourishes, sinister teeth-picking motions, that could be delivered from a sitting position, and they were back out on Sevier Street, the last streetcar had already left the carbarn.

Duke was the most visible of the boys Lucius knew, not so much at school—they were in no classes together—as in the neighborhood, and Lucius often ran into him swaggering around Market Square. So Lucius was with Duke more often than anybody else on his days off.

As they walked four miles home, failing to catch a ride hitchhiking, Duke kept Lucius fascinated with a long string of boasts that exploded like firecrackers along the sidewalk. The movements he made with his body to go with the boasts or fill brief spaces between them were almost as intricate as a Gene Kelly dance.

Within a few blocks of Lucius's house, Duke suddenly ran dry, and Lucius, seeing a boxcar parked behind W. W. Drummond's furniture factory, told him about the time he and Joe Campbell slept out in one. "You know Joe? Short guy, shorter'n me, got these buck teeth makes him look like he's always sneering at you, and big blue eyes and a black pompadour in his hair—always in a good mood, you know. We were good buddies all through fourth, fifth, and sixth, but I don't run into him much anymore. Ol' Joe hates to sleep at home because he has to sleep in the same bed with his three little brothers in this tiny room in the back of this tiny house, room almost as little as that old boathouse jacked up beside Mr. Lilly's Pond. They live right next door to it on Beech.

"So Joe's favorite fun's sleepin' out. Hell, we slept on his back porch a few times, on the tar-paper roof of his coal house, in the cab of the truck his daddy uses in his tree-trimmin' business, *under* the damned truck, in the bed of the truck, in empty trash cans, in a syca-more tree half of one night, the rest of it on a raft, floatin' on Mr. Lilly's pond 'cause he said he'd rather break a rule about kids on the pond than listen to us yapping in the trees. And we slept out up on Clayboe Ridge, on the steps of Clinch View school, and the last time, we tried the sewer but when a draft blew out the candle and the flashlight went so weak it made this weird light, we got scared and Joe climbed in the window into his bedful of brothers, and I went back to Mammy's at three o'clock in the morning, and this neighbor's chow dog almost chewed me to bits."

"I'd like to kill me a few people," said Duke, as if he hadn't heard a word Lucius had been saying. Tired of such talk, Lucius was eager to part with him. "Reckon could I spend the night at *your* house?" Duke's sudden pleading tone surprised Lucius.

"Don't you have to ask your momma and daddy first?" Lucius wanted to see what they looked like, and where Duke lived.

"Nobody gives *me* permission," he said, reaching inside his leather jacket for a Luger.

Lucius told Momma he was going to sleep out in the chicken house with Duke. Daddy wasn't in the bed beside her. Going to the kitchen, Lucius hoped to find Earl sleeping with Bucky, his stolen leather jacket draped over a kitchen chair, but only Bucky slept on the cot, sucking his thumb. Lucius pulled one of the quilts off and dragged it behind him out the back door. Duke was gone.

Somebody jumped on Lucius's back out of the cedar tree. "Teach you to be scared of the dark," said Duke, in his East Side gangster voice.

"I knew you was up there, just hoped you'd break your ass."

By the flame of Duke's Zippo lighter, they squeezed through the boxes and barrels and broken furniture, looking for a nest. "Smells like chicken shit," said Duke.

"Chicken house—used to be."

Feeling around in the pitch dark, they found some old bedsprings and a torn mattress and cleared the ground for them.

"Cold as a witch's tit," said Lucius, shivering under the quilt.

"Freeze balls off a brass monkey."

"Colder'n a well-digger's asshole."

Lucius felt the secret isolation of the place. The faint smell of an old chicken house—the lingering odor of straw and feathers, the sense of nestling—always excited him, like rain in the jungles on his ridge route.

"What you doing, Duke?"

"Nothin'."

"I'd always tell Joe a story before we went to sleep."

"I ain't camped out since Boys' Club on Lone Mountain," said Duke. He let out a jackass laugh. "Remember that time we got caught cornholing? You was in another cabin, and the director shined his flashlight on me and this big boy named Hobart and he made us go out to the parade ground and pull grass, and I thought we'd be the only ones, but there was ol' Lucius Hutchfield and about the whole rest of the camp, pulling grass in the moonlight."

"Stop playing with yourself, Duke. I can't get to sleep." Giggling, Duke went faster and faster, making the springs jiggle. "They can hear it all the way up on Clayboe Ridge."

Thinking of Duke playing with himself made Lucius get a hard-on.

"What the hell you doing, boy?" The way he said "boy" instead of Lucius—he'd never called him by name—made Lucius feel Duke was a stranger on the mattress beside him.

Because of his years of carrying papers on Sunday morning, Lucius still woke at five and couldn't get back to sleep. Looking around the chicken house, he began to think of it as a possible new sanctuary. Take a hell of a day's work to reshuffle the junk Momma had stored here—work that Duke might help him do.

The day was bright and warm out in the yard when Duke woke up. Remembering Tom Sawyer whitewashing the fence, Lucius said, "I hope Bucky doesn't wake up and come out here and start looking."

"For what?"

"Those dirty funny books Earl brought back from traveling with the carnival."

"Where? Where?"

"He hid 'em *some*where in here, but I haven't been able to find them. Guess I'll just have to move all this stuff out in the yard someday and make a more thorough search."

"If I help you, can I have half of 'em?"

"Sure. But I ain't guaranteeing we'll find 'em."

"*I'll* find the little fuckers."

While Momma and Bucky slept—and he hoped Daddy had come in finally last night—Lucius and Duke hauled all the stuff into the yard, aware that people going to church stared, disgusted, at the spectacle of a yard full of tacky furniture and barrels and boxes overflowing with clothes and other junk.

"Lucius, will you tell me what in the hell you're doing?" Momma stood on the back porch in her housecoat, the green latticework screening her from the churchgoers who drove the new cars that were coming off assembly lines for the first time since the war.

"I'm rearranging."

"You're embarrassing me to death. This is Sun-day morn-ing."

"We're almost ready to shove it all back in—neater. Tighter."

"*I'm* gonna shove it down your throat in about half a second . . ." Duke stood in the bright sun on the dying lawn, terrified of her.

"I'm fixin' me a sanctuary, Momma."

Duke gave Lucius a lip-curled, frowning look. "A what?"

"Clubhouse."

"I'll give you five minutes before I beat the socks off you."

Except for the desk that once belonged to all three boys and an old bed, they stacked all the furniture and boxes and barrels neatly in one corner and, between that and the coal pile, cleared and swept a space big enough for the bed and the desk.

"Bucky must have found them," said Lucius.

"Maybe Earl sneaked back and got 'em."

Wishing Duke would go home, so he could start fixing up his desk, Lucius ambled out into the yard.

A grey Chevrolet pulled up along the curb. Lucius recognized the face of the traffic cop who always stood in front of the Tivoli. Odd to see him out of uniform. Then he remembered he was Duke's daddy.

Mr. Rogers stuck his head out the window. "Hey, you!" When Duke saw his daddy, he seemed to change back into the runty, nervous little kid he was at Boys' Club camp. "Come here, you!" Duke looked quickly at Lucius as if pleading for help even as he ran, almost sideways, to the cement wall, dropped down to the sidewalk, crawled in the back seat of the car. His daddy reached back with one hand and, as the car moved away from the curb, pulled Duke over the seat into the front. The car wobbled from side to side down the street, almost ramming a streetcar—as if Duke's daddy were slapping him, steering erratically.

Lucius moved all his writings from Momma's bottom dresser drawer to the desk drawers, and he set his banana boxes of stills and movie magazines on top of two clothes barrels. Then Momma called him in to breakfast.

The sanctuary was a little cool, despite the warm sun in the yard, and his nose got a little leaky, but Lucius stayed at the desk, writing the synopsis of "The Unveiling of the Mask" by Will Cosgrove. Through the broken window of the chicken house, Lucius saw Daddy get off the streetcar. He hadn't been home in three nights and Momma had been going around the house threatening to divorce him. Lucius was relieved he was home, but he stayed in the sanctuary another hour, waiting for Momma's screaming to subside.

Bucky came out and stood in the doorway, whimpering, gravy on his cheek. "Wish they had the show on Sunday."

"Yeah, me too."

"Loan me a dime to get me a funny book, will you, Lucius?"

"When you pay me back?" asked Lucius, reaching for a dime.

"Ever when I grow up."

"Just promise you won't snake up to Emmett's house."

"Okay." Bucky stayed in the doorway, staring at the desk until he'd figured something out. "I want my drawer."

After three years, he wanted his drawer back—until Lucius paid him a quarter to rent it for a year.

As Bucky sat in the cedar tree blowing bubbles with the blow gum he'd bought with part of his quarter, Lucius made an entry in his diary for the day before.

Sat., September 21, 1946. Raine sang "Heartaches" at Bugs Bunny
Club. I love her. During my break, I met her and Peggy at the Tivoli

and Harry sat with Peggy when he got off for lunch. We ate popcorn
and kissed for lunch. Dragonwyck was on. Last of Tangier at Bijou.
Duke, the fabulous liar, came by the marquee and we slept out.
I am writing this Sunday afternoon in my new sanctuary.

The shouting in the house had stopped, so Lucius went in. "Where's
daddy at?"
"I turned him out into the street."
"What for?"
"Now, you just shut up, Lucius. It's none of your business. He's
probably headed straight for Barbara's, so you needn't feel sorry for him.
Save it till that husband of hers breaks out of prison and catches your
daddy in his bed, and I hope he blows his head off." Lucius saw him
do it.
Chicken gravy and mashed potatoes drooled down the walls very
slowly and a broken plate and chicken legs and green beans and corn
bread lay on the linoleum. Lucius was surprised that she'd saved Daddy
some dinner. He wanted to get the hell out. He wished it was six o'clock
so he could start getting ready for evening church services with Loraine.
"Well, I reckon I'll go out and write some more."
Bucky was not in the tree.

Sun. September 22, 1946. Dark. Momma came out to my sanctuary to
tell me to come in to get ready for church, but she told me she and
Daddy have separated. I cried and she cried and screamed, "You
love him more than you do me." Maybe I do. Wrote the outline for
"The Unveiling of the Mask." Went to church on Clayboe Ridge with
Raine and them.

Modulations of black and white pulsed fitfully from *Dragonwyck* as
Lucius turned to light the way for the tall, slender blond young woman,
wearing the same summery dress. Midway, not certain of the exact seat,
he turned his back to the screen and walked slowly backward, shining
the light at the young woman's feet. One seat in from the aisle, she
sat down. Glenn Langdan, a doctor, stands at the bedside of Vincent
Price's dying wife. As Price looks on coldly, Gene Tierney stares at him.
Light from the enormous pillow on the bed in the fabulous manison
lit up the young woman's flowered dress. Climbing the aisle to the Spot,
Lucius imagined showing her directly to her seat next Monday. She always came at five o'clock, in the middle of the feature, and when Lucius
returned from supper was gone. Watching the light play over her, he
wished he could remember where he'd seen her.
With each movie, the rhythm of light was different, rising and
falling over the rose and gold and the oak and brass furnishings of the
auditorium, and over the clothes of the spectators, fading now, except

for the blond woman, from bright summer to autumn hues. Feeling this pulse of color, controlled by the pace and lighting of individual movies, Lucius was sensitive to the slight, but distinctive variations of light intensity from one movie company to another—Paramount and Metro-Goldwyn-Mayer, Warner Brothers, Twentieth Century Fox, and RKO were very different from each other, and the differing tones of the background music affected the impact of the light. When he was stationed in the balcony, the shifts of light and dark within the single shaft projected from the booth window fascinated him. He was aware of a very different play of light and sound in the half hour before the movie started, when the curtain was illuminated and "Full Moon and Empty Arms" came from the booth's phonograph through the speaker behind the curtain. When the houselights came on as the last customers climbed the aisle, sluggishly, as if pleasantly stunned, he was aware of the vividness of the theatre's colors. When he did not concentrate on the images themselves, he felt laved in pure light and sound.

Going back to change into street clothes to go to supper, Lucius was aware of the dim yellow light backstage, of the forty-watt illumination of the corridor behind the steel door and in the dressing rooms. He felt a mild shock of transition stepping into the golden lobby, his neck free of the tight, clammy celluloid collar, and walking down into the even brighter intervening outer lobby, and on out under the fifty light bulbs that composed the star design in the ceiling of the outer foyer, and on out under the marquee's bulb-studded light border, repeated inward to the center, a round cluster of bulbs, he stepped out of a black and white darkness into a neon darkness. The two long display boards that hung on each side of the marquee and the fringed banner that hung over the curb created a realm distinct from everything beyond. Even though people passed under the marquee, he felt, standing on the sidewalk, that he looked out of a zone of light into Cherokee.

Watching the autumn rain pour down, feeling Minetta's eyes on his back, giving him that peculiar tingle in his spine he used to get playing cowboy, expecting any minute to feel the muzzle of a Gene Autry pistol in his back, Lucius wondered who sat by the drenched windowpanes, behind the yellow iron grille in the streetcar that passed. He dashed across the tracks toward Max's restaurant.

He was sitting at the counter waiting for the black coffee to-go that he was getting for Foster Bagwell the Christian projectionist—then he would walk up to Mammy's cafe for supper—when Momma walked out of the back region where the restrooms were. He was startled to run into Momma at this place in a sinister aura of danger and sinfulness, next door to the wrestling matches, across from the Jasper Hotel where he knew whores worked, near the courthouse where country people and whores and drunks and bums and a few decent but tough-looking laborers with their wives often sat on the lawn on hot summer nights. And Max sold beer, too. Lucius's awareness of not understanding much of what went on in the everyday world and his awe of the way *places* altered his responses to people gave him an odd feeling of imbalance, and watching Momma walk toward him with a radiant smile caused a flutter in his belly as though he hadn't seen her in weeks. He never noticed, except when he met her in public, how pretty his short, plump mother was. Her lustrous auburn hair.

When Momma walked behind, instead of in front of, the counter, Lucius was surprised, delighted, scared, feeling a sudden shift. She picked up some dirty dishes and put them in a pan under the counter. But she wasn't wearing a white waitress's uniform, she was in her best street clothes and had fixed herself up so she looked great, but why was she handling dirty dishes?

"Momma! What're *you* doing here?"

Her eyebrows went up, her mouth opened in a smile. "Well, honey! Glad you came in. I'm *working* here now." She put on a hoity-toity voice. "I'm the hostess with the mostest. Talk to you when you go to pay your check."

She went up to the cash register, and Max, a small man, got down off the stool and Momma, a small woman, climbed up on it, smiling at a man who stepped up to the cigar counter reaching for a toothpick. Lucius felt as though he were watching a brief scene from *Mildred Pierce*, when Joan Crawford went right to work in a restaurant in California after one of the waitresses suddenly quit. Before that, during the Depression, separated from her husband, Mildred had brought some money into the house by baking cakes. Lucius's mother had stayed up late herself many nights, making homemade fried pies for Mammy's and other restaurants, and almost went into business with a delivery truck.

Wanting to savor this new perspective on Momma, feeling a possessive familiarity about Max's now, Lucius went ahead and ate supper —hot roast beef sandwich with gravy and french fries and tangy coleslaw and light bread.

Lucius and Duke had walked out of Walgreen's several times without paying for their ice cream sundaes, pretending as they feigned a casual walk past the cashier that they'd only been looking for their mother. They'd stand outside in the bright sunlight or in the neon glow at night and look up and down Sevier a few times, to show they were innocent, and then, like Mutt and Jeff, walk off. Out of sight, they'd break into gyrations of delight. Lucius could never shake off the feeling that he looked suspicious as he approached cashiers, even though she was, tonight, his own mother.

"Do I get it for free?"

"Why, no, honey, I get *my* meals, but you'll have to pay sixty cents for this."

As she made change, she gave him a covert, significant look, and whispered, though no one could have heard, "Did you notice a woman in a flowered dress, blond young woman, come in the Bijou about an hour ago?"

"Yeah." Expectant, Lucius's heart beat faster.

"I seen her through the window. Honey, that's Luke's old girl friend, Ruby. She's married, and they had to meet secretly or her husband would've shot both of them." The thought of Luke made her tighten her mouth to keep from crying.

Walking backstage, Lucius saw the snapshot of the young woman among Luke's things: her legs apart, Ruby stood barefooted on two smooth rocks in a rapid stream, Chimney Rock Mountain over her shoulder, and heard, coming down the narrow stairwell, ". . . a tale well calculated to keep you in . . . Susssss-pense," then an eerie chord of music.

In the star's dressing room, lights out, two windows open behind them, revealing the dark courthouse clock tower, the sound of streetcars grinding around the corner into the carbarn, sat Gale, leaning back against the sill, and Brady and Elmo, cocked back in chairs against the wall, lighted cigarettes in their hands, the only other light the soft yellow dial beam on the table model Zenith radio. "Shhhhhh," they all said, with no smart-aleckness in their tone, "it's *Sus-spense.*"

Mon. September 23, 1946. Luke's girl Ruby still comes to the Bijou every Monday at the same time and sits beside an empty seat. I dropped out of band today because I couldn't read music good enough. Forgive me, Luke. Raine was in fashion show at Bonny Kate and was the prettiest. Harry won my lunch money playing black jack. I told Raine she looked cute on the stage. Dragonwyck. Max wears a suit and a towel draped over his Greek neck. Momma works for him now. Life is fascinating, God.

Tues. September 24, 1946. Took Betty R. to the Venice. Gale went too. Betty cuddled up close and I kissed her a few times after teasing her a little. She talked about marrying me. Dan Duryea and Peter Lorre were on in The Black Angel. It was really good. This song-writer doesn't know he killed his wife when he was drunk so he hunts down the killer and it's him. Lousy announcer on the Insomniacs show in place of Mark Fogarty.

Wens. September 25, 1946. Dragonwyk. Wrote some more on "Glory in a Sanctuary."

"Oh, I get tired of walking with just 'em ol' girls, Lucius," said Raine, as they walked down the hall be.ween classes. "They act so simple, and it gets me tickled so bad I need to go to the bathroom all the time."

Lucius blushed to hear such talk coming from such a beautiful mouth, as if Vivien Leigh, whom he couldn't imagine going to the bathroom, had said it. Sometimes Raine let a coarse sense of humor come out. But the sun, bright in her long blond hair, gave her an aura of purity.

"Well, let's just walk around for a while, then. I *like* to walk. *You* like to walk?"

"If it was with you."

"Honey, I love to hear you say stuff like that."

"You be looking when we come thew study hall?"

"Yeah."

"Sometimes you got your head down and you're writin' sixty miles an hour and miss me, and I feel sad all day, can't even eat my lunch. Else you're sitting in that ol' library at the same table with that Della Snow."

"She comes over to *my* table."

"I'm gonna nail a sign to it, saying, This Table and This Boy Is Reserved for Loraine Clayboe."

Sore from the straight-armed blow Sonny Hawn gave his shoulder, passing him in the hall in front of the entrance to the gym, Lucius stepped out onto the small concrete porch, posed a while in Luke's combat boots, and tried a new stance, one shoulder drooping, his fingertips touching his kneecap, casually, his eyebrows wrinkled against the pale sunlight like Errol Flynn.

Lucius met Raine under the mimosa trees. Alone, school let out, her friends, Harry among them, walking, more slowly than usual, away from her up Breedin Hill toward Clayboe Ridge, she looked strange, hugging her notebook. She wore his favorite outfit—blue skirt, soft white sweater, bulky white socks, and white and brown oxfords, a wide blue band in her hair. Intimidated by the occasion for enacting the convention of boy-carries-girl's-schoolbooks, Lucius decided to refuse to do as others did.

"Where you want to walk, Raine?"

"I like for you to call me Raine, Lucius. But maybe you better not in front of Cora and them. They might laugh."

"Let 'em laugh." Renaming her made her more his own. Like the elements in his stories, he re-created her. "Hey, you want to see where I used to live?"

"Yeah, *anywheres*."

Lucius followed Raine's searching look. "There they go." Raine waved but Harry and Peggy and Cora and Joy were too far, small on the steep hill.

"I used to watch you all from about here on my way to catch the streetcar."

On Holston, they passed the red clay field in the addition where houses were being built. "I used to play cowboy and army in that field —dewberry vines crawling all over it in the summer and little horse chestnut trees . . . . They used to be a big blackberry patch here. And we'd play in that WPA ditch and crawl through the sewer pipe and look up through the rain drain and go on under the street over to Crazy Creek. . . . Whenever things got too hot at Mammy's, I'd come down here and sit on the bank under the streetlight to be by myself."

Raine stumbled, and her notebook went flying out of her arms.

Lucius picked it up and carried it with his own. "There's my gran'maw's house."

"Is that where you lived when I first laid eyes on you in the tent by the river?"

"Yeah. We call her Mammy because she used to sing "Mammy's Little Baby Love Short'nin' Bread" when Earl was little and he started calling her that. She hates being called gran'maw. Lives there all alone now, but Chief Buckner out at the Oak Ridge fire department comes to see her—sort of her boyfriend—after she closes the restaurant and on Sundays."

"Who's the service star in the window for?"

"My uncle Luke." He wanted to tell her about Luke but he was afraid he'd start crying in front of her.

"I got four brothers that went and they all come back, meaner'n ever."

"What kind of work they do?"

"Well, Lennis's on the highway patrol, which makes it good for Creed, for he runs white lightnin' off Lone Mountain, and I got another brother—Buddy—he's a Trailways bus driver on the Louisville run, and my oldest brother, J. T., has his own trucks and a feud with the union."

"What about your daddy?"

"I thought everybody in Clinch View and all of Cherokee knew my daddy, I mean, *of* him. Bootlegger."

"You mean Feisty Clayboe's your daddy?"

"You ain't just a kiddin'."

'The one that said—"

"The very one."

"Aw, come on now, the one that the judge said to him, 'Feisty

Clayboe, did you shoot this man in self-defense?' and Feisty said, 'Hell, no, I shot him in the ass and he *jumped* the fence."

"Better hush or I'll do you like my momma done *him*—wash your mouth out with P and G soap."

"Why, me and Sonny Hawn and them used to sneak up and watch your house, waiting for the law to raid it, and I know I seen you one time out in the grape arbor playing dolls."

"Probably did. *I* didn't know what was going on. Not till they sentenced him, and my brothers offered to join up to kill Japs, and me and Momma moved to River Street till the war was over. Now, we're all back home. But I can't let you come see me because Daddy's afraid of people's mouth, and I have to go over to Peggy's to use the telephone, so you can't call me, because men are always calling in."

"Including my daddy, I bet."

Lucius was surprised Raine wasn't ashamed of all that and almost asked her why. Even though her name was the same as the ridge and he'd always known whom it was named after, she'd seemed so unearthly beautiful, he couldn't imagine her coming out of that wild two-storey house on top of the ridge. Looking up, he saw it.

"I never will forget how cute you looked in that uniform, Lucius. The way you just stood there, like a little statue, posing like you knew every girl in the Bijou was watching. And they were."

"I was just acting natural."

"And then in the revival tent. And then there you was in American history."

Lucius showed her the old neighborhood, calling out the streets and telling little stories about people in some of the houses. He stopped at a corner where he usually turned right to climb a steep hill, to go to the Hiawassee on the other side. "See that big house next to the jungle? That's where I lived when I was one year old. Momma tells about these big rats, came right up to the supper table." Wanting to show her the tile factory and veer on over into Clinch View neighborhood, where his life intersected hers, Lucius kept on straight ahead.

"Did I ever tell you 'bout the time the Tennessee Kid met Billy the Kid?"

"Un uh."

"Well, it was in Helena, Montana." He tried to tell her the story, but Raine kept asking questions about everything they encountered. He had little to tell her about the area they were walking through. Her attention wandered and she'd ask him to repeat what he said. He felt a need to fix her attention with his eyes, but they walked side by side.

"Hey, here's where I used to carry papers." He showed her Beverly

Taylor's house. Locked up, looked deserted. He pointed out the way his ridge route ran. "And it ended about there."

"My house ain't far from there, on down the ridge toward Oak Ridge Highway. See?"

Her house dominated the ridge. He told her where his other routes had been. Now the Tennessee Kid's story was lost.

"We used to play all the time in that tile factory. Come through here on our way to the Hiawassee from Beech Street in the daylight and come back in the dark. Scary as hell."

"Let's *us* go through there."

They turned off. Raine on the rails, her hand on his shoulder, they walked the tracks.

Inside the tile factory yards, Lucius felt embarrassed to be walking with Raine where he'd tightly rolled and screwed an extra paper at the end of his route so many times. But he wanted to share his child-hood scenes with her, and here all his buddies and brothers at one time or another had eluded the watchman, playing.

The factory workers, covered with white dust, carried empty black lunch pails in the bright sun.

"They knock off work at three o'clock here. Start about six A.M., I reckon."

"*I'm* dead as four o'clock that time a morning."

Raine climbed up on a formation of small cement sewer pipes and jumped over to a row of larger ones. Lucius put their notebooks down and ran over to where she'd jumped down between two rows. She wasn't in sight. Crouching, he went through a bottom tile in the row and looked up and down the next row. Doing the same thing in the next row, he reckoned she was playing hide-and-go-seek with him.

"Raine," he said, "I'm coming after you, Raine." He made a fiendish noise like Peter Lorre and crept along, in and out, in a weaving line, among the tiles, row after row, the sizes varying, the piles sometimes stacked four high. Entering one tile, at the end of a string of them lined up with each other, forming a rifle barrel effect, he sometimes got a view of Clayboe Ridge. Searching for Raine here where he'd spent so many hours of his life, with so many kids from five different neighborhoods, created an aura of his childhood, an ambience that was in the chill autumn air he inhaled, in the texture of the cool cement tiles his fingers touched gently, scraped hard, or trailed along as he slipped among them, calling, "Raine, Raine."

Even from up on the ridge where he'd looked down over the vast layout of geometrical shapes in strict patterns, and the black, tin-roofed, ramshackle buildings, and the brick kilns like Indian mounds or ovens, the tile factory exuded an aura of secrecy, an oasis in the middle of Clinch View. Walk in there and everything was sealed off. Inside one tile, feeling the presence of hundreds of others around him. Almost as isolated as crawling through the same kinds of pipes under the ground in different parts of town with Earl and Bucky and neighborhood kids. The pitch black, underground, then sudden sunlight at the end, was not very different from the feeling of being under the sun, but the difference was sensual, palpable, and when he was alone, always sexual, a good place to take a crap and wipe on a large leaf of one of the horse chestnut trees that grew in such places as wild as grass. This place always made him feel scared, sad, and happy simultaneously.

"Raine, Raine, Raine, come on out, I give up."

"Raine, Raine, go away, come back some *other* day."

Scared, he looked around, trying to locate her voice. On his hands and knees he peered through the smallest tiles. A little lump of cement landed on his shoulder. Turning his head, he looked up. Raine sat in a large tile on the fourth tier. The angle exposed her pink panties. Lucius turned, blushing, a little angry. He didn't want her to be here where he'd beat his meat and cornholed Joe Campbell and thought of doing it to twenty girls in a row.

"You're It again," said Raine.

"Come on down, honey, and let's walk over toward *my* house."

"Okay."

He was wondering how he was going to help her down—she looked so misty beautiful, she might break if she slipped and fell—when she jumped, her blue skirt ballooning, and landed on the gravel.

"You didn't even watch me," she said, her feelings hurt.

"Well, your dress—"

"You like it? Momma made it. How we get out of this joint?"

"Don't worry, Veronica," Lucius said, overtly imitating Ladd's voice. "I know every inch of this place."

"What's in yonder?"

"Where they make 'em."

"Gosh ding, let's you and me go in there."

"Night watchman might shoot us."

"He better not, I'll sic my four brothers on him."

Scared, as if he'd done something himself to make her four brothers come looking for him in trucks, buses, and fast cars, Lucius opened a little side door and Raine huddled up close to him. "Ooooooo. Gives me goose bumps."

The building was very old and many holes in the roof let in the sky, sunlight slanted through gaps among the boards, sharp, long rays cutting the dark, hitting pulleys, wheels, motors. Lucius enjoyed being scared among machines and levers and piles of sand and chutes and white gravel and lime and cement-encrusted buckets, and wheelbarrows and shovels, and warped boards that led from one platform to another and hairy ropes, rusty chains hanging from naked rafters and light bulbs hanging from long black cords.

"This where they mix 'em?"

"I reckon." Lucius seldom asked that kind of question. He knew that if he stopped to relate one thing to another, he could probably figure out how the process worked, but he didn't want to dispel the mystery. The brick building to the side, though, had an obvious function. "Want to see where they bake 'em?"

"Ooooooo. I bet it's scary in *there*."

He led her outside again and over to another building. "Help me," he said, yanking on the large handle of a heavy door that slid on a steel track like the one between the dressing room and the stage at the Bijou. As he pulled, Raine pushed. "Always make me think," said Lucius, straining, "of those gas chambers and," grunting, "ovens in the Jewish concentration camps," listening to the grating rattle and steely whine, "they all the time show in the newsreels."

"Ooooooo, Lucius, hush."

Lucius and Raine got it open far enough to enable them to squeeze through, but he kept his back against the door.

In there, the tiles, set on wooden racks, looked as if they were once alive and had turned rigid, baked to death. His heart pounded so hard, he couldn't speak. Raine took his hand, timidly. He smelled her hair, her cinnamon breath.

Slamming shut, the door scraped against his back. Screaming in the pitch black, Raine pressed so tightly against him he could scarcely breathe. Sealed in with the dead tiles, he yanked at the door, yelling, "Help!" the echo ringing in the long, low-ceilinged room. He tried to comfort Raine and still get free of her clinging body so he could take hold of the door handle and push. Discovering that he should have been pulling instead of pushing, Lucius panicked, then the rage he used to feel when Nazis hanged or shot the Jews or hostages in *The Moon Is Down* or *Hotel Berlin* or *Hitler's Children* broke through the panic, and he made a ferocious pulling assault and the door slid open enough for him to shift around and push and see Emmett King, jolting, slump-shouldered, rocking along the top of the highest tier of tiles out in the yard. Raine squeezed through, mashing her small breasts against the thick edge of the door where his hands had shoved. Lucius wondered whether Bucky was somewhere in the maze of tiles.

"I'm gonna kill your goddam ass, Emmett King!" Lucius screamed, running toward the row of tiles, angry he'd cussed in front of Raine.

"Where you running to, Lucius?"

"Gonna get Emmett King."

"*Who? Where?*"

Lucius couldn't see him either now, but leaping onto a low tile, reaching up, swinging up onto a bigger one, running down the row to a place where he could jump across the aisle into one of the largest, he felt that to Raine he must look really tough and swift to vengeance. Kid Eternity. He hoped Emmett would show himself so Raine could see how big he was. Run him down, beat him up, drag him back, sling him at Raine's feet.

Inside a large tile, Lucius came to a scrambling stop, stood up, tried to figure out how he could get on top of it and run after Emmett down the row. Then through a smaller tile, he saw Bucky, running down the railroad toward Peck's grocery store. Bucky stopped in the middle of the tracks, turned back toward the tile factory and waited, huffing and puffing.

Lucius saw Emmett running among the small tiles toward the kudzu-vine-infested red clay bank above the tracks. The impetus jumping out of the tile flung Lucius against the next row and scraped his knee, but he ran on, jumping over tiles, aware that Raine was coming in his direction.

When Lucius reached the bank, Emmett was coming back for a shoe that had come off. Lucius took a flying leap and landed on Emmett's back as he squatted to pull the shoe out of the dead kudzu vines. But when Emmett raised up, Lucius rolled off his back and hit his shoulder against a railroad tie.

"Run, run, run, Emmett, goddam it, run!" screamed Bucky, who from the angle at which Lucius lay looked as huge as Emmett, the sun, red, going down in a sycamore tree on the horizon where the tracks curved into the trees between some houses. Then Emmett's hulk got between Lucius and Bucky, and as Lucius rose, he looked up at the crest of the red clay bank, and Raine stood there in the blue skirt and soft white sweater, smiling, enjoying the spectacle.

Lucius took out after Emmett who had slowed down to a lumbering trot.

"Hit it! Emmett! Hit it! He's about to get you!"

Bucky ran up the other high bank across the tracks, fighting loose clay, and waved Emmett on. Lucius chased Emmett up the bank. Conner Street open and clear, Bucky and Emmett running straight down the middle faster than Lucius had ever seen them, because they must have known that Lucius was madder than he'd ever been. "I'm gonna tell Earl on you!" Bucky screamed back at him.

Bucky and Emmett ran through a yard, and Emmett stopped to take one big swing on a tire somebody had rigged to an oak full of coal smoke from a chimney close by, and the rope broke, and they jumped up on top of a pile of coal and over a fence and lit out down the alley, Bucky's mackinaw fading out of sight. Lucius lost them among garages, coal houses, hedges, and trash cans.

Lucius walked back down the alley and cut over to the clay bank. Raine was leaning against the guy wire of a telephone pole across the tracks from the tile factory.

"You ain't mad at me, are you?"

"Why, footfire, no, that was fuh-uh-un!"

"Fun? Where's my notebook?" He felt almost as panicky as when they were sealed up in the gas chamber.

"Where you left mine, I reckon."

"Wait here. Be right back."

Weary, Lucius hated to go back for the notebook. Red clay in his shoes, his shoulder still sore from Sonny Hawn's bully blow, the other sore from the railroad tie, his knee skinned and bloody, his whole body quivering with rage. Gritting his teeth, he cursed Emmett King, being more selective in what he called Bucky, to avoid throwing off on his own mother.

"Hey, boy, what you doing in this yard?" Lucius heard a bullhorn voice as he raised up, the notebooks in his hand.

The nightwatchman stood in front of the brick building, the thick, heavy door behind him. He wore a pistol, in a holster like the one Gran'paw Charlie was wearing when his enemy shot him in the back at the glass factory. Maybe this was the one, night-watching another factory.

"Just getting my blamed notebook."

"No cutting through the yard on your way home from school. Hear me!"

"Yes, *sir*." Lucius walked toward the bank.

"Go back the way you come."

"This *is* the way I come."

"Then go out the *other* way."

"But my girl's waiting for me up on the other bank."

"No fuckin' in the factory limits 'less *I* get some."

"Eat shit!" Lucius ran between the rows of tiles toward the bank, a feeling, concentrated on a spot as large as a gnat in the middle of his back. that the man was going to shoot him. He listened for him to yell, "Halt!" Lucius jumped off the bank, turned his ankle. As he limped down the track, the pain was sharp, stabbing.

"Raine, Raine, walk along the bank to where it comes out at Peck's store. I hurt my ankle. I'll follow the tracks."

"I'll kiss your foot for you." Raine laughed and skipped along the path above him, and, as the bank sloped gently to the street, came gradually down level with the tracks.

At Peck's store, where the streetcar turned around at the end of the line, Lucius bought Raine a Grapette and himself a Dr Pepper. "We almost in *my* territory now," she said.

Standing a moment at the screen door, Lucius looked at the house where, Momma once viciously pointed out, Daddy's girl friend Barbara lived. Large and white, a colored window over the door, fancy woodwork, like a fan, above it. Her son Fritz wasn't in the same room with Lucius at Clinch View, but he saw him often, though never near this house.

"I used to drag a wagonload of wooden baskets full of dirty bottles in here for show money," Lucius told Raine.

"Don't LaRue Harrington live down the street?"

"Yeah, but she's dead now."

"Dead?"

"To *me*, since I found *you*."

"Let's go stick some stinkweed on her grave."

They walked on down the railroad track, curving through the trees and houses, past the coal yard, to Lucius's house.

"Lucius," Raine read aloud the note on the table, propped against the melted butter going rancid that had specks of soot in the saucer from the window being left open, "don't for god's sake, don't forget to empty the ice pan."

Lucius bent over and, trying to slip the white, red-rimmed, chipped pan out from under the icebox, without tipping it, tipped it, as it hit a ruckle in the linoleum, and spilled over his shoes. He carried, spilling more on the floor, getting tickled, hearing Raine giggle and snort, and dashed it through the window behind the cot.

While Raine made some baloney sandwiches and lemonade, Lucius brought a bucket of coal in from the chicken house. He didn't want her to see the sanctuary.

Today was a good day to swing, but the porch swing was drawn up to the ceiling for the winter. As they sat on the front steps eating the sandwiches, drinking the lemonade, Lucius wished Raine would ask to read one of his stories, but she didn't.

Joe Campbell breezed by on his bicycle, and Lucius noticed that he looked like such a little kid. His own bike was stored in the chicken house now that he walked to school each morning with Duke or the Clayboe Ridge gang.

When Lucius saw Duke come strutting by, scraping sparks out of the sidewalk with his steel taps, grinning, leering, he hoped he wouldn't say anything smart or nasty. "Got to meet this man that's going to sell me a switchblade knife. Gonna have to cut some people up," said Duke, walking on.

As they watched Duke wait for a train to pass, Lucius thought of it passing the tile factory on its way to John Sevier Yards thirty miles away. He'd once hopped a freight out there. Remembering chasing Bucky back home when he and Pud used to go to the tile factory on Sundays, it occurred to Lucius that Duke looked and acted a little like Emmett King. The train cleared the tracks and the streetcar started growling.

Thurs. September 26, 1946. Day off. Me and Raine walked around. Beat up Emmett in the tile factory and went to see Angel on My Shoulder at the Bijou with Raine.

Fri. September 27, 1946. The world looked good today, but not as good as yesterday. God bless America. Angel on My Shoulder ends tomorrow.

Wearing her blue headband, a soft blue blouse and a white skirt, Raine came out onto the stage and sang "Heartaches," looking straight up into the balcony where Lucius had told her, backstage, he'd be standing.

"You looked so cute," Raine said, after the Bugs Bunny Club ended, delicately picking up the top blossoms of popcorn in the bag she held.

Lucius didn't tell her that Hood had shifted him to the other side and that, blinded by the footlights, she'd been singing to Bruce Tillotson, the albino.

"Hey, come on, Lolo, let's get goin'," said Cora, looking up from the first landing, her red hair wild.

"Lolo?" asked Lucius.

"Hateful thing's got everybody calling me Lolo 'cause *you* call me Raine."

"Thought you wasn't gonna tell 'em."

"Cora got in my things and read that letter."

"Dammit, Raine, don't you let people see what I write you."

"Well, you needn't fly up and cuss about it."

They stared at each other through the rest of the Paramount News.

"When you get off for lunch?"

"'Bout one o'clock."

"Why don't you meet us at Walgreen's?"

"I don't want to meet *us*. Why can't *you* stay here till I get off?"

"I promised Peggy I'd go with *them*. Besides, I already seen *Angel on My Shoulder*—wasn't so hot the *first* time."

"Go on, then."

"What's the matter, Lucius?"

"Who am I to keep you from your girl friends?"

"That's silly to be jealous of them, Lucius."

"I wanted to take you to a special place."

"Where?"

"Skip it."

"LoOOOlo! You coming or else not?"

"Cora's voice gripes me."

"I'll be waiting at Walgreen's," said Raine, backing toward the stairs.

"Don't be surprised if hell freezes over before I show up."

Peggy, Cora, and Joy charged up the steps and started dragging Raine down. Lucius knew that she, looking back up at him, where he stood in the light from the stairwell, could tell he was sad, and he imagined that to her he looked interesting, romantic, brooding, like Orson Welles as Rochester in *Jane Eyre*. She broke away from the girls and ran back up to him.

"You still yet love me, don't you?"

"I don't know."

About to cry, she turned, and the girls, following her up, seeing the look on her face, stepped aside, and followed her on down.

Lucius knew that he would be on Raine's mind all day, and she would lie awake tonight, conjuring images of him in many situations and postures.

Brady came up and took his place and Lucius went On the Spot, where he imagined himself as Raine would see him in her daydreams.

Gale glided slow motion across the lobby, slender in his tight uniform, a perfect fit. "Here's one for 'Believe It or Not.' " Surprised himself, Gale surprised Lucius when he told him that he'd discovered that Shirley Ford, the woman in lime, was only fifteen. "Big for her age." She was a cowlike girl—not cowlike, she *was* a cow, a big, luscious, pretty, soft, jolly cow, and the Bijou had become her meadow, where she munched and lolled and mooed, well attended by five boys in "cute" two-toned blue uniforms.

Too sad about Raine to run with the Bijou Boys at lunch, Lucius took off before they could change clothes.

Raine stood on the curb under the marquee banner looking straight into the main lobby, a band passing behind her on Sevier, playing "Stars and Stripes Forever."

"I slipped off from 'em," Raine said, taking Lucius's hand.

Between a white and a Negro high school band passing in the parade—kickoff for the football season—they raced across to Max's where he ordered steaks and lemon meringue pie. Max himself, dirty towel slung around his neck, served them, Momma waving and smiling from the high cashier's stool.

As he paid the check Momma took him aside. "If your daddy staggers in the Bijou drunk tonight, you tell him he better not dare come slobbering over to Max's."

"Okay," said Lucius, irritated that she harped on his daddy's probable crimes, on top of the real ones, feeling as if he'd done something wrong himself.

In Kress's, Lucius bought a silver ID bracelet. "Put Raine plus Lucius on it," Raine told the lady.

When the woman laughed at the name Raine, Lucius said, "Least she don't cry every time she looks in a mirror. Come on, Raine."

They went next door to McLellan's and he bought her another.

Raine was standing on the sidewalk admiring their names on the bracelet, when Lucius saw Peggy and Joy and Cora and Duke come out of Walgreen's. Raine didn't see them.

At the end of their roving, they went into the bus terminal and sat in a booth and took four-for-a-quarter pictures of themselves.

"Well, President Truman fired Henry Wallace," said Tillotson, leaning like the Tower of Pisa. A leering tone in his voice, he always broadcast the latest news as if he were telling about a sex orgy in broad daylight on Sevier Street that only *he* had witnessed. "The trucking strike is over, and then the East and West Coast shipping strike ended. You hear about that poison we developed that can wipe out everybody in the entire nation?" Lucius always felt stupid as Tillotson told him the headlines, even when later he remembered he'd already heard or read about the events himself earlier.

When the Paramount News came on, he noticed that the trucking strike was being reported. Humphrey Bogart and George Raft in *They Drive by Night*. Secretary of State Henry A. Wallace was saying, "Winning the peace is more important than high public office." When the cameraman swung around and dollied in on Lucius at the end of the news reel, he felt personally involved.

Lucius went over to Tillotson, "Hey, you hear about that duel between the Tennessee Kid and Billy the Kid in Helena, Montana?"

Tillotson blinked his pink eyes, sneering.

When Lucius returned to the Spot, Hood was draped over the balustrade.

Thelma came out of the main lobby. "The toilet's run over in the men's room, Lucius." He wished she hadn't told him that in front of Hood. He'd have to do it. His eyes stinging with the injustice of it all, he went backstage for a mop and pail. Every Saturday night since he'd started, the commode in the tiny, slant-ceiling room off the first landing to the balcony clogged up and overflowed and he, as the newest usher, had to swab it up.

In the backstage dark, he walked around in furious circles, cursing and slamming his fist into the thick curtains. Thelma, who kept an eye on the ladies' rest room, met him in the inner lobby. "What took you so long? It's dripping from the ceiling of the ladies' room! Hurry up!" He cleaned the men's room and then Thelma stood guard on the ladies' room while Lucius mopped. The ladies' room always smelled like left-over pussy and upstairs pee. Disinfectant, deodorizers, Tigress cologne, failed to eradicate the odor.

Drenched in sweat, Lucius returned to the Spot.

"Maybe you'd better take the colored balcony," said Hood, his nostrils flaring.

Lucius walked outside and around the corner and through the Negro entrance. When he reached the dark balcony where the lights were dimmer, he was out of breath, terrified of the dark shapes, afraid one of them would rise up and swoop down on him with a razor, gleaming from the light cast by *Angel on My Shoulder*. But after a while he liked the smell up there, exotic, strange, sexy, and stood with a hard-on. They needed an usher only on Saturday to keep order, usually the albino's job.

Lucius wished he could be the one to close the curtain and cut the lights, although the switchboard scared the hell out of him. When the last showing ended that night, and Gale turned up the houselights, Lucius was startled to discover that he was alone with about two hundred Negroes who jumped up and moved quickly toward him. He swung around and opened the fire escape doors.

When he reached the main floor, the boys were flipping up the seats for the Negro clean-up crew that worked all night.

A little girl came running back in. Her mother and father stood in the outer lobby. "I lost a lost article."

"You all find a Margaret O'Brien pocketbook?" Lucius yelled from the balustrade.

"Didn't know you owned one," said Elmo, snorting.

After all the customers were out, Lucius locked the front doors. Then he went backstage and walked the narrow, warped, wobbly planks that swayed and bounced above the empty dark, stretched across three two-by-fours over the pitch black basement forty feet below, shining his flash-light ahead of him, using the other hand for balance, toward the pale yellow shine of lights from the Fontana Hotel windows on the rain-wet street that he saw through the enormous open fan doors, like the gates to the village in *King Kong*. Pirates walking the plank. Jungle Jim trying to cross the gorge on a swinging vine bridge, cannibals pursuing, cutting the rope. Circus tightwire walkers. He paused a moment at the black sooty iron wire-mesh, three times taller than he and ten feet wide, enjoying the way the neon lights played over the rain-spattered pavement, the way car lights cut throught the mist, scattering needles of color, the lonesome sound of tires on the water, making him feel more keenly that he was inside and Cherokee was outside, and he was eager to ride the last streetcar home through the mist. He shut the massive, dirty red wooden doors through which the humid air of the Bijou was exhausted into the side street, and a suck of wind pulled him backward, flattened him out on his back on the plank. He rose slowly and turned slowly and, weak-kneed on the plank, walked, afraid of meeting a rat between, back to the small door in the beaver board wall.

In the main lobby, Elmo and Brady were spreading out on the carpet large posters that had come in the mail. Bette Davis in white mink, a smoking gun in her hand: "You'll see her deceive with all her cunning, so she could love with all her heart." Bette Davis, Paul Henreid, Claude Rains in *Deception*. "The star of 'A Stolen Life' steals another life!" Jeanne Crain, looking very wholesome in shorts, in *Margie*. An enormous black key, Gary Grant and Ingrid Bergman inside the round end about to kiss. "No risk too great for a love so enticing!" Alfred Hitchcock's *Notorious*. Robert Cummings and Michele Morgan in white, hiding in deep shadows from Peter Lorre, large Japanese characters on the gray wall. "You'll be gasping for breath at the end of the *Chase*."

New stills had come in, some of them in rich Technicolor, the tone a little different with each studio. Lucius read the information on the backs that would show up in the Cherokee *Messenger*.

Sometimes in the office, Lucius looked at the ad material, the mats for newspapers, as Hood unwrapped them, like a magician practicing out of sight of audiences. But he was always bewildered because Hood, who was in charge of the theatre and the stills, didn't seem thrilled about it, didn't seem to deserve his good fortune. He got magnificent ad copy for *The Big Sleep, Courage of Lassie, Of Human Bondage,* the whole layout arranged differently in black and white from the colored posters Brady put in the still-stands against the walls. Looking at the posters, Lucius liked to toll out in his head the names of the directors: William Wyler, Mervyn Leroy, John Ford, and producers, David O. Selznick, Mark Hellinger, Samuel B. Goldwyn, Walter Wanger, Darryl F. Zanuck, and the men who wrote music, Dmitri Tiomkin and Max Steiner, and a few of the scriptwriters: Philip Yordan, Lamar Trotti, Robert Riskin, Philip Dunne, W. R. Burnett, Ben Hecht. Though far below the stars, everything else had magnitude.

Coming into the main lobby, Mrs. Hood said hello to Clancy, Lucius's favorite projectionist, who was going out, taking two large film cans to the bus terminal to ship to Atlanta. Lucius had seen Mrs. Hood in the lobby of the Tivoli, maintaining strict discipline, Harry looking scared to death when he saw her coming, quickly escorting Lucius down the aisle, flashlight beaming. Under her suit lapels, she seemed to have perfect breasts, and, as she walked right on into Hood's office without speaking to the Bijou Boys, a cute butt.

Turning their backs on the Bijou, tightly closed up, Lucius, Gale, and Elmo went to the Smoky to catch the midnight burlesque show when Violet Lombard (he didn't like her having the same name as Carole Lombard) showed her pussy. Lucius had often seen the burlesque during the day and sometimes at night, but he'd only heard, frequently, about the midnight show. You had to be eighteen to get in for that.

"They gonna kick your ass out," said Elmo, who at nineteen looked twenty-nine.

"Watch me try."

"Paint on you a Jerry Colonna moustache," said Brady.

"One like Oliver Hardy," said Gale, and they all laughed and pushed at Lucius and goosed him as they turned left at Market Square.

The rain had stopped, and the after-scent of it coming off rooftops into gutters and the coal smoke from houses and factories accented the smell of autumn more intensely tonight. Farmers in overalls and rough men and tough boys stood around in front of the Smoky, squatting on the curb, smoking, rocking on the balls of their feet, or leaning against the still frames. Through arms akimbo and spraddled legs, Lucius glimpsed about fifty stills advertising the triple feature and chapter play they'd missed: Wild Bill Elliott in *Bitter Creek,* Erich Von Stroheim, Earl's favorite actor, especially as Rommel in this one, and Franchot Tone in *Five Graves to Cairo,* and John Garfield and Edward G. Robinson in *The Sea Wolf,* and Chapter 4 of *The Phantom.* These people evoked a feeling of Earl's milieu, and of Mammy's country past in Cades Cove in the Smokies. Lucius's heart beat fast, his mouth was dry, anticipating the hot sight of Violet's pussy. From the open door of the narrow lobby, he got the smell of stale piss and old clothes and layers of sticky spit and spilled "dopes" and Milky Ways on the floor, soot, dirt, and moldy curtains. The raunchy smells of such places simultaneously repelled him with an aura of death and excited his imagination with a sense of the possibilities of life.

"Give me thirty-five cents," said Elmo.

"Like hell," said Lucius.

"Goddam it, I thought you wanted to go to the show." He showed four tickets. "You all kinda blend in with them country hoojers when they go in, and I'll hand lard-ass the tickets, and maybe they won't notice you're only eleven years old."

That's the way they did it, and it worked.

In the rat houses, the stars lost much of their goddesses' aura, so their movies sometimes shamefully aroused him, and the burlesque shows gave him fierce, painful hard-ons, and he had to sit through three features.

a half hour of previews, a comedy, two cartoons, a chapter play afterward, suffering the ache of a severe case of the blue balls the long hard-on had given him.

Lucius sat beside Brady on the end of the rickety row, wishing he were sitting beside Gale, when the small orchestra started playing and the curtain parted.

As the boring comic routines dragged on, Lucius wished he hadn't missed the movies by coming in at midnight. Every seat was occupied and some men even stood around the walls under the NO EXIT sign and leaned on the rail up in the balcony. A cop older than Wade Baylis stood blocking the aisle in back. The sight of two women startled Lucius. The theatre got very hot. The girls came out and one of them stripping gave Lucius a hard-on. Lucius wondered what the Smoky looked like *back*stage.

Then, just as Lucius's eyelids drooped, Violet came out and she was the woman Wade Baylis hurt under the Bijou marquee. She pulled her G-string down an instant, let it snap back, quick as the shutter of a camera. They all felt cheated and booed and cursed and spit on the floor as they stalked out.

NIGHT RITUAL: Lucius stands with his daddy on the sidewalk in the hot sun in front of Hutchfield Bakery, quivering with fright at the streamlined black and white dog, taller than Lucius, that Mrs. Lucius Hatchfield, a tall, beautiful, blond-haired woman, holds by a taut leash, and Uncle Lucius, the man after whom Lucius was named, pats Bucky, who has long blond curls, and looks like an "angel," then Lucius, then Earl, on their heads, saying, "Well, what's new, small fry?" After that, the only time Lucius ever saw his uncle, whenever Uncle Lucius's name was mentioned—seldom in a friendly tone by Momma or Mammy who once worked for him—Lucius thinks of scrambled eggs frying on a hot sidewalk. . . . Lucius and Earl go to the small white church on the other side of the jungle. Lucius slips out of church and hides behind a tree in the back and looks up and sees a girl of about fifteen sitting on the running board of a black car, her legs apart, showing her panties. She calls him over to sit with her and asks what he does with his little soso and he says, "Pee," and she says, "Show me how," and he says, "Okay," and she says, "Not here, let's go in the basement," and he goes in, scared of the dark, but daylight stands stiff and bright in the low cellar doorway and he pisses on the cool, clayey earth, and they watch the puddle spread. Her daddy's sermon humming in the sun outside, she ding-a-lings his dong and gets it stiff by friction. She opens her legs and pokes it in a big red hole with hair around it. She giggles. Then she puts the nipple of her titty in his mouth. Three Sundays straight they do that, but on the third,

Earl and the Nickerson boys (who didn't believe Lucius about the pussy and titties) hide in the cool basement, up under the porch where they have to lie on their bellies among rats and snakes and spiders and worms and water bugs and alligators and look down into the pit where the cool pile and the furnace and warped wooden shelves of preserves are cobwebbed together. She hears them giggling and runs out of the basement, and Lucius has never seen her again and can't remember her name. He confuses her face with Fay Nell's. Even when they move to different places, Fay Nell comes to take care of them while Momma and Daddy work. . . . Huge, bare, chilly living room, dark except for kerosene lamplight from the kitchen. Rain pours down loud outside, and Earl laughs when lightning scares Lucius and Bucky. Earl, at bat, waits for Lucius to pitch the imaginary ball, Bucky, behind Earl, catching. Lucius pitches, Earl swings back and Bucky begins to scream and hold his head and roll in a spreading puddle of blood. Momma screams. The man next door opens his car door. . . . Lucius and Earl and about ten boys on Zachary Street are lying on the grass in the summer dusk, exhausted, burning hot from wrestling in a mean lady's yard, and Earl says he did it to Fay Nell, but Lucius doesn't believe him, and when they all laugh against her, he gets mad because she's wonderful. Then Percy comes out of the jungle rolling a big truck tire in front of him with a stick. Momma says stay away from Percy because he's a crazy man. Percy is talking to himself coming down the sidewalk. He lets his tire roll off the curb and down the hill while he unbuttons his fly and pulls out a big long, sloppy dodopeepeesoso, long as the pony's in the empty lot down the block where a house burned, and Earl yells, "Hey, Alice!" She looks at Percy, walking on the other side of the street. "Look, Alice!" says Percy. She sees it and giggles. All the boys laugh when Percy does. . . . Bucky falls off his tricycle and bursts open the nearly healed wound. . . . Bucky slips while walking a streetcar track and breaks open the new stitches. . . .

Momma's voice woke him, yelling, in a whispery, suppressed way, "Fred! Shut! Up! Get away from in front of this house!"

Lucius looked out the window. His daddy stood in the middle of the streetcar tracks, reeling, reeking, Lucius imagined, of white lightnin' that he got from Feisty Clayboe's, the rest of it in his rear pocket, bottle flat against his kidneys where it all got to finally, yelling into the numb night, "Irene! Irene! Goddam it, come out here. Yeah, you know it's me. . . . Fred. Irene! Goddam it. . . . Come out here . . . I want to talk to you."

"I'm calling the law on you right this second."

"Let 'em come. Hell, who cares?"

Tirelessly, he rambled on, repetitiously, mumbling, suddenly bursting louder, the breeze turning the leaves, showing their milk-green under-bellies, shivering cool behind him in the streetlight.

"See if *you* can shut him up, Lucius," said Momma, standing in the doorway, speaking as if she knew he was awake. "I don't appreciate even being associated with him. Everybody in Cherokee knows your daddy lives in that trashy L. & N. Hotel, chockablock with whores."

Buckling his belt, Lucius walked heavily across the back porch, down the three steps, his loose shoestrings clicking. Sleepy-eyed, limp-mouthed, he imagined himself moving in his daddy's red, bleary eyes, closer and closer, until the eyes saw nothing for the tears, then closed tight.

Lucius guided him to the steps of the Baptist church where he used to attend Sunday school with LaRue. Fred informed him that a war had been fought in Europe and that he'd been in it, and now it was over. Shirtless, Lucius listened, his elbow on his knee, his head heavy in his palm, shuddering on the cold step against the night chill.

Daddy took a swig, made a face, shook his head, suddenly turned to look down at Lucius, who sat beside him, one step below: "Lucius."

"Huh?"

"Patton's dead."

"Who?"

"General Patton. He was the greatest man who ever lived. Goddam jeep . . . coming around a corner and he hit this truck." Lucius remembered delivering the headlines in 1945. "Lucius, some of us thought he was murdered. . . . Somebody messed with his jeep. . . . Can't tell *me* he went through that whole war in Africa . . . France . . . Germany . . . then got killed in some little ol' accident."

"Aw, Daddy, who'd do a thing like that to Patton?"

"Lots of 'em. Patton made a lot of enemies because he was tough, mean. . . . But, Lucius, I don't believe what they say about him going in that hospital and slapping those two soldiers." Lucius remembered the report on the front page. Patton calling the wounded soldiers "yellow," malingerers. "He wouldn't *do* that. . . . I *served* under him. . . . You know what they used to call him?"

"Yeah."

"Blood and Guts Patton. Went around wearing pearl-handled pistols on his hip and riding pants and them boots."

"Did you ever get to see him?"

"I follered him right across France to Metz. We come rollin' into Metz, November, colder'n a witch's tit, and then we moved on into Luxembourg, and I went with him into Germany. . . . Patton's Third Army tank corps, by God."

"Did you ever get to ride in a tank?"

"Hell, no. I drove a ambulance, son. . . . That's what they give me the bronze star for. . . . Captain said, 'Who'll volunteer to go across those fields into the hills and bring back some wounded.' Nobody said nothing, so I said I'd do it. . . . Shells exploding all around, and it turned over once. . . ." Lucius's stomach lurched as he remembered riding with Daddy in the orange and white bakery truck down hilly curves. "And I just kept going. . . . Picked up some boys, come back across. . . . Gave the captain a Silver Star just for asking for volunteers. . . . But I don't give a damn . . . . I'm glad I done it."

"Were you scared?"

"Scared? Hell, yes, but I was a lot scareder after I got back. . . . Lucius, I ain't never gonna forget the . . . Patton said he loved war and he didn't know how he was going to live through the peace. But I wish I could forget the war. . . . All I want's peace. I keep seeing those guys dying. . . . It's not the dead ones that hurt, it's the ones that died because I couldn't do nothing *for* 'em. . . . Kept lookin' for Luke whenever I come to a bunch of 'em layin' on the ground, screamin', 'Medic! Medic! Medic!' "

Daddy looked at Lucius, tears bright in his eyes, and took a swallow from the bottle. "Son, you never knew when it was going to hit you. . . . This one time I was sitting under a tree cuttin' my toenails with a bayonet and limped over to the aid tent when I cut myself and started back for my boots and this shell exploded in the tree and killed three men. . . . 'Nother time, we had this second louie, kind of a sad sack, and so polite, he wouldn't even fart next to nobody. . . . He'd step off to the side. . . . Done that one time and stepped on a mine."

"Kill him?"

"*Kill* him? Blew him to Kingdom Come. . . . See, I can't forget them things. . . . And the drunker I get, the clearer my memory comes. . . . I keep hearin' the noise and the screamin' and the racket of them tanks, and thinkin' 'bout Patton, and I can't believe he's dead and I'm alive, after all he done for this world. . . . I can't seem to live up to my luck, son. . . . And look at Eisenhower and Bradley. Both of 'em served under Patton, and then during the invasion *he* had to serve under *them*. . . . I don't care nothin' for Ike. And Bradley, he was okay, but nothing could beat Patton's tank corps. . . . I'll never forget that Cathedral in Metz . . . through the mist, suddenly there she was. . . ." Lucius saw France and Luxembourg and Italy as the places where his daddy and Luke fought the war. "I don't know, son, maybe he did it deliberately. . . ."

"Did what?"

"Rammed his jeep right into that truck. . . . They say he always did the impossible. . . . Sure, he was mean, and he cussed worse'n any GI, but he was the greatest man who ever walked the face of the earth. I loved that man. . . . That goddam Eisenhower made him apologize to those two soldiers. . . . Hell, I don't know, Lucius, he told his wife he didn't know how he was going to live through the peace. . . . Some people called him Ol' Foot in the Mouth."

"I read once where he said America and England would rule the world. Said it was their destiny."

"Sonofabitches wouldn't promote him because he wouldn't kiss nobody's ass. They say he was his own worst enemy, but he was the enemy's worst enemy, by God. Ask Rommel. Ask Hitler. That wasn't no toy he wore on his hip. He used to do tricks with it like Johnny Mack Brown. . . . Son, I wish you could have seen Patton twirl."

"Me, too."

"Broke his neck. . . . I think he was murdered, myself. They was all jealous of him, and he had a lot of enemies."

"But didn't he tell his wife he didn't know how he was going to live through the peace?"

"How *you* know? Were you there?"

"No, I just . . ."

"Well, *I'll* never forget him." Laying his head on his knees, Daddy put his arms around his head, and his shoulders shook.

Lucius patted him on the back, saying, "I know, Daddy, I know, I know." But he knew that all he knew was what he'd seen in the movies at the Hiawassee.

Back in bed, Lucius remembered the time Momma sent him to the bakery to pick up a check she'd talked Uncle Lucius into giving her, to help out a poor soldier's wife during the war, and she'd been very bitter ever since that it was less than she'd asked for. Kitty, Great-uncle Lucius's secretary, who looked after Fred when she could, told Lucius about his daddy when he was a child. She'd heard it from Fred's brother, Uncle Hop, before he moved to Sante Fe. Kitty told Lucius that Fred would hang around the bakery when he was little, eating his favorite devil's food cake with white icing, and bum money from his Uncle Lucius to go to the old Majestic. And Fred would come across Sevier Street Bridge into South Cherokee at dusk, running, trying to beat the dark, but if dark caught up with him at the bottom of the ridge, he'd sit under the streetlight. Gran'paw Hutchfield would stand on the front porch—the roof of the world at night, with the lights of Cherokee spread out below, and call, "Freddie!" and threaten to whip him if he didn't answer. Then, finally, he'd send Fred's big brother, Hop, down to get him, and climb the pitch-dark ridge path with him. Hop seemed to have had Freddie to take care of the way Lucius had Bucky.

Sat. September 28, 1946. Took Raine to Max's to eat. Bought her a I.D. bracelet. The lady got smart and I told her off. Went to Smokey

with Gale and them to see Violet Lombard's ——. Wade Baylis put
her in jail few weeks ago. Daddy come by drunk. Dear Lord, take pity.
Angel on My Shoulder. Can't wait till Cloak and Dagger with Gary
Cooper.

Sun. September 29, 1946. Mammy's for Sunday dinner. Chief there.
Raine called me 6 times, 4 at Mammy's. I called her 2.

Dearest Darling, honey, sweet, lovely Raine,
It was like a breath of fresh spring air to hear your chanting voice
so early of a morning. Last night I dreamed we went to China
together.

    Last night when I went home from Mammy's house, I listened to
the radio. I was in the kitchen reading the funnies when the disk
jockey played Clear da Loon. I went in and sat on the davenport
in the dark. Used to when I heard it, I thought of Larue and realized
how much I loved her, but last night it was you, Raine, that I thought
of. As the music played on, I felt as if it was tearing something out
of me and I gripped the arm of the davenport and clenched my fist.
It was like pain, yet I felt good because I knew for certain by listening to that music, that I loved you beyond expression. It's you I
love, Raine, elevator going down for the rest of them, including
Larue. The Larue I once loved may just the same be pushing up
daisies. This morning I saw where my grip on the davenport had
tore a big gash in the material. Thats how much I love you. I go
and tare up all my mother's pretty furniture. Tsk. Tsk.

    People just naturally forget things, but don't ever forget that
I love you,
          Lucius

                    State of "Love"
                    City of "Kisses"
                    19 "Hugs"
                    46 "Kisses"
Hi ya "Sweet Stuff,"
    I'm going to write in and get that man to play Clair de Lune
for us. Lucius, my lucious, I love you so much it just can't be expressed in words so I'll just tell you & you can imagine it. We're
glued together and not anything can pull us a part. If you ever quit
loving me I hope it hurts you so bad you'll have to come back to me.
I used to be afraid to write you but now I'm not. I just write you
like I do Peggy only I lots rather write to you.

    I just came to the library and looked in study hall at you. You
looked so lonesome all by your sweet little self. (Except for Della
Snow) You look cute in your boots. You're different.

Golly honey I love you because your cute, handsome, sweet, nice, my type, "understanding," & so many ways. Honey, does your mother care for me calling you up? My mother knows I called you. She said "doesn't he care?" I told her I hope not. You know your the first boy I ever told I really loved. Gordon used to mean as much to me as LaRue meant to you.

I was going to read this book but you're more important than any old book. Cora is looking over my shoulder. Huh, the word she missed on the spelling bee was agrivate. She sure lives up to it. They're playing Indian Love call in music. I really in trully do love you. You come first on my list.

I'm a pretty slick chick. I've been chewing my chewing gum to beat the band all day and haven't been caught yet. Wonder I haven't got my head bit off by that old witch Mrs. Proctor. Peggy sent me a note just now. It said her "heart itched and she couldn't scratch it." Recon Harry can? It's a sin how much I love you.

I'm in English and that Della Snow's wolfing down Weathering Heights like it was jelly beans. She has a cold and so do you, & *I* don't!

Well, I've got to go to the unmentionable so I better quit.

The one that loves you the most,

Raine

Just as the OSS is about to rescue the woman physicist in Switzerland, her nurse, who is really her guard, a chunky, blond German woman, runs to her room and shoots her in cold blood, and Elmo stepped through the heavy curtains at the foot of the side aisle that led backstage, looking crisply official. Hood leaned on the balustrade. Gale stood at his post, next aisle over from Lucius. Hood loped back to his office, and Elmo, passing Lucius, suddenly broke into a Groucho Marx dip, trotted over to Gale, and as they gave each other significant looks and jabs, their excitement traveled across the carpet to Lucius.

"What's happening, Elmo?" Lucius asked, as Elmo passed, Gale following.

"Tell you in a few d'recklies," said Gale, gliding backstage.

Gary Cooper goes to Italy. Robert Alda, who played George Gershwin in *Rhapsody in Blue* that Lucius loved a few years before, is Pinkie, a partisan, and with him is a new actress, Lilli Palmer, in her slip in the bed of a truck approaching a German checkpoint. Regina—Lucius liked her name. Somebody lifts the canvas flap and Regina points a machine gun at the back of the truck.

Lucius escorted an old woman down the aisle. Noticing four good-looking girls on the front row, Lucius saw the curtain over the door in the orchestra pit move. Excited, he imagined Gale and Elmo looking up the girls' dresses.

Coming back up the aisle, he saw Luke's girl Ruby, in her usual seat, the one next to her on the aisle empty, and felt guilty, thinking of pussy with her under the same roof. On the Spot, he imagined Luke coming in, sitting beside her, taking her hand as if a war of Mondays had not passed.

When they came back up front, Elmo was in street clothes to go with Hood to make the Monday night bank deposit, and Gale was grinning and hiking his balls, making his pants rise, showing his white socks in the dim light.

"Go down in the fan room and sneak up to the curtain at the orchestra pit door if you want to see four puckered pussies!"

"Tell Hood I want to *take* a leak."

Lucius felt good that Gale stood where *he'*d stood On the Spot. Even before he passed the heap of tow sacks swollen full of raw popcorn just inside the stage door, Lucius had a hard-on. Feeling as though the girls heard each sound, knowing they couldn't, he eased down the rickety stairs. Afraid they'd see the sudden light of bulbs or a fitful flashlight, he felt through the dark, scared of falling into the big water troughs used in the air-cooling system. When he reached the curtains, his heart beat so hard he could scarcely breathe.

Looking through the rent in the red velvet curtain, he recognized Diana Brummett, one of the sisters he used to do it to on Beech, and the other three were from Marble Station, a tough bunch, and he'd seen them often at the wrestling matches or at the bus terminal or the Smoky, getting picked up by sailors or soldiers. From his angle, they seemed to rare back in their seats, their legs cocked up, their ballerina slippers and loafers resting on the railing, thrusting their breasts forward and up. They all wore leg makeup and silver ID bracelets on their ankles. Above their knees, their legs were stark white in the flickering light of morning by a stream where Gary Cooper shaved with soap. One girl's black hair curled out of the tight band of her pink panties. Diana's lacy blue panties caught in the crack, the cheeks of her ass showed, fuzzy with hair, hairless when he'd last seen it. Through the flyless uniform pants, Lucius rubbed his peter.

Lucius watched the girls open and close their legs in casual enjoyment of the images, responsive to the rhythms of interest on the screen. Modulations of black and white showed the whites of their eyes in a trance as they fed their rapt faces popcorn and candy, heads tilted back. Sensing their mood of intense concentration and anticipation, he felt a communion with them.

He felt ashamed of being a peeping Tom, but his dick pulsed against the thick material of his pants, his mouth dry, his hands sweating on the brass flashlight. Dimly, he saw Gale standing up at the front, and realizing that Elmo had crouched beside him, as Gale too had stood here with a hard-on, slightly disgusted him.

Gale led some people down the aisle. After he'd seated them, he deliberately came on down to the pit, flashed his light at the curtain, said, "Hey, Blue Eyes, what would you like to eat for supper?"

His face hot, Lucius jerked away. A popcorn bag hit the curtain and he started, guiltily, to laugh.

In the tiny cubicle, small as those solitary confinement cells he sometimes saw in movies, where a man could neither lie down nor stand up, Lucius stuck some tissue paper in the keyhole, dropped his pants, stepped up on the little platform, and sat backward on what Gale called the throne, careful not to let the split wooden seat pinch his ass.

He remembered discovering the window of the ladies' bathroom behind the Hiawassee theatre. Taking a shortcut among high weeds and garbage barrels, the corner dry cleaners steaming in the back, he sees a crack in the frosted window—a sudden rush of hot blood, knowing that the clouded glass means concealment of the forbidden, and scared, slipping up to it alone, he looks in, and a tall lady, long, brown hair, who resembles Ruth Hussey, walks in, past his eyes quickly, ducks into the booth, bending at the knees and swinging her butt in and down on the commode seat. The partition lets him see only her pointed high heeled shoes and a flash of panties let down, and he hears, immediately, a hard fierce piss, and flush. He'd always felt a warm affection for the woman pissing in the Hiawassee. Like a whisper, he spat in his hands, and using a little chip of Woodbury soap he kept hidden in a crack, worked up a lather.

Jacking off in the shared toilet at home, a dark, clammy room, the pregnant landlady in the adjoining kitchen, wondering if she knew what the rhythmic sound of the toilet seat meant. Then guilt. Headache. Insanity creeping into his head. Fearing the guilt more than pimples and blackheads. Proof on his nose and forehead, like the mark of Cain, he'd been pounding his pud. Backstage in the makeup mirror, he squeezed out the ones already there, wanting to rip his nose off his face. But knowing, too, he was handsome. The loveliest blue eyes.

Back On the Spot, legs weak, vision blurred, cold come drops sticking to his pants, Lucius welcomed a middle-aged man who carried a grey hat. Going down the aisle, he watched Gary Cooper, disguised as a German doctor, enter a palatial house in Italy. When he stepped aside to let the man into the row, he was gone. Then he saw Luke's girl rise and go up the aisle, quickly, and the man was sitting in Luke's seat.

On the Spot, Lucius sees the Tennessee Kid walking down the main street of Helena, Montana, Billy the Kid dismounting at the other end.

> Mon. September 30, 1946. Me and the boys went down and looked
> up these girls' dresses. Cloak and Dagger with Lilli Palmer.

Tuesday, his day off, Lucius went by the Bijou, to get a pass to the Venice
to see Mark Stevens in *Dark Corner,* but Hood was out, so he went up
to the projection booth and asked Foster Bagwell, a quiet, serious Christian who wore steel-rimmed glasses, if he needed some coffee and hamburgers from the Blue Circle. Foster said no, Bruce Tillotson had already
gotten him something, bless him.

Clancy had let Lucius pick up off the grimy floor of the booth the
pieces of film he'd cut out in the process of splicing. Most of the scraps
were from trailers of movies to come. Momma had given him an old sheet
that he tacked to the wall, and he stuck the large 35 mm clips into the
small aperture of his Keystone and projected portions of them, backing
up in the hall until the images filled the sheet and they remained clear,
and it was awesome to see the Technicolor images of great movie stars
in his own house.

"Care if I have the scraps off the floor?"

"Why should I? All movies should be scrapped anyway."

Feeling as if he were committing a new sin, Lucius picked up the
clips, rising at one of the little windows so he could see Gary Cooper
from way up here. "Where is Katerin Loder?" asked Gary Cooper, his
voice quiet, sad, but firm.

"Watch it ouside, Lucius. I've got work to do."

He sat in the balcony, closed to patrons at this hour, his sports jacket
pocket full of film scraps. Standing together in bright sunlight in an
Italian village, tall Gary Cooper in a soft grey hat with wide, dark band,
suit and tie, holding a white box in the crook of one arm, his large hand
splayed tensely against his coat pocket, the other hand holding Lilli
Palmer's arm. She wears a high-necked sweater, a tam, a black skirt,
carries a black coat, her hands together in front of her. The sight of the
gestapo has stopped them, Lilli coldly scared, Gary thinking of a way out.
A still in *Screen Romances* had caught that moment and turned up out
front next to the poster: "The Moment He Fell in Love Was His Moment
of Greatest Danger."

He remembered stills from *Boom Town* showing Clark Gable, Spencer Tracy, Hedy Lamarr, and Claudette Colbert and from *Rebecca* showing Laurence Olivier, Joan Fontaine, and George Sanders. He'd been
surprised to see them among stills for coming attractions. Perhaps an
earlier manager had loved them too much to part with them and they'd
just lain around. Nobody really needed them.

Lucius went quietly down to the basement of the Bijou. At the foot of the rickety, foot-worn steps, Lucius entered the dark still room, pulled the light chain, a 200-watt bulb hanging from the middle of the ceiling made the room very bright, shining on the whitewashed walls that closed it off from the rest of the vast basement. One side was old brick, painted white. He liked the sap smell of the raw white pine frame, visible on the inside of the room. The glossy stills in stacks on pine shelves caught the light. He spread one stack out on the worktable used for sorting stills, repairing still frames, painting occasional signs. Between shifts, Lucius often sat in the middle of the room on a high stool to be among the stills that showed scenes from coming attractions: *The Dark Corner, The Big Sleep, Notorious, Claudia and David.*

He'd seen *Rebecca* and *Boom Town* at the Hiawassee. The fight between Spencer Tracy and Clark Gable in the muddy street of the boom town and the one later when they were both rich, old friends from way back, and Gable locked the door of his fancy office and he and Spencer plowed into each other—he'd written many similar scenes himself. And he'd loved LaRue as deeply as Maxim De Winter loved Rebecca. These stills, he thought, as he spread them out on the worktable, belong to my life. My great love of them makes me the true owner. But when he saw the word "Re-Release" and the dates, he realized that they had just come in. His recent religious conversion made him feel he held all movies here in trust. Bucky had asked him, "Steal *me* some stills, Lucius." Thinking it might be stealing after all, no matter how much more intense his love was than anybody else's, he prayed to God to give him a sign. If the 200-watt bulb flickered, that would be God's consent.

Sitting on the high stool, the stills on his lap, he waited, staring at the brick wall. The intent of stealing made him feel he was being watched, perhaps through cracks in the wall or— An iron door, bolted. He noticed it consciously for the first time. He'd sensed vaguely other times that it opened upon another labyrinthine storage area. But something about the rusty surface and the old-fashioned bolt made his stomach flutter. Getting off the stool, he put the stills face down, walked over to the door, ran his hand over it. Rust flaked off.

He tried the bolt. Stuck, as if it had been many years since it was last opened. He forced it. Pried at it with hammer claws, then tapped it, but stopped, afraid Hood, up where Brady stood On the Spot, might hear it.

In the furnace room where daylight fell from a crack in the sidewalk far back on top of the coal pile, too perilous for peeking up women's dresses, he found some black grease in a grimy can. He spread it around the bolt and finally forced it to slide. Feeling like Jane Eyre in one of the stills Beverly had bestowed upon him, he pulled.

The door opened on pitch blackness: the mouth of the sewer pipes he'd crawled through on Beech Street, the baking oven of the tile factory.

Just inside, shelves and brick walls and piles of dirt and brick and then earth walls, rocks ribbing them, and slick, damp clay under his feet. Must have been a little storeroom long ago and the brick wall collapsed one day, exposing the cave, and they'd barred the door to keep people from getting lost. A coal mine shaft like the one in *How Green Was My Valley*. Turning his head, Lucius saw no light from the 200-watt bulb in the still room. He whirled around, ran back, crashed into the room, and stood trembling a while before shutting, bolting the door. He put *Boom Town* and *Rebecca* back where they belonged.

But upstairs, he went impulsively to the dressing room and came back with his flashlight and unbolted the door again. He followed the beam inside the dark, looking back now and then to make sure somebody didn't sneak up and slam the iron door.

Recalling the goofy he-men in the comic-strip ads who achieved great feats or rescues, Lucius shot the Eveready flashlight beam ahead of him. The cave wound and wound under the Bijou, like a dragon's guts, for what seemed miles. Then up ahead, he saw light coming down. He looked up at the varicose veins of an old country-butter vendor and recognized her face instantly. He was four blocks from the Bijou, looking up through a little drain in the concrete floor of the Market House. The clay was wetter, gluey on Luke's combat boots, and down the earth walls streaked beads of moisture.

The cave went on. Or caves. For it seemed to be a network of natural, underground caverns. As he walked, he saw images from *Cloak and Dagger*. The gestapo shoot two underground agents in France as they're transmitting messages—as the image faded, Lucius became aware of the narrowing of the tunnellike cave. Suddenly frightened, he saw Indian Joe, pressed between rocks in a very tight passageway, in Tom Sawyer's candlelight, and, wishing he had a brass door knocker, he felt the weight of Tom's in his hand. Tired from the nervous exhaustion of being scared every step he took, Lucius turned back.

If he had to be rescued, it'd be on the front page of the *Messenger* that Pee Wee, the new paperboy, would throw on LaRue's front porch, and she'd see his picture and call him up and tell him she was glad he got rescued.

The return seemed much longer. When he realized he was walking on silt and trash, he shone the light on the walls. They were corrugated steel, and ahead was twilight. He'd taken a wrong turn.

An iron grille, fastened into a wall of cement that he couldn't see now, but remembered looking back up at from the other end of the Sevier Street Bridge, covered the steel drainage pipe. Through the grille, Lucius looked across the river at the cliffs, bluffs, and hills of South

Cherokee and Hutchfield's Bakery where Daddy was working now, the slaughterhouse, the lumber mill, the houseboats, and the sand and gravel company and its barges, and straight down were the River Street slums. Among the rotting houses, once the homes of Cherokee's richest, stood the Old Cherokee Tavern, an inn for wanderers, hunters, merchants. Staring down at the banks of the Tennessee River where Cherokee began, Lucius had a powerful desire to know more about Cherokee's past, as if it would turn out to be his own.

He started back, eager to see the light from the still room.

The flashlight grew dimmer. Scared, Lucius said, aloud, in the tone of the narrator of "The March of Time": " 'While the Sea Remains' by William Cosgrove. 'Helena Street' by William Cosgrove. Alan Ladd in *This Gun for Hire*. Alan Ladd in *The Glass Key*. *And Now Tomorrow*, starring Alan Ladd. *The Blue Dahlia*. *Lucky Jordan*, starring Alan Ladd. Alan Ladd in *China*. *Salty O'Rourke*, starring Alan Ladd. *O.S.S.*"

Walking in water. Fredric March as Jean Valjean wading up to his neck in filthy water through the sewers under Paris, rats scurrying along the banks. Panicky, Lucius began to run. His left foot caught in a little gully, turned, threw him down on the damp clay. His foot hurt so badly he couldn't get up for several minutes. In the absolute silence, he thought he heard a streetcar pass above his head. The light was out. He felt around. The flashlight was wet. Rising, he took it with him, to slug rats. Limping, he prayed, talked with God, then started crying, and just as, in pain and fright, he was about to scream, he walked smack into an iron wall and hurt his nose. He pushed against the iron, the door swung open, and in bright electric light the poster for THE BIG SLEEP with Humphrey Bogart and Lauren Bacall greeted him.

Resting on the high stool in the still room, Lucius laughed—crashing into the iron door, like on the way to the lunchroom in Clinch View Elementary when he walked smack into a wall at a turn, imitating Curly, the bald-headed one of the Three Stooges, and sparked laughter all down the line. Then the pain in his ankle almost made him faint. He felt his entire body and mind as one constant throb. The pain eased up enough for him to climb the stairs on his good foot.

Lucius opened the stage door. Sudden light, a burst of warm air, a streetcar going by down on Sevier.

Tues. October 1, 1946. Found the lost caves. Springed my ankel. Cloak and Dagger.

That night, he lay awake thinking of the tunnel, the network of caves under Cherokee. He supposed they were his discovery, and felt no inclination to tell anyone about them. The faintly illuminated tunnel in *This Gun for Hire*, Alan Ladd and Veronica Lake running, and she sprains her ankle.

NIGHT RITUAL: The first morning after they move into the house on Avondale, Lucius looks out the kitchen window, sees Earl running in the yard under the trees, his wrist in a huge collie dog's foaming mouth. Lucius screams for his Momma. She laughs and tells him they're only playing. . . . The dog's name is Bozo. . . . Ernie doesn't want Bozo to run with Earl and Lucius, but Earl stands on a hill and yells, "Here, Snowsnake! Here, Snowsnake!" and Bozo runs to him, recognizing his voice. . . . Kitty Blond and Kitty Gray have litter after litter of kittens in the closet and on the back porch and in the flour bin of the cabinet during the two years they live in Avondale and when the babies die, Lucius, Earl, and Bucky wash the cobwebs and coal dust out of the fruit jars from the coal house and fill the jars with flowers and bury the babies in the red clay bank that runs alongside the house under the high windows of the sunroom where the boys sleep. . . . Lucius and Earl and Bucky and a bunch of kids watch a gang of men dig a long ditch out of the jungle and between houses and line it with jagged rocks stuck in cement. . . . Momma has a big belly and Lucius can't understand why. He and Earl are helping her carry the groceries, Hersheys and Dentyne gum concealed in the pockets of their mackinaws. Earl grins. While she is in the A & P, Lucius stands watch as Earl sneaks through a secret way still on the shelves. . . .

Lucius fell asleep talking with God.

> Wens. October 2, 1946. Ankle still hurts. Turned it again getting off the streetcar. Thinking up "Legion of the Double Damned." Hood told me I better keep my mind on my business. I keep letting what he calls patrons go by me, even while he's standing right there. Bad as when I used to miss people's paper. "Shape up or ship out," he said. Reckon he got it in the army. Almost fell off the plank that leads to the fan doors—afraid another rat was going to run up my leg and I turned my ankle again. Cloak and Dagger.

> Thurs. October 3, 1946. Dark Corner with Mark Stevens, but I didn't get to see it yet. Me and Harry went to Peggy's house. We sneaked away from blowhard Duke. Joy and Raine had to go to a party at the YWCA. Raine looked cute. As usall. Saw Humphrey Bogart in The Big Sleep at the Tivoli. My foot hurt the whole time. Springed it again in the hall at school.

Hobbling to school alone, Lucius remembered the time Momma made Earl help her clean out the basement on Beech, and he kept complaining his stomach ached and she thought he was pulling one of his work-evasion tricks and finally got so hysterical she beat him on his back with the broom she was using to sweep the yard, and he scampered down the alley hunched over. That night the old woman next door called her to the phone, and the hospital informed her that her son's appendix had been removed an hour after he'd presented himself at the emergency ward. Mammy loved to tell the story.

Halfway to school, Lucius, sick of the pain, turned around and limped back to the streetcar line. He'd been to General Hospital once before. With Bucky, he'd had his tonsils and adenoids taken out when he was nine. He was terrified that they'd look at his ankle and order immediate surgery and slap the ether mask over his face and the red devil would chase him again down the endless black tunnel, and while he was under, the doctors and nurses would stare at the hairs on his legs and his prong or he'd have a wet dream.

Sitting on a low stool before the high table where Lucius sat, the doctor, who resembled a civilized Groucho Marx, held Lucius's foot between his legs with both large hands, turning it this way, then that, asking, "Does that hurt?"

"Ohhhhhh!"

With a sharp pencil point, the doctor ran a new, weird sensation along the soles of Lucius' feet. He tapped Lucius's knee with a hammer, like in a slapstick comedy. "Hmmmmmmmm."

"Is that bad?"

"Loose knee cartilage, I expect."

"Is that bad?"

"Well, it only means that despite your broad shoulders, your dream of playing for the Rams is shattered."

"What are the Rams?"

The doctor looked up at Lucius, shocked.

"I think we may have a slight case of infantile paralysis." the doctor said to the nurse.

"Am I going to die, sir?" Lucius had often trembled at the news of the polio epidemics that had swept Tennessee in waves that summer.

"No. . . . Not if you drink your milk, wash behind your ears, and read by a good light. How can I reach your mother?" Lucius gave the doctor the number of Max's Restaurant. Listening, he gathered that the doctor wanted to know Momma's ability to pay for treatments. He came back to the table and looked down at Lucius. "Now, I want you to come to the Crippled Children's Hospital behind Fort Cumberland Hospital, next Wednesday—that's on Pershing past the college."

"On the hill above the Valencia Theatre?"

"The Valencia? Oh, yes, the Valencia. That's right. I want you to meet Dr. Koss from Sweden. Perhaps it isn't infantile paralysis. In any case, it's only a touch. You're fortunate."

Shaken by the doctor's uncertain diagnosis, Lucius knelt one knee on the Royal Crown Cola bench, so that cars passing would think he was only waiting for the streetcar, and prayed to Jesus that he didn't have polio.

The old lady in the principal's office didn't believe his excuse.

"Do I have to have a note from Sister Kenny?"

"I'll tolerate no sarcasm in this office," said Mrs. Fraker, raring back, flaring her eyes.

Miss Cline, in the middle of the Revolution, didn't believe him either.

"Wouldn't you even give a dime for my iron lung?"

Sitting at his desk, Lucius felt that in Raine's eyes, he must look like a sad and tragic figure. But then he realized that he hadn't told her yet.

She was waiting for him under the mimosa trees. Letting the girls go ahead, she walked with him to the streetcar stop and cried and promised to sit by his bed until. . . . And kissed him under the Texaco sign.

At Max's cash register, Momma fought back the tears. "He said it might not be, honey. Now, don't worry till you know for sure."

Minetta sat in her booth, looking sour, refusing to acknowledge his existence, even when he limped.

"The doctor said I had infantile paralysis," he told Thelma, who grabbed her pocketbook and dashed into the ladies' room.

"He said it was infantile paralysis," Lucius told the albino, the only usher on the floor.

"Well, don't forget FDR."

"Nothing. Nobody has—and nobody's going to," Mark Stevens says to Lucille Ball in *the Dark Corner.* "You either. . . . I'm clean as a peeled egg. . . . Now get out of here." Lucius was intrigued but mystified.

Gale came onto the Spot from backstage. Lucius ducked Gale's finger and he accidentally sparked himself.

Lucius told him. "I'm sorry, Lucius." The shocked look on Gale's face ignited tears in Lucius's eyes.

"Lucius." He turned. Her handkerchief at her nose, Thelma was leaning out of the main lobby over the threshold into the inner lobby. "Mr. Hood want to see you."

"What'd you do now, Lightnin'?" asked Gale, goosing him as he turned to go.

Knocking on Mr. Hood's open door, Lucius was worried that maybe he knew about his discovery of the tunneling caves. He'd not told anyone, feeling that the caves had waited for *him*, and he ought to keep them to himself.

"I noticed you limping."

"Doctor said I might have infantile paralysis." So many people had died or been crippled and so much radio time and newsreel footage and newspaper and magazine space had been devoted to the crisis lately that Lucius, in becoming one of the objects of such attention, felt somehow important, and, perversely, privileged. Mr. Hood's shocked expression confirmed that feeling.

"You look like to me you can walk pretty good."

"Oh, yes, sir, but my ankles hurt and my legs get tired easy."

"Well, I really need you on the job, Lucius, but if— Why didn't you just *call* in? Look, if your leg doesn't feel better, don't come in tomorrow. You gotta take it easy, young man."

A lump in his throat, moved by everyone's response to his tragedy and feeling a little guilty for not making clear that it might not be infantile paralysis and, fortunately, only a touch if it was, Lucius limped out of the Bijou, wondering whether he should buy a cane. When Minetta smiled sweetly and waved to him, Lucius knew Thelma, or he hoped Gale, had told her.

Weeping, Mammy set a bowl of vegetable soup before him, and sat beside him, and he felt as if she were spoon-feeding him.

When Lucius got to the house, nobody was home yet. He went out to the sanctuary to write a new story, but after he'd gotten a fire going, and had written only the title "Helena Street" and the new variation on his pen name—William de Cosgrove—that he'd thought up on the streetcar, his leg still hurt. To stop the pain, he knelt on the earthen floor, soft with rot, his head against the mattress of the junk bed, and unzipped his fly.

> Fri. October 4, 1946. The darkest day of my life. I have may have infantile paralyses. The Dark Corner ends tomorrow. I may not get to see the Bugs Bunny Club.

Alone in the house, Bucky staying all night at Mammy's, Lucius lay awake, hurting. Momma had gone with one of her girl friends to the Tennessee Barn Dance. Since she didn't like country music herself, she must have gone with Nola, who loved Red Foley and Eddie Arnold. Lucius had met two of Momma's boyfriends, Homer, a bartender who knew Daddy, and Norman, who was trying to bring a new business called Dairy Queen to the area. Neither liked to dance, so Lucius didn't know who Momma and Nola were out with. Not including Momma in the scene, although she'd be there, too, Lucius saw Nola making love to some strange man in the back seat of a car on a dark country road, when somebody knocked at the door. He jerked on his pants, aware that his hard-on was going down.

A man stood on the porch. "Reeny home?"

"No, she ain't," said Lucius, a little hostilely.

"You must be Lucius."

"Yeah."

"Your momma's told me all about you. My name's Dan Miller, good friend of your momma's." He held out his hand.

"Glad to meet you," said Lucius, opening the screen door. He liked the man's voice, his smile, his handshake.

"Mind if I come in and wait for your momma? She didn't expect me this weekend, so I guess she went on a date."

Lucius didn't want to get his mother in Dutch with one of her boyfriends, but this guy didn't seem to mind. When Lucius turned on the light, he saw that Dan Miller was a handsome man, and when he took off his well-shaped hat, he had wavy light-brown hair, with soft white streaks. He had been drinking, but he wasn't drunk.

"I tell you, Mr. Miller, I got a hurt foot, and I was almost asleep, but you're welcome to wait for Momma."

"You go right to sleep, buddy boy. Don't mind me."

Lucius crawled back in bed. He remembered how it was during the war. Momma and Daddy had separated even before he joined the army and Lucius woke up several times at night and found some man sitting in the living room, the lamplight casting a strange aura over everything in his sleepy vision. "He's a good friend, honey," Momma would say. "He wants to help me."

One night, when he was about nine, he couldn't sleep, feeling guilty about accidentally knocking a bird's nest down out of a slender tree he was climbing. The blue eggs broke and the sight of the yoke was like the spilled guts of a baby he'd murdered. Momma and the man assured him he couldn't help it, and Momma told him to go back to sleep. Then he dreamed that his mother was dying and the only way she could get well would be for her to take a magic serum or for him to "do it" to her. He still had that nightmare sometimes, and felt guilty all day, and everything around seemed hazy, alien, dreamlike.

Lucius had almost dozed off when he looked up at Dan Miller, standing in the doorway, moonlight playing over him. Lucius felt a pang of fear—the man might be a queer. He held a beer bottle. He must have gone out to his car.

"Your momma tells me you write stories all the time." Dan Miller's voice was deep and mellow and his tone implied that writing stories all the time was normal.

"Yes, sir."

"Dan. I'm only Dan. . . . Well, it takes a awful lot of hard work.

One of my best friends is a writer. Lives in Atlanta. You probably read some of his stuff. Jack Painter."

"No, never did."

"You never read Jack Painter? Writes for these Western pulp magazines." Dan sat on the foot of Lucius's cot and set his beer on the floor and lit a cigarette. Lucius liked the smell of the beer and the first smell of the struck match and the burning tobacco. "Yeah, ol' Jack. . . . You'd like him, Lucius. Cherokee Indian. Married to this Jewish girl. Been all over the world— Merchant Marines, soldier of fortune, cowpoke. Speaks five languages, and what a fanatic when it comes to religion and politics. He's an atheist in religion." The smoke hurt Lucius's eyes, made him feel logy. "Son of a gun writes three stories a day, speaks foul English, and never passed the eighth grade."

"I'd like to meet him."

"Sure. I'll introduce you sometime. And you never read none of Jack's stories?"

"I guess I've wrote more'n I've ever read."

"Wait." Very carefully, Dan set his beer down, put up his hand as if to implore Lucius to stay put, and tiptoed out, and Lucius heard the front door open and faintly a car door, then slam. He hoped his daddy wouldn't come down off Clayboe Ridge, full of Feisty Clayboe's moonshine, and stand in the middle of the streetcar tracks and call him out.

Dan stood by the cot in the moonlight, opening a magazine. "This one's in *Five Star Western*. He just gave it to me last time I saw him. 'Action-Packed Novelette of the Desert Land.' Called 'The Devil Rides West.' Says, 'Only one man knew the Devil was riding West—to Lightnin' Rock. Nobody suspected that the prosperous little town would vanish from the face of the earth before sundown. Only one man could save the helpless inhabitants—one man and a girl. But the town fathers had run the schoolteacher and her outlaw brother out of town.' That's to get you into it, see.

"Listen to this. Wrote it in two hours and got $100 for it. Says, 'Chapter I, Caught in a Sandstorm. With Lightnin' Rock in sight but still twenty miles away, Lock Jones felt no cause for alarm until he noticed little whirls of sand the wind lifted around the ankles of his horse. He longed to stand in the shade of the lone tree of Lightnin' Rock. In this open country, a sandstorm could delay a man with a mission too long—far too long. For Lock Jones was a man with a mission. He had seen the Devil drinking at Carson's Spring. Seized with a terrible thirst himself, he had by-passed the spring and rode on. To warn the good people of Lightnin' Rock that the Devil was riding through. Not the Devil of Pastor Stanton's fire and brimstone sermons—with his boiled red skin, red pointed tail, and pitchfork. No, it was the Devil of the Desert, who wore two guns and carried a whip instead of a fork. A terror they feared as much as that denizen of eternal fire."

Dan Miller's own excitement fascinated Lucius, and he was impressed that a man who was good friends with a real author was sitting on the foot of his bed. Three stories a day! Three hundred dollars! Lucius figured he could write that much too if he didn't have to waste time changing classes and devising ways to avoid detection by the teachers.

Dan read the novelette aloud to Lucius, chain-smoking, drinking five bottles of Miller High Life, "my favorite beer, named after me," making Lucius forget the pain in his ankle.

When Momma came in at two o'clock with Nola, she said, "Lord help us, we went around in circles, Nola. We're back in the Green Lantern."

"You reckon the house's afire?"

When she saw Dan sitting on the edge of the cot, Momma ran into his arms as he rose, and she acted like one of the silly society girls at Bonny Kate, and Dan responded with cool, debonair gestures and smiles and witty remarks like Gale Booth and reached over to stroke Nola's arm.

The voices of two women and a man in his ears coming down the hall from the living room—bedroom, Lucius drifted off to sleep.

Church bells woke him. Every morning, Lucius got up as soon as he opened his eyes, never lingering, too eager to plunge into the day's possibilities to wallow in bed. His mother's sluggish late-sleeping on Sundays was a partial inspiration. His opposite behavior was one of many ways of marking himself off as different from her and the rest of the family.

Wearing only undershorts, Lucius leaned over and looked through the doorway of Momma's room, afraid Dan might be sleeping with Momma and Nola. A mellow light flooded the bedroom, soft on the back of the davenport. Two brassieres looped over the back of an easy chair. Nola's bare arms showed outside the covers, and the delicate, pink strap of her slip lay curved above her vaccination mark. He heard the sound of their sleep-breathing. At least one Saturday night a month, Momma stayed out all night with Loreen Babcock or Nola Thornton or Gay Stokes, women she'd met in her various jobs. And sometimes Lucius woke up Sunday morning and found one of them in bed with Momma, after a night of dancing at some roadhouse.

Nola was the prettiest of Momma's girl friends. A tall, shapely blond who reminded him of Laraine Day. He thought of Gay, also tall, and luscious and auburn-haired. She gave him seductive looks and liked to tease him, saying, "Lucius is my secret love." Nola was divorced, but Gay lived on with a man she detested. Loreen was ugly in the face. Squinted, dark, heavily mascaraed eyes, puffed cheeks, rouged, puckered lips greasy with lipstick, hair dyed tangerine orange. But she had a very sexy body. Sometimes he thought she might be a whore. She had a loud, sweet-whiny, baby voice, worse than Thelma's, and lived with her mousy husband who ran the best cigar store in town. Lucius was ashamed of his desire to do it to her, because she disgusted him. When she stayed all night, he kept expecting her to sneak into bed with him. He lay on the cot again with a hard-on, thinking of making love to Loreen and Gay. He knew Nola liked him, but she didn't make a big production of it the way Gay and Loreen did. Nola was too pure to inspire thoughts of sex.

> Sat. October 5, 1946. Spent all day looking over and sorting out and arranging my stills and movie magazines. Met Dan Miller who knows Jack Painter the famous writer. The Dark Corner, but I was off sick. Never got to see it. Catch up with it later at one of the Market Street rat houses. Writing this Sunday morning.

> Sun. October 6, 1946. Wrote 3 stories—the last one, "Helena Street" almost finished. Westerns. Maybe $300 before long. Wouldn't talk to Raine on the phone even. Momma went to Mammy's for dinner. I stayed in my chicken house sanctuary, writing. Dan Miller took Mammy and them fishing at Lone Mountain Lake. Bijou dark. The Big Sleep starts tomorrow, helt over from the Tivoli.

A nonchalant lean to the right, the right arm hanging casually, the fingertips almost touching his kneecap—Lucius tried a new stance. Holding his black notebook, full of stories, in his left hand, he stood on the small porch outside the hall door, looking out over the moving heads of kids coming to school or loitering under the stripped mimosa trees, waiting for the doors to open. Lucius hoped Raine was looking for him, too. Wished he could track Earl down and get back his new leather jacket. Wished he hadn't loaned Luke's combat boots to Harry. The morning sun felt good.

Lucius called to some of the kids, shyly ignored others, shifting from one foot in his new stance to another. Then he saw Raine and them coming across the ball diamond. The bell rang, the doors opened. He was furious that they wouldn't have time to stand together on the little porch, leaning against the thin black iron railing: Lucius and his girl on display.

Raine wore a very gay red summer skirt, white blouse with red ribbons around the neck and the puffed short sleeves. In her hair, she wore a red ribbon and her lipstick was vivid red. He hated the clompy saddle oxfords and bunchy white bobby-sox around her delicate feet, but he felt so tender toward her, he forgot his anger—until she and her gang went inside at the lower door.

Lucius went in and cut down the hall, limping. They were coming toward him, laughing and knocking against each other, Cora exaggerating her own limp as if to mock his.

"Here comes Lucifer," said Peggy. "Cloud up and rain for us, *Lo*-raine."

"I thought her name was Gertrude," said Cora, calling Raine's middle name to tease her.

"You all hersh!" said Raine. "Hidi, Lucius."

"Thought you was going to *stand* with me."

"Thought *you* was going to call me."

"I was writing all day."

"I was sitting by the phone all day. . . . How's your leg, honey?"

"Meet me after your gym class."

"I'll try."

"Try, hell. . . . What you doin' wearin' a summer dress in October?" he asked, wanting to hurt her feelings.

"Come on, Loraine," said Peggy, " 'fore I beat his ass."

Lucius turned his back on them and went down the hall to his homeroom.

It was, according to alphabetical logic, Lucius's turn to read from the Holy Bible. He hated listening to the others drone through an entire chapter of their choice—usually the same choice—though the chapters were in actual length shorter than the ones he wrote himself, and he'd vowed to himself that when his turn came, he'd read with feeling and show his love of God's Word.

"Jesus went unto the Mount of Olives.
"And early in the morning he came again into the temple, and all the people came unto him; and he sat down, and taught them.
"And the scribes and Pharisees brought unto him a woman taken in adultery—"

"Stop!" commanded Miss Kuntz. "From now on, *I* will select the passage to be read," she declared.

Lucius swore to himself that he would never again read the Bible aloud in school.

While Miss Redding's English class studied the uses of the comma, Lucius wrote a note to Raine.

Dear Raine,
Did you like walking down the hall with the little girlies? I hope

you did. I hate to see you unhappy as you are when I *force* you to walk with me. It would have broke your heart to stand with me this morning, wouldn't it? Then I waited outside my art class but you didn't come. I reckon you met Peggy and them instead.

You acted sort of strange this morning. Maybe you don't care for me any more. If you don't tell me so and I'll leave you alone. If you love me, Raine, love me always. Is this the end of always? Girls like you leave a dent in me when you go.

> Love eternal, in spite of all
> Lucius

P.S. I'm sorry I got mad today but I hate to think you'd prefer Peggy to me. I want you all and all or nothing at all. Try to indure my foolish, hot-blasted talk. Answer this if you want to. I may lay out tomorrow and finish this story about The Tennessee Kid.

Then he returned to "Helena Street."

Lucius handed the note to Raine as she passed through study hall on her way with her English class to lunch downstairs.

In the library, Lucius sat at a table with Della Snow. He kept dropping his pencil, and when he stooped over to pick it up, Della spread her legs. When Lucius curled his index finger along his thumb and slid his pencil in and out, she got tickled, and smiled like she *would*, and when he wrote, "Are you *fer* it?" at the bottom of a page of "While the Sea Remains," she nodded vigorously, smiling radiantly.

Then Raine came in with a note to Mrs. Parker, permission to let her check out a book. Lucius behaved himself and smiled at her, and when Raine left, Della tossed an opinion book across the table. Gordon Puckett had written in answer to key question 8—"Who would you most want to be stranded on a desert island with?"—"Loraine Clayboe, but she'd probably get rescued by Lucius Hutchfield." Lucius wrote in the margin, "You damned right." But his own answer to that question was "Larue Harrington," to make Raine jealous. He knew that Gordon was grovelingly in love with Raine. She'd written in the book that Gordon was "cute as a bug's ear." She, who loved only Lucius, forever, and forever, as her notes declared, liked being groveled at.

As Lucius started to go into health class, Harry handed him a note from Raine. "Sell me these boots, Lucius." Harry had shined Luke's combat boots to a bright luster.

Raine's note was intricately folded, sealed with a lipstick kiss. "These lips aren't very good." A smaller note fell out of it.

Hon, I tried to call you two times. Hon, are you mad at us, you never do walk with us any more. Whats wrong, are we poison. I guess its Lucius and you want to be alone. I guess I better go, I have to study my spelling and go to church. Love always, "The Unloved" Joy.

Hi Sweetie,

Why in the do you get mad at me for walking with them? If I don't walk with them once in a while they get mad. Here's a note Joy wrote me last week. Those girls do get my goat sometimes, tho. Sometime I'm going to tell them that they're not running my life (slightly!). And they're not going to get me to like Duke either. I've got no notion for Duke.

Honey, please don't throw off on my clothes. It hurts me worse than anything. I know I don't have pretty clothes. I hate everything I got.

I just went in the library and you were in there. But oh! your so stuck up, my dear (stuck down I mean). You sure were interested in what you were writing. A love note to Della Snow maybe? I bet that ol Della Snow heard about you getting mad at me and thought boy here's my chance to get Lucius. I just was thinking, Huh, sister, no it shore hain't either. Lucius, don't let anybody brake us up. Don't be a sucker. Remember what it says in Proverbs about girls like Della Snow. Wormwood and gall.

I'm about to puke. Here comes that old Mrs. Procter.

Lucius, you don't like me now or you wouldn't have done me like that. You can't say your not mad because I know you are. I'm over my mad spell now. I was really just mad second & third period. No matter how hard I try to get mad, I couldn't stay mad long. You know I'm just a big fool. I've never admitted it to anybody else but I will to you. I love you so much it hurts inside out & you won't believe me. I'm going to slap you cross eyed one of these days. This is one of my tears. The others are on my arm or in my lap.

You know honey God done us right by letting us meet each other but he's punishing us because we fuss so much. What did God tell you in your prayers last night? I've got to say a real long prayer and pray for forgiveness for not praying. Let's get Preacher Horton to save us together so we'll never be far apart. Honey, let me stand out there with you every morning. I'll bet your grinning up a storm after you read this. Everybody can just go to and stay put. I love you better than any girl could ever love their boy friend. Our song is "It Had to Be You" but "Heartaches" is too.

Love Always, *because of everything*

Raine

Inspired by Raine's note, Lucius nearly finished "Helena Street" in health, while Mrs. Dakin wrote the basic causes and a three-step treatment for athlete's foot.

In the hall between classes, Mickey Stirewalt came struggling toward Lucius, lurching in her braces and strapped-on crutches, refusing help with a smile and a simpering tone. She gave Lucius the creeps. Cheerful cripples seemed monstrous to him, and he felt ashamed for sneering. She seemed to identify more with the most popular and normal and better-off kids in the school than with him or with Duke or even Raine. Why couldn't she be more like Quasimodo in that *The Hunchback of Notre Dame* movie? She had that slightly condescending way about her that some cripples have toward people who can do what they can't. When she spoke to him, he felt inferior. He'd sensed even a little pity for him when she asked, seeing his limp, if he had polio.

"I've been *laying* for you!" cried Hiss Cline, exultantly. As the class laughed at her accidental pun even before Lucius caught it, she ripped the last page of "Helena Street" from the steel rings of his notebook.

"Hey!" Lucius jumped up. "That's the end of my stor-ry!"

Suddenly, Miss Cline had his notebook in her hand and was leafing through it. "Sit down, Lucius Hutchfield!"

"That's private property."

"*I* am responsible for what goes on in my classroom and—Who, may I ask, is William De Cosgrove, for heaven's sake? Are you copying a story from some trashy pulp western? 'Helena Street!' "

"It's history, Miss Cline. About Montana in the frontier days."

Everybody was laughing at him, even Raine, as if this were just another of their almost daily battles. He didn't want to let her start one of her performances. Without his own controlled contribution, it would only scare him, make him say and do things that would surprise even himself.

"Give me back my notebook, Miss Cline!"

"Don't you get impertinent with *me*. 'Thunder struck and lightning lit the sky as Billy the Kid sadly rode away over the hill.' Such utter trash for a child to be filling his head with. You see too many movies, young man. I'll bet you don't even know what year Montana entered the union. If you'll promise to refrain from now on wasting class time piddling around with these stories, I'll return this notebook at the end of the year."

"Give it back *now*, Miss Cline." Trying to make his "lovely" eyes turn to blue steel through squinted lids, Lucius looked straight into hers, until she glanced away.

Miss Cline's face turned red. She thrust the black notebook into his hands and walked swiftly back to her desk, her heels the only sound.

The class held its breath, and Raine's eyes were large green. Standing behind her desk again, Miss Cline straightened her spine.

The sight of her legs pressed against the edge, her dress fitting tightly over her crotch startled him, but before he could get excited by the bold imprint, he looked into her face, the ugliest female face he ever expected to see in his life. She raised her voice, pointing to the door. "Lucius Hutchfield, get out of *my* room, and don't you ever darken my door again until you have been to the principal and obtained his permission."

Lucius had never seen her so angry, and the way the scene had played out frightened him. Trembling, sullen, he went out with his notebook, feeling Raine's finger graze the back of his hand as he passed. He left a room in which no one was breathing, and in the emptiness and silence of the hall as he walked numbly to the principal's office, he felt as if he were pulling away from a zone of stress.

Whether he'd done anything wrong or not, every time Lucius walked into the principal's office, he felt guilty. Grey-haired Mrs. Fraker ran the office from behind a high counter. The sight of only a third of her pigeon-breasted body enhanced the most frighteningly severe face he'd ever seen. Stiff-legged, Lucius approached the counter just as Mrs. Fraker moved away to deal with whoever had been so impertinent as to cause the telephone to disturb the mausoleum static of the office. Close to the counter, he was a little surprised that her body had a bottom part, but when she came back, he looked half aside, like a Negro yardman.

"What do you want?"

"Nothing."

"Why aren't you in class?"

"Miss Cline kicked me out."

"Sit down." Lucius turned, sat on a bench against the wall. "And I don't want to hear one sound from you." She stared at him a moment, her powdered bosom almost touching the counter, then she went in and told Mr. Bronson.

When she came back out, she continued making her mysterious motions, as adept as a spy with only ten seconds to find, copy, and conceal the plans to blow up Washington, D.C. And yet she seemed immobile, like a statue, endowed with human speech, but limited powers of motion. What went on behind that counter was more important than anything else in the world.

Nervous, tense, Lucius looked at the row of prisoners' chairs on the other side of the door. Another boy, his polo shirt rolled up tight to his shoulders, showing tan, muscular, but slender arms, his clothes old and messy, his hair fuzzy on the nape of a long neck with a sharp Adam's apple, sat slumped in a chair.

"You! Sit up straight like a human being!" Her mouth always

looked as though she'd tasted alum and found it delicious, though still puckerfying.

Hatred and throbbing contempt for the bitch made Lucius's eyes blink. When Mrs. Fraker turned, the lanky boy's wiry arm muscles jerked as he shoved a dull pencil into the air, as if up her ass. The thought that she might have an asshole made Lucius gag.

Lucius breathed a different air in this cramped place, as if all the natural air had been siphoned off, some synthetic gas, on which Mrs. Fraker thrived, pumped in. Maybe Mr. Bronson kept a bottle of clean air in the bottom drawer of his desk in the adjoining room and sniffed it on the sly, for his skin was not quite as pale and papery as Mrs. Fraker's. As if inoculated against the noxious fumes, the young students who assisted her somehow retained all their normal characteristics, except good cheer. Emanations from this woman seemed to creep down the halls, a slow, invisible, but penetrating vapor.

Lucius opened his notebook and began to draw a comic strip about the Tennessee Kid and Billy the Kid in "Helena Street." Himself thrust back into the days of Billy the Kid, the Tennessee Kid was his own creation. He loved Robert Taylor in *Billy the Kid* in Technicolor that he'd seen again last spring in the Smoky, looking very beautiful in black, wearing a black leather jacket. As he drew, his stomach began to hurt, his head to ache. He'd been constipated since Friday.

Suddenly, Mr. Bronson, a tall, burly ex-coach with a little wart on his cheek, looked across at him from behind the counter, Mrs. Fraker at his side. Lucius regarded them as two bodies with a single mind, the mind influenced by the bodies, the one with the bulge in front, like breasts, the stronger.

In Mr. Bronson's office, Lucius told what had happened in Miss Cline's classroom, and Mr. Bronson asked him if he was sorry, and when he said, "No, sir," Mr. Bronson commanded him to hand over the notebook.

"I can't, sir."

"You mean, you won't?"

"I can't."

"All right, then, young sir. Bend over and grip your ankles."

As the author of "Helena Street" and as Raine's eternal love, Lucius said, "Sir, I'm too old for that anymore."

"But you're getting to be just the right age for the reform school."

Mr. Bronson suspended Lucius until Wednesday morning, when he was to bring his mother with him at eight o'clock, to talk over solutions to his conduct at Bonny Kate Junior High.

Knowing that Raine, eager to learn the outcome, would expect him to be waiting for her at the top of Breedin Hill, Lucius went on to the streetcar stop on Grand Boulevard. He wanted her to daydream about him. Maybe she'd even come to the Bijou, a tragic look on her face. Remembering that he was exiled from school all day tomorrow, unable to see her, Lucius felt an aching sense of loss.

Dreading his mother's yelling and her dirty looks when he told her, Lucius decided to spring it at Max's so she couldn't collide with him full speed.

"Oh, for God's sake." She gritted her teeth. "If I have to go by the principal's office, I'll be late for work, and Max's already warned me. . . . First, your daddy hands me a headache. . . . Mammy said he came in the cafe and told her Earl stayed all night with him a few nights ago. He could've called me so I wouldn't worry. Never thinks of anybody but himself." Habitually, when she could, on the slightest pretext, she turned her private grievances into a public performance. As if all present knew full well the trials Fred put her through, she displayed a face and a tone and volume that assumed general sympathy. As she set peach cobbler before him, she whispered, "And I could just strangle *you*. Ain't it enough I have Earl and Bucky to worry me senseless? This is what your endless daydreaming and scribbling from sunup till sundown comes to. . . . Why didn't you just hand her the Goddamned notebook?"

Lucius turned on the stool and walked out, making a streetcar go slow as he limped across the track and stepped under the Bijou marquee.

Crossing the main lobby he remembered that *The Big Sleep* started today. Eager to see it again anyway. Take his mind off his troubles. He leaned on the balustrade like Hood. Bogart rises, taking off his coat, hanging it on the chair, reaching for his handkerchief. Dense greenery surrounds him. A stern old man sits in a wheelchair, a heavy rug over his legs, a striped shawl over his shoulders. He says, "It's too hot in here for any man who still has blood in his veins." Sitting again, Bogart wipes his face with the handkerchief. They are in a greenhouse that is very steamy. The old man says, "You may smoke too. I can still enjoy the smell of it, anyway."

"Well, they're gonna draft us when we get to be eighteen."

Smelling the Listerine breath, Lucius said, "Bruce, you got a bad habit of sneaking up behind a man and delivering the news of the day before he recovers from the fucking fright."

The old man in the hothouse is saying, "That man is already dead who must indulge his own vices by proxy."

"They let twenty-three of them niggers go."

"And that's another habit of yours. Talking right on as if nobody said anything to you. Which ones?"

"The ones that was in that race riot in Columbia, Tennessee. All white jury, by God."

Eager to get into uniform and see the rest of *The Big Sleep*, Lucius said, "Be back to relieve you in a few d'recklies," conscious of using Gale's phrase.

"Okay, Gale."

Negroes throwing popcorn down from "Nigger Heaven." "African rain," Elmo called it.

His eyes not yet adjusted, Lucius limped in fits and starts through the dark behind the box seats, his hands groping in front of him, the old man's voice saying, "You didn't like working for Mr. Wilde?" Bogart answering, "I was fired for insubordination—I seem to rate pretty high on that."

Approaching the gigantic, black amplifier backstage, Lucius heard Elmo's and Gale's and Brady's voices above him.

"Here comes Alan Ladd in person," said Elmo. "Ta dum, ta duh!"

"What you all doing up there?"

"Beatin' our meat," said Brady.

"Where the hell *are* you all? Can't see."

In the dark, a hand took his and pulled him up, another grabbed under his elbow and he was lifted. He held on to his notebook. He always hid it backstage, afraid to leave it lying on the shelf in the dressing room, where the boys might get into it and make fun of his stories. Against his knees through the fabric of his black corduroy pants, he felt the texture of tow sacks full of raw popcorn. A truckload must have come in today, and the boys were resting on what they'd stacked.

"Ain't you 'sposed to go On the Spot 'bout now?" asked Elmo, using his Captain of the Ushers' voice that he always held in reserve, but seldom used on anybody but Lucius.

"Yeah, but I got ten minutes yet."

"Take you that long to hook on your tie."

Lucius heard the old man's voice. "I'm being blackmailed again." Bogart asking, "Again?"

Lucius lay back and looked up at the shadows *The Big Sleep* cast against the brick wall above the purple-black backdrop. The Bijou Boys lay quietly awhile, shoulders touching. He wanted to announce that he'd gotten expelled today but he was afraid Elmo would ruin it with some ridiculing crack. Aware of the rumbling voice of Bogart and the old man in the hothouse, Lucius let the Tennessee Kid walk down the dirt street in Helena, Montana, toward Billy the Kid again, a church between them, hymn music coming through the open doors.

"Ow, Elmo," said Gale, "get your fuckin' elbow out of my back."

The rich old man says, ". . . my friend, my son almost. Many's the hour he would sit here with me, sweating like a pig, drinking the brandy I could no longer drink, telling me stories of the Irish revolution—But enough of this."

"Yeah, enough of this," said Gale.

"Enough of what?" asked Brady.

"I don't know. Man just said enough. . . . Damn good movie," said Gale.

"I can't figure out what the fuck it's about, myself," said Elmo. "Bad as that one at the Venice."

"*The Stranger?*" asked Brady. "Orson Welles thinks he's shit on a stick."

"Give me good ol' Errol Flynn in *San Antonio,*" said Elmo. Lucius reckoned he'd seen it at the Smoky last week.

"Talk about good stories. You all ever read a story called 'Helena Street'?" asked Lucius. "By William De Cosgrove?"

"William De Cosgrove?" Elmo brayed like a jackass.

"Goddamn it, Elmo, you wanna get Hood back here on our ass?"

"Hood's scared of the fuckin' dark," said Elmo.

"Sounds good, Lightnin'," said Brady. "What's it about?"

"Well. . . ." Lucius hadn't intended to tell it, just to get the thrill of saying the title and the author without their knowing the truth.

"Once upon a time," said Elmo, in a singsongy voice.

"Elmo, let him tell it, will you?" Brady got that hard edge in his usually pleasant voice that always made guys come to a full stop—and remember that "it's the quiet guys you better watch out for!"

"Well," Lucius said into the silence. "It's about the Tennessee Kid and Billy the Kid."

"I *hate* kids," said Elmo.

"I remember every bit of it, if you want to hear it."

"Hell, tell it," said Brady. "I ain't got nothing to do but walk the streets of Cherokee till I go on."

Lucius sensed that Gale was listening, as if he were glad Brady had taken the lead. Winding up to start, Lucius became aware of Bogart's voice: "Do the two girls run around together?" The old man answering: "I think not: They are alike only in their one corrupt blood. Vivian is spoiled, exacting, smart, ruthless. Carmen is still the child who likes to pull the wings off flies. . . ."

"It was early morning in the West and Lame-brain Gibson rode as fast as his horse would go, along the trail under the pine trees, and every time the horse went under a low branch it hit Lame-brain in the face."

"Sounds like Elmo," said Gale.

"He rode into a little clearing and reined in a halt beside a boy who was strolling deep in thought along a creekside path. His blond hair was long as a country boy's and he wore broadcloth and buffalo hide, kinda tan outfit with fringes on his sleeves. He was just a little over fourteen, but he looked older. He looked up calmly at Lame-brain, this tall, lanky, silly boy who depended entirely upon luck and God's pity to keep him alive. The blond boy said in a deep rich voice, compared to the voice of most kids his age, 'Be with you in a few d'recklies, Lame-brain. Gotta saddle my horse.'

"Lame-brain followed the boy to a green grassy spot alongside the creek, where a horse, pure white, gnawed at the grass."

"Damned if he ain't stold Buck Jones' horse," said Elmo.

"Elmo, you ever hang by your balls from them rafters?" asked Brady.

"No, never did."

"They's always a *first* time."

"Lame-brain says, 'Tunnessee, you gonna fight 'im?' The Tennessee Kid didn't answer at first. He led his horse, Ren, and Lame-brain's, too, over to the creek to drink. Then he says, 'You damn right I'm gonna fight 'im.'

"Got real quiet, watching the horses drink there, ol' Lame-brain leaning against a huge oak tree, scratching his rump at a pestering chigger, and the sunlight speckling the water and Tennessee's shoulders. Suddenly, Lame-brain pushed away from the tree and stalks over to Tennessee, this foolish grin on his face. 'Tunnessee!' and he's all excited. 'We 'uns kun kill 'im as he sleeps. He's stayin' at—' Tennessee gets madder'n hell at that, says, 'I know where he's a-stayin'. Damn you, Lame-brain! Tryin' to make a killer out of me? Well, Tennessee fights even and fair.' Walks closer to Lame-brain, his eyes trained on the eyes peering down at him. 'Don't ever fergit that. Let's be ridin'.'

"So the two horses carrying their human burdens gallop off toward Helena, Montana, and a date with bloodshed.

"And while they ride, the small, youthful mining town of Helena is just getting up from a summer night's sleep. Two hours early *this* morning, because it's a special day.

"In the Belmont Hotel, the keeper, Miss Devy, and the sheriff's brother, deputy Dudley Epps, are talking. 'Mornin', Miss Devy, honey, sugar baby,' says Dudley, and plants a kiss on her wrinkled cheek, stuck out by her tongue as she concentrates on her records. She draws back her head, shocked, puts her hand on her cheek, says, 'Dudley Epps, you tramp, you imbecile. Git on 'bout you bisness. I don't feel good this mornin'. My boy's a-gonna fight and'll prob'ly git kilt.'

" 'Your boy?' smirked Dudley.

" 'Yes, my boy,' she says. 'Tennessee's *been* my boy fer years.' "

" 'Aw,' says Dudley. 'He ain't *got* no mother.'

" 'I—I ain't gonna argue—I just ain't, that's all they is *to* it. Now git!' Tears come to Miss Devy's tired old eyes, and Dudley felt ashamed.

" ' Aw, heck fire, Miss Devy, I'm sorry. Well—I guess Tennessee *is* kind of your boy.'

"Miss Devy takes a handkerchief from her side pocket and dabs her eyes lightly. 'I just hope and pray he's out hidden som'ers. He didn't come home last night.'

" 'What about Billy?'

" 'Up,' she sniffs, 'up in his room, I reckon, sleepin'.' "

"Then Dudley—"

Recognizing Lauren Bacall's voice, Lucius listened: "So you're a private detective. I didn't know they existed except in books, or else they were little greedy men snooping around hotels. My, you're a mess, aren't you?"

"Then what?" asked Brady.

"So Dudley went looking around town for Tennessee, in miner's shacks and places where you can sleep overnight for twenty-five cents. Then he gives up and goes to the jailhouse where his brother, Sheriff Epps, is sitting calmly cocked back in a chair."

"What will your first step be?" asked Bacall.

"The usual one."

"I didn't know there was a usual one."

"Oh, yes," said Bogart. "It comes complete with diagrams on page forty-seven of 'How to Be a Detective in Ten Easy Lessons,' correspondence school textbook."

Getting a stomachache, Lucius didn't want to go on, but he was eager to satisfy Brady, draw Gale in, and triumph over Elmo.

"So Dudley leans up side the bridle tie and looks at his brother. They don't say nothin'. Dudley just watches his brother look at the town. Then Dudley gets up the nerve to ask, 'About Billy and Ten—'

" 'I hope they shoot each other's asses off.'

" ' Yeah, but we're the law and—'

"The sheriff looks up for the first time. '*You* wanna stop 'em?'

" 'Skip it.'

" 'You damn right.' Sheriff watches the sunrise get closer to time for the duel, says, 'They're both lawbreakers beyond my control. Which one dies, don't matter to me.'

" 'I thought you liked Tennessee.'

" 'I like to hear him about his far-off land.'

" 'His what?'

" 'His paradise on earth. Skip it, Dudley.'

"Dudley went inside the mud-built jailhouse and brought him out a chair. So there the two brothers sat, side by side, Dudley squirming, but his brother calm and patient as usual."

As Lucius told it, bowed backward over the rounded sack of popcorn, beginning to see the white hands and faces of the boys, clearly when Elmo took a draw on his cigarette, he saw images from "Helena Street" high up in the darkness of the catwalk and sandbags above the screen and the speaker. And off and on he saw the words, scrawled in pencil.

"I don't like your manners," says Bacall.

"I'm not crazy about yours," says Bogart.

"On the second floor of Miss Devy's hotel slept a very notorious young man. He was— Billy the Kid, the boy everyone was making such a fuss over. He slept peacefully and undisturbed. Then suddenly, he turns over on his side and—ut!—the sting of a porcupine needle that he placed there the night before wakes him up.

"Getting up at dawn after a drunken night was worse than getting dragged across the desert. That's what the Indians did to him one time when he cheated them in a trade. Billy pulls on his boots and goes to the window in his underwear. Then the dead silence of the early morning is broken by fast hoofbeats—and here comes—The Tennessee Kid and Lame-brain Gibson, riding into town.

"Billy quickly dresses while a queer and dreaded feeling lurks within his stomach. He checks his famous guns by the light from the window and starts for the door. But Miss Devy opened it, and stood there with a pistol in her two tiny hands, aimed straight out from her small breasts.

"Billy just grinned, his white teeth gleaming in the dim light.

" 'Mister Billy the Kid, you're not a-goin' out yonder to hurt Tennessee.'

" 'Ha!'

" 'Hoot all you want to. But Tennessee's gonna laugh the most.'

" 'Well, Miss Devy, honey, come on in. We'll have tea.'

"Billy backed into the room and Miss Devy stepped in—a hole in the floor, but Billy caught her before she went all the way through to the kitchen. He cut it the night before as a trap. He takes her gun and jumps over the hole and goes down the dim hallway, and steps out into the cool morning, and from the porch of the hotel sees the pale light behind the mountains of Montana. At the western end of the street, Billy sees the Tennessee Kid."

Lucius's stomach hurt so bad, he had to pause.

"To roll his overall legs up, Billy had to rest his foot upon the bridle-tie. He shifts his dark eyes, partly closed because of the cigarette smoke, toward the direction where Tennessee waited atop his white, dust-soiled horse, Ren, sucking on a straw, his hands resting on his right leg, crossed over the stout neck of Ren."

"How can you remember every *de*tail like that?" asked Brady, admiringly.

"Oh, just can. . . . Tennessee's blue eyes watched Billy the Kid step down from the hotel porch and walk crossways down the street toward the sheriff's office.

"Tennessee tilted his head toward the sky. Thunderclouds were gathering. From his buffalo hide jacket, he pulled a leather pouch and out of it took a small photograph of a girl, wrinkled around the edges. He remembered her long blond hair, her rosy, soft cheeks, her green eyes, pale red lips that had a velvety look. At the bottom of her picture was written her name: Rachel. He smiled, then put the picture in the pouch and slid it inside his jacket again.

"A little boy came running ahead of his fat mother out of one of the miners' shacks nearby. She yelled at him in a hoarse voice, to stop, but the boy ran until he reached Tennessee.

" 'Well, buddy, you'd better get some pants on, hadn't you?' says Tennessee. Little boy just looks down at his naked body and grins.

" 'Been sleepin'. Jest got up.' Little boy just stands there, swinging his arms back and forth. 'Mr. Tennessee, will you, uh—when you kill him, will you, uh—'

" 'Give you Billy the Kid's guns? Better wait and see who gets killed.'

" 'Won't be you, Tennessee Kid.'

" 'How you know that?'

" ''Cause I prayed for ye.'

"Suddenly, a sharp pain went to Tennessee's heart, and he almost did more than just sniffle. 'Well, dad gum, thanks, son. I sure will give ye his guns all right. Now you better git, I reckon.'

" 'See you when it's over, Tennessee.'

"Tennessee turns from the waist up and watches the little boy scamper back to the shack where his Momma's waiting impatiently, holding his overalls.

"Billy was near the porch of the jail now, walking very slowly, his holsters jolting on his bobbing hips.

" 'Mornin',' said Dudley, nervously, as Billy passes by.

"Billy waved his arm and walked on but stopped dead still when the sheriff said, gruffly, 'Wait there, Billy.' Turns his head slowly, pulls his hat further down over his eyes, says, sulkishly, the cigarette still dangling from his mouth, 'Yeah—Sheriff?' "

Hearing rain, Lucius stopped to listen to it hit the high roof of the Bijou.

"Then what?" asked Brady.

"A couple of hours," said a girl's beautiful voice out of the huge speaker, "an empty bottle, and so long, pal. That's life."

"What you stopping for?" asked Brady.

"Shhhhh."

"But it was a *nice* two hours," says Bogart.

"Uh, huh," says the girl, sighing. "There's Geiger's car, driving up."

Lucius remembered: Bogart talking to Dorothy Malone wearing glasses in a bookshop.

"So. . . . uh. . . . So then, Sheriff Epps just sits there, not moving a muscle, sucks on his Mexican cigar, says, 'Billy, I hope you get the hell shot out you.'

"Ol' Billy walks over to Sheriff Epps, stares at him over the bridle-tie rail, sheriff playing like he's just staring into space, and Billy takes his cigarette out of his mouth, wobbles his lips a few times, and spits right in Sheriff Epps's eye."

Lucius hears loud rain behind his head—it's in *The Big Sleep,* not on the Bijou roof.

"Then Billy walks off nonchalantly, while the Sheriff mutters under his breath, 'Slimy hellion!'

"Dudley uncocked his chair, and looks at his brother, who is calmly wiping the spit from his eye. 'Why don't you plug him, Dan? Git him while he ain't lookin'?'

"Sheriff sighs, says, 'He's watchin' me in the saloon winder 'cross the street.'

"Dudley cocks back in his chair again and watches every move Tennessee and Billy make."

"While they watch Tennessee and William the Kid," said Elmo, "let's go down in the orchestra pit and see if we can see us some pussy."

"I want to see how this comes out," said Brady. *"You* go."

"Let's go, Gale." Elmo sat up.

"I'm restin'." Gale bummed a cigarette off Brady, "Time out for intermission, Lightnin'," and lit it off Brady's.

"Now, 'fore I start shootin' at your feet," said Brady, "*tell* the fuckin' story."

"Yeah, tell a *fuckin'* story, Luscious," said Elmo.

"I *can't,* if Elmo's gonna keep innerruptin' me."

"He ain't gonna keep innerruptin' you," said Brady. "I'll stick this cigarette in his ear."

"And mine in the other one," said Gale.

Lucius got so tickled, he had to suck in breath to go on.

"Tennessee's sittin' on his horse, see, watching Billy walk slowly down the street towards him. Out of sight, the whole town is watching, miners, bartenders, saloon owners, storekeepers, women and children, even dogs that slept alongside the road were hid in alleys to watch history being written out in human blood."

Along his body, from skull to heels, Lucius felt the rumble of Max Steiner's music in the popcorn sacks.

"Lame-brain climbed to the top of the only tree in Helena, a big overshadowing oak that spread long gigantic limbs over the church house, and pulled from his undershirt a bottle of whiskey, took a gulp, then looked down on the street.

"Billy the Kid stood erect at the end of town—"

A woman screams in *The Big Sleep*. Somebody runs in the rain.

"—examining his guns. He holstered them as the Tennessee Kid, mounted atop his horse, watched."

Three shots came from the black speaker. Rain falls hard.

"Then Tennessee dismounts, strokes his horse's long mane, then starts walking tensely to the middle of the dirt street. Billy starts walking. Tennessee's blond hair swirls in the wind. The little boy hollers at Tennessee, 'Git him, Tennessee.' Tennessee gives the boy a kindly smile, then continues walking down the street."

Lucius was aware of running footsteps from the speaker.

"On down the street, Tennessee sees the church doors open for Mass, as bells begin chiming. He'd seen few churches like this in the mining towns in the region, but Robert Okindale, the young Dutch priest, was a persistent man, and he and his congregation had kept it going against all odds."

Lucius heard two cars going away in the rain.

"Tennessee seldom ever heard church bells, but when he did he always took a strange liking to the sound, it made him think of God and the beauty in life that he was seldom left alone to enjoy. He admired Robert Okindale's courage for opening his doors for church as usual, as if he was certain someone would attend. And sure enough, here come a small old woman sashaying down the boardwalk toward the church. The breeze was whistling about her ankles so that she skipped along ticklishly. She crossed the street directly in front of the Tennessee Kid and gave him a sweet trustful look as he passed, then tottled inside the church."

"Miss Devy," said Brady.

Lucius was fascinated to realize that he'd almost memorized some of the wording of the story as it had come to him On the Spot and writing in class over the past few weeks.

"Billy was sweating as he walked on, his eyes glued tensely on the boy walking towards him."

Somebody's face got slapped in *The Big Sleep*.

"Tennessee had a strange feeling that he often got when he faced a killer like this. Billy was trying to impress him with the way he walked, but he knew Billy was scared, too."

"You're higher than a kite," says Bogart. "Come on, let's be nice. Let's get dressed, Carmen."

"The breeze was now coming in harder," said Lucius, "and the sun was fading away."

"You tickle," says Carmen, giggling.
"Yeah, you tickle me, too," says Bogart.

"Dark clouds covered the sky. A cool breeze whistled about Billy's neck. He hated it, but loved the smell of rain coming on and the wind that tore his hair about his head and rippled his breeches legs and cooled his chest.
"Billy crossed his shirt and buttoned it around his neck.
"Thunder clashed in the sky. A wall of rain was coming over the dark, shadowed mountains, coming furiously but slow."

Lucius paused a moment. The gut ache brought tears to his eyes.

"Tennessee and Billy were now only a hundred yards apart. Their arms dangled at their sides, shaking with nervousness."

"I better take a stroll up front," said Elmo. "Case Hood's lookin' for me." Lucius heard him jump off the stack of sacks, five high.

"The church bells are still clanging, and Miss Devy prays, alongside Robert Okindale now. Lame-brain drinks his whiskey, his ragged hat pulled far down over his warty face. Dudley tries hard to roll a cigarette in the midst of the breeze and cusses each time the tabacca flies in his face, trying to watch Billy and Tennessee at the same time. Sheriff Epps tries not to let it show that he's worried for Tennessee. Thunder crashes, lightning strikes. A coyote howls in the distance and the street dogs start in barking. Horses neigh and stomp, and hugging close to the right side of the street where the church stands, Ren prances slowly, not far behind his master. The small miner's boy proudly watches his hero. Everyone is wondering foolishly why the duelers have not reached for their guns.

"Billy is dripping with sweat, despite the cool breeze. He don't fear any man on earth. But here is a mere boy, whose calm peaceful ways make him more nervous than any ten men alive. Ever since Tennessee shot one of Billy's gang in self-defense, the week before Wyatt Earp and his brothers cleaned up Tombstone, they'd been sworn enemies."

Lucius watched Elmo come backstage again and move, dimly, toward the stack of tow sacks.

"Tennessee was not sweating. He was doing what the little boy had taught him—he was praying, silently. But not for the first time. Tennessee was carrying, next to the photograph of Rachel, a Bible, very small. He was afraid, but he did have faith in God to pull him through. In his heart, though, he knew he deserved whatever Billy the Kid had in store for him. Tennessee had been both a bandit and a soldier. But wherever he was, whatever he did, he always had a touch of the Lord in his mind.

"And now as the two desperadoes walk to meet each other in unlawful combat, they realize that the day which has always had to come, *had* come.

"Billy was just beyond the jail. Tennessee neared the church. Candlelight flickering from within had brightened an area that lay nearly full way across the street. In the center of the lighted spot, a shadow stood out like a silhouette. Neither Tennessee nor Billy knew what the shadow represented. Billy wasn't interested. But Tennessee's concentration drifted from Billy to the shadow."

"Ain't you supposed to relieve Pink Eyes?" Elmo's Captain of the Ushers' voice spoke below.

"Yeah. Is it time?"

"*Past* time, and you ain't in uniform yet."

"Ah, shit, Elmo," said Gale, "let him finish the stor-ry."

"Hell, why not *read* the rest of it? Where'd you read it?"

"I forgot."

"I'd rather hear somebody tell it anyway," said Brady. "Reading gives me an assache."

"Elmo says I got to go on the floor."

The rain still falls in *The Big Sleep*.

"That crazy albino don't care if he's late," said Gale. "He can make it up tomorrow."

"All right," said Elmo, reluctantly. He leaned against the sacks, flicking his flashlight off and on.

"So Tennessee came alongside the church and he looked inside out the corner of his eye. Then his entire body slowly turned to face the entrance. His heart beat faster and in the place of fear, a wonderful feeling swelled his heart. His lips were dry. For inside the church, atop the dim candle lights, stood straight and high almighty, the statue of a man. Tennessee had never seen him, either in a picture or a statue, but he knew from the features presented to him in such magnificent glory and proudness that at last—he had seen—Christ.

"Without so much as considering the danger of his opponent's eager pose, Tennessee, due to an undescribable feeling which joyfully controlled him, slowly knelt down to one knee. The wind blew softly at his garments, at the dust, which whirled around his waist. There Tennessee knelt, one leg cocked back, and made the sign of the cross."

Elmo lit a cigarette, spewed smoke out loudly.

"Billy's brow ruffled and his dark eyes showed signs of bewilderment. What is he doing there on the ground facing the church, of all places? thought Billy foolishly. It's a trick. He isn't as religious as all that. . . . Now more than ever, Billy feared the Tennessee Kid.

"Everyone who saw wondered almost as foolishly and as misunderstandingly as Billy.

"It was now or never, thought Billy, as he dropped to one knee and drew, with lightning speed, two guns that blast out repeatedly, just as thunder boomed in the sky and the wall of rain reached Helena Street and began to pour down.

"Tennessee fell at the entrance of the sixth bullet. He was dead."

"That sonofabitch," said Brady, quietly, intensely.

"Billy rose to his feet, the guns still firmly gripped in his hands, and walked stiffly to where Tennessee lay. He looked, the rain beating hard upon his face and tearing his hair wildly, upon the greatest boy he had ever known. He knew now why his enemy had not drawn his gun. 'He was so excited at seein' Jesus, that *I* didn't even matter. I've killed a great man.' With those solemn words, tears came to Billy's eyes.

"The priest came out and carried Tennessee inside the church, first giving Billy a dirty look that was like he was cursing him to the devil. Billy watched the preacher carry Tennessee loosely in his arms, past Miss Devy, who was crying loud and asking God, 'Why? Why?' and on to the altar where he placed Tennessee at Christ's feet. This scene brought even greater sadness to Billy's heart.

"The little boy came running through the rain as Billy started eastward to where his horse waited, waited to take him away from his greatest and lowest injustice. In a moment, the small boy, who had loved Tennessee so much, began throwing rocks at Billy and calling him names. But Billy only walked on past the sheriff and Dudley, who sat in front of the jail, and mounted his horse. Even as Billy rode away, tears in his eyes, the boy was throwing rocks at him.

"After Billy left the street, the little boy ran to the church where Miss Devy was crying over her intended son.

"Dudley went to the church so he could comfort Miss Devy.

"Sheriff Epps, in utter disappointment and disgust, angrily set his chairs inside out of the rain.

"Billy took one last look back at the town from a hill and rode off in the midst of the furious rain. Thunder struck and lightning lit the sky as he sadly rode away over the hill toward the east." Half-mockingly, to cover his embarrassment at almost crying, Lucius imitated the symphonic melody of the music for *Gone With the Wind*. "The end."

"Amen," said Elmo. "And I'm docking you one half hour."

"Lucius," said Gale, sitting up. "You can't be an orchestra worth a shit, but that William De Cosgrove's pretty good. If you ever run across one of his stories again, save it for me."

"Hell, *that* ain't nothing," said Elmo. "Watch this." He struck a match and Lucius expected him to light another cigarette, in violation of the fire rules, but a loud fart ripped through the sound of rain from *The Big Sleep* and a foot-long blue flame shot out from the match. "Can you do *that*, Lucius?"

Loud knocking on a door in *The Big Sleep* came from the enormous black speaker.

II
Raine Eternal

Mon. October 7, 1946. Got suspended for protecting my stories. Told Gale and them "Helena Street." They all thought it was great.

Tues. October 8, 1946. Sanctuary all day, writing "River of Lost Tribes." Raine called 4 times. Woke up Mrs. Easterly's baby. Duke came by. Said Della Snow's not sick. She dropped out of school last week. Might not ever see her again on the face of the earth.

AFTER HE'D escorted Bucky halfway to Clinch View Grammar School, chased him the rest of the way, and threatened to throw a rock at him if he didn't run up the walk into the main entrance, Lucius returned to the house, where Momma stood on the curb, waiting. He was embarrassed to be seen walking to school with his mother. She griped viciously about having to beg him back into school and then beg Max to let her off to go to the Crippled Children's Hospital. "Your mother may be out of a job after today." Lucius felt ashamed, guilty, and angry. "I've had to run back and forth to juvenile court over Earl, and now *you're* starting on me with Bonny Kate."

As they entered Bonny Kate, Lucius was thankful they hadn't run into Raine and Harry and them.

Mrs. Fraker tried her North Pole freeze on Momma, but when she sensed that Momma was good at that act too, she eased off.

The conference with Mr. Bronson went well until he said, "Lucius, do you promise to stop writing stories in class?"

"I can't, sir."

"He *sure does,* Mr. Bronson," said Momma, flopping her pocketbook. Lucius still refused. She threatened to beat the living fire out of him. "It don't hurt to promise."

"Hurts more than a whipping does."

Realizing only tears would do it, Momma broke down in front of the whole world. "You're just as much a torment to me as Bucky and Earl *ever* were. Lucius is not my only problem, Mr. Bronson," Momma said, through her tears, a little coyly.

"Yes, I know. Have they tracked Earl down yet?"

"Why, what do you mean, Mr. Bronson?"

"Isn't he wanted by the police? Escaped from State Training School, didn't he?"

"How did you know *that?*" She was sincerely shocked. "I've not breathed it to a living soul."

"Why, it's common knowledge, Mrs. Hutchfield. A matter of public record."

But the tears won. Mr. Bronson left it up to Momma to extract finally a promise from Lucius before school Thursday. Meanwhile, he'd be allowed to return to classes this morning.

Mrs. Fraker was resentfully reluctant to accept Momma's request that Lucius be let off early to go to Crippled Children's Hospital. "He's missed enough school as it is."

"Mrs. Fraker, this child may have in-fantile pa-ralysis!"

Mrs. Fraker looked at Momma and Lucius as if they'd cooked up a lie between them. "Permission granted."

At recess after lunch, Lucius saw Harry coming out of the building, striding cockily in Luke's combat boots.

"Hey, Lucius, I heard Miss Cline got all over you in 'mer'can history."

"Yeah. Had to go see old man Bronson."

"He paddle your ass?"

"Wouldn't let him."

"Yeah, and I saw a rooster fuck an elephant, too."

Lucius, Harry, Duke, and Joe Campbell and a bunch of others sat under a lone, runty mimosa tree at the far edge of the vast playground playing blackjack for pennies saved out from lunch money. At their backs, hammering and sawing—twenty subdivision houses going up in the cleared jungle area where Lucius, alone, four years before, walking, one lonely afternoon, the smell of rain in the air, the green sap bursting through him, tried, under a giant oak tree that had vanished, to fuck mother nature through a dry dirt hole in the ground.

"Harry, when you gonna shuck off them boots?" asked Duke. "Lucius promised me *I* could wear 'em next."

"It ain't *next* yet."

Lucius saw the girls bunched around Raine under the naked mimosas, and in the cold shade of the building stood Gordon Puckett. Harry had pointed him out as the guy who had been in love with Raine since the fifth grade.

"Blackjack," said Lucius, the dealer, and raked in the pot. "Duke, take the deal for me, will you? Here's eighteen cents to *do* you."

Lucius stalked across the playground, past Raine and the girls, straight up to the boy, a short, blond kid, who stood in the shade as if on a little platform, deliberately, lovingly staring at Raine.

"Hey, you better stop that staring, buddyboy."

"I loved her before *you* did."

"How old are you?"

"Thirteen."

"So am I. Start walking, and I better not catch you slobbering over her again."

"I don't believe in killing." Gordon turned and walked away.

The girls gave Lucius dirty looks, and Cora said, "If I was *you*, Lolo, I'd tell him to kiss my rusty."

"Well, I *ain't* you." Raine smiled and Lucius smiled back at her. "I'm glad they let you back in class."

"Did you mean to touch my hand as I went out?"

"What do *you* think?"

Exhilarated by his power, he went back to the blackjack game under the skinny mimosa, and Duke had lost Lucius's eighteen cents.

The streetcar to Fort Cumberland Hospital passed the glass factory where Gran'paw Charlie was shot to death by the man whose job as night watchman he'd taken after the man was fired for being drunk on watch. Murderer's photograph in the clipping from the paper. Victor Jory's lean, dark face. In his Cherokee ramblings, Lucius had seldom wandered over this way. Going to the Valencia Theatre several times, he'd looked up the ridge at the hospital's white stucco with brown framing, like buildings in movies with Queen Elizabeth in them, a foreign look. As he limped up the steep hill, Lucius remembered what his seventh-grade teacher of Tennessee history had told the class. During the Civil War, they—he forgot which side—cut all the trees on the ridge, dug a wide moat and filled it with sharp stobs, poured water down the muddy, naked slopes so it would freeze. The attackers were cut to pieces. Fort Cumberland Hospital looked more like a rambling hotel than a hospital. A pre–Civil War mansion behind it had been converted into the Crippled Children's Hospital.

Along the curb out front, poor people sat in torn-up cars—a door was lashed shut with barbed wire—and rusty pickup trucks. Climbing the steps, Lucius was aware that he was walking between high Greek columns, afraid of what the doctor's further probings would reveal and of what the Swedish doctor, Koss, would do to him. Other waiting country people lolled in chairs and on benches around the front porch. More poor folks crowded the vestibule—wasted women holding babies, snotty-nosed kids. Most of the kids wore braces, casts, or tape on their legs. Lucius imagined River Street deserted.

At the far side of a wide aisle that extended into two wings of the building, a nurse sat at a desk, white in the dim light. "Yes?" Her voice conjured Mrs. Fraker.

"S'posed to meet my mother here." The whining screen door at his back made Lucius turn. Momma walked in, vivacious. "Here she comes."

"I'm Mrs. Hutchfield," said Momma, using her sweet, slightly aristocratic public voice. "My son, Lucius, has an appointment to see Dr. Summers."

"Take a seat."

"Honey, I had to take off from work—I'm the hostess at Max's restaurant—to come here, so I wonder, would it be possible to speak with the doctor now? I'm terribly upset. He said something about a touch of infantile paralysis, and I think from what Lucius tells me, he's just sprained his ankle."

"You'll have to wait your turn."

Momma looked them over. "Well, they don't seem to be working women. Maybe they have more time—"

"Mrs. Hutchfield, I can't take the time to ask them whether they're working or not, but I do know that *I* have a great deal of work to do. The rule is—"

"Well, thank *you,* very much," said Momma, pronouncing each word carefully with distinct facial enhancements. She took with a flourish some forms the nurse stiffly handed her.

Lucius and Momma sat along the wall. She stared straight ahead into next week, then commented on the bitchiness of the nurse, then expressed disgust for the trashy women sitting in the chairs, then great pity for the children walking in braces down the right wing to the examination room as their names were called out.

The way the people were dressed, the way they talked suggested they had full, mysterious lives. Lucius daydreamed brief episodes involving each of them.

Half an hour later, the nurse called Lucius Hutchfield, slushing it together. At the end of the right wing, a pleasant young nurse told him to step into a little booth, take off everything except his shorts, and sit on the table. Was it an operating table?

Momma was worried that Max might fire her for being gone so

long, but she said, "He can go jump in the lake," anxious to know what the doctor would say.

Finally, Dr. Summers came in, the nice nurse and a tall, handsome blond woman of about thirty-five behind him. His joking manner was so ambiguous Lucius was afraid that if he tried to link up to it— when he understood the wisecracks—his timing might be off, and the man might be curt instead of cute. A mock-severe frown, a full, black moustache, a deep, rich voice.

The tall woman stood at the doctor's side, staring straight down at Lucius's feet as the doctor handled them, telling her what he thought was wrong. But he wouldn't know until he saw X rays. "See to it that he washes his feet before coming next Wednesday."

"Oh, I'm very sorry, Doctor," said Momma, with sarcastic sweetness. "Will you need *me* next time?"

"If you're interested in knowing what your son's trouble is."

"He *says* he sprained his ankle backstage at the Bijou."

"What were you doing backstage at the Bijou?"

"I'm one of the ushers."

"That's a treacherous place back there."

"Did you used to usher there?"

"No, I attend the Cherokee Symphony concerts and every time I go back to congratulate Victor Savage, I sprain my ankle. And you'd better be glad you sprained *your* ankle, because otherwise we might not have found out whatever it is we're going to find out, until too late. Or will we?" Lucius bet Dr. Summers knew he resembled Groucho Marx.

"Could I just talk with you on the telephone about it next Wednesday?" asked Momma, carefully.

"Madam, I give my time free to this clinic each Wednesday, and I do not, therefore, hesitate to ask the parents of children on charity to be present when their child is being examined."

The tall, blond lady doctor followed Dr. Summers out, but the nice nurse stayed behind to tell Momma where to take Lucius to get his feet X-rayed. They went out the back and crossed the alley into the basement of Fort Cumberland Hospital.

Lucius was afraid of the X-ray layout, but when it didn't hurt, he felt tough—until he remembered he *still* didn't know whether he had "a touch of infantile paralysis."

Lucius rode the streetcar to town with Momma and they got off in front of the Pioneer. She went back to work, and Lucius, with an hour to go before he had to be On the Spot, bought a Mr. Goodbar at the Courthouse Drugstore and limped on down to Sevier Street Bridge, moved by an urge to look down on the slums, the river, the houseboats, the spot where he'd met Raine more than a month ago in the faith-healing tent, and to see if he could see where the caves ended at the sewer pipe in the cliff face. The smell of the river, swollen after last night's thunderstorm, led him on.

But as he passed the River Bridge Bookstore, he felt drawn to the window, full of magazines under a skein of Cherokee soot fallout, faded by the sun that burned through the pane all summer. The dimness of the enormous room, once a saloon, suggested he might find movie magazines from way back, maybe older than the ones Beverly bestowed upon him. He went in, roamed among the stalls, shelves, and tables, littered with all kinds of magazines and books.

The tall, thin old lady still sat at a desk in the middle under a weak light. His momma used to take him in there when he was little, and she'd exchange two back issues of *Cosmopolitan, Redbook,* or *Harper's Bazaar* for one, while Lucius, Bucky, and Earl plunged into the stacks of funny books and flipped through Big Little Books that had actual photos from *Call of the Wild* and Buck Jones and Charlie McCarthy movies, and some had drawings opposite each page of The Green Hornet, Tarzan, and The Phantom stories.

Looking for the movie magazine table, Lucius couldn't pass up the funny books. Spy Smasher's goggle-helmeted head behind a big city skyline, protectively embracing the buildings, watching himself, red cape awhirl, sock a German. *All Star Comics:* The Flash, The Green Lantern, The Spectre, The Hawkman, Dr. Fate, The Hour-man, The Sandman, The Atom, and Johnny Thunder sitting around a table, labeled The Justice Society of America, at their first meeting. Sheena of the Jungle. Red Ryder. *Classic Comics*—hey! *The Man in the Iron Mask.* "Coming At You!" Captain Marvel, Jr., "the world's mightiest boy," ripping through the cover, panels behind him showing him as Freddie, the crippled newsboy, a hook-nosed man about to shoot him. Popeye. *True Comics.* Archie. Mandrake the Magician. The Boy Commandoes. Mutt and Jeff. Flash Gordon. Batman pushes Robin out of the way as a mammoth yellow stone idol falls, breaking on a wide flight of steps. Seven yellow bolts of lightning stab different parts of Superman's body: "It tickles." Kid Eternity. Daredevil. *All Winners,* starring The Human Torch, Captain America, the Sub-Mariner, The Destroyer, The Whizzer, descending upon a monster, wired to an electronic device who is about to knife Toro and Bucky, who are strapped like Frankenstein's monster to an iron table. Lucius's own funny book collection had long ago dwindled, Bucky selling most of them to get in the show.

Absorbed in her work on the rolltop desk, the old lady, who looked exactly the same as the last time he came in with Momma, about five

years ago, seemed unaware of Lucius, as if he were a vague thought in
the back of her mind. He felt as he did when he was about to steal
something.

On the movie magazine table, he flipped quickly through stacks of
*Photoplay, Screen Book, Movie Story, Modern Screen, Movie Life,
Screenland, Motion Picture, Screen Romances, Screen Album, The New
Movie Magazine, Silver Screen,* finding no issue he didn't already have.

Their old mildew smell drew Lucius to magazines he'd been aware
of surrounding the movie magazines on the racks in the many drugstores he patrolled but had never really looked at closely. He enjoyed
the Norman Rockwell covers on *The Saturday Evening Post,* the girls
by Jon Whitcomb in *Cosmopolitan,* by Vargas in *Esquire.* He liked the
feel of the different grades and colors of paper in *Redbook.* The one-
page stories in *Liberty* and *Collier's* had a special importance. It was
odd that *Liberty* announced the time it ought to take you to read a
story. On the cover of *Reader's Digest,* no illustration, just a long list
of contents that made him dizzy to look at. *Omnibus,* that ran con-
densations of books: a cavalier stands beside a princess, watching a battle
near the castle. *Quick,* a new pocket-sized magazine. *Look. Coronet:*
a pretty girl in pigtails, tied with large ribbons, a cowboy hat hanging
over her shoulder, plaid boy's shirt, a straw stuck in her luscious lips.
A girl in a yellow bathing suit on the cover of *See* was sexy. *Collier's:*
young blond woman in a mauve suit, gloves, purse dangling from her
wrist, plays hopscotch, while two little girls and two boys watch, behind
them a wooden fence, a poster, almost obscured by her outflung arm,
advertising a western at the Bijou, a political poster on the other end.
He was surprised that other theatres in America were named Bijou.
Time: Einstein's white hair and moustache, foaming and billowing
like the atomic bomb cloud in the background: "Cosmoclast Einstein.
All matter is speed and flame." *Popular Mechanics* that Earl used to
bring home. *Argosy. Bluebook. Modern Romances* that Momma sometimes brought in, *True Detective,* with real photographs of murder
victims and the killers that Earl liked.

Four years ago, he'd sold *The Saturday Evening Post* and *Liberty*
door to door, taking up a job Earl had abandoned. He remembered
the smell of those fresh magazines, even more distinctive than the aroma
of fresh newspapers, and felt the long slender compact satchel against
his hip. Moving among the used magazines and books, handling them,
the old-house smell in his nostrils, Lucius began to feel as he did
when he rifled the stills in the Bijou basement, a sickening thrill—
eager to reexperience the briefly known and to explore the unknown.

The pulps seldom interested him, but Dan Miller's talk of Jack
Painter urged Lucius to look for one of his stories. *Ten Story Western*

Magazine: a cowboy with a match in his mouth shooting from behind a wagon wheel. *Double-Action Western:* fairly well done illustration showing a cowboy shooting from a steep wooden stairs coming up out of a stone quarry. *West,* featuring a Zorro story. *Ranch Romances. Western Action.* A Jack Painter story featured on the front, "Guns and Gold." Lucius set it aside. He found no others among the rest of the westerns.

Lucius had always sneered at the covers of pulp magazines, inferior compared with the artwork for movie posters, and the drawings inside were so crude, he was certain he could have done better. Spread out on a table of their own, the other pulps invited a brief perusal. *Captain Future. The Spider. Black Mask Detective. Startling Stories. Ace G-Man. Popular Love. Thrilling Wonder Stories:* a girl and a man in space suits, skiing away from a spaceship, the girl shooting at a creature whose claw only is visible. *Super Science Stories. Husbands. Space Adventure. Weird Tales. Football Action. Jungle Stories. Private Detective:* a man choking a girl, "Would You Like to Be a Corpse?" *Master of Man. The Ghost. Secret Agent.* Many issues of *Adventure,* one showing a cowboy, dripping oil, derricks in the background, carrying a man over his shoulder, shooting, gritting his white teeth. Handling all these, aware that the covers exaggerated situations he enjoyed in movies, Lucius feet superior.

The old lady had every magazine Lucius had ever heard of and many he'd never seen before. His hands black with soot and dust, he was excited, moving among so many magazines of the past and the present that gave him a sense of his own future more intensely than when he looked only at movie magazines.

Lucius had been aware of, but he'd seldom picked up paperback books because they had no pictures. Sometimes the covers were striking, but he felt remote from them, they were for other people. But the contrast between their covers and the pulps' was so obvious, he lingered at the table. Some of the covers seemed composed more of bold colors in patterns than depictions of real people. And the ones that were very realistic seemed more high-class than the pulps. *The Fog Comes,* Mary Collins, a giant figure, like the Shadow, moving in fog over the seashore, a cliff in the foreground, the illustration for the hardcover edition on the back, a map of the crimes inside. *Jurgen,* fancy cover, and James Branch Cabell on the back looked like a school principal. *Trio,* a triangle, two women and a man, crudely drawn, Dorothy Baker. First page inside: "We both want to be good writers," wrote Dorothy Baker of herself and her husband, "and to spend the rest of our lives working at it." Hey, *The Sea Hawk,* Rafael Sabatini, giant claws of a hawk about to snatch up a ship, Sabatini's face, shadowy, cigarette dangling from his mouth, like Bela Lugosi, on the back.

Destry Rides Again, very bad drawing, images of James Stewart vivid in Lucius's imagination. Max Brand—the pen name impressed him. A Charlie Chan mystery, *The Black Camel,* a camel and a dagger, Earl Derr Biggers—ugly name, why didn't he pick a better one? *The Heart Is a Lonely Hunter,* old-fashioned ink drawing of a boy, carrying a basket of fruit, a sort of fat-faced but intriguing girl on the back, her hands clasped over her head, a cigarette in one hand—Carson McCullers, nice name, a man's name, Jack Carson. "In the town, there were two mutes, and they were always together." *Thunder on the Left,* the title excited him, a pastel couple on the front, a fascinating, bearded, bespectacled man on the back, Christopher Morley, who looked imposing, like a real writer, the god who made the thunder on the left. On the back, Morley had written his own obituary, and Lucius was puzzled that a fiction writer wanted most of all to be a poet. Like some of the others, this one had a kangaroo on the cover wearing glasses, reading one book, another in his pouch. He set *Thunder on the Left* aside.

The Great Gatsby, crummy illustration of a woman's hand holding a champagne glass, people lolling drunk under an umbrella table, but F. Scott Fitzgerald was a great name for a writer. *The Summing Up,* an exotic emblem in white on a black background, inside various-colored rings, W. Somerset Maugham on the back, an interesting-looking aristocrat. He loved the pen name. "This is not an autobiography nor is it a book of recollections." What was an autobiography? Lucius set *The Summing Up* aside.

Bread and Wine, an iron fist clapped over the sun, a mountain village sketched below, a tough guy on the back, Ignazio Silone, Italian, one of the enemy's books. *The Saga of Billy the Kid.* Lucius was surprised to learn from the writing on the back that Tombstone and Billy the Kid had really existed. Maybe there really was a character like the Tennessee Kid, too, even if Lucius *had* made him up. Walter Noble Burns. He set the book aside.

On the cover of *Winesburg, Ohio,* a very sharp, unrealistic depiction of a small-town scene, with rocking chair, corncobs, whiskey jug, weather vane, and an ordinary-looking man's face on the back, Sherwood Anderson. "The writer, an old man with a white mustache, had some difficulty in getting into bed." He was excited to see *Mildred Pierce,* but James M. Cain looked like a professor, and he resented his claim to a movie that Lucius had possessed as his own a year ago. *God's Little Acre*—he'd heard about that one as a dirty book for a long time. Selling it right out in the open! Being old, worn, secondhand made it seem more sinful. Erskine Caldwell. A wooden fence board, a knothole knocked out, to show a view of a dirty farm, with a pump, a few scrawny pines, an old car, a green farmhouse, outdoor privy, and a heart with arrows sticking in it carved on the wood. Lucius didn't like Caldwell's first name, nor his looks much, but he set *God's Little Acre* aside.

None of the writers looked as great as Chopin. Graham Greene. Didn't they say he wrote *This Gun for Hire? Ministry of Fear. Topper* by Thorne Smith, whose naughty books Momma liked to read. *Wuthering Heights* by Emily Brontë, and in the back was an announcement:

HELP WIN THE WAR!

Don't waste *anything*. You can help by saving useful waste and scrap. Save all old paper, rubber, metal and rags. Give it to a charitable organization, such as the Boy Scouts or the Salvation Army, or the Police Departments in some cities—or sell it to a junk dealer.

Reading that, Lucius felt older, as if the war had happened many years ago. Maybe someday his children would feel about it as he always felt when Mammy took the old illustrated magazines that contained colored drawings and watercolors of World War I out of the bottom bureau drawer and spread them out on the bed and talked over them.

One with a strange shape—the spine at the short end, the paper thinner, the print in double columns. *Martin Eden,* Jack London. Oh, Armed Services Editions! Just for the boys overseas. Had boys returning from Europe brought these back in their duffle bags, having read them in the Philippines and the Sahara and Salerno and on the troopships, in airplanes, and submarines? Touching pages that had traveled, he realized that some men who had read them had not, unlike the books, made it back. Daddy and Luke had probably read them, too—maybe this one: *Hopalong Cassidy Serves a Writ.* He tried to spot more of these among the rest of the paperbacks, hoping to find Luke's name written inside the cover of *Penrod.* Booth Tarkington, a pen name he loved. On the cover, they showed a picture of the hardcover editions. *Let Your Mind Alone,* James Thurber, sissy name. I'll be damned, *The Green Years,* A. J. Cronin. He sniffed Zane Grey, *Western Union.* *"The Great American Novel"*—looked important, but Clyde Brion Davis was a sappy pen name.

He shuffled quickly through another stack of the regular paperbacks, looking for *Frenchman's Creek. Sunset Gun,* Dorothy Parker. Aw, shit, poems. *A Tale of Two Cities,* Charles Dickens, some boring old classic. *The Philadelphia Story,* Philip Barry, Cary Grant, James Stewart, and Katharine Hepburn bug-eyed in one still in his collection. Printed in an odd way. Oh, it's a play. They made the movie from a play! The discovery made Lucius feel disoriented. *Return of the Native,* a jungle story? Thomas Hardy. No, it's England.

The nervous excitement of going through the books with his hands and his eyes, smelling them, most of them old, food-spattered, cigarette-burned, finger-sweat stained, sneezed upon, pages turned by licked thumbs, left out in the rain, torn by dogs and infants—Lucius had to take a leak.

Lucius picked up the magazines and pocket books he'd selected and started toward the old lady at the rolltop desk. The weak yellow light shone on the cellophane covers of some hardcover books like the ones Momma sometimes checked out of Ringgold's Department Store at ten cents a week, and she often made him return them for her to avoid paying extra. Yeah, there was *Foxes of Harrow* by Frank Yerby. And she liked to read books by Francis Parkinson Keyes, *River Road,* and *Saratoga Trunk* by Edna Ferber, Gary Cooper and Ingrid Bergman in the movie. And there's *Tap Roots* by James Street and *Woman on Her Way* by Faith Baldwin.

Lucius's aversion to hardcover books carried over from his hatred of the printed word, created in Leon Hooker Grammar School when they lived on Avondale and the teacher discovered that he read too slowly and put him in a special class after school. He felt guilty for having to stay in, inferior and stupid, and blurred words through his tears lay inert on the page. He began to loathe anyone associated with stories and poems he "ought to read" because "they are by great writers" and "are good for you." Vaguely, the shelves of books in the Bonny Kate library at his back as he wrote his stories excited him, and he used to go into the branch of the public library next to the Hiawassee and look at magazines such as the *National Geographic,* thumbing through to look at the naked savages, and he knew the illustrations for *Robin Hood* and *Gulliver's Travels* and for the stories of Edgar Allan Poe were good, but he had no desire to read any of those books. Except for stories he was forced, under strict scrutiny, to read silently or aloud in class, he'd read very few, and not a single book in his life.

Sneering, he began to paw over the hardcover books. *A Tree Grows in Brooklyn,* Betty Smith—why didn't she choose a more dramatic name? He remembered every scene in the movie. On the cover, the Brooklyn Bridge, tenements, and a small, ragged tree. And there's *The Rains Came,* Tyrone Power and Myrna Loy in the movie set in India. Louis Bromfield—more like a writer's name. I'll be goddamned if it ain't *The Big Sleep,* but a sissy name, Raymond, like the man who introduces "Inner Sanctum." Movie stills in it. Great! Lucius set *The Big Sleep* aside.

Maybe the old lady had some more like that. *The Sea of Grass,*

Conrad Richter. *Forever Amber,* another dirty book. Kathleen Winsor. Sexy to think of a woman writing a fuck story. And *The Wake of the Red Witch* by Garland Roark, very colorful cover, with a sea captain, all kinds of little scenes in the jungle behind him, and a glimpse of a ship between the lush vegetation. It looked great, reminding him of "While the Sea Remains" by Luke Scott, which sounded even better than Garland Roark. "Prelude: I, Sam Rosen, have a tale to spin; and the reader is hereby warned:—" Piss on you, thought Lucius, admiring the writer's arrogance.

The Stories of Frank Stockton—Lucius remembered retelling "The Lady or the Tiger" to Bucky. *Sanctuary!* Lucius was thrilled by the title, and he liked the name William Faulkner. "From beyond the screen of bushes which surrounded the spring, Popeye"—named after Popeye the Sailor Man, that's funny—"watched the man drinking." Good ol' *Kings Row.* *For Whom the Bell Tolls*—damned good movie, fifteen stills in his collection. Ernest Hemingway.

W. Somerset Maugham again, *The Razor's Edge*—the title excited him, and there was that same exotic symbol again, this time gold, with the name in gold and the title white, against solid black. Maybe they'd make a movie of that one, too. *My Son, My Son* by Howard Spring. He'd never seen the movie, but he'd started his own version of the condensed story that appeared in one of Beverly's off-brand movie magazines. *The Chinese Room,* Vivian Connell. *The Man Who Was There,* sounded odd, and the author's name, Wright Morris. *Adventure,* Clark Gable and Greer Garson on the front, "a novel of truth and romance" by Clyde Brion Davis. He loved that movie. *Unmoral* by Jack Woodford, looked sleazy. *All the King's Men*—Lucius sneered at the reference to Humpty Dumpty—but he liked the author's name, Robert Penn Warren.

He'd seen Fannie Hurst's name before—a movie edition of *Humoresque,* but the movie hadn't come to Cherokee yet. He'd seen the same stills in *Screen Romances. B.F.'s Daughter,* John P. Marquand, sounded duller'n dishwater. By God, a movie edition of *Mildred Pierce,* with that little bitch Veda on the cover with Joan Crawford. He resented Ann Blyth because she distracted him from Joan Crawford the Goddess with a vivid sexuality that contaminated Joan. He set it aside.

The ones in good condition, with covers on them, seemed to be set off by themselves. Aware of shelves of jacketless books in the dark beyond the yellow zone of light—fucking classics, probably—Lucius reverently picked up *Leave Her to Heaven,* Ben Ames Williams, a name that sounded good when the announcer said it in the previews. Gene Tierney drowning Jeanne Crain's little brother, Daryl Hickman, in a lake in Michigan. "It stinks," somebody had written inside, above the title.

Although in many previews and at the start of some movies, they'd shown the covers of the books on which the movies were based, sometimes making the pages flip as if by an invisible hand, and sometimes by a real hand, Lucius had never realized until now that so many movies came from books. And the stills in the Tower Editions brought the movies and the books together. While he was writing stories based on movies, he'd been only vaguely aware that movies were often based on written stories. He looked quickly through the other books, hoping to find *A Song to Remember* before he had to show up at the Bijou. *Duel in the Sun,* Niven Busch. *The Moon Is Down,* John Steinbeck. *The Ox-Bow Incident,* Walter Van Tilburg Clark (remembering the hanging in the movie brought a pang of fear to his stomach). *Of Human Bondage,* Somerset Maugham (now, Lucius realized, he had a bum foot like the man in the movie). *Frenchman's Creek,* Daphne du Maurier! *There* it is, by God. Lucius set it aside, eager to compare it, by memory, since he'd lost it, with his own version. *Strange Fruit,* Lillian Smith, that somebody said had the word "fuck" in it. "Please return, if found, to Ramona Kappert, Chattanooga, Tennessee, April 4, 1944." Clarence Budington Kelland, *Arizona,* Jean Arthur and William Holden in the movie—he remembered illustrations for the serial in *The Saturday Evening Post.* A movie edition of *Gone With the Wind!* With reverence he hefted it, with awe, he looked at the pictures, and set it aside. No *Song to Remember.*

Well, a good place to stop. His heart beating fast, he felt as if the excitement that had been building up, thrill after thrill, would give him his first experience of fainting. He didn't mind passing up the nonfiction, but he'd return soon to look at every single magazine, paperback, and hardcover novel.

Lucius carried his stack over to the lady: *God's Little Acre, The Big Sleep, Dime Western, The Summing Up, Billy the Kid, Frenchman's Creek, Mildred Pierce, Gone with the Wind.* He put *Thunder on the Left* back to buy some other day.

"And *The Pocket Book of Short Stories,*" said the old lady.

"Oh, I didn't pick out *that* one. But it *looks* good." Because he'd written a stack of stories himself and wanted to see what other writers did, Lucius put it on the stack.

As the old lady put the books and magazines in a used A & P sack, she said, "You hear about that man burning up under the Sevier Street Bridge this morning?"

"No, ma'am. How did it happen?"

"Drunk. Crawled up under some old rags to keep off the frost, I imagine, and somehow caught fire to himself. Not the first time. Nor the last."

Worried it might have been his daddy, who sometimes hung out under various viaducts with bands of bums, Lucius paid her, and went out and looked down along the railing at a black spot under the bridge, built, he noticed on the plaque, the year he was born. But he was certain it couldn't have been his own daddy—the police would have come to the house.

The Mr. Goodbar aftertaste was nauseating, as he walked up the hill toward the Bijou. The smell of the river revived Lucius's spirits. He was glad his mother used to take him to that store when he was little. He wished he had Bucky's wagon full of books. Maybe he'd start collecting them. He was eager to rush backstage and flip through *God's Little Acre* to the part when this one guy was supposed to lick this girl's pussy.

Lucius limped past Minetta, whose granite face gave him the impression she'd forgotten his infantile paralysis, and into the Bijou. Sabra, the other box office lady, stood in the main lobby with her husband, talking to Thelma. He was a small man, handsome, his hair blond, darker than Alan Ladd's or Lucius's, but combed in the same long wave. Sabra radiated sex quietly, without tossing it around in front of the Bijou Boys.

Startled at the sight of Lucius, Brady looked at his watch reflexively, then did a mock double take, and a pugnacious crouch On the Spot.

Rain is still falling in *The Big Sleep* and Bogart is entering the building where he meets Elisha Cook, Jr. Eager as he was to get into *God's Little Acre,* Lucius let this special scene stop him in the inner lobby.

"Towards the front, please," he said to Brady.

"Towards my ass."

"Am I late?"

"Early."

Surprised, Lucius looked at Brady's watch.

"What's in the poke?"

"Trick or treat," said Lucius.

He sat just under the balcony. Bogart stands in an office, his hands on a wooden filing cabinet, listening through an open door to Bob Steele who holds a gun on Elisha Cook: "So you go to see this peeper, this Marlowe. That was your mistake. Eddie don't like it. And what Eddie don't like ain't healthy."

Something landed softly on top of Lucius's head. Must have been his imagination. Then something hit him lightly on the ear and he turned around but saw nothing, his eyes still a little daylight-blinded. Then two pieces of popcorn fell into his lap, and when he looked around, Shirley Ford was sitting five rows behind him. He picked up the popcorn and his sack of books and walked back and turned in at

Shirley's row, where she sat alone, in the middle of the theatre. "You dropped your popcorn."

"Pop it in my mouth for me." As Lucius pushed the buds of popcorn into her mouth, Shirley licked his fingers. "Don't want to lose the salt."

"What's you doing?"

"Watching that little man die of poison and waiting for Gale to shuck off his uniform."

"Fuck off his uniform?"

"Silly." Shirley slapped Lucius's leg, squeezed until he barked in pain.

"You got a grip like a bear."

"Better not let me get holt of it."

"Don't let *me* stop you."

Elisha Cook Jr.'s body thuds onto the floor.

"What you doing with your leg under my girl's hand," said Gale, behind them.

"Oh, hello, Gale," said Lucius. "Just keeping your sweetheart hot for you."

"I leave her alone a few d'recklies and every little boy in Cherokee comes sniffing around."

"I love to be sniffed," said Shirley, squinting her nose and her shoulders.

"Yeah? Well, let's move over to the dark side. Hood's liable to prop his head on the balustrade back there and wonder what I'm doing to the patrons. It was thrilling seeing you, Lightnin'."

"Come on *with* us, Lucius."

"You supposed to be with *me,* woman."

"But I like both of you, and besides, I ain't seen Luscious since the Bugs Bunny Club."

"Then you ain't heard about it?"

"'Bout what?"

"Lightnin's got infantile paralysis of the pecker."

"I ort to worsh your mouth out with P and G soap."

"Just swab it with your tittie and I'll curb my language. Come on."

"Come on, Luscious."

"So long, Luscious."

"Aw, let him come," said Shirley, holding Lucius's hand.

Gale pulled on her other hand. "No gang banging."

"Then I ain't going." Still holding their hands, she sat down.

"Come on, Lucius," said Gale, good-naturedly.

Shirley jumped up so fast she made her seat slap back and the patrons look at them. Holding hands, the three of them crossed the left aisle, Lucius toting his sack of books with his free hand, and moved all the way over to the wall, six rows up from the front, the curtained boxes just beside them, the smell of dust in their nostrils from the lack of traffic back there, rain falling in *The Big Sleep*.

"Cozy, cozy, cozy. I wish we was in a submarine and Humphrey Bogart was our captain."

"That was Cary Grant," said Lucius. "Bogart was in a tank."

"Who's got the popcorn?" asked Shirley.

"Run get us some popcorn, Lightnin'," said Gale.

"Okay, Errol Flynn."

"Oh, you ain't him," she said to Gale. "He's a movie star."

Lucius came back with a sack of popcorn and two candy bars. Sitting there hunched under Gale's arm, Shirley reminded Lucius of the black-haired, fat, broad-shouldered wild-eyed girl who lived on Beech and who had to be watched every minute or she'd wander away from the front porch glider. She was seldom seen out in the yard—he remembered her standing among a flood of buttercups in white patent-leather shoes. She was bigger than her brother, the most handsome boy in the neighborhood. Maybe she was dead by now. Lucius handed the popcorn to Shirley, "Thanks a whole bunch," a Baby Ruth to Gale, and started unwrapping a Butterfinger.

Shirley, bigger than Lucius or Gale, sat between them, hugging the popcorn bag in the crook of one arm, dipping into it with her free hand, pushing delicate blossoms of hot popcorn through her puckered lips that glistened with lipstick, salt, and grease, watching Lauren Bacall stare into Bogart's eyes as she takes a cigarette out of her mouth and puts it between his lips where he sits on a davenport, his hands tied, his face battered. "Why did I have to meet you? Why, out of all the men in the city, did my father have to call you in?"

"Is she going to screw the poor guy while his hands are tied?" asked Gale.

Lucius always hated, even from Gale, to hear such talk about the stars. The goddesses never made love. Men and boys whistled, stomped, cracked jokes, barked obscene noises when the goddesses removed a little of their clothes, but he never wanted them to take off more. Alive that instant was the moment in the Hiawassee when he suddenly realized, in horror and disgust, that Vivien Leigh had ears, a nose, and elbows. He'd never conceived that she had a vagina, like the one he had his finger in while watching Vivien Leigh. Like the marble and bronze statues of nymphs and satyrs in the Tivoli's lobbies and lounges, the gods and goddesses on the screen were peckerless and pussyless, smooth, seamless marble and bronze between the legs.

When Bogart shot Bob Steele, Shirley laughed and cheered loudly, raucously, and Gale looked around and ducked down in his seat, whispering, "Keep it down, Shirley."

Seeing Gale play with one of Shirley's breasts, Lucius put his hand on the other, surprisingly small for a girl so big, feeling it through her silky blouse. When Lucius put his finger in her pussy, he thought at first she had a pecker, but it turned out to be Gale's finger, and they got to giggling, and like Errol Flynn and Gilbert Roland in *The Sea Hawk*, they fenced each other inside her barndoor pussy. "Don't tangle the little hairs," she said, shoving popcorn into her mouth.

Lucius smelled pussy. Gale had put his arm around Shirley's shoulder and stuck his finger under Lucius's nose. "River Street," he said, "after a flood."

Bogart is in the hothouse again, talking to the old man, the butler standing nearby. "That's why I thought I should give you your money back—because it isn't a completed job by my standards."

"Here comes the boring part," said Shirley. She pushed the last blossom of popcorn into Lucius's mouth and blew up the bag and popped it. Lucius and Gale cringed.

"When you gonna let me *have* a little?" asked Gale.

"You can come to my house Sunday while they're all at church."

Lucius hoped Gale would invite him to share Shirley's pussy. He began to feel sad, though, knowing that all Gale wanted out of her was to do it to her, but Lucius himself didn't know what else was possible.

Gale kissed her. "You don't blow, do you?"

"I ain't letting nobody put one of them things in *my* mouth."

"Good, I'm glad," said Gale, and kissed her again. "Care if I pull off your bloomers?"

"Just down to my ankles."

Lucius hadn't really looked at a girl's pussy in four years, not since the Brummetts.

The popcorn packed into her round belly, Shirley was jacking Lucius and Gale with salty, greasy fingers when she suddenly plopped her hands in her lap, saying, "Zip up, quick, it's my brother."

Zipping up with lightning speed, Lucius caught a hair and yelped.

"Momma said you better git your ass home, Shirley," said a boy a little younger than Lucius, leaning across the aisle.

"I'm coming, Bobby, I'm coming. You run home and tell her I'm coming."

As Shirley followed her little brother up the aisle, Lucius thought of his own task of always having to look after Bucky.

Backstage, Lucius sat on the throne and skimmed through *God's Little Acre*, looking for the pussy-licking scene. All his life, he had heard that the nastiest thing, next to blowing a guy, was to lick a girl's pussy.

He'd never met anybody who admitted doing it, except Earl, who liked it, who said pussy tasted like pork and beans. Lucius wasn't sure whether he wanted to—certainly not Shirley's. He'd compared smells on his finger and noticed that some smelled less rank than others. As a captured secret agent, he'd often been forced by a gestapo officer to lick the pussies of twenty naked women hanging by their hands in a row.

In one intuitive rush, Lucius was aware of being surrounded daily by women, of whose presence, each and every one, he was acutely, sometimes painfully aware, and the degrees, kinds, qualities, and quantities of sensuality were simultaneously lucidly distinct and blended together into one morass of stimuli: not Raine, pure and sexless, but red-haired Cora, vulgar, Joy, dark and quiet, Peggy, cocky and tough, and all the girls he'd done it to before he was nine, out there somewhere roaming Cherokee, and all the stuck-up girls and the poor hard-eyed girls at Bonny Kate, and Kay Kilgore, but not Miss Redding, and Della Snow, and Shirley Ford, and Charlene, the musky Negro ticket girl, sexy Sabra, Thelma, evoking Carolyn, Mrs. Atchley, ambiguously handsome, hateful Minetta, her ass sloppy, the women customers of all ages, Hood's short, aggressive, blond wife, bossing a squad of ushers at the Tivoli, the Bitch of Belsen, the blond manager of all the theatres in the chain, her office in the Tivoli's basement, his mother's girl friends, the comic strip figures of Boots, the Dragon Lady in *Terry and the Pirates,* Blondie, Daisy Mae, the women in magazine ads and posters and billboards, and even some of the B-grade movie actresses in the Hollywood and the Smoky—some of the blond sexpots in the cheap comedies, contrasting with zanies like the Three Stooges, Penny Singleton as Blondie, a radiant beauty, but her zaniness implied a between-the-scenes sexiness. Lucius responded immediately, emphatically to all women in every conceivable perspective as though each, in her own way, were *presenting* herself, and one of *his* main functions in life was to register, accurately, like a seismograph each shock wave that slightly rearranged every cell in his body, every image stored in his brain. Lucius gave up trying to find the scene in *God's Little Acre.* Sitting astride the throne, feeling slightly melancholy, he got rid of the ache Shirley had left him with.

Each time he went backstage, Lucius glanced at his books again, noticing once with great delight that *God's Little Acre* was published in 1933, the year of his birth, and going home on the midnight streetcar, the last run, he held all the books in his lap, and felt armed against the world.

Wens. October 9, 1946. Got back in school. They took an X ray of my feet at Crippled Children's. Bought a whole bunch of books. Me and Gale sat with Shirley at the Bijou and——

NIGHT RITUAL: Earl wears a fuzzy, dull red sweater to school in winter until Christmas, and instead of buying milk at school, he carries some in a mason jar from home and hates it. . . . Lucius is swaying on a sagging honeysuckle fence, watching Earl come along the WPA ditch, two vague-faced dimes and nickels in his palm. "Momma said you and me can go to the show. She's sick." Lucius sees the red neon lights of the Hiawassee glowing like hot pokers through the thick trees of the jungle. Earl takes Lucius's hand and leads him along the flood-control WPA ditch that cuts through the dense jungle across from the house and they follow the path along Crazy Creek to Grand Boulevard. On the bridge, they lean over the rusty iron railing, looking down into the green water, and Earl tells Lucius about Fartso the Whale, who lives in the creek and is like Monstro in *Pinocchio*. He's mean but if you throw him presents, says Earl, Fartso won't hurt you. He might even help you beat up bullies and give you presents, if you're good, like Santa Claus does. "If I throw him a nickel, Fartso will tell his gremlins to bring you a Buck Rogers gun." Lucius thinks of Snow White's Seven Dwarfs. "Give it to me, and *I'll* throw it in." Then they cross the most dangerous intersection in Cherokee to the Hiawassee, the marquee's neon lights pulsing on their faces, and watching the Green Hornet's dark car swerve suddenly, forcing the bad guy's getaway car to smash into a gas pump and explode, Lucius wonders how it is that Earl hugs two bags of popcorn when he threw both their nickels into the creek. Going back home through the ditch in the steamy moonlight, leaving the Green Hornet and Kato in a fix until next week, Earl stops, puts his hand on Lucius's head. "Quiet. . . . I hear Momma cryin'." Lucius hears nothing. He follows Earl home, running. The doors are closed, the shades down. Teddie, who has a red face and gray hair, and takes care of them when Momma's working, leads them into the bedroom. Lucius can barely see the tiny red face peeking out of the covers in the crook of Momma's arm. It wiggles and explodes into crying, and Lucius sees the mobster's car crash again and explode and the baby is born in Momma's bed in the same moment. . . . Momma catches Earl trying to feed the baby a banana. . . . They all stand around the kitchen table between the cook-stove and the sink, watching Momma bathe the baby, and Bucky keeps calling it Baboo, but its name is Ronald Dennis Hutchfield. . . . Earl and Lucius and four kids in a tree in the yard at night singing "Home on the Range." . . . Baboo lies in a veiled crib on the porch in bright sunlight and Lucius says, "Ah, Baboo, you's gonna be a great man, wait and see. . . . Big, strong, and husky. I'll pull you around the park in my big red Fire Chief wagon I'm gonna get for Christmas. You sweet thing. You and me'll go out and conquer this ol' world. I got plans for us, yessir. You and me's gonna see all the whole, whole world together.

We gotta find out things. We'll always stick together. You're *my* little brother."

> Thurs. October 10, 1946. The Stranger started today—Orson Welles, Edward G. Robinson, and Loretta Young. Day off. Couldn't write.

> The Ambitious Author
> The ink upon the paper drys,
> The pen scratches as if it were wise;
> But when I finish it all,
> I have nothing but a crying squall.

> Fri. October 11, 1946. The Stranger. Saw a woman on the streetcar the other day who looks like Fay Nell who used to take care of us on Zachary, and a different one came into the Bijou tonight who was pregnant, and I can't figure out which one is Fay Nell and which is that preacher's daughter who used to do it to me when I was little. But when I remember her, I see Fay Nell's face.

> Sat. October 12, 1946. The Stranger. Good ol' show. Eddie G. tracks down Orson Welles who is a Nazi prison camp warden playing like he's a schoolteacher in a little town in New England. Can't wait to see Cary Grant and Ingrid Bergman and Claude Rains in Notorious—starts Monday.

"Well," said Mammy, as Momma stepped through the front door of good ol' 702 Holston, Lucius and Bucky behind her, "they come and got Earl," with that mountain tone of fate. Mammy and Momma had a way of announcing family, local, national, and world events as though presenting them solo on a stage or as the godlike voices on Paramount News.

"When?" asked Momma, in a high, dramatic voice, coming to a full stop just over the threshold, Lucius still holding open the screen, Bucky pushing at him from behind, scenting catastrophe, asking, "What's the matter?"

Over Momma's shoulder, Lucius looked at Mammy, sitting in her favorite chair across from the front door, her face contorted into mock crying, her voice a high whine, simulating a wail, "They just come right through my front door—didn't knock or nothin'," and she beat on the arm of her chair.

"*Who*, Mammy?" asked Momma, knowing the answer.

"The *po*-lice. And stomped through the house without a word to me, and me trying to ask 'em what it was they wanted, and on out the back door, and straight down to the coal house, and yanked him out and drug him through my garden up to the house again, and right *through* the house, tracking mud, and *out* the front door, and drove away just as my neighbors showed up on their front porches and the

Chief drove up in front of the hedge." Mammy bent and shook her head, pinching the bridge of her nose. "You just don't know, Irene, what I been *through* this mornin'."

"Oh, Lord, Lord, I thought we'd have a peaceful Sunday dinner for a change."

"They *ain't* no peace in this family, Irene. I thought when you all moved out, I'd be left alone awhile to get my strength back, and now this. Why couldn't they come for him at *your* house?"

"Moth-er," said Momma, standing on the exact spot where she'd stopped, holding the lemon meringue pie she'd carried in the mile walk from their house, "Earl has not *been* to my house."

"Last *I* seen him was when he did me a somerset over his head through the kitchen window."

"What happened?" Bucky held a bag full of bargains Momma had bought for Mammy at Ringgold's, his slightly buck teeth exaggerating the look of awe in his big brown eyes.

"Same thing'll happen to you, if you don't quit running with Emmett King."

"Kiss my rusty."

"Will you all hersh?"

"Well, for God's sake, Irene, come in and shut the door before I catch cold." Mammy pulled her quilted bathrobe tighter about her neck. Without his leather jacket, Lucius was chilled to the bone.

Momma came on in. "Take this in the kitchen."

Lucius put the lemon pie down on the kitchen table and brought a straight chair to the doorway and sat the way some cops do in the questioning room, resting his arms on the back.

"Didn't you ask to see a search warrant?"

"Irene, they come and went so fast, I didn't have time to notice I was *being* searched. *I* have to *live* in this neighborhood. You can move in and out as you damn please!"

"Mother, you *told* me to move—in fact, you said for us to get the hell out."

"I can't have *po*-lice cars roaring up to my door on Sunday mornings. Now that's all they is *to* it."

"Mother, *I* can't help it. Will you just calm down and tell me what happened?"

Mammy rared up in her flowered print chair, lips pleated like crimped piecrust, her finger pointing at Momma who sat on the edge of the davenport. "Now don't you sass me one time, young lady, after what I've been through—for *your* youn'un."

"Mother, let me get in the door before you start."

"Start? I'm finished. I'm finished takin' care of other people's youn'uns."

"Other *people*. Mother, I *am* your daughter, you know."

"We never had a lick of trouble with the law in this family until Earl—"

"You don't have to worry, you don't have to worry any *more*, Mother. This time, they'll put him *under* the jail and he won't see daylight for ten years." Momma was veering off anger onto the verge of tears.

Bucky sat bug-eyed beside her, his feet not touching the rug Mammy had brought back from their fine life in St. Louis before the Depression.

"And to have the Chief *see* all this."

"I thought he was going to be *with* us today."

"I sent him off."

"Why?"

"Didn't want him around. All this hell and commotion going on. I won't *have* it. I don't want no reflection cast on him for coming here, *po*-lice cars racing up and down Holston."

"Racing up and down?"

"Yeah, they took off up toward Bonny Kate and as I was standing at the door talking to the Chief, here they come flying back by, looking at us, and me still in my nightgown. I could have screamed bloody murder. Never was so embarrassed in all my life."

"What did the Chief say?"

"That sweet ol' thing wanted to jump in his car and run 'em down and ask for a warrant and take it up with the chief of police. He grew up with Chief Connor on River Street. But you know me, I had to fly off the handle at him and tell him to mind his own g.d. business." Mammy was about to cry. "It was just I was so upset, him seeing me in such a fix. And the sight of them dragging Earl out of the coal house had me on the verge of hysterics anyhow. That poor youn'un had nothin' on but his undershorts."

Lucius saw Earl again getting on the streetcar wearing his leather jacket and Elgin wristwatch, and undershorts.

"You mean they wouldn't even let him put his *clothes* on?"

"Irene, they was draggin' that youn'un through the house, and he kept saying, 'Least let me put my pants on, mister, least let me put my pants on,' and this big ol' fat one says, 'You shut your g.d. mouth.' "

"How many of 'em *was* there?"

"Three. Two in uniform and one a city detective."

"Oh, Lord, you don't reckon Earl's done something else since he run off from S.T.S."

Mammy's breasts shook as her head, bowed, nodded rapidly, but when she raised it, her eyes were bright, and she was trying to keep from smiling, "Euuuuuuuu, law! I'll never forget the sight of Earl—just as the po-lice car scattered gravel all over the hedge taking off—Earl tosses his undershorts out the back winder."

Bucky put down the package and opened the front door.

"Where you think *you're* goin'?" asked Momma.

"Play in the yard," he said, halfway out the door.

"Lucius, look out the bedroom window for any sign of Emmett King."

Not wanting to miss a word of what Mammy was saying, Lucius stepped into her room where the shades were pulled, and the old torn rose wallpaper hung down in long buckles from the ceiling and small tongues from the wall, and pressing his knee on the bed, let up the shade and watched Bucky go through the hedge and look up and down the street in front of the house. Emmett was nowhere in sight. Bucky came back through the brown, ragged hedge carrying a pair of shorts, looking at them as if Earl had sketched a map of a buried treasure on them as he was ripped off to jail. Bucky sniffed the cloth.

Mammy was saying, "I don't know whether they took him to the Safety Building or to the county jail behind the courthouse. They wasn't about to tell *me* nothing."

"Why, that's just like the gestapo, for crying out loud."

"Well, now you march yourself right down there and find out just what's what."

"I guess I better. I'll go to the Safety Building first."

"And get in touch with Freddie."

"Probably laying under the Sevier Street Bridge with a brigade of drunks. . . . Lucky he didn't burn up with that friend of his."

"Oh, Irene, I hate to see poor ol' Fred go down like that. Ain't they something you can do?"

"Mo-ther, what can *I* do? I work six days a week for a dirty old Greek to keep a roof over our heads and he squanders his pay the day Kitty turns it over to him."

"Well, he's been through the war, you know. . . ."

"I know that, Mother, but so have *I*. Who was it stayed home and took care of three kids?"

"And look how they're turning out. Kids needs their daddy."

"They're gonna be needin' a momma if I have to endure any more of this—wind up in the insane asylum."

"It ain't none of my business, but if it was me, I would have gone easy on him there at the first, till he was used to bein' back."

"Mother, please don't start that, I've got enough troubles on me as it is—I know, it's all *my* fault he's a slobbering drunkard, and I'll probably burn in hell for it."

"Don't you get sarcastic with *me*. I told you I'm in no mood to wrangle with you."

"Lucius, get Bucky and take him back home."

"Why, he'll do no such a thing."

Lucius picked up the bag of bargains. "Did you show Mammy what you bought her on sale at Ringgold's?"

"No, but she's showing her ass, and *I'm* about to *slap* it."

"Well, I don't know about you, Lucius," said Momma, standing up, "but your mother's not staying here, listening to that kind of talk from her own momma."

"Now, don't you walk out of my house in a huff." Between Momma and the door, Mammy stood up.

Bucky opened the front door and held up Earl's shorts. "Ta da!"

"What is the world is that?"

"Earl's shorts." Momma started crying. Bucky reached up and patted her shoulder. "Don't cry, Momma."

"You can't go in the jail all tore up," said Mammy. "Rest a minute before you go."

"No, I better get on. It'll take me an hour to catch a streetcar and get up there."

"You want us to go home, Momma?" asked Lucius.

"Why, no, honey," said Mammy, "you all stay here with Mammy and we'll have us a Sunday dinner and keep some warm for your Momma."

"Here's a dollar, Momma," said Lucius. "Take a cab back from Howell's Drug Store."

"Thank you, honey. Anything you want me to tell Earl?"

"Yeah. Ask him where's my watch."

"*What* watch?"

"My new Elgin."

"Did you loan it to him?"

"Well . . . yeah. Find out if I can visit him."

"Me, too," said Bucky. And he ran over to Momma and kissed her 'bye.

"Now you stick with Lucius today. Promise?" Bucky nodded rapidly. "And if Chief Buckner comes back by to see Mammy, you all take a walk, cause they got things to talk over."

"Well, it ain't likely he'll want to marry into *this* family after what happened today."

"Mother, *please* stop it."

"You quit that sassing me, and go about your business."

"Go to hell!" Momma screamed and slammed the door.

Mammy rushed to the door.

"Mammy, please don't fuss at her," said Bucky.

Mammy slapped Bucky and jerked the door open and yelled, "That's the last time you'll cuss *me*, you hateful bitch!"

"Come on, Bucky," said Lucius. "Let's go in the back room, honey."

His arm around Bucky, who was trying not to cry out loud, Lucius went back to Luke's room, where he and Bucky, and, for a while, Earl had slept during the last years of the war.

Lucius's leather jacket hung on the back of a straight chair, left behind when the cops took Earl. The room was cold as an icebox. He put the jacket on. Bucky sat on the bed, his face and mouth slack, a hurt look.

"She didn't have to slap me."

"Well, they're both tore up about Earl, Bucky."

"Lucius, you think Mammy really loves us?"

"Why, sure, Bucky. Don't be stupid. Think of all the trouble we've given her."

"What trouble?"

"Oh, God. Skip it."

"It's cold."

"Look what I found in the pockets of my jacket." Lucius showed Bucky fifty cents in change, a pack of Beech-nut chewing tobacco, a book of matches put out by the Inferno Roadhouse, a transfer with Rosalie Minton, 5–3321, written on it, five Ritz and Jewel ticket stubs, and a pack of Trojan rubbers.

"Can I have the chew'n tabacca?"

"You want to vomit?"

"I won't chew it, I promise."

"Then what you want with it?"

"Just to carry."

"Here."

The jacket smelled of Earl.

"You all come out of that cold room," said Mammy.

"Come on, Bucky."

The sun had come out and shone bright on the round kitchen table and on Mammy's fresh starched print dress.

"Want to help Mammy shell the shellies, Bucky?" she asked, in her gay voice.

"Oh, boy," said Bucky. "I like to hear 'em hit the bowl."

"Where's the Sunday paper, Mammy? Ought to be something good on the radio."

"Sit with *us,* Lucius." Mammy shoved part of the pile of shelly beans across to Bucky. Lucius sat between them and watched.

"I tell you now, Lucius, if you really want something to write about, let me tell you the story of Harl Abshire. Now, boys, that's a *tale.*"

"Tell it again," said Bucky. Lucius was as eager to watch the effect of the telling on Bucky as to hear it again himself.

"Well, sir, Harl Abshire was one of the most notorious desperadoes of the Depression. He come down out of the Chilhowee Mountains, 'bout forty miles from *here,* but it was just over the mountains from where *I* was raised. During Prohibition, they throwed his daddy, ol' Henry Abshire, in prison for making moonshine, and Harl's mother picked up the kids and moved to Sweetwater and she drifted on down to Chattanooga and went into a house of ill repute."

"What's ill repute?" asked Bucky, pushing shellies out of a pod.

"Where whores hang out," said Mammy. "Anyhow, that's not what this is about. What happened was that Harl and his brothers and sisters was left at his gran'mother's house, and they wasn't enough food to go around nor room to sleep all of them, so he being the oldest, they turned him out, told him to make it on his own. Which he did. Hopped a freight to Nashville, robbed a saloon, and got hisself throwed in the reform school."

"Where Earl is?" asked Bucky.

"Where Earl was, honey. But it was a worse place in them days than it is now. Anyway, Harl didn't like it in there, and one day they took a strap to him one time too many and he jerked it out of the man's hand and beat the living fire out of him—laid him up in the hospital, said, 'Ain't no man allowed to whup me but my sweet daddy,' and they throwed him in solitary, and when he come out, he looked like a ghost had took his place."

"I would've runned off, if id been *me,*" said Bucky, nodding seriously.

"Which is what he done, which is what he done."

"So did Earl."

"Yeah, well, Harl did, too—I mean before Earl. Way back yonder. Honey, this was in nineteen and twenty. And you know what Harl said to his buddy when he walked into the bean field, fresh out of solitary?"

"No, what?" asked Bucky. The way Bucky's interest in the story was expressed in his fingers working the shellies, his mouth and eyes related to his fingers, fascinated Lucius. The first voice Lucius could remember was Mammy's, telling him a story about the old man who used the money his wife saved for their twelve children's Christmas presents to buy himself a handsome tombstone. In winter, sitting with her feet on the fender of the Warm Morning heater; in summer, on a quilt on the grass. Firelit rug, moonlit grass—magic carpets. Her voice, acting out all the parts, like the sound track of a movie, and as she gestured, her body like a stage, the noggins of her spectators within reach. Watching Bucky's reactions, he remembered being aware, when he was four or five, of his own responses to Mammy's ways of telling a story—as if he were two people, one of them sitting apart from the other, observing, almost as absorbed in what was going on between the storyteller and the listener as he was in the story itself. And he'd understood why he loved to tell stories himself to Earl and the kids in the neighborhood. He'd already been telling stories for a year when he experienced that awareness of Mammy's deliberate method and his own response. And he'd felt keenly a desire to cause other people to feel as he'd felt, to make them live so vividly in the world created by his own imagination that spit drooled down their chins before they realized they'd forgotten they inhabited bodies. He wanted to do to others what Mammy and the movies had done to him.

"Let me get the water for the beans started first." Mammy got up and filled a big pot with water and stirred up the fire and set it on.

"*Tell* me, Mammy," Bucky bounced up and down in his chair, "you can tell me while you're doing it."

"Well, sir," said Mammy, sitting again, her eyes faraway and vacant, "He says," then suddenly filled to squinting with the presence of Harl Abshire, " 'I've seen my last cell. They'll never get me in one again.' And don't you know that youn'un was halfway to the Chilhowee Mountains by nightfall?"

"How'd he get out?"

"Why, honey, *I* don't know. I wasn't there."

"Then what?"

Mammy closed her eyes. "Nothin'. Nothin' happened for two years. Nobody heard *of* him, nor *from* him, nor *seen* him, nor knowed a *thing* about him. We thought he'd disappeared. Sometimes we'd hear a noise out in the yard and my Momma'd go to the winder and whisper, 'Harl, is that you outsyonder? You git yourself in here and git something *in* you, boy.' She felt sorry for him. Me and Gran'paw Charlie had moved in with Momma to take care of her and Paw—they was both bad off that summer.

"Well, then it happened. We got news—hardly ever seen a newspaper up in them mountains where we lived, but we heard about things from folks that went into Maryville with their produce, and we heard Harl Abshire had robbed a bank in Sevierville."

"Did he have a gang like John Dillinger?"

"No, sir, he did it all by his lonesome."

"How'd they know it was him? Didn't he wear no mask?"

"No, sir, he was too proud. I *done* it, now try and *get* me for it."

"That's what he said to 'em?"

"No, that was his attitude. Shell them beans, Bucky, keep your trap shut and your ears open. Now. Where was I? . . . Oh, yeah, that bank. Well, sir, then it was another one, and another one. Still the Lone Wolf, and his face as open for all the world to see as a baby's ass. 'Cuse me, children. Got a little too hot for him in Tennessee. And reckon who it was with him in Indianapolis?"

"John Dillinger!"

"Shorty Luttrell, his ol' buddy from the reform school, the very one. Three days after they let him go, he was riding country roads with Harl Abshire.

"So from 1923 to 1934, twelve years, it was the Abshire gang—for he took on first one and then another, and then another, twill he had ten or more, and they branched out an pulled a few jobs and split up, so we'd hear about the Abshire gang robbing a bank in Tennessee and another in Missouri—on the very same day. Got to be like the A and P, with business going in more places than one. One time they did put him in jail in Jonesboro for a few hours, but he broke out and stole the sheriff's big black mare and rode out of town on her, bareback, him bare chested, a gun blazin' in each hand.

"And we kept up with him all that time, and in the meantime, me and your Gran'paw Charlie and your momma and little Luke had moved to St. Louis and they was something in the paper all the time about Harl Abshire.

"You all don't want to hear the rest of this ol' story, do you? I've told it a hundred times."

"Yes, I do!" said Bucky.

"Well, okay. . . . It all comes to an end, in nineteen and thirty-four, right here in Cherokee. Harl had been laid up in some little town in the mountains with T.B. I mean, he'd *had* T.B. for years, but that way of life had finally come down on him hard, and he'd been hiding out for two years, and his gang had sort of wandered off, and he decided he better get help—for that T.B. Must of heard about the sanatorium we got here, and just made up his mind—the way he did about anything—to get *well*, even if he had to go to jail afterwards.

"So, way it come out was, he contacted this old friend of his—a sheriff who was raised in the Chilhowee Mountains with him. Said, 'Sheriff, I'll strike up a bargain with you. If you'll get them to promise to let me go into that sanatorium and get treatment for my T.B., I'll give myself up in Cherokee.' So, the way they tell it, the sheriff said he would, and he contacted somebody, nobody ever found out who, that promised, and he took Harl in his own car all the way over the mountains, about a hundred miles, and they went in this house on the bluffs in South Cherokee near where your daddy was raised, and waited for the law."

"And reckon whose house it was? Reckon whose it was?"

"I got my eyes open and my mouth shut," said Bucky, giggling.

"Belonged to Beaver Cooper, my nephew. Harl was his hero and he wanted to ride with him so bad he could taste it. He didn't seem to know what was going on, because he was coming in at the end of Harl's robbing days. Anyway, Harl was sitting in the kitchen listening to Amos and Andy and eating catfish my nephew had caught out of the Tennessee River when in walked the sheriff, and three *policemen right behind him. And one of them was his own cousin, Cool Abshire. Now don't that beat all?"

Mammy got up and dumped the shellies in with the green beans and stirred. Lucius heard the bubbling of the green beans stop.

"Tell about them shootin' 'im," said Bucky, squirming.

"Well," said Mammy, in a tone that said there wasn't much to tell, wasn't much to it, "Sheriff just said, 'Harl, looks like they follered me here,' and Harl said, 'Hello, boys, we got a deal?' and his cousin, who'd never laid eyes on Harl before, said, 'Mr. Abshire, this ain't no deal. You're under arrest,' and Harl looked at the sheriff and the sheriff said, 'These ain't the ones I was dealin' with, Harl. They follered my trail, I reckon.' Harl stood up like it was the end of the world and when he raised his hand to wipe the fish grease, one of 'em clapped the cuffs on him and they marched him out the front door.

"Standing on that front porch, all poor ol' Harl could see was blue— blue sky and blue uniforms and blue cars. Most peaceful scene you ever saw. When all of a sudden, Harl grabbed a gun from a *policeman's holster and before he could fire it, it was like ever' gun in the world went off at once and quick as a wink, he was laying in the dust, dead."

They listened to the green beans and shellies boil.

"Tell it again," said Bucky.

Mammy laughed and patted Bucky's cheek. "You all wait a minute, I got something I want to show you." Bucky followed her into the bedroom, and Lucius ambled after them.

Bright sun poured through the window upon the lid of the old pine box Lucius and Bucky had slept in years ago, staying all night, and that Lucius had stored his writings in. Mammy had brought it back into the house out of the circus wagon coal house after they'd moved and when she lifted the lid, the room went dim. She dug around in the dark box, and Lucius, glad to be going through the ritual again, anticipated the picture of Snow White and the Seven Dwarfs in color, a slew of pictures of World War I, of the Quintuplets of Canada, who looked weird, the sweet pictures from ladies' magazines of sleeping babies or reprints of paintings of charming old-timey landscapes and children dressed up like adults, and kittens dressed up like people, posing for real-life scenes, with funny captions, Mammy showing them with an air of exclusiveness, as if some of them weren't available anywhere else in the world. And the news clipping about Gran'paw Charlie being found shot to death and a picture of the accused—that face like Victor Jory as Injun Joe.

"Now, I ain't never showed this to you before, because it ain't fit to show children," said Mammy, "but I reckon since I've done told the story, it won't hurt. . . ."

Mammy spread the Cherokee *Messenger* out on her white bedspread, smoothed the yellow wrinkles gently, and when she pulled her hands away, Lucius saw, stretched out across the front page, under the banner, beside the headline, the body of a man riddled with bullets. " 'LAW'S GUNS RUB OUT ABSHIRE,' " Mammy read aloud, tracing the words with her finger, sounding as if she were reading it for the first time. " 'Notorious Bandit, Drilled 32 Times, Grovels in Dust.' Above the picture: 'Abshire meets Pay-off: "The Wages of Sin Is Death." ' They say," said Mammy, "John Dillinger come through Cherokee once, and my grandmother swears she once set next to Jesse James on a train out of Chattanooga. Tuesday, August 3, 1935. Law, Lucius, you was only two years old, and, Bucky, *you* was just a dishrag in heaven."

Lucius was amazed that such a historical event had happened in Cherokee during his own lifetime.

"Slaying Seen by Small Boys. Now ain't that terrible? Thousands Jam Funeral Parlor for Glimpse of Notorious Bandit. Mountain Folk Had Predicted Fate of Harl Abshire. 'They'll Never Put him in a Cell,' said Chilhowee Mountaineer. Well, he was right. They never did.

"Oh, there's poor little Beaver Cooper." Lucius looked at a picture of a man who resembled young Rudolf Hess. "He was my nephew. They found him in the bathtub tremblin' in his own dirty water. Sentenced him to Bushy Mountain. Got in a fight on the chain gang and this ol' boy hacked into him with a scythe."

"Did it kill him?" asked Bucky, bouncing on the bed.

"Bucky, I've told you and told you not to wear out them springs." Bucky bounced backward off the bed. "Deader'n four o'clock. Now, that's what comes of runnin' with the wrong crowd. Ort to show this to Earl before *he* run wild." Idly, Mammy turned to the next page and Lucius was thrilled to see an ad for the Bijou: Carole Lombard and John Barrymore in *Twentieth Century*. Despite her comic vitality, Carole Lombard was among the rarest goddesses because of her beauty and because she died in a plane crash and Clark Gable, her husband, had climbed the mountain to rescue her. Five more pictures distracted Lucius: A crowd

across from the Smoky outside a funeral parlor. A shot of the sheriff. The
white house where Abshire was caught. The spot where he fell. The three
policemen who shot him, one of whom Lucius had seen in the Bijou,
looking for Baylis.

Lucius read aloud: "City Police Claim Abshire Didn't Shoot. Say
He Broke Away After Snatching Officer's Gun, Turned and Lifted It,
Perhaps to Shoot Himself. One Policeman is Outlaw's Cousin."

"Now, ain't that awful! Had to be told he'd shot his own cousin.
Lord have mercy," said Mammy, "now ain't that one more sight! Children, it just don't pay to go up agin the law."

"Yeah, I *know* it," said Bucky.

"Oh, gracious! My beans is burning!" Mammy ran out of the room.

Lucius sat on Mammy's bed and looked at the show page. He looked
for the Majestic but couldn't find it. A mysterious theatre he'd not had
a chance to become familiar with. It had eluded him, slipped away before
he could ever willfully reach for it. He felt cheated and bereft. Resent-
ment that something had been there in Cherokee and gone before he
was born.

Mammy, passing the doorway, said, "Now, you all be careful how
you turn the pages, Lucius. I wouldn't take the world for them papers.
Bucky, want to lick the butterscotch pie bowl?"

Bucky ran out after Mammy. Lucius scanned the other headlines,
fascinated to know what was happening at the same time as the Abshire
killing, trying to focus himself at the age of two, living on Park. "Friends
Wonder If Doug and Mary Will Kiss, Make Up. Hitler Is Ready to Bury
Hatchet Against Vatican. Infantile Paralysis Situation Improves. Political
Dictator Huey Long Silent on Foe. Judge Clears Representative Arlington
of Prowling: Coeds Testify—Not Peeper." Except for noticing a cartoon
ridiculing Roosevelt, Lucius passed over the editorial page. "Evangelist
Jailed After Kidnapping Hoax. Cuba Scheme Nipped in Bud. Siamese
Twin Marries, Sister Not Upset. Batista's Troops Quell Plot on Govern-
ment. Washington's Shaft to Undergo Cleaning. Kentucky Farmer Slain
in Ambush."

Going back, reading all the news stories about the killing of Harl
Abshire, Lucius was amazed that Mammy had remembered so much, even
the things people actually said, amazed at how much she'd left out or
added. Leaving the papers spread out on the bed, Lucius felt more
satisfied with Mammy's version, and already the newspaper's effect on
him was fading.

After dinner, Bucky said, "Mammy, get out the pictures and stuff,
will you?"

Sitting between Lucius and Bucky on the davenport, Mammy went
through the old family pictures, regretting again the burnt condition

of some of them, promising again to take Bucky and Lucius to the mountains glimpsed in many of the shots.

Bucky found a Victory letter from Luke and began reading it out loud very slowly: ". . . and when I come home, Mom, I'm going to art school and learn how to be a cartoonist like—"

"Let *me* finish it," said Lucius. Bucky handed it to him. "—Bill Mauldin. You've seen his cartoons, haven't you? G.I. Joe. All I ask is that you have faith in me, Mom, and if you will, I know I can do anything. I've dreamed about this all during the war, and I've made up my mind. So please don't try to talk me out of it. Please understand that I am a big boy now, and when I come home I'll prove it to you and Hazel, too. I want you to be proud of me, Mom. Even if they send you a telegram that I'm missing, look for me to show up at the screen door. Well, that's all for now. We're moving out."

Lucius felt a pang of shame. He'd just had no feeling for the clarinet, and when he dropped it, Momma had gotten only half the money back on it. He started to cry.

"Honey, Luke was just reported missing. It ain't for certain. . . . I just know he'll come back. Why, one day we'll all be sitting at the dinner table, and sure 'nough, he'll slip in the house and scare the living daylights out of us all."

Bucky parked himself at the end of the davenport to listen to Gene Autry. Lucius went outside and sat in the cold circus-wagon coal house and looked at Luke's busted sled. Remembering its effect on Gale and them, he imagined getting "Helena Street" published in *The Saturday Evening Post.* He took the sled down off the wall and sat on it, inhaling the cold smell of coal dust. He demanded nothing of anyone in his family as a condition of love, but he felt guilty for the sadness each of them felt. To atone, he'd become a great writer and they'd share in his fame, his glory, his fortune.

> Sun. October 13, 1946. They come and got Earl. Mammy told about Harl again. It was good. Bijou dark. Wanted to work on "River of Lost Tribes," but promised Raine I'd take her to skating rink at the park.
> Mon. October 14, 1946. Notorius. Gale and Brady said they picked Della Snow up in the bus terminal.
> Tues. October 5, 1946. Notorius—one of he best of the year! Raine wrote me two notes. Thank you, God, for sending me Raine.

"Get these trucks moving. The Japs are just a few miles down the road," said Lucius.

Today was Lucius's turn to strut in Luke's combat boots. Harry was getting to where he acted as if he owned them, and the way he walked made them seem such a part of him that Lucius, putting them on later, felt as though he were wearing Harry's boots. Waiting for the Grand Boulevard streetcar, Lucius looked slowly around, holding his head up, just right, putting on one expression after another, not satisfied with any of them, self-conscious but enjoying the effect. " 'Desert Romance' by William De Cosgrove. Have you read 'Desert Romance' by William De Cosgrove?"

Everybody else still in school with two more classes to go, and Lucius was free—it was a good feeling. Riding the streetcar to the Crippled Children's Hospital, Lucius prayed again that he didn't have infantile paralysis. He finished a chapter in *God's Little Acre* and dreamed up part of a story about a movie projectionist in Chicago who wants to join the mob of a famous gangster, but the hood only uses him as a patsy in a revenge scheme.

Getting a drink at the fountain in the left wing of the Crippled Children's Hospital, Lucius saw a ward full of kids, lying in beds, some of them strung up. There ought to be something he could do for them. When he realized that soon he might be lying among them, he felt scared and nauseated. He wished Momma would hurry up and get there.

This time the pleasant nurse took Lucius into a classroom where desks for elementary kids and a few for kids his age were loaded with patients, the parents standing by, shifting from foot to foot. A short, heavy, but very pretty woman seemed to be the teacher. Clearing out a few of her things as medical examinations began, she explained to a mother that there was so little space even this classroom had to be used for examinations and checkups.

He enjoyed watching Dr. Summers talk with the children and their parents, but when he got annoyed with one of them, Lucius felt apprehensive, afraid he'd get angry because Momma wasn't there, and counted the people ahead of him, dreading his turn, but wanting to get it over.

A brace-bound, pretty girl sat trancelike across the aisle from Lucius in a tiny red chair.

"Do you know what happened to *her*?" Lucius asked the nurse who was realigning some desks.

"Well, since it was on the front page last spring, I guess it's okay. She jumped off the Sevier Street Bridge."

"How come?"

"She was going with this older boy and he got married on her. She was only in the ninth grade. She didn't walk out far enough so she didn't hit the water. The kudzu vines on the bank broke her fall a little." The nurse joined Dr. Summers and Dr. Koss, the tall, beautiful woman in white who looked like Ingrid Bergman.

Lucius wished he could help the girl. He would talk to God about her tonight. He realized that if she were well now, she wouldn't be there, someone interesting for him to think about. But he might end up like her himself with polio.

Lucius tried to hear Dr. Summers talking with the girl. "Well, now, I had hoped today, I'd get a smile out of you, my dear." He looked down at her, smiling, apprehensively, his hands crossed in front of him. She made no sound. "I said, I had—"

"I have no reason to smile."

"How about the mere fact that you're alive?"

"I didn't ask to be."

"Your legs are much more eager than *you* are to return to a normal life."

"I don't care if I never walk again. I told you that the *last* time. If I *could* walk, I would go right back to that bridge."

Her mother seemed bored by the conversation, even when the doctor looked at her now and then for some response or help.

"So many children, Dr. Koss, who want more than anything else in the world to walk," the doctor said to the tall, beautiful woman, shaking his head, sadly, "and this little lady wishes she were at the bottom of the Tennessee River. Legs that *may* mend, a heart that refuses to." Then he spoke to the girl. "And here's your mother, who loves you."

The girl looked Dr. Summers straight in the eye: *"Please shut up."*

Dr. Summers's face turned red, but showed that he knew she was right. He was talking nonsense to her because he knew nothing to say that would make sense. In a low voice, he gave more instructions to the nurse, then said, louder, "Return two weeks from today."

Dr. Summers stepped crisply over to Lucius. "Well, Lucius, how does the world look to *you?*"

"Pretty good, sir."

"Not in love, I hope."

"Yes, sir."

The girl turned and looked at Lucius, and he smiled, but she turned back around, and allowed her mother to help her get up off the little red chair.

"The X rays," said Dr. Summers, looking at them against the bright October light from the row of windows, "indicate no infantile paralysis. What you *do* have is clawfoot deformity."

"Where?" A lump in his throat, Lucius stared down at his dangling feet that looked perfectly normal.

"It's incipient. Lucky for you you sprained your ankle. . . . Tell me, what had you planned to do with yourself when you get out of high school?"

"I might not go to high school. Might hit the road before then."

"Hit the road?"

"Yeah, see the world, you know, go in the Merchant Marines or something."

"Yes, well, I meant, what do you want to *be?*"

"Oh, detective, I reckon. Private."

"Hard on the feet." Dr. Summers worked the joints in Lucius's toes and twisted his foot until he gasped. "What do you do when you're not spraining your ankle in the dark recesses of the Bijou?"

"Oh, I draw—and—write—stories."

"Write stories?"

"Yes, sir."

"And draw. Well, that's good. Very good. Keep that *up.*"

Something future, something ominous in Dr. Summers's voice made Lucius ask, "What's gonna happen, sir?"

"Well, this is an unusual deformity, Lucius, and we will just have to try a few things. Maybe we can control it. It's very early. Grip the floor with your toes, Lucius. . . . You see how your toes grip the floor? Also, notice how high your instep is, Lucius, and how wide your foot is."

"Momma always had trouble getting wide enough shoes, but my feet are little."

"Yes. . . . I thought, at first, it might be clubfoot."

"I've heard of clubfoot," said Lucius, thinking of Philip in *Of Human Bondage,* "but not clawfoot."

"I know it sounds awful, Lucius, but if you help us, perhaps we can make an operation unnecessary. We're lucky to catch it so soon. Now, I want you to go with Miss Reed and do as she says, and when we've finished making our rounds, Dr. Koss will tell you what you are to do."

"Thank you, sir. I really appreciate you helping me."

"Well, it's not every day we get to work on a clawfoot, so we're even."

Lucius was relieved that the doctor hadn't said anything sarcastic about Momma's absence.

Miss Reed took Lucius to a room down the hall, a gymnasium sort of place, a large tank in the middle.

"Put this on," she said, handing Lucius a pair of black fuzzy wool trunks. "Then wait for Dr. Koss." Surprised, Lucius watched her turn several valves and water rush into the tank.

Miss Reed went out, and Lucius took off his clothes and pulled on the trunks, then sat listening to the steam heat pound in the radiator. He wished Momma was there. Seeing iron lungs and oxygen tents, imagining contraptions he'd never seen, worried about needles and ether and wet dreams, Lucius talked with God.

But when Dr. Koss finally came in, Lucius was staring out the window at bare sycamore limbs, thinking about Earl and his strange, wandering life.

"You are ready?" For the first time, Lucius heard Dr. Koss speak— the accent sounded German.

"Yes, ma'am." Maybe she was an impostor. She reached over and with slender wiggling fingers tested the water in the tank. It *looked* like water, anyway. Maybe she was one of the women who helped run the concentration camp—on trial now in Nuremberg. He wanted to slip out the door behind her. But she turned, "Come," clapped her hands, "Get in!"

Lucius climbed steel steps and slipped over into the tank. The hot water made him catch his breath.

"Too hot? It must be as hot as you can stand it."

"That's about what it is."

Dr. Koss brought a rubber bag to the edge of the tank where he stood. "Sit." As he sat in the hot water, he wondered whether she'd try to shove the bag down over his head. The fuzzy itchy wool trunks were creeping down over his hips. He wished he'd tied the string tighter. She was taking ordinary marbles out of the bag, dropping them into the pool. "Make your feet go back and forth. Yes. Correct. Now. Turn over." As he turned over on his belly he held on to the trunks. "Now grip the edge of the pool with both hands." He did. "Now kick. . . . Hard. . . . Harder. . . . Harder. . . . Faster. . . . Yes. . . . Faster." When she stopped, her voice high, he quit, waited a second, and when she didn't give another order, rolled over—and saw the woolly trunks floating in the middle of the tank. Thrashing in the water, he squatted. "Don't be an idiot. I've seen naked boys before. Put on your trunks and stand up."

Lucius dog-paddled over to the trunks, pulled them on under the water, and stood up, tying them, tight.

"Now pick up the marbles with your toes."

She had a few more tricks up her starched sleeve, none of which seemed to Lucius the right way to deal with a clawfoot, but then he realized that he didn't have one yet.

"Out of the pool, child. Now. Each morning, this is what you must do. Listen carefully." Ingrid Bergman in *Spellbound* talking to her patient Gregory Peck—about his mind, not his feet. "As soon as you get out of bed, sit in the bathtub and run it full of cold water, *ice* cold, and as it fills up, swish your legs back and forth sideways. When it is full, turn over and kick! kick! kick! Do you understand? Good. Return next Wednesday and we will do the whirlpool treatment again. We have made a start."

Lucius pulled on his clothes, thinking that if she were a Nazi in disguise, they might track her down before next Wednesday, and he'd visit her in the Safety Building, or maybe they would put her in the county jail where Momma had located Earl. And Earl, especially if he discovered she was an ex-Hilter's child, would find a way to do it to her.

On the streetcar to the Bijou, Lucius continued reading *God's Little Acre*. His response to it was influenced by the place where he bought the book, its cover, the author's picture, and the decision of the court on charges of obscenity printed in the back, and by the fact that he'd started reading it on the throne backstage, continued it in school, except in American history because he didn't want to read a dirty book in Raine's presence, and waiting for streetcars, concealing it everywhere. Very slowly, absorbing each sentence, he was reading a novel for the first time, in the way and in the places where he'd sustained running reveries, spun stories of his own.

During supper break, he read it in the still room, on the high stool, under the 200-watt bulb. Gale came down, and then Brady, to read a few passages over his shoulder. He expected Bruce to come down, too, but hoped he wouldn't, afraid it would hurt his feelings to read about Ty Ty and Buck and them capturing the albino who was supposed to have some weird power to divine where gold was buried. "Send up a flare when you come to the fucking part," said Elmo from the stairwell, not even deigning to come down. Lucius sneered. There was much more, he'd discovered, to *God's Little Acre* than sex. Looking for the sex, he'd gotten seduced by the story. Still, he wondered whether he'd come to the part where Will licks Griselda's pussy. Maybe the rumors were lies.

> Wens. October 16, 1946. Notorious. Didn't go on the spot after supper, had to go up to the Negro gallery. I don't have infantile paralysis, just a touch of clawfoot deformity. Cary Grant again tomorrow in Night and Day.

> Thurs. October 17, 1946. Night and Day. Next Thursday is Alex Allison the Magician at the Bijou. Brady says Bijou has plays, too. All kinds of shows, not just movies and amature nights.

Jack stands by the window in the moonlight reading the letter. It's from Smitty, his old army buddy, who visited Jack's farm in Maine a few months before. Smitty vows his love for Cathy. Jack is certain now that Smitty made love to her. He puts the letter back in the bottom drawer under Cathy's slip where he found it the day before. Cathy is watching him from the bed. Jack stands over her a long time.

In the fishing village nearby next morning, Jack mails a letter to Smitty, pretending it's from Cathy.

A few nights later, Jack and Cathy climb the cliff from swimming in the ocean. At the top, he says, "Smitty's waiting for you in the fog. You can go to Smitty or stay with me. I'll wait here while you decide."

Hearing the inspiring melody of "Night and Day," Lucius smiled at the appropriateness. Cary Grant says, "It's yours, Linda. Without you, I could never have finished it." Although Lucius usually read the story of the movies in *Screen Romances* or pieced together from one source or another a sense of what a movie was about, it was pleasantly strange to see most movies now in fragments.

Cathy goes back to the farmhouse and lies on her bed, trying to decide what to do. She's pregnant by Jack. She knew about it even before Jack wrote to Smitty for the tenth time and finally persuaded him to come up from New York to visit them, but she hasn't told Jack. Smitty kissed her only once in the orchard. But she knows Jack's too jealous by nature to listen to her or to understand. She hears Jack calling to Smitty in the fog near the orchard. Cathy runs out of the house.

"If you ask me," said Bruce, coming up behind Lucius, his hot Listerine breath going full blast, "I think the Chinese Communists are going to run Chiang into a shack."

Lucius groaned. "Stop. Stop. It ain't funny."

"Naw, all joking aside, Lucius, I thought you'd like to know, they hung ten more in the prison gymnasium at Nuremberg. But guess what?"

"Doodley squat?"

"No, Hermann Goering cheated the hangman by swallowing poison two hours before he was due to hang."

"Yeah, I heard it on the radio backstage day before yesterday."

"Well, I get behind. We don't have no radio and the paperboy misses the porch half the time."

"I bet it's great living in a houseboat."

"We hate it. They won't *rent* to us."

"Who won't?"

"People all up and down the Mississippi and the Ohio River and the Tennessee. We float like Gypsies. We get run off by people when they get tired of staring at us." Us? Lucius hadn't realized that the whole family was albino. "They play jokes that end up hurting us. They cut the mooring ropes and we wake up on a foggy morning and we're out in the middle of whatever river it is, and it's lucky some oil or sand barge didn't cut us in two during the night. My daddy says sometimes he feels like shooting us all right between the eyes. How would *you* like to live on a houseboat?"

"You still like it better here than with all those cadavers at Randall's Funeral Home?"

"I ain't seen much difference so far."

Bruce walked back to his post on the left aisle, flicking his flashlight on and off.

Daddy came in, smiling, as though shyly aware he was lovable, but slightly conscious of the fact that not everybody around knew him. Here in the Bijou lobby with his boy, among other people, Freddy seemed to have the same half-apologetic, but basking look on his face as when Lucius walked through the bakery with him. Thelma said, in that sweet-sweet voice, "Freddy, tell Lucius to get a haircut." And then after Freddy sat down on the back row with his sack of peanuts, bought in the Negro business district along Crazy Creek, Lucius, standing apart now, felt the carry-over of the bakery feeling to the Bijou. Momma hardly ever came in, nor Mammy with the Chief, but it was good though embarrassing when they did, the atmosphere lurched, and the lobby was a dim boat, drifting in the middle of Cherokee.

Eager for a roast beef sandwich and mashed potatoes at Max's, Lucius went backstage to see what was keeping Gale. Nobody in the dressing rooms. Going back up front, he collided with somebody in the dark, dusty passageway behind the thick curtains that backed the two box seats. "Hood's looking for *you*."

"*Me?* Let him look for Gale."

"Hurry up, Elmo."

Brady with Elmo, and Lucius felt their excitement, rapid breathing and little jerky laughs. "What you all doing?" asked Lucius, jealous.

"Gale's got Della Snow at the stage door," said Brady.

"Aw, you're kidding."

"See for yourself."

Lucius followed Brady back up the three steps to stage level where Elmo opened the stage door, letting in grey light and cold air and Della, who wore a rough-textured green coat, Gale following her, wearing the flight jacket with sheep's wool lining that he bought at Army Surplus last Saturday. Elmo shut the door, leaving only the dim yellow stage light on them as they came down the ramp, Brady stepping forth to help her because she seemed surprised by the ramp and awkward.

"Where's Lucius?"

"He has to stay at his post a while longer, then he'll be back," said Elmo.

"Want to see what it looks like backstage?" asked Brady.

"Yeah, I'd *like* to see it backstage. His dressing room back here?"

As Elmo and Brady led Della back behind the curtains and the giant speaker, along the high brick wall, as if she were blind, Gale saw Lucius standing beside the front teaser, and skipped over to him. "Listen, I know I was supposed to relieve you about ten minutes ago, but we run into her at the bus terminal again and talked her into coming *with* us. Let us get her hot for you, and I'll be up in a few d'recklies. Okay, good buddy?"

"Yeah, okay."

On the Spot, Lucius saw the Bijou Boys train-fucking Della. Waiting, thinking, Just like 'em to play a trick on me, somehow. Do it to her and take her out before I can get back there. Hell, she promised me way last year I could have it someday. Gale had met her at the Union Bus Terminal last week where Earl used to pick up girls who weren't having luck picking up sailors and soldiers returning home from Europe and Asia. When he said he was a Bijou usher, Della had asked Gale if he knew Lucius Hutchfield, and that was how he got in good with her. She'd shown Gale a picture she carried in her wallet of Lucius sitting under the scrawny mimosa tree with Harry and Duke, playing blackjack. Lucius was surprised, and a little scared, to know she'd taken it on the sly. Gale had walked her to the building near the Market House where she lived. Odd to live uptown. Lucius didn't know anyone else who did.

Staring at the screen where Cole Porter is riding in a storm, very sad, trying to forget Linda, Lucius imagined Della's face, too dimly lighted to see backstage when she came in, and saw only a light sprinkling of pimples, but he knew she was pretty underneath the look of sin she had about her, and her figure was voluptuous, and her body and clothes had a faint odor of poverty and sin.

Suddenly, a spike of yellow light showed through the thick curtains over the entrance from the basement to the orchestra pit. Cole Porter rides fast. A tree falls. The horse rears, slips, falls on top of him. Lucius remembers Cary Grant as Devlin the secret agent, riding a horse with Ingrid Bergman past Claude Rains, a scheme to put Ingrid and Claude together. Cary all week, as two different men, in a Hitchcock suspense and then a movie biography. Cole Porter's legs are so crushed, they may have to be amputated.

Lucius turned toward the bright lobby and lidded his eyes. Cathy hears a shot. Someone falls off the cliff into the sea. She doesn't know whether it is Jack or Smitty. She runs to the garage. Old Luke, the foreman, is there. He advises her to go ahead and run away.

Weeks pass and Cathy is a waitress in a tavern in Portland, Maine. Luke comes in. He refuses to tell her which one of them is alive. For the baby's sake, she hopes it's Jack. But if he's dead, she can love only Jack's best friend, Smitty. She goes back. In the living room of the farmhouse, she sees smoke rising above Jack's chair. She cannot see who it is. Is it Jack or Smitty? "The End," whispered Lucius.

When Cole and Linda are reunited at the end of Night and Day, Lucius, hearing the theme song at his back, cups his hands over his mouth, saying, "One of the great motion pictures of the century, 'Souls Under Conflict' by William De Cosgrove, starring. . . ."

Gale in uniform, grinning, hiking his cods, scuffing his feet to work up a spark. Lucius dodged. "She's in the basement, Lightnin'. Brady and Elmo's getting it, but by the time you get out of uniform, you'll be next in line."

Lucius went backstage and was changing into street clothes when Brady came in, saying, "*Man,* o man! Was that good! Was that good! Man, o man!"

As Lucius was going down the narrow stairs, Elmo was coming up, grumbling, "Fuckin' rubber busted. Had to jack the hell off."

Cavey smell of the storage room, chills along his neck, imagining rats. Failing to find her in the still room nor in any of the fan rooms, Lucius panicked, thinking, as he had feared, that she was gone. Maybe they discovered the cave and she was in there. But he found a fan room he hadn't seen before, very cramped. A gigantic, silver-painted steel drum, humming, took up most of the sooty room. In a dark corner, Della Snow lay on some hairy tow sacks and posters on the cement floor. The room was hot and steamy and smelled of oil and hot wires and hot fan belts and burnt, grinding bearings. Looking down at her as she looked up at him in the beam of his flashlight, lying on her back, her dark winter coat flung back, her legs cocked up, a flowered summer dress pulled up over her white belly, Lucius felt the shadowy intricacy and secrecy of the basement, the coal pile, the heavy curtains to the orchestra pit, beyond which sat a theatre full of people, watching Cary Grant, as the picture started up again, explain to his mother why he must drop out of Yale: "Every time I pick up a lawbook, I hear a tune instead."

"Hello, Lucius," whispered Della. But he hadn't seen her face yet. How did he know she wasn't Raine, slipped in as a joke.

"Is that you, Della?" He lifted the beam to her face.

"Yes—finally."

Lucius took out the rubber Earl had left in his jacket at Mammy's, and slipped it on, the first he'd ever *used,* though he'd tried on several, getting hairs caught now, too, as he unrolled it over his prong. Feeling around in the dark, his hand touched her soft warm thigh. He knelt between her legs, one palm on her knee, like a porcelain doorknob. Startled, he felt her groping hand take hold of his peter, stroke it, guide it in. Shocked, scared, he felt her hairs—nothing but peach fuzz on the last girl he'd done it to, four years earlier. And shocked again when he felt how hot her pussy. Had it melted Elmo's rubber?

Della's breath smelled like pinto beans. Afraid now the rubber might break and he'd knock her up, and they'd put him in the electric chair—no, he'd learned that that was only if you raped them.

"I've always loved only you, Lucius," Della whispered in his ear, and hugged him so tightly just as he was about to say, "I love you, too," that he felt smothered, his nose and mouth mashed against her coat. "The bird of time," she said, "hath but a short while to flutter, and the bird is on the wing."

Fucking Della, Lucius knew he was defiling her as the other Bijou Boys did, but loving her while others reviled her, purified her again. Like going up front to be saved. To be washed in the blood of the lamb.

"Don't you have a sweetheart?"

"No."

"How many boys you done it with?"

"I don't know."

"You can't remember?"

"I can remember the boys, but I never counted 'em up."

"You like to do it?"

"Not *too* much."

"Then why you let 'em?"

"They won't come and see me, if I don't."

"When was the first time?"

"Bout nine years ago."

"How did it—I mean, how did the boy talk you into it?"

"It wasn't a boy—it was a man."

"Who?"

"My daddy."

Lucius rammed his fist against the steel drum. "I'd like to kill his goddam soul!"

"Don't say that, Lucius." Della turned loose of Lucius's hand.

"Honey, don't you know Jesus doesn't like for you to do it to boys?"

"Jesus?"

"Yeah. You don't *have* to do it with boys to have a friend. Think of Jesus when guys try to get you to do it. Read the Bible and pray. The world is a beautiful place, and you've got your whole life to live, and if you keep letting all these boys do it to you, it'll just ruin your whole life. You want to get married, don't you, and have kids?"

"Lucius, you think Jesus don't love me?"

"Yeah, he loves you, and he forgives you, but think of how much he *would* love you, if you just showed him how much *you* love *him?* Wouldn't that be wonderful? If Jesus is in your heart, you don't need guys that go with you just so they can do it to you."

"But *you* did it to me."

"I know, and I'm ashamed of it. You know what they call it, don't you?"

"What?"

"Being a whore. And—Listen, honey, promise Jesus you won't do it no more."

"Will you be my only sweetheart? Then *we* can do it."

"Did you like it when we did it?"

"If we could do it in a bed like we's married, I would."

Lucius hugged her. "Shut your eyes." Della put her arms around his waist. The top of her head fitted just under his chin. "Now pray with me."

"Okay."

"Dear Jesus. . . ."

"Dear Jesus. . . ."

"Please forgive me for committing fornication with all those boys, including Lucius. . . ."

"Please forgive me for committing fornication with all those boys, but I hope it was okay with Lucius."

"And I promise to be pure from now on and to walk with thee."

"And I promise to be pure from now on and to walk with thee."

Shining his flashlight, feeling silly, as if he were showing a patron to her seat, Lucius led Della out of the fan room, through the basement.

"Do you ever go to the library—the one uptown?"

"The one in that big old-timey plantationlike house?"

"Yeah."

"No, I don't care too much for books and stuff."

"Promise you'll come there sometime. I go there a lot. I live only a block from there. We can kiss in the stacks. Promise?"

"Okay."

Lucius led Della up the steps, took her hand, helped her walk, sore from fucking four boys, behind the curtains, behind the speaker, led her through the pitch dark to the stage door ramp and the weak yellow light, Errol Flynn in his flight jacket waving her on viciously, afraid Hood would catch them. Lucius handed her up to him, Della slipping on the ramp, busting her knee, as she reached for Gale's grasp, and Brady helped him shove her out into the freezing rain.

"You didn't have to shove her," said Lucius.

"A stiff prick hath no conscience," said Gale.

As Lucius passed Gale On the Spot, Daddy jumped up on the back row and bummed a dime off Lucius.

Run down by the physical and emotional stress of doing it to Della, Lucius, On the Spot, was so weak he could hardly whisper loudly enough to make himself heard as he told, then begged patrons to "step back out of the aisle."

Wade Bayliss, out of uniform, walked past Miss Atchley without a ticket, and every time Lucius came back up the aisle from seating patrons, he covertly sneered at Bayliss, who sat on the aisle seat on the back row. The post was between Lucius's head and Bayliss.

The fire marshal Lucius had seen at the Pioneer during wrestling matches across the street came in and was roaming around, and Lucius kept saying, "Step back out of the aisle, please, step back out of the aisle, please," the celluloid collar sticking to his flesh.

Suddenly, Bayliss's seat clapped against the half-wall, and Lucius saw him jump up, massive, step down in the aisle, and saying, "Didn't you hear the kid? *Step back out of the aisle!*" shove with his two enormous hands the whole tight pack of them back out into the bright main lobby. Then he sat down again.

Shyly, Lucius thanked him, mutely nicknamed him Samson.

"Merry Christmas, Cole Porter. You're crazy. You write beautiful music, and you're forgiven."

Lucius was eager to see again the part where Cole sits down in the middle of a bombed building in his uniform, his trench coat over his shoulders, and writes "Begin the Beguine" on the top of a keg.

Fri. October 18, 1946. Night and Day. Gale and them brought Della Snow backstage and we ——. She said she loved me. I felt sorry for her. Forgive me, Raine.

NIGHT RITUAL: Telling Bucky and Earl stories under the covers, all three in the same big bed on Avondale. About Buck Jones and Zorro and the Green Hornet and Straight-hair and Fatsi, who forget to put on their clothes in the morning and get on the streetcar and these old ladies say, "Eoow! Butts and dodos!" . . . Lucius runs to a neighbor's house and asks to use the phone to call a doctor. Baboo lies convulsed on the ironing board, a padded plank stretched between a chairback and the table, Lucius and Momma waiting for the doctor to come. Bucky sleeps peacefully in the boys' bedroom, Earl is in the Hiawassee alone, watching *Gunga Din.* The doctor bends over the ironing board under the kitchen light bulb, a siren coming nearer. "You're a smart boy," he tells Lucius, because he knew how to use the phone in an emergency. . . . A brown and yellow police car—"A tisket a tasket, a brown and yellow basket," they sang to passing patrol cars—pulls up in front of the house, that bright Sunday morning, and Momma goes out with Daddy's grey and black speckled bathrobe so he can get from the curb to the living room without the neighbors seeing that he has on only his shorts and a hangover. The cops found him under the Sevier Street viaduct, stripped of all but his shorts, into which he peed in fright as the muggers stripped him. Lucius runs back to the bedroom. He hears Momma crying. Hearing the creak of the door, Daddy looks up and the light from the many small high windows in the room where Lucius and Earl and Bucky sleep make the tears on his face glisten. Daddy is sitting on the edge of the bed in his undershirt and shorts, one skinny white arm around Momma's plump humped shoulders, she in her nightgown, crying, looking up, red-eyed, and says, "Baboo's dead." Daddy's big toes claw at the floor. Lucius sees again the Green Hornet force the gangster's car into the gas pumps, and Baboo dies in the explosion. "Lockjaw." The Green Hornet's mask, the hornet at his lips. Lucius sits on the bed, hugging Momma and she hugs him, and Bucky comes in and wedges between Daddy and Momma. "Why for you all cryin'?" "You wouldn't understand, honey," says Momma, hugging him, kissing his mouth. "Tastes like salt," says Bucky, licking his lips. Earl stands in the doorway, and Daddy waves him toward them, but he stands there, trying to look serious, trying not to laugh. . . . Baron, the bald-headed boy next door, laughs at Baboo's funeral. . . . Lucius sees Baron on the street next day and beats him up.

> Sat. October 19, 1946. Raine was at B. B. Club. She talked me into
> going to church with her tomorrow. Night and Day ended.

Sunday morning, at five thirty by the kitchen clock on top of the stove, Lucius woke and, halfway into his pants, remembered he wasn't carrying papers anymore. But drifting back to sleep, he realized that, in a sense, he would carry them forever.

Bells and bright sun woke Lucius later. Except for bells on a record pealing "Softly and Tenderly" over a loudspeaker from the belfry of the Second Baptist Church out over the neighborhood, and the cars going as slowly as a funeral cortege to church, nothing moved. The new pane beside his head felt warm to his palm.

Lucius fed the cookstove kindling and coal and splashed coal oil on it, and the explosion singed the hair on his arm. Wrapping a towel about his waist, he went across the hall to the bathroom, feeling as if Dr. Koss herself drove him to his morning therapy. He hooked the hall door, then the one to the landlady's kitchen, and got into the tub, ice-cold against his naked butt. Shivering, he pushed forward, flesh squeaking against the porcelain, and, his back touching the back of the tub, barked, "attt!" He reached his foot out and gripped the faucet handle as he'd gripped the marbles in the therapy vat, and cold water rushed into the tub, splashing his legs, spraying his balls. He squeaked, squalled, and huffed rheumily, remembering Mammy's tales about nuns forcing little girls into tubs of ice water.

Momma woke up bitching, making Bucky itch to get out.

"I'm going to Mammy's," he said, defiantly.

"No, you are not. The Chief's over there, and they need to be alone."

Bucky put all the chairs together in the hallway and played train.

Lucius put on his leather jacket, a scarf, and Luke's combat boots and went out to his sanctuary in the chicken house. Sitting in a shaft of warm light that came through where Bucky had tromped too hard on the roof, he began to write "Souls in Conflict."

"Lucius, you want to freeze your fanny off?" Momma stood in the doorway to his sanctuary, wearing her quilted housecoat, her hair helmeted down with glinting bobby pins.

"It's not too cold."

"Well, listen, honey, I promised Earl I'd visit him today at the juvenile, but Max was on such a rampage last night and I had to spend my lunch hour begging and pleading with people to help me get Earl *out* of that fix, to where I just am too sick and nervous to make it. *You* go, will you, honey, and take him some stuff? Tell him I'm comin' tomorrow anyway for the hearing."

"Okay. I'd like to see him anyway."

Momma pressed a fresh blue shirt and tan whipcord pants for Lucius, then attacked his forehead and cheeks with her fingernails to squeeze out blackheads and burst pimples, leaving his face a red moonscape, oil slick, while Bucky watched, giggling.

"After I come from Earl's, I'm gonna go to church with Loraine."

"Oh, Lucius, I wish you wouldn't go to those Pentecostal churches. She's a sweet little girl and I just love her, but I have a good friend who lives at the bottom of the ridge and she might see you go in."

"Momma, I don't *care* what other people think."

"That's okay for you, but I *do* care, and I'm telling you not to go over there. Why can't you take her to a decent church? I don't want you up on that end of Clayboe Ridge to begin with. Honey, they's people robbed and murdered up there every night."

Putting on his leather jacket, Lucius said, "Reckon I look nice enough to visit my brother in jail?"

"Talk like that and you won't be *able* to visit him. Lucius, what's got into you lately—sassin' your mother like that? You used to be the *sweetest* boy . . ."

"Skip it, Momma. I'm *going.*"

"No, forget it, just go on right now and waller on Clayboe Ridge and to hell with Earl. After all, he's *only* your brother. Lucius, if you roll your eyes like that just one more time, I'm going to smack you clean into next week."

"Momma, it's time for the streetcar. If I miss it, visiting hours'll be over."

"Get out! Get out of here and leave me alone!"

His legs wobbly, Lucius walked out on the porch into the chilly air and bright two o'clock sun. He heard the streetcar coming behind his house. Leaping off the porch, dashing across the yard, swinging on a limb that let him down on the walk, he ran after the streetcar, but it passed the stop. He chased it half a block, and gave up.

Lucius walked seven blocks over to Oak Ridge Highway. Standing across from Phelps' drugstore where he once got caught swiping a Tarzan funny book, he thumbed a ride to town.

As the car passed Old National Cemetery, he saw Daddy loping along toward town, looped on white lightnin'. Probably been up to Feisty Clayboe's and was walking back to his room in the L & N Hotel across from the depot. He waved but Daddy didn't see him.

A police car parked outside the gate, its motor running, made Lucius wonder whether Earl had already escaped. He was still too young to be kept more than a few nights in the jails uptown, but he'd already escaped from this place when he was ten. When Lucius stayed there, Earl was well remembered, and some said it was because of his escape they'd strung three strands of electric barbed wire along the top of the fence. For Lucius, all barbed wire was connected by a phantom circuit to the movies about German concentration camps, making the Juvenile the most forbidding place in Cherokee.

Lucius hesitated to push the buzzer at the gate, afraid it might be connected to the barbed wire and he'd get a shock, and they'd examine his pecker and discover he'd fucked a girl the day before and throw him into pitch dark solitary with corn bread and water.

Rolling up *Batman,* Lucius used it to press the black button—the ring was loud as an alarm clock. Quivering, his Alan Ladd jacket giving him little courage, Lucius stood at the steel gate, waiting a long time, imagining somebody walking down and around many corridors through many steel doors, unlocking and relocking, and when the guard saw Lucius he'd be angry.

A very fat man—Lucius thought of the fat armless, legless man Earl took care of in the carnival—came to the gate with a key ring over his wrist.

"What you want?" The fat man's voice was like a crabby old woman's.

"I come to see if I could see Earl Hutchfield."

"You his brother or something?" His voice and manner seemed to change.

"Yes, sir."

"Where you *get* such a mean brother?"

"I don't know." Such questions always seemed stagy, conjured up a cluster of associations, and he never knew what to reply.

The fat man opened the gate, that looked too narrow for *him,* and stepped aside to let Lucius through. When he locked it back, Lucius felt shut in.

Inside the building, the fat man took Lucius to a little schoolroom and told him to park himself at one of the tiny desks. He'd forgotten this room, where he'd gone to school for two weeks. It resembled the place at the Crippled Children's Hospital where Dr. Summers examined his clawfeet.

Earl came in, grinning, maybe sneering, a piece of adhesive tape stuck to his forehead, Lucius's gold-plated Elgin watch around his wrist.

"Hi, kid, how you doing?" He stopped grinning, but he didn't seem sad, only resigned, and low keyed.

"Momma and me sent you this stuff," said Lucius, handing him the white bag. Lucius felt guilty wearing the leather jacket, as if he were throwing it up to Earl that he'd swiped it off him.

Earl sat on the desktop, raised two feet above Lucius who stayed on the seat until he began to feel silly. Thinking of asking for his watch, Lucius stood up and looked down at Earl. Making conversation, he asked, "How'd you get cut?"

"Three pigfuckers tried to jump me in my cell last night and take your watch off my wrist. Bastards dropped it on that steel floor."

The watch had stopped at nine o'clock. "Goddam it, Earl!"

"Well, I *tried* to protect it for you. They near 'bout killed me, but I got it back, by God. Damn guard beat us *all* with a belt. They gonna pile his ass before they ship us to Nashville."

Scared, Lucius asked. "They sending you back to Nashville?"

"Looks like it. Be glad to ditch this town. Cherokee is the asshole of the world."

Kids who'd been there had told Lucius about the Reform School since he was seven. In *Crime School*, the Dead End Kids got locked up in such a place and Humphrey Bogart tried to reform them. Lucius wished Earl had listened to Bogart the reform school principal instead of Bogart the gangster in *Dead End*.

"Ain't you scared?"

Earl shrugged. "They caught me."

"You gonna try to break out again?"

"Not with that hot barbed wire out there." Then he grinned. "Course I got one angle that might work. Might just walk right out the gate, easy as you."

"How's that?"

Earl smirked and nodded his head and wrinkled his eyebrows, making Lucius feel left out of something special. "Know that fat guy that let you in here?"

"Yeah."

"Well, *watch it* when he goes to let you *out*."

"How come?" Earl leered and licked his fingertips and sleeked back his eyebrows. "Oh."

"If I make it, I'm heading for Uncle Hop's in Sante Fe and then on down into Me-hi-co." He smacked his lips the way he used to in grammar school, eating stolen pineapple from a can at the lunch table. "Hey, kid, who was that cute little gal I saw bending over you out on the sidewalk?"

"Which one?" Lucius didn't want to talk about Raine with Earl. Least reference to a girl, his tone dripped lechery.

"Angel tits."

"Oh, that was Peggy," said Lucius, knowing Earl meant Raine. "Say, Earl, did you really sell that man a cheap ring for a hundred dollars?"

"What do *you* think? Wouldn't *you* help a poor little kid get home to his mother's funeral? And ain't I a master con artist?" He started digging into the white bag. *"Batman?"*

"Thought you *liked* funny books."

"I outgrew Batman long time ago. Why'd you waste your money on *True Detective?"*

"Didn't you used to read 'em all the time?"

"If I did, I don't remember. Candy! I don't like sweet stuff." Earl used to have to help churn the homemade ice cream on Sundays in the summer but he hardly ever ate any because it hurt his teeth and gave him a headache. "I can *use* this candy, and the other junk, too, I reckon. Trade it off for cash."

"Where you spend it?"

"It's to get things done for me. How come no chew'n tabacca?"

"Didn't think they'd allow it."

Feeling guilty for wasting the cash on candy, Lucius gave him his last dollar. Earl took it without a word.

"Try winding the watch to see if it'll go," said Lucius, hinting to get it back.

"Naw, I tried it. Why didn't Momma or Daddy come?"

"Oh, Daddy's drunk and Momma's sick and in a bad mood."

"She drive *anybody* crazy."

"Watch how you talk about Momma, Earl."

"Okay, Momma's boy."

"Kiss my rusty."

They were quiet a long time, Earl smoking a cigarette butt he took from his shirt pocket. What Earl could get done for those fresh Philip Morrises was a mystery to Lucius.

"Momma tell you what the doctor said about my feet?"

"Well, kid, I better get back to my cell."

Hurt that Earl didn't care that he might have polio, Lucius said, "Yeah, I guess I better be going, too. If I don't see you before they send you to—" Lucius tried to keep from crying.

"Yeah, yeah, kid, okay. Send me some a that money you get from ushering each week. Okay? Promise?"

"Okay."

"And here, you mize well take your watch back." Earl held out his wrist for Lucius to slip it off.

Thinking Earl would want something to remember his brother by, Lucius said, "Naw, *you* keep it."

"What *I* want with it? Can't do *me* no good broke."

Pulling the watch off Earl's wrist, Lucius imagined the cops approaching the circus-wagon coal house, and Earl stepping out wearing the German iron helmet Daddy sent back from Brussels, barking, "Heil Hitler!" a coal dust stain under his nose, his hair combed down over his forehead, looking the spitting image of Adolf Hitler, Earl's hero.

Earl walked down the corridor ahead of Lucius and spoke to the fat man, and they laughed and pushed at each other in a theatrical way that made Lucius feel inferior. Coming out on the electric bus, Lucius had imagined the guards dragging Earl, crying and kicking, back to his cell. Lucius waved, but Earl walked away, swinging the white bag full of stuff in his hand, the neck twisted. The fat man shut the door on Earl and locked it, then led Lucius down the other end of the corridor.

Kids played on the swings out in the yard and in the sandbox, wearing mackinaws and leather helmets like fighter pilots, and the little girls just stood around, as the old women were doing. One of the old women looked at Lucius and he knew she recognized him. "How's little Bucky doing?"

"Fine."

"Well, you bring that child by here to see his old aunt Maud."

As Lucius stepped through the gate, the fat man patted him on the ass. Walking down the steep hill between the kudzu vines, his face was scalding hot with embarrassment and rage. At the electric bus stop, looking back, the sight of the building on the hill in the winter evening light so depressed him that he started walking.

Doing it to Della made Lucius want to be with Raine in church. He didn't feel guilty because of Raine—she was completely separate from that, and he had an urge now to experience that separateness. But fucking was sinful, and thinking of how guilty Della was—letting four boys in an hour do it to her—thinking of her burning in hell, made him feel sad, and as he climbed the steep gravel road up Clayboe Ridge in a buffeting wind, he asked God to forgive her and Jesus to make her into a good Christian. Maybe she'd turn into a missionary, and in his own wanderings over the world, he'd see her again in Africa.

Lucius saw the lights of Raine's house. The rusty water reservoir stood black against the sky. Out of commission since before Lucius was born, it had hovered over most of his childhood, and when he was little, a high school kid drowned in seven feet of rusty water on graduation night. A few years ago, Lucius had turned away from Sonny Hawn's dare, afraid to fail in front of the kids and spark ridicule, but climbed it early one Sunday morning at the end of his ridge route just to prove to himself he wasn't a coward.

The cars were roaring away, spewing dust and gravel into the wind. Harry and Peggy walked on toward Peggy's house and Raine spoke to Cora and Ruth, asking them not to tag along with her. "Why don't you cloud up and rain, Lolo?" yelled Cora, her red hair wild in the wind.

Lucius and Raine walked alone, under bare oaks that creaked in the wind like rafters.

Lennis in uniform slowed his highway patrol car alongside Lucius and Raine. "I ain't done nothing," said Lucius, kidding.

"And you better not, either," said Lennis, kidding the way Sonny used to just before he'd bloody Lucius's nose.

Lucius looked down in the valley where a passenger train's window lights flickered, passing over a viaduct.

"Wouldn't you love to be on that train," said Lucius, "going to Manhattan or Boothbay, Maine?"

"Ouuuuu, no, I'd be scared silly. I don't never want to go beyond Cherokee."

"What? Honey, think of the *world* out there—the places we could go."

"You mean run off together?"

"If we was married, we'd just go when we felt like it."

Loraine stopped and looked into Lucius's face. "Lucius, don't trifle with me. Don't say nothing about getting married, 'less you mean it." Raine kissed and hugged him hard. "I'll never love nobody but you, Lucius. You ain't like none of the boys I ever knowed."

"I hope not. I hate being like other people."

"Why?"

"Gives me the creeps. Most people all act the same, believe the same, and talk about stuff like the weather. I have thoughts—I always did—that makes other people think I'm crazy. Well, nobody else sits around and writes stories all day." He hoped she'd ask to read "Souls Under Conflict."

"That's what I know. You're the only boy I ever heard of that wrote even *one* story. You look funny when we're in Miss Cline's room and you're writin' them stories. Makes me feel funny, and I keep hopin' you'll look back at me."

"I want everything to be different—new. The same thing keeps happening over and over. One time when I was in the second grade living over on Avondale, I was walking home from school in the leaves in the gutter and I smelled leaves burning and I could smell a house nearby that'd burned down over the summer, and it come to me that I'd walked this way before, down this same street, in this same gutter, with the leaves and the smell of smoke, and it was like death— the smell—and I realized that I had to make every second of my life special and new and different. You know?"

"I reckon," she said, her heart not in it.

"I even feel different about religion."

"Lucius, you're Christian, ain't you?"

"Yeah, I reckon, but, it's got so I don't like to go to church no more—'cept with you—and worshipping by a schedule makes me sick, like it's wrong—against God." Lucius was aware that even though Raine went to church three or four times a week and had a ministry to sing and play the piano for Jesus, she didn't seem deeply affected. "Because see, I talk with God and Jesus and pray to them off and on every day all day long, and every night I go off to sleep talking with them, and I take long walks on my nights off, through all kinds of neighborhoods, just talking to God about life and what all I want to do when I grow up and about the way people act and stuff. If the spirit comes over me, wherever I happen to be, I pray, even if it's walking down the street."

"I never knowed anybody like *that* before. You talk different from Harry and the other boys I know."

"You like Harry?"

"He's okay."

"You sure talk about him often enough."

"Lucius, Harry is *Peggy's* sweetheart."

"Way you talk to him and look over at him sometimes, bet you wish he was *yours*."

"Listen, here, son, you want me to beat the everlastin' fire out of you?"

"No," said Lucius, laughing.

"Then hush that talk, or I *will*."

"How about Duke?"

Raine slugged him on the shoulder harder than Sonny Hawn did in the halls at Bonny Kate.

They reached the front of her house. It was two storeys and had once belonged to a rich man, but now it was a wreck, like the two pre-war trucks and three of the seven cars in the bald, rutted yard. He wished he could see inside, but Feisty Clayboe, afraid he might see something and tell, wouldn't allow him to come farther than the front steps. Lucius looked up into the giant oaks where the wind racketed and felt an aimless spirit thrashing inside him. He was alone in the world, and Raine was his only hope of keeping some contact with other people. She was more beautiful than Vivien Leigh, her face unblemished, and she loved him.

"When we getting married, Lucius?"

"You have to be fifteen even in Georgia, Whistle-britches."

"Two more years! I can't stand it that long. My Momma got married when she was fourteen. I wish we could get married this very night. I love you so much it's downright pitiful—I really in truly do."

Lucius hugged her and they leaned against an oak, lights coming from tall, bare windows up at her house, limbs falling in the wind, the sound of cars passing on Oak Ridge Highway echoing in the marble quarry by the creek. When he married her, they'd go away to Maine and live on a farm by the sea and while she plowed, like Betty Field in *The Southerner,* he'd sit under an oak and write.

"If you love me, Raine, love me always."

"I'd sweep all the streets to China for you."

They kissed until their mouths got sore, their lips chapped.

"You're too good for me, Raine."

"Don't say that, Lucius. You're the best thing God ever give me."

As Raine walked backward up the step, flagstoned walk to the high steps, waving, under the blowing trees, Lucius walked sideways down the gravel road, the lights of Cherokee below, until tall trees obscured the house, and he felt a pulsing ache in his chest, and, wishing he could fly with the wind, he began to run and leap, until gravel in his shoes slowed him down at Peck's store, at the intersection of the paved street where LaRue lived in the nice neighborhood.

Sun. October 20, 1946. Dark. Wrote on "Souls Under Conflict." Visited Earl as Juvenile. Went to Church with Raine. She said, "You're the best thing God ever gave me."

Hiya "Sweetheart,"

Maybe someday I'll get to say husband: I dreamed last night that we were married. A dadgummed dream. Of all the luck I have it. Honey, I'm not dreaming when I say "I love you." Popular boys just don't interest me. Why did you say I'm too good for you? Because you cuss sometimes? I hate for you to cuss, honey. I get so sick I could lay down & cry all night when I hear anybody shoot out one.

I'll get about two letters put down and there's somebody to look over my shoulder. Mind your own business, Cora. She gripes my goat.

Lucius, are you kidding me when ever you say you want to marry me? Honey, don't kid me. There's no doubt when you say you love me, though, because I'll always believe every word you say. Well, honey, we've got to do some more adjectives so I guess I'll go now.

I'm in the library now. My foot is about to kill me. Cora stuck half of a straight pen in it right before I came in here. You just now came up to the door. Cora said, "I have reference work to do." I said—there's *my* reference work.

When you said if you love me, Raine, love me always, it made a pain run all the way through me. And that proved I loved you more than God could even offer himself. You said only God knew how much you loved me. Well, I know it, too. I belong to you and you belong to me. God knows everything. Everything, honey. Everything.

Lucius, honey, when we were talking last night and kissing funny fillings ran all through me. Maybe that's the sign I love you. I'd sure give a million dollars to be standing under that oak tree with you right now.

These old crazy books. Here's one named *Boots and Saddles*. My gosh who cares about that may I ask?

I love you more than I loved anybody since I've ever been old enough to love a boy. Gosh ding I can't express it.

Loving you always,
Raine

P.S. A rattlesnake got in the chickens last night and woke up everybody on Clayboe Ridge. I hope it woke up Larue, too.

In every class, hearing hardly a word any of the teachers said, Lucius wrote, in a trance, undisturbed, except when Raine came into the library on a pass to pick up a book she didn't really want.

He stood On the Spot from 3:30 to 7:00, intensely absorbed in "Souls Under Conflict," while *Courage of Lassie* moved on the screen at his back.

After midnight, in his sanctuary, Lucius answered Raine's note.

Dear Raine,
Last night I was out with a very charming, beautiful young lady who helt my heart in her hand the whole time I was with her.

That —— of a Mr. Chadwick took your note away from me and tore it up. Everybody probably thought I was going to hit him, I looked at him so hard. He said he wouldn't read it and I said "You're damn right you won't read it." I told him it was none of his bisness and he said he'd have to do something about me. I said, "That's all right with me." I really gave him down the road, that made me so mad, I'm not over it yet. I thought about putting that trash can over his pointy head but I would've look like a fool after waiting so long, so I just hoped he'd get smart again so I could do it later, but he started reading a book called "The Midnight Ride of Paul Revere," and after lunch, the flat-footed, pickle nosed, B-B eyed, cabbage eared, weed haired, snagle toothed, son of a decaded string bean, asked me if the note was from my best girl. I said yes, of course.

I was supposed to hear Rubinoff second period with you all but they didn't tell the English class. His violin carried down the hall good though.

You said you would sweep all the roads from here to China for me. We'll sweep them together. If the bondage that keeps you and I together, loving each other intencely as we do, should ever be broken, I'd more than likely join the forein lejun.

When you said, last night, "Lucius, you're the most wonderful thing God ever gave to me," I couldn't seem to get it out of my head. By now you have become a part of my bewildered life and I cannot even imagine you apart from me.

I think of you my dearest, as a distant promise of beauty untouched by the world. Before I met you I was suffering from heartaches, yet I knew that I would find a real girl that I could love. It was terrible, waiting for you, Raine. But finding you was such great and wonderful miracle that anything I suffered seems only a small payment in return. My love for you is to me a beautiful thing and to lose it would smash my heart to smithereens.

I love you now and till the end of time,
        Lucius

He closed the *Screen Romances* that carried the story of *Love Letters* with Joseph Cotten and Jennifer Jones. He'd read it soon after Beverly bestowed her magazines and stills upon him, and one of the love letters struck him as the most beautiful he'd ever read. He adapted the passage into the last paragraph of his letter to Raine. Taking his diary out of the bottom drawer of his desk, he wrote:

Mon. October 21, 1946. Courage of Lassie. Alex Allison the Magician coming to Bijou Thursday.

When he left the chicken house and went into the kitchen, it was almost one A.M. As he lay next to Bucky, the cold windowpane rattled in the wind a few inches from his ear.

> Wens. October 23, 1946. Courage of Lassie. Whirl pool therapy. It snowed. "The Bird of Time hath but a short while to flutter—and the bird is on the wing."

> Thurs. October 24, 1946. Alex Allison the Magician's plane crashed in a tree top on Clayboe near the old water tower but he was really good at the Bijou. Wore a cast on his leg. He told a reporter: "The show must go on. I will appear tonight on the Bijou stage if I have to break the other leg getting into a taxi." Bucky went up on stage naturally. Dark Mirror was very good. I couldn't figure out which sister died. Maybe Lew Ayres ignorantly married the murderess at the end. Writing "Souls Under Conflict."

"How did he *do* it?" Bucky asked Lucius, as they were getting ready to go to school.

Impersonating Alex Allison, imitating his voice and gestures, Lucius reenacted some of the tricks and tried to hypnotize Bucky, sending him out into the backyard to pick a four-leaf clover. He came back in with a snowball that skittered on the cookstove.

"No, I mean how does he *really* do it?"

"Watch this," said Lucius, annoyed that he'd not convinced Bucky. Covertly sticking one of Bucky's crayons in his ear, Lucius showed him how to make it disappear.

"How'd you *do* it?"

Lucius pretended to scratch his ear. "Watch." He reached and plucked at Bucky's ear and opened his hand to show the green crayon rolling off his palm onto their cot.

The third time around, Bucky caught him, because he couldn't make it reappear. Stuck in ear wax. Lucius had to get Momma's tweezers, and while Bucky held a hand mirror beside his ear in front of the mantel mirror, Lucius dug the crayon out.

"Where's he gonna do it next?"

"Somebody said Atlanta. Why?"

In Kay Kilgore's art class, Lucius drew a picture of Alex walking out into the lobby of the Bijou, where Lucius himself stood in his usher's uniform. Behind him a display stand, a poster in the middle, four stills in each side panel, advertised a movie called "While the Sea Remains," starring Alan Ladd and Vivien Leigh, Coming Thurs., Fri., Sat. On the opposite side of the lobby, behind Alex, "Glory in a Sanctuary," starring Cornel Wilde and Hedy Lamarr, coming Mon., Tues., and Wed. Kay Kilgore, still looking like a flat-chested, skinny Jane Russell in mouring, suggested that Lucius find a more ordinary subject for his life sketches.

Fri. October 25, 1946. Dark Mirror. Nothing much happened. Daddy bummed a buck off me. Finished God's Little Acre by Erskine Caldwell—the first book I have ever read from start to finish. Wasn't just sex. The story got me. Loaned it to Gale. Promised Harry next.

Saturday at lunchtime, Lucius set out to see his daddy. Clancy was standing in front of the little Jasper Hotel next door to the Bijou, picking his teeth, watching the people go by, as he did every chance he got—maybe being in the projection booth so many hours alone reminded him of the German prison camp.

Resisting the temptation to stop off at the used book store, Lucius walked across Sevier Street Bridge to Hutchfield Bakery. After Chief Buckner declared, on one of his inspection tours before he got transferred to Oak Ridge, that the old bakery on Sevier was a firetrap, Uncle Lucius had moved it to South Cherokee on the bluffs.

Lucius liked the sight of the vast parking lot full of bread trucks, the multiple giant images of the Lone Ranger riding Silver on the sides, unseen on the radio. Visible only in comic strips and funny books, and blown up on bread trucks. His daddy had bummed a dollar off him the night before, coming into the lobby when there was a big Hold Out for *Dark Mirror,* promising to pay him back Saturday.

"Lucius, he comes sauntering in here with those big Clark Gable ears mashed down under that hat, and that shy grin and says, 'Aw, hell, Kitty, all I need's a few bucks,' and I give in," said Uncle Lucius's secretary. "Came in here bright and early this morning and swore up and down that he'd go to work today if I'd just give him a few dollars to get some breakfast so he could sober up. I'll tell you what's the truth, Lucius, I'm disgusted with your father, and if you find him, you can tell him I said so."

Kitty had been watching after Freddy as if he were her own brother or husband or father or lover ever since she went to work for Uncle Lucius when she was only seventeen.

The phone rang. "Okay, Lucius. Well, yes, I think they signed all ten copies. Okay." Lucius had not seen his uncle since he was very little. He felt dislocated, standing in the outer office of the president, who was his great-uncle, and yet not feeling free to go in and see him, having slept in the bed of his uncle on his mother's side. He'd met few of the rich Hutchfields, and never lain eyes on his grandparents. Only one photograph—of his grandmother, her face cut out to put in a locket that nobody could track down. Maybe Uncle Hop had it in Sante Fe. Lucius had never seen *him* in the flesh, either. All the poor Hutchfields, and Momma and Mammy, too, had worked in the bakery at different times.

"Lucius, I'm worried sick about your daddy," said Kitty. Younger than Lucius's mother, she was a pretty woman from the bluffs of South Cherokee who'd worked her way up in the world out of a family of twelve. Being with her in the flesh embarrassed him, because she was often in Lucius's fantasies. "He's much worse with that drinking than before he went into the army. I think he's brokenhearted that your mother threw him out. I watch over his money for him—dole it out a trickle at a time, so he'll have something to do him through the week, but he needs more than that. Lucius, you're the only one in the family who can help—since it looks like your mother's abandoned him to his weaknesses. He needs help.

"He's always been too dependent, Lucius. Ever since Freddy was a kid, your Uncle Lucius just forked over. Anything Freddy wants. . . . Well, don't you know that's bad for a kid who's lost his daddy and momma and's the baby of a big family and who's left to an older sister to raise? Spoiled rotten—for the rest of his life. To your uncle, Freddy is the exception to every bakery rule. No matter how often he lays out drunk under the L & N viaduct with the Clanton boys and others whose names I forget, Mr. Hutchfield will never fire him. But by now, being dependent must be part of Freddy's nature. He was probably perfectly happy in the army—before they scared him half to death overseas. Then when I try to watch after him, he gets mad and says the awfullest things about me—I mean when he's drunk. Sober, he's the sweetest man that ever walked the streets of Cherokee, ask anybody. We all love him around here.

"And now, I'll tell you something I've never told a living soul. Don't you ever repeat this, Lucius. When I first came to work here when I was only seventeen—fresh out of business college—I took one look at Freddy Hutchfield—that was before he walked into that ice cream parlor where your momma was dishing out sundaes—she'd just come back from living in St. Louis. . . . But then I noticed pretty quick how he hadn't the least spark of ambition, and I said, Kitty, if you want to throw your life away, there's one quick way to do it. So I became his sister, right quick, and sure enough, he hasn't changed one iota. Of course, I don't mean to speak against your mother, honey, but if she'd just go a little easier on him. . . ."

"Reckon *you* could talk to her about it?"

"Lucius, people tell me I got a nice head of red hair—Freddy can't keep his sticky hands *off* it—and I want to *keep* it."

Lucius looked for his daddy at the pastry-cutting tables. Ott, a young cutter who worked with Freddy, said, "Lucius, he's probably at one of these beer joints down by the bridge."

"Which one?"

"Let's go. I'll help you look for him—shave off my lunch hour a little."

They found Freddy in a booth in a rattly little joint that was about to collapse into the Tennessee River.

"Freddy."

"What, Ott?"

"Let's go home."

Freddy winked at Ott. "Now I *know* you're crazy."

"Well, I got to get back. See you later, if the pink elephants don't get in the way." As he went out, Ott said to the bartender, jacking his thumb back at Freddy. "Take care of him, will you?"

"If I don't, who will?"

Freddy looked up suddenly, bright tears in his eyes, as if seeing Lucius for the first time, "People always tryin' to help me. I've helped a lot of dyin' people in my time, son." He bent his head again. Suddenly, he looked up. "Lucius. . . . Lucius. . . . That's my uncle's name, too. . . . I ain't hardly even seen him since I got back. He don't walk through the bakery like he used to." Daddy reeked of beer and cinnamon. "Lucius, I tried to go back and get him, but they wouldn't let me. Orders. Yes, sir, fuck *you*, sir."

"Who, Daddy?"

"Should a run *over* 'im with my ambulance. Got it turned around to go back for him, but it was too late. Demolition blew the bridge." Lucius waited for Freddy to go on. He kept holding the empty bottle to his mouth, tossing back his head. "Eisenhower ordered one woman shot by the firing squad. You had to take orders. The captain gave me a direct order to hold one of her arms."

"Who's this, Daddy? The one on the bridge?"

"So what if she was a kraut? She was just a girl not much older'n you. She didn't know what we were doin' in that little village. She hated our guts. She'd lure the G.I.s into bed and when they was asleep, she'd strangle 'em with piano wire. Captain said, 'Hutchfield, grab her arm, stretch her out.' I thought he was kiddin', trying' to scare her into confessin' or something—like in the movies or something—and this other guy held her other arm, and we stretched her out against the wall, and I thought, What a dirty joke to play on a kid, and this sergeant opened up with a machine gun and cut her in half. I wasn't supposed to have nothin' to do with killin'. I was a medic. They had to pry my hand loose."

Without asking him for the dollar he owed him, Lucius left Daddy in the Bluff View Bar and walked back across the bridge to the Bijou.

For lunch, he bought a Fifth Avenue candy bar from Thelma.

"Hood's looking for you," said Elmo, trying to scare Lucius with his tone.

"What for?"

"I don't know. Better make it snappy."

Lucius knocked on Hood's office door, scared, wondering what he'd done wrong now, ready to promise again not to daydream On the Spot.

"Come in. . . . Hi, Lucius. . . . Listen, how'd you like to put in a little overtime?"

"Be okay."

"Quarter extra per hour. I want you all to paint this theatre between now and next Sunday. Start backstage and come right on out to the inner lobby. Professionals'll do most of the front and all the lobbies. But don't say yes 'less you mean to stick."

"I'd like to do it, sir. . . . What's it for?" Lucius thought maybe they were finally releasing Jane Russell in *The Outlaw*, premiering it in Cherokee.

"Don't you read the papers? City voted to let theatres open up on Sunday, and it starts *next* week."

Most of his life, Lucius had spent Sundays wishing theatres could be open, but the news that they would made him feel nervous and slightly nauseous. Going back to get into his uniform, Lucius saw Olivia de Havilland as Terry hang up the telephone, the background music roar suddenly, and the camera move in to show her name pin on her breast—Terry. Lew Ayres and the audience had thought he was talking with the good sister, Ruth. Lucius felt the fear running through the audience as it gasped—because now Terry is leaving to meet Lew, pretending to be Ruth, intending to kill him.

When Lucius went over to Max's for supper, sick on the candy bar, Momma told him that General Hospital had just called to inform her that Bucky was in the emergency room with a crayon in his ear about to rupture his eardrum.

"For God's sake, Lucius, what in the world was he doing with a crayon in his ear? They sent an ambulance to Emmett King's house. I'll bet that idiot stuck a crayon in poor little Bucky's ear, and when he tried to get it out, it just jammed in further and further. Honestly, I've come to the end of my rope with that boy."

Back On the Spot, Olivia at his back saying, "Look closely. Are you so sure you know whom you have kissed? Look closely," Lucius imagined Bucky in the tiny, low-ceilinged King house, showing Emmett magic tricks, imitating Lucius's imitation of Alex Allison, and somehow Earl was mixed up in it, as if Alex had learned all his tricks from him.

Sat. October 26, 1946. Dark Mirror. We started painting the dressing rooms. Some negro women come about 5 o'clock to clean up, polish the brass, dust the coming attractions stands, vaccuum the carpets, sweep out the theater. Momma used to warn us that negro women carry razors. Hobart Pickard, one eyed stud, is their boss. I love the way he acts. Me and Elmo took a cab to Clinch View. The sky through the kitchen window looked like Sunday mornings when I used to get up to carry papers. Bucky stuck a crayon in his ear and is in the hospital.

So tired he couldn't sleep, Lucius drifted into his nightly ritual: Momma sends Lucius to the store because Earl always loses the change—Lucius knows and Momma suspects he spends it on chewing tobacco—and Bucky's too little, so Lucius is always the one to go. . . . The boys call Earl "Big Chief Chew-Tabacca." He always has a wad in his mouth. Nobody else in the family chews. The boys push him around, bully him, call him names, but he takes it silently, never cries, just looks at them, quiet, as if to say, "There'll come a day." He won't fight back, but he doesn't seem to fear anything. . . . Lucius and Earl and two other boys sneak into the tall weeds behind L. T. Dobbs's, pulling Bucky's red wagon. Earl is the first to go in the secret way. It's broad daylight. They wash in Crazy Creek with Lifebuoy soap and sit on the bank eating potted ham and corned beef out of cans. . . . In a vacant lot on the hill in the hot sun, Earl beats up a tall skinny boy whose parents give him everything he wants, and Lucius helps him pour red dirt down his pants. . . . A red-clay path drops down the side of a little bakery set into a slope. Earl is always the first to slip down and come up with a Moon Pie from the boxes on the sidewalk.

About to go to sleep, Lucius wondered where Daddy was wandering, and went to sleep talking to God.

Sun. October 27, 1946. No streetcars were running yet, so had to walk, after only 1 hour of sleep. The stores were ghostly. The light grew brighter on the deserted streetcar tracks as I got closer to the Bijou. I walked straight down Sevier, down the middle of the tracks. We started painting again at eight o'clock. Bucky's out of the hospital, but he hasn't come home yet. He's okay now, but they said he may go deaf in one ear some day. Please, God. Hood turned us loose at supper time and Gale took me home with him over near Ephraim Lee Institute for orphans and problem kids and me and him and Brady and their cousin Lufton and Jane Cardin and Treva Ritter who live down the street played tackle football in the cemetery where Gran'paw Charlie and his momma's buried. Treva has thick, moist lips and you could see Treva's hairy —— when Lufton tackled her. She is dark as a gypsy. Jane told Gale that she likes me for a boyfriend. I reckon Treva's hot for Lufton.

Mon. October 28, 1946. Bucky still hasn't come home. The police are looking for him. Hood let me off the floor to paint with Gale. I got the last streetcar home. Had to wait a long time in the cold and then it came. Black Beauty. Got paint on Luke's combat boots.

Tues. October 29, 1946. They found Bucky on the stage of a theater in Atlanta where Alex Allison went. The cops put him on the bus and I met him at the Union Terminal. Black Beauty. Bought Screen Romances. Deception with Bette Davis looks good. And Jolson Story is in it, and the Razor's Edge by W. Somerset Maugham, with Tyrone Power and Gene Tierney on the cover. Leaning against the mailbox, front of the Venice, waiting for a streetcar, and this queer walked up to me and said, "You go out Bluff Street?" I didn't even look at him, I just said, "Get away from me you damned queer before I kick your teeth in." I wish I had hit him. He looked creepy and sinister, like a mad scientist, and talked with a blamed Yankee accent. Gale likes God's Little Acre that I loaned him.

As Lucius was drying off, Dr. Summers came into the therapy room. Lucius clapped the black woolly trunks over his pecker like a fig leaf. Dr. Koss came in a few moments later and stood behind the doctor.

Looking at Lucius's feet, Dr. Summers shook his head. Lucius felt a moment of panic, thinking Dr. Koss had deliberately fouled up his foot muscles. "Advise metatarsal bars for both feet and continue hydrotherapy," he said, to Miss Reed, the nice nurse, as she came skipping in. "Lucius, my boy," he said, in a stern but kindly voice, "Dr. Koss and I have studied your X rays more carefully and we feel we should begin immediately to supplement the hydrotherapy with metatarsal bars."

"What—what are metatarsal bars?"

Dr. Summers picked up Luke's boot and laid his finger across the sole as emphatically as if it were nailed. "Here, we place a thick piece of leather. This forces your foot, when you walk, to press down and exercise those incipiently deforming bones to function the way God meant them to. You see the odd way you're wearing down the heels of your boots—all to one side?"

"These friends of mine wear them, too."

"Nevertheless, you're the one with clawfeet. Your feet don't grip properly. And get rid of these oversize boots—they don't provide the proper support."

Lucius went by Max's to borrow some money from Momma until payday and at Thom McAn's bought some snazzy military shoes with a strap and a buckle on the side. They looked very streamlined and dramatic.

Then he took the prescription to the orthopedic shoe store behind the Cherokee National Bank. He sat in his sock feet awhile, surrounded by braces, crutches, high shoes for people with one leg shorter than the other, grim posturpedic shoes that looked like the Gay Nineties, and other weird contrivances. When he saw the strips of leather across the bottom of his brand-new shoes, he gulped, they looked hideous. When he stood up, he was a little taller. He didn't mind that, but as he walked along the street, he felt a stick under every step he took. He'd never resorted to taps such as Duke wore. Now, he was forced to wear these gadgets. Hobbling along, he felt like Philip in *Of Human Bondage* which was starting tomorrow at the Bijou in a new version.

Hood, Elmo loping along a little behind, both carrying sacks, went into the Cherokee National Bank. Lucius knew they did that each day, and again at night, but it was odd to *see* them do it, unseen himself.

A little more aware of books, now that he'd visited several bookstores and read his first book, Lucius responded more consciously as he approached Matthews's Bookstore. The windows displayed only new books with shiny covers, mostly Bibles and religious publications. He'd always passed it feeling it was one of those places that were too good for him. Even more than the public library in the marble mansion on the hill, Matthews's—the very name made him think of St. Matthew and the Bible—seemed beyond his world, and he'd never entered either place. But today, having moved among books, though secondhand, he paused to let the new books excite him: *The King's General,* Daphne du Maurier. Taylor Caldwell, *This Side of Innocence. The Roosevelt I Knew,* Frances Perkins, *The Egg and I,* Betty MacDonald. Frederic Wakeman, *The Hucksters. Peace of Mind,* Joshua Loth Liebman. Thomas B. Costain, *The Black Robe. I Chose Freedom,* Victor Kravchenko. *The Snake Pit,* Mary Jane Ward. *The Miracle of the Bells,* Russell Janney. Ernie Pyle, *Last Chapter.*

Even though he felt more unworthy than ever because of the conspicuous way the bars made him walk, his recognition of some of the author's names gave him enough familiarity with the world glimpsed through Matthews's window to urge him through the door.

New books—a whole store full—smelled very different from old ones. He felt more comfortable in River Bridge Store and liked its smell better, but Matthews's excited him because it offered a fresh angle of experience. The saleswomen were nicely dressed and almost as severe-looking as the school librarian, but he moved in awe and reverence among the tables. He saw no paperbacks. He was aware of but did not really look at racks of greeting cards and whole tables full of religious books and Bibles. Feeling the slick flesh of the new books and inhaling their aroma made him nervous, scared, and his heart pounded.

Many copies of each of the books in the window were stacked on tables. A few others caught his attention: *Ulysses S. Grant* made him sneer, and another called simply *Ulysses* made him wonder what justified two books on Grant.

He wondered what the row of books called Viking Portables meant. *The Portable Dorothy Parker, The Portable Hemingway, The Portable Mark Twain, The Portable Thomas Wolfe.* He liked the name. He pulled Thomas Wolfe out and gazed at the cover. Mustard yellow, dark green, mostly bold white lettering. And a bold drawing of a man with wild long hair, a massive forehead, deep, dark eyes, a strange mouth, sensitive but strong—a thin upper lip, a thick lower lip, and a cleft chin. "Episodes from Wolfe's four great novels. . . . integrated into a continuous work which tells the story of his life." Was it just what they call a biography? No, novel meant made up. *"Look Homeward, Angel,* early life in the South." Lucius was glad Wolfe was southern. *"Of Time and the River.* Adventures at Harvard, in Manhattan, London, Paris." The titles were wonderful, making him feel jealous and possessive. *"The Web and the Rock.* Success; the life of wealth and culture in New York. *You Can't Go Home Again,* Retreat to Brooklyn; return home." This was the story in brief outline of Lucius's own life, as he intended to live it. *"The Story of a Novel,* complete and 6 complete short stories. Selected, arranged, and introduced by Maxwell Geismar." Why didn't Thomas Wolfe select the stuff himself? Lucius looked at the spine. "The Story of His Life. . . . From His 4 Great Novels. . . . With Other Writings and Stories."

Trembling, Lucius put the book back and moved among the other tables, aware that one of the salesladies was hovering close enough to swoop down on him if he made one false move. As if every move were false, he felt guilty. Thomas Wolfe. The name rang on an anvil. He tried to see the titles in his imagination. He wanted to look at the book again, more lucidly, but deliberately saved it for the end of his look around: Gore Vidal, *Williwaw.* Eudora Welty, *Delta Wedding.* Howard Fast, *The American.* James T. Farrell, *Bernard Clare.* Ann Petry, *The Street.* Erich Maria Remarque, *Arch of Triumph.*

Near time to go to the Bijou, hurting to piss, Lucius eased back to Thomas Wolfe. The longer he contemplated it, the more deeply the green cover moved him. He was overwhelmed with awe of the man's dark, granite looks, and of the titles listed, like deeds chiseled on a monument, on the front. The book felt sensual in his hand. Almost guiltily, as if picking fruit before it was ripe, he read the titles of the stories: *From Death to Morning,* "The Face of the War," "Only the Dead Know Brooklyn," "Dark in the Forest, Strange as Time," "Circus at Dawn," "In the Park." *The Hills Beyond,* "Chickamauga," the name of a street in Cherokee. "Only the Dead Know Brooklyn"—the title made him feel as if background music as in a movie preview was suddenly swelling.

He wanted to save even the introduction, but his eyes fell on ". . . since he was so tall, he wrote, standing, upon the top of his icebox door days on end, adding up episodes of 50,000 words each. Or how he filed his manuscripts in huge wood packing cases—that is, when he was not recording the endless flow of his reveries in those huge accounting ledgers: ledgers that contained every impression of his lived and remembered experience, and packing cases that contained every ledger he had ever compiled." Lucius, too, had kept everything he wrote, and he wrote in a chicken house. But never about anything that really happened, much less his own life. Seemed strange, to write fiction about your own life. He felt a compulsion only to create other worlds and people. How could you make up, tell a story about something that really happened?

Two dollars. A lot of money. But he had it. He could buy it now. The book belonged to him already. But he was so strongly attracted to him, Thomas Wolfe seemed too remote, unattainable, beyond the power of two bucks and somehow the desire to own the book seemed disrespectful of Wolfe. Feeling a living presence at his back, Lucius turned.

"Are your hands clean?" asked the old lady who'd been circling the tables, zeroing in on him now.

Lucius reflexively put Wolfe down and showed his hands, dirty from used book stores, sweaty from Thomas Wolfe's impact.

"Look at that! You've stained the nice new cover of this brand-new book."

"Sorry." Lucius turned and walked out. But he paused on the sidewalk in front to demonstrate his innocence. He had not stolen anything. That time he was caught stealing a Tarzan funny book made him walk wobbly-legged across the threshold of stores where he'd only been looking at stuff. He limped off toward the Bijou, intoning, " 'Only the Dead Know Brooklyn' by Thomas Wolfe," wondering what his real name was. Warner Brothers music. " 'Souls Under Conflict' by William De Cosgrove, alias Lucius Hutchfield."

Lucius came in out of the bright sun and the theatre was pitch black until an atomic bomb lit up the screen, filled the theatre with blinding light. "Bikini Atoll," the godlike voice of Reed Hadley on *The March of Time* said, as foaming atomic mushrooms glared in his eyes, making him anticipate the brassy smell of his flashlight.

Wens. October 30, 1946. I can pick up all the marbles with my toes in whirlpool therapy. Had to get bars put on my new shoes. We moved the dressing room upstairs but it was too cold. Bruce got off to paint. Glad Black Beauty is over. I hate those boresome classics. But I love to look at Evelyn Ankers.

Thurs. October 31, 1946. Halloween. Raine gave me a picture of her it was a big one. Painted on my day off. Mr. Hood's mother dyed so we didn't paint the floor of his office. Elmo went home with his cousin. Of Human Bondage, Eleanor Parker and Paul Henreid. Not as good as the old timey one with Bette Davis and Leslie Howard.

Fri. November 1, 1946. Painted till 3 a. m. Me and Elmo took a taxi. Of Human Bondage.

Sat. November 2, 1946. Bugs Bunny Club was good. Raine sang "Heart-aches" to me, my favorite. Swept and painted until seven o'clock this morning—Sunday. We got dirty and lazy and grouchy. We went over to Max's and ate breakfast.

Stepping down from the streetcar and entering the Bijou at two o'clock, Lucius was a sinner unsure which sin he was committing. Something indecent about the sight of Minetta majestically walking out to the ticket booth, Hood following her, carrying the cashbox. All his life, Sunday was the day you had to go to church and were denied the show. The day you read the colored comics. The day the streetcars ran an hour apart. In *The Reader's Digest* he'd read once that if you wash your horse in the streets of Cherokee on Sunday you'll go to jail. Everybody walked and talked on Sunday the way they did when Roosevelt died. The Hiawassee was always as blank dead Sunday afternoons as when he passed at five A.M. on his way to pick up his papers.

Lucius was surprised to find himself the only usher. On the Spot. He'd expected a full force, as on Saturday nights when they had the biggest holdouts. But Hood was so certain the audience would be light, he told Thelma to tear tickets at the candy counter.

Two hours after the churches closed theirs, the Bijou opened its doors for the first time on Sunday. Lucius and the first customer, a man in a mended overcoat, about fifty, the kind who sat in hotel lobbies listening to "Amos 'n' Andy," were very shy with each other, as Lucius showed him a seat, as if ushering him into the waiting room of a cat-house.

Daddy came loping in, looking like Clark Gable with his big ears, lopsided grin, one eyebrow crinkled, his hat in one hand, a bag of popcorn warmed over from Saturday night in the other. "Kinda spooky, ain't it, Bub?"

Piped down from the projection booth through the speaker behind the screen and the closed gold curtains, Dick Haymes singing "The Girl That I Marry."

Everybody walked and talked very softly, guiltily, as if moving in a shameful dream, from which each knew he would awake separately, so his public shame was low-keyed. Lucius resented the sparse turnout. He'd expected people to flock to the theatres to make up for all the Sundays they'd missed.

> Sun. November 3, 1946. Bijou opened on Sunday. Painted till early this morning. Slept from seven till twelve, then had to go to work at two. Hood had to wake me up On the Spot at nine. Let me come on home. Raine called. She said it was a sin to go to the show on Sunday. Sister Kenny.

> Mon. November 4, 1946. Momma went to Juvenile Court with Earl. Earl pleaded his own case, and lost. The judge sent him back to the reform school in Nashville for one year. Sister Kenny.

Proud of his contribution to the brand-new look of the freshly painted theatre, Lucius touched the gold on the stuccolike wall as he passed. A little came off on his fingertips. He waved to Gale, who was On the Spot, and to avoid running into Hood, who might put him to work before time to relieve Gale, he entered the inner lobby by the left door.

Sister Kenny in army nurse uniform tends to Dean Jagger, the captain who loves her. Wounded in the leg.

Wade Baylis's bull-like back leaned over the balustrade the way Hood's leaned on the other end of the lobby. But Wade seemed to be talking to somebody sitting on the back row. The leather belts around his waist and over his left shoulder shone in the light from the main lobby, and the way he stood made the butt of his pistol stick out dramatically. Lucius felt an impulse to slip up, stick his finger in Wade's fleshy hip and say, "Stick 'em up, Copper," but didn't, afraid Wade might show his temperamental side. Thinking of jerking the pistol out of Wade's holster was pure fantasy. "Hi, Mr. Baylis." He paid Lucius no attention.

Lucius sat in the middle section on the back row, eager to see part of *Sister Kenny* again. Glancing at it yesterday had been like a fitful dream. Sister Kenny is talking to her old friend Dr. MacDonnell, Alexander Knox, whom Lucius can't forget as President Wilson in the movie biography. She's back from the war, still in khaki, wearing the wide black Australian hat. She wants to quit nursing and marry Dean Jagger, who has waited for years already, but Dr. MacDonnell shows her the newspaper: POLIO EPIDEMIC IN TOWNSVILLE.

"He gave me down the road last night!" a loud, woman's voice, slightly familiar, made Lucius turn, look across the aisle to see who was sitting directly beneath Wade's chin as he leaned over the balustrade. His eyes not fully accustomed to the dark of the theatre and the silver light from the screen, all Lucius saw was the dim shape of a woman wearing a hat. Attendance was usually light this time of day but that nobody else was in the theatre was odd. "Called me everything but a human!"

"Well, you needn't broadcast it!"

"I don't *give* a rat's ass!" she said, out loud. Maybe she'd run off the rest of the patrons. Lucius wished she'd shut up, but afraid of Wade, he didn't tell her to hush.

Sister Kenny has a new clinic going. Rosalind Russell is very beautiful, but the real Sister Kenny looked ugly in her pictures, like Mrs. Fraker in the principal's office at Bonny Kate. Dr. Koss was beautiful, too, but nothing like Rosalind Russell, the way she talked to crippled kids. Sister Kenny tells Dean Jagger, "I don't think I'll *ever* be finished." She doesn't want to waste his life, too. But he vows he'll wait. Then they close her clinic, as they'd done before the war. Lucius liked the first time better—when the doctors took the kids to hospitals and walked past all the crutches and braces Sister Kenny had thrown away. Seeing parallels between his Crippled Children's Hospital and Sister Kenny's, Lucius settled deliciously into his seat.

A racket made him look over and see the woman getting up, Wade gone. When she stepped down from the slight elevation onto the red carpet and the light from the main lobby struck her, Lucius recognized her as the woman whose arm Wade was bending that rainy night under the marquee, and who turned up again on the Smoky stage, showing her pussy, Violet Lombard.

Lucius's favorite part was coming up—where Sister Kenny goes to confront her enemy, the famous authority on infantile paralysis who ridiculed her methods and got her clinics closed. But he wanted a better look at Violet Lombard.

As he reached the doors to the main lobby, a scream made him freeze. Then he whirled to look at the screen. Sister Kenny stands in the balcony of a medical auditorium, listening to Dr. Brack lecture to a large audience of doctors against her methods. Lucius remembered no such scream in the movie. For a moment, he thought somebody was clowning in the main lobby. He stepped out there, saw Violet Lombard crawling under the rope chain and sign that forbade people to sit in the balcony, and as she climbed the carpeted steps on her hands and knees, clutching her pocketbook, her shaggy fur coat making her look like a bear, her red hat flashing out like the leaves of a lush plant, an Orange Crush delivery man rushed at her. Followed her right up the stairs and out of sight.

Lucius ran up the opposite stairway and caught sight of Violet and the man as they emerged into the balcony. The light from the screen was dim. The medical audience laughs at Sister Kenny as Dr. Brack ridicules her. Someone banged frantically on the steel door to the projection booth. A man sitting on the front row, his feet cocked up on the brass railing, illegally, smoking a cigarette, looked back at the racket. Across the theatre from Lucius, stood the Orange Crush man, pointing up toward the projection booth.

A shaft of bright light shot out of the booth over the backs of the seats, casting rounded shadows of the seats and the shadow of Violet Lombard's hat. Suddenly, fire spurted, out of the man's finger, it seemed, and the roar of a gunshot in the empty balcony deafened Lucius as he dropped down on his belly. Violet rolled down the steps into Lucius's view, and the steel door to the booth slammed, making her a dark bulk in the aisle at the feet of the man in the Orange Crush uniform. Without a sound, the man looked down at Violet, blue smoke drifting from his hand up into the flickering shifting shaft of light from the projection booth window. From Lucius's angle of vision, the Orange Crush man looked like a giant. "You are no longer a nurse," says Dr. Brack.

"Drop the gun, Lombard!" Lucius recognized Wade's booming voice, but couldn't see him.

On his belly in front of the fire escape doors, about to jump up and escape through them, Lucius heard the pistol clatter on the buffed linoleum floor. Suddenly, the houselight went on, and Lucius blinked at the stark sight of the man and Violet.

As Wade walked up to the man, his pistol aimed at his back, his face looked strange. When he saw Lucius, his expression changed instantly, startled, then angry. "What the fuck *you* doing there?"

"Nothing," said Lucius, getting up, brushing the grime off the front of his leather jacket.

"Then get the fuck *out* of here!"

Lucius jumped up and clomped down the stairs. Hood, Minetta, Thelma, Miss Atchley, Gale, and Bruce stood at the foot of the steps.

"What happened?"

"He murdered her," said Lucius, and began to cry.

Wade trounced the man down the stairs and told Hood to call the station, but three cops ran in just as he was dialing. They took the man out, handcuffed.

The ambulance came. As the men carried Violet out, Lucius saw her bright red dress under the coat, thought of the last scene of Dillinger where the mysterious woman in red points out Dillinger as he ambles, in disguise, out of the Biograph Theatre in Chicago where Clark Gable had just walked to the electric chair in *Manhattan Melodrama*. Except that the movie was black and white and you had to imagine the red dress. Lucius couldn't see whether Violet was still breathing. He wanted to tell them to put a mirror up to her mouth.

Wade stayed behind to take names.

"Lucius Hutchfield. What happened, Mr. Baylis? Was that her husband?"

"Shut up. You'll be subpoenaed to appear at his trial." Baylis gave him a stern look, as if Lucius had been involved himself.

Hearing the background music for *Sister Kenny* swell, sensing the emptiness of the theatre, Lucius went back into the auditorium. The lights bled Rosalind Russell's face, but he listened to her disappointed voice as one investigative committee after another, in London and America, rejected her, and as the crippled children, gathered on the lawn outside her window, began to sing "Happy Birthday, Sister Kenny," Lucius cried again, for Sister Kenny, and for Violet Lombard. Gale turned the lights on again as the show ended, and Lucius prayed for Violet's life.

> Wens. November 6, 1946. A man shot Violet Lombard in the balcony of the Bijou. Wade Bayliss was talking to her. Sister Kenny ends today. Whirlpool therapy. Hedy Lamarr in Strange Woman tomarrow. Writing "The Trail to Maine."

"Don-ald," said Mrs. Rogers through the ajar bathroom door, "I told you what my answer was."

"But, m*other*," said Duke, standing in the living room, leaning against the doorjamb, talking across the freshly mopped linoleum of the kitchen. "We just want to go uptown to the Venice and come straight back."

"The answer is no." Her voice was strict, cold, distant, but not hateful. Leaning against the other side of the doorjamb, Lucius imagined Duke's mother standing in the bathroom—or maybe sitting on the toilet—in her slip. Duke aimed a submachine gun at the bathroom and, quietly making an ut-ut-ut noise, riddled the door with bullets.

"Beg her, Lucius." Lucius often persuaded Duke's mother to let him out of the house.

"Mrs. Rogers?" Lucius watched the door open, hoping she'd present herself naked. She wore a starched white, red-striped nurse's aide uniform. Raising her arms, she began to pick the bobby pins from her hair. The expanse of green linoleum, gleaming with rubbed wax and the light over the sink in the bathroom, separated them. "I sure wish you'd let Duke go *with* me. It's my day off and I don't hardly ever get to see him." Whenever Lucius ran into him uptown, Duke had slipped out of the house.

"I'm sorry, Lucius, we just can't let Donald run loose whenever he gets the notion." She was always very polite and sweet, but the tone of her voice suggested something withheld.

"Please, ma'am, just this one time," said Duke.

"If it's not this, it's something else, Donald. Now you know what your father said last night, and he made you repeat it three times to make sure it sunk in."

"We'll be careful, Mrs. Rogers," said Lucius, alluding to the fear of accidents she'd expressed in earlier wrangles.

"So many things could happen." She was looking in the mirror over the sink, combing out her curls. She wasn't pretty, but a little sexy. Duke had sucked her titties when he was a baby.

"One of these days they'll be sorry," whispered Duke to himself. Like when Aunt Polly thought Tom Sawyer had drowned?

"Don't talk back, young man." She didn't seem to have really heard what he said.

"Could he go if we stop by Mr. Rogers' corner and let him know we're all right?" asked Lucius.

"Lord, no, he'd fly into a fit if you distracted him while he's directing traffic. It's like his religion. No, you all can just find something to do around the house."

When Mrs. Rogers went out the front door, Duke bent each one of her bobby pins out of shape. "Just because I once had this nervous condition . . . It's like being sentenced to life imprisonment." Then he bent each pin back to its proper shape again. "They look right to you?"

"Yeah."

When they hit the street in front of Duke's house at the foot of Clayboe Ridge, Duke took command by sheer velocity, verbosity, and nervous energy, and by Lucius's willingness to act as straight man to his lies and postures, gestures and poses, stances and plunges. Lucius, continually fascinated, wondering what next, responded to Duke's every nuance and word.

Uptown, they made the rounds, hitting all the places that set off Duke's conception of himself most glamorously. Up one side and down the other of Market Square, past the stores—Duke showing he looked old enough to buy Trojan rubbers in a little hole-in-the-wall tobacco store—and the Ritz and the Jewel and the vegetable and flower trucks lining the curbs. And through the enormous cave of the Market House, up one side and down the other. Lucius had to argue to make Duke stop long enough for him to buy some good ol' country butter with an eagle imprint, made by a wooden mold the lady, her hand stained from shelling walnuts, showed him, letting him touch and smell Mammy's origins in the mountains. But Duke said he wouldn't walk with Lucius if he bought a big mayonnaise jar of fresh-churned buttermilk to carry back home. Lucius put the butter in his jacket pocket.

Past the Smoky on the next street over. They avoided the corner in front of the Tivoli where Duke's father directed traffic. They ate a sundae and french fries in Walgreen's and, making a flourishing show of looking for, failing to find, a friend, left without paying. Up and down Sevier Street, Duke striking up sparks with the steel taps Lucius had permitted him to put on Luke's combat boots, since Lucius couldn't wear them anymore without the metatarsal bars. Wearing his leather jacket with Duke's white silky scarf, Lucius had trouble keeping pace because of the leather bars on his military shoes.

They entered the Union Bus Terminal through a grey concrete facade that looked like Pharaoh's Tomb, down a wide arcade past many little shops, to the waiting lobby, a regular stop, where Duke loved to check all the pay phone booths for left-behind-in-a-hurry nickels and dimes and quarters, where they sat, doors open, hands on the brass handles, smoking cigarettes, blowing the smoke out of the half-dark toward the first of the pewlike waiting benches, as if posing for cameras, then stood beside bus drivers and passengers making a rest stop en route to Chattanooga, Miami, Atlanta, New York at the row of reeking urinals. Cheek to cheek, they sat in a booth, staring into the lens, grinning into blinding flashes of light, and got four sepia-toned photos from the dispenser outside, then, whooping over the sight of themselves, strutted downstairs, outside, walked among buses, motors running, Lucius noticing the newspapers, rolled and wired, he used to steal and sell, then back up to the waiting room and swaggered back down the arcade toward the giant *Messenger* Milk Fund bottle on the curb outside, beyond which, on across the street, the lights of the Hollywood told that Sunset Carson in *Red River Renegades* was showing, when suddenly, Duke veered right, into Gamble's department store, and Lucius, disgusted by this dashing move meant to throw him off his own stride, almost kept walking, but bored, sneering, decided to follow.

"Let's go, Duke. They ain't nothing in here."

"Gobble a goot, Shit-hook."

"I ain't following you around, Duke."

"Just take a minute, then we'll go watch Sunset Carson plug a few." Duke stopped at a counter full of necklaces. "If you was Peggy, which one would you beg for?"

"You ain't got the money for *none* of 'em."

"Who needs money? Watch *me* and you'll loin something," said Duke, imitating Leo Gorcey in the Bowery Boys. "Anybody lookin'?"

"Yeah, the whole damn town of Cherokee. Knock it off, Duke, you ain't gonna steal nothing."

"What can I *do* for you all?" asked a snooty clerk as she turned to them, finished with a lady customer.

"I want to take a look at that bracelet on the other side of the counter." When the woman turned, Lucius turned to the next counter, embarrassed. "Looks lousy. I'll come back when the building boins or something."

Lucius felt a jab in his side, and turned to follow Duke, his hands in his jacket pockets, the mold of cool butter riding in one palm. Outside Gamble's, in the arcade, just as Duke broke into a dance of triumph, a voice behind them said, "May I see the receipt for that necklace, please?"

"She didn't give me none. What necklace?"

"The one in your coat pocket. Fork it over."

"It belongs to my girl."

"Come with me."

"I'll sue for false arrest."

The man took Duke's arm and reached for Lucius's. "I'm coming."

The floorwalker, a tall, skinny, young man, with the looks of a tough kid from River Street but wearing a suit and tie, took Duke and Lucius to a small basement room, cluttered with stacks of boxes and papers and office equipment. Heat poured in through a duct in the ceiling. He locked the door. Trembling, Duke sat down. Lucius was more angry at Duke for getting him into this fix than scared of the floorwalker, who seemed to ignore him anyway.

"I didn't invite you to sit down."

Duke jumped up, as if afraid sitting had added to his crime. The man held out his palm and wiggled his fingers. Duke took out the fake diamond necklace and let it dribble into the man's hand. "Sit down." Duke sat. "Not you, him." Duke got up and Lucius sat, and the man went behind the desk and sat, and leaned back in the swivel chair, locked his hands behind his head, and braced the soles of his feet against the desk, with an air of posing. "So you think you're smart, huh?"

"No, sir, I—"

"Shut up."

"Yes, sir."

"What's your name, Squirt?"

"Uh, uh, Harry Marcum."

"He's my own brother, you ain't *him*." Lucius knew he was bluffing. "Fork over your real name."

"Donald."

"The ass end of it."

"My parents don't claim me, so I picked a new name. Hughes."

"After Howard? I don't see Jane Russell. You steal it for her?"

"Yeah." Duke laughed, to be buddies with the guy.

"That's it, laugh. Have your last laugh, Squirt."

Lucius looked up at Duke, tall and skinny, looming over himself and the man.

"Ever been caught before?"

"No, sir."

"Smart guy, huh? Sit over there."

Duke looked at the boxes of typing paper in the only other chair. He picked them up and sat and held them on his lap.

"Gonna steal them, too, huh?" Duke started to put them on the floor. "Keep 'em on your lap. What else you stold in here?"

"Nothing, sir. . . . I was just borrowin' it. I was gonna bring it back, mister."

"You were *what?* What's the matter with you? Where's your old man work?"

"I don't know. He never told me."

Lucius listened to the man's voice, looking at him through his jacked-up legs. He wore a ruptured duck pin in his lapel.

"I ain't never seen one like you *before*."

"I didn't mean to steal it, sir."

"If I believed you, that'd make two idiots in this one room and your buddy would be Einstein."

"I was gonna bring it back."

"Aw, hell, Duke, why don't you cut it out?" said Lucius. "He caught you red-handed. Own up to it. No use lyin' to him."

"You run around with this lame-brain?"

"Yes, sir."

"You ever rogue anything in here?"

"Yes, sir."

"When was it?"

"Last time was 'bout four years ago. I turned Christian."

"Ever get caught?"

"No, sir."

"What's wrong with your buddy here?"

"I don't know."

"Who dropped a rose?" Lucius and Duke looked at each other. The man's nose was crinkled. "Ort to send you to Nashville just for *that*. Stand up." Duke stood up and set the boxes on the chair and scrambled awkwardly to keep the stack from tipping but the top box fell. Lucius picked it up and made a neat stack. The room was hot and somebody had farted and fear made Duke's breath stink.

"Empty your pockets on the desk."

Duke put the contents of his pockets on the desk and the man let his feet hit the floor and leaned across and picked over Duke's belongings. "Come over here." Duke did as he was told. The man frisked him. "What's that?"

"Nothing."

"Feels like it. Fork it over." Duke tossed the gold-foil-packaged Trojan onto the pile. "Rapist, huh? We're gonna give you the electric chair for that."

Smelling Duke's feet in Luke's boots, Lucius looked up. A tear gleamed in the bright light on Duke's cheek.

"Let's see, what's that number at headquarters." The man dialed. Lucius wondered why he was acting. What was he *really* going to do?

"Please, mister," said Duke, crying. "Don't turn me in, sir. I promise I'll be good. I'll never do it again. I'll go to church on Sunday. Please. . . ."

Lucius felt a hard lump in his throat.

"Line's busy. What's that, Squirt? Gonna confess now?"

"Yes, sir, I did it, and I'm sorry. I'm sorry," he cried, through gritted teeth.

"Okay, now what's the number at your house?"

Someone knocked at the door. "Come in." He got up and unlocked and opened it. A pretty blond stood outside, holding her pocketbook.

"Ready for supper, Bill?"

"I'll meet you at the Market House, same place, honey." She smiled and nodded and turned to go. The man closed the door. "What's the number?"

"I don't know it, sir. Never learned it."

"What?" He stared dirty at Duke.

"Seven–six thousand."

The man started dialing, stopped, flabbergasted. "Mind telling me how long you lived there?"

"Oh, all my life, I reckon."

"All your life. Born in a cell, huh? Who's your mother? Sergeant McNally, maybe?"

"Huh?"

"You're the lousiest liar I ever run into, I ain't *never* seen 'em as dumb as *you* are. That's the fuckin' police station! And that's what I'm gonna dial right now." He dialed. "Busy. . . . Okay, look, seems how you're such a lame-brain, such a lousy thieving liar, I'm gonna break down and let you go."

"Gosh bum, mister, thanks a lot."

"Because you're bound to get caught again, and I only hope the next guy is meaner'n snake shit. Only one thing, and that is—your friend here has to promise to coldcock you every time you pop off one of your stupid lies. I'm paroling him in your custody, Kilroy."

"Yes, sir," said Lucius. "I promise he won't ever do it again."

"Okay, pick up your stuff. 'Cept this. Come back and claim it when you can raise a hard." He put the Trojan in his own wallet.

"But *that's* stealing, too, sir" was on the tip of Lucius's tongue. He left it there. "Thanks a lot for letting us go, mister."

"Yeah, thanks, sir. I'll pray for you at church this Sunday."

"Thank your buddy here. If he'd been as lousy of a liar as you, I would've sent you up for life." He unlocked the door and let them out.

"Who's your favorite movie star, sir?" Lucius asked, guessing Zachary Scott.

"Woody the Woodpecker."

As soon as Duke's feet hit the arcade again, he broke into his gyrating walk. "That shit hook! How'd you like that act I put on? Cut the mudduhfugguh's nuts out! Better not catch him out after dark."

"I ain't in the mood for that crap, Duke."

"He thought I was really crying."

"I'll be seeing you, Duke." Lucius turned out of the arcade and walked toward the Tivoli.

"He better keep lookin' behind him, by God."

"I'm going down to the Bijou," said Lucius. "See you later, Duke."

But Duke ignored him, talked a blue streak of threats all the way down Sevier to the Bijou.

"I got to see Hood," said Lucius.

Relieved to be rid of Duke, Lucius scraped his feet to work up electricity and was about to spark Gale, who was watching Hedy Lamarr On the Spot, when he heard Duke's taps on the tile floor of the main lobby. He was handing Miss Atchley a ticket. Lucius kept moving on backstage.

When he slipped his hand into his pocket to touch the mold of butter wrapped in the waxed paper, it was mushy. He plopped it into the toilet and flushed it into the Tennessee River, and imagined Duke sitting out front watching Hedy Lamarr in *Strange Woman*, still muttering threats.

Thurs. November 7, 1946. The man hanged himself in the city jail with his own belt. He was her husband. Violet Lombard didn't die. Doctor said she could dance again before spring. They caught Duke stealing in Gamble's. Strange Woman—good ol show. I love Hedy Lamarr. Writing "Trail to Maine."

Prince Karl kisses Belita good-bye and leaves her in the Duke's garden. In the moonlight by a waterfall deep in the Norse woods, the Prince's white horse grazes. The prince takes his outfit from the saddlebags and rides off, wearing his Black Lash mask. When a coach comes along the road, carrying a shipment of gold to Count Olaf's castle, the Black Lash holds it up. Suddenly, a whip lashes out of the darkness and jerks his guns from his hands. Belita, dressed up to look like the Black Lash, deepens her voice and commands the coach to continue. Belita rides away and the Black Lash chases after her.

Somebody slugged Lucius's shoulder, knocking him off balance against the lockers set in the wall. Two kids accidentally walked on his notebook—Raine + Lucius on the cover—before he could snatch it up. Looking down the hall, he saw Sonny Hawn glancing back, grinning, as if mildly amused at the spectacle of somebody lying flat on his ass.

Lucius ran after Sonny and slugged him on the shoulder as hard as he could.

Turning, Sonny pointed at Lucius. "I'll see *you* in the parking lot, after school, and you better *be* there."

Blood boiling in Lucius's brainpan made him walk almost drunkenly to art class. He was too angry and afraid to answer Kay Kilgore when she said, "Lucius, you're as white as a ghost. What's wrong?"

To keep from imagining the scene after school in the bicycle parking lot, he drew the Black Lash. He was afraid not to show up. The idea of Sonny Hawn hunting Lucius down, not knowing when or where he might appear, suddenly around the corner of the Market House, out of a little patch of jungle, cocked back in one of the little round-backed chairs backstage, the ushers' uniforms hanging behind him, terrified him more than showing up in the lot and getting the inevitable over with.

Lucius hoped Duke wouldn't be watching. Maybe he could get Duke to help him pile Sonny. But no, Duke was not the same person today as he was yesterday. He couldn't count Duke's descriptions of fights he'd won, with no help from Lucius, but had Lucius ever seen him in a fight?

He thought he might ask Harry to help him, but if he was afraid to, Harry might tell Raine, and the whole gang of them, including Duke, would show up to see the fight. So Lucius told no one.

In English, Lucius projected the fight through his imagination over and over, wearing the faces of Alan Ladd, Cagney, Bogart, Ladd, Paul Muni, Clark Gable, Ladd. Insistently, lucid images of Lucius himself getting mauled, dragged, kicked, slugged, stomped, picked up and thrown down, interrupted his fantasies of victory. He started listing all the movies he'd seen in his life, and all the movie stars he could think of.

In the cafeteria, his lip curled at the sight of steamed wienies and sauerkraut. Covertly, he glanced out the window, through the iron mesh, at the winter light in the bicycle lot that sat between two wings of the building, closed at this end by the cafeteria. The killing ground.

The bicycles—last year, his own blue Western Flyer leaned there, awaiting his foot, to go pick up papers—looked conspiratorial, as if Lucius
would move among them as an alien in Sonny Hawn's world.

Recurrent images of Sonny's past meanness interrupted the persistent image of slaughter. When they lived in the same block on Beech
Street, Sonny's house was the nastiest—dog squat in the grassless yard
and on the rotten front and back porches. Flies swarmed in thick black
clouds. Black tar paper covered the slanting, leaking roof where the
summer sun blazed, and red tar paper covered the walls. Rain formed
pools of warm water under the house, built low on the ground in a
sunken area, and spread around it and seeped up through the floor.

One time at twilight, Lucius was sitting under an Indian cigar tree
with the Brummett sisters and their brother, when Sonny came across
the street, saying, "Hey, Lucius, come here!" Lucius didn't move, suspect-
ing a trick. "I got something to show you." Lucius went over to him.
"Look at my hand." Fist, turned palm up. Lucius stepped back. "Naw,
look, I want to show you something. It won't bite you." Lucius sensed
that Sonny was really trying to be friendly, going out of his way to
single Lucius out. Maybe he was sorry for knocking him off his green
trike that made him feel like the Green Hornet. A new, good, feeling,
this sudden change—Sonny being friendly. Lucius looked. "Closeter. It
might get away fore you can see it." Lucius imagined a butterfly, but
hoped it wasn't crushed in Sonny's hand. He put his nose almost touching Sonny's fist. Then Sonny opened his hand and quickly put his head
down as if surprised to find it empty, and Lucius was about to say, "Ah,"
in sympathy for Sonny's loss of his butterfly, when he heard "shooosh,"
and a cloud of pepper flew into Lucius's eyes and nose.

The more he thought about this and other scenes, re-creating his
moods of hurt and shame and fear and vulnerability, the angrier he felt
over the injustice of a boy two years older than he treating him as if
he could do anything he wanted to him and get away with it.

Lucius felt a slight chill, smelled cold wind on skin and hair, and
mustard on somebody's breath at his ear, "Hey, Lucius, somebody told
me you fucked Loraine Clayboe in the elbow." Even before he saw the
face, not recognizing the sneering voice, Lucius whirled around, his fist
flying, and socked Sonny Hawn square in the mouth.

Before Sonny could get up, Mr. Chadwick stood between Lucius
and Sonny, slapping his palm with a ruler. "What started this?"

Lucius's heart pounded so hard he couldn't speak.

Mr. Chadwick coached basketball and football, but taught math
and English instead of gym classes. The army rejected him, and people
said it broke his spirit, and everybody loved him because he put on an
act of being meaner'n a pregnant rattlesnake, but most of the women

could stare and snarl more viciously than he. As he talked to them, he
hitched his cods, and if he was outside, spat off to the side through his
teeth.

Harry walked up, unwrapping an ice cream sandwich. "What started
this?"

"Said—some—thing nasty towards—Raine."

"I better not *ever* catch you saying nothing against *Peggy*," said
Harry, bending over in front of Chadwick, pointing his ice cream sandwich at Sonny.

"Peggy *who?*"

"That's all right *who*."

In study hall, Lucius was still trembling, enraged over the fight
that was over, still scared of the fight to come, when he heard, "Hummm!"
looked up, and Raine was past him, looking ahead in her class's lunch
line that was filing through, her hands behind her back, holding her
notebook, a sheet of paper braced against it, MY HEART ACHES FOR YOU,
printed on it.

By the time school was out, all kinds of kids were coming up to
Lucius, asking him if he was going to fight Sonny Hawn over Raine.
At three o'clock sharp by Lucius's repaired Elgin, he almost rushed to
the parking lot, afraid Sonny would be more ferocious if kept waiting.
But Lucius was eager, too.

Boys were taking off on their bicycles, some with stylistic flourishes,
others with bored matter-of-factness. Lucius did not wave back to the
boys from the old paper corner. He had to concentrate on finding Sonny
in the moil of bodies rising up on pedals suddenly, settling down on
seats raised rakishly high. When he didn't see Sonny, he had a moment
of panic, afraid he'd come, looked for Lucius, then gone, and he'd have
to worry for days, wondering when and where Sonny would jump him.

But the longer he stood there in the cold wind, wearing brand-new
leather gloves, folded back once at the wrist, exposing a little rabbit's
fur, his leather jacket collar up, his black corduroy trousers, his red
turtleneck polo, Luke's combat boots that he'd made Duke swap for
Lucius's military strap shoes, the more his Alan Ladd image hardened
and shimmered.

Lucius was disturbed to see the Clayboe Ridge gang come out the
door near the cafeteria windows, Duke hobbling behind them, Lucius's
shoes too tight.

"We'll help you put him back together again," said Harry, grinning
like a gopher.

Down on the concrete walk with two other boys, Sonny was walking
right past Lucius, as if not seeing him. He touched the handlebar grips
of his bicycle.

"Hey, Sonny!" Lucius used his Alan Ladd voice. Sonny looked up, not surprised to see Lucius, but as if he only half-remembered. "You said for me to meet you."

"That's *right*, Shit-hook!" Sonny let go his handlebars and walked toward Lucius. His looks didn't stimulate the terror Lucius had been feeling all day.

Encased in leather, Lucius waited for Sonny, who wore only a black and white fuzzy mackinaw, no gloves, ordinary shoes, to reach him.

"I don't want to hurt you, fart-blossom, so listen," said Sonny, softly, trying not to be heard by the frieze of girls and boys behind Lucius. "I'm gonna play like I'm beating the piss out of you, and you just yell and scream all you want to, hear? And then take off running, okay?" Lucius just looked at him. "I hate to beat your ass, see. I'll give you three to run." Lucius stared hard at Sonny, "You ready?"

"Are *you?*"

"What you mean?"

"I'm giving *you* three to run."

"Ha! You all hear that?"

"If you didn't," said Lucius. "I'll say it again. I'm giving him three to run. One."

"One!" yelled Sonny. "Two!"

"Three!" said Lucius, and hit Sonny in the mouth.

Sonny fell back against a bicycle that knocked over three more. Lucius let him get up, feeling like Errol Flynn in *Gentleman Jim*. But it was Sonny who seemed to know how to make the gestures and movements of a boxer. Lucius was afraid he was secretly a member of the Golden Gloves. He looked a lot like Billy Conn. That made Lucius Joe Louis.

"Cut the dancing, Hawn!" said Duke.

"Shut up, Duke!" said Lucius.

"Yeah, shut up, Duke!" said Sonny. "Hey, look up there at that blimp!" yelled Sonny, stopping suddenly, looking up, pointing. Lucius hit him in the stomach. "Hey, no fair!" Sonny abandoned his boxing performance and ploughed into Lucius, swinging wildly. Lucius was glad they were down on the gravel, wrestling. "Hey, be careful of my arm," said Sonny, as Lucius twisted it behind his back, "I broke it in my childhood."

"Then you give up?"

"Hell, yeah!"

Lucius stood up and stepped back. The sight of blood from Sonny's nose made him sick.

"You won, Lucius. Shake."

"I ain't forgot that pepper."

"What pepper?" The look on Sonny's face convinced Lucius he really *had* forgotten, so he put out his gloved hand and they shook.

Sonny rode off on his bicycle, jacked-up seat jammed into his tail.

Lucius enjoyed Raine's and Harry's and Duke's and Joy's and Peggy's and even Cora's praise as they started to walk over the two steep hills to Peck's, where the streetcar turned around. He was glad when Raine said, "We're gonna cut through the woods, you all."

They stopped under a sycamore tree and smooched until their mouths hurt and the raw air chapped their lips, and they had to keep blowing their noses.

Fri. November 8, 1946. Beat up Sonny Hawn for talking nasty about Raine. Sprung my wrist, so I bought a leather wrist guard today. Looks great. Wish I had me a black eye patch. Going to get me a corncob pipe like General MacArthur smokes. Strange Woman.

Sat. November 9, 1946. Raine played Clear da Loon on the piano at BBC, and won the prize again. We ate together in the Market House. Strange Woman ended today.

Sun. November 10, 1946. Canyon Passage with Dana Andrews and Susan Hayward. Dan Miller came to see Mother. He has a new yellow convertible. He took her to see Norris Dam. Me and the boys went over to the Pioneer to look up some girl's dress through the grille in the sidewalk. Betty Rankin was at the show but I didn't talk to her. I should go to bed. I shall. Goodnight. I have gone.

"Hey, Lightnin'," said Gale, pulling the curtain on *Canyon Passage*. "Reckon I could get you to work in my place tomorrow? All that sawin' on fiddles makes my ass crave cold buttermilk."

"What fiddles?"

"It's the symphony tomorrow. *Canyon Passage* ends at seven."

"Say, didn't they use to have it over at the Pioneer?"

"Yeah, till the wrestling matches stunk it up. Ain't even fit for wrestling anymore. Condemning the damn place."

"Aw, they wouldn't do that."

"*Do* it, hell. Didn't you see the signs they nailed up today? Condemned by City Ord'nance." Lucius's frowning stare and open mouth made Gale say, "I ain't birdin' you."

As if he'd felt the balcony of the Pioneer give under his feet, Lucius was dizzy. "I can't believe it."

"You *better* believe it. Boarded up. Arrest your ass if you even go in the lobby."

"I don't see how they could do it to such a old theatre."

"What do *you* care? That thing's old as the fuckin' Tennessee River, 'bout near."

"Maybe they'll condemn the fuckin' Tennessee River."

"Listen, dammit, you gonna work for me?"

"I ain't too crazy 'bout symphony music myself."

"Who *is?* Brady and Elmo turned me down and Hood won't let the albino. You don't have to *listen* to it. Hood just likes you to stand by, in case they *need* you for something. Then when it starts, you can hide in the still room."

Or sit behind the rusty iron door and rig up a table and a candle in the cave and write some of "The Black Lash" to the symphony background music. "Okay."

Mon. November 11, 1946. *Canyon Passage.* A good day. I pray for God's blessing.

At seven o'clock the next night, Lucius pulled the curtain on *Canyon Passage.*

In his brown two-toned sports coat, wearing one of Luke's bow ties, his military buckled shoes shined, Lucius helped Spit and Pete shove the black speaker on its rollers back against the brick wall. Strange to watch the screen ascend into the loft on sandbagged pulleys. Gale hadn't told Lucius that Pete and Spit would be ordering him around, putting him to hard work, clearing the stage. "What we clearing the *stage* for?"

"For the music," said Spit.

What the hell was going on? He was eager to see how an orchestra would look in the orchestra pit.

As they worked, he noticed some men wearing heavy coats, scarves, and hats coming in the stage door, carrying big cases containing their instruments, like gangsters concealing machine guns. "Fuckin' sissies," he muttered.

"Lucius." He jumped at Hood's voice, sudden, behind him, on the stage, where he'd never seen him. "Stay by the stage door and keep out anybody who isn't with the orchestra, and sort of help out if somebody asks you."

"Yes, sir." He walked away from Spit and Pete, glad to be free of their grouchy commands.

Asking people without instruments if they were with the orchestra and helping the ladies down the dim ramp, Lucius felt important. He was surprised to see women in the orchestra. Some were old battle-axes, but a few were tall, good-looking girls of about high school age. He helped a blond girl and a white-haired man scoot a large trunk like a mummy case down the ramp. "What's in *here?*"

"A harp," said the girl, a lovely voice.

"Ohhhhh," said Lucius, impressed, thinking of Harpo's serious moments.

Spit and Pete were setting up thin, black, spiky, steel music stands on the stage. Lucius glanced into the pit. It was dark.

Up in the lobby, some pretty girls in evening dresses, wearing corsages, held armfuls of programs. Nobody had come in yet, though.

"Hood said for you to put out the sign." Spit pointed at a fancy, colorful standee with sparkles on it, and a picture of Victor Savage. He carried it up the aisle and out into the main lobby and Hood told him to set it out front in the middle of the sidewalk under the marquee.

A streetcar passed, and Lucius hoped somebody he knew saw him putting out the sign: The Cherokee Symphony Orchestra Presents VICTOR SAVAGE. It looked good. A drunken soldier came up and looked at the sign, disgusted. "What the fuck happened to *Canyon Passage?*"

"Avalanche." Lucius went back in, leaving the corporal staring at the sign, sneering.

Lucius was eager to see Victor Savage. Several times, on the front page of the Cherokee *Messenger*, Lucius had seen pictures of Victor Savage, the new, young conductor, arrested for speeding or drunk driving. Tall, dark, handsome, very distinguished-looking, too sophisticated to breathe. Those reckless driving charges stimulated Lucius's imagination.

As Lucius entered the lobby, eager to get backstage again and watch the procession of strange-looking people, who knew all about Chopin, George Gershwin, Cole Porter, and Freddy Martin, he heard a loud voice.

"I don't give a god*damn* what the agreement says," said a tall, husky man with a thick moustache, a tiny triangle of hair under his lower lip. His eyebrows peaked in the middle and curled up at the ends, and his dark eyes flashed. Victor Savage, by God. In his white tie and tails, he had Hood backed up against the lobby wall. A handsome, slender lady in furs stood off to the side, looking around as if she belonged to the scene, but had been through it enough times not to be overwhelmed. Hood's look of fear made Lucius feel a flutter in his own stomach. "You can't tell *me* that the ladies of Cherokee who come to this concert will not be allowed to use your goddam restrooms."

"Mr. Savage, we have to *pay* the maids to clean up, and the rental fee is too low to cover that, so we let them off for tomorrow."

"What do you expect—that the people who come to our concert are going to shit on your precious floor?"

"Oh, Victor," said the aristocratic-looking woman.

Lucius was shocked that such a high-class man would say *goddamn* and *shit* in the lobby of the Bijou where in the old days mainly rich people came to see classical plays.

Lucius thought of the times the men's room upstairs had flooded, leaking down into the ladies' room, and was glad he wouldn't have to clean it up in front of these people.

A strange-looking girl whose skin was pure white and whose long hair was dark blond appeared in the doorway from the inner lobby.

"Don't talk to me about keeping your lousy restrooms clean. That hole in the wall backstage is much worse than what we had at the Pioneer. Would you want your wife to sit on that toilet seat?" Lucius's face turned hot. "Come back there, I want to *show* you—"

"Lucius," said Hood, trembling. "Go back with Mr. Savage and clean up the toilet for him."

Savage didn't even glance at Lucius, but the dark blond girl did. Her eyes were large and brown and seemed unused to light.

"Yes, sir," said Lucius, running backstage to catch up with Savage, hearing his powerful voice all the way down the left aisle and up the steps onto the stage.

After Lucius in anger and humiliation had viciously swabbed out the backstage toilet, he returned to his post at the stage door. The held notes made him nervous as the musicians tuned their instruments, but he was eager to watch Savage perform. Through the stage door, he heard the voices and respectable laughter of customers passing, going around to the front entrance. Some of the players walked around in the shadows, trying not to look nervous. A few did look like sissies, talking in a prissy way. The men wore tuxedoes and black ties, the women wore long black dresses, some with corsages pinned under their chins. They seemed so grave and slow, but gave each other quick smiles and touched each other delicately. Lucius hoped they'd play "Rhapsody in Blue," "Deep Purple," and "Claire de Lune."

An old fogey behind the kettledrums seemed to be smiling sardonically, as he tightened some screws and tapped the drums a few times and listened, the way Lucius tried to pick up the hum of a distant train with his ear on a railroad track. Then he and the few other players out there left their big instruments behind, and only a short man with a long, flowing moustache putting sheet music on the stands remained onstage.

People were sitting in the seats out in the auditorium now. The beautiful girls in white evening dresses stood at the posts to greet the people coming in, many of whom wore evening clothes, and led patrons down the aisle, the way Lucius and Gale did. He was delighted to see Dr. Summers approach the Spot.

Lucius spotted the dark blond girl, sitting with Mrs. Savage, probably her mother. The girl sat back in her seat while the woman in furs leaned over a seat, talking to a man and a woman who were raring back to look at her while they talked and laughed and patted each other on the arms and shoulders the way Negroes did, but much more lightly, their gestures sharper. All these people acted very intelligent, and rich, and important. They were and they weren't behaving the way symphony audiences in movies did. It was too dark up there to tell whether Negroes sat in the second balcony.

As Lucius started back to the stage door, the man who had set out the music came over to him. "We are about to begin. Would you guard that door? Lock it, and don't let anyone in, under any circumstances."

Lucius didn't like taking orders from a stranger, no taller than himself, but he enjoyed being a part of the production. From where he sat, he looked at Victor Savage standing in the wings on the opposite side of the stage, talking to the harpist. The players filled the stage now, tuning up.

Then one of the violinists stood up, a dark, slender, handsome man, eyes set deep, suggesting he'd had a sad, but heroic life and was playing to soothe the tragedy in his past. Lucius thought he was going to play a solo like Rubinoff who'd come to play in assembly at Bonny Kate earlier in the year. But the man's back was to the audience, facing the players. He struck a note on the violin and the rest of them played a note. They did it again, and then he sat down. But in a few moments, he stood up and all the other players stood up and the audience applauded. It must be a little joke they all had before it got serious.

But then Victor Savage strode with vigorous, strict motions between the curtain and the violins and walked to the podium, where he bowed, baton in hand, to the applause. Lucius reckoned it was like cheering for the team when they came out, to encourage them, but here it was only the captain. Lucius hated that kind of thing. But Victor Savage looked very dashing and romantic and almost tough.

Savage turned his back as the applause died down, and Lucius saw him, in profile, bend over at the waist, his baton lifted. For a moment, he held time and all breathing on the tip of the baton, then he thrust it down and the poised instruments sounded all at once. The difference between the sound of an orchestra on the screen, that now hung over their heads, and the actual sound smote Lucius. His heart beat faster, his body thrummed.

When the music stopped, Lucius was surprised. Victor Savage bowed to the audience and walked off and came back out again at the tall dark violin player's signal. The houselights stayed dark, so Lucius waited, seeing Savage still moving around in the wings. Then he came out again and the audience clapped.

Lucius was delighted when they played the theme song of the chapter play *The Riders of Death Valley*. "We ride, we ride," sang Dick Foran, as Buck Jones and his band rode into the titles.

Bowing at the end, Victor Savage looked like a prince, dignified, in absolute control, but sweating so hard it dripped off his forehead and sparkled in the light as it fell to the podium, making dark spots.

Then all the players filed out, Lucius thought the concert was over, but one of them told him, "No," there was much more to go. "The best part," he said, sarcastically.

Lucius found a program on the floor and saw that the first piece had been Mozart's Symphony No. 40. He felt tricked—the whole idea of Mozart and all those old-timey composers had always made him sneer. The *Hebrides* Overture opus 26 (*Fingal's Cave*) by Mendelssohn was listed as the piece they'd just finished.

Going back to the dressing rooms, hoping to get a glimpse of one of the girls undressing, Lucius asked a trombone player if they hadn't made a mistake in the program. "Wasn't that the theme song for *The Riders of Death Valley* with Buck Jones?"

"Yes, of course," the man laughed, condescendingly, "but Mendelssohn stole it from them between episodes."

Spit called Lucius over to help him and Pete shove a grand piano out onto the apron.

Lucius caught a glimpse of Victor Savage through the half-open door of the main dressing room where Lucius's own uniform hung. He felt honored. Wiping his face with a thick white towel that hung around his neck, Savage looked like a dignified boxer. "Folks, it's snowing outside," a sissy man said, as if he'd told them so before. And here was Savage about to burn up. But he looked very happy and excited, and the girl with the long dark blond hair stepped into view and kissed him on the mouth. "Hello, Gaile," a lady wearing a diamond necklace said to the daughter. Without smiling, Gaile Savage murmured something from deep inside herself. Then Lucius realized what the lady had called her. Coincidences beguiled him.

When Gaile walked out front, Lucius went out to the lobby, too, and mingled with the patrons, who seemed to hold their cigarettes like people in Lubitsch's movies about the rich. The candy case looked ghostly, shut up, the popcorn machine padlocked, as if these men in tuxedoes might try to rob it. People kept coming up to Mrs. Savage and Gaile.

When the concert resumed, Lucius was surprised to see the handsome, dark, young violinist, who sat in front of the row of violinists on the left, emerge from the wings carrying a baton, the audience applauding. When the man mounted the podium, Lucius was a little shocked, as if he were a prince trying out the throne. Then Victor Savage came out, empty-handed, bowed to the increased applause, and sat down at the piano. Lucius stepped over to the crack between the doors to catch the light from the main lobby and was thrilled to read that Savage was about to play his own piano concerto—as if Wolfe or Caldwell or Twain had suddenly appeared on stage to tell one of their stories. Playing, Victor Savage was almost as handsome and dashing as Cornel Wilde in *A Song to Remember*.

When the concert was over and everybody—Victor Savage, Gaile, and the players, and all the people who'd come back to congratulate him—had left, and Lucius had finished helping Spit and Pete fold the music stands and put them in the back of a car and helped them lower the screen and push the black speaker back in place, Lucius stood in the middle of the stage, looking out at the empty, dim auditorium. In the lighted main lobby by the door, Hood and Spit and Pete were ridiculing the hoity-toity people who'd invaded their theatre, even though they'd worked with the symphony for three years. "That Victor Savage is gonna get his block knocked off one of these days," said Spit, "acting like he's the Prince of Wales."

Lucius turned his back on the auditorium, stepped up onto an imaginary podium, said, "I dedicate this song to Raine Hutchfield," lifted an imaginary baton, and struck up the theme song that Buck Jones stole from Mendelssohn.

Tues. November 12, 1946. I saw Gaile Savage. I love and fear God.

Wens. November 13, 1946. Canyon Passage. In English, I told about my most exciting experience. Wade Bayliss and the man who shot his wife in the balcony. Mrs. Redding was fascinated but Tippy Harper didn't believe me. Whirlpool therapy.

Thurs. November 14, 1946. Margie. Last night, I dreamed there was women and girls in the bathrooms and it was normal. And they came into the shower.

> If man had left well enough alone,
> He would now be living in caves.
> L. H.

Fri. November 15, 1946. Margie, Jean Crane. Elmo got a good luck letter in the mail.

For weeks, the titles of Thomas Wolfe's stories, evocative of many moods, characters, and places, had haunted Lucius. During his lunch hour, he went straight to Matthews's and picked up the *Portable Thomas Wolfe*. "A stone, a leaf, an unfound door, of a stone, a leaf, a door. . . ." Without understanding what the words meant, he was as impressed by them as by the Lord's Prayer. "And of all the forgotten faces." With his pay in his pocket, he had more than enough, but still, he wanted to delay buying the book. From the cash register, the woman who'd been shocked by his dirty hands gave him a dirty look. He held up his clean palms and the old woman rolled her eyes and shook her head as Lucius left the bookstore.

At Baylor's record shop, Lucius bought a twelve-inch recording of Chopin's "Polonaise" played by Jose Iturbi, whom he'd heard in *Holiday in Mexico*. He imagined that Dr. Summers had listened to Victor Savage play it in the Bijou.

Elmo and Brady made fun when they saw the record in the dressing room.

"Hell, you ort to *see* Victor Savage lead that orchestra one time."

"Most them kinda musicians is queer," said Brady.

"I'd like to see *you* wave 'at stick around for two hours," said Lucius, taking it personally.

"If I waved *my* stick around in front of all those people I'd get throwed in jail."

"Elmo," said Lucius, "you got belly-button lint for brains," and walked away mad.

Eager to listen to Jose Iturbi play Chopin's "Polonaise," Lucius dug his Western Flyer out of the chicken house and rode over to Mammy's. The Chief had bought her a Philco console radio–record-player combination. "He's starting to move a few things in, 'cause it won't be too long 'fore we'll be getting married. . . . But I want some money of my own laid back first. For I'll never be dependent on no man again as long as I live."

Before he left Mammy's, he hid the record behind the phonograph, afraid Bucky might come by to see Mammy and find it and break it.

After supper, Momma went off in a car with Norman Upchurch, a man she met at Max's. He was trying to get some ice cream stands started, selling Dairy Queen, a new kind of frozen custard. Momma loved frozen custard, and the man was very nice, big, smoked cigars, and drove a new Packard. She was going along with him to visit his sick sister in Jonesboro. "I can't wait to get out of this g.d. town—even if it's just for a few hours." Lucius was resentful, knowing she planned to divorce Daddy as soon as possible.

Sun. November 17, 1946. Deception. Norman the Dairy King was here.

Mon. November 18, 1946. Deception with Bette Davis.

Tues. November 19, 1946. Read "Haircut" by Ring Lardner in my book of stories. Cleaned up the house. Had to go to Bijou for fire drill. Deception.

NIGHT RITUAL: Lucius and Earl carry their lunches in lard pails, their own milk in Mason jars. But at the lunch table, Earl takes a can of pineapple from his pail and, with a big taunting smile on his face like the

Joker in Batman funny books, opens the can with a stolen can opener and eats the pineapple, smacking his lips while the well-to-do kids watch enviously. . . . Lucius sits in a small room after school is out, trying to learn to read better. The teacher looks at him severely when he misses a word. "You want to end up digging ditches all your life?" He imagines being deep in a ditch and somebody shoveling dirt in on top of him. . . . Momma screams at Daddy because of Barbara, who works in the bakery with him, and whose husband is in jail, and she throws a plate at him like the women in the movies. And after he runs out the door, she tells Lucius that Baboo wouldn't have died if Daddy hadn't spent the money she gave him for medicine to get drunk with Barbara. . . . Lucius tells Earl that as soon as Momma goes over the hill to catch the streetcar to town, he's going to meet Louella in the WPA ditch in the jungle and "do it to her." Momma stands at the open kitchen window. She calls Earl into the house. Earl's screams as Momma beats him come through the sooty screen. She thinks Earl put Lucius up to messing with Louella. She stays home. Earl runs off from home. . . . Watching a return of *Snow White* in the Hiawassee, Lucius is thrillingly terrified of the queen, but aware of a sinister sexuality.

> Wens. November 20, 1946. Deception was very good. Bette Davis was Claude Raines mistress, but she fell in love with Paul Henreed. She is a music teacher and Raines is a famous composer and conductor and Henreed is a cello player. Raines is jealous and gets even trying to wreck Henreed's career. But Bette shoots him. Great music in it. Got a good luck letter one like Elmo got. Harry got first hand info that Della Snow laid four boys. I had reformed her. Lousy job. Whirlpool therapy.

> Thurs. November 21, 1946. Nobody Lives Forever started today. Raine and I fussed on the way home from school because she made fun of Joy. At church we wrote notes. She loves me. In front of her house she was sweet.

"Well," said Mammy, when Lucius came into Jane's Cafe for supper, "they come and got *Bucky*."
"Oh, my God! Where'd they *take* him?"
"Juvenile."
"They come to the house?"
"No, they knew just where to look. They waltzed in here like Pharaohs and plucked him right off that stool at the counter. I'd just put a plate of chicken 'n' dumplings before him, poor little starved youn'ern, and he was grinning from ear to ear." Lucius imagined his slightly buck teeth showing, his big ears sticking out, one of them full of cotton because the crayon had bruised his eardrum.

"Good God. . . . I kept trying to *tell* him they'd get him, if he didn't quit layin' out of school."

"Lucius, we *all* told 'im and didn't do no good. Well, now, he's fixed his little self, and they're—" Suddenly, Mammy turned her head toward the steaming kitchen, resting her cheek against her shoulder.

"Don't cry, Mammy, we'll get him out of it."

"He's such a pitiful little feller. We all love him to pieces . . ."

"I know . . ."

"But seems like we can't control 'im, and if your momma or you can't look after him, they're gonna put him in a home where he'll be *made* to go to school. A body can't get *nowhere* in this world without a high school diploma. But little ol' Bucky can't see that. He's too young to see the consequences. The Chief's *tried* sitting down with him, to talk to him, but it don't sink *in*. So they finally *come* for him. We all *knew* it'd happen one day."

"I know, Mammy, I . . . We all . . . God!" Lucius went through the kitchen and out the back door, into the cindery parking lot for the apartments in the old green and white YMCA building. He leaned his arm, flung across his face, against the leafless mulberry tree and cried.

When he went back in, Mammy was serving chicken and dumplin's and hot corn bread to four firemen in a booth. Lucius sat at the counter. Kitty Wells and Red Foley stopped singing "Honky Tonk Angel" on the radio and Lum Cody himself came on: "Now, folks, I want you to do me a big favor this Thanksgivin', if you've enjoyed these programs all along, of gospel songs of the ol' time religion, I want you to do me the favor of going down to your good Ol' Lum Cody stores, at the sign of the crossroads—just like your old country store—and don't forget, I's raised deep in the Smokies and had to walk it twenty mile to the nearest one—and just kindly take a look at them turkeys we brought in from Tellico Plains this week." Mammy came over and started pouring four cups of coffee.

"Momma know about it yet?"

"We ain't tellin' her till she gets off work. No use to get her all tore up when they's nothing she can do till Monday."

"I'm goin' to the Juvenile." Lucius saw the fat man approaching the electrified gate.

"No, you stay away from there. Don't go off." Mammy served coffee to the firemen. Five others were getting loud, raising a cloud of cigarette, pipe, and cigar smoke over the wobbly booth. She came back to the counter and started wiping while she talked in a low voice, like a bartender in a James Cagney movie, passing on information. "But now we're not breathing a word of this to the Chief."

"Okay, Mammy, okay. . . . Daddy doesn't know either?"

"Lord, honey, your daddy don't know his own name after six o'clock on Fridays." Talk against Daddy, even from Mammy, always made Lucius feel as if he were to blame for Daddy's actions. "He staggered by here ten minutes ago—on his way, looked like, to that hive of niggers down along Crazy Creek. Gonna get his throat cut open one of these days, hanging around that bunch. Harl Abshire's old stomping ground."

When Lucius came in at midnight, Momma was crying and she cried all night, cussing Daddy.

> Fri. November 22, 1946. They come and got Bucky. Laying out too much. Nobody Lives Forever. Damned good show. John Garfield was a big mobster who turned against the mob.

> Sat. November 23, 1946. Nobody Lives Forever. BBC was lousy. Raine didn't sing. Momma visited Bucky on her lunch hour, come back late. Max threatened to fire her again. Daddy came by to bum some money off me while I was eating at Max's and Momma stayed in the ladies' room. Momma said we got to move again. Easterlys kicking us out. Too far behind in the rent. It'll be better anyway if we can move on the other side of town—keep Bucky away from Emmett when he gets out. Old Lady at Matthews told me to quit pawing over the books. Bought Story Pocket Book at River Bridge store.

"No, Lucius, they's no point in you or any of the family going to see Bucky today," said Momma. "Let him sit there by himself one day. It'll do him good. You can visit me before long at the State Asylum, or maybe in jail, for I just might take a notion to shoot your daddy or Emmett King, one—whichever crosses me first."

"Poor ol' Bucky. I'm gonna try to be nicer to him from now on. . . . I feel like strangling Emmett King myself."

"I feel so helpless. I never hoped it would be much better when your daddy got back from Europe, but I never dreamed it'd get worse than before. . . . Lucius, turn off the radio, honey. It's Bucky's favorite song."

Lucius turned off Gene Autry singing "I'm Back in the Saddle Again" and went out to the chicken shack sanctuary and built a fire in the old stove and worked on "The Black Lash." In The Story Pocket Book, Lucius read "Sherrel," by Whit Burnett, the editor of the anthology. The narrator is haunted by the death of his little brother, who is somehow partly the cause of his becoming a writer, and he uses his brother's name as a pen name. Moved to tears by the story, Lucius remembered his own little brother. Named after Ronald Colman, Momma's favorite actor, especially in Random Harvest. "He's such a man of the world, but so gentle and kindly." Lucius struck out William De Cosgrove and wrote "Ronald Hutchfield," struck out "Hutchfield," wrote in "Birchfield."

More keenly now than other times, he felt a surge of new power as he looked at the new name. In a sense, he had resurrected Ronny, or made him less dead, and Lucius himself was just a little more alive, and would be immortal. Glancing at the dedication, he remembered that he'd renamed Loraine, too.

Sun. November 24, 1946. The Best Years of Our Lives started. I have a new pen name, Ronald Birchfield.

Mon. November 25, 1946. The Best Years of Our Lives. The Juvenile Judge gave Bucky a card that says he has to go to school every day at the Juvenile, but he can come home at night. If he lays out one more time they're going to commit him to Lee's Foster Home.

Tues. November 26, 1946. The Best Years of Our Lives. Had to ride 5 buses, looking for a place to move. Bought Screen Romances—has story of the Yearling by Marjorie Rawlings. Wish I'd won that contest to be in it.

When Lucius came in from the Bijou, he found Bucky standing naked on one of the green, round-backed kitchen chairs. Momma stood before him, washing his pecker, the foreskin pushed back, the bright kitchen light overhead falling directly between them. Lucius had watched her do that all his life, glad he'd been circumcised when he was a baby.

"I found us a wonderful little house," said Momma. "Bucky! *Hold still.*" She slapped his leg and Bucky started bellering. "Shut up! Shut up!"

"Well, I hate to leave my ol' chicken shack."

"If I never see Clinch View again, it won't be too soon. There's too many sad memories here. And no more g.d. apartments. I'm sick of living in a rat's nest."

Lucius was eager to wriggle out of his old skin and pull on another. If he couldn't run away to Maine or New Orleans or Palestine because it would add to Momma's burden of worries, he could move across town. Lying in bed, he enjoyed the sadness of leaving the scenes of his best childhood adventures. Just as he sometimes felt drawn in his wandering walks back to Beech and to Avondale and to Zachary and Park streets, he could come back to Rader and Trescott and gaze at the house made strange by new occupants of the apartment where he now began to review his life before falling asleep talking to God.

Wens. November 27, 1946. The Best Years of Our Lives ended today. Three Wise Fools a dumb ass Christmas story, starts tomarrow. Momma found us a house. Whirlpool.

Lucius got up early Thanksgiving to start packing. Bucky snuck off before noon. Momma screamed at Lucius forty-'leven times, and he had

to go out to the sanctuary and shatter lumps of coal at the wall before
he could stop trembling enough to take down her bed.

At two o'clock, the Chief came by in his old 1941 Packard and drove
them over to Mammy's for Thanksgiving dinner. When they went in
Bucky was reading a Donald Duck funny book by the heater. "You *better*
hide behind that funny book," said Momma. "And wipe that silly grin
off your face."

After dinner, the Chief drove Bucky to the Hiawassee Theater and
Momma to the streetcar stop. Lucius thought it unjust that she had to
work even on Thanksgiving. Mammy and the Chief wanted to see the
new house so they drove on over to Camelia Street in East Cherokee, an
area where Lucius had never lived. Momma had forgotten to give Lucius
the key, so they stood on the front and back porches and in the dead grass
at the sides, peering in windows, and then Lucius found one unlocked
and crawled in, and they tiptoed like housebreakers through the rooms.
Lucius staked out one for his sanctuary, and wondered which one
Momma intended for the roomer who would help with the rent. Maybe
a waitress from Max's.

Thurs. November 28, 1946. Three Wise Fools. We packed on Thanksgiving. Ate dinner at Mammy's. Went by the house. Took Raine to
see The Strange Love of Martha Ivers at the Venice with Elizabeth
Scott, Van Heflin, Kirk Douglas, a new guy, and Barbara Stanwyck.
Great.

Fri. November 29, 1946. Three Wise Fools. Our new house burned clear
to the ground. Two little boys got in and were smoking cigarettes and
some old magazines caught on fire. The fire trucks were there and it
was still burning when our moving truck that belongs to one of
Raine's cousins pulled up. It's parked in front of his house now. Me and
Duke bought us two pearl-handled switchblade knives. We're going up
there in a few minutes and sleep out in the cab of the truck. I'm
afraid somebody will take off with my stories and my movie magazines
and stills. They better not try it, by God.

Sat. November 30, 1946. Three Wise Fools. Raine's cousin parked the
truck in front of Mammy's, and I slept on the couch last night to
keep an eye on it. Last night it snowed but Raine's cousin came down
at 2 a. m. and threw five old ragged tarps over the top of the truck.
Written Sunday morning.

"Dear Lucius," said Momma's note, stuck to the sooty screen with a
safety pin, "we have moved to 1845 Bluff Street above the river. Near the
River Street slums, God help us. Key in the mailbox."

Lucius stuck his hand in Mammy's rusty mailbox. No key. She must
have meant the mailbox at the new house. Mammy's bedroom light
went on.

"Didn't mean to wake you up, Mammy."

"Lord, I wasn't asleep, honey. Sergeant Lovell come for Bucky, and I've been tore up ever since. He run out the back door and hid in the coal house, and Sergeant Lovell had to drag him kicking and screaming into the *po*-lice car. And that big lummox Emmett King was already sitting in the front seat. Well, we can't say that man ain't tried his best to keep Bucky out of an institution."

"What'd they do this time?"

"Lord, Lucius, I never got the straight of it. It had me so nervous and tore up, I couldn't concentrate on what the poor man was saying, and Bucky was a-bellering and begging me and your Momma not to let them take him—I tell thee, I am— Well, it was something about tangerines, snitching tangerines from the fruit stand in the Market House."

"Tangerines? Is that all?"

"It don't take much when a body breaks the law."

Lucius walked on up to the corner at the old house to catch the last streetcar back to town. Wanting to see what it looked like in the cold moonlight, he climbed the short concrete wall by the sidewalk and looked in the window Earl had tossed him through months ago. Moonlight gleamed on the floor. Four rusty leg prints where the Home Comfort cookstove had set. Momma always cleaned up before she left the rats' nests they lived in, so that the next brood could start from scratch with their own sticks and spit. He wanted to look in the other window and walk in the backyard one last time, but the ghostly moonlight on the emptiness scared him and made him feel more deeply sad about Bucky. As he boarded the last streetcar, marked CARBARN, he felt the endedness of his life in the half-empty house.

Lucius rode into the carbarn, dark like the Horror House at the Park. The Coca-Cola neon sign mounted atop the Indian mound in front of the courthouse was off. Crossing Sevier Street, he looked back at the unlit Bijou marquee where the letters he had handed up to Elmo announced Barbara Stanwyck and Van Heflin in THE STRANGE LOVE OF MARTHA IVERS.

As he turned onto Bluff Street, the thrill of living in a strange new house near the River Street slums and the Tennessee River and the River Bridge Bookshop and the Bijou competed with his sadness about Bucky and leaving the house on the corner of Rader and Trescott. He passed the oldest church in Cherokee. Two blocks on up the hill, he found 1845 Bluff Street, a dull green house, a picket fence with a little low gate and two front doors and a wide porch. On the mailbox on the left: IRENE HUTCHFIELD. He dipped his hand into the box, feeling rust and a smooth key. He unlocked the doors, delighted they were French, like the ones in "Black Dust," and stepped into a new apartment for the first time in a house he'd never seen before.

Scared of the dark house, even though light would reveal familiar furniture, he groped along the wall for the light switch, found it, and there was the old furniture in strange relationships, making a strange room look partly familiar. Sheet music on Momma's piano: "I Can't Begin to Tell You," "Oh, What It Seemed to Be," "Doin' What Comes Naturally." The shade was off the floor lamp and the bare bulb sticking up reminded him of the work light Spit and Pete used on the Bijou stage when they were setting up or taking down a stage show.

Lucius paused in the dark doorway of the bedroom. "Momma? . . ." He turned the light on. On one side of the kitchen door, his mother's bed, empty, made, on the other, the cot, empty, made, not folded out to create room for two. Lucius stepped back, as if he'd entered the wrong house. But the boxes and barrels stacked to the ceiling in the four corners of the room testified that he was in the right house, where some things would always be wrong. An eerie sensation in his belly, Lucius looked around. Tired from working and late walking, Lucius moved as if on sponges, blinking at the new nest. Afraid, he turned on the light in the kitchen. An electric stove! He felt sad to lose the old yellow and green enameled cookstove, but excited at the idea of cooking with electricity. The kitchen was small but it was a kitchen that was *not* also a bedroom. Same old table, though. With a note propped against a stack of dishes, still wrapped in the Cherokee *Messenger*. "Dear Lucius, Honey, the cops come and got Bucky again. Now they'll send him to Lee's Foster Home. Dan called and I begged him to take me for a ride to put Cherokee City limits behind me for a few hours. Go on to sleep. Your mother."

Lucius saw a small room just off the kitchen—high windows, a glass door along the back wall, about chin high. There sat the icebox but nothing else. The sight made him giggle and dance, exhilarated. He stepped into the room, and stumbled, not having seen the one step down. Then, through a small hole in his left shoe, he felt ice water. Pulling the brass chain above him, he saw the floor flooded. A saucepan set down to catch the drip had run over. Then he realized he was lucky he hadn't electrocuted himself. He made out that the porch had been built onto the back of the house—the two sides without windows were made of exterior overlapping white boards. He let out a window-rattling yell. This was *it*—his sanctuary. For the first time, he would have his own room in the house—not in a chicken house outside.

Lucius mopped up the ice water, then emptied the pan, spilling most of it on the floor he'd mopped, dousing his shoes. But he wasn't upset. Having mopped the floor again, he dragged the cot into the little porch-room, then the desk he'd shared with Earl and Bucky from the front room. No phone there. Dan must have called her at Mammy's.

Over his desk he draped the tapestry with the spot of blood that Daddy had brought back from Belgium. On the tapestry he set the polo player someone had donated when he and a bunch of kids in the fifth grade, let out early, went on a scrap drive, pulling Bucky's wagon, during the war. He always felt guilty for holding back the statue, sneaking it home. It could have been melted down into a bullet. And now he often wondered whether some American soldier, maybe Luke, had run out of bullets because of his filching. Beside the polo player stood the little boy pissing that Daddy brought back from Brussels. When a nobleman's son got lost, the prince vowed that wherever he found his son, there he'd erect a statue showing the boy doing whatever he was doing when he was found.

A single shelf ran along the wall against the kitchen. He put all his books up there on eye level. Turning out all the lights, he looked out the windows of his sanctuary. A wooden fence surrounded the little backyard. In one corner was a small apple tree. Under it, he saw by the light spillage from the kitchen, sat the old Home Comfort wood stove, snow melting and dripping off the warmer. Across the alley stood a slummy three-storey house alone against the sky. Behind it was, he knew, a sheer cliff, then a narrow road, the railroad tracks, then the river. He saw the lights of the slaughterhouse, of the bakery, of the little airport island, of houseboats.

Harry lived in a shotgun house, where he was born and raised, next to the rambling tin sheds of the White Star tobacco warehouse, three blocks down the hill. Inside the Bijou, Gale was Lucius's model, friendly but distant. Outside, the boy Lucius most enjoyed watching and wanted most to run with, as a friend, was Harry. Gale and Harry were similar in build, looks, and the sort of gestures they favored, except that Harry looked more like Bogart than Flynn. But Harry's style was a little more conscious, more in-the-making, than Gale's. Gale was older and his scope smaller—the radius of the Bijou. But Lucius could observe Harry everywhere except the Bijou. On his own carpets, in the Tivoli's dimly lighted lobbies, chandeliers overhead. At school. And now in this neighborhood along the river.

Only five blocks from the Bijou, the neighborhood seemed impressive. An exciting part of town, in the middle of many buildings Lucius had long known and felt were important and that made him feel inferior, but exposed to possibilities. "Thank you, God."

Lying on the cot, he realized that the privacy of his sanctuary depended on Earl's and Bucky's being in the reform school and the foster home. The cot, which wouldn't open in the small room, and the desk, which he would fill with his writings, were exclusively his now. He swallowed against a knot in his throat. "I didn't put them in jail," he said, to the mooncast patterns on the wall. "*I* didn't put them in jail!"

Sun. December 1, 1946. The Strange Love of Martha Ivers. I am writing
this on Monday night. We moved to Bluff Street Yesterday and I set
up my sanctuary.

Monday, December 2, 1946. The Strange Love of Martha Ivers is a great
show. I tacked some stills up on my new wall, and sorted out my stories
and put them in the drawers of the desk. Momma said I have to leave
the icebox out here and to keep an eye on the drip pan. She said I'll
freeze my ass off out here but I don't care. Raine called 3 times. The
landlady doesn't care if we use her phone. My little chicken house
sanctuary. Gone. Miss it. Love it. Always remember.

Tues. December 3, 1946. Coming back from the Hiawassee, stopped
by Mammy's, saw Walt get off his motorcycle, delivering for Howell's,
and he looked like Luke coming back, and I run like greased lightning
to get to see the look on Mammy's face.

Inspired by a photograph of Thomas Wolfe that he'd found in a reference
book in the Bonny Kate library, Lucius went by Matthews's on his way
to the Bijou. He went to the table often, as if visiting a grave to read the
noble, stirring epitaph, the tributes over and over, paying homage to a
dead giant whose spirit lived on in Lucius. He stood in reverence, aware
that everywhere else in Cherokee kids and grown-ups were looking at
funny books, pulp westerns, and mystery stories. Ignorant of this great
writer, they passed by on the sidewalk outside. Lucius carried the book
to the cash register, his money in the other hand, but impulsively turned
back to the table and replaced it.

He let it stay there, as if allowing a rare wine to age—wine stolen
from vengeful gods. And he was a little afraid of Thomas Wolfe, the
marble brow, shadowed cheek-hollows, the glowering stare—as if he expected great things of Lucius if he bought the book—and the pouting
lower lip, and chin-propping, massive fist. Realizing that he'd been thinking of Thomas Wolfe as if he were dead, Lucius scanned the introduction. "In July 1938, after having delivered a new manuscript of more
than a million words, Wolfe became ill with pneumonia. He died that
September, at the age of thirty-eight." Saddened, Lucius left the bookstore.

Wens. December 4, 1946. The Strange Love of Martha Ivers. I think
the big house on the corner is a horehouse. Whirlpool.

He liked this house better than the one on Rader, but he'd forgotten to
empty the icebox pan, and he realized that everyday life would always
be pretty much the same.

He plugged in Momma's hair dryer and set it on the sill to heat his sanctuary, and began reading "The Windfall" by Erskine Caldwell in *Story Pocket Book,* "Domestic infelicity in Maine." Most of the books Lucius bought at River Bridge, and now in drugstores, and at the Iowna across from the Smoky, but never at Matthews's, he read no further than the information on the back about the author and the page of entice-ment on the front about the book, and the title pages, and stray sen-tences as he flipped through. Despite his sense of possessiveness, he never presumed to write his name in the books, and his feeling of reverence was so keen he made no marks in them, except light crosses beside passages he expected would prove immortal. He felt himself becoming more and more immersed in published stories, in pages, which, being a poor reader who'd suffered remedial courses, he read very slowly, but savored thoroughly.

The bawling of cattle across the river made him want to explore the riverbank. Leaving "Windfall" unfinished, he walked down the cobble-stoned alley, cut between two fire-gutted houses, descended a slick red-clay path. People had tossed garbage, trash, and junk down the cliff over the past half century. He came out of the kudzu jungle at River Street, crossed it, crossed the railroad tracks and started walking.

Looking across the river at the lights of the packinghouse, he said, aloud, "In the summer they slaughtered cattle." Make a good title. He walked between two tobacco warehouses, corrugated tin, where boxcars were parked empty, and approached the factory where the marble they gouged out of the hills was cut into slabs. Then up ahead, he saw the smokestacks of the water plant and off to the right, across the river, the red lights of the little island airport. Where the tracks swung left and curved just ahead, two long rows of round-domed kilns, bricks stacked in front of each, pulsed fire. He walked between the hot kilns and down the bank to the edge of the water and looked upriver, then down, and there stood a tower, back of the marble yards, hidden among giant oaks and willows. On the bank above it, a huge crane held a massive, drill-grooved block of marble high.

In the moonlight the tower, a sandy color, looked small. Marble dust and little chips and chunks and broken blocks of marble, white, some a little green, surrounded the tower. Lucius couldn't figure out what it had been used for. Maybe a sentry box during the Civil War. Maybe a lookout for Japanese submarines during the last war. The little room on top looked just big enough for one or two people.

Walking over the marble debris, he stumbled and fell and turned his ankle and stood at the base, kneecaps bleeding, looking at a metatarsal bar that had come loose. Walking around the base, he looked up and found rusty iron, handlelike ladder rungs beginning halfway up. He couldn't reach the bottom one. He tried stacking shards of marble but they slipped loose under his weight. A piece of driftwood leaned against the wall brought him within a few straining inches of the first rung. Backing off, he ran up the log and jumped against the wall. The shock almost made him turn loose of the rung that he snagged with three fingers. Grabbing it with the other hand, he pulled himself up to barbed wire. But he squeezed through, ripping his flannel shirt.

The ceiling was low, he had almost to squat. A breeze blew through the two narrow windows as through the eye of a needle against his hot, perspiring body. He liked the smell of himself and of the river and marble dust. Then his foot stepped in something soft and another smell filled the room. As he looked out over South Cherokee and up and down the north bank, a cloud drifted across the moon and hovered.

He had to pee, but couldn't get his pecker up as high as the ledge of the window. His body bent like an S, he thought he had his prong pointed so it would shoot out in an arc, but the arc curved backward into his face. Cursing, feeling that fate was mocking him, he wiped with his handkerchief, then draped it over the pile behind him. Then the moon came out again, and he imagined his glorious future beyond the hills of Cherokee.

Thurs. December 5, 1946. Wake Up and Dream. Found a tower! Bing Crosby's singing "I'm Dreaming of a White Xmas" on the "Insomniacs."

Fri. December 6, 1946. Wake Up and Dream. John Payne and June Haver. Met the old lady in the apartment next door Mrs. Maggard. She owns the house. This old Negro woman named Blue lives with her. She has been in the family since she was a child. She doesn't talk like most Negroes, but she looks like Aunt Jemima. Saw a windup victrola in the radio repair shop window behind Crockett Hotel. Looks good.

"Nobody tells me what to do, Marco." Waiting for the light to change, Lucius kept his eyes on the cars, expecting one to swerve against the curb, somebody in back to open up with a submachine gun. He imitated the rumbling tones of Warner Brothers' background music.

On the Bluff Street Bridge that spanned Crazy Creek, he leaned against the iron rail and looked down into the gorge where the lights of shacks along the banks glowed warm. "Lillian, I must go away for a while. . . . I don't know. Maybe I won't be back for ten years. I'm searching for something. . . . I don't know. Will you wait for me?"

Lucius kicked the page of a newspaper, fluttering, into the air, caught it, read the headline about India's dispute with Pakistan in a Constitutional Conference in London, saw Earl's picture in the bottom left-hand corner. Earl stood in front of bars in the Safety Building, his arm around a smaller boy, both of them grinning. The boy was wearing

a dark knit toboggan cap, and Earl wore only a tee shirt. FUGITIVES SUR-
VIVE TREK ACROSS MOUNTAINS, Hutchfield Saves Comrade's Life.

Eager to show Momma the picture, Lucius ran up Bluff Street hill
and rushed through the dark front rooms toward the kitchen light. A
note on the table, written on the back of the last page of "The Trail to
Maine," ripped out of his notebook, said: "Dear Lucius, Gone dancing
with Norman and Gay. See clipping. What next? Love, Momma." The
picture, scissored out, lay on the table.

The new apartment stimulated sweet melancholy moods in him
when he was alone, but tonight he was a little scared. He wrote in his
diary:

Sat. December 7, 1946. Earl escaped. Picture in paper. Wake up and
Dream. Stopped by to look at Portable Thomas Wolfe. Almost bought
it again. Pearl Harbor Day.

Then he went to bed, reviewed his life: Lucius, Earl, Bucky, and
Momma sit in the summer doorway, lights out all over Cherokee, stars
bright over Beech Street, listening to Lucius tell ghost stories, listening
for the motors of Nazi planes, hearing at last the all-clear siren from
W. W. Drummond furniture factory where Sonny's and Jim Bob's
momma works. . . . They all give little Judy Brummett a nickel and
she gets under the tarpaulin and shows Lucius, Earl, Sonny, and Jim
Bob her pussy. . . . Lucius squats at the edge of the jungle and crawls
through the weeds, briars, and honeysuckle vines and slinks between little
trees to the ditch and crawls inside the sewer pipe alone, to prove to himself he's as tough as Sonny, who won't do it alone. . . . Peggy Ann Garner
in *A Tree Grows in Brooklyn* is like those snotty little girls in the
neighborhood that he wants to screw but who act as if they're too good
for anybody. . . . Lucius and Earl and Sonny and Jim Bob wrestle in
the long front yard of a little red tar-paper shack among the red clover
and wild onions and buttercups, and twilight is chilly, and Jim Bob
and Sonny get mad at each other and Sonny sticks his rusty penknife in
Jim Bob's back, and hugs and kisses him and begs him not to tell their
momma, and they pull it out, and Jim Bob goes around with the blue
shadow of the tip in his back close to his spine. . . . And fell asleep,
talking to God.

Lucius woke, hearing his name called out in the alley. Momma stood
beside his cot. "Lucius, go out there and make him shut up."

"Do what?"

"Your daddy's been out there in that alley yowling since one o'clock.
'I-reeeene. I-reeene.' God! What will the neighbors think? Miss Maggard'll
probably ask us to move, if you don't pacify him."

"Lucius! Ho, Lucius!"

"See, now he wants *you*. I raised the window and told him to hush or I'd call the cops, but he won't let up."

"What time is it?"

"Two o'clock in the blamed morning."

"What's the *matter* with him? He hurt?"

"You needn't sound so worried about your precious daddy. The S.O.B. is weepy drunk. 'We got to help Earl, Irene.' Where was *he* when Earl got into trouble in the first place?"

"Overseas in the war, Momma."

"You want me to smack your face?"

"Momma, it's two o'clock in the morning."

Lucius put on his pants and his leather jacket and shoes. When he hit the porch, he wished he'd put on his socks and shirt, too. Under the streetlight down the hill, frost covered the cobblestones.

Lucius looked around. "Hey, Daddy!"

"What you want?"

Lucius found him sitting on the curb in front of the isolated three-storey house behind Lucius's, gangly, stoop-shouldered. Somehow the Mason jar of white lightnin' looked elegant.

"Sit down, Bub."

"Daddy, I got to get some sleep. Don't you reckon you ought to go home before we *freeze* to death out here?"

"Have some splo, Bub." Daddy held out the jar.

"No, thanks, I'm too young."

"Sit down." Daddy drank from the jar, patting the curb. Lucius sat on it, then got right back up and squatted on the edge. "What we going to do about Earl, son?"

"I don't know."

"Walked all the way cross the Cumberland Mountains."

"I know. I read about it in the *Messenger*."

"Saved his pal from freezin' to death. They'd shaved the poor little feller's head."

"I could use that toboggan cap right now myself."

"He's a hero."

"Yeah, that's right."

"The heart of winter. Took the shirt off his own back. Kid woulda died." Daddy began to cry. "Lucius, I *had* to blow that bridge. It was a *di*rect order."

"I know." Lucius wondered again why Daddy was so obsessed with having blown a damned bridge.

"Take a swig."

"No, thanks. Look, why don't you get some coffee in you and go to bed?"

"You got a dime?"

"Here."

"Thanks. Need it to go with my forty cents. I know where I can get me a shot in the morning for fifty cents."

"We gonna *get* shot, if we don't move from in front of this house." Once magnificent, now slummy, why had they built it on a street as narrow as an alley?

"It said they broke out of the reform school at Nashville and crossed the Cumberland in three feet of snow."

"*Two* feet." Against the silky lining of his leather jacket, Lucius's nipples were hard as the tips of icicles.

"They beat it here?"

"What?" A light snow was beginning to fall on Lucius and Daddy.

"Takes after me. Don't mind walking."

"You *walk* over here?" asked Lucius, trying to make conversation.

"Why, sure." Daddy looked at Lucius as if he thought he was stupid.

"I'm getting frostbit, Daddy."

"Just be glad you don't have to cross them mountains in the snow, without no hat on your head or a shirt on your back."

"Well, right now Earl's in a warm cell and we're *freezing* our ass off." Still, Lucius was moved by the story, more hearing it from Daddy than reading it in the paper. As a news story, it sounded like *The Call of the Wild*. Having always thought of Earl as selfishness in its purest form, as a person who never did anything for anybody else, much less sacrifice himself, Lucius was glad this streak, buried deep in his brother, had finally surfaced.

Lucius watched snow come down, faster, thicker, and their breath make clouds over the gutter where beer bottles and cigarette butts and a broken Yo-Yo and Popsicle sticks and leaves were all matted together.

"Want the last swig?"

"No, thanks. *You* take it."

"Thanks. I can *use* it."

Lucius went inside and woke up Momma to tell her it was snowing. "Can Daddy sleep here tonight?"

"Hell, no. Let him freeze. Nobody told him to go out traipsing around Cherokee at two o'clock—my God, it's *three* o'clock—in the morning."

When Lucius went back out to tell Daddy he couldn't come in, he saw him walking under the streetlight down the hill, leaving black footsteps in the fresh snow behind him, and the clear glass jar sitting on the curb.

Lucius took off his pants and jacket and put on his socks and got in bed, but his cold feet kept him awake almost an hour, seeing Daddy

as a kid, sitting under a streetlight at the foot of the bluff in South
Cherokee, waiting for his big brother, Hop, to come down and walk
back up in the dark with him, and when Lucius woke up at noon Sunday, he felt groggy, as if he had a hangover.

> Sun. December 8, 1946. The Show Off with Red Skelton. They trans-
> ferred Earl to the Juvenile. Bucky's still there, too, but in the part for
> little kids where we stayed that time Momma was in the hospital.
> Momma went to see them. Read "A Passion in the Desert" by Honore
> de Balzac. Called Raine.

South Cherokee Junior High across the river was closer to Bluff Street
but Lucius couldn't stand the thought of not seeing Raine and them
every day, so he caught the Grand Avenue streetcar at the Indian Mound
and rode out to Bonny Kate. He just wouldn't tell Mr. Bronson he'd
moved.

As he approached Bonny Kate from a new angle, he saw a crowd
gathered under the huge oak at the entrance to the bicycle parking lot
where he'd whipped Sonny. They were gazing at Howell's delivery motorcycle, one of the few in town. He wondered if Walt had just come from
delivering something to Mammy's. No, she'd be at the cafe by now.

He couldn't find Raine in the crowd. When Lucius heard the motor
strike up and saw the kids stepping back, one of them on his foot, Raine
sat behind Walt, her hands clapped on his hips. The motorcycle scattered
gravel over their feet and climbed the steep hill toward Clayboe Ridge.

"If you start out running," said Cora, behind him, "you might can
catch up with 'em, Poet."

Ignoring her, he went into the building through the door beside
the cafeteria.

When Raine came through study hall with her class, going to lunch,
Lucius didn't look up. She tried to speak to him in the hall between
classes but he walked on. In American history, he consciously frowned
fiercely, stared at the title "The Road: His Only Freedom," his lower
lip thrust out, his jaw mashed against his fist, and refused the note she
tried to pass by Lard. When school let out, he didn't walk with her, but
went on to the Bijou.

> Mon. December 9, 1946. The Show Off. Raine did me dirty. Momma
> said she called four times. Earl escaped from the juvenile. But he
> didn't take Bucky with him. The Killers coming.

Lucius hid out in Spofford's grocery near Bluff Street, drinking a
Grapette, until he thought Momma'd be gone to Max's, then went back
to the house. As he was unlocking the door, Blue called him to the phone.

"Lucius?"

"Yeah?"

"Ain't you coming?"

"Hell, no," he whispered, aware of Mrs. Maggard's dark house.

"You don't have to cuss about it. . . . Please don't lay out."

Lucius wondered where Raine was calling from. "What do *you* care? You got that motorsickle, ain't you?"

"Oh, shoot fire, Lucius, he's just an old boy that lived on River Street when *we* lived down there. Used to alla time try to get a date ever before Momma allowed me to *go* with anybody, and now he thinks he's so hot, running around on that motorsickle, delivering paregoric."

Lucius heard Cora bark a laugh.

"Then why'd you let him take you for a ride?"

"Cause I ain't never *rode* on one before."

"Well, you can ride till doomsday for all *I* care. I'm leavin' Cherokee and hittin' the road." Lucius hung up.

The phone rang again as he started to open the front door. Blue held it out to him, haughtily.

"It's worth another nickel," said Cora, "just to tell you that Raine said she could ride with whoever she *wants* to," and tossed the phone into its cradle.

They'd probably walked down to the drugstore on Grand and would be tardy.

An old lady almost a century old, Miss Maggard had lived in the house since the First World War with Blue. Making only a few little noises a day, Mrs. Maggard and Blue crept around on the other side of the wall. When Lucius saw Blue come out on the back porch, dressed like Aunt Jemima, but never smiling, something about her way of walking and looking at him, and her soft, impersonal voice, her impeccable diction and white-folks sentence structure made him feel he was poor white trash that had moved into one half of the old plantation. But she was polite and so was Miss Maggard, and they were interesting. Even though Momma had found out that Blue grew up with Miss Maggard in a big fancy house upriver, they seemed slightly sinister and he was a little scared of them.

Sitting at the little desk in his sanctuary flooded with winter morning light, wishing he could run away to Maine and work on a fishing boat, Lucius dreamed up a village in Maine that he called Greenbay.

Tues. December 10, 1946. Show off. Raine called. We fussed. Layed out.

Laying out again, Lucius stayed in the house, shivering in his sanctuary, trying to write, brooding, too restless to read. When time for his whirlpool therapy neared, he decided to go only because he could stop by Matthews's bookstore on the way.

Walking along the street, Lucius spoke loud his part of dialogues he imagined with Raine and them, what he should have said and was going to say, and imagined what he should have done and was going to do, and tried to forget what actually had been said and done.

The Portable Thomas Wolfe stack had not diminished. He was contemptuous of everyone in Cherokee for failing to see the greatness of this man. Wolfe belonged to him. But the reverence with which he handled the book still baffled him. He carried it around the store while looking over the new novels, passing up the nonfiction. *The Neon Wilderness* by Nelson Algren, *The Victim* by Saul Bellow, *The End of My Life* by Vance Bourjaily, *Knock on Any Door* by Willard Motley, *The Harder They Fall* by Budd Schulberg. Through a kind of osmosis, he'd picked up authors and titles out of an ambience, responding to surface sheen, and thought of himself as being in the swim.

Ghosts of other thefts in other places made him feel guilty, as if he were about to steal the Wolfe. He felt weak in the knees, as when he walked toward a pretty girl on the street. What a risk he would be taking. Three Hutchfields in the Juvenile at once. Then he realized that this very risk enhanced the value of the book. Going to put it back, he saw the mean old woman bent over, picking up some dropped change, and he stuck *The Portable Thomas Wolfe* inside his leather jacket.

Feeling steamy and hot inside his jacket, his forehead sweating, his trousers causing his legs to itch, his shoes hot, he ambled around a while, pretending innocence, then went out and stood in front of the shop a while to show the lady inside he was guiltless.

To punish himself, he walked all the way to the Crippled Children's Hospital. Exhausted from nervousness, he didn't go in, but caught a streetcar back to Sevier, and walked home.

Sitting in a one-armed easy chair, broken in moving, he stayed in his cold sanctuary reading, gazing every few paragraphs at the drawing on the front, setting his lip like Wolfe's.

Reading "The Story of a Novel," he got a great urge to write. While he stared at the blank lines on the notebook paper, Blue called him to the phone three times, but he didn't answer, and he was still staring at the paper when Momma came in the front door at eleven, and reported that the cops caught Earl halfway to Atlanta.

Wens. December 11, 1946. The Show Off, but I wasn't there. To-marrow starts Ernest Hemingway's The Killers. I laid out of school again today, and skipped whirlpool therapy, and didn't go to the Bijou. My ass is mud. Read Wolfe. "Bums at Sunset" and "Circus at Dawn" and "The Story of a Novel" in a book which I ——. Tried to write but couldn't. They caught Earl.

Thurs. December 12, 1946. The Killers. Mr. Bronson didn't say much only said I had to stay in for 2 weeks. Ignored Raine. Ignored the damned teachers. Saw Wuthering Heights at the Cosmopolitan way out on the Smoky Mountain highway. Beatiful. Tragic. Took a rope down to the tower and cleaned it out. My secret place. Like the caves.

Friday. December 13, 1946. The Killers is Great. Wonderful. Introducing Burt Lancaster and a new girl named Ava Gardner was good in it. Hemingway is a great writer. I've got the Killers in my book. I just read it. One of the best stories I've every read. Almost as good as the movie. Read "Seeds" too, by Sherwood Anderson. Wuthering Heights is lousy. The book. Hood gave me a warning not to lay off work again.

"And now, boys and girls," Miss Potter announced, "one of your old favorites and mine, who has won your applause and first place several times in the past. . . . Loreen Clayboe, to sing, "Heartaches.'"

As Raine came out to the microphone, Lucius walked impressively down the aisle, told some kids on the front row to take their feet off the orchestra pit railing, and as he turned, looked straight up into Raine's eyes, caught her watching him, then he went back up to the Spot, as if unaware of her.

A crippled girl who wore only one brace, making Lucius imagine she'd cast off the other in Sister Kenny's clinic, asked him the time, and thanked him in a very sweet way that seemed forced. The happy cripples at the Crippled Children's Hospital and in Bonny Kate's halls embarrassed him, made him feel guilty for the way he felt about them.

When she turned to him again, he was afraid she'd seen his sneer. "Didn't recognize my voice, did you?"

"Are *you* the one that calls sometimes and just hangs up when I answer about four times a day?"

"I cannot tell a lie," she said, coyly.

She turned again, and hobbled down the aisle.

"Your girl friend's cute," said Gale, elbowing Lucius's ribs suggestively. "I can just hear you clinking your braces together."

"Up yours, Cheeta."

Between the Bugs Bunny Club and *The Killers*, as the kids milled around, moving to the balcony or from the balcony to the main lobby, and to the bathroom and the candy counter, Lucius slipped backstage and walked about with a businesslike air. He strode past Raine, who'd won a mirror and brush set for second place.

"Hi, Lucius," she said, moderately friendly.

"Hi, Loraine," he said, using her real-life name to cut her.

He'd envisioned her worrying about him, afraid he might have left town. Because he didn't want her to think he'd chickened out of running off, he said, "I had to go to Chattanooga to get some parts for the projector last Tuesday and Wednesday." Though she seemed to suspect the truth, she didn't throw it up to him. Still, he passed up this opportunity as he had passed up others in the last week to attempt a reconciliation with her. Uncertainty and pride held him back and he sensed they kept her own gestures and expressions from encouraging him.

Sat. December 14, 1946. The Killers. Daddy talked Uncle Hop into letting Earl stay with him in Sante Fe to help him in his radio repair business and learn a trade. Momma got the Judge to say okay. Bucky got jealous and tried to run off but the fat man caught him at the gate. God have pity on poor little Bucky.

Sun. December 15, 1946. Tarzan and the Leopard Woman starts. Momma called Raine and invited her to Sunday dinner and I went out to Clayboe Ridge and got her and we fussed walking across the bridge tords the house and it began to rain. She met Dan and liked Momma on the piano. We ate privately in my sanctuary, used my desk as a table. And listened to NBC Symphoney but she kept horsing around. We went to see Alan Ladd in Two Years Before the Mast at the Tivoli! Saw Harry. We kissed. In front of her house, too, sitting in her brother's taxi while he was asleep. Bruce Tillotson took my place at the Bijou. This picture of them tearing down the Pioneer was in the Messenger. They got a fence out front so I didn't know they had tore out the guts of it, and the walls in back are half-way down. Showed this crane with a iron ball on a chain. Looked like the London blitz or the ruins of Berlin. Momma just came to the door of the sanctuary and said, "Bucky was bright-eyed and thrilled to pieces to see me. Wasn't the least sign of a fever. Either he passed through the worst while I was riding the streetcar out there or it was all put on. I could have wrung the little dicken's neck. And then Max fired me for taking off to see Bucky, the greasy sonofabitch. I could cut his throat without batting an eye."

Hi Sugar,
  The best way to start a letter is I love you. I feel as close to you as my skin is to me. Honey, I don't love anybody but "You." Not one soul. Oh, yeah, I love God but I mean on earth. Sometimes I think just really how much I do love you & I get right sick.
  Lucius I hope you're over your madness. If we ever really broke up I'd just run off (to Maine). If we were only old enough to get "hitched." Lucius I can't seem to make you understand how much I do care for you. When you got mad that hurt me worser then it did you. Lucius I care for you as much as I do myself. I'm not writing this just to be writing.
  I rode on Walt's motorsickle to make you jealous. If you will forgive me, I'll never try to make you jealous again, because I can't begin

to tell you much I do love you. I'm jealous, too. And I'm jealous of the following: Larue Harrington. Della Snow, and a few more. I'll never get that "engagement ring" you promised me if I keep on making you jealous. I hope you love me as good as I do you, and if you do that would be saying a lot. If you do, it will tell by the type of note you write back. If you was to ever leave & go off like you said on the phone last night, that would hurt me a lot. If we are mad and do remain that way it would take me a long time to forget you, and your presence. I don't like Walt. And I don't like Gordon, neither. I played sucker for him last year but I sure won't this year because I have the cutest boy that ever was.

Seems like when we're with each other we fuss a terrible lot. I think we should discuss that part together and not on paper. Do you think we should stop now or go on? You can have it either way you decide although it does mean every thing to me to be with you. But this trouble we got won't last. Things always come out. Last night I would have given $50 dollars if I had it for you to have been with me. And too, lets not go with any other boys or girls. By that I mean lets not date any body but just me and you go together. I believe that's the only way we can get along, don't you? I've had some of the best times with you that I didn't have with other boys. The band just went out and Billy Timmons was with LaRue Harrington. He was carrying her musical instrument, they looked cute together, me & you do to, I think. I just love to hear them play the Star-Spangled Banner. Prissy Cobb just put Teeter Letner in in front of the room because all he did was blab. She'd cut my water off if she knew I was writing this note. Wow she's rough as a Cobb. I wonder whats ailing her. I'm going to finish my outline. (I hope) I've got to do 18 more sections. You can read this in detention hall. I wish you was in here and nobody else was. Honey, I'd kiss you cross-eyed. Miss Cobb is just *looking* over here. Hope she can't read what I put.

I just got through reading every slap-dab one of your notes. Lucius, I'm half crazy because I'm so much in love with you. Sometimes I'm just setting here & I just shake & wring my hands. Lucius, let's get married. You can't back out now because I just right now talked to you by your locker, and you asked me to.

Raine, who now loves you and always will no matter what.

Dear Immortal Love,

When I love someone I never quit. Like Larue, I still like her deep down in. Nothing too real though. Someone out of a life gone long ago, never to return. With each girl comes a new life, a phase in the major life, a life that must fulfill my dreams, wants, and desires. As the saying goes—The Bird of Time has but a short while to flutter—And the Bird is on the Wing. I love you darling while the Bird is on the Wing sailing cheerfully through the quiet arches of my life, you shall be the warmth and sweetness of the time with which it has to fly. The bird will never tire for you and me as long as you love me even half as much I love you. Sometimes you think I don't love you. Well, my dear, it's this way. There is a wall between you and me. A wall that failure, disgust, sadness, sin, and Larue has built with stones of glass. On my side of that wall there is much love, beauty, and devotion waiting solely for you, at the will of God. It is up to you to tear down that glassy wall. That was just an illustration.

They're singing some pretty music in music class and it makes me think of you. I wish you and I were down in Florida now, together, inwoven in the bounds of holy matrimony. You as Mrs. Lucius Hutchfield, wife of that amazing young and talented writer and illustrator, author of all those wonderful books. We walk down the beach clad with many famous people.

We were destined by the wonderful will of God to love each other, so if we ever broke up, our love someday would bloom again like a turbulent flower of unsurpassed beauty, from out of the muck, black earth of lonelyness and dispair, we may someday be a part of, should a great and terrible sword cut the lovely bonds that hold our loves together.

My love, such words of beauty that linger in my fluttering heart so perpetuant with its cherishing love for you, my soul will not let free, for it loves and adores such words that describe you, and it cannot bare to lose them. Fore, my darling, my soul drinks the wine of life and love from those words telling of my love for you, and it drinks on and on becoming most lustful and again more passionable as every drop it swallows. Yet the wine is never all taken.

There are somethings you cannot say merely on paper, so some of the most induring things I must say to you will have to explode from the massive inferno of my heart when we are together.

Always in your arms,
Lucius

Tues. December 17, 1946. Tarzan and the Leopard Woman. Bought The Heart Is a Lonely Hunter at River Bridge. Read "A Municiple Report by O. Henry." Raine and me wrote each other letters. Gale and me went to the Venice to see Singing in the Corn with Judy Canova and Allen Jenkins. Set behind Barbara Cotter and Barbara Arnett, and Mary Ed. Reading "Big Blonde" by Dorothy Parker when Raine called. Turned out the light in Mrs. Maggard's living room. Cars passed by out on the street and girls laughing past by the house. I felt very close to Raine over the phone. We talked very nice to each other. It was wonderful and we are in love. May God let it always be with Raine and me. I've lost God since last summer. I must find him again. I need him.

Wens. December 18, 1946. Tarzan and the Leopard Woman. Dr. Summers was mad because I missed Whirlpool therapy last week. Writing "April Tragidy" in school.

Thurs. December 19, 1946. Alan Ladd in Two Years Before the Mast, started today. Saw Blue Dahlia with Raine at the Hiawassee. She loves it, too. Read "Paul's Case" by Willa Cather.

Fri. December 20, 1946. Two Years Before the Mast. Their going to send Bucky to Ephraim Lee Institute when they have room. Last day of school until next year.

When he wasn't On the Spot at the Bijou, Lucius ran with Raine and the Clayboe Ridge gang. They covered many miles, aimlessly walking the streets, dashing into Kay's ice cream parlor or the Blue Circle or Krystal Kitchen or a movie theatre out of the cold, and spent many hours lolling around Peggy's living room, down the road from Raine's, their legs looped over furniture, listening to Peggy and Raine play duets on the piano and sing gospel and popular songs, listening to Boogie Woogie on the radio, watching the girls jitterbug together, listening to each other squabble over trivia, watching Peggy's momma and daddy and big sister and her husband and their little kids traipse back and forth through the room. Because of the way they did it, everything they did impressed Lucius.

But when he was alone, roaming, or at home, he was aware that very different things mattered to him, and in very different ways. Sometimes, he didn't want to wander with them. He winced when they talked about ways to "kill time." But then he felt empty for missing whatever they were doing while he was writing or reading or making stops at bookstores and record shops.

Lucius had permanent passes now to most of the theatres, and he loved to flash it and go in and stand by the aisle and watch a few minutes, then go back out, and on about his business. Sometimes he wove in and out of four theatres that way, and throughout the run of movies over a three-day period, he liked to come in on shows at different points, as if the life being shown went on continuously and he'd just walked by and glanced through a window. And then when they came to the Bijou he saw them again, brokenly, until he'd finally seen or at least overheard them, all the way through.

In Lucius's absence, Duke had begun running regularly with the Clayboe Ridge gang. Peggy thought he was the berries, but made fun of him, behind his back, sometimes with Lucius and Harry. Loraine seemed impressed by him. Lucius looked at Duke more closely now. Although she never broke off with Harry, and showed no overt signs of taking up with Duke, something implied about Duke came between Peggy and Harry.

"Let's get together, just you and me," said Harry, tossing a dixie cup into the trash can, "and hunt us down some pussy on the hoof."

"This one girl I know might be fer it," said Lucius, thinking of Shirley Ford.

Sat. December 21, 1946. Two Years Before the Mast. Alan Ladd's not as good as he is in gangster pictures. Elmo sat with Shirley in the Venice and ——.

Sun. December 22, 1946. Me and Harry —— Shirley at her house while her mother and brother was at church and her grandmother was in the back room sick yelling for her to come empty her slop jar. Sinking springs sag, zigzagging rumps of labor love. Then I visited Bucky before work. Same vat of lard answered the buzzer. "Well, won't be long 'fore we get the whole family behind Earl's electric bob-wire." Said they were putting Bucky in Ephraim Lee's Institute next week. Mr. Hammer used to tell us when we complained about St. Thomas that we ought to thank our lucky stars we weren't at E.L.I. Bucky was swinging on the swings where I used to swing with him when we were there together, dragging his feet in the dust to stop the swing when Mrs. Ailor told him I was there. He looked pitiful in that old pilot's helmet with the flaps flopping and his mackinaw open, all the buttons off, his corduroy trousers legs rolled up at the bottoms, whorping against each other, the string of one shoe untied. It hurt my feelings when Mrs. Ailor said all he talks about is his big brother. Earl. We even set at the same desks as that time I visited Earl. Except he loved the Bugs Bunny funny book and the suckers with cherry stuff inside, and the pecan log, and juicy fruit chewing gum. The Brummett girls are in there, too, because their momma ran off to Baltimore with some old man and their daddy don't want them. All the kids are either too big or too little and he doesn't have any friends. When I told him it looked like he wouldn't get to come home for Christmas, he cried and it made me cry too. Lard ass listened in while I was telling Bucky a Zorro story. The Chase with Robert Cummings, Peter Lorre, and Michele Morgan.

Mon.–Tues. December 23–24, 1946. The Chase. Read "The Monkey's Paw" by W. W. Jacobs. Harry's worried he caught the clap off ——. Bought Tragic Ground by Erskine Caldwell, River Book Store. Read

part of The Chastity of Gloria Boyd by Donald Henderson Clark.
A lot of his books on the shelves. Mix him up with James M. Cain
sometimes and Walter Van Tilburg Clark who wrote The Ox-Bow
Incident.

Chief Buckner sat in Mammy's chair, in his fireman's uniform, smoking
a big Dutch Master, and on the arm of the chair sat Mammy, dressed
up fit to kill, and through the flowered drapes, Lucius saw the kitchen
table, loaded with food, the bowls steaming. "Merry Christmas," she
said, a jolly female Santa Claus.

Wens. December 25, 1946. They didn't let Bucky come home for
Christmas. Momma called Uncle Hop's and we all talked with Earl.
He didn't like the presents we sent him. Rather have money. Momma
screamed bloody murder when I asked could Daddy come for Xmas
dinner. He didn't call. "No telephones under the Sevier Street viaduct, I recon," Momma said. Everybody felt sad because Bucky, Luke,
and Earl was missing. I got sick on too much turkey and mince meat
pie. Chief drove Mammy and Momma to Ephraim Lee, but Mammy
stayed in the car with the Chief. I didn't go. Bad enough imagining it.
Gave Raine a big box of candy. She ate so much she puked over
Peggy's banister. She said I got something for you. It was a camera.
One of her sisterinlaws took a picture of Raine and I in front of
Peggy's house. We were sitting in the swing, crammed together, and the
red ash of my cigar the Chief gave me burnt the lob of her ear. She's the
sweetest girl alive. Had to go On the Spot at 4:00. Gale showed us this
surplus army jeep he bought. After work he gave us all a ride home.
It was great. I always wanted to ride in one. If I had the money to get
there, I'd be in Jerusalem right now, looking toward Calvary from the
window of my room, and it full of rifles and TNT to fight the British
and the Arabs. The Chase.

Thurs. December 26, 1946. Took Raine to see I've Always Loved You
at Bijou, with Philip Dorn, Catherine McLeod, and Vanessa Brown.
This musician loves Catherine but when she gets to be better than he
is, he tries to destroy her, and even works on her daughter years later.
Raine didn't like it, but I did. I loved it. While I was there, Hood
made me help Elmo put the valence up. Gave Raine "Souls Under Conflict" to read. We ate at Mammy's cafe. Momma has a new job now
as practical nurse to the invalid wife and new baby of the councilman
who owns Randall's funeral home.

NIGHT RITUAL: Lucius and the Hawn brothers play fox and hounds with
the Brummett girls and finger them in the weeds. . . . The Beech boys
hop a freight to Bull's Run or Beaver Creek or Powell Station. . . .
Mammy shows Lucius Gran'paw Charlie's shoes, saying, "They still in
good shape. Won't be long fore you'll be able to wear 'um, they so
small." He sits down beside the clothes box and tries them on. They ·

feel a fit. He throws his own wet shoes onto the back porch. . . . Walking to Luttrell's farm and playing in the hayloft and riding the mean horses and eating mulberries and crabapples. . . . Lying on one of his quilts with Jim Bob in the jungle across from Lilly's Pond, waiting for the Brummetts' pretty cousin to pass by from the streetcar stop, trying to jack off as she goes by, unable to come. . . . Taking over Sonny's paper route and Sonny collecting each Friday anyway and beating up Lucius when he complains and he turns the other cheek and Sonny slaps it, too. . . . Breaking into L. T. Dobbs's at night over on Grand and stealing soap and sugar and dopes and fizzing them against the large Orange Crush sign painted on the side of Fisher's store. . . . Playing jungle with the Brummett girls, taking turns being Tarzan and Jane and Boy and Cheetah, and always two left out—Bucky and Judy, too little. Then Bucky and Judy go off and play Tarzan and Jane all by themselves. And Alice says I ain't going to do it anymore, and Earl gives her a dime, and she does, and Sonny and Jim Bob gang up on her and take the dime away from her and she cries and Lucius stays with her when they run. . . . Suddenly, but too late for pride or safety to run or hide, seeing Sonny walk toward him down the street. . . . Thinking of the story of Sonny's daddy coming home drunk in a snow blizzard and going to sleep by the pump. . . . Earl talking Sonny out of beating him up. . . . Earl running when he sees Sonny coming down Beech. . . . Sonny, the only bully Earl really fears. . . . Watching Sonny fuck his bulldog. . . . "If I have to lie, cheat, steal, or kill," said Lucius, squinting his eyes at the sky, shaking his fist at the forces of uncertainty, "I will nev-er—go—hun-gry—a—gain!" . . . A boy in the auto graveyard said Joseph did it to Mary to get Jesus, and Lucius smeared his ass. . . .

> Sun. December 29, 1946. Till the End of Time with Guy Madison starts today. Ate dinner at Mammy's. Visited Bucky at Ephraim Lee. Its a string of old mansions and farms strung out over a long ridge. Took him some stuff and told him and some boys a Straight Hair & Fatsi story. After I left Bucky, I was too sad to write so I walked on the river. Climbed up in the tower and watched the sun go down beyond the Sevier Street Bridge and the Grand Street Bridge and the L & N tressle.

> Mon. December 30, 1946. Till the End of Time. Read "Bliss" by Katherine Mansfield. Not so hot. Went to see High School Hero at the Hollywood. Wrote some of "Through Heaven and Hell." Raine called. Ruby, Luke's secret sweetheart, was at the show.

Coming out of the Tivoli after seeing *The Locket,* Lucius stepped into Wygle's department store and went up to the balcony to listen to *Orpheus in Hades* by Offenbach that he'd heard one Sunday afternoon on NBC Symphony. Then he walked down Sevier Street toward the Bijou, stopping off ritualistically at three other stores to listen in booths to the part of Tschaikovsky's Piano Concerto that Freddy Martin had stolen. Playing the records, he began to feel as he did when handling the stills, or handling the used books in the River Bridge store or the new ones in Matthews's. He slipped "Clair de Lune," played by Jose Iturbi, up the front of his leather jacket. But before he left the booth, he took it out and paid for it at the counter where an old lady treated him like scum.

Around the corner from the Crockett Hotel on Bluff was a radio repair store in an old house next to the mansion of the first resident in Cherokee, now a public monument. For weeks, he'd stopped to look through the grimy window at a portable windup victrola, shaped like a suitcase. Yesterday, a little card with a price showed up on the turntable, as if the repairman had noticed Lucius's unrelenting curiosity. Lucius paid the man three dollars to "take this junk off my hands" and set the suitcase on the curb in front of the first residence in Cherokee and listened to Debussy's "Clair de Lune." It was so beautiful and sad and glorious it hurt. Not until he stood up to go, did he see three Negro kids listening from a rooftop, clustered around a leaning chimney.

> Tues. December 31, 1946. Till the End of Time. Perry Como did
> the background music on a record. Taken from Chopin's Polanaze.
> Bought me a new diary at Woolworth's. Red. On sale—last year's.
> Start tomorrow.

The few weeks alone in the Juvenile Detention Home after Earl went to Sante Fe only made Bucky mean and sullen, so at Ephraim Lee Institute, he was always in trouble, letting the cows let out onto the Pike, sassing the house fathers, breaking dishes when he had to work in the kitchen. The big kids beat him up and the superintendent punished him so much, Momma looked around for another place to send him.

> Wensday, January 1, 1946⁄7. Read "The Necklace" by Guy de
> Maupassant. Unforgettable. Put a dollar in savings at the Cherokee
> National Bank across from the Venice. They give you a dime bank
> shaped like an old-fashioned book for starting up a savings account.
> Looks good. Going to save enough to run off if I fail the 8th grade.
> Went to Paradice to see, China's Little Devil wih Paul Kelly and Harry
> Carey. Worked a little on "Storm," a radio drama. Till the End of Time
> ends today. Whirlpool. Hood told me to go to the Gallery and relieve
> Gale.

"Say, you write pretty good stories, Lucius," said Raine. "Did you just make 'em up, or copy 'em out of a magazine? Well, you needn't give me such a dirty look."

Thursday, January 2, 1947. The Locket starts today, with Loraine Day and Robert Mitchum and Brian Aherne. Bought Beau Geste at River Bridge. Raine didn't want to go in. Took her to see a real live Vaudeville show at the Bijou. Larue was there with her Momma. They let Bucky come home for a while.

Sunday, January 5, 1947. School starts again tomorrow. Humoresque with John Garfield and Joan Crawford is on. He plays a violinist out of the slums—like William Holden in Golden Boy. The Chief drove Bucky to Cold Springs.

Momma had found a place near Lone Mountain, twenty miles from Cherokee, called Cold Springs, that had been a summer resort hotel for wealthy people from the Gay Nineties until before World War I. Mammy and Gran'paw Charlie had ridden horse and buggy out there in the last year of its decline. Before Bucky went, he had been allowed a few days at home. Somehow, Bucky managed to break a window. At the end of "Helena Street," in the space left at the bottom of the page, he drew a picture of a face and under it wrote "Lucius." Lucius said it was good and tried to keep from getting mad that Bucky had messed around in his desk drawers, but he felt sorry for him, and guilty that he wanted Bucky not to come home to stay, imagining what a pain in the ass he would be. Even for the two days, Bucky insisted on having his drawer back, so Lucius took his stuff out, and Bucky put a nickel Mammy had given him and a bag of marbles he'd stolen in *his* drawer. The day after the Chief took Bucky to Cold Springs, Lucius erased Bucky's drawing, but the imprint of the hard pencil remained.

Monday, January 6, 1947. Humoresque. School started. I was eager to see Miss Redding. She looks like she's going to have a baby. It was strange to walk into Miss Kuntz's homeroom again. It was like prison and the guards looked and acted like they made a New Year's resolution to clean out the place by putting everybody in the electric chair before the week ends. The nicest part was getting our report cards. I thought I'd get all F's except in Art. But when I *saw* all those F's except for C in Art I couldn't hardly keep from crying. But I don't give a —— I'll be in Palestine this time next year.

Lucius had held in his hand many times the Penguin edition of W. Somerset Maugham's *The Summing Up*, which featured the exotic symbol on the front—white, with green, yellow, red circles around it like a whirlpool. "Perhaps the feeling for pattern can explain the mystic significance for Maugham of the Moorish symbol against the evil eye which appears on the cover." said the note on the back "About the Author." He'd been disdainful of the book because it was only nonfiction. But in the River Bookshop, he read: "It is only the artist, and maybe the criminal, Maugham says, who can choose his own life." The application to himself and to Earl and Bucky made Lucius put his hand in his pocket for money.

He had become bored with the burlesque shows at the Smoky and didn't want to wait ten minutes anyway, so he didn't stay after *Captain Fury*, with Victor McLaglen and Brian Aherne, was over. He was eager to get home to finish his second radio play, "The Sorrows of Hell," about two French gangsters, one of whom lies dying in a Paris warehouse. He was up to the point where Harry, the experienced gangster, has just learned that the love of his life, Regina, was once in love with Frenchie, the young gangster who is hiding with him in the warehouse, and that she is now dead and buried on a hill that can be seen from the window of the warehouse. And now Harry persuades Frenchie to shoot him, to put him out of his misery. Walking toward Sevier Street, Lucius listened to Frenchie and Harry.

> Promise me something, though, Harry.
> Yeah, Frenchie?
> I want you to go to sleep—praying. Perhaps—
> Sure, Frenchie. . . . I know what you mean. Thanks.
> After I shoot you, *I* am going to pray. Then I am going to give myself up to the police. And I am going to ask them to bury you and me out on that summit—under the great oak and poppies with Regina. They will do it if I pray. And perhaps—
> I hope you make it, Frenchie, to heaven, I mean. . . . You know, you might read something out of that little Bible you carry around—after you shoot me.
> I will, Harry. I did it for her.
> I'll try to sleep now, Frenchie. . . . I'm very tired.

Tuesday, January 7, 1946⁄7. The new projectionist, Monday Wise, is a ——. The Christian projectionist told Thelma the movies were too big a sin to waller in day by day, so he quit. I strolled in on my way home and Hood made me take the new projectionist some coffee and stuff. The balcony was closed. He's tall and wears glasses and loud shaving lotion. He let me have some cuts from Humoresque for my projector. I was watching the part where John Garfield is playing the violin in a concert and Joan Crawford, this rich society lady who helped him in his career, is in her beach house, drinking alone, and it goes back and forth from him to her, and she sees herself in a long dress in the window with the sea outside and breaks the glass and the wind comes in and blows these thin drapes, and she goes out to the surf in this long black, spangled gown and walks into the sea, my favorite part, but it looked sadder from up there in the booth, and Monday Wise come up to my ear and said, "How would you like to stick your pork in that?" and I almost hit him for talking dirty about Joan Crawford. The screen went dark and he had to jump to switch it over to the Paramount News. And then he pulled out some of those dirty funny books that Earl always said I ought to learn how to draw to get rich, and seeing Popeye, Moon Mullins, Andy Gump, Maggie and Jiggs, Barney Google, and Tillie the Toiler doing it made me feel like when I'm in the jungle and its about to rain, and he said he bet I had a —— and I said I didn't neither, but when he reached over he caught me in a lie. Tomarrow is Rebecca. "Last night I dreamt I went to Manderlay. . . ." It's a new series. What they call classics from the past every Wednesday from now on. How can you call a movie a classic?

Wensday, January 8, 1946⁄7. Rebecca. "Last night I dreamt I went to Manderlay again. It seemed to me I stood by the iron gate leading to the drive and for a while I could not enter, for the way was barred to me." I made a basket in gym. Whirlpool. "I feel like a rabbit with his balls caught in a sewing machine." Erskine Caldwell. Harry is reading God's Little Acre in school. I loaned it to him.

Every time he wrote Ronny Dennis Hutchfield at the head of a sheet of notebook paper, everything stopped. Then while mild Mrs. Dakins, standing against the windowsill, the winter light soft on her rust-grey hair, dictated a test to the health class, Lucius wrote "Ernest Hutchfield" and loved the look of it. He went all through the recent stuff in his notebook and erased the other names and wrote in Ernest Hutchfield.

Dear Lucius,
Lucius, sometimes I pity you because I love you so much. You yelled at me to turn you aloose the other night when we were on Peggy's devanet. I got so tickled. I'm setting here about to freeze to death.
Honey I just read that story you wrote. I read the last page twice. You know I wish you hadn't let me read that. It gives me a feeling like I had yesterday. I mean a really wanting feeling. You know, honey, I'll give you the honest words right here and every word is true. It's the first time I've ever felt that way. It's been in me all day today and when I was with you yesterday. I wish I could get rid of it because. . . .
Now I'm in the kitchen. Practically on top of the stove. I do love you but gosh ding! I lots rather tell you out to your face as in a note. I can still hear you say you love me, just every move you made. Don't you say I loved you if I set & hug a blamed pillow every night: I got down today & just imagined it was you. If I had you now I'd kiss the fool out of you. I had to get up to fix the fire. I was just thinking about you so hard I let it burn down and nearly

froze. I've been listening to a murder story for about 15 or 20 minutes. Awwwww it's so scary but aawwwww lala its so good. I'm so cold I wish we were in Maine in our house. I keep all your letters in the Christmas candy box you gave me.

We've got to learn some rules. The first 10 that learns them gets double A. If I don't get one I'll die.

No wonder I fell in the creek today. You couldn't at least waited until I got across to kiss me? After four days of not kissing, it really got me. Lucius I said last night I was going to quit acting silly when were together and I'm going to quit acting silly any way its 25 after 11. Where's my pillow? I wish that was us instead of Carol and Mark in that story you wrote. Except for the divorce.

Love "Always" Raine (Whistle Breeches)

Suddenly realizing that "Whistle Breeches" was what you call somebody who's always farting, Lucius blushed.

Thursday, January 9, 1947. Temptation. Bought the Avon Annual at River Book Store. Short stories. There's one by Irwin Shaw, "The City Was in Total Darkness" where this guy says "He wants a character out of Thomas Wolfe." Strange to see Thomas Wolfe's name in somebody's story. My other book has too many old writers in it, Stevenson, Bret Harte, Tolstoy. But I like *it*, too, anyway.

My Darling Raine,

My thoughts love you, darling. They wander from other things to you. I told God that there wasn't any use in letting me live any longer if I ever quit loving you, which is, my dear, past the impossible. I love you. That is the only thing in this hell-of-a-strange world that I am positively sure of. I love you very much. That is the most absolute statement of truth I have ever made and I mean it from the pit of my heart. Words are weak, they are not fit to discribe the love that burns like a torch within me. The walls of my mind echo night and day of the love, adoration, and yearning that screams from my heart. In paris under the great Arch of Triumph burns a flame in dedication of the unknown soilder, night and day, beyond storm and war and hunger, the flame burns on. This is how my love for you goes, on and on, the flame never ceasing to glow.

I'm writing a new radio play. "The Limping Corpse." For Molle Mystery Theater. Imagine me and you setting before the radio and listening to my play being acted by some famous actor—Lawrence Olivier. And then at the close of the program the announcer says, "Our play tonight was written especially for this program by Ernest Birchfield." I'd really be a snob then, but not with you, Raine.

Being an author is like being a big shot gambler, you win or lose, and whether you have a steady streak of either depends on the writer's talent.

My love for you is even worth going to the reform school for. You know, that wouldn't be bad. I could at least have plenty of time to write. Gosh, I could write four books in two years. It would be a classic joke. The principal gets me sent up the river. I come out rich, famous, and marry you.

When I am with you I forget the hell of life and I live. I wish sometimes I could live like some of my characters: such as Dan Fontaine, Rhett Darcy, Sam Gulliver, Lamarr Haven, Parris, and Chad Havlin. But I can only write, and there find the emptyness of life quite filled.

Love forever and then some,
Lucius

Friday, January 10, 1947. Temptation. Merle Oberon and George Brent is on. We had a show at school. As in study hall I'm reading The Summing Up by W. Somerset Maugham, this boy asks, "What do you get out of *that* shit?" "I get out of being ignorant." Saw a man get beat up in front of the Bijou. Ate hamburgers with Gale and them in the still room. "I may kiss your ass today but I'll be aiming to kick it tomorrow." Adria Locke Langley, A Lion Is In the Streets.

Saturday, January 11, 1947. Temptation. Earl ran off. Uncle Hop called. They caught him yesterday. Guarded the stage door at BB Club and Christine this gril from South Cherokee came to sing. She looks like Evelyn Keyes. Three grils, friends of her, and she too talked to me backstage. I kinda like one of them whose name is Frances, but Christine the best.
To Raine
Her love is sincere, her beauty divine,
I lover her deeply now—till the end of time.
L. H.
P.S. Harry just came by at midnight and sat on my bed and talked about Peggy and cried and I patted his shoulder about it. He prays to have Peggy—she's in love with Duke.

Uncle Hop called Daddy at the bakery to tell him the hell Earl had put him through, and Daddy came by the councilman's house where Momma was a practical nurse and tried to tell Momma, while she tried to give him the bum's rush, for the judge had forbidden him to try to see her at home or at work. And, his story half-told, he'd tried to find Lucius, Thelma reported, but he was out to supper. And they just missed each other at Jane's Cafe, where Daddy told Mammy the rest of the story.

Then she told Momma, and when Lucius got home that night, Momma told him, and the next day, the heat from the coal heater hit him like a wool blanket as he came in Mammy's front door and he began to sweat, and they sat around all day, Momma sat on one side of the heater, Mammy on the other, their feet up on the fenders, toasting themselves, telling each other the bare outline, each filling in the gaps with variations of her own.

According to what Aunt Lou told Uncle Hop, Earl woke Aunt Lou up last Tuesday morning just after Uncle Hop had gone to work and asked her for some money to get him to Mexico and when she said, "Honey, I ain't got it to spare," he said he knew she didn't have anything in her purse, but he was also certain she had some hidden away, and she said what she had hid was to get her a new set of teeth, and he said if she didn't give it to him, he'd kill her, and she saw he had a golf club in his hand that *her* nephew left behind when *he* came for a visit. So she gave Earl her saved-up fifty dollars and he took off.

Then a few days later, Aunt Lou left the house to get the balance of her teeth pulled, and when she came back, all the furniture was gone. The house had been stripped of every stick, and the radio was gone and her new double-wringer washing machine.

The police checked all the used furniture stores, and sure enough a woman had called and told Liupa's Used Furniture Store to bring a truck and buy up a whole houseful of furniture, that she was moving to Alaska on the frontier to start a new life and didn't want to drag all that furniture, and that her invalid son would be there to let them in and take the money.

The police caught Earl in Las Vegas, asleep on the twelfth floor of a fancy hotel with ten cheap rings in a little jeweler's display case that cost far more than the rings and a hundred dollars in bills in the wallet in his new suit. He denied everything, saying he inherited the money from an old man he'd befriended in Rockport, Maine, but the police figured out that he'd been robbed in Flagstaff of the fifty bucks he took from Aunt Lou, then he'd doubled back, waited for her to leave the house, broken in, and imitated Aunt Lou's voice, and sold all the furniture right out the front door.

Aunt Lou and Uncle Hop were buffaloed. They couldn't understand where a seventeen-year-old boy learned such tricks. No, they weren't going to press charges because when they found out that the New Mexico State Police wanted him for passing bad checks in Albuquerque and Gallup three weeks before, they understood why the poor boy did them the way he did. He was "despurt."

Sitting on Luke's busted sled, in the circus-wagon coal house, Lucius daydreamed ways of bringing all three of them together—Earl, Bucky, and Daddy—of solving all their problems, reforming them, by starting a bakery and making them partners, or buying a farm and raising steers.

Sunday, January 12, 194⁄7. My Darling Clementine, with Henry Fonda, Victor Mature, Linda Darnell. About Wyatt Urp and Doc Holiday. Ate at Mammy's. Chief didn't come.

Loraine,
This morning I noticed out of the corner of my eye that you were gazing admiredly at that drip of a Gordon Puckett. Being the jealous person that I am, I knew that you still loved him and not me.

Lucius Hutchfield

Dear Lucius,
That note I got from you today I was shocked. And Lucius if we aren't sweethearts anymore, we can speak. It would have made you mad if I'd went up the hall and got with a boy and walked by you with him like you did me today. You was walking with LaWanda and Duke and Peggy were in front of you, walking together. I tried to laugh it off, but it made me so mad I saw sparks, and that's the reason I didn't care how much I talked to Gordon today. I wouldn't have done you like that, I'd have had a little bit more pity for your feelings. But I'm not mad. I like Gordon for a friend, but I don't like any boy like I love you, I don't appreciate what you wrote in that snotty Jeanette Lobertini's opinion book, after all I wrote about you.

Have you ever felt you could take something and break it into a million pieces with one little finger? Well I'm going to have to knock you in the head to let you know I love you, and NOBODY else. If we can't believe in each other's love then maybe we better quit. It sounds easy to say quit but I've never tried to really write it before. It just pulls at my hand & something says don't write it. It makes every muscle in my body ache because it would kill me if we did but it's got to be said sometime so now or never. Put yourself in my place and think it over. And if you don't still yet love *me*, stop broadcasting it that you do, Buddy Boy. Are you still mad? You sure act it.

Are you going to the Minstral Show their having Thursday at Bonny Kate? Though I would go. I'm buying my ticket today. Lucius, I figure on getting you something nice for your birthday even if it is 8 months off.

Love till Doomsday, "Raine"

Monday, January 13, 194⁄7. My Darling Clementine. Fuss with Raine.

Tuesday, January 14, 194⁄7. My Darling Clementine. "Granny" Mitchell caught me and Raine in the hall when I was jerking her arm asking if Gordon really gave her a bracelet. I had to stay in for it. "Granny" exaggerated. Went over to Peggy's after school. I told Raine to give back the bracelet. We had a good time at Peggy's. Joy and Cora was there they fussed. I rode Peggy on my back. Cora said Gordon didn't really give Raine a bracelet, she was just trying to make me jealous. I pinched Raine and she bit a piece of skin off my knuckle. I started to leave but she stopped me. I barely kissed her good-night. I still love her very much. Jesse James classic comes tomarrow.

Lucius turned off the furnace. The whirr of the motor stopped, he felt an inrush of silence, the presence of the gigantic pile of coal. Even the shovel, shoved into the pile where Brady had left it, looked threatening. He heard Gale and Elmo, who'd been changing the marquee from *My Darling Clementine* to *Jesse James* and *The Return of Frank James,* stacking leftover red and silver aluminum letters. Cutting off all lights behind him, Lucius walked back toward the stairs. The lights ahead went out. Lucius turned on his flashlight. "All right, Elmo, goddam it!"

A fiendish laugh. "Who knows—what eeee-vil lurks—in the hearts of men. The Shad-dow knows!" The fiendish laugh again.

Lucius went on up and turned out all the dressing room lights. The moldy smell of the dark empty rooms made them sexy, scary.

Elmo and Gale, out in the auditorium, were yelling up to Brady, who was checking "Nigger Heaven." Lucius stepped out onto the stage, dark behind, below. Elmo, his head thrown far back, whispered loudly up to Brady, who leaned over the crooked railing in the second balcony, throwing a flashlight beam straight down on Gale and Elmo: "Check the Fontana Hotel while you're at it."

"Roger, Kemosabe."

"Help us turn back the seats," said Elmo, seeing Lucius come down the steps beside the stage.

Starting at the front, Elmo took the middle section, Lucius the left, Gale the right, and they turned back the seats, working toward the lobby, where Thelma was saying goodnight to Hood. Up in the first balcony, Clancy slammed and locked the steel door to the projection booth, then went down the stairs, carrying the reels in their transport cans. Elmo would take them to the bus terminal to go on the one A.M. Greyhound to Atlanta.

Bent over the seats, flipping them back, scanning the filthy floor for lost articles, the squeak and clap-clap-clap and thudding of the seats in his ears, clearing the way for the predawn maids—all these late night, empty-theatre activities made Lucius move with grace and style, a feeling of being part of an important activity.

A beam shot down from the second balcony. Brady stood just inside the fourth exit door. He flashed his light on and off, three times. Scurrying down the row, Elmo ran behind the box seats to his special dressing room by the steps to the stage as Lucius and Gale crossed the auditorium. Hood was in his office, the only entry to the Negro balcony from inside the main theatre. So they had to go out the fire door and through the Negro entrance and up four flights.

"Shhhhhhhh, Lucius! Hood might hear us. Walk softly."

"Well, wait, dammit, it's dark."

Elmo caught up with them.

From the fire escape, they scanned the windows of the Fontana Hotel.

"Oh, hell, don't tell me she's gone," said Brady.

"Better not be, Shit Hook," said Gale.

Out of breath, his stomach hurting, Lucius felt dizzy from the climb and the outdoors height.

"There she is! God!" said Elmo.

"Where, dammit?" asked Gale.

"There! Fifth window from the back, second floor!" Elmo looked through his spyglasses.

"Shut up," said Gale. "She might hear us."

"Worshing her cock," said Lucius.

"Cock?"

"Yeah. Cock."

"That's a pussy," said Elmo. "Don't you know the difference between a cock and a pussy?"

"Well, we called pussy 'cock' where *I* used to live."

"If you're dying to see a cock, I'll show you one, but not till I get done looking at her pussy."

"How you like them titties?" asked Brady.

"I wouldn't kick her out of bed," said Elmo.

"Hey, there's a *man*," said Lucius.

"Look at his pus-sy!" said Elmo.

"Kick your ass off this fire 'scape," muttered Lucius. "You see him fuck her, Brady?"

"She's getting dressed," said Elmo. "But he's just sitting on the bed smokin'."

"We can see," said Gale.

"Why don't he screw her again?" asked Brady.

"Lucius's got a hard-on," said Elmo.

"I ain't done it."

"Hey, everybody, look! Lucius got a big-ass hard-on."

"*Big?*" said Brady. "Hell, his pecker's so little, he once't pulled out a hair by mistake and pissed in his pants."

"She sure is fast," said Elmo. "Hey, he's *paying* the bitch."

Suddenly sad, Lucius wished they wouldn't talk about her that way.

"Hey, why don't we *get* some of that?" asked Elmo.

"I'd rather jack off on Sevier Street," said Brady.

"Make you bust out all over with pus," said Gale.

"Blind your ass," said Elmo.

"I ain't never had it," Gale told Elmo. "But I guess *you* know enough about it for *both* of us."

The door in the room shut, and the man stayed on the bed, smoking a cigarette. When he lay back, out of sight, smoke spewed into the window frame.

"Ow!"

"Shut up!" said Elmo.

"What's the matter?" asked Gale. "Got grit in my eye," said Lucius.

Elmo grabbed Lucius's arm and twisted it until he cried: "What's you do *that* for?"

"You still got the grit in your eye?"

"No."

"Worshed it out for you."

The Bijou Boys turned their backs to the hotel, leaned against the railing, and talked back through what they'd just seen.

Lucius had noticed that ever since the symphony concert, the things he told them about, his ideas about girls and God, made them ridicule him with less and less of the friendly manner that had kept him from being too hurt in the past. He began to detect a cool attitude, covert looks, hear overtones, catch secret allusions that brought laughs. Reminding him of the way people treated Duke. He'd been in on that himself.

Lucius leaned over the railing and gazed at the mellow glow of lighted shades, like the radio band in Mammy's old console radio. Feeling dizzy from the open height, he saw a young blond-haired woman turn on a light and start taking off her green dress. She hung it up very slowly, neatly, on a hanger, on a hook, on the back of the door, covering up a small, square, white sign. Then she took off her pink slip, folded it neatly. Bending over to drape it on a chair pulled her panties tight in the crack of her fanny, showing the cheeks, firm, round, a bruised place on one. Tender, pink marks on her bare legs where her garters had pressed into her skin. She reached back and, unhooking her brassiere, released her small breasts. Then she pulled down her panties and stepped out of them. She lit a cigarette and lay back on the bed, naked. She reached over and picked up a magazine. Lucius tried to make out what kind it was, hoping to establish some kinship, but couldn't. He imagined her reading *Cosmopolitan*. But she shut the magazine, bored, tossed it down to the foot of the bed, and reached for a book that lay on the lamp table. Casually, she stroked her breasts, then her pussy, stretched, yawned, turned out the light. In the dark, she smoked. None of the Bijou Boys saw her.

Walking home, sleepy, Lucius saw the girl lying awake. He saw Raine asleep, naked, but felt ashamed and shut off the image.

Wensday, January 15, 1946̸7. Jesse James and The Return of Frank James. First double feature since I been there. Jesse James is in technicolor but Frank James isn't. Never saw it before. Almost as good as Jesse, which is one of my favorites. We saw this man and woman over at the Cumberland Hotel. Whirlpool.

NIGHT RITUAL: Thelma's mother, ironing in Lucius's mother's kitchen. Her wrinkled face, her creepy walk, scare him, like the cartoon witch in *Snow White* that he often confuses with the live one in *The Wizard of Oz*. He discovers an odd electrical connection between the switch on the back porch and the iron. When he flicks the switch, the iron cools. The tall, gaunt old lady, hair pulled back tight in a knot at the back of her head, walks around in the dim kitchen, bewildered, a country woman used to heating her irons on a hot cookstove—as Lucius's family had, only a few years before. Then Lucius lets it heat up again. She must think the iron is cursed. She is an intruder, a specter, who came to live with Thelma several months before. Lucius enjoys teasing her every time she irons. . . . He steps into the hall to go to the bathroom. She is sitting on the commode, letting the door hang open, her old-timey, tiny-floweredy printed cotton dress hiked up over her hips, the hem wadded in one hand, exposing thin yellow shanks and a stark white belly—odd that an old woman has a belly button—her hair let down, long, thin, and stringy like a mop dried in the sun, and she raises her head, a glazed look, her toothless mouth agape in a frozen grunt. Disgusted, horrified, contemptuous, frightened, Lucius goes out and pisses behind the collapsing garage, but then the image excites him, persistently, and he pretends a little later to have to go again. She is still sitting there, her panties bagged around her ankles, groaning. An hour later, he peeks. She is gone. When he happens to glance in there again, an hour later, she is there, exactly as before. . . . Then he goes to the Hiawassee to see a rerun of *Frankenstein* which he'd missed, although he'd seen all the sequels. Because of the monster's kindness to the little girl, Lucius's fear of him undergoes, despite the fact he finally kills her by the lake, a transmutation into comradeship, and by an effort of will and imagination, Frankenstein (as he calls the Monster) who years ago terrified him more than any other creature becomes his companion, warding off Wolf Man, as he walks unafraid, through the dark stretches between streetlights and through the tile factory in the two miles home—before, it was the specter of Franken-stein himself and nameless and faceless other monsters that had hovered in the shadows. . . . When he comes into the high grass in his front yard, a weak light is burning on the back porch. Momma, Bucky, Earl, and a strange, tall, black-curlyheaded man in a blue shirt are out there eating watermelon. "Ain't none left for you, Lucius," says Bucky, pretending sadness, over his smugness. "Lucius," says Momma, "Thel-ma's Momma's dead, honey." She and Mammy have such a deadpan theatrical way of announcing disaster that Lucius can't grasp it. "Earl come in and found her on the bathroom floor, out cold, and after they pumped out her stomach, she died, poor old thing." "What did it?" Something, he knows, connected with electricity. "Honey, that poor thing was so blind she put rat poison instead of sugar on her fried apples. Offered 'em to Caroline when she came home from swimming. Thank God, Caroline didn't want any." She'd offered some to Lucius, too, but because he hated her, he couldn't stomach the idea of eating anything she'd fixed. He starts crying. "Don't cry, honey. It's probably for the best. She was old, old, old, honey, and feeble." Lucius stares at the light switch, thinks that if someday he went to the electric chair for fucking the Brummett girls, *he* would know that God was really making him suffer for Thelma's mother's death.

"Better stand back, here comes Trigger," said Duke, stepping up beside Lucius to the urinals, between English and art.

"Saw some great pussy last night."

"*You* didn't see no pussy."

"Fontana *Ho*tel. Purtiest little ass, and she had blond hair on her pussy." Lucius realized he didn't feel about her the way his voice sounded.

"Reckon she was one of 'em that got burnt up?"

"Got burnt *up?*"

" 'At fire last night."

"What fire?"

Zipping up his pants, having only flourished his dong, Duke looked at Lucius astonished, then grinned, possessed of information he was delighted to deliver. "The fuckin' Fontana Hotel, boy, it burnt down to a spot of grease last night."

"You 'pect me to b'*lieve* that?"

"Take a look as you go home 'iss afternoon."

"God, Duke, you ain't *kid*ding me?"

"No, fucker, I'm tellin' you, fifty damned people burnt up. You might been the last to see 'at girl's pussy alive." On the platform, his back to the urinals, Lucius stared at the commode in one of the doorless stalls. "I'd love to go see it. . . . What the hell's the matter with *you*, Lucius? You know somebody staying there?"

"Yeah. . . . See you, Duke."

"See you later, Alligator." Duke went out, taps on Luke's combat boots racketing in the hall. "Okay, Joe, I *told* you I was gonna *get* your ass!"

Lucius stared at the living, pulsing winter light that shone on the commode through the window. "I'm the lowest goddam sonofabitchin' bastard—shit!—in the world!" Enraged, he hit himself in the cods and sank to his knees. When the pain had subsided, he saw himself kneeling on the latrine room tile floor and the realization that he was trying to present a dramatic tableau to an unseen but attentive audience filled him with sickening self-hatred that made him almost too weak to get up. He began to cry, not just for the girl whose real life he'd imagined last night and who'd inspired a story this morning in which he named her Rosemary, but for all the others, whose names, real or fiction, he didn't yet know.

All day, wind rumbled in the windowpanes, made the shades flap, and rattled the bare branches of the mimosa trees outside as Lucius sat in class after class. The sky slate grey, but the wind warm for January, the atmosphere almost muggy for a while, then chilly.

Swaying on the bench, staring, Lucius ate lunch in a heavy, sluggish trance. On the playground, the way the trees waved, shimmered, and shook in the wind excited him. When he caught himself embellishing his feelings about the fiery deaths with stances, strides, postures, gestures that would look dramatic and profound if someone happened to glance at him, wishing someone would ask what the matter was, he hated himself. He knew he wasn't completely playacting, but for the element of self-dramatization that was there he felt contempt that was new to him, and the realization that he was reveling in a little self-dramatization even in his self-contempt left him miserably helpless.

Everyone was aware of the sound of the wind and the feel of the atmosphere and watched gusts thrash branches and yank off dead twigs and suck them up and whirl them around, push them along the ground and around the huge oak near the bicycle parking lot and under the pines at one end of the grounds, surrounding the greystone clubhouse, where Lucius had failed to learn to play the clarinet, and into the woods and the yards outside the school grounds.

In line with her math class, passing through the auditorium, on her way downstairs behind the stage to the cafeteria, Raine kept trying to get Lucius to look at her, but he kept his head toward the window and the grey sky. In American history, Raine kept looking back at him, her face sad, and tried to pass him a note, but he spurned it, and when she got Lard Fogel to hand it across the aisle to him, Lucius took it, shoved it in his pocket unread, but imagined every line in five or six versions. As the rest of the students read passages aloud from the history text, Lucius prayed to Jesus and to Rosemary for forgiveness for having peeped at her and promised that he'd never peep at another girl again. He didn't hear a word the teachers said, ignored everyone else, and didn't open his notebook once. Near time for the bell, he realized he was feeling eager for school to let out, so he could see the ruins of the hotel and brood over them, and despised himself.

When Lucius walked out of homeroom into the hall, Raine, and Joy and Cora were waiting to escort him to the streetcar stop at Peck's store. At the end of the hall, he saw Duke and Harry and Peggy silhouetted against the sky that had turned eerie green.

"I think I'll go by myself today, Raine," Lucius said, feeling free of poses, wondering whether the dropping of poses was itself a pose, hating himself for wondering anything at all. He walked away, toward the daylight at the end of the clean-dungeon corridor.

"If you don't walk with me, I'll get Duke to," Raine called after him.

"He's goin' off in a corner sommers and write a stor—ry," yelled Cora, laughing and making her feet slap as she walked around in circles. "Too good to walk with us. Hey, Poet!" Lucius glanced over his shoulder and Cora gave him the finger.

He walked on, shaking his head, ashamed to be alive.

The cold air hit him and his mind cleared and wind stung his eyes, and he wondered if Raine really would walk next to Duke. Wind blew in the trees, and kids scuffled in the leaves, making a very distinct rustling. Wind lifted dead leaves into the lower branches of the mimosas. Approaching the tree at the end of the double row, Lucius glanced back. Raine and them stood on the small concrete landing between the thin black porch rails. Raine was looping her red scarf around Duke's neck while he laughed, affected condescension. Lucius wanted to run back and tell them all about Duke's hour of shame in the basement of Gamble's. Duke had probably already impressed them with his own lying version.

Impulsively, Lucius threw down his notebook and attacked the mimosa tree as if it embodied all his conflicting frustrations—the devil that let the fire burn Rosemary and forty-nine others to death, Duke who told him about the fire, Cora who mocked him for being a writer, Peggy who was sexy, Joy who was holy and good and not in love with him, Raine who made him jealous, the world that made Bucky have to go to Ephraim Lee Institute, and just life that made Luke missing in action. And himself. He slammed his shoulder against the rigid trunk of the tree, as thick as his thigh, and felt the jolt throughout his body. Leaping for a limb, he rode it down, and, standing on the ground again, pulled it back hard, his eyes shut tight against the exertion of his muscles, feeling the heat rise in his body. When he opened his eyes, he saw Loraine and Duke and the others through his tears—they had come down closer—let the limb fly, making them jump back, their mouths open in astonishment.

"Go to hell, every damned one of you! I hate all you damn people! I hate the whole world! I wish I was dead!" Everything he said sounded stupid, he wished he could stop, he went on and on, until he noticed that Raine was looking around him at something happening behind him, and, turning, saw that the wind was plucking the pages out of his notebook.

Panicked, Lucius chased after the pages as they flew out over the ground, dashing here and there, stumbling, bending over to snatch them up as if they'd deliberately let themselves get caught in the wind and he wanted to hurt them, as if grabbing a child viciously by the arm when she steps out in front of a streetcar. They were all laughing, pointing at him. He stopped some pages with his foot, cursing them, as though they were whirling away of their own will, to spite him. Grass bent in the wind. Rain started coming down. The wind and the wet wrapped some pages around the tree trunks, and he pulled them free and hugged them to his chest, bent over, to keep wind and rain from getting at them again. He dashed over the field, bending, stumbling, stumping about on his knees, wadding pages against his chest, crying, cursing, begging God to help him, feeling his impotence against such an act of nature, such an accident, such a stupid mistake. He chased some pages into the street, imagining the people in cars and the kids on the bus watching, laughing, glad. Then he realized that he'd left the notebook on the ground, and ran back through the pelting rain and muddy water.

Raine and them stood in the doorway and kids stood at windows in classrooms, out of the rain, watching, grinning. Another gust of wind lifted the pages rapidly, the sound like the wings of frightened pigeons. As he ran toward, reached for, the notebook, wind plucked pages off the three steel rings and flung them against his chest and face, and he fought them and tried to catch them at the same time. He grabbed the notebook and ran into the hallway, pushing kids aside. He hated them all. Knowing he'd never forget the look of those flying pages, he put them all back in the notebook as the rain slackened.

When he went back out, the air was freezing, the rain had stopped. Cora yelled, "Want us to help you pick 'em up, William De Cosgrove?" Only Raine could have told her about his pen name.

"Fuck you, Cora."

Suddenly, Cora's face changed, she charged toward him, her tall, skinny body and thin red hair thrashing the air in a gyrating plunge. She slapped him, kicked him, pulled his hair, slugged at him, as he tried to beat her off with his notebook. "Don't— you say— 'fuck— you'— to— me! You little shitass— I'll kill you— goddamn sawed-off little sombitch!"

Lucius backed off and pointed his finger at Cora. "All right, goddamn it, Cora, you just stop right there, don't you call *me* a sonofabitch. I don't give a damn if you *are* a girl."

"Well, don't you say 'fuck me' then."

"Nobody wants to fuck you, anyway."

Cora started crying. She picked up a rock. Shielding himself with his notebook, Lucius backed away. Cora threw it at him. He found the rock and threw it back at her, but it skimmed off a mimosa tree and hit Harry on the leg.

"Watch it, Hutchfield. . . . By God!"

"You all just leave me alone! Who asked you to come around me?"

"Come on, Cora," said Joy, "let's all go, and quit acting so stupid. They ain't no need in all this." When they didn't respond she turned to go. "Well, for *my* part, I'm going. *You* all can *do* ever what you want to. . . ."

Reluctantly, they gradually followed her, and she kept looking back to see if they were coming. Lucius had always liked her, she was always the quietest, the gentlest, the softest, and seemed older, but too tall, and he realized now that she was the sweetest and maybe the prettiest of them all, and he loved her.

On the streetcar, Lucius sat down next to a Cherokee *Messenger*, spilled out over the seat, some pages trampled in the aisle. He looked at the horrible pictures of the fire, and wondered if one of the firemen had been Chief Buckner, then remembered he was stationed in Oak Ridge, then read that it was such a big fire, they'd had to call on engines from Oak Ridge and Alcoa, too. The names of the dead were listed, among them Rosemary Ammons! But she was fifty-two, so she couldn't have been the girl he watched undress. Helen Bradford, twenty-two, nurse, was listed. Rosemary wasn't wearing a uniform. But maybe she was off duty. Ten bodies were yet to be identified. Six separate stories, with eyewitness accounts, telling how they supposed it started and what they supposed happened.

When Lucius looked up, finished, he saw that the streetcar had passed the hotel and was all the way up to the Hollywood. He almost ran back, hating himself for being eager to see the ruins.

Seeing sky where he'd never seen sky before was strange. The street in front of where the hotel had stood was full of water that the sudden cold was turning to ice. Thinking of Buck Jones perishing in the Coconut Grove fire, he watched thin wisps of smoke coil up from the black level area. It looked small. He'd expected something like Hiroshima, but this was like a little parking lot. Smoke had blackened the entire three-storey side wall of the Bijou.

Policemen were standing guard, and many people stood on the sidewalk, looking over the chain that surrounded the area, into the ruins. The icy wind thrashed the valance hanging from the marquee where GILDA in red and silver letters had melted in the heat. The front was grimy from soot and smoke and dirty water. Watching cars and streetcars pass as they always had, Lucius was shocked that while Jesus wept, life went on unchanged after such a holocaust.

Too sad and nauseated to see Gale and them, Lucius walked on across the bridge over Crazy Creek where it emptied into the Tennessee. He set Momma's hair dryer in his sanctuary to take the chill off, and changed into dry clothes, and ironed the muddy wet pages of his stories dry, and sorted and arranged them, and put them back in his notebook where they belonged, lamenting the missing ones.

Somebody knocked at the door.

"Come on in, Duke." Lucius didn't want him near his sanctuary, so he sat down on the living room davenport. Duke took a tightly folded note out of his jacket pocket.

"Lolo begged me to bring you this note."

"And she means it, too, you——fill in the blank. Cora," was written on one side, "Amen. Peggy," on the other.

"Ain't you gonna read it?"

Lucius unfolded the intricately folded letter and read:

Dear Lucius, The person who brings you this letter is the boy I love. I can't help it. He is the one I love. I have always loved him and I will never quit. But he doesn't love me. He loves Peggy and she loves to torment Harry by wrapping Duke around her finger. But I am going to make him my boyfriend if it's the last thing I do. I'm sorry if this hurts your fillings, but I can't help it. Please always be my friend. I will need it. Your friend, Loraine Clayboe. P.S. You can show this to Duke if he asks to see it.

Lucius handed the letter to Duke. He read it. "Huh. She'll play hell, too. Well, I'll see you."

"See you."

After he'd mopped the floor where the ice pan had run over, Lucius lay on his cot and shuddered until he began to cry and couldn't stop.

Thursday, January 16, 1946/7. God let me down but many other times
he has picked me up out of the dust of dispair.

Quietly, Lucius climbed the steps to the front porch, listening to
Vaughn Monroe sing "Dance, Ballerina, Dance," and to the sound of
Loraine's voice above the others. He knocked and Peggy came to the
door. "Hi," she said, coolly.

"Joy here?"

"Yeah. You want to see her?"

"Would you ask her if she'd come out on the porch?"

"Just a minute." Peggy was trying to be nice, but she was still mad.
"Hey, Joy, Lucius is out here. He wants to *see* you."

"*Me?* What's he want *me* for?"

"Maybe he wants to scream dirty talk at you," said Cora, loud,
so Lucius could hear. He listened for Duke's voice.

Joy came to the door and looked out. "You want to see *me*, Lucius?"

"Yeah. Can you come out a minute?"

"Somebody shut the dadblamed door," said Loraine. "It's cold on
me." Lucius tried to see her through the lace curtain over the door.

"Okay, Lucius," said Joy, "but it's freezing out here." She shut
the door and leaned against the wall, hugging herself. "What you
want to see *me* about?"

"I thought you might could help me get back in good with
Loraine."

"She's pretty mad at you right now. Why don't you wait and let
things kinda die down?"

"Couldn't you just talk to her, get her to—"

"She won't listen to *me*. Why don't *you* talk to Loraine?"

"Reckon she would?"

"Well, I'll ask her, if you want me to."

"Okay. Thanks, Joy." She opened the door, and started to go in.
"Hey, Joy?" She looked back through the sooty screen, her eyebrows
raised. She was awkward doing this whole thing and seemed to want
to be back inside, warm. "I want you to know that I think you're a
good person, and I wish more people was like *you*."

"Well, I'll tell Loraine to come out." She shut the door.

Lucius stood on the edge of the porch, staring at the cold moon,
then into the bed of the red truck Peggy's daddy, Buggs, hauled junk
in. He wanted to make up with all of them. In a world where fire
could suddenly, like Hiroshima, obliterate so many people, he felt
a profound desire for everybody to love each other.

Somebody pecked on the glass, and Lucius turned. Peggy signaled
him to come in, but the door was locked. He felt like smashing the

window. Then, unseen, somebody threw the latch and he went in. Vaughn Monroe was loud, and all of them were sitting—Duke in a low blue easy chair, doilies on the arms, in a corner, Luke's boots sticking out in the middle of the room, Peggy on the davenport, Joy beside her, their mouths full of fudge, the plate, half-full, on the black piano bench beside Loraine.

"Where's Cora?" Lucius asked, to start talking.

Loraine leaned over the plate of fudge and the butcher knife they'd used to cut it and asked Duke, "What did he say?"

"He asked where was Cora?" Duke was weirdly quiet tonight.

"What you want with Cora?" asked Peggy.

"Nothing. Just wondered where she was."

The music stopped. "She hates the sight of you, so she went in the back room," said Peggy.

"That ain't the way *I* heared it, Johnny," said Loraine, imitating the old man on "Fibber McGee and Molly." Lucius couldn't speak to her. He looked all around the room, only glancing at her. "Way *I* heared it, she *loves* Lucius, and always did."

"You shut your damned mouth, Loraine Clayboe," said Cora, through the tiny roses on the wallpaper.

"I wanted to tell her I'm sorry for what I said."

"Well, she's hiding under the bed back there," said Loraine.

Lucius went down the hall and spoke through the brown door, "Cora?"

"You better not come in here. I got me a butcher knife."

"I just wanted to tell you I'm sorry."

As Lucius came back to the living room, Loraine and Peggy scurried back to their seats, as if they'd been talking against him.

"Want some fudge?"

"No, thanks, Joy, I don't feel very good."

"You look sick in the face," said Peggy.

"How you doin', Duke?" He didn't *look* like somebody Loraine could love.

"Okay, Lucius," said Duke, wiping his fudgy fingers on the blue arms of the easy chair.

"Where's Harry?"

"We had a fuss," said Peggy.

"What about?"

"None of your damn business."

"Play 'Zip a De Do Dah!'" said Duke.

"We ain't got it," said Peggy.

"Why don't you do your imitation of Vaughn Monroe for us, Lucius?"

"Why don't you shut up, Joy?" said Cora, through the wall where a lone wolf howled on a snowy hill above a lighted house, a smoking chimney.

"Make me." Joy spoke too low for Cora to hear. Surprised to know that Cora had secretly loved him, Lucius wished Joy did.

"I got somebody I bet would like to meet you, Joy."

"Who?"

"Gale Booth."

"Oh, that cute usher that works with you at the Bijou? I'd be scared of him."

"You're scairt a your own shadder," said Loraine.

"Oh, leave her alone," said Peggy, and hugged Joy.

"Maybe Lucius wants to hug her, too," said Loraine.

"I didn't *say* anything, did I?"

"No, but you sure been talking sweet to her tonight."

"'I might talk sweet to somebody else, if they'd talk sweet to me." Lucius was suddenly hot in his red flannel shirt, green scarf, and leather jacket.

"I'd rather play than talk. Come on, Peggy."

Peggy got up and handed the plate of fudge to Duke, then sat beside Loraine. They played "Power in the Blood" together.

"Play some Boogie Woogie, Lolo," said Duke.

Before they finished playing "The Bumble Boogie," Harry came in, carrying a brown paper sack. He ambled over to the red easy chair across the room from the blue one where Duke sat, scrunched down in it, his knees sticking up, his feet thrust out into the room, his black wavy hair hardly visible.

"Who's that sitting over yander in the corner?" asked Loraine.

Surprised, Peggy said: "Looks like B. O. Plenty to me."

"What you got in the poke, Harold?" asked Loraine.

"Suckers." Harry unwrapped one very slowly and started licking on it. He left the bag open in his lap. He looked so self-isolated nobody went over to look in the bag or to get a sucker.

"What you say, Harry?" Lucius still dangled in the middle of the room under the tulip-shaped, frosted glass light shade that hung from the ceiling.

Harry saluted Lucius with the grape sucker.

"Hey, Duke," said Lucius, "when you gonna get done wearing my uncle's boots?" Every word he spoke echoed distinctly in his mind, but seemed also to echo in the room and hang like icicles.

"Wish I had me a big orange," said Peggy.

"Want me and Loraine to go get you one?" asked Lucius.

"You and *who?*" asked Loraine.

"Come on, let's go to Peck's."

"I got no notion of going to Peck's with *you*. Me and Duke'll go. Come on, Duke."

As Lucius watched Duke and Loraine collect money for some big orange drinks, Duke avoided Lucius's eyes.

"Quit staring at me, like that, Lucius," said Loraine, buttoning her blue coat in the middle of the room.

"I'm not staring at *nothing*."

"So I'm nothing, huh?"

"*You* said it, not me."

"Let's go, Duke." Loraine opened the door and waited for Duke to pull on his coat and cross the room to her.

"Stay right where you are, Duke," said Lucius.

"Just going with her for some big oranges."

"No, you *ain't*, neither."

"Whose gonna stop him?" asked Loraine.

Harry loudly sucked his sucker and stared across the room at Peggy.

She stared at the label on the black Vaughn Monroe record. "What are *you* lookin' at?"

Harry didn't answer. Distracted, Lucius turned to Loraine again and stared at her.

"I'm about to freeze, you all," said Joy, cringing on the davenport.

Ain't nobody care if you *do*," said Loraine.

"Okay if we go out on the porch? I just want to *talk* to you a minute."

"Oh, Loraine," said Peggy, "it won't hurt you to *talk* to him."

"Okay, but it ain't as if I *wanted* to." She flounced out onto the porch, slamming the door in Lucius's face.

"Thanks, Peggy," said Lucius, and went out.

Loraine was sitting in the red cab of Buggs's junk truck. Lucius walked around in front of the blank headlights and got in behind the wheel. He sat next to her in the cold awhile, their breath smoking as they stared through the windshield at moonlit rooftops.

"Loraine, reckon why God let those people get burned up?"

"What people?"

"In the Fontana *Ho*tel."

"How should *I* know?"

"Didn't it make you wonder?"

"Wonder 'bout what?"

" 'Bout God—I mean, I still b'*lieve* in him, but seems like. . . ."

"Listen, I ain't gonna sit here in Buggs's truck and listen to *no* talk against God."

"I was just wonderin'."

"Well, you needn't wonder around *me*, for *I love* God. And I don't even want to think about them people, so you can just hersh."

"Why did you write me that note?"

"'Cause I do."

"I bet."

"I do, too."

"Say it."

"I will if I *want* to."

"See."

"I love him. Now shut your trap."

"Why can't people love each other and not have to fuss?"

"'Cause some people don't act right. You alla time writin' them ol' stories or goin' round frownin' 'bout something or starin' at the sky like a air raid warden or something. You ain't *like* everybody else."

"I don't *want* to be like everybody else."

"Why you have to be so different? Writing stories alla time!"

"Now you sound like Miss Cline."

"You take that back, or I'll slap you cross-eyedit."

"I don't mean looks, honey—"

"Don't 'honey' *me*."

"I thought you *liked* me writing stories."

"It was okay at first—kinda funny—but it gets old. And seems like you always moody and jealous, if I even *look* at another boy."

"I thought we was going to get married."

"Maybe we was and maybe we wasn't."

"You said you'd love me forever."

"I can't help it if I did."

"People ought to mean it when they say things like that. Even if we was to break up, *I'd* still yet love *you*, until I die—even if I was to get married to some other girl."

"If I was *her*, I'd cut your throat for lovin' another girl. "

"But I promised I would, and I mean it."

"Lucius, you talk silly—I never knowed a boy that talks the way you do. I tell Cora and Peggy and Harry and Duke some of the things you say and they bust a gut."

Lucius gripped the steering wheel tightly, turned it viciously, glared at her: "You laugh together at what I say, behind my back?"

"Oh, stop acting dramatic. You think you're so hot. It makes me sick. I like to laugh and cut up, and you always look so serious, going around trying to walk like Alan Ladd."

"Least I don't get to giggling so bad I start staggering all over the street and rolling on the grass."

Loraine got tickled. "Oh, hush, you gonna make me fall out of Buggs's truck."

"What's so great about you and *them* that you can throw off on *me?* Can *you* all write a story?"

"No, and ain't nobody wants to, neither. I don't even like to *read*. It makes me squirm. I'd rather play the piano with Peggy and sing before the church."

"Church! Can't you live without the church? Don't you wish— Aw, I don't know. . . ."

"Well, I know one thing—I ain't about to sit here with you and freeze to death talking simple. I'm going after us some big oranges and *you* can come, if you *want* to."

"I ain't hanging around with people that laughs at everything I say or do."

"Not *every*thing—just *some* things."

"I'm going away from here and never coming back."

"I'll bet."

"I'm going to Palestine and fight with the Jews."

"Jews? 'Em ol' nasty Jews? You're crazier'n hell, Lucius. Jews!" She started laughing, jumped out of the truck, ran up on the porch, opened the door, leaned in, and said, "Hey, you all, you know what Lucius just said? Said he was gonna run off to Palestine and fight with them Jews."

"Shut up, Loraine!" said Lucius, getting out of the truck.

"*Make* me. I can say anything I want to. You ain't got no right to tell *me* how to act. It was them Jews that killed Jesus!"

"Jesus was a Jew his own self!"

"He was *not*. You better not broadcast it on Clayboe Ridge, mister. That's a good way to get lynched."

"Jesus was a Jew!" yelled Lucius, then looked at the windows of the houses, scared.

Peggy ran up to the door, a sucker stick poking out of her mouth. "You better get *away* from my house, boy! We don't want no cross burned in *our* yard!"

"Don't worry, I'm gonna run away from Cherokee and never come back to this town as long as I live!" Lucius walked down the street. A man in coveralls stepped out on a high porch and looked down at him.

"Lucius, you 'uz just *kiddin'*, wasn't you?" yelled Loraine.

Lucius looked back. She stood out on the sidewalk. The sight of her looking worried spurred him on to end the scene. He kept walking.

Feeling a desperate urge to stay all night with Mammy, Lucius cut over to Prater Street. He wanted to feel the fear of walking down the steep hill into the absolute black of the narrow dip in the road, surrounded by dense jungle, and then climb the gentle slope on over to Mammy's alley. That black pit he'd run through in fear after the show at the Hiawassee when he was little, and last summer walked through rapidly, pseudo-brave, under God's or the Frankenstein monster's protection.

Looking down into the blackness, he felt, more deeply now than after that first day in the second grade walking through dead leaves in a gutter, a sense of death and the brevity of life, the futility, the sorrow, and the anguish. Still steeped in the emotions people had stirred up in him during the past few weeks, Lucius looked up at icy stars, and felt that each person on earth is alone and that he knew it better than anyone had ever known it before he drew breath. "Dear God, I want to live forever," he whispered, and for the first time his words to God sounded a little hollow, because he knew he wouldn't. The ache cut off his breath, but as he sucked in the cold night air, a sudden sense of his own future greatness overwhelmed him, filling his eyes with fierce tears, and he scooped up a handful of dust and gravel from beside the road, shook his fist at the stars, and, referring to himself in the third person for the first time, screamed out of the black pit, "Someday—Lu-cius Hutch-field will leave his mark—on the world!"

III

In the Cave

Friday, January 17, 1947. Laid out of school. Laid off work, too. Went to see Raine. It is over. Raine is dead. Mammy's house was dark, but Chief's car was parked out front. Nobody came to the door. I walked all the way across Cherokee to Bluff, remembering all the outstanding things of my childhood. . . . Nostalgia, wanted to cry, but I ran to keep from it. "Someday I will make my mark on the world!" Lucius Hutchfield.

WHEN HE walked into the Bijou, he would make no impression because to the boys he would *look* the same. He wished he'd been in a shootout or something, returning with his arm in a sling, his cheek gashed by a bullet, limping because of a leg wound.

Lucius walked down to the Southern Railroad viaduct and went into the little store next to WLUX where all kinds of tricks and jokes were sold (and dirty funny books under the counter). He paid a quarter for a black patch. He saw himself wearing it and his leather jacket and faded blue work shirt over a red turtleneck polo as he walked up Sevier Street through falling snow, trying to ignore the stares he inspired. Raine and the Clayboe Ridge gang and the Bijou Boys would be awed by such a sign brought back from mysterious adventures.

The hotel fire had scorched the side wall of the Bijou.

"Lucius," said Mr. Hood, "I'm afraid I'm just going to have to let you go."

"You laying me *off*, sir?"

"No, I guess you'd have to call it firing you."

"Well, I tell you, Mr. Hood, I really need the job. I wanted to make it my career."

"I know, but so far, you haven't acted like it. Besides laying out yesterday, you can't break the habit of daydreaming all the time."

"I promise to try, sir, if you'll let me usher again."

"Sorry, Lucius, I've already brought in another boy that's had his application in for several months."

"But the rest of 'em don't care nothing *about* movie stars."

Hood's face went blank, his eyes blinked. "Sorry, Lucius."

Lucius was about to cry, watching Hood shuffle papers on his desk. Shutting the door softly behind him, he went out into the lobby.

Thelma pretended to be arranging Powerhouses and Baby Ruths in the candy case, waiting for Lucius to speak first.

"Can I have a Milky Way, Thelma?"

"What did he say, honey?" She handed Lucius a Milky Way.

"Fired me." Thelma's face, soft with sympathy, made Lucius feel eight years old. On Beech Street, she'd hugged him when Sonny Hawn bullied him or Momma cussed him or Bucky broke one of his toys.

"Oh, Lucius, I'm just as sorry as I can be."

"Well, I'll see you, Thelma." Lucius unwrapped the candy bar, his lips trembling. Nobody seemed to notice his eye patch.

"Don't be a stranger, honey."

"I won't." Glancing at Rita Hayworth as Gilda giving Glenn Ford an enigmatic smirk, he felt as if he'd slipped in. He started out the left doors to avoid Mrs. Atchley, but she smiled and he waved.

Biting into the chocolate-caramel-marshmallow, he tasted the sickening sweetness and the salt of his own choked-back tears at once, and the outer lobby suddenly looked strange, future, rather than past, something leaving his life, lost, like Raine, but never forgotten. The winter sunlight on the streetcar tracks clear among the snow outside seemed alien. As he stepped into the outside lobby, the lights under the marquee went on as if to mock him. Like a guard at Alcatraz, Minetta, her marked cheek flaming red, perched high in the ticket booth, stared out into the street over his head, without deigning even to sneer in victory, merely raising one greasy eyebrow a hair. Lucius had stood his last watch On the Spot.

Feeling the piercing humiliation of expulsion from the Bijou and isolation from the thriving life of the ushers inside, Lucius stood across the street in front of the rough wooden fence surrounding the demolition of the Pioneer. He hoped for a glimpse of Raine, who was coming to the Bugs Bunny Club to compete for the $25 Savings Bond.

Saturday, January 18, 1947. Hood laid me off. Said I couldn't break the habit of day-dreaming On the Spot. Duke said Loraine sang "My Adobe Hacienda" on the Bugs Bunny Club. She didn't win. Momma

is gone dancing with Nola. I'm alone. I wandered all over Cherokee.
I hate the looks of Cherokee.

Sunday, January 19, 1946 7. Went to Mammys. Found one page from
"While the Sea Remains" wrapped around a dead cornstalk in Mammy's
garden. Blew all the way over there from Bonny Kate. A sign God
means for me to be a writer. Hood called and asked me to come in
and sign the payroll. Undercurrent is on with Robert Taylor and
Katharine Hepburn but I didn't get to see it. Reread some old stories
of mine. Excellent.

Lucius's confrontation with Mrs. Fraker was worse than he'd imagined
it all day Sunday. He thought she'd shown him her worst side until
she snarled, with a confidence that almost convinced Lucius, "You'll
end up just like your brothers, wait and see."

Bronson only said, "You're suspended until you bring your mother
with you."

"But, sir, she'll lose her job if she has to come."

"And you won't have to look far for the person to blame."

Crossing Sevier, Lucius walked and looked past Minetta as if she
didn't exist, feeling twice as real himself because he knew the way she
was staring at him. She stopped him in the outer lobby but let him
go on in when he told her he'd come to pick up his pay.

Bruce Tillotson, On the Spot, was the only usher on duty.

"Hey, Lucius, you hear about them finding the polio virus?"

"Yeah, they found it between my toes."

The look of evil in Robert Taylor's eyes as he walked toward
Katharine Hepburn in *Undercurrent* shocked him.

"You come to see me, Lucius, you hear?" said Thelma. "And
bring little ol' Bucky *with* you. And you tell that Earl he better get
himself in here and *see* ol' Thelma." She didn't know about Earl and
Bucky being in the reform school and at Cold Springs. Momma and
them tried to keep stuff like that away from relatives and friends.

Passing Duncan's Office Furniture and Supplies Company on his
way to look at the stills for *The Personality Kid* at the Hollywood,
Lucius saw a ledger in the window, soot-dappled, lying on white paper
where dead flies of autumn lay scattered. Reading "The Story of a
Novel" made him want a ledger like the ones Wolfe used when he
wrote *Look Homeward, Angel* in Paris and London. On the front
of the ledger: *Records*. He went inside and asked to see one. The young
clerk gave him an odd look, as if he were the first person who'd ever
bought such an item. He wanted to tell him what he was going to
use it for, but sensed he'd get only a dumb frown. The wording in the
front: "Standard Blank Book." It was tall, slender, official-looking, pale
bluish gray, large stark blue numbers in the top corner of each page.

Eating lunch in one of the stands in the Market House, Lucius borrowed the waitress's pencil. He wrote his name in the front. Then: "What dull beasts we all would be, if, on this unbright cinder, we lacked a memory." As she brought his pinto beans, baked macaroni and cheese, corn bread, and country steak with gravy, she said, "You got the prettiest blue eyes ever I seen." Then he wrote, "A Stone, A Leaf, an Unfound Door" and "Vigil Strange I kept on the Field One Night. Thomas Wolfe."

In his sanctuary, Lucius copied into the ledger all the entries he'd made in the new red diary and stored it away with Luke's old diary in the bottom drawer of his desk. He read nothing, wrote only a few titles. In the tower by the river, he brooded on Life and Death, Chance and Destiny, and God's Mysterious Ways. He would go on a safari into Africa and teach the natives to read, then he'd hand out copies of his books and their lives would be transformed.

The next morning, Momma called Mr. Bronson from Councilman Randall's house and told him she could say what she had to say over the telephone, that she couldn't afford to be running over to Bonny Kate every time Lucius popped off at some teacher or laid out of school. Bronson wasn't satisfied. Then Momma armed Lucius with a long letter to Mr. Bronson apologizing for talking smart and promising to keep Lucius under control.

"If you get suspended one more time," said Momma, "over writing those silly stories, they can just cart your little ass off to the reform school."

"Well, you take up for Bucky and Earl, don't you?"

"I'm not one of your teachers, Lucius, so don't think you can sass me without expecting to get your teeth knocked down your throat."

NIGHT RITUAL: Lucius and Diana get in Momma's bed and play like they're married and Lucius is certain they *will* get married. Her breath always smells like corn bread. . . . Lucius runs away from home because everybody says Sonny Hawn is looking for him, to beat his ass, and he climbs the mountain highway toward Oak Ridge, Clark Gable, his protector, a miniature figure on his left shoulder, Vivien Leigh, his goddess, on the right. . . . The Beech Street Gang wanders around the Indian graveyard and the slaughterhouse down on the highway to Oak Ridge, then hop a freight to Bull's Run. Walking home along the tracks, Sonny notices a solitary boxcar on the opposite rails, and says, "I'd like to ride *that* around the neigborhood," and a little later, they miss Earl, and look back down the tracks, and he is running toward them, the boxcar in flames behind him. . . . Sonny pushing Earl around, Earl talking him out of beating him up, Jim Bob, another time, kicking Earl, who doesn't run. . . . Sonny beating Earl up on the corner across from Fisher's store. Suddenly Earl is pushing Sonny's face into the red dirt, trying to smother him. Jim Bob kicks Earl in the back and he jumps up and runs down Beech Street toward the house. . . . Sonny is crying, his tears streaking the red dust into clay on his face, Jim Bob, Carl Brummett, and Lucius walking down the street toward the house. . . . Lucius is scared, proud of Earl for turning on Sonny, but waits to see what will happen, as if it is a movie. . . . The boys beat on the door, finally break the lock. Earl stands behind the kitchen table where all kinds of knives are spread, leaning back against the cabinet, arms crossed, a sarcastic grin on his face. The boys stop, back out the door, turn and run, Lucius with them. . . . In the large, bottom drawer of the cabinet, where Momma stored paper bags, the tiger-striped cat shits mice that turn out to be kittens. . . . Sunday, and the Beech Street Gang lies in the grass beside the tracks in the train yard. A hobo walks up, sits with them, and tells about his travels. He shows pictures of his wife and kids and speaks with a Yankee accent. At sundown, he gets up and Earl follows him down the tracks. . . . Sonny squirts a whole tube of Pepsodent toothpaste on Carl Brummett's dick while he sleeps on an upper bunk with a piss hard-on at Boys' Club camp on Lone Mountain. . . . Earl tells about working for the armless, legless fat man in the circus, being his servant, and leers, suggesting the man is a queer. . . . Meeting Momma at the streetcar stop, helping her lug the week's groceries home through the black dark, passing Lilly's Pond in the hollow like the one he passes through on Prater Street going to Mammy's. . . . Earl lifts the sewer grating in front of Lilly's Pond, Lucius crawling with the Beech Street Gang through the concrete pipes, under the jungle, coming out in front of some houses, several blocks away. . . . Momma tells him as they pass Lilly's Pond about the houseboat in the middle of the water. That Mr. Lilly was born in it, his grandmother, his father and mother, and his wife died in it, and he rented it for ten years to a Negro family, then when he retired from the railroad, he dug a pond and hauled the houseboat off the Tennessee River near the River Street slums across town. The only person he's got to talk to is the little replica of the Charlie McCarthy dummy that rode his shoulder like a little kid, dressed in a black tie and tuxedo and top hat and monocle that scared Lucius when Mr. Lilly appeared in their doorway to collect the rent when Lucius was three. Charlie McCarthy always gives Lucius the creeps, and he can see Edgar Bergen's lips move. . . . In dreams and in sudden daytime reveries, Lucius often sees the green slime of Lilly's Pond, gone almost dry, the weeds dripping off the faded red, rusty barrels, and the old boathouse, mounted on rusty oil drums, sagging beside the once magnificent pond, now a corpse of the old man's years of labor and loving care, and imagines himself being born out of that slime, and sometimes confuses his own face as a baby, living in the house Lilly owned, with the face of the facsimile Charlie McCarthy dummy. . . . Lucius stands in the middle of the street across from the pond, sees no one, no running children, not even a dog or a cat.

Mr. Bronson reluctantly accepted Momma's letter. "One more suspension and you are expelled—you're already failing your courses. The juvenile court might then very well put you in Ephraim Lee Institute."

Miss Redding seemed saddened by Lucius's status as a student, and Miss Kilgore was no more severe than usual, her unsmiling strictness being a front for her own timidity as a new teacher. Out on the playground, Miss Cline said she was certain he was now well on his way to becoming a spot of grease on the road of life, and Miss Kuntz nodded her head. His hatred of them so physical it was almost sensual. Next year, he'u have to repeat American history with Miss Cline. From all the other teachers, who seemed to have been informed of his unauthorized absences, emanated the quiet hostility of vindicated prophetesses.

Loraine and the Clayboe Ridge gang stared at Lucius from a distance, and even Harry and Duke seemed to avoid him.

The girls in the halls seemed to refrain from speaking to him. In English class, a pretty girl Lucius had always admired and considered too good for him said, "Lucius, why don't you get a haircut? You look like Nature Boy," and he looked around at all the boys with burr cuts and butches and a few football players with Mohawks, and decided he'd let his hair grow as long as Errol Flynn's in *The Sea Hawk*. To hell with *all* of them, he didn't need *any* of them.

Lucius withdrew into a passionate reverie about a boy named Damon Redding who is forced to wander all over the United States, Canada, and Mexico because he shot his mother's lover, pursued by detectives and two hired gunmen like the ones in *The Killers*.

Tough in posture, clipped in speech, icy in gesture, Lucius shunned everybody, blunted himself against everything, stared at nothing, in class after class, and in detention hall after school, and walked to the streetcar stop on Grand in a daze.

He went by Hutchfield Bakery but couldn't get up nerve enough to ask his uncle Lucius for a job.

Walking back across the Sevier Street bridge, imagining himself as Dillinger fleeing over America from the G-men, he planned a robbery of the Cherokee National Bank.

The Bijou marquee, advertising *Undercurrent*, which he'd missed at the Tivoli, seemed to spurn him.

In his sanctuary, he wrote down titles of stories the plots of which he'd not yet thought up: "Summer Tragedy," "Rain in Their Coffee," "The Wine of Destiny," "Sand in Their Navels," "The Cosgroves of Destiny." Remembering that W. Somerset Maugham had written of the importance of the writer taking notes, he wrote in his new ledger: "The weeds are high in the back yard, scraping the rotten dry fence when the wind blows. Even up to the back steps grows grass that sheds millions of tiny seeds, which as I tread the swollen path by frosty morning, stick to my socks and trousers cuffs. The steps lift to a locked door. I always have to go around the house to the basement to tend the furnace. At night, the windows of my tiny room open light patches upon the yard, and my shadow breaks the yellow ground as I pass to the basement entrance."

In art class, he sank even deeper into the continuing reverie about Damon Redding, and in study hall, he began to do up a long list of all the types of people he'd make Damon encounter in his wanderings, types Lucius expected to encounter himself some day. The rest of the school day, he ran through possibilities for a new pen name and hit James Austin Frank, then immediately conjured a title for Damon Redding's odyssey: "The Yearning Heart."

More than ever, he craved the subtle adoration of good girls, the brazen adoration of bad girls. And he was alert to softening attitudes of inaccessible girls whom he considered better than he, and even revived his old hopes of a miracle response from LaRue. Several girls, sensing that he and Loraine were sadly, reluctantly ignoring each other, began to speak more hopefully to Lucius, yet hesitantly, as if they weren't sure they wanted to subject themselves to the moodiness, the strangeness that went with this particular "cute" boy. As he passed where she sat on locker guard in the hall, Jody Carmichael, who used to sing a duet with Mary Stinnet, "I Love You Truly," each Friday in music class at Clinch View elementary, gazing at him, said, "Lucius, you walk just like Alan Ladd."

On the racks at the Courthouse Drugstore, Lucius discovered something called *Writer's Yearbook*. He wasn't sure what it was, but it looked like something he might want to get. It carried articles by famous writers and descriptions of magazines that would buy your stories and how much they paid. Three cents a word. Was that good? How many words in "Helena Street"? He'd never thought of that. And places to sell radio and play scripts and what they looked like. "How to Write 'Fillers,'" paying from $10 to $100, appealed to him as a way to make money so he could hit the road, though the kind of thing that was wanted didn't excite him—"Most Unforgettable Character I Ever Met" and book quizzes in something called *The Saturday Review of Literature* that he'd noticed often but had never felt the urge to look at closely. And ads for agents and schools that offered to teach him how to write salable stories.

Ledger: "No rage hath heaven like love to hatred turned." (Arabian propherb)

As he was leaving to go to the Crippled Children's Hospital for his whirlpool therapy, Lucius saw Miss Redding walking down the empty hall. He loved to watch her walk. Springy. The look of her shiny brown hair from behind—it swayed and swung—made him ask her to look his stories over, tell him which one she thought was most likely to be the basis for a best seller.

Thursday night, after spending all afternoon skimming back and forth through *The Writer's Yearbook*, Lucius decided to drop all his stories in progress and work hard and fast on a novel and send it to a book publisher. A rich and famous writer, he wouldn't even have to go into the ninth grade. Because of his writing in class, his absences, suspensions, and his attitude, he'd probably fail the eighth grade anyway. And the possibility of taking it all over again made him vow, in nausea, to join the Jewish rebellion in Palestine. So he got out all his writings and looked through them for a synopsis for a novel.

As if he were looking over the writings of a stranger, Lucius was fascinated to observe the different pen names he'd used: Cidney Cornel Chesterfield, Ladd Hutchfield, Tennessee Hutchfield, David Hamilton, David H. Scott, David Scott Hamilton, Luke Birchfield, Ronny Birchfield, William De Cosgrove, James Austin Frank. He noticed that he'd had a special fondness for a certain kind of notebook paper at different times, that he no longer wrote on the backs of pages, that the way he made quotation marks had changed, that his handwriting was very different now, smaller, with a different style "t." He never wrote in ink, and his handwriting was badly smudged from the number two pencil he favored.

Part of "Black Dust" was missing, blown away. Lucius set it aside as a possibility. Maybe he could resurrect it. Picking up "The Face of a Chinaman," Lucius felt sad. The first five pages and about ten here and there had been lost in the wind that day under the mimosa trees. He read the synopsis, badly muddied and mangled in his desperate snatching. Lucius looked over the few drawings he'd made of scenes from "While the Sea Remains," then set it aside as a possible best seller that would be made into a movie, premiered at the Bijou, and he'd come out on the stage to receive the applause and thank everybody for coming. With a stack of possibilities before him on his desk in his cold sanctuary, Lucius could not decide.

Excited by his vision of himself in the future as a famous writer, Lucius drew some self-portraits, such as might go on the back of his novel, in place of a photograph.

Ledger: Old, bent, slim negro woman going down Sevier street in front of the Hollywood wearing two grey, battered, felt hats, pencils sticking out between.

"Well, Lucius," said Miss Redding, sitting at her desk, after school Tuesday. "First of all, there's no doubt that you have a fertile imagination. I can't comment on your ability to use words because you're only showing me outlines for stories. And very interesting outlines they are. It's strange the way you mix elements of westerns and crime and love stories and historicals all together in a single story sometimes. But I wonder why you're so attracted to events in the adult world—I don't mean, of course, the every*day* adult world, but there's not a single person your age in these stories. What I'm trying to say to you is that I think you would do well to write about what you know."

"Oh, I know all about this stuff, Miss Redding."

"Yes, but where did you pick it up?"

"I don't know."

"In the world you live in?"

"I reckon. . . ."

"No, I mean, from your family life, the neighborhood. . . ."

"Some of it. . . . But I think these are the ones that will sell."

"Don't be so eager to sell a novel, Lucius. You've got a long life ahead of you."

"Well, I know it'll take time, but I'm gonna work hard—day and night, every day until it's finished—ever which one we decide I ought to hit—and if I'm lucky it'll be in Matthews's Bookstore by spring, at the latest."

Miss Redding smiled and patted Lucius's knee. "Well, don't be disappointed if it's a little later."

"Well, if it's not till fall, that won't be *too* bad, but I'd hate to have to go through the summer."

"You could be working on some of the others."

"Yeah. I could. Or something else. I get a new one every day, seems like. Get started on one, all of a sudden another one starts raging."

"I've never heard anything like it."

"Which one you think I ought to work on?"

"Well," she said, picking them up. Lucius liked the way they looked, each paperclipped together. "I liked 'Face of a Chinaman' least."

"But didn't you like it where Greg forced this surgeon to change his face and he double-crossed him and gave him the face of a notorious Chinaman?"

"Well, I must admit it's clever, but—"

"I should've given you the pages I got wrote on it. What you think of 'Black Dust'?"

"Exciting, but not coherent enough, and it's not quite finished, is it?"

"No, ma'am. I got to dream up the ending."

"Don't you think there's a little too much violence in it? For instance, the scene where the detective kicks the girl downstairs after taking her money away from her."

"But the money belongs to Lew." Lucius was embarrassed, talking about a whore, sitting next to Miss Redding.

"Then there's 'Adventure Beneath the Sun,' but I believe it's a little too much like *Gone With the Wind*. It reads like an analysis of movie scenes. Although your additions do take the story far beyond its inspiration, still, Margaret Mitchell might sue you for plagiarism."

"What's plagiarism?"

"That's when you use another writer's material."

"Well, where'd *she* get it from?"

". . . Come to think of it, most of the books and movies you see *are* just a restructuring of events, a realignment of characters, a variation of dialog, aren't they? And your story is as different from *Gone With the Wind* as *Reap the Wild Wind* is."

"You see that one? That was really great where the octopus tried to strangle John Wayne, wasn't it?"

"Yes, very effective."

Lucius wondered whether they could get Mammy for plagiarism for the stories she told him.

"Well, that leaves 'Reap the Poor.' "

"Don't forget 'Desert Romance.' "

"Yes, that's a good one, but the backgrounds of your characters are so colorful and complicated they hardly have anything left to do in that African village except talk about the past and wait."

"Yeah, that's the one thing I didn't like about that movie that made me think it up—*Green Hell*. All that waiting they did."

"I must have missed that one."

"On at the Smoky. You wouldn't be caught dead in the Smoky. But it was real good." In a three-minute gush of excited recollection, Lucius told Miss Redding the entire plot, how Douglas Fairbanks, Jr., and

George Sanders and John Boles and all the other men on the expedition fell in love with Joan Bennett who had journeyed through the jungle to see her husband at the Inca ruins, but he was dead and she was too sick to return to civilization, and all the men fought over her, and the natives became hostile and attacked, and Douglas Fairbanks, Jr., got shot with a poisoned arrow, and George Sanders shot himself to escape capture and torture, but then a friendly tribe rescued them. "How 'bout 'While the Sea Remains'?"

Miss Redding was staring at him as if she were in the Smoky, watching *Green Hell*. Then, she said, "Yes, very good, but I think, 'Reap the Poor,' despite its similarity to *Scarface* and *Public Enemy* and *Little Caesar*—"

"And *Show Them No Mercy*—"

"I don't remember that one. . . . Anyway, your version has its own complexities. . . ."

"And maybe a little of *Dead End*."

"No, really, the ingredients may make you think of certain movies, but the combination is really a lot of fun, and the characters have many possibilities. Your outlines are incredibly involved, but I became intrigued by the relationships—Vivien Sterippi's love of her brother, Maxim, the mobster, and how that conflicts with her love of Calvin Hunter, the cop who goes to work for Max, and her love of Gil Lawrence, the outcast doctor who sets up a wildcat hospital in the East Side slums, and how Vivien's love of her father complicates her relationship with Max even further when the father returns from prison and Max vows to kill him for killing his mother, and then you've got another brother-sister relationship between Livia Hammond and Hal, and how she's always trying to persuade him to quit Max's mob, and meanwhile she's in love with Gil, who, along with Cal, is in love with Vivien. I kept saying to myself, No, no, no, this just won't work, it's too wildly intricate, but here I am telling it back to you and enjoying my memory of it, wanting to know more about them in a well-developed story."

"Then, you think I ought to do that one?"

"Of the six, I would choose 'Reap the Poor.' "

"I know all about the people in that one."

"Though there's still too much sex and violence, and the movie version will have to be censored. . . . Well, there's no rush. But I must, as your English teacher, Lucius, it's my duty not to pass up this opportunity to tell you that you simply must learn to spell, spell, spell."

"You should have seen me before I got in your class."

"You can't draw the veil of flattery over *my* eyes, young man."

" 'The veil of flattery.' . . ."

"I suppose I read it somewhere. . . . Despite the worst spelling I've ever encountered, I must say that I'm surprised you don't make more grammatical mistakes than you do. Writing in such haste, as I know you do—because you often write a blue streak during grammar lessons."

"I'm sorry. I promise to not do it again."

"Don't make promises you can't keep."

"Well, I promise you one thing," said Lucius, touching Miss Redding's knee with the same gesture she'd used on his, "I'm dedicating this first novel to *you*."

"Won't Raine be jealous? I saw her name on all the stories—and you drew a line through poor LaRue's name on 'The Face of a Chinaman.' "

"Me and Loraine Clayboe broke up."

"I know. . . . Lucius, why not write about yourself sometime?"

"Never thought about *that*."

"I know how you feel, Lucius. I know it's not just two kids—well, maybe for her, it's . . . Oh, look! It's starting to snow again."

Miss Redding stood up to look out the window, her belly bulging in outline against the light. Lucius wondered whether she was pregnant, but remembered she wasn't married.

"Now, you promise about the spelling?"

"Yes, ma'am. And after I've written one all the way through, reckon you could read it over for me and correct the mistakes?" Miss Redding's head was turned toward the window. She nodded. "'Cause, I guess editors are like schoolteachers, they don't like all those misspelled words. Well, I'll have three hundred pages for you by Easter. Hey, maybe you could be my agent!"

Miss Redding looked at Lucius, smiling, but her eyes were red. Looking out at the snow, she'd seen something that had nothing to do with Lucius and this room.

In his sanctuary that night, Lucius dedicated "Reap the Poor" to "a girl unknown," and wrote the introduction to the novel:

When the twenteth century came the nineteenth century of course died and was recorded in history just as the eighteenth century. But many insidents took place that history does not, possibly will not, tell in more than a few words, which may be—in the nineteenth century crime riegned in all filth of the word. Here I attempt to tell what I imigined went on in the dark shadows which history avoids.

The depression was hitting the american people solidly below the belt and East New York was getting most of the pain. On the east side imigration was knee deep with Jews, Greeks, Italians, and Chinese. The rackets varied from robbery, the bookies, the protec-

tion racket, boot-legging, and the smuggling of dope. Maxim Sterippi, a tall greasy hair greek with a mixture of irish, took profitable advantage of these easy ways to the electric chair.

Ledger: I wanted to see Ingrid Bergman and George Sanders in Rage
in Heaven, the movie classic, and good ol' Wallace Beery in The
Mighty McGirk, but it makes me feel bad to think of going back to
the Bijou. Blue Skies are on now, with Bing Crosby and Fred Astaire,
but I saw it at the Tivoli, and the part where they meet on a stage and
recall the time they played the old Bijou together almost made me
cry. And they go into this long duet song and dance, a routine with
many parts, and all through the movie Fred is reading the story of
their lives, being in love with Joan Caulfield all the time, on the radio.

"Why don't you go take a flyin' fuggut the moon?" (John Steinbeck)

After whirlpool therapy, Lucius went into the Courthouse Drugstore.
Looking over the magazines depressed him. If he was to fail the eighth
grade in the blaze of glory he imagined, he had only four months to
finish a novel and get it published. Maybe he could get a job and save
enough money to run away, carrying all his stories in a knapsack.

This Wednesday's classic, *No Time for Comedy*, with James Stewart, as a struggling young playwright, and Rosalind Russell, was a good
excuse for Lucius to return to the Bijou. When he plunked down his
quarter, Minetta looked at him as if she'd never seen him before in her
life. But Miss Atchley and Thelma danced around him, plucked at his
sports coat.

James Stewart was sitting glumly in a cafe near the theatre where
people were laughing at his serious play.

Coming back up to the Spot from seating an old lady, Gale asked
Lucius, "How far down?"

"All the way to hell, if I don't do better."

Thelma called to Gale and Lucius sat in the first seat on the back
row, across from the Spot. Smoke from the hotel fire still hung in the
air of the auditorium. He was beginning to savor the strangeness of
being now and forevermore an alien in the Bijou, while enjoying the
show, when Gale sparked his cheek. "Hood wants to see you."

What've I done now? Then Lucius remembered he wasn't an usher
anymore.

But ten minutes later, he was in uniform, bound by a solemn promise not to daydream On the Spot and never to lay off work. The new
boy had refused to clean up when the men's toilet upstairs overflowed,
and he'd been scared of the dark backstage.

Ledger: Earl escaped from New Mexico reform school. Hood hired
me back. Got off early from school to go to CC hospital. Dr. Sum-

mers was P.O. at me for missing and for tearing loose my metatarsal bar. Might have to operate. Whirlpool not fixing it up. Maybe a brace first. I wish he wasn't mad at me. Seems like that little school desk I sit on when Dr. Summers checks my feet is a harbor from the rest of Cherokee, even if it does remind me every Wenesday that I might end up a Quasimoto cripple for the rest of my born days. Then Dr. Koss says in her Nazi voice, "By missing steps number 14 and 15, you have seriously jeperdized the effectiveness of the series"—worse than all the hatefulness of all the teachers at Bonny Kate combined. I don't care if she *is* beautiful. They painted bright red the side of the Bijou the smoke from the Fontana Hotel fire turned black. Even inside the Bijou you can hear the trucks hauling away the ruins. Rosemary's ashes. Are they in the wind? Do I breathe them?

In a stupor, Lucius mourned the loss of Raine. He knew it was final. The world was dead to sight, touch, hearing, and no smell, no taste penetrated the gloom. He tried to think of a story—a new one, an old one, to pull over him like a sack and tie the mouth, but he couldn't get the images started. The teachers' voices were distant, and Raine herself only *looked* near. He didn't attempt to speak to her.

But, suddenly, during American history, as he was drawing a picture of Thomas Wolfe, a realization struck him with such force all his senses came alive and he saw, heard, smelled, tasted everything within range very vividly in one instant: his love letters, more than a hundred pages of them! He'd beg her to give them back to him. After he was famous and dead, the world would want to read them, and they'd learn of his great love for Raine, one of the greatest love stories of all time.

When the bell rang, he rushed into the hall and waited for her to come out. He knew she saw him, but she dodged about among the kids. "Loraine, I got to see you a minute." But she almost ran, her face red, shy again, as if he were a stranger trying to ask her for a date. But she seemed ashamed of herself for having hurt him. And as she walked toward Peggy, Joy, and Cora, who stood in the bright light that came through the doors, she had an aura of belonging to Duke.

"Loraine, I just want to ask you one thing."

Without turning, she said, "Lucius, it hurts me to have to talk to you. I'm sorry."

"I ain't trying to get *back* with you."

She stopped, turned, hugging her books in her arms. "Then what you want?"

"My letters back is all in the world I want." He was afraid she might want hers, but he would stall her, and figure out a way to keep them.

"I ain't got 'em. Burnt 'em up last night."

Lucius seized her shoulders and shook her until the chewing gum she shared with the gang flew out of her mouth and she dropped her books. He stared at her. "Oh, Loraine, honey, I'm sorry!" Trying to pick up her books, he scrambled around her feet, her shoes emanated an aura of death. He was aware of Peggy, Cora, and Joy charging down the steps to the lower hall.

"My brothers'll kill you, you pegleg—asshole!"

The girls jumped him before he realized they were close enough, and kicked and scratched and yelled, and Lucius didn't resist. Taking hold of his blue shirt, they slung him against the lockers. Loraine just picked up her books and walked away. Cora spat in Lucius's face.

Peggy and them caught up with Loraine, put their arms around her, and took her books and carried them for her.

The slaps and scratches began to hurt. Lucius's shirt was ripped down the side. When he started to limp away, he felt Loraine's chewing gum stuck to the bottom of his shoe.

Ledger: Fuss with Loraine. Keep listening for her brothers to crash through the front door to get me. I shook her too hard and I shouldn't have done it. Saw The Southerner with Zachary Scott and Betty Field at the Hiawassee again. Tacked For Whom the Bell Tolls stills all over the walls of my sanctuary. Wrote letters to five literary agents from the Writer's Yearbook to get them to work for me. Going to get my stories typed up neat.

Dear Loraine,

God has turned against me because he won't let you love me. Laugh if you want to but I'm a fool anyway. I am so lonely I feel that at any moment my heart will break into uncountable pieces. . . . I miss you and yearn to hear your inchanting voice, so sweet and clear. I miss your calls. . . . Sinatra is singing a love song and I can feel tears stinging in my eyes which exist longer only for another glimpse of you, my darling. If I heard Clare de Loon my heart would go from me . . . I feel like going to Asia.

No one can cut you out of my heart as my eyes can freeze and crack and fall like sun-blasted icycles, or my ears be bitten off by hyenas, my teeth plucked out by a door slamming in my face. You remain with me even when the clods of dirt thud upon my coffin lid, echoeing in my dead brain, and even after the sun had killed the grass over my eyes and winter has cracked my over-coat of earth like the wrinkles of old age: you remain in my smoking heart, even until and after it has wrinkled into a stale fig, my heart shall smell of your sinamon breath. The tight waded cells of my brain shall rot, but the images of you it so cherished shall nourish the roots of daisies. Your breath in the flowers that grow from my gaping bones shall intoxicate sun blinded bees.

Last night I went with Duke to a party. There was a little baby there, about 10 months old, she liked me and I got her to giggling. She cried when anybody else helt her.

I'm working on a novel now. You can read it when it comes out as a serial in Saturday Evening Post. I'm writing off today to get it copywrighted.

I love you till after doomsday,

Lucius

P.S. Answer this sometime if you want to. I hope you do.

Ledger: Took "Helena Street" to the Letter Shop that Miss Redding told me about to get it typed up. I thought it would be only about a nickel a page, but Writer's Yearbook says The Post pays a thousand so I can afford 25¢ a page. The four women that type there look like school teachers but they were friendly to me.

February 1, 1947

Percy Pryor

Literary Agents

Dear Mr. Hutchfield:

Thank you for your recent letter of inquiry about my agency. If you care to send us what you feel are your best short and short-short stories, we will read them and let you know whether I consider them marketable. Sales to motion picture companies are undertaken, by the way, only after publication of manuscripts. Best wishes,

Yours sincerely,

Percy Pryor

Already late for work, having missed the streetcar, Lucius ran to the Letter Shop to pick up "Helena Street," eager to see it typed—the next best thing to publication.

"There you are," said Mrs. Hawkins, a rather plump young lady. The two copies of the manuscript felt exquisite in his hands. He put them down and took off his gloves, so he could feel them. "That's really wonderful. I'm gonna get *me* a typewriter someday." All the ladies were looking at him now, listening, delighted with his reaction to their craft. "Is it hard to do?"

"Not really. But you *do* have to work hard at first. I liked your story, by the way."

"So did *I*," said the old-maidish, teacherly looking lady in the back.

"Oh, we *all* did. At first we thought you must have copied it out of a magazine."

"It's certainly impressive for a boy your age."

"You all really liked it?" He realized they were his first readers, not counting Loraine and Miss Redding, who'd seen only scenarios.

"Oh, yes."

"Oh, yes."

"Indeed we did."

"I *loved* it. It'd make the best movie."

Lucius caught his breath. "Well, I got a whole bunch more at home. Enough to keep all of you busy till Christmas and this agent wants to see them."

"I bet you're going to be a writer when you grow up," said Mrs. Hawkins.

Lucius buttoned up his jacket and rearranged the white satin scarf Duke let him wear, saying slowly, "A writer is what I *am*."

Leaving, Lucius felt that all the women were looking at a young man who was different from the one who walked in several days before. "Bring us another story, James Austin," said Mrs. Hawkins.

Ledger: Sent "Helena Street," and "Union Station" and "Hesitation and Temptation, No Combination," a short short, to Percy Pryor. Hope he doesn't mind about bout the ones in pencil. City for Conquest with James Cagney and Ann Sheridan is on—classic. Read "The Enemy" by Pearl S. Buck in Avon Annual. Whirlpool. Writing "The Corn Huskers." "There are three things you cannot hide: Love, smoke, and a man riding a camel." (Arabian propherb). Al Jolson Story is finally coming to the Bijou.

In Miss Redding's class, Lucius made a list of all the books he'd bought, the few he'd read, and the ones he'd almost written.

Then he daydreamed of winning Raine back, of their doing many beautiful things together. Taking long rides on the streetcars, discovering new places in Cherokee. Seeing a swarm of movies. Raine asking, finally, to read another of his stories. Showing her the ones Miss Redding liked best.

In art class, drawing the book jacket for *Look Homeward, Angel,* his response to a commercial art assignment, Lucius daydreamed himself into a new life, a saga of roaming over the United States, Raine searching for him, having her own separate adventures, discovering, in spite of herself, a new and better kind of life. "The Whiffenpoof Song" came across the hall from choir class, now and then Raine's lucent voice above the others. He asked permission to go to the bathroom so he could stand outside the windowed back doors to the large room. While they were singing "Holy City," Lucius gazed at Raine, tragically. Her suffering in his daydreams all day affected the misty glow around her eyes and mouth, making her more beautiful than ever.

Walking outside the invisible fence around Bonny Kate always made Lucius feel free when he got off early each Wednesday to go to the hospital.

After his whirlpool therapy, Lucius didn't return to Bonny Kate to continue serving time in detention hall after school. Eager to see *Kings Row,* the classic rerun, Lucius hurried to the Bijou. It was much more dramatic than when he'd first seen it in 1943 at the Hiawassee. What he'd remembered most vividly was Ronald Reagan waking up in bed after getting run over by a train, Ann Sheridan at his bedside, and suddenly realizing that both his legs had been amputated: "Where's the rest of me!" In memory, Lucius had confused *Kings Row* with *The Magnificent Ambersons.* But now the characters—Robert Cummings as Parris Mitchell, his elderly grandmother, his friend Ronald Reagan, and Ann Sheridan who marries Reagan, and Claude Rains as Dr. Tower, Betty Field as his strange daughter Cassie, and the sadistic doctor played by Charles Coburn, his hysterical daughter, Nancy Coleman, and Judith Anderson as the doctor's wife, and the situations and conflicts among them, set up in a small town and worked out over many years, became clear, and Lucius was so moved he became nervous.

Cassie says to Parris: "I'd hate God if I could but there's nothing I can reach!" and Gale said, "You're *on,* Lightnin'."

Lucius rushed backstage, quickly got into his uniform and came back out, and when Hood leaned on the balustrade or walked nearby in his stride-and-dip way, Lucius closed his eyes, listened carefully to the voices, felt his emotions rise with the music, and saw vividly scenes he'd first seen when he was ten. But the noise of bulldozers clearing the black area where the Fontana Hotel had stood jangled his nerves.

Off for supper, Lucius was so nervously elated and depressed, he didn't want to go out. Still in uniform, he sat in the wings and watched the last ten minutes of *Kings Row.* The news came on, showing French soldiers attacking Hue, trying to drive out Viet Nam armies, as he roamed nervously about the backstage area, in and out of the dressing rooms, then down into the basement.

He walked aimlessly around the still room. Then he saw the door to the caves and suddenly felt a longing to see them again. He opened the door. Finding a light bulb, he screwed it into the ancient outlet just inside the cave. He dragged two stools inside and, using the back of a new poster advertising *Sinbad the Sailor* with Douglas Fairbanks, Jr., and Maureen O'Hara, began to write. With the door shut, the cave was stone dead still.

All This He Did For Raine (1947)
By James Austin Frank

The shock was terrible, the feeling painful, the right side of his upper lip trembled as his blood slowly seemed to grow hotter. His eyes knew but little vision and his fingers, doubled, pressed hard at his palm so that red marks appeared where his finger-nails dug in. He had been jelous many times before but that was only because of what she had *said* about Duke, who now held her in his arms kissing her. What he saw brought blood to his eyes and the liquid of jelousy raced madly through his veins.

Luke stood in the doorway, his feet apart and his fist trembling. Hate and jelousy raged like a storm within him. Then suddenly he walked over to the davenport and pulled Duke to his feet. Luke changed his hand from the back of Duke's neck to the collar of his shirt. Then his fist cocked back and suddenly pushed out with blinding speed and landed hard upon the center of Duke's face. The might of the blow sent Duke reeling backward and out the huge window of the living room onto the porch, wet with the rain that so furiously poured down from a dark sky.

Raine said nothing she merely stood there beside the davenport and watched. Then her eyes wandered about the room when Luke began walking toward her.

"Think I'm going to kiss you don't you?"

"Luke, I—"

"Skip it. I'm leaving this—this damn town like I've always wanted to and should have before I met you. Good-bye, Loraine and I mean for good."

When Luke came to the door Raine began crying and said in the mist of her tears. "Go on I don't care. You needn't come back either, because I won't even know you. You're nothing but a silly something that I've never been able to understand. Go on and see if I care. I least won't have to put up with the silly things you always saying."

When Raine's voice faded away, Luke was on the road outside overlooking Cherokee. But he had heard every word and each thing she had said was even more terrible to bare than seeing Duke kiss her. He stopped at the bend in the ridge road and looked back at Peggy's front porch, while the rain came down harder and harder. Lighting flashed in the sky and just as it did Luke saw Raine lean through the open window, which went as far as the floor of the porch, and help Duke to his feet.

Every vien in his body pounded to the rythm of hate and jelousy. Until midnight he walked, strange visions of what the out come of it all would be, focused before the mirrow of his mind in a thousand different forms which sometimes repeated themselves. Many times he had told her that he didn't know what he would do if they ever really broke up. But in his heart he knew and had it all planned out.

It wouldn't be anything drastic but he would leave Cherokee and roam the hills and plains in serch of a land unknown where he could forget her if such a thing was ever possible. But as he walked a new idea flashed in his mind. If ever he were to die, her believing it to be her fault, if she ever loved him that old love would rise again and lay claim to him. Of course he wouldn't actally kill himself but he would make it appear that way.

It was 8:30 the next morning when he reported for work at the Bijou where he was an usher. His manager, Mr. Hood, was very glad that Luke had layed out of school. A stage show was coming in that day and he needed someone to help Elmo, the head usher, get things ready for their arrival. So Luke worked. But very little as thoughts of Raine never left his mind, and even as he ushered people down the aisle he was hearing her voice and seeing Duke as he had kissed her. Luke would at times let the people go by without sitting them and Mr. Hood called his attention to it he merely repeated the same answer over again, "Yes sir."

At 3:30 Mr. Hood called Lucius into his office and gave him his weeks pay. He also gave Lucius a sermon on ushering and warned him about letting the patrons go by without ushering them. This didn't bother Luke he was quiting anyway. Now that he had his pay, Luke went back stage and got out of uniform and into his street clothes. He left by the stage door with sound of the vaudeville preformers music and jokes loud in his ears.

The next day the papers told of a boy who had drowned in the river having found no trace of the body. A railing had gave way and sent him hurling down. On the Sevier Street Bridge was found his coat with identification papers inside the pockets.

And so Luke having aroused extreme grief and sorrow within his beloved took to the open road with all its advantages and mostly disadvantages. Hoping or more so intending to return some day to Raine who he prayed would then love him.

And many was the time by railroad tracks or mountain trail or the bow of a ship that he remembered the day he frist met Raine in the tent by the river. And the day in school their acquintance frist began, causing a fond feeling to blosom within Raine. She dropped her American history book and Lucius picked it up for her. She smiled and thanked him and that was how it all began. As simple as the falling of a book. Little did either realize that a great love was soon to be expressed.

Through the stage door, Lucius remembered, as if it had happened years ago, he'd only last week looked out into the misty, rain-wet street between the Bijou and the walls of the Fontana Hotel. That those walls had gone up in smoke, that the fire escape he'd stood on with the Bijou Boys was now painted rust red again, covering the smoke stains, that Rosemary and forty-nine other people were dust, seemed incredible. The Fontana Hotel. Hiroshima. The Pioneer Theatre. Hiroshima.

Ledger: Whirlpool. Kings Row classic. Started "All This He Did for Raine" in cave. Did without supper.

* * *

This space is dedicated to a day forgotten, a day that need not have been lived. I enjoy life, however.

* * *

Three cops came to the door, looking for Earl. Momma and me got mad and told them off, and they almost arrested me. Homer came over for Sunday dinner and Momma baked a cherry pie. Helped us rearrange some boxes in Momma's bedroom.

Lady in the Lake, starring "you" and Robert Montgomery says the poster. They fixed the camera so it never shows Philip Marlowe's face unless he looks in a mirror—we see everything through his eyes like we are him. Worked on "All This He Did For Raine."

Old woman with a very sad, deathlike, white, powdery face wearing bright colors, walking across Sevier Street Bridge, had a terrible sore on her nose. A retired whore, wasting away in the web of her sins?

* * *

Harry and Peggy had a fuss over Duke.

The whistling mouths in a pool room scattered with cigaret butts. Old man, dressed nice, asleep in one of three theater seats against the wall. Negro racker with side burns slams foot loudly on platform, awaking old man. Good humor (externally) among them all.

NIGHT RITUAL: Lucius and Diana are doing it in the basement and Earl sneaks through a hole in the bricks at the side of the house and catches them and makes Dianna let him have some and she keeps saying it hurts. . . . Momma screams at Earl to admit he stole cigarettes from Howell's Drug Store, but he won't. She pushes him down on the floor, sits astride him, takes hold of his ears, bangs his head against the floor, crying and screaming, but Earl doesn't cry, his eyes look at her, astonished. . . . Momma cries as she gets ready to go to juvenile court to plead for Earl. . . . Lucius comes into the bedroom and catches Earl trying to persuade Bucky to play with his pecker for candy. . . . Earl loves to tease

Bucky by saying big words like "municipal" in a high falsetto voice, bouncing his eyebrows and leering, making Bucky think he knows something about him that not even Bucky knows, and Bucky whines and cries and beats on him with his little fists. . . . Lucius and Earl and Sonny and them are playing marbles and Earl suddenly stands up, says, "Well, I'll be seeing you guys. I'm going swimming." They all laugh as he walks down Beech street into the October sunset. . . . In the cramped lobby of the Hiawassee, rowdy girls slap open the ladies' room door—a whiff of women. Entering the urine-Lysol reek of the men's room. Inhaling the dust of the aisle carpet. In August, only a large fan whirring beside the screen. Melted Milky Ways, Hershey Kisses that leather and bare feet grind into the concrete. Sweating bodies of children, parents, old people— soiled clothes, saturated with coal smoke. Lucius sits on the front row, pads of chewing gum stuck to his sooty bare feet, stale blossoms of popcorn nudging his toes, watching Rhett Butler carry Scarlett O'Hara up the wide, red-carpeted staircase for the fifth time in his life, knowing Gable will make love to her but refusing, out of respect and loyalty, to project onto the beaded screen in his head images of that god "doing it" to that goddess whom he worships above all women, even though it shows in her face after she wakes up smiling the next morning. A dark-haired girl from an old neighborhood comes up to him and asks if he remembers her and the time they were five and he "did it" to her among dandelions one spring behind her white coal house, and he tells her yes, but no, he's forgotten. Even when he was five, he understood perfectly the love story in *Gone With the Wind* and began to think of himself as a combination of Rhett and Ashley and sought and loved girls who were a blend of Scarlett and Melanie, and did it to girls like Belle Watling.

> *Ledger:* I showed Don Dobbs at the Messenger a plot for his Judy comic strip, but he said he couldn't use it. Amazement at my age. Went to Olympia and saw '"East Side of Heaven" and "Imitation of Life" with Irene Dunne which was a great picture.
>
> Bought Thunder on the Left. Looks good. The thing in the front says its about a ten year old boy who imagines the future of his playmates who have all the faults of the adults around him, but *he* keeps his childhish qualities, though he moves among them in the body of a man, and he is a stranger that they presume is an artist.

In the Cave, Lucius finished "All This He Did For Raine."
"I ain't fit to walk God's earth that he made for men not fools."
At this Raine rose and put her arms around his hulking neck, kissed his cheek then asked. "Luke, what are you saying, what do you mean?"
"Raine I wish I could explain but if I try to I might change

my mind about something I have to do. Something that has to come sometime and it mies well be now. Raine, I gotta leave here, leave you, and never come back. I couldn't stay here remembering what I've done. I was a damn fool for every coming back."

Raine was completely ignorant of all that Luke was saying but she worked it out well enough so that she could determine he was going to leave. And the thought of it was unbearable a morbid feeling loomed inside her, a feeling that terrirized her.

For a minute Luke just looked at her yearning to kiss her but he had within him a certain strange pride that kept him from it. It took every once of strength in him to say to her. "Good-bye, my darling and forgive me as I hope God has."

Luke walked slowly away feeling that he was one of the greatest if not the greatest fools or fiends that ever loved as he had. To imagine how he must have felt, how she also must have felt and the things that went on in their mind, would be impossible even for the greatest poet.

Raine screamed for him to come back but he kept a steady pase as he walked on down the road, trying desperitely to fight off the pleading screams which beckoned him to the one he loved so gloriously but couldn't have because of that strange misterious feeling which revealed plainly to him all of the terrible reasons which lured him away from her and pushed him on down the sunburned highway topped at the hight of the hill by a colorful beaming horizon which offered him nothing but pain and heartaches.

Then suddenly that bright horizon reflected before him something else. As it came into view the more it looked like a vision. Luke was so startled that when he saw it all he automaticaly looked up and asked God what it was.

Strange though it may seem a faint voice sounded high above him and seemed to echo amist the red stained sky possed with swipes of blue where clouds were now rolling lazily along & and said in a voice hearable only to him. "Go back my lamb, you have succeded the test. Bless you both for you have been a great demonstrator and a great example of jelousy and its outcome has been expressed through you."

Actually Luke had only imagined it all but somewhere God was watching over and had willed it. Through the stillness of the sky and its beauty always admired by Luke, God had expressed his words of guidance.

Luke in turning saw Raine standing before him like some earthly Angel. God had blessed him and then put her in his arms ready to be kissed and forever to be loved. Luke silently thanked

God then lead Raine back to the house. Both hearts were overflowed with a new feeling of love as they gayly walked hand in
hand away from that new and terrible horizon to a new one unseen but imagined.

The end

Percy Pryor
Literary Agents

February 11, 1947

My dear Mr. Hutchfield:

I was pleasantly surprised, upon reading your scripts, and examining your drawings, to see work of such high character from
a youth of your age. You deserve much praise, and encouragement.

It seems to me that your three manuscripts entitled "Helena
Street," "Union Station," and "Hesitation and Temptation, No
Combination" have much promise. They should, however, Mr.
Hutchfield, be strengthened before submission, and certain better-
ments should be made. May we recommend an analysis and criticism
from this office on each in the interests of presenting a professional
script free from defects which now exist?

Our fee-cost in the matter would be $7. for all three mss. and
work will commence immediately upon receipt of your letter of
authorization to proceed, together with remittance to cover the
costs involved.

Your work indicates potential talent, and we are glad to
cooperate with you.

Yours sincerely,
Percy Pryor

P.S. After the analysis of your work is completed, as above, I will
have a proposition to make to you on the subject of permanent
collaboration and representation of you in the New York market.

Lucius grabbed Gale by the lapels of his fur-lined flier's jacket.
"Percy Pryor likes my stories, you sonofabitch!"

"Well, don't blame *me*," said Gale, pretending terror.

Ledger: Got letter from Percy Pryor, my agent. He said I have great
talent. I took it to the Councilman's house but Momma said he was
just trying to get my money and I better not waste $7 on it. But I
called up Miss Redding and she said same thing.

*   *   *

Bucky run off from Cold Springs Home for Children. Drew some
very good pictures in Kay Kilgore's class of Thomas Wolfe and Ernest
Hemingway and Somerset Maugham—kids all fasinated. This girl

Rebecca in Health asked why I never talked to her. I finished "Sunday Dinner at Granny's" today, the summary that is. Just all kinds of stuff that happens when all these country folks get together. Fantasia was the classic. Whirlpool. "A woman can run faster with her dress up, than a man can with his pants down." (Confusus)

* * *

Walking down Market, Bucky was selling newspapers he stole from bus terminal in front of the Ritz, trying to get money to see Song of the South. I took him. When we came out of the Tivoli, a cop car pulled up and I had to go with him to the juvenile. I think I talked Sargeant Lovall into giving Bucky another chance to stay at home. They kept him tonight, though, and I got to ride home in the cop car.

After visiting Bucky, Lucius walked all over West Cherokee, thinking of Bucky and Earl, Momma and Daddy, and Raine, dreaming up stories about himself in the future, talking to God, praying, looking at every object, listening to every sound as he wound along the streets and the railroad tracks in the general direction of Sevier Street. On a hill above the tracks, a woman wearing an apron came out on her back porch, cupped her hands to her mouth: "Herrrrrmannnnn! Herman! You get yourself home, you hear?" She sounded angry but sad. Lucius imagined Herman trapped in a sewer pipe. At Fountaindale Pike, Lucius's feet hurt too much to keep walking, one of his metatarsal bars had come loose, and it was getting dark, so he impulsively caught a streetcar.

Negroes—men, children, women, as if they composed several families —occupied the seats extending from the rear to the third seats from the front. Lucius, mildly thrilled at the unusual number of Negroes at one time congregated in a streetcar, took a front seat, noticing that, halfway down the aisle, one white man sat by a window next to a black man. That's good.

As the streetcar stopped for more riders, the number of Negroes increased, and when a few white workers got on, Lucius felt some tension. The Negroes chatted, but the whites were quiet, glancing at the Negroes, concealing their thoughts. Lucius tried to daydream about Raine, but he couldn't concentrate. He unzipped his jacket.

An elderly, one-legged Negro, limping on crutches, got on in front of the Unique Theatre for Negroes. As whites and Negroes stepped aside to let him pass, the old man quietly begged pardon. When the streetcar, starting again, began to jolt and when it jerked at a curve, four Negroes rose just as Lucius did, to offer their seats. The old man cheerfully thanked them, but declined. As the streetcar jarred and rumbled and the crippled old man swayed over them, blacks and whites shifted uneasily in their seats.

"Stop! Stop this streetcar, conductor! Stop it!"

Lucius turned and looked back at the white man who'd been sitting back with the Negroes. He was standing, pushing the bell button, his face red, his eyes blinking nervously. Heavy, in his late fifties, he wore spectacles and the clean, starched clothes of a lower-class workingman. The streetcar jolted forward, then backward, stopped.

With calm astonishment, the young Negro who sat next to the white man rose and stepped into the aisle. In his late twenties, he was well groomed and wore clean, well-pressed clothes.

The conductor ambled down the aisle. "What's the trouble, mister?"

"I want to know what you're goin' to do about this, conductor?"

"What?"

"You know what! These niggers sitting beside me! What's so many doing on this streetcar, anyhow? He came in and set right down beside me!"

"Why didn't you say something about it *then?* He's been *on* this streetcar since Dawson Street."

"Well, I *started* to." The white man moved into the aisle and stood staring at the young Negro.

"You should have said something *then,*" said the conductor, his hands on his hips.

"Well, I studied about it."

Tightly gripping the edge of his seat, looking at the mouths and eyes of the people, Lucius began to feel an anger so intense, he could barely catch his breath.

"Well, they's three empty seats up front now," said the conductor. "One of 'em yours if you want it." He started up the aisle to take his seat behind the throttle again. The white man started to follow, his lower lip trembling.

"I didn't mean no harm, mister," said the young Negro. "But I'm just as tired as you are. I'm a hardworking man, too."

The white man whirled around. "Don't you sass me!"

"In Naples, didn't nobody care if I sat beside them."

"I'll throw you out that winder!"

The Negroes looked up at them from their seats.

"I'm sorry, mister, you ain't gonna throw *me* out no window."

The white man flipped back his coat and Lucius saw the butt of a revolver. The man drew it from a holster, pointed it at the Negro. "Don't you sass me, nigger! I'll fix you good! Now shut up!"

The young Negro did not move. Negro kids began to push the bell button, yelling: "Let me off here, man, 'fore you shoot!" "Hurry up, mister conductor, open the door." Women screamed and a few men rose and mumbled among themselves. The crippled man said: "Man, can't you see they's women and children on this here streetcar?"

"Shut up!"

The white man had backed up alongside Lucius's seat. Impulsively, Lucius slowly rose and said: "Here, mister. You can have *my* seat." The man looked down into Lucius's eyes hard. Lucius's eyelids quivered, but he didn't look away. "Pardon me," said Lucius, quietly. The man, revolver pointing at the ceiling, awkwardly stepped aside. Lucius sat by the window in the seat the white man had vacated. The young Negro jerked, as if awakening and sat beside Lucius.

The conductor was talking to the white man, who stared at Lucius. Then he put his gun away and sat down in a seat across from the one Lucius had vacated.

Ledger: Went to see Bucky. Got Bruce to take my place. Walked all over. Man on streetcar pulled a gun—hated to see so many Negroes on the streetcar. I thought it was going to be the start of another race riot like the one in 1921 that Mammy always tells about. Soldiers with machine guns on Sevier Street.

Lucius was keyed up to see *Sea of Grass* again, but wished he didn't have to stand through the Bugs Bunny Club that was beginning to make him sick at his stomach every Saturday morning. But maybe Raine would sing "Heartaches" and dedicate it to him. As he was about to slip backstage and pretend casually to glance around, Hood came out of his office and said, "Keep an eye on those kids over by the box seats."

Planted On the Spot to greet the Saturday night throng, Lucius began to see again the hostile look in Loraine's eyes, and saw more clearly an attitude that had been growing among the whole Clayboe Ridge gang, including Harry, and among the Bijou Boys. He sensed that they were tolerating his strange ways reluctantly, but, slowly, they were beginning to avoid him.

Walking home, images of the dark tower by the river consoled him.

Ledger: They let Bucky come home for a trial period. Sea of Grass was great. It was a saga. I'd like to write one like it.

*   *   *

Bucky brought a stray puppy left to drown in the river home. 13 Rue Madalaine with Cagney is on. Wrote poem about Thelma's mother.

*   *   *

During Sunday dinner at Mammy's, Momma started crying. "Ronny would have been seven years old today." Homer, the bartender, who serves daddy beer in the Red Wagon Saloon, came by Mammy's and took us home, and Norman Upchurch, the frozen custard

man, came by later. At least, I got a King Edward out of Norman. I
hated the sight of both of them.

*   *   *

Today is the turning point in my life. I met Mr. Finestein,
a middle-aged man, surely a cusser and a fine guy who was staying
next door to the Bijou in the Jasper Hotel. I showed him some of my
stories—"The Raven" and "Big Dogs Don't Last." He met Momma
when she worked at Max's, and she told him I was a writer. Me
and Mr. Finestein hit it off right away. We talked for hours. I now
have a job as reporter and story writer for the *Taxi-driver's Companion*.
Read "Disorder and Early Sorrow" by Thomas Mann. Not so hot.

*   *   *

Bucky swallered a quarter. He draws religious pictures. Good.
The puppy is sick. Bucky locks him in the basement and forgets to
feed him. Gary Cooper in *The Plainsman,* classic. Whirlpool. Bought
Screen Romances. *Ramrod* looks good.

The class stood to recite the Lord's Prayer. Lucius's turn to lead, but
Miss Kuntz took over, and he stood there, mute, and felt the insult to
God of a bunch of clowns mumbling every morning at exactly 8:45,
rushing, when the shrill bell interrupted them, to "amen."

Miss Redding had come to school every day for the past week ex-
tremely nervous, irritable, vague, and defenseless against the kids. Monday and Tuesday, her freckled face and her eyes and nose were red from
a cold and when she lifted her hand to write on the blackboard, the
delicate tail of a handkerchief peeked out of her clenched hand. "She's
got a handful of snot," Lard had said, and Lucius had whirled around
but missed hitting him with his grammar text.

Today, she kept bending over at the board, her back to the class,
as if she had cramps. And when she walked toward them, staggering, her
eyes were still red from what Lucius guessed was night long crying. "Bitch
is drunk." Lucius turned. "Lard, I'm gonna do you a favor and change
your ugly looks, if you don't keep your mouth off Miss Redding."

"Nonrestrictive clauses (or phrases)," said Miss Redding, "and other
parenthetical elements (interrupters) are set off by commas. Restrictive
clauses (or phrases) are *not* set off." It looked as though what she'd just
said made her start crying. Turning toward the door, she murmured,
"Excuse me," and leapt in a fast walk out into the hall. Lucius went to
the doorway and saw her rush into the girls' lavatory instead of the one
for faculty women farther down the hall.

Suddenly, the class was open and swarming like a stump full of ants.
The giggling and jabbering got on Lucius's nerves, he wanted to stand
up and tell them to shut their traps, he hated the sight of them. Thinking of Miss Redding in there hurting, maybe vomiting, he felt nauseous.

Bob Founds ran up to the front of the room and started to write something on the board. "Bob Founds, *get* your ass back in your seat," said
Lucius.

"Who *you* supposed to be—the principal?"

Lucius started smacking his fist into his palm, and Bob Founds sat
down. Lucius felt some girls nearby frowning at him. "No need to talk
nasty," said Linda McPheeters.

"If you don't like it," said Lucius, lamely, "you can stick it in your
ear."

Miss Redding came back in, her eyes misty, her movements languid,
as if the effort to shake off cramps had left her feeling dopey. "Now, let's
return to the rules of the parenthesis. Class! Please, class, settle down."

When Lucius held up his hand, Miss Redding looked a little startled,
as if she expected him to set off a chain reaction of smart-aleck remarks
that would leave her totally out of control. "Yes, Lucius?"

"Miss Redding, why don't we knock off the grammar today and you
sit down and rest, and we can do something that's *connected* with English
but that's not so boresome."

"Grammar is very important, Lucius, as you, above all—"

"I know it, ma'am, but we can see you don't feel good."

"Well . . . what did you have in mind?"

Lucius didn't have anything in mind, but he started an answer: "I
don't know, we could do something, like. . . . Well, maybe we could. . . .
Hey, *I* know! We could put on a radio program, and ask questions about
stuff that's going to be on the test Friday."

"Yea!" the class cheered. And Miss Redding, trying to suppress her
delight, mixed with obvious suspicion, shushed them. "Well, I don't know,
I don't know, Lucius, there's no room in the lesson plan for a thing like
that."

"Wasn't you going to have a review tomorrow anyhow?"

"Well, yes."

"That's what *this*'ll be—only funner, and we can pick up parentheses
tomorrow where we left off."

"Well . . . I don't know." The effort of thinking made her eyelids
droop and she stood there swaying, then suddenly came awake, her eyes
large, and smiled nervously. "You promise to be real quiet, and not disturb Miss Cline? Because Mr. Bronson—"

"Don't worry. You just sit in the back of the room and watch."

"Now, Lucius, don't start bossing your teacher around," she said,
shyly, and walked to the back of the room, sat where the glare from the
sunlight on the snow outside wasn't so bright.

"Okay, Folks," said Lucius, warming up his announcer's voice, like
Mark Fogarty's on WLUX. Up in front of the class, his book in his hand,

Lucius was suddenly scared and nervous, but exhilarated by the sight of all the faces turned up to him, expectantly. A few kids sneered weakly, some cocked their heads skeptically, but most were simply grateful for the rescue. Miss Redding rested her elbows on the desk, put her face in her palms, and looked straight down the room at him. Opening the book, he looked at a strange page. "Who's got a microphone?"

They offered him a Yo-Yo, a little hand mirror, a pack of cards, a wallet, and a pocketknife to do for a microphone. He chose the hand mirror that had a little handle. Now that he had control over his body and his voice, a sense of power welled up in him and came out in his first official words: "This is the National Broadcasting Company." Changing his voice, he said, "And this *is* WLUX in Cherokee, Tennessee. The correct Eastern Standard Time now is—three thirty." The class cheered, and some faked getting up to go home. "Stay tuned for the Quiz Kids. But first . . . when you go to your grocery store tonight, be sure to pick up a loaf of good ol' wholesome Hutchfield Bread, which brings you each weekday at six o'clock, the adventures of the Lone Ranger." Somebody trilled off the theme music. "And now, ladies and gentlemen, WLUX presents—The Quiz Kids, brought to you directly from Bonny Kate Junior High School by the makers of Garrett Snuff. This is your announcer, Lightnin' Hutchfield, and we're going to roam over the class this afternoon, folks, and ask some real head-crackers, and the prizes are as follows: A, B, C, D, and S."

"What's S stand for?" asked George Woods, sarcastically.

"Stupid, Stupid. And now, our"— Lucius fumbled through the pages, which looked strange to him—"first question . . . isssss . . . One moment, ladies and gentlemen, for our . . . first . . . Ah, yes! Which of the following is correct: Everybody stood on *their* chairs or everybody stood on *his* chair?"

Hands went up. "Yes, young man, and your name, *please?*"

"Jeff McFarland."

"Tell us, Jeff, which is correct, *their* or *his?* No coaching from the audience, *please.*"

"How many tries do I get?"

"One," said Lucius, giving Jeff a vicious stare.

"Uh, uh. . . . I don't know, sir."

"Thank you for trying. And now, young lady, I believe you had *your* hand up."

"Yes, I did. My name is Gloria Stoddard and I say *his* is correct."

"Right, and you win one point toward a grand total of A." Lucius looked at Lard. "Monitor, will you put her name on the board and mark one?" Lard rose. "And now, the next question. Are you ready, Contestants?"

"Yea!" they all yelled.

Miss Redding was sitting up straight, looking at Lucius, her eyes bright, and she was smiling.

Lucius held their attention and elicited their participation until the bell rang, and they stayed around for the accounting, some risked being late to Miss Kuntz's and Miss Cline's and Mrs. Sisk's classes, and Mary Roberts won the most points.

Lucius was aware as he ate the sawdust meat loaf in the lunchroom that he had robbed them all of their identities for a while, but the method was mysterious. Thinking back, he realized that the same thing presented by Harry or Duke or even Gale might have bored the kids to tears. The working element seemed to be the contagious personality and enthusiasm of the performer. Recklessly depressed when he walked in, Lucius had felt responses from the kids and Miss Redding as he talked and then something had happened to all of them, including himself, until for a while they were one person. Being able to do that awed him.

Ledger: Bought "The Great American Novel—" by Clyde Brion Davis. Whirlpool. They measured me for a leg brace. I get it next week. "Give light and the people shall find their way." Masthead of Cherokee Messenger.

The world is too near me to write great poetry.

Lucius Hutchfield

Bucky stole my book bank full of dimes. Ran in the house, yelling that he chased a Negro man down the alley who was coming out the back door. Stanley and Livingston, Spencer Tracy classic.

*   *   *

A substitute teacher was in Miss Redding's class today. She made us read The Reader's Digest without looking up. I gave her hell.

Heard that Harry and two Tivoli ushers train fucked Shirley at the island airport. I feel sorry for her. Turn her toward you, Jesus, I pray.

*   *   *

The substitute teacher gave us Miss Redding's grammar test.

Bucky's puppy was whining. I went down to the basement. Stuff was coming out of its mouth. He was dying. I hit him with a poker to put him out of his misery and buried him in the side of the bluff.

Momma spent the night with her girl friend Gay, so she told Lucius and Bucky to stay at Mammy's and she'd come on out for Sunday dinner. She didn't like them staying by themselves all night on Bluff Street where the niggers could cut their throats. Lucius woke at near eleven o'clock, hearing Mammy's and the Chief's voices in the kitchen. Carrying his shoes and pants, Lucius cold-footed it into the living room and dressed, huddled up to the stove. Sleeping in his red, turtlenecked polo had stretched it sloppy. The Sunday morning *Messenger* was already scattered over the davenport. Lucius read the funnies and the show page. He realized he'd never really noticed the book page before. He read about *The Moneyman* by Thomas B. Costain, *Lydia Bailey* by Kenneth Roberts, and *Kingsblood Royal* by Sinclair Lewis, recognition of the names making him feel a part of the world of books.

"Lucius, go wake Bucky for breakfast," said Mammy.

Luke's bed was empty.

"Wouldn't be surprised if Emmett King didn't sneak right up to the winder," she said. "Irene said Sergeant Lovall was working on a way to let him stay home, but if he commences to run with Emmett again . . ."

Between the new house on Bluff Street above the river and Beech Street at the foot of Clayboe Ridge near the city limits lay most of Cherokee, but Emmett drew Bucky relentlessly back to the old neighborhood. Lucius had seen Bucky and Emmett bumming pennies on Sevier Street in front of the Hollywood, going in and coming out of the Union Terminal, running up and down Market Street on each side of the Market House, or pawing over stuff in Kress's.

"Hey, Lucius, wanna take a spin around the block?" asked the Chief.

"Sure." Lucius seldom got to ride in Luke's old Dodge.

"Don't want her to get out of tune."

Just as the Chief went out the front door, the phone rang. Lucius put on his deep, mellow, radio announcer's voice. "Hello."

"That you, Chief?"

"No, it's Lucius. That you, Daddy?"

"Yeah, Bub." Daddy laughed in his nervous, jerky, deep voice. "What's you all doing?"

"Getting ready to limber up Luke's old Dodge."

"Son, he ain't never gonna come back. . . . Listen, jump on the streetcar and meet me in front of the Pioneer, will you, son? I lost my key."

"What key?"

"Key to the storeroom at the bakery, and if I don't find it, Kitty'll catch hell."

"How come?"

"I ain't supposed to be *in* there. L & N *Ho*tel kicked me out cause I set my bed afire last Saturday night, so I been sleeping on sacks of flour all week. Don't nobody but Kitty know it, see, 'cause she let me use the key. I'm just coming off a toot, Bub, and can't remember nothing."

The Chief carried Lucius on down to the car stop at Grand in Luke's Dodge. Lucius imagined wandering all over Cherokee until dark, looking for a damn key. No telling where Daddy lost it—maybe even at Feisty Clayboe's. Daddy was more of a Cherokee roamer than Bucky and Lucius put together. Everybody knew him. Everybody liked to give him a free ride of some kind. Being lovable was what did it. Got him into the football games for nothing, and Mrs. Atchley even let him in the Bijou free, trusting a movie to sober him up. Everybody took care of him. By the time Lucius got to the ruins of the Pioneer, it was a golden key. Humphrey Bogart in *Dead Reckoning* on the Bijou marquee.

Across Crazy Creek Bridge, a muddy road followed the bank. The snow was crusty and ice in the ruts reflected the bright sky. Lucius looked up at the high back porches of houses perched on a steep hill. Two storeys in front, they were three storeys in back. The stairs hanging from porches looked dangerous. Tow sacks covered some of the windows. Soot from the plumes of coal smoke coming out of the chimneys speckled the snow and grimed the windowpanes. A few oaks, sycamores, and beeches stood in the fallow ground behind the houses. In the summer, little gardens flourished by the creek. Crate boxes functioned as chicken coops, hideouts for kids, and cart bodies for the adults who gathered cardboard from the alleys uptown.

"God, I've seen everything," Lucius said, wanting Daddy to regard him as a writer evaluating raw material.

"Huh!" Daddy chuckled. "You haven't seen everything *yet*."

"Intriguing place, isn't it?"

Following Daddy up a steep slope from the creek road toward peeling paint on a basement door, Lucius began to get scared. Maybe somebody like Harl Abshire or Harvey Logan was hiding out in there. A Negro woman stepped out on the back porch two storeys up and tossed slop over the banister into the yard. It splashed far behind Lucius and Daddy.

Daddy looked about. "Boy, we can't let nobody see us. It'd be *ever*'body's ass." He knocked twice, then opened the door.

Lucius expected a basement full of Negroes. "Reckon they don't mind if I come in?"

"Naw, they don't *give* a happy horseshit." Daddy shut the door and they were in total darkness, an overwhelming smell of cigarette smoke, whiskey, musty rags, crap, and coal dust. Lucius stumbled over a tin can. Opening a door, Daddy let in enough light to see by. Lucius tried to appear calm, looking at the people in the room. Through the ornate head of an iron bedstead that faced the door, Lucius saw a Negro man in overalls lying propped up on his side on a torn mattress. On another bare mattress on a blond Hollywood frame lay a fat, grey-haired white man, propped on his elbow, in need of a shave, a hat shadowing his eyes. In the middle of the room, within reach of both beds, a middle-aged, maybe older, woman with short, dyed red hair sat at a scarred metal kitchen table, smoking. Around her ankles, stockings hung loose. At her side stood a man in striped coveralls. Lucius listened to four slobbery pronunciations of "Fred." Boards kept the light of day from flooding the room through the only window. Almost every strip of green wallpaper buckled from the ceiling and hung down from the walls like the blades of jungle plants.

"Mickey, I lost a key somewhere. You seen one around?" Daddy was pretending he was still drunk, too.

On the red-haired woman's table stood tin cans, Vaseline, snuff, rags, and a ripped, unclothed, headless doll carcass. Cigarette butts garnished the load.

"Lost a key? You lost it *here?*" She was goo-goo-eyed and her voice was unsteady. "Aw, you come here and drink up all the whiskey, then you say we—you lost a key—You didn't lose a key here."

"I lost it on the floor somewhere around here. See, it's to the factory, and if I don't find it, I put Kitty in dutch, 'cause she's the secretary, see?" Daddy walked over and sat on the bed beside the white man who wore a hat. Lucius noticed Daddy didn't wear a hat. The man on the bed wore it.

"You're a cross-eyed lying bitch, you are," said the tall man in coveralls who stood next to the red-haired woman. His hair was coal black, close cropped, his face was lean, his chin dark with whiskers.

"Who's a cross lying bitch?" asked the red-haired woman, coughing.

"You a bitch up one side and down the other, with the only cross-eyed pussy in Cherokee." Lucius was shocked into delight to hear grown-ups talk that way so casually to each other. "I wouldn't fuck you with *his* dick," said the man, nodding across the room to where Lucius stood on the threshold.

"Whose?"

"That red turtleneck boy's."

"Hey, honey, I didn't even see *you*. What you mean talking like that in front of a little kid in my house?"

"It ain't your house, it's Lyle's."

Lucius wondered if he meant the black man on the ornate bed.

"What you doing here, son?" asked the woman, who did seem to act as if she owned the place.

"With my daddy."

"He your boy, Fred?"

Fred grinned. "Gonna grow up to be a artist. Draw funny books better'n Batman."

"Draw me a picture."

"Well, I'm really going to be a storywriter."

"I keep telling him funny books is where the money is. But he won't listen to me. Tell him, Mickey."

"If you want to write stories, you come to the right person."

"You can write about Harvey Logan," said the man wearing Daddy's hat.

"Did you know Harvey Logan?" asked Lucius.

"Sure. He used to hang out down along this creek whenever he come through Cherokee. Him and Harl Abshire, too."

"Tell him about Harl Abshire," said Mickey, coughing violently.

They all told Lucius about Harvey Logan and Harl Abshire, Daddy throwing in, too, only the Negro remaining mute, and then they all sang "The Ballad of Harvey Logan."

Another man came in, wearing Daddy's overcoat. "I tried it on Cherokee National Bank," he said, holding out the key, "but it don't fit."

Lucius walked with Daddy across Sevier Street Bridge to the bakery because Daddy wanted to show him where he slept, and he gave Lucius a package of cinnamon buns and went to sleep.

Before he went On the Spot and during supper break, Lucius, feeling that he had a sacred obligation to record raw life as it happened with absolute fidelity, wrote down in the cave, where he'd hidden a notebook full of Blue Horse paper, the entire mesmerizing conversation, word for word.

> *Ledger:* Went with daddy to the slums along Crazy Creek to get a key he left. Harry came down to the Bijou to give Hood a message from his wife and told me Raine's house burned down last night. She's okay, except her face is red from standing too close watching it burn. Maybe that's why Daddy was laying out on the creek. He could have been burnt up at Feisty's. But everybody got out okay. Dead Reconing with Humphrey Bogart and Lizabeth Scott.

Sitting in assembly watching *Les Miserables,* which he'd first seen at the Bijou, years ago, Lucius projected himself and Raine and Harry and Duke into the future in an epic story. Deeply moved now as before by *Les Miserables,* he was simultaneously obsessed with his own, untitled, story. Fredric March wades in water up to his chin in the sewers under Paris, rats watching him. Earl comes to Lucius in the middle of the night, begging him to hide him. Lucius breaks into the Bijou and hides him in the caves under Cherokee. He saw only the back of Raine's head, but she was much more vivid and alive in the story of their future. He hoped she was moved by the tragic story of Jean Valjean. Images from "Glory in a Sanctuary" intruded upon those on the screen and in his epic daydream—fitful but intense bombardment. On the screen, Inspector Javert steps off the dock into the fog over the water.

> *Ledger:* Miss Redding was absent. Writing "A Little Child Shall Lead Them" for Taxi-driver's Companion.

Bucky went to General Hospital and asked them to circumsize him and they called Momma and she said okay and he came home walking inch by inch and yelping each step as he came into the house.

When Lucius came in from school and reached behind his windup phonograph for "Polonaise," a broken half of the disc came out in his hand.

Too crying mad to write or read, he went out to the Valencia to see Tyrone Power and Gene Tierney in a rerelease of *Son of Fury*. The Valencia, at the foot of the steep hill to the Crippled Children's Hospital, was a little prince of a theatre, neat, clean, compact, cozy, in a high-class neighborhood near the college. The manager resembled Sterling Hayden, with an Ashley Wilkes gentleness. Lucius felt as if he had to meet mysterious qualifications to belong in there. Suddenly, there was Frances Farmer, his favorite mystery actress. Ever since he saw a picture of police dragging her away, her panties showing, when she resisted arrest for dunkenness, he'd had a love-lust for her, and eagerly followed each clue of her wild personal life.

All the way back on the streetcar and walking home, Lucius imagined beating the hell out of Bucky for breaking "Polonaise."

"Where's Bucky?" he yelled, coming in the front door.

"They come for him, honey," said Momma.

"Who come for him?"

"Sergeant Lovall of the juvenile department. Claimed Bucky laid out of school all last week and stold some wallets today from McClellan's. And Emmett King trudging right along with him. Dan just called, so don't breathe a word about this when he comes by."

She was always ashamed to let people know, even the Chief. Even though it had always hurt when people made fun of him because of his brothers, Lucius had never felt ashamed.

"Why, why, why," wailed Momma, "does Bucky *do* me this way?"

"He likes the way we talk about Earl."

"I don't know what you're talking about, Lucius. All I know is the poor thing's back in that awful Juvenile. And now he's got the reform school staring him in the face. I think about him locked in and —" She started crying.

"Well, he may be locked up, but he sure runs loose in our heads."

If he hadn't been working at the Bijou, he could have watched over Bucky. Now they'd send him to the reform school. Lucius felt sorry for him, and knowing what anguish Momma was suffering, experienced her feelings, too, and guilt for his failure to prevent events or change situations.

Ledger: They did Bucky a dirty trick. Swiftly cast out of freedom's warm belly back to dispair and darkness. "The physical events of life

are of no future importance, only in the nostalgic sense are they."
(Lucius Hutchfield)

Lucius rode the Grand Boulevard Streetcar to the Hiawassee on Thursday to see Janet Gaynor, for the first time, and Fredric March in *A Star Is Born,* a movie he'd often read about in his movie magazines and from which he had several stills in color. One of the first Technicolor movies, it had a soft focus that lent the characters a mythic and spiritual quality. When March walks out to sea to drown like Joan Crawford in *Humoresque,* Lucius cried.

He seldom wrote in the tower, but read there in the daylight on his days off, brooded there at night, scared of the dark, of bats, hiding his rope under a triangular slab of marble. In the tower, he enjoyed being isolated from Cherokee, withdrawn into himself. He took *Sanctuary* by William Faulkner into the tower. Its cover excited him, the author's name in mauve, the title in white, against a pockmarked, gangrenish stucco wall, with a splash of blood and a ripped photo, a hatpin sticking in it, a girl wearing a mauve gown. In the picture on the back, the author looked like a French postmaster in World War II movies. The titles of his other books were intriguing, and the note about the book appealed—a horror story, a kind of gangster novel, but, he imagined, something more than that. The novel itself was hard to read.

Ledger: Miss Redding was absent.

* * *

They let Bucky go back to Cold Springs for one last chance. Bought Serenade by James M. Cain. Cover looks good. Boom Town comes tomorrow, classic, Clark Gable, Spencer Tracy, Hedy Lamarr.

Lucius dreaded going to Crippled Children's Hospital where a gleaming brace waited to clamp its leather jaws around his leg.

"Today the following pupils will go to Mrs. Waller's room, two-oh-seven, instead of *Miss* Redding's."

Lucius asked Miss Kuntz why.

"Miss Redding will not return. Period."

From his desk in the back, Lucius stared at Miss Kuntz as if she'd cut Miss Redding's throat.

As regular study hall supervisor, Mrs. Waller was always harassing Lucius. Since there was a need for only three classes in cooking and sewing, she taught one class of eighth-grade English to fill out her schedule of duties. The students had to sit on high stools at electric stoves and brace their books against the tops. Mrs. Waller spent most of the period yelling at people who opened the ovens to give themselves knee room, or for playing with the switches, and at Lucius for setting off a timer.

Between the Crippled Children's Hospital and the Bijou, the brace had already rubbed a sore on Lucius's leg and he limped.

"Turn into Captain Marvel Junior for us," said Gale.

Spencer Tracy and Clark Gable are brawling in two feet of mud in the main street of an oil town. Lucius knew they would have another fistfight in Tracy's plush office in New York after they became rich.

"Where's all the pee-pul?" Lucius was a little hurt that the revival of one of his old favorites from the Hiawassee's golden age hadn't drawn a crowd.

When his brace made too much noise as Lucius led patrons down the aisle, he went backstage and hung it on a hook in the dressing room.

Younger than in *Strange Woman,* Hedy Lamarr in *Boom Town* looked incredibly unreal, a pure, angelic love goddess. Lucius was struck again by the amazing fact that she and other goddesses had ears and nostrils like other women and that they had to eat, but he couldn't imagine them going to the bathroom. He didn't want to think about it.

A hand in front of Lucius's eyes startled him out of a fixed stare, shattering a static image of Raine standing on a mountaintop beside him.

"Hey, Duke, ain't seen you in a *long*-assed time," said Lucius, as Duke swaggered a circle around him.

"Hey, mudduhfugguh, out my way, out my way!" Duke did a flamboyant gesture, pointing at his pecker, and Lucius looked around, afraid some of the customers might see. The act seemed to have something tangible behind it tonight. Duke huddled up close to Lucius, and, leaning conspiratorially, his eyes covertly casing the joint, rain sparkling in his hair, said, in a mock-tough tone that half-convinced Lucius, "Fuck with me, get y' goddam ass blowed cleeeean *off!*" Lucius sneered at the hammy performance until Duke flashed open his leather jacket. Stuck in his ruby-studded belt, a gun glinted in the light from *Boom Town.*

"Is that a toy gun or something?"

"*Try* me. Guess where I got it?"

"I give up."

"Raine's old house. I was poking around in the ashes and found it. Good as new."

"Got any bullets in it?"

"One muddah*fugguh.*"

"Listen, stick around till I get off. I'd like to see it."

"Okay. Guess I'll see the show. Any 'count?"

"One of the greatest of all time."

Duke sat on the back row on the aisle in the seat Gloria Fletcher used to sit in, and Raine when she came alone. Giving Lucius knowing looks every ten minutes, he made him feel silly.

Lucius resisted the urge to tell Gale and them about the gun, enjoying the tight zone of secrecy, knowing that of all the people in the Bijou, only he knew Duke was packing a rod.

After the Bijou closed, Duke walked on the wet sidewalk down Sevier Street with Lucius. When a police car passed them, Lucius broke into a tough-guy stride matching Duke's and felt an aura of contained menace emanate from him like body heat.

In the alley behind Courthouse Drugstore, Lucius used Duke's Zippo lighter to see the gun more clearly. Duke let Lucius hold it and aim it at the moon, where rain clouds were racing, thinning out.

> *Ledger:* Miss Redding is never coming back. Maybe she was pregnant and they run her off. Who was it? I pray it wasn't Bronson. I loved her. Duke brought a pistol to the Bijou. I got to aim it. *Boom Town.* Back stage, Elmo told me what was wrong with me—I'm too sassy, can't take orders, and stuff like that. I asked Gale, and he said he agrees, but he was nice about it.
>
> This is a rotten, lousy world, but dear God, please save me and let me live. I love thee but it is all so far away.

Something about the way Duke walked toward him from the far end of the hall told Lucius that he had the gun on him. In the lavatory, Duke said, "Feel," and put Lucius's hand against his belly. The gun was stuck between his pants and the curve of his hip. "Snuggled right next to where my ruptured appendix was."

"How about letting *me* carry it, Duke."

"What you give me?"

"You already wearing Luke's combat boots."

"That don't equal."

"I'll buy you some bullets."

Too excited to work on "The Yearning Heart," Lucius carried the gun the rest of the day, enjoying the ignorance of the people around him who knew nothing of the deadly object that moved in their midst. When the teachers talked hateful, he thought, if you only knew what a risk you're taking, and felt that he'd spared them.

"Whoever heard of snow in the middle of March?" said Mrs. Waller in a bitchy tone, a disgusted sneer on her face, making everybody in class feel uncomfortable and slightly guilty as if they were somehow at fault.

By the time school was out, the sun was out, and the snow had stopped. The air was still cold. The snow stuck. Thinking everyone was looking at him as he walked down the street, the brace creaking loudly, making him walk awkwardly, Lucius wanted to be inside the Tivoli in the dark, watching Gregory Peck and Joan Bennett in *The Macomber*

Affair. Then Duke caught up with him, let him carry the gun, and he felt light afoot.

Lucius had to pay the rent at a real estate office in the Clinch Building. Duke went with him, carrying the gun himself now, between his belt and shirt, covered by his buttoned jacket.

As a lady wrote a receipt for Lucius, they watched a clerk open a safe. "All we got to do is pull out this gun, man, and we're rich."

"Shut up, Duke, you wanna get our ass in trouble?" Lucius got scared, more fully aware now of how dangerous it was for a boy like Duke to carry a revolver.

"Let's *take* this place, man."

"Goddam it, Duke!"

"We can be in Baghdad by nightfall."

"They got burglar alarms. They's cops in the lobby of the bank downstairs."

"We can blast our way out."

"With only one fuckin' bullet? Let me buy the bullets and we'll plan it, boy. Okay?"

"I ain't scared a *none* of these people," said Duke, as if talking to to himself. It suddenly occurred to Lucius that Duke had never called him by his name—only mudduhfuggah and other obscene epithets.

As they got on the elevator, Lucius began to feel that to Duke he was just one of many imaginary extensions of his own personality, mixed up with radio and funny book characters and a few movie characters from the Hollywood and the Smoky. When they hit the ground floor, Lucius's mouth was dry.

As they passed Red Wheel Saloon where Homer was bartender, Duke said, "Let's get us a beer, man, and plan the robbery."

"You know they won't sell us no beer."

"Blow their fuckin' heads off, mess with me, 'i God."

Duke asked Lucius for the money to buy bullets and Duke went inside a hardware store alongside the Market House while Lucius looked at the still for *The Spoilers* and *Wake Island* set out front of the Ritz on a standard board.

"Wouldn't sell me none. Said he didn't like my looks. Put on a mask, 'i God, rob his ass blind."

In front of the Tivoli, Duke, saying, with no consideration for Lucius's feelings, that he was going to a party at Cora's house on Clayboe Ridge, jumped on the Clinch View streetcar.

Vultures eating a carcass on the African plains. Gregory Peck and Joan Bennett and Robert Preston in wide-brimmed black hats and khaki pants with high boots in a canopied jeep, their heads clustered, her face so beautiful Lucius, coming in, paused in the aisle as a conscious act of reverence.

His brace pinched his leg and pulled at the hairs. Preston shoots a lion. They follow it. Under a stark tree, Preston and Peck talk it over, and Preston wants to let it go. Peck tells him you can't leave a wounded lion. "Isn't done." Joan looks great, sitting in the jeep by herself, watching through spyglasses as Preston, her husband, runs when the wounded lion goes berserk. They come back to the jeep and she kisses Peck, their guide. She kids Peck about his red face, says hers is red today, too. Preston gets mad at a native, hits him. "I wouldn't miss something like today for anything," says Joan Bennett. She is a very sophisticated, absolute bitch, and Lucius feels the power she radiates, almost sexual, and likes her name Margot.

Every time Harry led a patron down the aisle, Lucius admired his style. The thick, padded leather strap just under his knee made his leg swell. It felt the way he always imagined a tourniquet would feel if a rattlesnake ever bit him. His other leg went to sleep. People seemed to be watching him constantly shift in the seat. He pulled up his pant leg and unbuckled the brace. The raw new leather and his sweating feet reeked.

Coming out of the Tivoli, hobbling down the half-block-long outer lobby, where he often used to stand in a packed crowd between velvet ropes, feeling the firm buttocks of girls in front of him during the long "holdouts," he stopped to look at the poster: GREGORY PECK MAKES THAT HEMINGWAY KIND OF LOVE TO JOAN BENNETT! . . . "Only Ernest Hemingway, author of 'The Killers' and 'For Whom the Bell Tolls' could have written of love like this."

The Clinch View streetcar opened its door at the end of the concrete platform beside the tracks.

As he started up Clayboe Ridge, a fine rain fell. Peggy's house was dark. As he approached Cora's house, the mist turned into snow. The windows were lit and "Managua Nicaragua" throbbed inside. As they jitterbugged, the fire in the grate cast their shadows on the golden shade.

Standing behind the telephone pole in front of the house, Lucius stared at the window, hoping for a glimpse of Raine. She could be as mean a bitch as Margot, but he knew he'd always love her. The brace and the cold air hurt, he was hungry, his hair was full of snow, and his shoes were wet. He pushed his fist against his mouth to keep from crying.

Somebody put "Linda" on, then the shade went up and a dark cluster of heads filled the frame. They cupped their hands around their eyes to see out. Lucius hid behind the pole. But the streetlight above cast his shadow out over the snow-covered street.

The window went up. "Hey, is that *you*," said Cora. "William de Cosgrove the third?"

Lucius didn't move. Let them think it's *only* my shadow. If he walked up to the porch and let them see his brace, they'd feel ashamed.

"Shut the winder," said Loraine. "It's cold."

IV

In the Tower

Ledger: Got to carry the gun in school. Duke wanted to stick up real estate off. Saw The Macomber Affair at Tivoli. Can't wait to see it again at the Bijou. I'll Be Yours, with Deanna Durbin and Tom Drake started today at the Bijou. Went by Cora's in the snow to see Raine. Stayed all night at Mammy's. Wrote essay "Adventure." "Someday I will absorb every mood, action and theme of which adventure is the master. Meanwhile, I have the inspiration to create my own adventures in endless stories." Lucius Hutchfield.

D UKE CARRIED the gun all day Friday. While they were talking about how they'd rob the real estate office, Lucius told Duke about the trips Hood and Elmo took to the Cherokee National Bank.

Lucius found no novel called *The Macomber Affair* in the Bonny Kate library nor in the used-book stores. He was late for work.

Journalism Institute of America
Established 1923
Twenty Park Avenue
New York

March 12, 1947

Dear Inquirer:

For one so young you have done some very good work with our Writing Aptitude Test.

We believe, however, that you had better wait until you are at least eighteen before enrolling as a member of the Journalism Institute. By then you will have had more background and experience with life and will be likely to get more out of the training we give.

With best wishes,
Stanley L. Vickery,
Vice-president

NIGHT RITUAL: Eager to see the next chapter of "Spy Smasher," Bucky runs ahead of Lucius as they walk up the long narrow outer lobby, and the ticket man grabs him and rips his shirt off and Lucius picks up a cigarette butt urn and threatens to coldcock him. The man says he thought Bucky was trying to sneak in. After they've seen it twice, Lucius drags Bucky out from under the legs of some women where he's trying to find spilled popcorn, but he doesn't want to go and Lucius slaps him and pulls at him and he screams in the lobby and some man comes up and says he's going to beat hell out of Lucius if he doesn't quit slapping that sweet little boy. . . . Jacking off in the jungle, Lucius remembers Bucky saying he caught Carl screwing Diana one morning when he went over to play with Judy. Lucius imagines the house that always smelled of poverty, the bedroom, full of beds, where all the girls and boys, about ten, kin and all, were packed into the five-room house during the housing shortage, the bare, torn, pee-stained mattresses, and envies Carl having three sisters to do it to anytime he wants. . . . Lucius and Bucky stand on the bridge, leaning over the rusty iron railing, watching Crazy Creek. Lucius wants Bucky to get rid of the bag of popcorn he has picked up off the floor of the Hiawassee, crawling all over under seats. He tells him about Fartso the Whale. "And he has gremlins, and if you throw him popcorn, you might get a new Gene Autry pistol, with a red-pearl-handle like Oogie's got." "Like Sanny Claus and his helpers?" "Yeah." Bucky gobbles a mouthful of popcorn and sprinkles the rest over the moving muddy water. . . .

Lucius got Bruce Tillotson to work for him, and went to catch a Greyhound bus for the first time in his life, at the Union Terminal where Earl used to look for pussy, and Bucky often bummed show money, and where Lucius himself had bummed. He carried the camera Raine had given him for Christmas and a picnic lunch in a cardboard box. He stumbled over the wired rolls of newspapers piled against an iron railing that he used to swipe when he was nine and sell around Market Square, barefooted, grimy all over.

It was a bright day and everybody had windows up to catch the sweet, fresh smells of the country after a winter of Cherokee soot and the rotten egg smells of the new plastics factory. The bus passing the landscape of small towns and farms and wild country aroused a melancholy in Lucius for all life, and fragments of his own stories, of a new story, of things he'd read, movies he'd seen flickered through his mind, himself observer or participant. His head leaning against the glass, his hand cupped over his mouth, he simulated symphonic background music to the images swarming in his head, superimposed over the long, sad panorama of the landscape. Lucius pictured Bucky sitting on his cot all day, waiting for someone to tell him his brother had come to visit him. He wanted to live in all the deserted houses that attracted him, to visit folks in the ones still occupied, to ride a horse or walk over the terrain, sit on one of those stark white rocks in the fields where new grass had sprung up.

Passing through a small town, Lucius was surprised, thrilled, a little jealous to see *Calcutta,* with Alan Ladd, Gail Russell, and William Bendix on the Roxy marquee.

Lucius got off the bus at Cold Springs. It went on to Washington, D.C. The dead grass was high, vivid little shoots of green starting out of the loamy soil. He imagined how splendid the sprawling hotel once looked, the wide front porch, painted white, looking like the one in *Saratoga Trunk* with Gary Cooper and Ingrid Bergman. Passing the bandstand, he heard ghostly sounds. A hill of green pines rose behind the hotel, and then he smelled them. A few windows along the front were broken, and out of some of them, little boys and girls stared, and their staring brought a woman to one of them.

Feeling the presence of the rich, glamorous people who used to come here on vacation, he kept looking around, hoping to catch sight of Bucky. The pillars above him made him think of *Gone With the Wind,* until he climbed the wide stairs with the easy grace of Rhett Butler.

The lobby he entered was dark, but he could see what it must have been long ago. The kids' names were attached to the little mailboxes as if they were guests who might call any moment for a message. A lady came out from behind the lobby desk to greet him. He asked her for Bucky. "I'm his brother."

"He's had a terrible earache lately," she said, ringing a buzzer. Lucius expected Bucky to open the doors of the elevator nearby and step out.

"You a new boy here or just visiting?" asked a man who was dressed like a preacher.

"Come to visit Bucky Hutchfield. I'm his brother. Not Earl, Lucius."

"Never heard of none of you, but you favor a boy we had here long ago that got killed on Wake Island."

"Bucky's got kinda buck teeth and thick lips and pretty blue eyes and sort a puny."

"Oh, Bucky. Sure. He's out cleaning the barn. Or ort to be. Hey, Kippy, you know Bucky Hutchfield?"

"I reckon."

"Run get him."

The boy lit out before Lucius could say, "I think the lady already went."

"I'm the superintendent, Mr. Macabee." Short, fat, black curly hair, smoking a cigar.

The place smelled a little like an elementary school building. The man didn't smile but he seemed nicer than most of the teachers at Bonny Kate.

Still, the place was dingy and grim and nobody was smiling. At Ephraim Lee Institute, he'd felt a sense of energy, about to break out any moment, spontaneously, and the people running the place also seemed busy and involved in a complicated network of relationships. But here everyone was languid and dull-eyed and neither moody nor pleasant.

Bucky came down the once-elegant stairway, looking very small, his nose runny, wearing new steel-rimmed glasses, his leather helmet with the busted goggle, and the fuzzy little mackinaw that Lucius discarded a few years ago, speckled corduroy trousers, shoes worn down in the back, his laces untied as usual. Seeing Lucius, he was very surprised, smiled, showing his baby dimples and snaggled teeth, and shuffled down the steps, in his jogging way.

"How you doing, Bucky?"

"Not so hot, Lucius. Why didn't Momma come?"

"She had to work."

"I wish Momma'd let me come home."

"Momma can't help it, buddy."

"Yeah, she can, too. Mr. Macabee said it was up to her, and she told 'em to keep me for a while because she couldn't take care of me." In the middle of the lobby, under the rod where a chandelier once hung, he stared into space, pouting.

"Momma has to work, Bucky. She can't look after you."

"*You* used to."

"And you'd run off from me and roam around with Emmett. Besides I'm—" Lucius muttered, thinking he would be hitting the road before long.

"Why didn't you never play with me, Lucius?"

"I played with you."

"When did you?"

"Allatime."

"You screamed at me for even touching your stuff, and you used to throw rocks at me to make me go home when I was little and tried to foller you and Joe Campbell when you all sneaked off to play commandos."

"Bucky, I'm sorry I did you that way." Looking at Bucky's thick lips and buck teeth, moist with sadness and sulk, Lucius tried not to cry. "I didn't mean to. See, when I had to take care of you all the time when we lived with Mammy, and Momma was working, it made it so I couldn't ever do anything by myself. I didn't have many friends, either."

"Yeah, you did. A whole bunch."

"Yeah, but not a real friend like you and—"

"Yeah, Emmett was a better friend to me than any friend *you* ever had. He never screamed at me and he never hit me one time. He'd even let me beat him up, just like you did, and he never got mad at me." They dangled silently in the middle of the lobby. "I promised not to run with Emmett, though, but she said she couldn't do nothing, and then I found out she didn't want to. We got to go in yonder."

Bucky led Lucius, feeling silly, being led by a little boy, into a room big as a barn, with many kitchen chairs. The old ballroom, huh. Bucky looked sad and mistreated, thinner, and his face and hands and clothes were filthy.

Lucius saw one family kissing around good-byes, and they went downstairs, leaving a girl of about twelve by herself looking out the window, holding a play-pretty of some kind. He didn't know there were older girls here too. He imagined slipping off behind barns with girls and sneaking into their dormitories. There'd been girls in one half of St. Thomas's, too, and none of that happened that he knew about, but somehow this old hotel on a hill, isolated, out in the country, seemed a lair of possibilities. He stood by a window for a good view of the sad face of the girl left behind as she watched her family's car go down the long, winding drive past the bandstand to the highway.

"Lucius, our family ain't like it used to be when we was little."

"Ain't you hot in that outfit?" Sweat beads under the rim of his helmet above his scar where Earl hit him with the baseball bat.

"And this place ain't like St. Thomas was. I hate it here. They make me shovel cowshit all day just because I didn't make my bed this morning."

"*There* you are," said the little boy Mr. Macabee had sent for Bucky. He pointed his finger at him. "Mr. Banghardt said he gonna tear your ass *up* for walking off the shit pile."

"The kids don't keep as clean here as they did at St. Thomas's, do they?" asked Lucius.

"Most of 'em ain't nothing but trash from out in the country, meaner'n rattlesnakes."

"You know that girl standing by the window?"

"She won't fuck."

Even though Lucius was "doing it" to the Brummett girls when Bucky was six years old, it seemed sinful and dirty for a little boy his age even to *know* about such stuff. But he knew Bucky knew everything, even about queers, and felt guilty that he'd not protected him against such filth.

"What'd you bring me?"

"Some Tootsie Rolls and a Donald Duck."

"And what else?"

"Buddy, I don't get paid till next Friday and I have to help Momma on the rent."

"Got any cigarettes on you?"

"When'd *you* start smoking?"

"I didn't, but you can trade 'em for stuff."

"I don't carry 'em, Bub."

Setting plumply between his feet, the open sack stared up at Bucky.

"I heard you got kicked out of school."

"That was a few months ago. Just a suspension."

"How come they don't put *you* in Cold Springs?"

"Oh, Bucky. . . ."

"That's okay, I bet Earl comes for me and me and him's gonna go to Mexico. I always wanted to be like Earl and go off with the carnival."

"Now, don't you go running off, boy, or you'll end up like *him*."

"Well, he has fun, don't he? He gets to go all over."

"You want to end up in Nashville?"

"Mize *well* be in Nashville. They treat you mean here. Lucius, promise you'll talk Momma into letting me come home."

"Okay, Bucky, I didn't know you could."

"Okay, now, tell me a story."

"Well, maybe 'fore I go. . . . Reckon we could take a little look around and have us a picnic on the lawn?"

"I reckon."

Across the long room, Bucky led him through a door.

"That your brother, Bucky?"

"Yeah," said Bucky proudly.

"When you gonna tell us a story?"

Lucius smiled and waved to the three kids. "Oh, sometime."

"See the one with the sores on his mouth?"

"The one that keeps looking back?"

"Yeah. They turned him loose last month and his momma bought him a brand-new bicycle. Know what he done? Got on that brand-new Western Flyer and rode it fifty miles back here. Said, 'I didn't have nobody to play with. And my momma kept pushing me out the door so's she could fuck this old man that *gives* her stuff allatime.'"

Lying in the sun on a concrete slab over an old cistern were two boys, much older than the kids Lucius had seen so far. One of them had his head in the lap of the other who was squeezing blackheads out of his face, using the tail of his undershirt to wipe them off in disgust. His face was red and raw. The three little kids stopped to watch.

"Hey, Lucius," said the kid who was squeezing blackheads for his pal, "why ain't you like Bucky and Earl?"

Lucius was thrown off, his name being called so casually by this strange boy, as if he were part of a family and this were a reunion where he was meeting for the first time cousins he'd only heard about. "I don't know."

They were very friendly in a slightly mocking way, and Bucky seemed to enjoy the tone they used when they said his name.

"Mind if I take your picture?" Lucius was fascinated by the tableau of the two boys on the cistern.

"Shoot."

As they walked around, Lucius sighted other girls, good-looking, but tough.

"And right through that door yonder's where they take you when you're mean or run away and they make you pull down your pants and bend over a barrel and take a strop to you."

Lucius felt queasy. "S'urt?"

"S'urt? You ort to see my ass."

They spread the fried chicken and Bucky's favorite cake, apple-sauce with orange icing and bananas between the layers, under an oak, the bandstand roof just below.

Aiming so as to get as much of the hotel in as he could, Lucius got a shot of Bucky beside the bandstand.

"This is the worst place I've ever seen," said Bucky. "They don't never do nothing here but sit and cry." Lucius tried every way he could to turn the black things Bucky said toward a little sunlight, but Bucky didn't believe him. But when he made up interesting things to distract him, he believed every word. "Will you tell me a story now?"

"I ain't in the mood right now, Bucky. Next time."

Bucky pouted, folded his arms tightly, wouldn't talk. Then he wound up to cry and Lucius gagged on the applesauce and banana cake. "Which you rather have, Straighthair and Fatsi or Zorro?"

"What about Johnny Mack Brown?"

"You want Johnny Mack Brown?"

"Make it Zorro."

"Okay, then."

Bucky reached in the bag and handed Lucius a Tootsie Roll. "Here. *You* can have one."

"Thanks. . . . Once upon a time, there was a man who lived in old Mexico who always left a Z mark on the cheeks of crooks with his sword. He was dressed all in black and leather and a silk black mask and his name was—"

"Ain't you gonna do the other one first?" asked Bucky, almost shocked.

"What other one?"

"Mighty Mouse."

"But you always cry when I do that."

"But that's part *of* it."

"Okay. Once upon a time, there was a little Mouse and his name was Mighty Mouse. . . . The end."

"Hey, Kippy, wanna hear a story?" yelled Bucky.

"Yeah, boy!"

"Go tell ever'body Lucius is going to tell a story like I promised."

Under the domed roof of the bandstand, Lucius told twenty girls and boys, the girl by the window among them, a story about Zorro, and they begged him to tell another one, and he told them "The Palestine Story," but their interest lagged and he slipped into a Straight-hair and Fatsi "butts and do-dos" routine and they filled the dome with ricocheting laughter.

Fascinated by the rambling, brooding look of the place in the late melancholy sunlight, Lucius asked Bucky many questions about the hotel. "What did they use that towerlike place in the middle for in the old days?" But Bucky showed absolutely no interest in the hotel now nor as it once had been. He related everything to his everyday life. Lucius was a little contemptuous of such lack of interest, disgusted that Bucky was not a little happier to be living in a romantic old hotel than at Ephraim Lee or the Juvenile or the reform school.

"Hell, I'd rather be in Nashville with Earl than in *this* old place. It's haunted, Lucius. They's a man killed his wife in the room down the hall from our dormitory, and at night, we can hear her walking up and down. . . . And the week 'fore I come, a whole busload of kids from here got killed right out front, coming back from the show in Bristol."

"Show me where the man shot his wife."

In the hall on the fourth floor, Bucky showed Lucius the blood-stain. He envied Bucky living in such a strange place. From a round window in his dormitory, he saw five lakes, the Smokies beyond.

"When I get rich and famous from my novels, I'm gonna buy this place and live in it."

"It'll burn down by then. They's a fire gets started 'bout ever' week. I wish the Chief'd give 'em a bad inspection. I wish I could go home. Lucius, call up Momma and ask can I go home on the same bus with you. Please?"

"I wish I could, Bucky." He knew he was in for a long, tangled wrangle about why Bucky couldn't go home. He was angry at Momma for not finding some way, but still, as ever, he didn't want to have to put up with Bucky's messes and his antics and the trouble and worry.

He told Bucky that Mammy said to tell him they were going to come see him next Sunday, maybe in a new car, and Bucky asked questions about the car, and hoped he could go home in it.

On the wide porch steps, Lucius took Bucky's picture, while ten other boys and the girl stood far off to the side, out of the frame. Then Bucky snapped Lucius in the same place.

Bucky stood on the wide porch between the high white columns and waved to Lucius as he walked down the long grey gravel road to the highway, and as he waited for the bus, he saw Bucky still standing there, the others gone now, in the dim seven o'clock light, watching him, jumping up and down every once in a while to attract his attention, and as the bus, marked *Atlanta*, moved away toward Cherokee, Lucius lost sight of Bucky behind the screen of leafy boughs.

Lucius asked God why life had to be so sad, and the lump in his throat made him cry.

On the journey back, smoking a White Owl, he finished dreaming up "The Yearning Heart."

Monday was Lucius's turn to carry the gun. Duke had scrounged around. It was fully loaded. But Lucius was not so overwhelmed he couldn't concentrate on writing "The Yearning Heart."

New York harbor was foggy and dark that morning and at 5:30 not a soul could be seen anywhere near the damp docks along the shore. At 6:00 a huge frieght boat was to set sail for French Indo China, however, its distination was then unknown to its crew. The voyage was of no importan sugnifigance except to deliver goods in the catigory of luxuries to the high-rankings of that Empire.

Within fifthteen minutes sailors began to appear on the deck, duffle bags shouldered. The thought of it all to some was merely routine, but to others it meant, boredom, lonelyness. The money didn't matter, it was escape most of all. From an unruly wife, the police, mobsters and disgrace. The young boys were mostly country hoojers, adventure seekers and reform school veterns.

Among these sailors there was a young boy and this was his frist voage. As he walked through the alley outlined by garbage cans, his duffle bag bobbed upon his back protected from the early morning chill by a thick black seamans jacket. He was the picture of strength as he sniffed the air and examined the poverty stricken homes that bordered the river Hudson. Blonde hair with a wave slanting in front beset his head possessed with bold cheeks and serious blue eyes set in deep pockets topped by brown brows thick and wavy. His mouth was full and well-shaped, his nose straight and round at the tip, his round chin dimpled. Had he been naked one would observe with admiration the muscles of his body. He appeared to be at least sixteen but was actually only 14. He walked like a sailor, though a ships deck had never been under feet, he had that certain wobble, unstable walk. The truth was a physical defect in his feet.

Suddenly out of the darkness of an adjoining alley two sinister figures creeped out and fell upon the boys back but were instintly thrown off. The boy flung his duffle bag at the one with a gun. Then whirled around to hit the other when a black-jack landed hard and painful upon his jaw. He saw colors, very bright, then total darkness.

Lucius asked the Bonny Kate librarian, a fairly nice lady, if there was such a thing as a novel called *The Macomber Affair*. "No, it's a short story. I'm not certain Hemingway is appropriate for your age level, but we do, in fact, have that story in a collection. . . ." So she gave him an anthology of modern stories. "The Short Happy Life of Francis Macomber" was a better title than the movie's. All Hemingway's titles were impressive to say. He started reading it in study hall, eager to encounter the part near the end of movie where Wilson needles Margot for shooting her husband, Francis, and she keeps begging him to stop, and he says, "Now I'll stop," like Rhett telling Scarlett, "Frankly, my dear, I don't give a damn."

But halfway through the story, Lucius had an urge to write his own version of it, to capture the look and feel of the movie and the sound of Hemingway's style.

"I'll give you five dollars," Alfred Lonas said, over Lucius's shoulder, interrupting his story, "if you'll write me a fuck story." Alfred had been in the reform school and, with a constant leer on his face, said something nasty about every girl in study hall and every girl who passed through to the lunchroom, except Raine and LaRue, knowing that Lucius would fight anybody who said the least thing out of the way. Lucius despised Alfred Lonas, but the idea sexed him up. He'd never read a fuck story. It would be his first sale.

"Maybe."

Ledger: "Doesn't do to talk too much about all this. Talk the whole thing away. No pleasure in anything if you mouth it up too much." (Ernest Hemingway.) The Macomber Affair is at the Bijou now.

This girl told me Kay Kilgore wears black in mourning for her pilot husband who was shot down over Berlin. She's Catholic—used to wear a cross, but not now, maybe they told her to take it off. Writing Macomber Affair.

Duke came to school naked. His father had found the gun. Like a victim of malaria, Duke wandered in a yellow fog from class to class. Lucius was relieved. He imagined what his life would have been like if he'd gone ahead with Duke and robbed that real estate office. But Duke still talked about robbing Mr. Hood, as if he still had the gun. "Guns! They're a dime a dozen, ass. She-ut!"

Lucius was sitting at the little desk, the mildly chill March wind blowing through the high windows, wearing a stiffly starched cotton shirt, without an undershirt, because Momma didn't have time to wash clothes before going off with her friend Loreen and her husband, Kyle, for a drive last Sunday, when he made a startling discovery. As his hand moved over the page writing his version of *The Macomber Affair* the shirt chafed his nipples, making him feel strangely sad.

He kept thinking of Margot Macomber and Wilson, the hunter, seeing and hearing what the movie only implied. Although he could use Alfred Lonas's five bucks for his runaway fund, a more immediate stimulus made his mind wander back to the safari. With a raging hard-on, he began to write:

"As Asses Rise and Fall" or "A Night of Bliss"
by Mr. X
From a short story by Mr. X

"Francis Macomber is dead," she said coolly.

Robert Wilson jumped up and threw his cigarette down and took her in his arms. Her nice fluffy titties rubbed against his chest and she tilted her head covered by a mass of blonde wavy hair and he felt her soft sweet breath saunder through his nostrils and he knew that soon the smell of things would change trimendously.

"Are you sure he's dead?" Robert asked pearing deep into her eyes waiting to be reassured.

"Doubly sure. I felt his heart and pulse. And even his prone drolled down when the poison got him. Oh, he was fucking the hell out of me when it happened. He seemed more interjetic or something. As if he had fallen in love with me all over again. It was a shame to kill him just when he was the happiest in all his life. But you and I have our lives to live. And how we will live!"

"We've waited, it seems forever, but now we can do anything we want to!"

"Just anything!" she sighed with contentment and rubbed her body closer to his. She felt his dick throb through his corduroy trousers. She yearned to shed her black satin negleja and let him take her good. "Let's go walk under the stars, Robert. It's beautiful outside."

"Alright. We'll walk in the pasture by the stream."

"And for once Francis won't be watching. And we can do anything. Take me by the waist and don't hesitate to play with my ass."

"Let me get my-ha-well you know." Robert walked across the dirt floor of the tent to a small rough painted utilities cabinet and opened it, withdrew a small package and put it in his pocket. Margot hurried to his side.

"To damn nation with those things. I'm your's Robert. Take me. Take me bare. We want every ounze of living we can drain from this wonderful earth."

"I like you because of your deep feelings, Margot."

His blood and imagination running ahead of his pencil, Lucius felt cold dribbles of jazz against his leg, and jacked off into a sock. Feeling guilty for desecrating Hemingway and Joan Bennett, Lucius left the story incomplete, and missed his first sale.

Ledger: Les Miserables, classic re-run. Whirl-pool. Doctor gave me some salve for the brace sores on my leg. Said my feet was doing okay, but might still have to operate. Till the Clouds Roll By about Jerome Kern with Robert Walker and Judy Garland starts tomarrow.

TENNESSEE WILLIAMS'
GLASS MENAGERIE
COMING TO BIJOU

Reading the article at Mammy's house, Lucius sneered, for he'd never heard of Tennessee Williams, and he was jealous that a man raised in St. Louis and New Orleans, who, according to the *Messenger,* had spent only a few summers in Tennessee visiting relatives, was known by the pen name Lucius used himself during the time he daydreamed of being the Tennessee Kid. The article said the guy was already famous for his first Broadway play, *Glass Menagerie,* set in St. Louis, where Lucius's mother grew up. Lucius had never heard of the actors either. Hood hadn't yet told the ushers it was coming. A "road show," the article called it. Sounded sleazy, like vaudeville.

"Well, I look for Bucky to come through that front door before we get up from the table," said Mammy. "I had bread and took bread." Lucius felt guilty every time Mammy or Momma broke out crying over Bucky, and a little jealous.

Lewis Stone talking in dead earnest to Mickey Rooney at his back, Lucius imagined Tennessee Williams walking into the lobby and demanding they stop *Love Laughs at Andy Hardy* so he can inspect the stage for the play. It would be fun to meet a real live playwright, but he hated plays. He'd seen three short ones at Bonny Kate.

> Cherokee, Tennessee
> 1845 Bluff St.
> March 24, 1947

Dear Miss Redding,

I suppose your wondering what that old pest, Lucius Hutchfield is doing writing you. The fact is that I regret not having treated you with gratitude inacount with your fine help and support of my ambition to write profitable and famous novels. I was looking forward to futher help from you but when I discovered that you had left Bonny Kate I was very shocked. Mrs. Kilgore gave me your address. By the way my vocabulary has increased. This also came about as a result of your cautions. I know a good vocabulary is very useful in this profession. I am reading *Sanctuary* by William Faulkner and marking all the words in it that I don't know, quite a lot.

I take Miss Waller's class now and we have English on top of stoves. I miss you infinitely, and wish you were still my English teacher. Sometimes you probably thought I wasn't learning much, but someday I hope you will see good results for all your labors. As I look back now I appreciate your help very much and in dedication to you I am going to dedicate my first book to you. By the way what is your first name. If I ever become anything in the field of authorization I will always remember your fine consideration and will speak of you in a thankful tone. Nobody else at Bonny Kate shows any interest in my writing. They ridicule it and spend all their time endeavoring to make me into there enemy. I think some of them need to learn how to teach like you.

You seemed unhappy a paramount of the time. I hope you will forgive me if I contributed in any way to your unhappiness. Sometimes I get carried away and try to make the kids laugh. But you always tried to help me anyway, like that time you read all my litterature.

I am writing a new novel. It is called "The Yearning Heart" under the pen name of James Austin Frank. I have many other stories waiting to write: "Searching Restlessly," "Blind Dagger" (a radio play), "Life from Death," "Fruitless Obsession," "Beyond

Sorrow Lies Our Paradise," "Portrait of Jennie" (radio adaptation), "And Nothing After," "Life from Death," "Three Fascinating People."

I am confident that by the end of school, I will sell a story to The Saturday Evening Post or my novel to a big publisher.

I hope you are happy now and not so sad, and that you think of me sometimes. I remember you very clearly, and will never forget you.

The teacher is watching me so I will close for now.

Eternally grateful,

Lucius

After his whirlpool therapy, Lucius went straight to the Bijou. He'd looked forward for a week to seeing again the long-remembered scene where Jimmy Stewart as Destry straps on his gun after Little Joe is shot down, and Destry strides along the wooden walk to the saloon to kill Brian Donlevy, and the sad part where Marlene Dietrich as Frenchy run in front of Destry to warn him and Donlevy shoots her.

But Destry Rides Again was canceled for The Glass Menagerie. And suddenly, there was the stage, transformed into a room, with doorways, curtains, windows, tables, chairs—real. Mellow lights like in a dream or the soft focus of an aged Technicolor print. An old woman, a young woman, and a young man, dressed oddly, sat at a table, talking, but they weren't loud enough even to be heard in the inner lobby. It was a sensation that he was totally unprepared for. He'd gotten used to what had once seemed strange—working in a movie theatre. And just when glamour had become routine, the exotic banal, suddenly a magical transformation, more magical than Alex Allison's tricks.

People were scattered among the seats, some stood in the lobby, behind the half-partition, leaning on the balustrade. In the middle of the auditorium, a man in a double-breasted suit, who had a moustache and wavy hair, stood up and, in a mellow, rich resonant voice, spoke to the man and the women on stage. The young man squinted against the footlights, as if to see the man in the auditorium would enable him to hear better. The three played with spoons and glasses idly as they looked out, then down, listening. "Okay, take it from 'In what way is she peculiar—may I ask?'"

Suddenly, all three stood up and the girl backed away from the table and the older woman and the young man came forward into the living room and the kitchen area became shadowy and the girl seemed to be washing dishes. Lucius realized that he'd not walked into the middle of a scene in the play, but a rest period of some sort.

The movements and voices of the old woman and the young man seemed very different now. The young man told the woman who seemed to be his mother that the girl lived in a world of her own—little glass animals—and played phonograph records and that was all. Then he said he was going to the movies and his mother got angry and said she didn't believe he went to the movies every night. When he was gone, she called "Laura," and the girl came out of the kitchen, and her mother told her to wish on the moon. There was a realistic pause, but then the old woman slapped her forehead and said, "Line!" disgusted.

A female voice in the darkness of the auditorium said in a monotone: "A little silver slipper of a moon. Look over your left—"

The older woman shifted into a different stance and said, "A little silver slipper of a moon. Look over your left shoulder, Laura, and make a wish."

Lucius sat in the aisle seat at the back and listened to the two women talk. They did the whole scene again, and just as the young man was going to the movies, a man in coveralls came out on the apron and looked up toward the balcony, his hand over his eyes like an Indian, and Lucius recognized Spit, who was still standing there when the curtain closed behind him a few moments later. Jealous, Lucius wondered whether Brady or Elmo was back there pulling it.

Having changed into his uniform, Lucius watched the entire rehearsal, not always alert to the transitions from the play into real-life talk *about* the play. During a scene, someone would wander in and fiddle around with the walls or the table. He thought he recognized the man they called the Gentleman Caller. "Used to act in a lot of Republic chapter plays as a kid," said the man Lucius asked. When he told Lucius they were going to "run through" the whole play without interruption because the actress playing the mother was an understudy for the regular actress who was sick, Lucius went up into the Negro gallery to watch it alone.

He loved watching the brick wall turn into a thin curtain, and another such curtain divided the living room from the kitchen. Tom came out dressed like a merchant seaman and stood on a fire escape and talked right at Lucius.

"Yes, I have tricks in my pocket, I have things up my sleeve. But I am the opposite of a stage magician. He gives you the illusion that has the appearance of truth. I give you truth in the pleasant disguise of illusion. To begin with, I turn back time. . . ." He pointed to a portrait on the wall of a man with a big grin wearing a World War I doughboy cap. "This is our father who left us a long time ago. He was a telephone man who fell in love with long distance." Watching Tom walk through a wall into the kitchen was jarring, but then the scene became realistic. Lucius felt close to Tom because he was fired for writing poetry on the lid of a shoe box in the factory where he dusted shoes. But Tom was a little like Earl, too, because he was in the Merchant Marines in New Orleans. Lucius wondered if Earl, deep down, looked back on their family as Tom looked back on his. Tom's mother looked back from the limbo of the present on the good old days of her girlhood the way Momma did. And the way they talked about him, Tom's daddy was like Lucius's. And strangely, Laura seemed like Lucius himself because they were both blond and lame. He wanted a sister or a sweetheart like her.

" 'Blow out your candles, Laura—and so good-bye. . . .' " said Lucius, as he felt along the wall in the dark, going down from the Negro balcony after the run-through.

He moved among the actors and the workers during the break as they sat around, the houselights on bright, drinking coffee, eating hamburgers, working on sound cues over the speaker system, and making adjustments in lighting. Lucius felt left out. He asked the young man who played Tom when Tennessee Williams would arrive, and he laughed, his mouth full of slaw.

In uniform, Lucius stood in the lobby and watched the people coming in, looking for Gaile Savage and her father, Victor. Girls from Cherokee High drama society showed people their reserved seats. Lucius and Gale were mere decoration.

"Lucius, somebody wants you on the telephone," Hood whispered in his ear after the play got going. "Tell Gale to hold down the Spot."

Scared, Lucius shined his light over to the second aisle into Gale's eyes. He struck a melodramatic pose as if he'd been blinded and began to stagger toward Lucius.

"What?" Gale reached out but Lucius ducked too late and caught a stinging spark on his ear.

"How 'bout taking the Spot a minute. I got a phone call."

"I've had to put up a solitary battle all these years," Mrs. Wingate was telling Tom. "But you're my right-hand bower! Don't fall down, don't fall!" Just what Momma always told Lucius.

His heart beat fast, he expected something terrible—Bucky dead. Momma sick. Hood glared at Lucius as he walked into the bright office. "Tell him this is a business phone, Lucius," whispered Hood, not looking at him. As if this weren't the first call he'd received at the Bijou.

"Hello," he said, using his announcer's voice.

"Lucius?"

"Yeah."

"How can I get hold of Mammy or Momma?" It wasn't Uncle Luke, it was Earl. Lucius wondered if the FBI or somebody was tracing the call.

"Where are you?"

"Bus terminal in New Orleans."

"New Orleans? What you doing down there?" Lucius remembered the time Earl showed up at the screen door in a merchant seaman's outfit, just up from New Orleans.

" 'Bout to go back to the base."

"What base?" Lucius didn't know what he was talking about.

"Who's on second, stupid. Air Force. Hell, I'm a fly-boy, now. Listen, I want you to tell Momma something for me."

"Okay. What?"

"Tell her I'm desperate, *I am desperate,* for some money for my wife—"

"Your what?"

"Carla here. We got hitched. But see, she's pregnant and her mother's threatening to kill me if she catches us, so— They're Catholic, see, Italian Catholic, like the Pope, you know, and Murder Incorporated. So, I got to get her out of here, and I'm already AWOL from the base."

"I'm sorry, your three minutes are up, please signal when through."

"Okay, operator," said Earl, with the authority of a company president. "I'll notify you. . . . Lucius, you listening?"

"Yeah, I'm listening." Hood's stare as he drummed his fingers on the glass top of his desk intimidated Lucius. Somehow, staring at the poster, half-rolled on the side of the desk, advertising Bogart in *The Two Mrs. Carrolls* helped him concentrate on the voice from New Orleans.

"I'm about to get kicked out of the Air Force."

"Kicked out? When did you get kicked *in?*"

"Tell him this is a business phone," said Hood, not looking up.

"This is my brother, Mr. Hood," said Lucius hoping to impress him. "The one that won the talent contest."

"*What* talent contest?"

"You remember, don't you, the— Yeah, Earl, I'm paying attention."

"I lied about my age, see, so when they go to court-martial me for being AWOL, I'll tell them I'm only fifteen and my name isn't really Fred Hutchfield."

"That's right, Earl, always tell the truth."

"Okay, you got it straight, kid?" His accent was even more Yankee now, even though he was as far south as he could get, and he sounded like some of the guys who came with the stage shows to the Bijou.

"Yeah. . . . Well, Earl, I hope this means you've given it up for good."

"Lucius," he said, solemnly, "I've learned my lesson. I'm through. I'd rather die than go back to the reform school."

"You know, Earl, the thing that's always scared me is that when the G-men are tracking you"—Hood looked up—"you might take a gun, and—"

"Lucius!" hurt in his voice, "you think your own brother'd do a thing like that?"

"No, I just. . . ." Hood looked interested.

"Well, here's your new sister, wants to say hello."

Lucius felt awkward, wondering what he could say in Italian.

"Hello."

"Hello, you speak English, huh?"

"Why, of course." In fact, she had a Yankee accent, too, that made her sound sophisticated, and Lucius saw her wearing a fur piece and a fashionable hat and diamond earrings.

"And you can give the bride a kiss," said Earl, suddenly back on the line, his tone evoking a naked girl with long black hair.

"Earl, why don't you just catch a ship like you done that other time?"

"What other time?"

"When you was in the Merchant Marines."

Earl was silent, then he said, "Kid, I ain't never been in no Merchant Marines. I just wore that uniform so I could hitchhike across country easier. Well, I better hang up now and go face the music." Without waiting for Lucius to catch his breath to speak, Earl hung up.

At intermission, Lucius watched Victor Savage and his wife walk regally up the aisle to smoke in the lobby. Gaile remained in her seat, staring at the closed curtains.

"Lucius," said Hood, startling him, "I'm docking your pay two dollars and four cents."

Lucius turned. "What for?"

"That operator called back, said your party walked off without paying for the overtime."

After the play, Lucius stayed to help "strike the set," as Spit called it, so Momma was asleep when he came in, but he deliberately let the icebox door slam, and told her about Earl's long distance call. She was appalled but fascinated, and wondered what Carla looked like, and worried about the outcome of Earl's scheme to elude military justice. But she said sarcastically, "I'll send him five to pay for a cab to the hospital, and I'll ride with her."

Ledger: Earl called and asked for money for his pregnant wife. Yeah, I'll bet.

"At one time Oscar Wilde was beaten and dragged to the top of a mountain by some fellow class mates at colledge. At the peak they let go of him. Oscar stood erect, straightened his clothes and said calmly and admiringly, "Yes, the view is wonderful from up here."

Glass Menagerie by Tennessee Williams was something fine.

Nick was sitting in his easy chair, the one with the arm missing, smoking a cigarillo as he read *Look Homeward, Angel,* when into the grey light of the room—

After Duke had gone, Lucius relit his Robert Burns cigarillo and, reverting to a discarded pen name, started something fresh, the fictional biography of Earl Hutchfield.

"The Call of the Wild Goose"
by Ronald Dennis Birchfield

Though the sun shone brightly, snow fell. It lit upon the ground softly, drifting on the air with dream-like movements. I could smell the heather, high, bent by the wind, in the raw air. Strange, it wasn't even cold that day, though snow fell and the wind swept over the countryside from the ocean. "Here in this valley," his wife, Eileen, told me, "Ben finally found peace."

I looked out over the valley, and could feel its infinite calm, peace. Somewhere in the distance a train whistle blew, strange and hollow as if from the very bowels of the earth.

Standing beneath the curving, reaching finger-limbs of the giant oak with the heather at my feet, my brother dead and cold forever numb from the bitter sting of death under the soil, I tried deliberately to relive the past.

Lucius began again.

Ben entered the house quietly, and the following morning his family awakened to find him asleep on the davenport. That is the way he always came, suddenly, like summer rain, and was gone in the same manner.

The tough, the perverse, the wild, the weary, the strange, the defeated, the curious, the adventurous were his constant companions. And his brothers looked at him as though he were an interesting visitor. On the road, wandering aimlessly from state to state, into Mexico, into Canada, he hungered for the unknown. Cities, people, experiences he had not known were many, and he pursued a mad desire for realization of them all.

On the Spot, while Robert Mitchum and Teresa Wright in *Pursued,* a strange western, played at his back, Lucius played out "Call Herman in to Supper" in his imagination, turning every once in a while to try it out on the Bijou stage. He'd never read a play. He decided to track one down so he could see how it was done by professionals.

"Lord, Lucius, you sure *you* ain't in some kind of trouble. Ever'body else is."

"Naw, I'm just having trouble getting started on this play I'm writing."

"A acting play?"

"Yeah."

"What's it about?" Mammy asked, absently, fixing chicken and biscuit dumplings. "Too bad it ain't quite warm enough, we could eat outside under the mimosa. Did you see that marble table the Chief set up?"

"Yeah, saw it last Sunday. Looks good. . . ." Easter Sunday, and the backyard full of clover and violets and buttercups, the garden freshly plowed by an old Negro who came down with his mule and wagon off Clayboe Ridge every spring to plow all the gardens in the neighborhood. The Chief'd torn the wall out of the front room so it could be extended six feet, and the smell of fresh lumber stacked outside by the hedge drifted in. "What do you think of my title?"

"Your what?"

"My title—of this play I'm writing. I named it "Call Herman in to Supper." Sound good?"

"Yeah, I reckon so."

"It's about this little boy named Herman, and he lives up in the Smoky Mountains with his momma and daddy and his gran'paw, who's blind and deaf, but he can talk, see."

"Lord have mercy, I meant to tell the Chief to bring some country butter on his way in."

"And his daddy—whose name is Will—"

"That was *my* daddy's name . . ."

"I know it."

"Now, listen, I don't want you writing nothing about *my* family."

"No, Mammy, it's just the name. But he works in this coal mine, see. . . ."

"Well, my daddy wouldn't go *in* a coal mine if you vowed to shoot him."

"But what he really wants to be is a farmer, like his daddy was."

"Now, you're gettin' hot. My daddy owned half of West Cherokee at one time, had it all planted in corn."

"Let me tell you, now. . . . So his wife—Cora's her name—thinks she might have cancer."

"She's a goner. Ain't no cure for it."

"Except she's probably pregnant."

"Now, you hush that kind a talk in my kitchen." Hurt, Lucius sat down at the table and played with the broken shells from the boiled eggs Mammy was shearing into the dumplings.

Shortly, Mammy said, "Is that all they is to it?"

"To what?"

"To the story."

"No, it goes on to where it's a day in the fall and supper's 'bout ready, Cora's fixing it, and Will comes in, and he ain't found no job and they're poor and hungry and all she's got on the stove is beans, and Will starts talking mean about Gran'paw, 'cause all he does from morning till night is rock in the rocker and spit tobacco juice in a lard can, and when it comes time to eat, and he smells beans cooking, he calls for Herman to come lead him to the table. So Cora tells Will to call Herman in to supper."

Mammy went over to the stove and fiddled with the candied sweet potatoes, and Lucius followed her and stood by as she bent over the oven to put the corn bread it.

"And Herman doesn't answer, so he says he's gonna give Herman a whuppin' for being late, and Cora says he better not be down there at the creek again. See, he's just about four years old. And Gran'paw keeps calling Herman to lead him to the supper table, 'cause he smells them good ol' beans cooking, and it bothers the fool out of Will. Will keeps talking about blowing up the mine, and it worries Cora, then he'll threaten to shoot himself, then *all* of them—"

"Don't, Lucius. . . ."

Lucius didn't know what she meant by that, but, a little confused, he went on. "He dreams of growing stuff next spring, and when Cora finds a bottle of whiskey in his pocket, he tries to get away from her as she comes at him with a stick of firewood for wasting what little money they got on moonshine, and she hits him with the stick where he's got the bottle in the back pocket of his overalls, and gran'paw smells it and whines for a swaller of it. Then Will gets worried about Herman, so he goes out looking for him, and Cora looks at herself in the mirror and talks to her daddy about when she was young and happy—"

"I thought he couldn't hear?"

"Well, he can't, but she just gets to talking to him—sort of to herself. . . . Then she gets out this wedding dress. . . ."

Mammy rattled coal from the bucket into the cookstove. "Chief's gonna get me one of them 'lectric stoves, soon's we get married. Boys, won't that be the berries?"

"Want to hear the rest?"

"I'm listening."

Lucius followed Mammy around as she moved about the kitchen, running water, stirring stuff in pots.

"Well, she looks at herself in the mirror and it starts her to crying to see how run down she looks."

"Them mountain girls goes fast, honey. Your gran'paw Charlie took me over the Cumberlands to Harlan in nineteen and twenty-one before the first railroad, and girls five years younger than me looked old enough to be my mother."

"Anyway, so— Really? I always like to imagine what it's like in Kentucky. Did you see *Trail of the Lonesome Pine?*"

"Sure did, but it ain't like that."

"Oh. . . . Well, so, Will come back in, and he didn't find Herman. And so they dream about things, how it might be if he was to plow in the spring, and then they fuss again and ol' Gran'paw cranks up to whine for Herman again, and then this neighbor of theirs, named Hank, comes in, and he sort of beats around the bush, but Will and Cora feel what it is he's going to say, and—"

"Better not nothin' happen to that little Herman, now. . . ."

"Well, wait and see—And so, he says, he was fishing down at the bridge and he saw something in the water, floating—"

"Now, Lucius, you hush."

"Mammy, it's just a story."

"I don't care! That poor young'un!"

"So Cora and Will run out to the car—it's a old-timey T-model Ford—and Hank sorta ambles out, and it gets real quiet on the stage. . . ." Sensing the fear and sadness he had excited in Mammy, Lucius was thrilled, eager to make it show even more in her mouth and posture and gestures. "And then ol' Gran'paw stops rocking, and he says, 'Hermie, Hermie, boy, Gran'paw's hungry.'" Imitating the old man's voice, Lucius noticed Mammy stopped turning the sweet potatoes and held a dripping fork, looking at him, her mouth open, the heat from the oven making sweat burst out on her forehead. "'Come on over, and lead ol' Gran'paw tuh the supper table. Aw, man! Smell 'em beans, son? Ummmmph! Come on over, Hermie, boy, Gran'paw's a-waitin' to eat. Got good ol' beans fer supper. Hermie. . . . Hermie, boy. . . .' And then he slowly leans back, relaxes, moans a little—as the curtain comes *down*."

Lucius and Mammy looked into each other's eyes.

"For the Lord's sake, Lucius, will you tell me where in this world you *get* sich stuff as that?"

"Oh, I was just walking down a railroad track past these ol' poor people's houses, and the sun was going down, and it was real chilly and

I could smell the coal smoke, and I heard this voice calling Herman to come in to supper, and it just *got* me."

"I never heared such a tale in all my borned days. Do you *have* to make it so sad? Can't the little feller turn out not to be drownded after all?"

"That would spoil the whole thing."

"You already got the story wrote?"

"Play. No, I sort of made up part of it as I was telling it to *you*."

"Then it ain't too late to change it. Why can't it be a log?"

"Why can't *what* be a log?"

"That the man saw a-floating towards the bridge."

"Oh, Mammy. . . ." Lucius drifted into the living room, sat on the flowered davenport, hunted for the book and the show pages among the Sunday paper spread out around him.

The Chief at the wheel of a Packard, puffing on a King Edward, slid into view at the break in the hedge.

"I don't see why the little feller has to get drownded," said Mammy, from the kitchen, as the Chief stepped over the sill.

Bewildered, the Chief asked Lucius, "What's she talking about? What did you say, Jane?"

Mammy came to the door. "Well, good morning, sir. . . . Oh, I's trying to dream up a new ending for Lucius's play. Joe, that youn'ern has cooked up the awfullest tale ever you heard in your life," said Mammy, in her mock-crying voice.

"I seen a lot of 'em," said the Chief, "at the old Pioneer, when I was fire inspector. They'd bring a whole stage full of horses out there. *Ben Hur,* it was."

Ozark College
Mt. Galilee, Arkansas
March 28, 1947

Dear Lucius,

What a delightful surprise to find your letter in my mailbox this morning! I was sorry to have to leave my Bonny Kate students so abruptly. Since I left Cherokee, I have often thought of my students and wondered how they are doing. I have missed you all. So it warms my heart to have your letter and to know that I am not completely forgotten in Cherokee. Lucius, you must not feel that your teachers are your enemies. I am sure you know I am your friend, but perhaps you have among the other teachers friends you know not of.

I am glad you are as determined as ever to become a famous writer. Your vocabulary has indeed grown. That comes from writing so constantly. I never practiced the piano as diligently as you practice your writing. My! And you can imagine how pleased I am that your letter shows some improvement in your spelling. (The sweet things you say about me are also heartwarming.) I hope you don't mind my being a teacher even after I've left your classroom. But I do want to stress the importance of your working on the vocabulary you now have—and I know few boys your age who have such a large one—so that you can feel confident you are using your words properly.

I am impressed by the list of projects you have set for yourself. I was always so amazed at the scope of your interests and the vividness of your imagination. Persevere, Lucius! And don't shirk the hard work. I know you thought English grammar a drudgery! Still, you will discover that a command of the necessary language skills will help you make the most of your plots.

Your letters will always make me happy. Give my warm regards to your classmates.

Sincere best wishes,
Shirley Redding

Ledger: Letter from Miss Redding. Her first name is Shirley! Boomerang! is great. The cops just seem like ordinary, hardworking people. Dana Andrew and Arthur Kennedy.

"I didn't want to tell you before, Lucius, because I was afraid you'd get to thinking about it too much, endanger your schoolwork, you see. But since you tell me you expect to fail—and with only two more months to go—I can see you're scared stiff. Well, don't be. It'll hurt after the operation for a week or so, and then the casts will bother you for six weeks, but the results will change your life."

"What you gonna do?"

Running a pencil over Lucius's high instep, Dr. Summers said, "We'll go in here with a long incision, another along the inside, and a cross on the great toe. The same thing on the left foot. We're going to transplant some bones, Lucius, locking the two great toes so that they cannot bend."

"Forever?"

"No, my boy, in heaven the crooked shall be made entirely straight."

Breathing fitfully, Lucius was unable to laugh with everybody else. He trembled, thinking of the hairs on his prick, the wet dreams, the ether, the red devil chasing him down a tunnel.

"Still ushering at the Bijou?"

"Yes, sir."

"You can keep ushering right up to the day before you're admitted to the hospital sometime early in June. Meanwhile, continue to wear the brace and bars. You know, I used to go to a nickelodeon called The Bijou Dream in my hometown Rochester in 1914. Never quite forget that place."

As Lucius put on his brace, imagining the operation formed a hard lump in his throat. But he was a little relieved to know for certain now, and he began to wonder what it would be like. Raine would hear about it and grieve for him and finally come, risking his rejection of her, and she'd find some other girl there. Maybe Gaile Savage. Lucius stood up, his legs wobbly, hurting already.

Lucius rode the Clinch View Streetcar to Peck's store where it turned around. The Clayboe Ridge girls wouldn't speak to him, but they didn't seem mad at him anymore.

Mrs. Waller made Lucius stay in for writing during the grammar lesson. When she released him, he cut through the auditorium study hall, heading for the back exit. He felt that he was the last student in the building. He'd never been in the auditorium this late in the afternoon. Silence buzzed in the sunlight that lapped the backs of seats the study hall students had shined with fidgeting. The curtains on the stage were drawn. A large gold BK in Gothic script was sewn to the curtain that skirted the top of the stage. Feeling the pull of the empty stage, Lucius walked straight down the wide middle aisle and jumped up onto the stage, and as he turned toward the seats a thrill ran through him. He imagined something more momentous than the few sappy little plays he'd seen here. But it was not yet clear what. "Call Herman in to Supper." Then, his own adaptation of *Gone With the Wind,* a five-hour epic play, himself as Rhett Butler and LaRue Harrington as Scarlett, and Loraine would sit in the audience and see that their own romance was like Scarlett's and Rhett's, except Lucius was also a little like Ashley. He'd *do* it, by God! But then, he realized that he hadn't enough time this year, and he was going to fail the eighth grade, and by next fall, he'd be shipping out of New Orleans or Maine in the Merchant Marines.

Made of the Tennessee marble that went into the post office and the Statue of Liberty, the Aldrich-Carnegie Library on Catholic Hill had always seemed alien to Lucius's life. He passed it as a little boy running around barefoot and filthy in coveralls uptown with the Hawn boys, stealing papers at the bus terminal to sell around the Market House or running in and out of the Boys' Club. The library was impressive, like an outdoor vault or a big tomb for the Aldrich family. Reminding him always of Henry Aldrich, the contrast between the way it looked and the name made him sneer. It was for rich or especially smart kids. "Public" made him think of "Public Utilities."

A cold, scary, mean-school feeling from the atmosphere reached all the way out to the front brass-trimmed doors. Entering the lobby, he climbed more marble steps inside, with brass railings on the sides. The fact that as far as he knew there were more books in this building than in any other in Cherokee, and that he was a writer of books himself, and knew and read and felt possessive of some of the best writers, did not give him any feeling of belonging in this place. He felt self-conscious, as though he'd come to steal or had stolen before, and the old women sitting and standing and walking around, looking severe, were waiting to spot him to call the police. He saw Clark Gable talking loud in the library in *Adventure* and Greer Garson, the librarian, trying to shush him, then Lucius himself, like Gable, standing on a pier in the Merchant Marines. One librarian, flipping through a book as thick as her waist, looked up, gave him a stare as if to say, "I would like to hang you by your balls from the ceiling." His face and scalp burned and itched.

He'd come to look up some stuff about New Orleans and Maine. He took notes on black-water streams, spruce trees, sawmills, chief crops, boatbuilding, shoe factories, fishing, largest ports, whales, spear cannons, dolphin, barking sharks, coral reefs, the ice industry, and other facts to authenticate his fiction.

Looking them up in a book called *Covering the Continent,* Lucius accidentally stumbled onto, "Cherokee is the ugliest city I ever saw in America." But the guy loved Maine and New Orleans.

Lucius looked for Wolfe's books. He was astonished to see physically on the shelf all his works. That one human being in so short a life could write so much was incredible. But then he realized that since he intended to live past a hundred, he could produce twice as much as Wolfe's span of books, for he died young.

Sad, sick-sad over Loraine who'd sworn to love him forever but who'd so soon mocked him, Lucius walked Cherokee, talking with God. He vowed always to tell the truth, to speak only memorable phrases, and imagined future consequences in dramatic scenes of conflict with the world he lived in now and the glamorous world into which he soon would go. But a more profound response to the world's lies and hypocrisies might be utter silence. He would listen, he would not speak. Only his eyes and the expression on his mouth would reveal his feelings about people and events, and his writings would express what he thought.

Having lost Loraine, Lucius had become very religious—but he was ashamed because the need was so obvious to Jesus. He wanted to love Him purely, without necessity. He thought as he walked of his ideal girl that he'd asked God for many times, the dim figure who came more and more often into the reveries of the future that he put down as novel scenarios. She had many names and came from many different places and settled with him in Maine on a farm or in New Orleans on a boat.

Because he hated group prayer, he'd thought often recently of how it would feel to pray in a church at night when it was closed. He found one of Cherokee's largest churches near the Hutchfield Bakery. From the high steps he saw a large house on a hill, one such as he'd wanted for his own retreat, after years of labor and writing on a farm or a boat. Afraid someone, a night watchman perhaps, would hear him, call the police, or shoot him in the dark, he opened the door and went into the outer lobby and knelt on the carpeted steps that led up to the inner doors. Feeling guilty toward Jesus for being timid in his approach to Him, Lucius walked, defiant of possibilities, into the auditorium, down to the altar. Kneeling, he heard the faint sounds of traffic outside, and many mysterious little sounds in the quiet, deserted church. On one side, the stained glass windows were dark, on the other, slightly illuminated by the fitful lights of cars coming over the river bridge.

"Dear God, please let it be that the girl I have dreamed and written about all my life will come into my life soon, and dear God, please let her be near right now, lying in her bed, dreaming of someone like me, who will take her out into the glory and adventure and beauty of the world thou hast made. I love life, dear God, and I love thee and Jesus, and I love the girl you will send me. In Jesus' name, I pray. Ah-men."

STORYWEAVERS GUILD 3415 Hollywood Blvd.
Hollywood 28, California
Personal Report on Personality Quiz and Aptitude Test
The New Carlton Cramer Course and Service in Storyweaving

March 31, 1947

Dear Lucius:

Your name has been placed on my **ACCEPTED** list for reasons which I shall explain to you. First of all, Lucius, please understand that this preliminary work is intended to reveal to me only your possession or non-possession of natural talent and aptitude. Your answers to the Questions and your treatment of the Exercises offer ample evidence that you can learn to write well.

You started proving your fitness for the study of story creation in your work on Exercise Number One. In this you tell simply and with deep feeling of the death of your baby brother Ronny. You have built this up convincingly, realistically to its conclusion, and you have made your emotion very clear to me. That is the essence of good writing! The ability to project emotion through *words on paper.*

I like the straightforward, matter-of-fact manner in which you have performed Exercise Number Two regarding your remorse for having teased the old woman who came to do your mother's ironing. These little incidents in our lives, upon which we look back with regret, are always difficult to set down dispassionately, but here you have "come through" in fine autobiographical fashion.

Your description of Raine is fine indeed. The simple, sincere manner in which you have written this is a manifestation of good writing. Your Exercise Number Four displayed some good logic. Your work in connection with Exercise Number Five reveals a splendid quality of imagination. You have painted a picture of a place you have never visited in person—the rocky coasts and rugged mountains of Maine. You have reduced your imaginary impressions to *words* on paper. Imagination is indispensable to the writer!

Millions of readers are indirectly paying thousands of dollars weekly to writers who can create imaginary scenes and situations, presenting them convincingly, entertainingly. That is what you have done here.

It is necessary to read currently published magazines in order to study the methods of currently popular writers. The basic technique of modern fiction is to be found in any class periodicals. I further recommend reading of the Bible for writing style and technique, among other virtues.

I adhere to a rule of not accepting applicants under eighteen with few exceptions. In view of the potential ability you have shown, I am inclined to make an exception of you, providing one of your parents will approve your desire for Storyweavers training.

I am convinced you can make a successful writer of yourself. I strongly urge you to continue your writing whether or not you decide to enroll for training in Storyweavers Guild. I see no reason why you should not be successful, if you will work as diligently in your future studies as you have in these Exercises.

I shall be glad to work with you, Lucius, if you do enroll, and am therefore enclosing a copy of our Membership Agreement.

Yours sincerely,
Carleton Cramer,
President

Ledger: Emmett King was waiting for me under the mimosa trees. Told me my mother was dead. Jumped off the Sevier Street Bridge. Said he heard her say she was going to do it one day. I called Councilman Randall's house, and she was fine. Emmett better start praying.

We're doing career books in school. Mine is on journalism. Got letter from Storyweavers. Song of the Thin Man, William Powell & Myrna Loy. Writing out "The Yearning Heart."

Lucius left home early and took the Clinch View streetcar in front of the ruins of the Pioneer and rode to the end of the line. Harry was eating a Butterfinger, washing it down with an RC. Lucius showed him the letter. "Yeah," he said, handing it back. He sucked the last of the foam down just as Raine and them burst through the screen door. Peggy ignored Harry and Raine ignored Lucius.

Peggy read the letter, walking very slowly, bent over, crossing one leg before the other as she trudged up the hill toward Bonny Kate. "Are they going to pay you any money for it?"

"For what?" said Lucius, irritated that she was missing the point.

"I don't know. Ever what it was you mailed to 'em." She made it sound as if he'd sent in cornflakes box tops.

"Skip it."

"Okay, I will."

Lucius wanted to show all his teachers, even the secretary Mrs. Fraker, who treated him with contempt. See, see, this man in Hollywood, the president of the school, thinks my writing is good. But he imagined their cold looks. Still, he watched Miss Kuntz's face, during homeroom, for a sign of good temper.

His turn, Harold Vaughn read the Bible. As he muttered through the Sermon on the Mount, Lucius listened carefully to the words themselves, trying to hear what Mr. Cramer had in mind when he recommended reading the Bible, which people all his life had made so dull, despite widely spaced moments when some verses inspired him. "The light of the body is the eye: if therefore thine eyes be single, thy whole body shall be full of light. But if thine eye be evil, thy whole body shall be full of darkness." Yes, the words were beautiful.

"Why do you mumble like that, Harold? That's not the back of a cornflakes box you're reading."

Miss Kuntz shot up as if somebody had given her a hotfoot. "Mr. Hutchfield, stand in the corner until the bell rings." Lucius stood in the corner. "Judge not, that ye be not judged."

Love thy neighbor as thyself, thought Lucius. It ain't easy, said Humphrey Bogart.

Lucius looked all day for openings but not even Kay Kilgore was in a mood good enough to encourage him to take the letter out of his notebook where it was pressed between an illustrated title page of "The Yearning Heart" and the first chapter.

Mrs. Waller seemed the most likely person, for they were on a letter-writing unit. But some girl had burnt a cherry pie in the class before and the smell in the air and the still warm stove under Lucius's elbows made him sick at his stomach, and he didn't feel like risking a glazed-eyed dismissal of his triumph.

Lucius sat on the new grass, watching girls play kickball, the smell of wild onions stirring in him a melancholy sensuality. He sat with Harry, Duke, and three other boys under the lone mimosa tree that had somehow gotten started two years ago at the far edge of the vast playground. Under the noon sun, the feathery, fernlike leaves cast little shadows over them that waved in the April breeze.

Playing blackjack, everybody was surprised at the amount of money Duke put down to back up his loud bravado. Harry, the dealer, seemed unusually quiet, smiling enigmatically as he raked in everybody's money. A few boys thought the smile meant he was cheating, but nobody tried to prove anything.

His mind only half on the game, Lucius was aware of the hammering across the macadam behind him where new houses were going up.

"What're you smiling about?" Duke asked Harry, beginning to lose his bravado as his funds shrank.

Lucius became aware of the invisible fence that surrounded the Bonny Kate grounds. If you took one step into the street, a teacher was immediately at your heels, first with shouts, then with a grip on your sleeve. It seemed strange that a real, electrified fence had kept Bucky inside the juvenile detention home, while an invisible fence kept Lucius inside Bonny Kate. Cars passing, women hanging up wash, trees budding on Clayboe Ridge, life apart from this stupefying, monotonous, and grim life inside the invisible fence, seemed strange.

"Blackjack your ass," said Harry, showing his cards.

"I quit," said Duke, jumping up.

"I reckon so. You can't play with nothing on you but belly-button lint."

The other boys still in the game said they heard the bell ring and Harry went in with them, jingling his money with a thrill-giggling dance.

As Lucius walked alone across the deserted playground, late for class, the wind blowing in the mimosa ahead of him, he was aware of the solitary tree behind him.

Sitting in study hall, bitterly conscious of his separation from the kids around him, Lucius began to write:

ON LUST OF THE MIND
by James Austin Frank

What goes on in their minds, what hidden things that not even death could tell? Thoughts whose actions would, perhaps, burn them in the firey pits of Hell. Behind those misty eyes there dreams a dream that few men dare to give reality.

What strange and God forbidden desires they nurse, the plays that dark thoughts preform on the stage of the mind, plays that never see the light of day, lest due punishment soon befall.

In the domain of our minds we committ countless acts of adulitry, rape and murder. Education abolishes ignorance, true, none the same for murder and its ken. There swells within all born yet and to be born, primitive desires, passions.

Deeds imigined, not permitted to know action—thus is God within us all—none too many know it. . . .

Ledger: Almost late to work. Had to stay in for Mrs. Waller for sassing. Planned chapt. seven of "Yearning Heart." P.S. Mr. Bronson gave a lecture on electives for the ninth grade. I elected "speech and dramatics," but I will be in Maine or New Orleans.

Lucius sat in the tower, shivering in the night air. Duke was out running with Raine and them. At first when they made fun of Duke, Lucius, who had admired and been fascinated by him, was hurt, felt ashamed, as if they were ridiculing him, too. And then, even when he contributed to the network of subtle and overt ridicule, he had felt silly himself when Duke lied and acted stupid. And when they'd teased him, Lucius had hated Duke for bringing it all on himself, sensing that none of the others really disliked Duke as he did. Lucius was struck suddenly with the insight that Duke's antics were a sort of travesty of his own inclinations and aspirations. Self-contempt kept him in the tower by the river.

NIGHT RITUAL: Lucius is living at Mammy's with Momma and Bucky, and Earl is in the reform school in Nashville and Daddy's in the army overseas, and Lucius is in the house alone, too late to go with Mammy and Momma and Bucky and the Chief to put flowers on Gran'paw Charlie's and Baboo's graves on Decoration Day. He played too long down in the addition, in the WPA ditch, and the rain pipes. Feeling guilty, he digs into the clothes box where he used to sleep when they stayed all night, and finds the clipping of the man Mammy says shot Gran'paw Charlie at the Peerless Glass Company when he was a night watchman, charging Charlie took his job from him, and remembers they never sent him to jail. He puts on Gran'paw's old shoes, and takes Luke's Daisy BB rifle and starts to set off on his Western Flyer but it has a flat, and walks down the railroad tracks, and crosses the river trestle at sundown, scared to death and hungry and chilled, and slips into the factory through a hole in the fence, and is trying to take a crap when the man opens the door, the same one that shot Gran'paw, and scares the shit out of him, and the man calls the cops and they drive him home, and Momma takes Gran'paw's belt to him. . . . In the jungle behind the Hiawassee, under a tree limb that undulates like Sabu's python in *Jungle Book*, trying to poke through June's panties that she won't take off—an older girl whose frequent innuendos in fifth-grade geography have led to this crusty red clay where ants are driven among crawly dewberry vines. . . . Lucius mows lawns and collects enough money to take LaRue to see *Gone With the Wind* at the Hiawassee, turns to ask her at the water fountain just after taking a drink, but water comes out of his nose because his adenoids were removed the week before, stinging, a feeling like drowning, strangling, as he once almost did in Lone Mountain Lake at Boys' Club Camp. . . . He's watching *Mrs. Miniver* for the second time on the front row of the Hiawassee and Diane comes up and reminds him of the times they did it on Beech and he fingers her to the end and all through the next showing, and coming out blinking his eyes against the six o'clock August sunburst, sees his finger bleached white, wrinkled at the tip, as if he has stayed too long in the YMCA chlorinated pool. . . . Lucius goes to a birthday party at LaRue Harrington's house and he is so excited and thrilled to have been invited, to be playing the games, supervised by her beautiful older sister, that he, finally, after a week of enduring severe stomach pain, can't hold it in. . . . Having fucked his extra paper between two boxcars at the end of his route, he takes out his pecker to pee in the men's room of the Hiawassee, and is horrified to see it swollen large, red, wrinkly. Every ten minutes he goes to the bathroom to check his peter, relieved more and more as the swelling subsides, dashing back into the audience to miss as little as possible of Joan Crawford in *A Woman's Face*. He promises God he won't beat his meat ever again. Then he buys some popcorn and a pecan roll and when the six o'clock sunlight strikes his eyes outside, he's sick as a dog. Stomach aching, arm sore, peter tingling, head aching slightly, he walks to Mammy's. When he wakes the next morning, it's normal again. . . . He stuffs his satchel with extras Tuesday morning after the bomb. The front page is pink. He wanders all over Cherokee, lingering in the Negro districts because it scares and fascinates him, yelling into the empty streets at 5 A.M.: "America Drops Adam Bomb on Japan!" That evening Chief Buckner comes by Mammy's from Oak Ridge, says, "Well, Jane, we done it! Now we know what we was making out there!"

Ledger: Homer Davis came to see Momma when I was putting pics in my scrapbook. Drew a pic of the Swede in The Killers. We made ice cream and Homer was not eager to do it. Smash-up started today— Susan Hayward and Lee Bowman. Writing "The Cosgroves of Destiny."

JOURNALISM

B+

CAREER BOOK

Lucius Hutchfield
Copyrite 5/5/1947
Table of Contents

Preface: "My Fitness for the Work"

When I first began in elementary school and up until I reached the sixth grade I had always regarded books as in the same catagory as poison, boredom or a foolish waste of time. This applied to fiction but generally to non-fiction. Although I had this point of view towards books and stories (in some cases I still have a distaste for various types of litteture), I enjoyed telling stories of my own orgination or stories about moving pictures I had seen. These stories I told to my brothers, my friends and even a few grown ups, all of whom seemed to injoy them and after hearing one hounded me to tell another. In those days and more so now, I had a very broad scence of imigination. It always gave me pleasure to put these imiginations down on paper, but I never did this until I luckily reached the sixth grade, before then telling them gave enough satisfaction.

The only barrier between me and my sucess is discouragement and the teachers in school who furnish most of it, and difficulty in getting the novels published. Short stories aren't very hard to sell—if thier good. Many times a teacher has distroyed a tediously acquired piece of manuscript before my face. This angers and discourages me more than anything else.

I expect to be a forgien correspondent, too, or a New York news commentator something on the line of Walter Winchell. A bit headstrong I must admit. I like the idea of taking up for the common people and thier common ways. I like to bring out the finer charateristics of somewhat hostile nations or individual people. All this I can do through the field of Journalism.

For three years I have practiced daily along the field of litteture towards the goal of success. I intend to continue dispite any possible obstickles. Most of my many stories I have not finished through lack of intrest or time. I have in all, sixty two story summeries from which I hope to produce saleable novels by June, 1947.

Momma and Daddy had been separated so long that putting the official seal on the divorce the day it became final came as no great shock. But Lucius went around all day sad, choked up.

He'd not gotten around to thinking up the story about the man who smuggled arms into Palestine to aid the Jews. Inspired partly by the pictures on his sanctuary wall of Gary Cooper as Robert Jordan in *For Whom the Bell Tolls.* But in his own story, he saw himself. The newsreels and the newspaper stories and the magazine articles had stimulated him to respond to an aura about the "Holy War" that made him want to become a foreign correspondent, free-lancing from places like Jerusalem. So he wrote some sketches in Health class.

WRATH OF WAR

The child screamed and her tears dampened her mother's bosom. The blast had torn the woman's dress half from her plump body. Her black hair lay in the dust and her eyes were open but saw nothing. The child screamed and tugged at her mother's body and the sun dried the blood in the dust. Two men came with a cart and the woman was lifted into it with the others. The men went away with the cart and the child was too young to walk and it screamed and the war went on in the street.

Realizing that it might be several years before he would become accepted as a correspondent, Lucius imagined what it would be like in the future:

PALISTINES LAST STAND

reported by Lucius Hutchfield

A. S. P.

Jeruseleum, Palistine, Dec. 7, 1950–Soon, perhaps before dawn, the bloody fuedal war between the jews and arabs, will be over. Jeruselum, the final battleground, will lie in numb silence. But what an awful city that silence will know. On every torn street the bloodstained, disfigured bodys of arab and jewish soilders, women and children and feeble creatures will plainly show the folly of the whole massecur. Very few living beings will observe the spoils. The city of the dead.

It is high noon. I typed this in a small, filthy room over looking the choatic city, I have clear view of the intire display of violence which is the hottest since Iwo Jima.

That night, Lucius went down the red clay path and across the tracks. Hiding his brace under a slab of marble, he climbed into his tower, and listened to the bawling of cattle and watched the full moon's reflections on the rain-swollen Tennessee River.

Hearing a thrash of branches down on the bank, Lucius froze, listened keenly, then squatted and looked over the windowsill. From the direction of the Sevier Street Bridge, somebody was coming through the weeds and horse chestnut trees. White, slender hands parted the vines and a girl with long dark blond hair stepped out naked onto the scraps of marble. Her breasts were small and her hips round but narrow, her belly button made a dark shadow, the hair below her navel was frizzy but pale. The sharp scraps of marble must have hurt her bare feet, she kept whisper-crying, "Owwwww! Ow! Ow!"

She eased back against the large, cracked triangular marble slab that leaned against a pile of big chunks. Her buttocks touching the cold marble set her shoulders shivering, and as her back touched, she shuddered. But then she smiled and sighed and looked up at the moon and reached her arms out as if to embrace it. "Moon, Moon," she whispered, intensely. The moonlight full on her face now, her long hair spread out around her white shoulders, she was Gaile Savage, the symphony conductor's daughter. "Gaile Savage is dead! I am reborn like the phoenix as Reva Tamargo!" she whispered to the moon. Lucius understood why she was here, even if what she was doing wasn't quite what he'd do, but wondered why, with the name Gaile Savage, she was changing to Reva Tamargo.

She lay sprawled in the moonlight on the slanting marble slab that hid his brace, the pointed end of the triangle sticking up, aimed from her angle of vision at the block of marble hanging from the crane high above her head, beside the moon. She spread her arms, and when she placed her palms flat on the marble, Lucius felt the touch in the center of his own palms, and then her toes gripped the slick surface and she arched her back, and aimed her body like a bow at the moon, and cried, a little louder: "Moooooon, I am the moooooooon goddess!" She was so beautiful Lucius couldn't speak. He imagined how he would feel to get caught by a voice from a dark tower. She lay there a while longer, basking like a sunbather, then rose, as if in a slow-motion movie, and stepped off the slab and started walking toward the vines again, crying, "Ewwww! Owwww! Aowoh!" Two round moons of marble dust on each reddened cheek. The vines swallowed her. Silence. Then from the darkness came a shrieking, female version of the Tarzan yell. It floated out over the river and echoed on the south shore among the houseboats. Silence again, and from the packinghouse down the river came the bawling of cattle.

Lucius took off his clothes and hung them over the window ledge and climbed down without using the rope, cutting his feet when he dropped from the last ladder rung, and lay down on the marble. His body absorbed Reva Tamargo's warmth. Realizing that looking at her had not even given him a hard-on, he was bewildered, but the smell of the river and the breeze chilling his nipples and tingling the hairs on his cods made his pecker rise. He didn't reach for it.

He wished he'd used the rope. He tried running up a log, but kept slipping off and became so exhausted he couldn't reach the ladder. Bruised and tired, he started crying. But walking along the bank, trying to find her footprints, relaxed him. Was that Mars Bar wrapper hers? Then he found an old paper sack and pulled down a kudzu vine and wrapped it around his waist and hung half of the sack over his butt, the other, that had the A & P insignia, over his prong, and strapped on his brace and sneaked, creaking, up the trash-strewn red clay cliff, then up the alley and through the back door of his house, and for the first time in his life, went to bed naked.

"I love you with all my heart, Gaile," said Lucius, "and I will love you till the end of time." What about Loraine Clayboe? "Loraine Clayboe is dead."

He got to thinking about Mrs. Waller, contemptuous of her attitude toward English and the way she taught it and the hateful way she talked to him and most of the boys, and her fat body disgusted him, but the more he looked her over in his nocturnal reverie, the more readily involuntary images came to him, finally giving him a hard-on, and he kept letting his pecker go through the hole in the sheet and rub against the wool army blanket.

Ledger: We heard a lecture on art today by my old art teacher. Miss Kilgore asked me to take art again next year. I said O.K. but I may be on the high seas. *Great Waltz,* classic, Louise Rainer.

April 10, 1973

Dear Mr. Cramer,

I wish to thank you for your persistent intrest in my writing. If it ever comes to be that I can afford to take your courses in writing I will do so, for I have the deepest confidence in your courses, that they would make me a better writer, quicker.

But now I do not desire to break off with a man who has given me my first affective encouragement. If it would be possible for you to be my agent, I'm sure that we can be successful together. What I mean is, I have a great number of story synopsis, that is the outline of novels I haven't written yet. An item on writing original stories for the movies which I read in one of your hand books really interested me. Going by what I have been told, I can freely say that my imigination as a whole is far betten than the way I express it.

I have in my possession near 30 book size stories which haven't yet went past the stage of synopsis. You said in one of your books that the movie Co. wants new material. I think I have just what they or at least something will consider purchasing.

With your influance in Hollywood and my stories I think that we can crash the field. If I were to sell at least one story, through you or if you didn't want to put up with me any further, I could make out on my own, but I would not very much like that.

If this proposition intrests you, and I deeply hope it does, please write back—please do so whatever your desicion on the matter. Tell me in your replying letter wheter or not you would like for me to send you one or two of the stories.

I look egerly forward to your reply.

Sincerely yours,
Lucius Hutchfield.

Ledger: I think about assembly and "Call Herman in to Supper" being presented, me sunburned and proud and thanking God before all those people. It'll take a lot out of me to finish it. God, please. *Guilt of Janet Ames,* Rosilind Russell. Melvyn Douglas.

*   *   *

Got one of Bucky's stories typed and sent it to him at Cold Springs. *My Favorite Brunette,* Bob Hope and Dorothy Lamour.

Wrote letter in the cave to Uncle Ben, playing like I was Bucky, asking for $25 to buy the secondhand typewriter in the Grand Avenue Used Furniture store. I hope he reads it on the air. The audience is sure to vote for me. It tells about my braces and how I told stories when I was little and write stories all the time, and need a typewriter while I'm bedridden after the operation.

The stout blond schoolteacher at the Crippled Children's Hospital asked Lucius where he went to church, and when he said, "God is everywhere, even if I prayed in a cornfield," she was shocked and urged him to attend her church, Cumberland Pentecostal.

"I don't believe in regular church anymore. I talk with God all the time. I don't need to go to any one place at a set time and carry on with a bunch of other people," he told her, firmly, proudly, but in a friendly way, and was delighted that she didn't get mad at him, as most grown-ups would, and it made her seem a little younger.

She gave him a little booklet from her purse. "Take it. No charge. You try to sell your product, so do I, though my efforts may be feeble and impressionless."

Ledger: Discovered that Reva Tamargo alias Gaile Savage lives high on the hill near the church where I prayed for my ideal girl. Thank you, God.

*   *   *

"I complained because I had no shoes until I met a man who had no feet." (In this circular a holy-roller preacher handed me on Market Square.) Earl wrote Momma from Germany. Still in air force. Wanted her to borrow $100 from the Chief to get married on. Daughter of a former Nazi colonel named Erica—if he can smuggle her out of Germany. He said his other wife Carla met some banjo picker in a hillbilly band and run off with him.

*   *   *

This blind man came in with a white cane and black glasses and left his German police dog in Hood's office and paid him ten dollars and paid me three to sit with him and tell him what was happening on the screen. Duel in the Sun with Gregory Peck, Jennifer Jones, Joseph Cotten, and Lionel Barrymore was on. It was wierd. But halfway through, he told me to shut up, because he could see it okay in his imigination, but to sit with him. Duel in the Sun is one of the greatest shows I have ever seen.

NIGHT RITUAL: His small hand dipping into a pickle jar, eating with the baby next door, a whole economy-sized jar of dill pickles. . . . Autumn, in the kitchen on Coker Street, Momma cooking dinner while Otto's Momma watches, drinking coffee. Otto says, Momma? What, Otto? Whyfore's Ducious got a bigger dodopeepeesoso than me do?. . . . Summer. Blossoms. Warm sunlight. Along Coker walks a dirty, humped Negro woman. . . .

Ledger: This road show put on *Hamlet* by William Snakesnot with this sissy-looking guy named Evans as Hamlet. I watched some of it through a crack in the door from the lobby. Shitty. Some parts were good. Went backstage at intermission to get some water to mop up some vomit and this guy that play's an old man, Plutonious, grabbed my ass. International Lady, the classic, with George Brent and Raymond Massey showed only 3 times, and I came in on the tail end of it. Looked good.

On the streetcar, one old woman said to another, "The poor ol' Bijou has really gone down since the golden years."

The pictures of burlesque girls on the standee out front were much more glamorous than the ones at the Smoky, but they struck Lucius, too, as a dramatic departure from anything else he'd seen at the Bijou. *Corsican Brothers* classic went off at seven o'clock for the burlesque show, the first ever presented on the Bijou stage. Burlesque, Lucius felt, belonged in the Smoky, a filthy hole, the natural habitat of sexual sin.

"Lucius," said Mr. Hood, "when's the last time you had a haircut?"

Seeing a strange policeman sprawled out along the balustrade, Lucius realized that Wade Bayliss had never returned to the Bijou.

Having found a reason for going backstage, Lucius just happened to be climbing the steps to stage level when the main attraction skipped out of the bright light into the dusty wings, stripped of most of her costume. The contrast between her movements on stage and the way she slumped into a slouchy listless walk the instant she was out of the light made Lucius feel a sense of imbalance, and to see the soft naked flesh of a tall woman, jacked up on high heels, made even taller by plumes shooting up out of her head, back here where he'd experienced dull routine, where he and the boys had lain on popcorn sacks, talking about pussy, where they had peeked out at girls sitting on the front row, and where Raine and other girls had performed in Bugs Bunny Club —it was almost as if she were walking around in his own house. Seeing the girl in her performance on stage, he got a hard-on, but somehow catching her backstage where she saw him face to face seemed sinful and disgusting.

The girls were very haughty and spoke to none of the ushers, and the way they walked around half-naked and talked so casually to equally casual men bewildered Lucius, and made him feel invisible. How could men stand to be near girls like that without fondling them at least? Their perfume lingered in the dressing room for days.

"Stand, people, for the morning prayer," said Mrs. Kuntz.

Lucius felt the rush of bodies, the cluck-click of desks as students all around him stood up. Lucius stared at the desktop.

"Lucius Hutchfield?"

"Ma'am?"

"We are waiting."

All the kids in the front kept their heads down, turned them to look back at Lucius.

"Are we going to have to wait all day to give thanks to our Lord?"

"No, ma'am. You all can give thanks any time you feel like it. And if all of you just happen to feel like it every morning at exactly three minutes before the bell, and one minute before the reading of the morning bulletin, that's okay with me. But I don't feel like praying now, and even if I did, I wouldn't toss my prayer into a stewpot with everybody else's."

Some giggled, some laughed, nervously, some sighed deeply, some made sounds of shock. Lucius thought for a moment the mean look on Mrs. Kuntz's face was a deliberate imitation of the Witch in *The Wizard of Oz* to get a laugh.

"Do you realize that what you have just said," said Mrs. Kuntz very slowly, "is blasphemy?"

"No, ma'am. What's blasphemy?"

"Do you know what sacrilege is?"

"No, ma'am."

"Lucius, I want to tell you something in front of the whole class, I want them to know that in all my years of teaching, I have never, repeat, never had a student like you. I have never even heard or read about any such thing as a child who refused to pray." Guilty and proud, Lucius tightened his mouth to keep his lip from trembling, but his eyelids fluttered. "And furthermore, I think you are one of the most contemptible human beings on the face of God's green earth."

Ann Carmichael, her head still bowed, her shoulders hunched, a long hank of her peroxide Veronica Lake hair hanging down almost to her elbow as she leaned sideways and turned toward him, her face red and streaked with tears, asked him in a clear voice, "Lucius, don't you believe in God?"

Shocked, moved, he was glad to say, "Yes," but felt obliged to add, "but I don't believe in churches and praying in public. And I'm not going to do it ever again in my whole life."

"Then you will never again set foot in my classroom, you—you ungodly heathen! Get! Out! Get! Out!"

"Yeah, go on," said Lester Henderson.

Lucius gave him a cold stare as he walked out.

Because Mr. Bronson wouldn't return until three, Mrs. Fraker let Lucius go on to English. "I don't deserve the punishment," she said, "of having to look at your sullen face all day long."

"Lucius," said Mrs. Waller, "it's your turn this Friday to give out the *Reader's Digest*s." Lucius groaned. "And don't groan about it. It's not going to kill you."

Lucius went to the glassed case behind her desk, squatted, pulled out a stack of ragged *Digest*s that sat next to the cookbooks and passed them out. He'd read in sources he respected that *Reader's Digest* was superficial and that a condensation ruined a book.

The aroma of devil's food cake hovered over the room.

"Stick *that* in the oven and bake it," Lucius said to Mary Sue Lobertini, handing her a *Digest*.

He sat at his own stove, the oven still too hot to open so he could have knee room, and flipped through the *Digest*. He was staring dully at "The War Waifs Arrive in America," when Mrs. Waller left the room. Every Friday, while she went into the model housekeeping room next door and supervised end-of-the-week projects, some of them special jobs for school activities—mending band uniforms, making banners —the *Reader's Digest* babysat for Mrs. Waller.

She passed, a distorted apparition, beyond the screen door between the rooms, moving from light to dark. Sunlight flooded the kitchen and glared off the porcelain coating of the fifteen stoves.

THE PALISTINE STORY
by James Austin Frank

For Gaile, alias Reva

(Summary)

I went to the apt. house and met Ramona. Max came in, his brother was dead. They had the guns on a garbage barge. I was supposed to be an agent for Grandis Satgaris who was buying the rifles from Max to arm the arabs. Actually I was an agent for Carlos Sabitini who was a Jew. I had delayed the real agent by killing him at the docks. I found Max very charming and I knew that though fat he was Ramona's lover. I gave him a small down payment then left.

As I expected, the police found the agent's body and tracked him back to Grandis. Meanwhile our men got the rifles from the boat and set out for the high seas to meet the seaplane. I went back on the garbage boat and paid Max's man.

Max came out of the opera with Ramona and three men made him ride to Grandis' hotel. Grandis thought Max killed his agent, then Max explained and both rode to meet the garbage tug. I had counted on this so before we landed I swam to shore and slept in a Negro's flat so I would be above suspicion.

There was a fuss at the docks and Max shot his way out, leaving Ramona. I heard about this and went to Max and offered to help. This was the proposition: both of us would get her out but one of us may die or get caught. He did not love her but he wanted her back so we went after her. Max's boys were under Grandis' watch so they were unuseful. Me and Max got into the hotel and found Grandis in bed with Ramona. She had stuck a ice pick in his back. Max shot me, then they beat it. I woke up and crawled down the steps to the street.

When I was released from the hospital I went through court and was sentenced to the federal penn. But Carlos was on the train and helped me escape.

Carlos said that I had reservations on a ship to Palistine, there the jews would care for me. I helped the jews and fought Arab's. Then a big attack was made on the city and I found Ramona in the ruins. Our men nursed her and a certain jew gril that loved me tried to murder her but I caught her. Ramona became one of us and I fought for her love. I tried to be as courageous as Max was.

One day Ramona and I was trucking some amunition to some jews ambushed in the hills. A pack of beaten arabs attacked us and Ramona took to a machine gun. One arab was still alive after the others had fled. We found from him that the arabs were retreating. He died. But what we didn't know was that they fell off by the road as they retreated and our truck wrecked over a machine gun hole. Ramona hid under the seat cover and I gave up.

In the camp of the great arab bandit Sorius Cerello I found Max as the cook, a worn-out man with dreams of Ramona. They tortured me and Max slipped me food. Then one day when Sorius went out to make a raid, Ramona came. She said to leave the disfigured man behind. When I told her it was Max, she weeped at his feet. I went outside and lit a cigerette. Then I heard a shot and she came out holding a gun. She couldn't bear to see him like

"Lucius Hutchfield, *what* do you think you are doing?"

"Writin' a story."

"I've warned you not to waste class time with such trash."

"Trash? Mrs. Waller, this story will still be here when you and me's both gone."

"You and *I*. You see, you can't even *speak* the King's English, much less write it. They warned me about you before you came *in* my class. When are you going to learn to do as you're told?"

"Who am I hurting?"

"You shut your notebook and your mouth, young man, and get back to reading your *Reader's Digest*."

"Can I just finish this one sentence?"

"No, you *may* not finish anything except what everybody else's finishing." Staring down at "She couldn't bear to see him like" Lucius didn't move. "Lucius, I am *telling* you to shut that notebook."

"Talk about trash. That's what the *Reader's Digest* seems like to me."

"And who do you think *you* are?"

"I'm Lucius Hutchfield."

"And Lucius Hutchfield thinks he knows more than his English teacher what is good literatoor and what is not. Lucius Hutchfield— who is every bit of thirteen years old. You make me laugh."

Lucius was not so angry that he didn't notice Mrs. Waller was at least willing to argue with him. But he couldn't resist taking that much leeway and running with it. "No one person is better than another, Mrs. Waller."

"I am your superior, and you will do as *I* say in *my* classroom."

"Nobody is superior to anybody else, Mrs. Waller. We were *all* born naked."

"That will be more than enough, young man. Now, you can just march yourself right down the hall to the principal's office. You have a reputation for thinking B.K.J.H.S. teachers are 'old fogies' who don't know anything."

Everybody clapped.

Lucius shut his notebook, handed Mrs. Waller the *Reader's Digest,* and, all eyes watching, walked out of the room.

As he walked down the hall to the principal's office, he had a feeling of inevitability, certain that for the third time this year, he would be suspended, and so expelled. He dreaded what Momma would say after they called her at Councilman Randall's house.

As Mrs. Fraker looked up, intuitively knowing, it occurred to Lucius that his own behavior *in* school paralleled Bucky's habit of laying out of school, and he felt a little guilty that his form of disobedience did not land him in Cold Springs along with his brother.

That night, Momma opened the door when Lucius's feet hit the front porch.

"You and Bucky and Earl and Mammy and your precious daddy and the town of Cherokee will put me in the State Asylum. One of these days, you'll wake up and find me gone," said Momma, prophesying as she often had before.

Ledger: "We were all born naked." To Mrs. Waller. "This above all, to thine own self be true/ and it must follow as the day the night. Thou canst not then be false to any man." (Shakespeare) *It Happened in Brooklyn,* Frank Sinatra, Katherine Grayson.

April 18, 1947

Percy Pryor, Literary Agent
Dear Mr. Hutchfield:

I appreciate greatly your friendly comments. You will get a square deal here at all times.

Answering your specific queries:

Your stories basically have merit; of course, there is never any guarantee of sale. If they were my stories I would proceed with the professional report of analysis and criticism because that would enable you not only to place present work in marketable shape, but would save you time, energy, thought—for the future as well.

We hope that you will forward your remittance as soon as you receive this letter, and you may count upon first-class work from this office, at all times.

Yours cordially,
Percy Pryor,
Literary Agent

Ledger: The air force arrested Earl for selling supplies on the black market. Put him in stockade in Munick.

*   *   *

Keep dreaming about Thelma's mother, that she's buried under some old house in the River Street slums and they tear it down and find her and I was the one killed her.

"Pessimism is the fertile ground for revelation." Lucius Hutchfield.

*   *   *

It has rained all night. The windows in my sanctuary are open and I hear the spring rain. There are things in my heart that want to be said—but I like them where they are.

"Lucius," said Mr. Bronson, "you are expelled for the rest of the year. Next year, you will repeat the eighth grade." And may God have mercy on your soul.

*   *   *

Ledger: Momma tried to cry me back into school, but Mr. Bronson said I need to be taught a lesson. Okay.

*   *   *

Ledger: Made a list of stories to get into shape to sell, estimated a price for each, also added a list of scenarios. Total: $133,744. I sleep naked every night now.

*   *   *

I got up the nerve to go down and sit beside Luke's girl, Ruby, who comes to the Bijou every Monday at 5:00 and sits in the same seat, second from the aisle. She got up and left.

*   *   *

Got nostalgic for the old paper route and rode the streetcar out Grand Boulevard to Whedbee's drugstore. Seeing Pee Wee carrying papers on the old route was weird. Walked in the woods up on Clayboe Ridge. Saw *Black Narcissus* with Deborah Karr, way out at the Cosmopolitan. Takes place in India! Might run off and seek Greenbay, Maine.

Painfully but deliciously lonely in the house on the bluff above the Tennessee River, Lucius imagined himself into the future, wrote a sketch of himself waiting to meet Ernest Hemingway at a sidewalk cafe in Paris to say good-bye before setting out for India.

Hem and I delighted in sitting at a table on one of those Paris sidewalk cafes. We sat in the sun all day, talking and drinking beer. Many of the people who passed us knew and spoke to Hem. Some stopped and talked, had a mug of beer, then went busily on.

"When do you sail, Nick?"

He had asked me that ten times.

"At dawn."

Ledger: Walked up on Clayboe Ridge today—part where Raine used to live. Just started roaming up that way and couldn't stop. The houses are exciting and the people look different. See kids playing at Bonny Kate. Cheyenne, Dennis Morgan, Jane Wyman.

There are so many yellow horses and bloody menestrating whores in this hollow vaccuum where sin's whining voices echo, deafening the frightened ears. Once my feet are healed, I'm going to go to New Orleans and join the Merchant Marines.

They hanged six more Gestapo officers for the massacur in Lidice.

Keep looking for Reva Tamargo, hoping I'll see her coming toward me on some street.

San Francisco, California
April 22, 1947

Dear Lucius,

I loved you so much I couldn't stand it, so I just quit school, and finally I run off from home with a sailor, it hurt so bad. I'll always love you, no matter who you love. Someday I'll be a famous poetess, then will you love me?

Sincerely yours,
Della Snow.

Postcard: Cable car. Addressed to the Bijou. There'd been so many girls that year. He'd never forget Della, but he'd forgotten the names of a few already. Who was that girl who . . . ?

April 30, 1947

Dear Mrs. Mayorga:

Here is a one-act play entitled *Call Herman in to Supper*. I am well acquainted with your yearly collection of one-act plays, and via the latest I was informed, in your introduction, of the fact that you would endulge in personal readings of unsolicited scripts. I hesitated to send you this play, since it is rather removed from conventionality, though not unique of its kind. However, the inclusion of Tennessee Williams "Unsatisfied Supper" in your last collection encouraged me. Certainly it was "brave" of you to enclude such a modern, complex piece. Not to say that I approach at all Tennessee Williams. I, a mere boy of thirteen! But I have plenty of time to outdo him, not that that is any ambition of considerable sincerety of my repertoirie of ambitions.

Please read my play and if it merits let me hear from you in a critical attitude, the more cold-hearted the better.

Thank you for your time; I hove my play makes it enjoyable.

Yours sincerely,

Lucius Hutchfield

YOUR LITERARY I QUE
by Lucius Hutchfield

Many great novels have been turned into great movies. Given below are the great writers who wrote the novels and the famous stars of the movies made from the books and the names of the characters they played. Can you guess the names of the books?

1. John Stienbeck: Henry Fonda: Tom Joad
2. Henry Bellamanns: Robert Cummings: Parris Mitchell
3. Ben Ames Williams: Hedy Lamarr: Jenny
4. Will James: Fred McMurray: Clint Barkley
5. W. Somerset Maugham: Leslie Howard: Philip Carey
6. Raymond Chandler: Humphrey Bogart: Philip Marlowe
7. James Hilton: Robert Donat: Mr. Chips
8. Kathryn Forbes: Irene Dunn: Mama
9. Margret Mitchell: Olivia de Havilland: Melanie Wilkes
10. James M. Cain: John Garfield: Frank Chambers
11. Daphne du Maurier: Lawrence Oliver: Maxiam de Winters
13. Charlotte Bronte: Orson Wells: Edward Rochester
14. Graham Greene: Alan Ladd: Philip Raven
15. Frank Yerby: Rex Harrison: Stephen Fox
16. Ernest Hemingway: Gary Cooper: Robert Jordan
17. Walter Van Tilburg Clark: Henry Fonda: Gil
18. Nevien Bush: Jennifer Jones: Pearl Shaves
19. Charles Dickens: John Mills: Pip
20. Clarance Day: William Powell: Father

The Letter Shop typed it up for him, and Lucius sent it in to *The Saturday Review of Literature.*

Ledger: Went back to Aldrich Public Library. Somebody left this book *Ariel* by Andre Maurois on the table and I checked it out. Biography of Percy Byssche Shelley. First Chapter was most important in my life. Shelley walked alone, refused to be like everybody else, and had trouble in school. Guys bullied him and called him "Mad Shelley," and he was kicked out of college for writing *The Necessity of Atheism.* I skipped ahead and found out he drowned because he never learned how to swim off the coast of Italy, and his friends burned his body on the shore, and Byron jerked his heart out of the fire and it was still beating. Hot damn!

Having reviewed his life until he felt he was about to drop off, Lucius went to sleep talking with God, and dreamed he was walking down the hall at Bonny Kate, saw through the little window in a classroom door a tall woman in black, wearing a large black hat. Something about the way she stood in front of the unseen class was so sad, Lucius woke up crying. Asleep again, he dreamed that she turned and looked at him for an instant, and he saw only her eyes, misty and ineffably sweet and sad. He thought of Shirley Redding, but the woman wasn't her.

Greenbay, Maine
Spring, 1953

My Eternal Love, Raine,

As Time goes by I'm loving you more and more. Yet if Time stopped dead still my love for you would go on as gloriously as ever. If the end of the world should come, my last thought would not be of death and the dying but of you, my darling. And when you would be taken to heaven and I possibly to hell, I would fight my way to you. For even as I burned in the purpetual furnaces of hell, among theives, murderers, and sinners, a sweet, gentle and induring Love for you would give me nameless powers so that I could find you and hold you again.

If I can impress and influence *one* person as deeply as Thomas Wolfe has impressed and influenced me, I won't lie in a restless grave after a life of desperate, tragic struggle, having had no success. If that *one* person should be you I would dance in my dust with inhuman joy.

I often unravel stories in my mind about you and I in the future, married and happy, struggling and discouraged. They are wild yet beautiful yarns that often warm my heart, actually bringing me to tears. I see you as inhumanly understanding, patient, and lovely. You quite me in my rage with intelligent methods for which I and others admire you intensely. You tell me what is good and what is lousy in my writings, you discourage me at times but there is encouragement even in that, and I love you for it.

All my love always and forever,
Lucius

In the mornings now, before he began writing or reading, Lucius felt deprived of the sight of Raine and them. He read in *Duel in the Sun* and *The Wayward Bus* and *Sanctuary* for a while, then, out of a melancholy compulsion, wrote: "There is within me a mute voice. I seek in the far distances of earth a tongue with power to speak for my heart. There are many things I must write about someday, somewhere—but not now. When and where will it be? Death remain forever in the shadows. I live in the dust and yearn to breathe a clean air of wisdom and understanding. Upon which tiny mote in the sunlight am I to find the tongue

I seek? Perhaps there is no tongue. Oh, God, why is there no answer? Why is ignorance so mute and like a vacuum? Within what naked flame of inexistence can I find the true heart of unfound, long desired knowledge? Ah, dispair, utter, blind, bitter groping, when shall it all end in victory's bright noon? If I had a place in which to work where people are missing and the modern world is shut away in another room, where birds sing freely, and the trees are without the stain of soot, I could tear down the dam before my creative river. Peace, solitude, Lonliness, my—"

Hearing someone creep up the back steps, Lucius turned. Nobody at the window in the door. Then Duke's face jumped up. Grinning, snapped his fingers, pointed his thumb at his prick.

"You have to go around. The bed blocks it," said Lucius. He got up and opened the side door. "Laying out of school, huh?"

"*No*body tells Duke Rogers what to do. You got that?"

Lucius didn't feel like listening to that kind of talk, but he was glad to see Duke. Duke draped himself on the cot.

"How'd you like to drive your own car?" The sun was so bright through the window on Duke's face he let his eyelids droop. "Head for New York City."

"I can't drive."

"I'll teach you. We can go in together on this car I seen in the Buick company's secondhand lot. Thirty-nine Buick limousine in mint condition, by God."

"Where we gonna get the money?"

"Stickup."

"Yeah."

"Yeah. I been follerin' Hood past two days. I know just how to work it."

"What you gonna use for a gun?"

Duke glanced around the sanctuary. "Put your hand there." Duke took Lucius's hand and he thought he was going to feel a hard-on. It was the handle of a revolver.

"Where'd you get *that* thing?"

"See?" Duke unbuttoned his shirt, revealing the handle.

"I thought your daddy took it away from you."

"I found where he hid it. You gonna help me get Hood?"

"I don't know about that," said Lucius, laughing.

"Chickenshit."

"Don't *call* me that. Let me think it over."

"Well, don't take your time because I want that car."

"Let's go look at it. I want to see what I'm risking my ass for. I'm already in the shadow of the reform school."

At the top of the steep Bluff Street hill that dropped to the bridge, Duke said, "Let's practice running—barrel ass."

"Watch it that pistol don't jiggle down your britches leg."

The Buick used car lot was on the Grand Boulevard streetcar line a few blocks past the decaying old two-storey house Raine's family had bought after the fire.

"How's that for a getaway car?" asked Duke, putting his foot up on the running board of a long, black, sleek '39 Buick limousine.

"Get away from what? You plannin' a crime wave?"

"I bet you think John Dillinger's great."

"You reckon Hood'll have eight hundred on him? What if he don't?"

"This pistol ain't gonna wear out in one robbery."

"They might sell her before—"

"They better not, by God, I'll track the fucker down and steal it."

Duke got in the car and sat behind the wheel. Lucius shut the door and tapped on the window and Duke rolled it down, snootily, and Lucius leaned in, "Listen, there's one thing we got to get straight, Duke."

"Look at that! Only twelve thousand miles."

"Listen! You're carrying the gun. Right?"

"Less you think you can shoot better'n *me*."

"No, the gun's yours, so you got to carry it, but you got to promise you won't fire it off."

"Not unless I *have* to."

"You want to go to the Tennessee 'lectric chair?"

"Nobody's goin to the 'lectric chair. Too bad we don't have this car for our first getaway."

"How many times I have to tell you to keep your ass *out* of that car," said a bullnecked salesman, yelling from the doorway of a little blue shed in the middle of the lot.

"Okay, mister," said Duke, getting out fast. "Just looking it over. This guy might buy it."

"If he's eighteen," said the salesman, "I'm Margaret O'Brien."

"He says that every time," said Duke, sneering.

In the drugstore on the corner, Duke bought some Camels. Coming out, he said, "Hey, we better walk over the territory. Rehearse the damn thing."

Lucius and Duke caught a streetcar back to town and got off at the Cherokee National Bank across from the Venice where Dick Powell in *Johnny O'Clock* was showing. Lucius remembered that he had not walked through those shiny brass gates to put a red cent in the white marble building since he opened his savings account in January.

As they walked past the brass night deposit slot, where an old blind couple sat against the white marble wall, they kept their eyes straight ahead but talked out the scene as it would go Saturday night when Lucius would lay off sick. In the alley, they started running, pretending to grab a previously stowed A & P paper sack to put the money bag in.

At the Smoky, they bought tickets to see how long it would take to make it to the roachy latrine, where they pretended to hide the money bag behind a rusty radiator. When the Smoky opened Sunday afternoon, they'd retrieve the money.

"If the rats don't eat it," said Lucius.

"Okay, let's go over this again," said Duke.

"Hey, *I* got it," said Lucius. "You be Hood and I'll come up to you at the deposit slot."

"Hot shit! But I get to rob."

"Me first. *Then* you."

"Okay, I'll walk from the Bijou and reach the slot at exactly twelve thirty. Synchronize your watches, men."

"Hey, what bout your daddy directing the damn traffic?"

"Naw, he goes to lunch by the noon whistle."

Lucius waited at the Orange Julius stand across from the Tivoli for Duke to pass. *Ramrod* with Veronica Lake and Joel McCrea on the marquee looked good. Ten minutes later, Duke came by. Lucius followed him to the night deposit slot where the blind couple was sharing snuff. When Duke stopped to pick up some change he deliberately dropped, Lucius stooped to help him.

"I'll count to ten," whispered Lucius, "then run to the Smoky, but I won't go in, 'cause second time 'round she'll wonder."

Lucius counted to ten, then walked to the alley, then ran past a man and a boy who were crushing and stacking cardboard boxes onto a cart.

His heart beating fast, Lucius waited for Duke under the Smoky marquee, seeing Dillinger get mowed down at the mouth of the alley by G-man machine guns. Duke walked past as if he didn't know him. Lucius followed him as he circled back past the YMCA.

"Okay, now *you* be Hood and I'll be *us*."

"I'm tuckered out, Duke. These metatarsal bars and 'iss brace are hard on walking, much less running."

"Hey, I like the way them bars look. Reckon I could get some to go on my boots?"

"*My* boots. You need a prescription. In other words, you gotta have the clawfoot deformity to go with them."

"You can have 'em. Where's *your* clawfoot deformity?"

"It don't show yet. That's what the metatarsal bars do—help keep it down."

"You got *me*. Well, take off—your turn, by God."

Lucius took the back streets to the Bijou. Then imitating Hood's brisk Harry Truman-like jauntiness, imagining Elmo loping along behind him, Lucius set off up Sevier Street. Passing the Orange Julius, he saw

Duke out of the corner of his eye take his last gulp of foamy orange. The Tivoli ticket girl must be noticing something funny by now.

At the night deposit slot, Lucius dropped his change and noticed as he bent over that the blind couple became alert again and turned their heads his way. Then Duke was helping him pick up the silver, counting aloud. Then a man in a business suit was helping pick up the change, and a little boy put his foot on a nickel and scraped it in a stiff-legged way, as if he had to go to the bathroom, then bent over quickly, snatched it up, and ran. Just then, Duke turned into the alley.

"Hey, I think that boy ran off with some of your money," the man said, pointing not toward the little boy, who only Lucius had seen, but toward the alley. "I *thought* he looked suspicious."

The alley magnified the explosion of a bullet. Lucius ran to the alley, saw Duke running scared toward the other end. The man and the boy by the salvage cart jumped out of Duke's way.

"We better call the police," said the well-dressed man, who helped Lucius pick up his change.

"Well, that's all right, sir, it was only a nickel."

"Yes, but a nickel's a nickel these days, and that boy had a gun. He must've tried to shoot that junkman. You never know what some crazy kid like that will do next. I'm calling the police as a citizen." The man started off, looking up and down the street.

"I'll chase after him," said Lucius, and ran down the alley, imagining Duke's daddy chasing them. The cardboard man and the boy jumped behind some trash cans.

Duke wasn't under the Smoky marquee.

Lucius ambled all over uptown, looking for Duke, and, failing to find him, went on home, sweating and trembling, and tried to get started on "Two People," a saga of Lucius and Raine in the future.

When somebody knocked on the door, Lucius was afraid it was the cops. Who walked in was Duke, his pecker out of his fly in an enormous hard-on.

"Where *was* you?" asked Lucius, as Duke pranced around the living room. "I was looking all over town for you."

"In the goddam Smoky."

"Listen, I said not to go *in* there."

"That trash man raised up from behind them barrels and scared the living shit out of me and the gun come loose and went off when it hit the alley and whizzed right by my fucking ear."

"I told you you'd drop it, if you didn't watch out. That man went looking for the blamed cops."

"What man?"

"One that was helping us pick up the change. And when you lit out, he thought you was rogueing my money, so he went for the cops."

"Hot *damn!* You shoulda *been* there when that pistol went off. Sounded like a cannon in that alley. I run right into the Smoky without paying, and then I finally paid the man and just sat there, right through *Dakota* and *Fallen Angel* and *Life Boat* and that red-assed stage show. Kept looking around for you to come *in,* goddamn it."

"Well, I just thought you kept on running—off the face of the earth, for all I knew."

"Well, there goes my Buick limousine."

"*Our* Buick."

"Well, I saw it first."

"Let's *sell* that damn pistol or throw it in the river, one."

"What pistol? I dropped it in the damn alley."

"You mean, you left that pistol behind in the alley?"

"Hell, I wasn't 'bout to pick that thing up after it went off at me like that."

Duke found Lucius's Momma's plastic apron, something new on the market, that Duke's own Momma had bought, too, and swabbed it with soap. It was icy cold at first, but the friction warmed it up.

Eager to see Duke, and glad of an excuse to walk close to Raine, who was staying all night with Peggy, Lucius was waiting at the top of the hill when they got out of school.

Raine told them about the cops waking her big brother up in the middle of the night. They'd found his pistol and wanted to know what it was doing in the alley behind the Cherokee National Bank.

"Had to go down to the police station this morning and see about it."

Lucius and Duke looked at each other, scared. They kept dropping back behind the others to piece together a conversation that sought some solution to the problems they would have if fingerprints were found on the gun.

"They'd be mine, yours, and your old man's."

"Want to help me swipe that Buick?"

"Want to kiss my rusty?"

Wondering whether there would be anything in the *Messenger* about the mysterious alley incident, Lucius bought a paper from the legless man in front of the Courthouse. Finding no mention of it, almost disappointed, Lucius headed for the Bijou.

Saturday, Lucius ran into Duke in the Market House at the Blue Goose lunch stand, where he was eating a barbecue sandwich.

"They give Raine's brother back his gun," said Duke. "Figured somebody must have found it in the ashes of her house when it burned down, and far as they can tell didn't nobody use it to kill nobody, so they let him have it back. Carries it under his seat in the Ford he uses to run whiskey out of Kentucky."

Sunday morning, Lucius and Momma rode the streetcar from the Indian Mound out to Mammy's neighborhood. Mammy wanted them to see the new wallpaper and two new windows in the extension to the living room the Chief had built.

"Lordy, Granny Foster wouldn't recognize her little old shack, would she, Irene?"

"Not that *I* do either." Momma tried to look delighted, but she seemed uneasy. "It was only one room when she built it, Lucius. Then Mammy and Daddy added three rooms to it."

" 'Fore the Chief gets done with it, it's gonna be one of the cutest, neatest, snuggliest little houses on the block."

"Gonna cover them old grey boards that ain't never been painted with white slate shingles," said the Chief, "and put on a new roofing and build a patio in the back with big slabs of broken marble from the quarries, and lay a new floor in the bathroom, and move that circus wagon off to the side, make it my tool shed, and build a nice garage, and turn that ragged garden into a grassy backyard with flower beds that won't quit."

"And Chief's gonna bring furniture from his old home in South Cherokee, so Irene, you can start putting your brand on some of *this* stuff."

"Most of it came out of our house in St. Louis, Lucius," said Momma, stroking the arm of the davenport, "when Daddy was doing well."

"I've got pictures of the way it used to be," said Mammy. "But most of 'em got scorched when your daddy set the coal house afire."

The transformation of the house made Lucius and Momma feel a little insecure, but Mammy felt more secure than ever. Even the changing of the house number last week by order of the city to 2234 was slightly threatening, but Mammy still referred to it as "good ol' 702 Holston."

"It's the only permanent home any of us ever had," said Momma. "Me and Charlie left it to go live in Harlan, Kentucky, awhile, and St. Louis, but other than that . . ."

Mammy's was the only house Lucius had known throughout his life. All the rooms of all the other houses were superimposed upon these familiar rooms, enriching his responses to Mammy's house, as if, in its oneness, it were many. Momma's apartment was a nomad tent in the desert. Mammy's little house was the old lady's shoe, the pioneer homestead, a cluster of such clichés, real as rock.

While Momma was turning the chuck roast and the Chief was taking

Luke's Dodge out to tone up the rubber and the engine, Mammy promised Lucius again in a low voice that she'd take him to Cade's Cove in the Smokies this summer after she and the Chief returned from their honeymoon in Florida—and that wouldn't be long.

"Well, they ain't much to it anymore, with all those tourists overrunning Gatlinburg," said Momma, appearing in the doorway, holding a dripping spoon.

"Well, I promised Lucius since he was a little feller to show him Cade's Cove." During the war, Mammy used to sit on the long grey bench under the oak tree, resting in the evening after working her victory garden, and she'd tell him about the Smoky Mountains and how she longed to go back someday in a fine automobile and see her ancient, blind momma and her feisty sister. "We gonna climb high up on Rich Mountain and look out over mountain ranges and mountain ranges and moutain ranges, blue, and grey, and misty—smoky, smoky—and some places where the sun hits, and others in cold dark shadder, and nothing but mountain wilderness all around for miles and miles and miles, and then down we go into Cade's Cove—little farms scattered all over and two white churches with their little graveyards and a mill."

Haunted by what she and her brothers and sisters had left behind, Mammy talked of it as something vague in her people's past, but to Lucius the trees and wooden fences and log cabins and beehives and even the horses and cows were things of that past vividly alive today, and he responded to the images as if they'd come down directly to him, as palpable as the grass and the mimosa trees and the sticky green stalks of flowers coming up in Mammy's backyard now.

"And coming back, we'll eat us a big meal in this hotel in Sevierville where the Ku Klux once hanged a man and where the Chief put out a fire years back and ate in the grand dining room in his big muddy boots."

Since her services were no longer needed at the councilman's house— the mother healthy enough now to care for herself and the baby—Momma had begun looking for another job. She was invited to return to ladies' ready-to-wear at Ringgold's, where she'd worked several years before, and she was about to accept, but one of her traveling salesman boyfriends told her about a job as cigar counter lady in one of the best hotels in Nashville and she was tempted. "I can be near Bucky that way and Earl when they transfer him back from Germany to the reform school and if Lucius keeps acting up the way he has here lately, he won't have so far to travel to see his brothers."

During dinner, Mammy told a string of anecdotes about Luke, and Lucius went down to the circus-wagon coal house and communed with his uncle's things. He hoped the Chief wouldn't paint the old sled—

or throw it out. Starting back up to the house, he heard Momma and Mammy arguing.

"I feel like Luke's ghost, Mammy," said Lucius's mother, crying, "that's just how I feel."

Without going back in, Lucius went on to the Bijou.

Ledger: The Jewish terrowists blasted holes in the walls of a big prison in Palistine and freed a hundred Jewish and a hundred Arab prisoners. Wish I had been with them when they did it.

Bucky ran off from the reform school. They called Mammy's.

*   *   *

Gale can't make payments on his jeep so he enlisted in the Navy today. Lied about his age. Hope they kick him out so he'll come back to the Bijou. It won't be the same. Walking in the country down the river—in a field—graves. Cold and alone neath slim, stark tree, a small, stained stone slab.

*   *   *

The army's sending Earl back to the U.S. May send him back to Nashville. Still a juvenile.

I have this burning desire to invent a language that only I can understand, and I can respond to the words of the world with strange syllables and musical sounds that would confound and astonish and put people in awe of me as a strange unique being.

"Love is a pair of wet bloomers hanging on the line to dry." Lucius Hutchfield.

The Sea Wolf, classic, John Garfield, Edward G. Reading *For Whom the Bells Toll* by Ernest Hemingway.

On the verge of sleep, Lucius imagined a young woman with short blond hair, wearing a brown dress, coming through the dark front rooms to his sanctuary. Her stride is strong and aggressive and alien to Tennessee and she wears no makeup. She leans over the cot, pressing her thighs firmly against the mattress, imprinting her soft brown silky dress with her pudenda and her belly button. The dress is tight across her breasts, the neckline tied with a darker brown ribbon, and sleeveless, and her arms are plump, coming out of the torso of her dress. She has an odd but pleasant odor that somehow makes Lucius think of the parade grounds in *Hitler's Children* with Tim Holt and Bonita Granville. "I have come from your brother, Earl." Her voice is like a hard stream in the black forest behind her icy smile. She seems very aristocratic. Lucius sees naked, fleshed bones stacked like wood, and a dark room full of teeth and human hair, and he is aware of the shadows in his sanctuary, and feels that Momma's bed in the dark room beyond the kitchen is empty. "They came in my house in Berlin and arrested Earl," she says, the slow way she spaces each syllable making him see the peaks of Austrian Alps and gulp the cold air. "They arrested him at my grandmother's house, too, one time." "My father knew nothing of the crematoriums. Ze war is over. Correct?" "Correct." "*Auf Wiedersehen*," she says, putting out her hand, but in it she holds an ether mask.

Lucius woke, unable to remember where his waking dream had merged with sleep.

Percy Pryor

Lucian Hutchfield   MSS
Subject: Report on criticism and analysis

I have just finished rereading your manuscripts, and I remain impressed with your work.

I suggest you cut the entire ms. of "Helena Street" quite a bit; it contains much dead wood which does nothing but slow the action and dull the reader's interest. If you cut everything after the shooting, the ending would make a very nice surprise twist.

In "Union Station" you have a good idea and theme, but the point that weakens the whole story is that it lacks conflict and plot. The soldier and the girl simply meet and talk. You should try to make Mary and John more interesting people in themselves; it is not enough that they are in an interesting situation. Also, define the situation earlier and more clearly, and make their part in the story clear and brief. Remember, Mr. Hutchfield, that you must be constantly on the watch for material which lacks the power to keep the reader's interest.

The beginning is very rough. In that first paragraph you have too many sentences of the same length. If you have trouble with it, try reading it aloud, and listen to the rhythm.

You know, Mr. Hutchfield, I am sincerely impressed by your work. I believe that you need help, however, before we can put your scripts into salable shape. I think I can offer you a plan which will aid you in your writing career and also save you the expense of individual reading fees or costly revision charges.

I'll make a protégé of you and handle all your work personally for the next year. There is no contract to sign and you are in no way obligated to us. We can make this offer because we know that our services will be profitable to you and that you will be satisfied with the high caliber of our work.

Percy Pryor

THE WINE OF TRAGEDY

Outline of a movie script by Lucian Hutchfield
This movie shows how ignorance tends to destroy the struggling in-

tellect. It can convey a profound meaning to those who are sensitively minded. It's meaning to each individual may, or surely will, vary. However this picture may be intercepted, we can be sure that its significance will not lie merely in the virtue of entertainment, but seriously done, as it shall be, make a vital impression upon all those who see it.

The story:

One afternoon Johnny tries to get into a football game in a field near his home. The boys sarcastically consent and proceed to gang up on him in the course of the game. (Thus, first symtom of his change, namely his need of companionship.) His mother scolds him for getting dirty and scarred, yet nags him for his inactivity in the past time matters of other boys. He meekly goes off to his room and we have admission to a few of his thoughts. He is in desperate need of friends and understanding.

He gets a job as an usher in a downtown theater. There he meets two boys who at first make fun of him but later go out of their way to gain his friendship. He is greatly flattered and his joy is undescribeable, especially when he is asked to join in their card game backstage.

The card game, inflated with beer, produces to us the real intentions of the two boys, Jack and Hank. They wish to rid themselves of poverty and the dull existance of going to high school. Therefore, they submit a plan to Johnny whereby an expert job could be done of robbing the theater manager of the day's intake. Their three musketeer attitude overwhelms the lonely Johnny, who, for the sake of friendship consents to take part.

We are shown the proceedure by which the three complete their aim, and drive away with the loot. Later, when they are counting the money, Johnny becomes disgusted with himself and airs his discomfort to the boys, who, mission completed, treat him with far more indifference and disrespect than he has ever encountered. He realizes that all his convictions have become polloted by cheapening himself to accept the friendship of anyone who comes along. Unendurably angry, he snatches up the gun and shoots them both, aiming wildly. A neighbor rushes in. Johnny sits in a chair and his countenance reflects the confusion within him.

He goes to jail. The two boys were merely wounded. In jail he asks for a book by Thomas Wolfe and is given comic books instead. Johnny flings them through the bars into the gaurds face.

The trial is brief. He goes to the reform school. In there he becomes popular. He is a leader now and greatly respected, for to these imprisoned boys he offers release from depression and loneliness. He tells them stories, talks endlessly of the many aspects of life, instigates the presentation of a play, encourages the boys to read. The superintentant becomes angry with him for having so much influence over the boys. Their mind is not on their work and they continue to talk and read long after "lights out" is ordered. Johnny stops associating with the boys; forced to treat them unkindly. They gradually become depressed again and eventually a series of runaways begins.

Johnny and the superintentant's daughter, Gaile, become good friends. She is sent away to school and consequently Johnny escapes to go to her. But Gaile convinces him that he is needed at the reform school, that the boys need him. He realizes his mission and returns. The boys cheer him as he comes from the whipping chamber with RUNAWAY painted on the back of his shirt.

Ledger: Last night I dreamed my grandmother was dying. For my mammy to die is the most impossible thing. My mother met me at the busline on Grand Boulevard. She had a serum. It was for Mammy. It kills you. She would have to drink it too. But only a little, not enough to kill. I met Mammy walking to the bus. She wore a damp guaze blindfold and she knew what was coming. She was the same as dead. Obviously before you die they blind you with a needle applied near the eye. Then you have to take the serum. It isn't difficult. I embraced her and spoke brave words of love. She was very brave as she disappeared down the street, unshaken, resolved to her destiny. I've never seen her face like that. When I woke the feeling of depression was there as though waking dispelled nothing. It took time to wear off. I'm too young to bare the ordeal of the death of my grandmother. How could such a thing be possible?

*   *   *

Wrote some sketches about the Bijou as it really is. Momma's boyfriend Dan and I were drinking beer at the kitchen table. Momma heard someone on the stairs.

"I'll bet it's Gay." Moving to the door.
"Let's go see."
Tiptoeing. Peeking.
Daddy!
Drunk.
Needing haircut. Shabby.
Mother charming.
Handshaking.
"Hello, Fred."
Return to kitchen.
"Is my face red?" To Dan.

Their backs to us, as Daddy sat on bed, legs over footrail. Me in one-armed chair in sanctuary. Daddy worried about Russians. Earl.

"I'm going to ask your mother to marry me again."

"Let's go down to the street and talk."

Sunny. Bench. Wind. Talk. Streetcar.

Mother on bed crying.

Supper with Dan.

Johnny O'Clock, Dick Powell, Evelyn Keyes.

*   *   *

Got up at four thirty Sunday morning to go to the Bijou to open the doors so the college theatre group that was putting on Juno and the Paycock next Tuesday evening could have its dress rehearsal.

THE DEAD LEAVES OF AUTUMN

For Her

1st writing Sunday
May 11, 1947

by Lucian Hutchfield

Autumn leaves were falling, brown and crisp. The sky was pale blue and clear that day, the air barely chilly. Nick wore a mackinaw coming home from school, schuffling along, seeing beauty in the season of death. His long wool socks sagged down around his dirty ankles. Let them sag. Into his lungs he drew the air filled with autumn smells—leaves burning, turning to ashes, having been green and glorious all summer. His underwear kept hiking up the crack of his buttocks. Bowing his legs as he walked, he tried to wiggle it out. Through the naked branches and swigs of an Indian cigar tree he could see the sun and the ragged blotch of orange red on the sky around it. Nick shoved his hands into his pockets and, strolling along in the middle of the narrow street, he stared at the sunset and through a hole in his pocket pushed his forefinger over the tiny hairs growing around his loins. They stick. Why do you need to have them?

Nick could see the high ragged hedge, barely see the roof of his house. Hope Momma's home. He walked through the hedge and went up to the screen door. His mother was sitting on a chair. Aw, she's cryin' again. Wish she wouldn't cry so much. He opened the screen door and walked in. The room was dim, and Momma was wearing a faded, flower print dress, crying, her face covered by her hands.

"Momma, what's uh-matter?"

She looked up, her eyes red. Her eyes had tenderness with the sadness. At that moment, Nick, standing before his mother, could see Mammy sitting at the kitchen table with her wrinkled hand on a piece of brown paper. She was crying. Nick had never seen Mammy cry before. She stared down at the piece of paper. The light of sunset came through the front door to shine upon the kitchen floor, recently mopped.

"Luke's dead," said Momma.

Nick didn't hear at first. The words went to his brain. Slowly the terribleness swept to his heart. Oh, God, oh, God. Luke! Dead! In Nick's mind: a German soilder with green, gritting teeth charging through mud, leveling his rifle, firing, and Luke falling into the mud dead. Dead. . . . Life gone from my unckle. Curly, brown hair. Luke in his undershirt shining his infantry boots, letting Nick help. Nick beside the drugstore kicking around inside a huge cardboard box, Luke suddenly standing there in his uniform, giving Nick a nickel. Pepper in his buttermilk over on Avondale Street. Luke under ground cold, rotting, dead, dead, dead. . . . Oh, God! Nick cried.

*   *   *

Ledger: Thought of a way to get back in school. Going to write a book report on the Thomas Wolfe Portable, so good they can't turn me down.

The Chief didn't come for Sunday dinner because he had to go to a funeral. Mammy told me the Chief used to be married to this woman who had cancer and that's why they didn't get married years ago.

High Barbaree with Van Johnson and June Allyson. Started story about Luke being missing and another one about when he was little that Mammy told me. Reading *A Farewell to Arms.* Frederick Henry drove an ambulance like Daddy.

They found Bucky in Florida walking around this old fort in St. Augustine. Traveler's Aid sent him back, and me and Momma and the Chief met the bus. The cops were sitting in a patrol car and they took him to the juvenile.

House, old, on Grand Boulevard. Night: Small boy naked, sitting in dirty window sill. Woman standing there, the cries of little children. Bought *A Passage to India* by E. M. Forrester.

Elderly iceman, always happy, comes in trying to whistle every day, only rythmic air sounds come out. Last of Mohicans, classic, Randolph Scott.

Talked with Mrs. Fraker on the phone, she said Mrs. Waller read my review of Wolfe and they all had a good laugh and tossed it into the trash can. She didn't even bother Mr. Bronson with "such trash."

Writing a lot of scenarios about me and Raine and Gaile in the future.

*   *   *

The UN urged Palistine to reframe from violence till autumn, 1947. Then why don't the British let them alone? Bought *Georgia Boy* by Caldwell. Heard a rumor they were going to scrap all the streetcars and put buses in their place. I don't believe it. Maybe I could buy one and park it by the tower on the river and live in it.

*   *   *

Blaze of Noon with William Holden about early air mail pilots.

Planning to write a biography of Thomas Wolfe's life. Made outline on new kind of notebook paper, the size of a book. I'll show them all.

Saw James Cagney at Smokey in Lady Killer, old, old movie where he's fired as a movie usher and becomes the brains of a gang in Chicago.

THE IDIOT WHO FOLLOWS YOU
by Lucian Hutchfield

I often wonder, in the final analysis, was Bucky a mischivous boy or was it that his curiosity, his desire to experience, and his wonderlust spirit had merely found expression in taboo enterprises.

The youngest of three boys, Bucky was frail and small and often ill. Since his mother worked all day (his parents were divorced), he was entrusted in the care of his next oldest brother, a dreamer. The dreamer was often rigid with Bucky, whose curiosity and unruly mannerisms encouraged little patience. His excapades, in the early stage of his "mischivous" nature, inspired an "isn't he cute" attitude in most people. To this day, people are usually awed when confronted with the details of Bucky's eventful life, even the dreamer and his mother, who suffered by the wild abandon of Bucky's "mischivous" career; but perhaps not the older brother, Earl, who answered the call of the wild goose when he was ten, and who set an example for Bucky.

At first he roamed the city alone, and later in company with the neighborhood idiot, a dark giant of a boy. The two became inseparable, and as a team they reaped a harvest of dubious deeds. They stole from ten-cent stores and played hookey. Bucky failed the first grade twice because of eyesight; and he later lost sight in one eye, and became deaf in one ear. No force on earth could keep him in school. His teachers must have prayed very hard, for he was finally committed to a detention home.

The idiot couldn't follow, since they don't put idiots in a home with normal boys. Once out of the home on good behavior, Bucky returned to his old habits and in time acquired new ones. The dreamer often found Bucky in odd situations: sitting on the head of a statue on the courthouse lawn; begging for show money on Sevier Street; eating dinner with some businessman in the best restaurant for he had a magnetic personality.

Bucky began to broaden his interests beyond the city limits, indulging in jaunts to Chattanooga and Atlanta. His absense was welcomed in the classroom, but frowned upon by the truant officer, who soon became a friend of the family. All the while the giant idiot's shadow lay upon the whole skeme of things.

Bucky was sent from orphanage to orphanage, endured and rejected or withdrawn, while the idiot ran loose.

Bucky had a knack for finding money and other objects. People marveled at his luck, but soon stopped to wonder. Consequently he was found out.

His adventures, meat for a meaty book, were innumerable. They finally landed him in the headquarters of his contemporaries in Nashville. He took spur of the moment vacations from the institution as often as he thought necessary to his morale. He broke the record for distance, once reaching Miami before he was caught and retrieved.

Oddly enough he's always liked policemen and was ever in awe of any type of uniform. He had a tender heart too, for he was never cruel, though unintentionally inconsiderate. He never rebelled, he never resented, he never bore malice. The world existed for him, and he used it to satisfie every random or intense motivation.

Perhaps there is something too complex in a boy like Bucky for anyone to really understand, something profoundly beautiful that is in all of us to a lamentable degree. He was merely following his adolescent whimsies, forever trying to satisfy his curiosity, and giving vent to his pent-up restlessness.

Someday when the weather is right, I'd like to take a Sunday afternoon stroll through Bucky Hutchfield's mind.

$$*   *   *$$

Ledger: Ate supper at Mammy's cafe. Sad to see For Sell sign in the window. Bought *Alabam* by Donald Henderson Clarke.

The sun was bright shining into my sanctuary this morning when I awakened at eight o'clock. God was shining upon Cherokee today.

I finished "Souls Under Conflict" the revisions and it is ready to be typed for Percy Pryor. Please God—this time.

I mopped floors this morning. I love my little room.

A 1:00 I went to see "Stallion Road" with Zachary Scott and Alexis Smith. It was good. I was dressed up nice and felt good, like a writer who cannot discribe the things he feels and doesn't especially want to.

The sun was very nice on Sevier Street bridge. I looked down on the river and the people and houses on River Street and a boat on the tobacco-yellow-brown river, for a long time. People down on the thumb-like piece of ground out on the river were pitching horse shoes where the faith healer's tent once was and enjoying Sunday in the sun.

I took a picture of the spit and the boathouses with the camera Raine
gave me for Christmas. I stood on the bridge and got drunk on a Robert
Burns cigarillo.

I thought of girls and between their legs. I thought of the hole
and all men did to use it. But watching rubbers floating down the
river below under the bridge, I kept saying, "It's only a hole, it's just
a hole, that's all it is." Then why was I so blue-balled about it?
I was disgusted yet fascinated. On the bridge I dreaded to go back
into the city and when I did the people frightened me yet I enjoyed
watching them. Why are we here, God? Why? Yet thanks because I am
here among them and maybe thou wildst let me have Raine again.
Or Gaile. I went On the Spot at 4 o'clock. *Undercover Maisie* with
Ann Southern.

Momma told me that Mammy and the Chief had a fuss and broke
up for good.

Where the Fontana Hotel had once stood, a raw pine-planked screen
had hidden construction for a month. When Lucius started to go into the
Bijou Monday afternoon, the screen was gone, and he saw a new building
with CHEROKEE NEWSSTAND in large gold and green letters across the top. As
he entered, he saw a smaller sign over the door: GATEWAY TO GOOD
READING.

The smell of thousands of brand-new magazines, newspapers from
all over the country, and paperback books and the sight of all the shiny
faces and scenes on the covers hit him so hard he became nauseated with
the excitement of anticipation. Tyrone Power and Gene Tierney on the
cover of one of them. The title *The Razor's Edge* struck him again, but
he was jealous, perversely, he realized, that he didn't know the book itself,
so he wouldn't buy it. And there was W. Somerset Maugham's intriguing
symbol again.

After an hour of handling the paperback Penguins and Bantams
and the latest issues of the *Post, Cosmopolitan, Liberty, Collier's, Redbook, Argosy,* and several movie magazines, he hurt to *go.*

Ledger: Wrote a long, long 25 pages letter to Raine, the first one
I ever mailed to her. Quoted some of what Romeo said to Juliet.

Bought *Innocent Voyage* by Richard Hughes.

Dear Lucius,
Your letter inspired me. It's the most wonderful thing you ever
wrote. Duke better not read this or I'll kill him with my bear hands.

I want us to be sweethearts again. Will you? It just isn't the
same without you loving me the way you did. I get so dad-blamed
lonesome in this big old house so far from you and everybody. I
could scream bloody murder. Peggy and them don't hardly ever come

over. I sit in the library and keep hoping I'll look up & see you standing there but I can't. I've set & looked 50 thousand times. I'm going to write me a 25 pages letter to go with yours.

I got done stringing the beans so I can write you. I'm setting here all by my little self in the kitchen with the sweet sound of potatoes frying. I've got to read this con sarned book, *Debbie Debutante,* but I lots rather write you. *Your the only one for me!* I'm not kidding either. I'm telling the truth if it was ever spoken before in my life.

My legs are so sore. I stayed all night with Peggy and that running down the hill I did to school this morning caught up with me. Even if I did beat Cora, it hurts. We got dogged in basketball pretty bad today. In choir we sang "Let Us Walk in the Light of the Lord" and "Waltzing Matilda," and were they pretty! But she had to ruin it all by calling in that old bag of a La Rue to sing "Danny Boy." Nobody asked me if I ever won first place at the Bugs Bunny club singing that one, oh, no.

Here's "Inner Sanctum." It's so scarry I wish you were here. I'm laying here on the bed. It always seems scarier here. Shoot, I wish I had some chewing gum. I'm just chewing an old tooth pick.

I shifted over to Mark Fogarty on Insomniacs show and reckon what? "Heartaches"—dedicated to me and you. Recon who called it in? You know it's a sin to like a song as much as I do that one.

Peggy's momma gave us their sofa cause all our stuff got burned up. You know I get a funny feeling just setting on the sofa because I think of the good times we had just kissing & hugging on it over at Peggy's.

Honey, go to church with me on Sunday. I've gone Monday and Tuesday and I'm going to try to go every night of the revival. That preacher is so good & just love to hear him. Please go with me. Will you? Well, honey, I've really got to go take a bath and wash some things out and roll my hair.

Your stinkin' little wife,

Raine

Ledger: "They stood there, silently, with the two days of random conversation behind them and Brazil and Athens behind them, and five hundred flights behind them, and Jerusalem and Miami behind them, and the girls from Vienna and the American Embassy and Flushing, Long Island, behind them, and the Greek mountaineers behind them and Thomas Wolfe's funeral—And, ahead of Stais, home and a mother who had presumed him dead and wept over his personal belongings, and ahead of Whitejack the cold bitter mountains of

India and China and the tearing dead sound of the fifties and the sky full of Japs. . . ." (Irwin Shaw, "Gunner's Passage.")

Me and Raine sat on the front porch a long time, overlooking the lights of Cherokee, and at midnight, she waved to me from the high porch as I boarded the last streetcar to the barn.

The Sanctuary
2 a.m.

Dear Eternal Raine,

When we are plowing the earth of Maine or France under the sun, the rich brown furrows shall smile at our love for each other. The strange devotion that I have for the earth, for the life that I am seeking but have not yet found, comes from the will of God and the core of all my loneliness is death and I go on looking for elements of the future, because, I have you and your love. That and faith in God is all I have for success. I love you always, until the return of Christ, and even after. For whether we be in heaven or hell, you shall hear my voice calling among the flames of hell or from the quiet pastures of heaven.

Someday, after we're married and farming on a big rich stretch of fertile land in Maine, and I am a great author & we are old, we will laugh about LaRue and Duke as we watch our grandchildren play about the farm. Through all the years that we will live together until death, you will help me to go on writing, believing in people, God, and the good things that I have to write about.

Love beyond Eternity,
Lucius

Ledger: I was on the streetcar and I saw Raine talking to some boy. I got off the streetcar and beat him up and she just acted innercent, sitting in her brother's highway patrol car. I walked off. I nearly died of mortal pain for two hours until Raine called. We talked, she cryed when I said we would brake up. She asked me to kill her. That done it. After a while we made up and I told her about "Now and Forever," the saga of our future. She was thrilled to pieces. Just heard on the radio that all 28 white men that lynched a Negro in Greenville, S.C., was let go by the jury, which was all white. The Judge refused to thank the jury for their services. I admire that man.

Duke brought me another letter from Raine. No greater love hath any man than me for her.

The Two Mrs. Carrolls, Humphrey Bogart and Barbara Stanwyck.

Dear Raine, My Love,

Loving you and knowing you love me causes roses to grow from the mock dust, and the dreary, tragic thoughts of my mind. I see the world as a mud-pie made in God's youth, thrown aside into the infinite limits of the sphere by Him and forgotten like all youth's broken toys. Upon this tragic, unbright cinder, I have found only one in whom I see no evil, no utter lack of beauty, no aimless desires. You are the one.

I'm beginning that story about you and me "Now and Forever" today.

> I'll Be Loving you as Time Goes By
> Lucius

I plan on marrying Raine soon as I sell my first novel.

*   *   *

Duke shot his Momma and Daddy with his daddy's shotgun. They were doing the dishes together. Duke begged to go to the wrestling match at the Smokey (because the Pioneer's gone) and they wouldn't let him. His daddy's face is shot away and they don't know whether his momma will live. They'll probably send him to Nashville. He still has Luke's boots. Maybe if I had been a better buddy to him. . . .

Raine and them were at the Bugs Bunny Club. Joy met me in the Market House at the Blue Goose and told me that she was the only one that ever loved Duke. That Peggy and Raine both told him a few days ago that they had just played like they loved him to make Harry and me jealous. That he was nothing but a big blow hard. When Joy told him she really did love him, Duke thought she was only making fun, and said he was going to burn all their houses down and mine, too, while we slept. How could God let such a thing happen?

Today was Gale's last day. He's going in the Navy Monday. I'll miss good ol' Gale. No more sparks.

Momma got a letter from Earl yesterday. He's out of the air force and back in the reform school with Bucky. Bucky's in the reform school's hospital and Momma took a bus this morning to Nashville. Going to see about the job at the cigar counter in the hotel, too. Bucky enclosed a letter with Earl's. They stenciled RUNAWAY in white letters on the back of his coveralls.

"The city is a germ, one of a million germs in the gigantic infection." (Lucius Hutchfield)

V

Slow Train to India

THINK we ought to give him another chance, Elmo?"

"If he promises not to just sit around with his thumb up his ass, dreaming up stories."

"I swear to God, I won't," said Lucius, afraid the third threat, like the one at Bonny Kate, would become a promise made true.

"Okay," said Hood, "with Gale gone, we need you. Get back On the Spot."

That night after supper at Max's, Lucius led a long-haired blonde and a long-haired redhead down the aisle almost to the front row, fairly sure they were two of the Smoky burlesque dancers. A strange dislocation, to think of them sitting there, looking up over the stage at Humphrey Bogart in *The Two Mrs. Carrolls.*

At the top of the slope somebody sitting in the back row on the aisle caught hold of his sleeve and light from the screen showed Daddy's face under a wide-brimmed hat that folded his ears down in the way that made Momma cross over to the other side of the street when she saw him coming.

"Hey, Bub."

"Hi, Daddy."

"Shhhhhhh!"

"What's the matter?"

"Bend down, I got something I got to tell you."

"*I* tell you, move over to the side aisle by the wall. Mr. Hood's liable to *jump* my ass."

As Lucius walked along the half-wall toward the fire exit doors at the side, expecting his daddy to follow, he saw the heads of patrons in the row bobbing up and down as they let Daddy get by. But no empty seat on the other end. So Daddy huddled with him in the curve of the wall by the lighted still stand.

"Too much light here, Bub."

"What you mean?" Lucius was afraid he wanted to toss a bottle, maybe even a Mason fruit jar of splo.

"Listen, they's somebody after me."

"*After* you? What for?"

"This girl's husband broke out of Petros penitentiary and he's roaming the streets of Cherokee with a gun, out to get me." Either Daddy wasn't drunk or he was scared sober on top of being drunk.

"*Whose* husband?"

"Barbara," he said, as if she were as inevitable as rain and he had no control over the way she'd woven in and out of his life over the past decade.

"And it's her husband that's out to get you?" Daddy nodded. Lucius was scared, afraid any second a man would leap into the lobby and start blasting. "Why don't you hide someplace?"

"That's what I come to see you about." That seemed odd, since Daddy knew every open sewer and crouching place in Cherokee where, on winter nights when the wind howled, he huddled next to one of the drunks he roamed with. "I thought you might know of a good place I could hide." Then Lucius realized that what Daddy was really saying was that he'd already thought of a good place to hide. Lucius didn't want to embarrass him by making him come out and ask, so he said,

"See that curtain at the end of the aisle?"

"Yeah, I see it."

"Walk right through there, but make sure nobody notices you. I'll be back in a few d'recklies."

Daddy started walking. As Lucius crossed the narrow inner lobby toward Brady, he bounced on his toes several times to see over the balustrade and saw Daddy walk through the curtain without even feigning.

"Beauty is worth any sacrifice," Humphrey Bogart told the cold beautiful rich bitch Alexis Smith, who'd come to visit him at his house in Scotland. Lucius liked this moment. He paused, listening for the other line that thrilled him even before Bogart got it out. "I *always* tell the truth." Somebody said he was ruthless. "I paint what I see."

"Take the spot for me, will you, Brady? I got to *spring* a leak."

"Think you can find it okay?"

"Want to help me look?"

"No, thanks, I just got *over* the syph."

As Lucius turned to go, Brady goosed him with his flashlight.

"Where *are* you?" Getting no answer, Lucius was suddenly afraid the convict had knifed Daddy when he stepped into the dark. But he found him onstage at the head of the short steps, light from *The Two Mrs. Carrolls* flooding him.

"Looks funny from the side, don't it?" He held a bottle of white lightnin' in his hand. "I just had to have me a little one, son."

"Okay. Follow me, Daddy. I got the damn best hiding place in Tennessee."

"Long as it's one *he* can't find," said Daddy, following the light Lucius held at his side, shining at his heels, down the steps into the basement.

In the still room, Lucius opened the steel door.

"What's this? Some kind of a storeroom?"

"Come on in," said Lucius, grinning. As he reached for the light, he was suddenly apprehensive that the convict was hiding around the bend of the cave with a pistol aimed at his heart. "Shut the door."

Lucius turned on the light.

"I'll be damned."

"How you like it?"

"Looks like it goes on back."

"It's the Cherokee caves."

"I was borned and raised in Cherokee, son, and this is the first I ever knew of any caves."

"Didn't you ever hear of any caves that run all round and under the uptown?"

"You ain't shootin' me the shit, are you?"

"They hell, no, it winds and winds and winds, and they's a hole under the Market House right at Calvin's Meat Market."

"Sounds like them caves under Luxembourg."

"Which ones is that?"

"Didn't you ever hear of the *Bock?*"

"Un-uh."

"Prince Sigsimond built 'em under his castle in thirteen and something and his ancestors kept adding to 'em until they ringed all of Luxembourg, which—the old town anyway—is built on a big rock—and it was their defenses, see, and no army ever stormed them until the Nazis blitzed 'em."

"Really?"

"I wouldn't shit you," Daddy said. "What do I do now?"

"Well, you just take it easy, like Ali Baba. Go anywhere you want to and can't nobody find you."

"Any way to get out the other end?"

"Maybe they is, but I ain't found it."

"This is a new one on *me*."

"I'll have to lock you in because the boss might see the latch up, and wonder."

"Okay, Bub. Wake me when it's over."

"Take my flashlight. I'll borry Bruce's."

"They ain't no dragons in here, is they?"

"No, I already cut their heads off. I'll come back before the last show's over and see how you doing."

"Okay, Bub. I just hope they run him down by then. Ol' Sergeant Foley told me Cool Abshire was on his trail."

"Ain't he the one shot *Harl* Abshire?"

"Yeah. Don't think I don't feel sorry for ol' Sid."

"Well . . ." Lucius started to go.

"Lucius . . ."

"Yeah?"

"I *had* to blow that bridge."

"You never *told* me what happened."

"Yes, I did, a hundred times," Daddy said, sounding drunk now, as if safe from Sid, it had suddenly come back over him, and with it, the reason he drank. One.

"Tell me again before I go."

"Bud Tibbs, this Indian friend of mine from Oklahoma. Went into the village to get some more poontang and wine before we had to pull out, and he got between the panzers and the bridge, running like a fuckin' wild Indian, grinning, war-whoopin', his arms full of bread and wine for all of us, and the captain give the order to blow the bridge, Bud in the middle, never suspectin' nothing, didn't even hear the tanks, he was so drunk on wine and poontang and gifts to give us. Went up in the sky like a bird above the blast."

"You keep saying it was *you* blew the bridge. You was in the medical corps."

"That's what I know. But ain't I in the human race, too?"

"You never told me that story before."

"Yes, I did, a hundred times."

"Well, don't brood about it, Daddy. . . . You're safe from Sid, anyway."

"Oh, yeah. Oh, yeah. Good night, son."

Locking his daddy in, Lucius felt silly, as if he'd locked him in with Bucky and Earl, too, in the family dungeon so he could rule the castle alone.

On the Spot, aware of his daddy's presence down in the caves, Lucius thought of the caves of Luxembourg, and remembered the only time he laid eyes on Barbara Thomas, Daddy's girl friend since the days they lived on Zachary. Hot Saturday in July, the first summer after they moved on Beech, when Lucius was nine, and he was roaming uptown with Jim Bob and Sonny Hawn. His clothes and his feet and arms and face were grimy, and the sidewalk was hot under his bare feet. The Hawn boys had stolen something from Kress's and sold it to get money to go to the Hollywood to see Roy Rogers and chapter seven of the *Riders of Death Valley* with Buck Jones in sepia tone, but Lucius had been afraid to steal, so he decided to bum a penny from nine people, claiming he already had eight and needed only one to make nine, the show fare. As Lucius stood in front of the still slots, Daddy walked by with Barbara and her son, Fritz, a boy Lucius knew and liked at Clinch View elementary, and Lucius ran after him, hurt, and asked him for a penny, and Daddy gave him one and went on. It hurt so bad Lucius forgot it, until now. He'd never held it against Daddy, and now it seemed only interesting. Suddenly realizing that Luke's girl had never returned to her seat on the aisle since the time Lucius sat down beside her, he wondered what made him think of her at this moment.

Only a few people in the theatre. Lucius leaned against the pillar On the Spot and watched Bogart setting up the poisoning of Barbara Stanwyck because she knew too much and also because he wants to switch over to Alexis Smith now. Bogart's little girl and the housekeeper go to London and he pretends to go, too. Barbara is alone in the house, sick, but her old boyfriend who lives nearby has given her a gun. There's a killer-burglar loose in the area. Bogart comes back unexpectedly. "I'll bring your milk up," he says. Lucius always thought hot milk before bed was a very aristocratic idea. She says she'll have it downstairs. The phone rings. She throws the milk out the window into the rain. When she goes to her bedroom, she takes the gun along. The wind blows the windows open and Bogart sees the milk spilled. He prepares to strangle her, making it look as if the burglar has done it. He is dripping wet from the rain and turns out all the lights in the big house. She is calling her old boyfriend. He cuts the wires. Suddenly the windows of her bedroom fly open and he is standing on the wide sill, his arms flung out, shadows on his face, looking like a vampire as she screams. Then they talk frankly, and he says, "My painting of you is finished. The Angel of Death. You made my work live again at first. Now Cecily has done the same." He is about to strangle her with the sash, when she pulls the gun. Then her old boyfriend and the cops crash in. "I had to kill her so I could go on with my work." He has the eyes of a psychopath now. They take him gently away. But on the wide staircase, he pauses. "Before we go. You gentlemen like a drink. Glass of milk perhaps?" THE END.

He paid Brady, who was off the floor to change the marquee, to get him some stuff at the Blue Circle. Lucius sneaked backstage with a sack full of hamburgers and two black coffees.

Daddy wasn't in sight. Panicked, Lucius ran, yelling, then screaming, through the caves, the beam of Bruce's light bouncing. Then he was scared and mad, too, as when he used to lose track of Bucky back in the years when he had to take care of him, and Bucky would wander out of the Hiawassee and Lucius'd find him hours later playing on the creek bank where he was liable to fall in, calling for Fartso the Whale, wanting to join his little helpers, not just to help, but to get next to all the goodies Fartso had to dispense. Lucius stumbled on an empty whiskey bottle. The green radium dial on his watch showed he had been in the caves ten minutes. The Bijou Boys would be looking for him, and they might find the door open and discover his caves. Panicked both ways, Lucius stopped and screamed his throat raw. "Goddamn it, Daddy, I know you're *in* here, so answer me."

He ran on back to the still room. Just as he was latching the rusty steel door, Elmo came loping in. "Hey, you hear somebody screaming down here?"

"Nope, why?"

"Sounded like Barbara Stanwyck when Bogart swoops down on her like a fuckin' bat. Hood swears you're down here raping one of the patrons or something. What you doing with the door?"

"Nothing. Just fiddlin' around."

"Hell of a time to fiddle around with that damned door. Besides, you can save your breath. We tried it one time and it won't budge. How 'bout shutting the fan doors, Shorty?"

Exhausted, his legs wobbly, Lucius started up the stairs. He walked the narrow, buckled plank over the black gulf of the basement and pulled the huge red wooden doors shut over the sooty chicken-wire grill, watching people who'd parked for *The Two Mrs. Carrolls* get in their cars. Turning around was always the crucial move, and this time he was certain, nervous and hot as he was, and dizzy, that he'd fall. Or that Emmett King would reach through the door and shake the plank. His metatarsal bars scraped on the plank and his brace creaked. A phony fiendish laugh startled him, then Elmo's half-assed imitation of the Shadow, "Ooooooooooo, the Shad-dow knooooooooows."

"Eat shit, Elmo."

"It isn't Elmo. It's Mr. Hood."

"Eat shit, Mr. Hood."

"What did he say?" Sounded as if Mr. Hood had just walked up.

"Nothing, sir," said Elmo, covering up.

As soon as Hood dismissed him, Lucius ran to Market Square. The Salvation Army was banging and singing and shouting on the corner across from the Market House's main entrance. On the opposite corner, a preacher was raving. Dark against the TVA building, men leaned, listening, the same sort who'd go to the Smoky down the street a little later to watch wounded Violet Lombard flash her pussy at the stroke of midnight.

"Ain't they pitiful?" a woman said to her little boy as they skirted the spectacle. "We may be down, but thank God we ain't like that."

A girl knelt in the gutter as the preacher beat the April night air with his Bible. Were the man and woman and little boy who stood against the wall, watching in rapt immobility, the girl's momma and daddy and little brother? They were ragged and dirty, having crawled up the steep, kudzu-vine-choked bluff from the houseboats or walked to town from the jagged hills beyond South Cherokee, he imagined. Lucius was afraid of the preacher's throbbing tongue and deep-socketed eyes.

The Smoky lights were bright, as country hoojers walked toward the midnight strip show, and cop cars and taxis prowled.

On the side of the Market House that he figured was closest to the crack in the cement floor that opened into the cave, Lucius put his mouth to the crack in the locked double doors, and whispered, "Daddy?" Imagining Daddy trapped in the cave, sewer rats chasing him all night the way they chased Jean Valjean, Lucius kept it up. "Daddy? *Hey, Daddy!*"

"No use trying to break in there, son." Cop behind the wheel of a patrol car. "Ain't nothing left but fish tails and pig knuckles and nasty sawdust and wilted cabbage."

"I think I dropped my wallet in there at lunchtime."

"How about getting in the car and you can look for it in the Juvenile."

"Sir, do I *have* to?"

"No, you can resist arrest and we'll put a slug in your ass."

As Lucius reached for the door handle, the other cop said, "What you want to scare the kid for, Vaughn?"

Lucius laughed along with the joke. "Say, you all seen Fred Hutchfield rambling around?"

"Fred Hutchfield? Ain't that the guy they 'lectrocuted ten minutes ago, Ed?"

"Naw, we ain't seen him, son, but if you see him first, better get him in off the streets cause Judge Corey swears he'll put him *under* the workhouse next time he shows up in morning court."

"You all lookin' for Sid Thomas?"

"*Ever*'body's looking for Sid Thomas. You know where a feller can lay hands on him?"

"Naw, sir, I just wondered. I *heard* he was runnin' loose."

"Come on, Vaughn, we got more important work to do than scarin' kids."

"Okay, Blondie, but if you find that wallet, it's mine."

On a fast start, they burnt rubber. Lucius waited until they turned the corner of the Market House, then he cut loose running, took a short cut down an alley, ran six blocks, doubling back past the Bijou, and on down the steep hill to the River Street slums. He looked around, back up the kudzu-infested hillsides between the houses for the place where the large sewer pipe opened in the cliffside. Sighting it, he ran between some houses, stirred a dog up to barking, and, afraid of snakes, climbed on up the rugged cliff.

Clinging to the cliff face just under the rusty grill over the pipe, he yelled, "Hey, Daddy, you *in* there?" His voice echoed back out over the rooftops and he imagined Bruce in one of the houseboats recognizing his voice. He kept yelling, "Daddy, you *in* there? Say!" Then a voice came across the river from the jungle on the south side: "No! So shut the hell up!"

The kudzu around him suddenly took sharp shape and below he saw a lighted back porch, a Negro at the screen door. "Who's *up* there?"

Lucius shut up, didn't move. When the light finally went out, he sneaked back down the cliff, past a horse tied to a tree.

Dirty, scratched, weary, he walked home, crying, his legs aching.

Ledger: Daddy is lost in the caves under Cherokee. Momma called the cops to look for him.

"What is this world that you cling to it?" (Irwin Shaw)

To keep from waking Momma, Lucius pulled out his cot to unblock the door and squeezed through the back door and down the steps. He was about to go around to the front to look at the Sunday morning *Messenger* to see if there was news of Daddy, when Blue came out on Miss Maggard's screened-in back porch and said, "Lucius, there is a gentleman to speak with you."

He was embarrassed to go into Miss Maggard's house so early, and Blue was wearing only a housecoat and her red turban. Did she ever take it off, even for bed? "And last night a young lady called and wanted to speak with you. She said her name was Stella Snow."

"Thank you. I hope it's her. . . . Hello?"

"Hey, Bub."

"Daddy!"

His nervous shy laugh. "They got him."

"Got who? Oh, that Thomas guy?"

"Yeah. Run him down over in South Cherokee. Don't know what he thought I'd be doing over there that time of night."

"Daddy, where *are* you?"

"She don't like me to tell anybody, son." In a louder, phony voice, he said, "Oh, I'm using the phone at the L & N *ho*tel." Then he whispered, "Barbara's. I waited till she started running her tub to call you and tell you. I just thought you'd like to know."

"Yeah. Glad they caught him."

"I got to get some sleep. I been riding around in a patrol car all night. Ol' Sergeant Foley took pity on me and let me ride with *him*. He don't *say* nothing, but he knows about me and her, and that Sid broke out to get my ass."

"Well, Daddy, tell me one other thing, will you?"

"Sure. Shoot."

"How'd you get out of that cave?" The line went dead. "Daddy?"

"Cave? Jesus, Bub, how'd you know I was in some cave?"

"How do *I* know it?"

"Yeah, I dreamed I was wandering around in this cave and then I was somewhere down on Crazy Creek and—How did *you* know I was dreaming about some cave?"

"Daddy, that was not a dream cave, I hid you in there myself."

"Like shit. They *ain't* no caves under Cherokee. I know I was looped, but I wasn't that looped. Listen, Bub, I gotta hang up. I just thought you'd like to know about ol' Sid Thomas. They sending his poor ol' ass back to Petros. It's *in* this morning's paper. Bye, Bub."

"Bye, Daddy."

When Lucius went out on the front porch, he couldn't find the paper. He opened the little gate in front and looked up and down the street. The whores in the big house down Bluff Street were reading the paper on their front porch, but he didn't reckon one of *them* had taken it. The damned paper boy had missed.

The sight of a new lime green Lincoln Mercury Zephyr parked in front of Mammy's little house startled Lucius. It was as if the Green Hornet had stopped by. Alone in the house thinking of Duke in the juvenile home, Momma gone to visit Earl and Bucky in Nashville again in Dan Miller's convertible, Lucius had longed for Mammy's on Sunday afternoon. Now this fancy car, a rare model on the streets of Cherokee, parked in bright sunlight outside the dark green hedge, the yellow fireplug at its bumper, declared that a part of Lucius's life was past, because for the most important adult in his life there had been a great change. He'd passed Jane's Cafe again yesterday and the FOR SALE sign and the dark windows setting high up the bank at the top of a steep flight of warped wooden steps, the cafe huddled up against the gigantic Avalon Arms, had made him feel as if he were looking at a funeral wreath.

Sensing that other things were missing, too, Lucius picked up the Sunday morning *Messenger* and timidly knocked on the door.

"We eloped last night," said Mammy, shyly, "and we're off to Florida in about two shakes. I whupped us up some cowboy coffee to send us down the road. Want some, honey?"

While they dressed, Lucius read the book page and Kerry Drake and the show page. He couldn't imagine Mammy on a honeymoon with the Chief for two weeks in Florida.

Going into the bedroom to use Mammy's phone to call Raine, he saw the Chief's uniform hanging on a coat hanger on the back of the door and his fire chief's cap on a peg on the wall, and knew that this house would never be the same.

He called Raine, told her to be standing out on her front porch, he'd be passing by on the streetcar to the Bijou d'reckly.

"Lucius, your ol' Mammy's starting her a new life, and they's—well, a few things—you're old for a boy your age, and practically the man of your family—few things I want you to know, for we can't keep it from you forever."

"Well, tell me, Mammy. I want to know."

It was like the way she'd do when somebody was hiding in her bedroom to surprise him, except that she was suppressing tears of shame rather than smiles of exhilaration.

"Honey." Her voice was rhythmic with love, and he wished he could keep that and not have to endure the rest. "We've *always* thought Gran'paw Charlie wasn't murdered by no mean night watchman, that maybe—he done it hisself."

She walked out of the room, leaving Lucius stunned.

A while later, she came back in and said, "Well, we better go 'fore dark catches us halfway there."

The car had a fat spotlight, a snappy aerial, no running boards, and, instead of door handles, large silver buttons. A rose from the garden in his lapel, the Chief opened the door of the fancy Lincoln Mercury Zephyr and Mammy, like a queen, slid in.

After he'd waved them out of sight over the hill, Lucius felt a vast emptiness around him.

Uncle Luke's little green Dodge was missing.

The hedges had been cut down from above his head to below his knees. Now he knew why she'd let them grow wild and high after Gran'paw shot himself.

In the living room window, the service star flag did not hang beside the ice card.

Lucius sat behind the circus-wagon coal house, his feet in the alley, the smell of grape vines from Mr. Stookesbury's arbor contradicting his efforts to imagine suicide.

On the Grand Boulevard streetcar, Lucius wrote a poem for Raine, using a scrap of brown paper bag he'd found beside the road.

Raine waved to him from the porch, dressed in shimmering blue, and he threw the poem to her through the window.

Ledger: Wrote a wierd story. "You Name It." Just wrote down a description of everything on my desk, every little move and all my thoughts and everything Raine and I said when she called, and what Momma said when she came in from uptown, looking for a job. Right in the middle I got a idea for a story. But I might can sell this one, too.

P.S. Raine just called back. Her house burned down again. The cops accused "Feisty" Clayboe of arson.

*　　*　　*

Mammy and the Chief are on their honeymoon in Florida. Bought Great Stories of Today.

*　　*　　*

I must have solitude. A place in the mountains. Austria or Switzerland or an apartment in the Paris slums. Sidewalk cafes, sitting in the sun in summer and autumn and drinking cold beer from a mud mug; an elm beside my favorite table or a willow like a green waterfall, and when it rains there is mist mingling lovely in the limbs, and my table there with rain drops and tiny green leaves on the dark green marble top. I'd sit there after a summer shower with my white shirt open and drops of rain would fall from the leaves and the air would be coooool and clean and sweet-raw in my lungs and sitting in the mist, leaning back against the trunk of the willow, I would smoke a slim cigar and drink beer and think of Raine and our children Tom and Vivien and plan for them and day-dream of them and increase with lovely thoughts my love for them, and I could think of God and the glory of Jesus and would let my self go, cut away the chains that bind my thoughts to a state of unity and let them flow like a bubbling stream with a bed of clean brown pebbles and sand, deep in a virgin forest, and every thing would be lovely and I would think "I'm in Paris. God is lovely!" what a strange feeling to know you are in Paris and home is far away. The waiter comes now and then, a red-faced, bald frenchman with thick lips and a moustache and a belly big as a barrel and a joval air about him, and I would get drunk on ice cold beer and fall asleep in a wicker chair and while I slept the sun would shine again, warm breath on my sleep and the rain drops on the leaves would now and then fall and plock softly against the damp earth, and I would still be asleep when the sun went down and all heaven's glory kissed the colors of dusk.

*　　*　　*

Earl escaped from the reform school. Bucky's still in there.

*   *   *

Minetta quit. Thelma thinks she's pregnant. I didn't do it. A beautiful girl named Regina was in the ticket booth when I went to work. About 18. Used to work part time at the Valencia. I am in love with her. I'm going to use her name in a radio play I'm writing. She talks to me very sweetly. Brady and them were talking about doing it to her in the dressing room, but I didn't join in. But I can tell they know she's different. Special. Rare. Wonderful. Black hair and green eyes.

I Stole a Million, classic, George Raft, Claire Trevor.

"Like Jews, they wandered as though stung by a wasp that had fed on the burst heart of Wolfe." (Lucius Hutchfield)

*   *   *

Daddy and I had a can of beer in my sanctuary and I asked him to read "Nostalgia" about our children. He went histerical crying. "This is poetry." He said. I hugged Dad. "Don't, Daddy. I'm sorry. I didn't mean to. I don't hold anything against you."

"There is no beauty," Daddy said.

Why do the things that hurt Daddy and them to remember seem beautiful in some ways, no matter how terrible, to me?

I was waiting for Raine and them at the top of the hill when they got out of Bonny Kate. Walked Raine to Peggy's house where her family's staying until they move to another house. Coming home on the Grand Boulevard streetcar, I saw them tearing down the burnt out ruins of Raine's house, exposing the scorched walls of their living room. Momma says they're going to put up a Dairy Queen where her house was. Raine said they're going to move into the Old Cherokee Tavern on River Street, a block from Harry's house. She's going to lay out of school tomorrow and I'm going to help her clean it up. Called Brady and he said he'd work for me.

"Listen, honey, can I turn this stuff off?"

"No, don't, I love church music," said Raine, raising clouds of dust, sweeping.

"It's too loud."

"Brother Ed's gonna be on d'reckly. He's a wonderful preacher."

"Hey, I know, let's me and you go up to the River Bridge Bookstore and use their phone and request "Heartaches" on Mark Fogarty's 'Insomniacs.' "

"I'd be embarrassed to go in a bookstore."

"It's fun, honey, I wish you'd go with me one time."

"They ain't got nothing good."

"Why, they do, too."

"What?"

"Shakespeare. Know what Hamlet said to Ophelia?"

" 'Doubt thou the stars are fire,
Doubt thou the sun doth move,
Doubt truth to be a liar,
But never doubt I love.' "

"Why don't you just sit and read the telephone book while you're at it?"

"You trying to make fun of me again, Raine?"

"Footfire, no. Don't fly *up* at me, Lucius."

Raine had fixed a pickle jar full of lemonade at Peggy's house. They set the radio in the windowsill and sat on a rusty glider, and Lucius held her hand, his feet not quite touching the floor.

"Listen, can I turn Brother Ed down a hair?"

"Okay, but it don't seem right to turn a preacher down."

To get his arm around her, he had to sit back, but then his feet left the floor. Raine's feet touched and she made the glider move back and forth, mingling its whine with the bawling of cattle across the river.

Ledger: "To lose the earth you know for greater knowing; to lose the life you have for greater life; to leave the friends you loved, for greater loving; to find a land more kind than home, more large than earth." (Thomas Wolfe, *You Can't Go Home Again.*)

Duke, who was probably in Nashville by now with Bucky, and Earl, if they'd caught him, intruded upon Lucius's reverie, and he started a new story, imagining that Duke was with him that Saturday in August when he saw the first Bugs Bunny Club show.

"Run"

For Raine

By Lucius Hutchfield
Chapter One

Nick and Tex stood there on the landing of the balcony. The Bijou was filled with yelling, screaming, booing, cheering—flirting kids. Nick leaned against the wall under a tiny yellow wall light. He had a headache and had not had any breakfast so he felt sick at the stomach. The crowd was unusually loud this Saturday morning. Down on the brightly lighted stage the mistress of cere-monies, Mrs. Potter, was asking final applause for the contestants. A decision was trying to be made as to whether a small boy or a small girl should receive a watch for best performance. Nick and Tex were rooting for the little boy although neither had seen either performance.

Nick wore a bright red turtleneck pullover and

Disgusted that he was unable to capture in words the total reality of that Saturday long ago, Lucius wadded the paper and tossed it at the coal bucket in the kitchen. He took the miss as a sign that God meant him to keep everything he wrote. Having unwadded it and put it in his notebook, Lucius went down to the tower by the river to watch the sun go down over the island airport.

Ledger: "A writer is a flower that grows by intellectual sunlight." (Lucius Hutchfield)

"Wake up, Lucius."

"What for? I don't have to go to school."

"One of these days you'll wish you did."

"Let me sleep. I was up till three o'clock writin'."

"Well, *I* tossed and turned all night long. . . . worryin'. Even if I do find a job, where I'm goin' to get the time and the energy to pack and move again, I don't know. Listen, Lucius. . . . You listening?"

"Yeah."

"Well, answer me then."

"Answer you what?"

"Since you don't have to go to school, you can pick up the morning paper and start looking for us a place to move."

"Momma, I was going to work on my story this morning."

"*To* hell with your damned story. We're going to be without a roof over our head, and you worry about those silly stories."

"They're not silly damned stories," said Lucius, turning over, staring up at her. Her dress looked to have come fresh out of a Sanitary Cleaners bag.

"Lucius, I'm beginning to worry about you, the way you spend all your time writing stories."

"They thought Thomas Wolfe was crazy, too."

"I don't give one damn about Thomas Wolfe. It's not good for a thirteen-year-old boy to hole himself up the way *you* do."

"I do a lot of other stuff."

"I am *not* going to argue with you, Lucius. I've got three minutes to get out there and catch that streetcar."

"Just don't talk against my writing. You sound like those teachers at Bonny Kate used to."

"You've failed the eighth grade because you wouldn't straighten up and fly right."

"I don't give an iceberg in hell if I did."

"Honestly, Lucius, here lately you've got so you're almost as much of a worry to me as Bucky or Earl."

"Thanks. Maybe they'll send me to Nashville for writing stories, then you'll stick up for *me* the way you do *them!*"

"Hush! Will you hush!"

Lucius jumped out of bed and brushed past Momma who stood on the raised threshold of the sanctuary and slammed the door of the bathroom just off the kitchen and turned his cold bath water loose to gush.

"Lucius, you open this confoundit door. I have to get *in* there before I go." As Lucius stormed out, Momma grabbed his arm. "Now you just stop that yelling! You're trying to send me to work all tore up, and me already so weak from lack of sleep. . . . If you *ever* yell at your mother about something as stupid as writing stories, I'll slap you winding, boy. You hear me?" She shook his arm, a vicious look on her face.

"Yes, I hear you. But one of these days you won't think it's so stupid. I'll show *all* of you."

"Lucius, nobody in *our* family ever went in for stuff like that. I don't—"

"Maybe I'm different."

"You sure the hell are." Momma stepped into the bathroom and slammed the door. Lucius went into his back porch sanctuary and stared at Errol Flynn gripping Ann Sheridan by the arms, Walter Huston and Judith Anderson watching, in *Edge of Darkness*, carpet-tacked to the wallboards.

Momma came to the threshold again, her purse over her wrist. "I've got one more thing to say, then I don't want to hear another word about it: One of these days, you'll learn that dreams don't put bread and butter on the table, a roof over your head, and clothes on your back."

"You earn the food, I'll earn the fame."

"You hateful thing! Get out of my sight before I knock your teeth down your throat."

Lucius jerked his cot clear of the door and went out and sat on the back steps in his undershorts, so mad he couldn't even cry or curse.

When he heard the streetcar go by, three blocks away, he imagined Momma sitting up front across from the motorman, telling him her troubles.

Without taking his cold bath therapy, without eating, hating the sight of the kitchen table and all the other malignant objects in the house, Lucius got dressed and walked out.

Walking east along the riverbank past the boxcars, the tower, the marble mill, the brick kilns, Lucius talked with God, imagined himself and Raine into the future in Paris. He turned north through poor

Negro and white neighborhoods, and climbed a high red clay hill above the Avalon where he used to see *Tarzan* when he was little across from the Cherokee Knitting Mill, and sat under a walnut tree and looked out over the city. He hated the rooftops and the people squatting under them. All they thought about was what his mother spent her every waking minute worrying and talking and whining and raging about: food, a roof, clothes. In the distance, the Great Smoky Mountains stretching blue, from one end to the other of the horizon, made him feel there was something better beyond Cherokee and that he could find it. He began walking toward the mountains, not intending to go to them, simply to feel nearer them.

Walking south down Sevier Street, he felt drawn to *Bush Pilot* with Jack LaRue, playing at the Hollywood, to *Suddenly, It's Spring*, with Fred MacMurray and Paulette Goddard, playing at the Venice, and then he saw the Tivoli marquee: TYRONE POWER and GENE TIERNEY in THE RAZOR'S EDGE.

The posters and the stills out front made a sudden, strong impact, and his response was instant, total. Around Tyrone Power hovered the aura of *Jesse James, The Rains Came* (that he once thought Maugham had written and in which the exoticism of India first made an impression on him), *The Mark of Zorro, Blood and Sand, The Black Swan*, and around Gene Tierney the aura of *The Return of Frank James, Tobacco Road, Belle Starr, Laura, Leave Her to Heaven*. Although Lucius had read only "Rain" and "Red," and browsing through Cherokee stores had seen his books in paperback and hard cover, each stamped with his exotic symbol, W. Somerset Maugham had a magical sound every time. The poster resembled the paperback book he'd seen in the new Cherokee Newsstand.

When Lucius walked into the auditorium, a Bugs Bunny cartoon colored almost a thousand empty seats. Impatiently, he watched the News of the Day—Senate hearings about a U.S. experimentation with a radioactive cloud-making device, and the hanging of more Nazi concentration camp guards. His feet hurt from walking on the metatarsal bars. He unlaced one shoe, and took the other, brace attached, off.

People dressed in early twenties style. A luncheon party in a Chicago country club. Black and white tones as luminous and lush as the early Technicolor of *Jesse James*. Herbert Marshall enters, limping, introduced as Somerset Maugham! He's like me, thought Lucius, excited by a similarity between himself and W. Somerset Maugham, but then he remembered that Marshall limped in *all* his movies. The idea of the author being portrayed in a movie adaptation of his own book thrilled Lucius.

Tyrone Power comes in, wearing black, looking stunningly handsome.

The music enhances everybody's movements and speech. In the garden, an iron bench around a huge tree strikes a romantic response in Lucius. Tyrone Power is Larry Darrell, a fighter pilot in World War I. Gene Tierney is Isabel, a rich young society girl who expects him to marry her and go to work and get rich. "What do you plan to do?" "Loaf." Larry contrasts with Clifton Webb as Elliott Templeton, Isabel's playboy uncle just over from the Riviera. He exudes disdain for Larry.

Isabel wants Larry to accept a job he's been offered, selling bonds. He loves her, but he can't. "Oh, Larry, darling, you're so different to what you were before you went away to France! Are—are you terribly unhappy?"

"I don't think I'll ever find peace until I make up my mind about things. I saw men die, Isabel—many men. And it's all so meaningless. You can't help but ask yourself what life's all about—whether there's any sense to it, or whether it's all a stupid blunder—"

Lucius knew when the movie ended, but when the Bugs Bunny cartoon ended, he was surprised that he'd sat through it again. Wanting the experience of the movie to continue, but not by another run—it wasn't a movie, it was real life—Lucius got up.

When he stepped through the doors of the Tivoli, the sight of Cherokee made him nauseous. Under the marquee, he stood on the sidewalk unable to move, without impulses. Nothing seemed desirable or even necessary.

Like a patient coming out of ether, he started down Sevier to the Cherokee Newsstand. He sneered at James Stewart in *It's a Wonderful Life* on the Bijou marquee. Cherokee soot had turned the fresh paint job on the side of the Bijou dull red again.

At the Cherokee Newsstand he started to buy the paperback edition of *The Razor's Edge*, but feeling disloyal to Larry compared with Wolfe, he stole it.

The look, the heft, of the book sustained him. He'd postpone reading it. Approaching the Tivoli again, Lucius realized how to make Raine understand. He'd be waiting for her at the top of the hill when she came out of Bonny Kate, and he'd take her straight to see *The Razor's Edge*. Listening to Isabel, she'd recognize herself, and listening to Larry, she'd finally understand Lucius. On the raised concrete platform in front of the Tivoli, he caught a Clinch View streetcar.

He wanted to go to India now, not Maine, or New Orleans, or Palestine, and he wanted to go today. But he was afraid. India would be final. Not just miles would cut him off forever from Cherokee but the discoveries of the spirit that he'd make on the holy mountain, and his contact with his family's world, with Raine's, would end. He'd not forsake Maine, his heaven on earth, the wandering hero's final home, but henceforth it would be in India that he'd imagine discovering his own soul. Until then, Maine would be uninhabitable.

The June breeze coming through the grill over the open window of the streetcar, Lucius pondered the title page: "The sharp edge of a razor is difficult to pass over: thus the wise say the path to Salvation is hard. Kathat-Upanishad." Convinced that reading this novel would change his life, Lucius turned, trembling, to page one: "I have never begun a novel with more misgiving. If I call it a novel it is only because I don't know what else to call it." This approach intrigued Lucius, but impatient to hear about Larry Darrell, he skipped ahead, and was disappointed to discover that the early pages dealt with snobby Elliott Templeton. He decided to wait until he had time to read attentively through the boring beginning.

Stilled by awe and wonder, leaning against a giant oak, waiting for school to let out, Lucius noticed that if he were still in school, he could look out Miss Cline's window and see this spot. Perhaps some dreaming student, maybe even Raine, was looking at him now. He stood to be looked at from far down there. He felt sad that he'd never darken the doors of Bonny Kate again.

The sun went in, the wind started blowing in the limbs of the oak over his head. Then a boy ran out the side door as if shot out of a circus cannon, then two more boys, then a girl, more boys, then a steady stream of colors. Kids began trudging up the hill against the wind, dresses and shirts ballooning. Then he distinguished Raine and the Clayboe Ridge gang, Harry and Peggy and Cora. Poor Duke gone. Where was Joy? Soon they'd see him, and wonder, then start waving. They were very tiny, more color and movement than people, but somehow recognizable by movement and color.

Lucius stared down at them as they climbed nearer, grew larger and larger, still not seeing him. And then he detected by the way they walked that they knew he was up here but that they were conspiring to pretend not to see him, giggling, jabbing each other, wisecracking about him. Furious, he almost turned to walk back down the opposite slope into Clinch View.

As they came alongside, Raine looked up, pretended to see him for the first time. "Oh, hi, Lucius."

"Come here, Raine."

"You come over here."

"Skip it."

Raine stopped and looked at Lucius, then shrugged her shoulders and started to follow the others, who were weaving drunkenly from one side of the street to the other, hanging onto each other, giggling.

"Stop pulling at my arm, damn it!" Harry told Peggy.

At the rounded crest of the hill, Raine stopped and looked back. "You *said* you'd come by and walk to schoo' with us. What'd you do 'iss morning?"

"I made the greatest discovery of my life." His voice sounded like Tyrone Power's.

"You did the what of your what?" asked Peggy, with that look of mirthful scorn that easily cut him down. But today a buffer of airy steel seemed to hang invisible between them.

"Raine, stay with *me*, will you?"

"I can't."

"Why not?"

"Got to go to Peggy's."

"Okay, I'll walk you."

"It's a free street, Lord help us," said Cora, lamely.

Lucius pushed off from the rough hide of the oak tree and caught up with Raine. "Hi, Harry."

"Hi, Lucius."

"Let's let them go ahead, Raine."

"But I was walking with *them*."

"Well, why can't you walk with me?"

"Why can't we all walk to*gether?*"

"I just want to be with *you*. What's the matter, don't you love me anymore?"

" 'Course."

"Then let them go on."

"Oh, hell's bells. All right. You all go on, he wants me to be just with him."

"Too good for us, huh, Poet?" asked Peggy.

Harry paid no attention. Cora sneered, and they all walked on, deliberately cutting down a different street. The absence of Joy made Lucius feel off balance, but he didn't want to ask Raine and set her sarcasm off.

"Well, what did you want?"

"Nothing. Just to be with you."

"Listen, how come you don't beg Mr. Bronson to let you back in schoo'? We only got till this Wednesday."

"I'm *never* going back."

"Yeah, I'll bet," said Raine, imitating a braggart tone.

"You trying to say I'm talking like—" He didn't want to get on Duke. "—all mouth?"

"Don't be so touchy."

"Listen, honey, I came just to *get* you. I want to take you uptown to the Tivoli."

"I can't, Lucius."

"Why not?"

"Promised Peggy I'd give her a Toni."

"A Toni? Please, honey, I really need you to *go* with me."

"What's so important about some ol' movie?"

"You'll see. It's all about us, honey."

"What you mean 'about us'?"

"Let me take you, and you'll see."

"What's the name of it?"

"*The Razor's Edge*." Echoes of the background music rang in his voice.

"Oh, I seen the previews. Looked to me like a silly'un."

"It's the greatest movie ever made on the face of the earth. See. Here's the book of it. See?"

Raine glanced at it. "Gene Tierney looks kinda buck-toothed."

"Let's go, honey, and see it together."

"Looo-shush," she said. "I prom-isssed Peg-gy."

"Well, when in the hellfire you goin' to promise *me* something? You promised you'd love me forever. Remember?"

"Well, forever ain't over yet, and I still like you."

"*Like* me?"

"Lord love a duck! Okay. *Love.* . . . Lucius, what say, let's just hold hands and hersh."

Lucius jerked his hand out of hers. "You can't stand to hear me talk, can you?"

"If you'd just talk about stuff a body could understand. Sometimes you sound *put* on, and it's got worse since we started going together again."

"Okay. I'll shut up then."

Wind blew his hair. He felt too sad to speak.

"Well, what did you want to talk about?"

After a moment, he said, "If you'd just let me tell you about the movie. It's like it really happened."

"Okay. Shoot."

"Well, it's about this guy named Larry Darrell who was a fighter pilot in World War I and he comes home to Chicago and all his friends are only interested in making money and getting rich. They invite him to this ritzy party. And guess who's there?"

"Rockerfeller?"

"W. Somerset Maugham, the British author."

"Oh."

"He's *in* it. . . . Well, Larry has this long talk with Isabel, this beautiful rich girl who loves him, but he tells her he has to search for the meaning of life."

"Don't he ever read the Bible?"

"Raine, he probably read the whole thing, but he's *still* confused. So Isabel promises to wait for him until he *finds* himself."

"What if *she* finds *her*self first?"

"She ain't lost. She *knows* what *she* wants—him and money and babies and a high-class house."

"She ain't gonna get it from *him*."

"But she hopes he'll turn out just like their friends. So Larry sets out for France on a tramp steamer. He figures that the best place to start his search is in France, where he fought in the war and first started worrying about the meaning of life. . . . You listening?"

"Yeah. . . . I was just watching that cat jump out of that tree."

"Here, kitty, kitty, kitty. . . . But after a whole year in Paris he was no closer than before to finding what he was looking for."

"What was he looking for?"

"I *told* you."

"I forget."

"The meaning of it all. Then Isabel came over with her mother on a visit, and he had a good time escorting them around Paris. But when she saw his room, she was shocked. Crummy, but clean. And nearby I could hear somebody playing Chopin's 'Polonaise.' Anyway, she begged him again to give up his search. He says, okay, I'll marry you, let's go right now and get married. They'll have to live in poverty, see, but they can wander all over Europe—even with their kids. Ain't that a beautiful idea, honey—just you and me wandering all over the world, not caring where we live or what we eat or what we wear?"

"I want to have fun, I don't want to search for no meaning of life."

"See? See, there. That's just what *she* said."

"Who?"

"Isabel."

"I ain't her. She's rich."

"She looks just like you when she's mad."

"*I* ain't mad, and I ain't got buck teeth, neither."

"Well, she's used to the best, so she refuses to do it, and says, 'You've had your fling—your *fling*. So come on home with us now.' And Larry says, 'What you forget is that I want to *learn* about life just as much as Gray Maturin (that's their childhood friend) wants to make money. I can't stop now. It may be that when I'm through, I'll find something to give other people and they'll be glad I have it to give.' "

"What?"

"Wait and see. It comes in later. But you see how she's like you and Larry's like me and Gray's like Harry?"

"When's the shootin' start?"

"Raine, stop horsing around now, and *listen!*"

"I am, I am!"

"So later on, Larry gets this picture—wedding picture of Isabel and Gray, and there's ol' Somerset in it, and Sophie, their childhood playmate with her own husband. That hurt me as much as that letter you sent by Duke.

"Larry's working in this coal mine near the Polish border and in this sooty old tavern he meets an ex-priest who's been defrocked, they call it, for some mysterious sin, and he's sort of a philosopher, and he tells Larry that knowledge can only make you unhappy."

"Makes *me squirm.*"

"Hush, honey. Please. . . . Larry tells him he's lost confidence in the accepted values of society, and the man tells him it has to come from within you. Well, he tells Larry he met a strange man in India. A saint. People come from everywhere to tell him their troubles, and listen to his teaching, and they go away strengthened in their soul, and live in peace. Made me want to see what this man looked like myself, and when Larry starts off to look for him, it's really exciting, you know?

"So finally, he climbs this mountain in India to the simple dwelling of the Holy Man and his disciples. And don't this sound like— And Larry says to him, 'To my friends, I'm just a loafer—afraid of responsibility. I've studied, I've read everything I could lay my hands on, I've traveled a lot—but don't none of it seem to satisfy me. I try to get excited about settling down, but that only makes me more eager to move on. But I know that if I *do* find what I'm looking for, it will be something I can share with other people. But *how* can I find it? And *where?*' And the Holy Man said—"

"Go and sin no more."

"This ain't Jesus, this is—" Lucius took a deep breath. "What he said was, 'You got to live from within yourself, from your own heart, which is where God is.' "

"I could have told him that."

"But there's more to it, Raine, than anybody can *tell* you. . . . So the Holy Man let Larry stay with him and they talked and talked. Then come the Depression and wiped out all Gray Maturin's empire of wealth, and this friend of theirs, Sophie, her husband, and child were killed in a car wreck.

"Then the Holy Man sends Larry higher up in the mountains, alone, above the clouds, where he could be completely isolated and alone from the world in his own little sanctuary—this hut made of stone and mud, like it was part of the cliff. He let his hair grow, and I wish I had me a sheepskin-lined coat like he wore. So months later, the Holy Man visits him and Larry tells him of this vision he had one morning watching the sun come up. Says, 'I felt that if it lasted another minute, I'd die. Yet I was willing to die. Because, for that one moment, I had a feeling that—that—' 'That you and God were one,' says the Holy Man, real soft."

"Was he dead?"

"No, Raine, he was not dead. He was more alive than he ever was in his life. Then the Holy Man told Larry to return to the world and love the things in it for God is in those things, and His vision would stay with him forever." Lucius remembered the soaring music as Larry left the mountain and wandered across Europe to Paris again. "And you know how *long* he was in India?"

"Lucius, you really think this is a good movie?"

"Seven years! What if *we* were separated seven years?"

"You just try it, buddy boy!"

"Wait till you hear what Larry did. See, he runs into Somerset Maugham—he keeps coming into the story, almost like a god in disguise —and they talk in this sidewalk cafe, and he tells Larry that Isabel and Gray and their children are living with her snobbish cousin Elliott Templeton, so Larry goes to see them.

"Gray is wearing these dark glasses and he's depressed because he lost all his riches and these violent headaches are driving him crazy. Larry uses this method he learned from the mystics. It's a Hindu coin. It helps Gray to cure himself, somehow."

"Well, how?"

"I don't know, honey, it's this mystic method. But it works. And Gray feels good enough to go with all of them to dinner. Ol' Somerset offers to take them. He says to Isabel that Larry looks strangely aloof, and, honey, she says, 'I've never stopped loving him.' "

Lucius hoped Raine would say, I know how she feels, but she didn't.

"Well, so, after dinner, Isabel insists that they all go slumming. In this apache cafe, they run into Sophie, who's with this greasy apache in black, and she's a sluttish sot now, and wears this black band around her neck."

"What's apaches doing in Paris?"

"No, it's this certain kind of gangster they have. Dances with a knife in his teeth."

"Oh, I've seen them in a whole bunch of movies."

"And this little orchestra's playing 'Mam'selle.' "

"Number three on the Hip Parade. Ta da!"

"So Sophie comes over and gets everybody all shook up, and Isabel gives her a cold but polite look, and Larry reminds her that she used to be a good shortstop when they were little kids, and she reminds him that they used to read Keats's poems together, and some poems *she* wrote. Isabel insists that they leave.

"In the car Larry says Sophie had a lovely purity, and he stops the car and goes back.

"The next day, he takes Sophie in a rented car on a picnic. When Isabel returns to Paris about a month later, she calls Larry, and he tells her he's going to get married to Sophie. It makes her so mad she hangs up. And she rages against Sophie, and Somerset Maugham says, 'I call a person bad who lies and cheats and is unkind.' And to quiet her down, he praises everything about Isabel's face and hair and says, 'Kiss me on the lips.' I loved that part. I loved the way everybody seemed to close to each other, like they'd lived together all their lives. It wasn't like they were acting it."

"And that's *it?*"

"No, a little bit more, then I hope you'll want to *go* with me. What happens is that Isabel thinks up this scheme to get Sophie drunk. There's this really ugly scene where Isabel's wearing a black hat that's flat and flared out in the front, and she sets Sophie up so she can't resist taking a drink, and we can hear 'Mam'selle' playing. Meaner'n a snake, just like she was in *Leave Her to Heaven.*"

"I hope you're through comparing her to me, mister."

"No, no, honey, that's just the way *she* turned out. Then the next day, Isabel calls Larry and tells him that Sophie started drinking and now she's missing. So, Larry goes to search for her, wearing this black tam and raincoat, and he finds her in an evil bar where an *A*rab and a Corsican are trying to pick her up. They jump Larry and knock him out. A year later, he's still searching for her all over France, and, honey, he learns that her body was found in the river in this small town, and guess what? She was murdered."

"I hate to say it, but it was Isabel."

"That's what Larry thinks—tells her in the— Honey, let *me* tell it, and then we'll *see* it. So in her room, Larry finds this book of Keats's— 'The day is gone. . . .' And the police pick Larry up and at the station he finds Somerset Maugham, too, because some things in her room connect both of them with her. I'd love to be like Somerset Maugham, and have people tell me stuff they wouldn't tell anybody else—Well, Harry used to sometimes. . . ."

"What did he tell you?"

"Why? . . . Why . . . Then Somerset asks Larry to go with him to Nice, where Elliott Templeton is very sick. Templeton gets invited to this duchess's ball and he writes back that he 'can't accept due to a previous engagement with his blessed Lord.' Then he dies."

Raine laughed so hard, she had to stop and catch her breath.

"Why were you so eager to know what Harry told me?"

"Lucius, tell it."

"Well, Gray and Isabel are there, too. And Gray offers Larry a job, because now Isabel will inherit Templeton's money, and Gray can start his business up again. Larry says no thanks."

Within sight of Peggy's house, Lucius persuaded Raine to sit on the running board of a wrecked T-model on the edge of a patch of jungle for the end of *The Razor's Edge.*

He's going back to America, but to buy a taxi and make his living *that* way, so Isabel and Larry talk about his future. Isabel gets madder'n hell, says, 'Sometimes I think you're completely out of your mind! Doesn't it mean anything to you that I love you—that I've never loved anybody else but you? That my children might have been your children?' She begs Larry to love her now. But even though her beauty still stirs him up, he suspects it was her that fixed Sophie up with whiskey. Very slowly, he accuses her, until she finally admits it. She'd do anything to win him. But she's shocked when he says Sophie was murdered. 'Do they know who did it?' He says, 'No, but *I* do.' And so he tells her good-bye.

"And the last thing we see of him is on deck a tramp steamer again, at sea in a storm, the wind and ocean lashing against him in his black raincoat. Now will you go with me?"

"I got to go in now, Lucius. I promised Peggy I'd give her a Toni. She's been looking forward to it, and I just love to do it. Why don't you stick around and watch, and then while it sets, we'll make us some good ol' homemade fudge."

"Raine, don't you give a damn about your own soul?"

"You better watch your mouth, son!"

The wind blew in the high limbs of the two giant oaks in Peggy's front yard. Lucius's heart was racing and his stomach throbbed. "Well, I guess this is the end, Loraine."

"The end? What for? What brought *this* on?"

"You. The way you act towards me."

"Why, I didn't do nothing. I listened all the way through that silly-assed story, didn't I?" Sounding like Cora.

"That's it. That's it, by God. All you care about is boogie woogie and church and Tonis and running around with a pack just like yourself and making fudge and reading funny books. Good-bye, Raine." He hoped she'd beg him not to go, beg him to explain his vision of life, then go with him now to see *The Razor's Edge,* and that it would change her life.

"Where you goin'?"

"Far away, and never come back."

"Don't talk simple, Lucius."

"Good-bye, Loraine. Forever."

"Where you going?"

"To India."

Loraine burst out laughing. Lucius turned swiftly and walked away, down the gravel road, under the blowing trees of Clayboe Ridge.

"Send me a postcard from Baghdad, Poet!" she yelled. "Lucius, don't be silly! Come back here and stop acting like a lum-lum."

Lucius didn't look back until he was a block away, expecting to see her standing under the blowing trees, watching him walk out of her life into an unknown future. But Loraine had gone in.

He walked all the way across town to Bluff Street as if streetcars had never existed, and went to his sanctuary, and took "Helena Street," his first typed story, out of the drawer of his desk and folded it lengthwise and put it in his two-toned brown sports jacket pocket, *The Razor's Edge* bulky in the other pocket, his middle button pulled tightly against his belly. He wrote a note to his mother and left it propped on the kitchen table against the rooster saltshaker:

Dear Momma,

I am going to India to search for the meaning of life, even if I have to go to the end of the earth I will find it. Cherokee is dead to me. Loraine is dead to me. Someday you will understand. Tell Mammy I love her when she gets back, and I love you and Daddy, and someday when I am a famous writer we will all meet again in New York or Paris or Calcutta. Loraine can tell you why I am going away. And now I belong to the world and God.

                              Your son,
                              Lucius Hutchfield

On the tracks by the river, he snuggled down beneath a giant chunk of marble. An hour later, the freight train began to move.

Lucius had seldom wandered far beyond the brick kilns. Still, the landscape, the houses, and buildings the train passed seemed as familiar as any he'd ever looked upon, but his intention of never returning made him feel isolated and estranged from what he saw and cast over it an aura of images recollected in reverie, as if he were watching a movie he'd seen six years before many times over at the Hiawassee and knew every image, every word, every note of background music, and seeing it now a seventh time reminded him of his life when he first saw the show. Lucius's senses, his brain, so hummed from stimuli, he felt numb. He was on a boat that had lifted anchor, pulled in its mooring ropes and chains and was beyond the lighthouse, and as the houses of Cherokee became fewer and fewer, until the swarming green of the countryside slid by, he felt adrift on the ocean. He remembered the time he hopped a freight with Sonny and them from a trestle over a creek in the country to beyond the opposite side of Cherokee, and he held on, his legs and arms spread wide between boxcars, stretching him as if on a rack, the cars jerking and swaying, and he was certain he'd fall and prayed dear God he wouldn't, and it didn't stop going through Cherokee, and passed by the waterworks, just as this train was now, and carried him to a gigantic train yard about ten miles beyond.

"Reminds me of the time," Mammy would begin, "they used to tell about Gran'paw Charlie when he's little—runnin' off that time. Only tin years old and he ended up in Chattanooga. Went all that way by one means an t'uther and the *po*lice picked him up wanderin' the streets way early one mornin', and took him in and kept him at the station house three days 'fore they got hold of his paw, and put him on the train home. Captain wrote an' told how Charlie was such a little gentleman the whole time. An Charlie wrote him a letter thankin' him in the most high-tone terms for treatin' him so good."

And Luke telling how *he* ran off one day when Gran'paw Charlie whipped him, struck out down the railroad tracks and along about dark he was cold and scared and he looked up and there was a lumberyard, and who was it but Gran'paw coming through the gate and saw him standing there on the rail, trying to get his balance, his mouth wide open.

Looking back as the train crossed a creek that flowed into the river, Lucius felt as if he were leaving his childhood behind. He hummed "Till the End of Time," then, his hand cupped around his mouth, sang, low, lulling himself into a stupor of departure.

Not until he hit Marble Station, the biggest marble quarry in Tennessee, that he'd heard about but never seen, did the numbness of leaving fade and thoughts and images begin to flow. Over and over, he relived the scene with Loraine, then imagined the future. Married, with five kids, she'd see, in the newsreel at the Tivoli, Lucius arriving in New York on the *Queen Elizabeth* ten years later, a famous author, a hero of the Palestine war, carrying a cane, his new novel under his arm, wearing a moustache, a black patch, and a trench coat. And lurking in the background would be Tamara, a beautiful Arab girl, who resembled Hedy Lamarr, and Loraine would wonder who she was, and she'd cry. And her husband would ask, What's the matter, honey, and she'd say, Oh, leave me alone. The train whistled through Morristown.

Lucius saw Harry lying on his cot in his sanctuary, talking out his misery over Peggy. Comforting him was like Larry Darrell helping Gray Maturin find peace. The train passed through Witt. And trying to make a Christian out of Della Snow was like Larry Darrell trying to pull

Sophie up out of the gutters of Paris's Left Bank. As a fine rain began to sift down, Lucius, huddled under the slab of veined marble, imagined finding Larry Darrell, still as young and godlike as Tyrone Power, somewhere in his travels. Perhaps he'd returned to India. Lucius would slowly work his way down to New Orleans and from there sign on a ship to India. Thoughts of his future as a wanderer made his heart beat faster, his mouth go dry, his stomach hurt. Now he was doing what he'd imagined Damon doing in "The Yearning Heart." The train passed through White Pine and along the edge of a vast lake.

His cheek against the marble slab, Lucius felt the naked cheeks of Reva Tamargo's delicate fanny. Maybe at this moment Reva Tamargo was leaving Gaile Savage behind. As her train passed his, she looked out the window of the passenger car at him. He'd not see her again until Calcutta.

Cupping his hand intimately around his mouth, Lucius improvised fitfully, brief scenes out of *The Razor's Edge* and other movies, his stories, and real events of the past, spacing them with Warner Brothers background music, dreaming out of the past, out of Cherokee, into other places, future times.

Lucius and Raine argue over her pretended love of Duke and she confesses her secret love of Harry. In Buggs's scrap junk truck in front of Peggy's house, she makes fun of Lucius's expression of bewilderment about the meaning of life. He takes a bus to Atlanta, where he sees a rerelease of *Gone With the Wind* and searches for Margaret Mitchell's among the faces of people leaving the theatre, but doesn't see her. He sleeps on somebody's front porch the first night and in a church the second. He begins to find what he is searching for, but love of Raine draws him back to Cherokee.

They are reunited in Peggy's backyard under a giant oak with a wooden bench around it. For months, they are happier than ever before. School lets out for the summer. Lucius passes everything, Raine fails English. They hike out to the country where he used to go with Sonny Hawn and them. He tries to explain about his search, and asks her to come with him, but she laughs, and he gets mad.

Early the next morning, Lucius calls Peggy and tells her he's leaving. He hops a freight train bound for South America. That night at church, Peggy tells Raine that Lucius has left Cherokee forever. Raine cries so hard, she can't sing, and walks home alone. Raine calls Lucius's mother and they cry on the phone. And Momma calls Mammy, but Mammy understands better than any of them. Raine asks God to help her understand Lucius's wanderlust.

Rankin. Mountains ahead. The train whistle made Lucius feel he was in a movie.

One night about five months later, Raine is alone in the house, reading over Lucius's love letters. She wonders if she could find him out in the world. The lights go out and a strange vision causes her to leave the house. She thumbs a ride and a nasty old man picks her up. When he stops out in the country and starts to rape her, she coldcocks him with a rock and takes his money and catches a bus on the highway to Atlanta.

As the train passed through Del Rio, crossed over into North Carolina, and entered the mountains, Lucius felt the marble against his cheek turn chill.

In Cuba, Lucius joins the Merchant Marine. Bill Easterday, the bosun's first mate, picks on him because of his youth and his reading. Lucius fights him, and all the men are for Lucius, but Bill wins, and becomes an outcast on the ship. Later, Lucius and Bill become good friends.

Hot Springs.

In New York, Raine finds a job singing in a nightclub, but is later fired when she hears Chopin's "Polonaise" and can't go on. A drunk on the street in Greenwich Village tries to pick her up. She struggles and kills him. A detective finds Raine working as a waitress in a sidewalk cafe in the Village and follows her home. She suspects something and sets a trap, but he foxes her. When an autopsy reveals that the man really died of drinking, Raine is released.

When the boat docks in England, Lucius deserts. Bill finds out and deserts, too. Lucius persuades him to return to the ship.

Lucius locates W. Somerset Maugham, and they have a good long talk about literature, life, and Lucius. He's surprised to learn Lucius is only thirteen. Maugham tells Lucius where Isabel Maturin lives.

Lucius goes to Isabel's house in London. Gray is dead and she is in awful condition. She still loves Larry Darrell.

Marshall.

"This is WLUX in Cherokee, Tennessee," Lucius said, imitating Mark Fogarty. "Correct Eastern Standard Time now is six o'clock. Stay tuned for Walter Winchell—next, on the National Broadcasting System." Lucius imitated an orchestral bridge, then a telegraph racket, noticing the train was entering Newport. "Good evening, Mr. and Mrs. North America and all the ships at sea. Flash! Rumors report that world famous foreign correspondent and novelist Lucius Hutchfield will arrive in Hollywood by seaplane tonight for the world premiere of *The Yearning Heart,* based on his international best seller, written while living high in the Himalayan Mountains of India. But Lucius—as I call him— has informed yours truly that, on the contrary, he will arrive at La

Guardia airport tomorrow morning to begin directing his new play, *In the Summer They Slaughtered Cattle.*"

Alexander, high in the mountains. The train was moving along a river, steep bluffs along the other side. As it crossed a bridge, Lucius saw a city up ahead and watched for the sign. ASHEVILLE. Surprised, thrilled, feeling God-placed, Lucius jumped off while the train was still moving, ripping loose one of his metatarsal bars, turning his ankle. Pounding his shoe against the railing to knock the bar's nails back into the sole, Lucius smiled to see the sun setting in the direction from which he'd come. " 'Bums at Sunset,' " he said, and looked around for bums beside the tracks, and, seeing none, walked. Reva Tamargo, his spiritual love, walked beside him toward the streets of Asheville, a beacon south to India.

He didn't want to ask anybody to tell him the way to the house where Tom was born and the other one, the boardinghouse, where he was raised. He'd walk about the town and when he saw it, he'd know it for Tom's.

His legs and ass sore from the long ride on slabs of marble, Lucius walked in a spell of mingled emotions and moods, fascination, bewilderment, fatigue, sweet loneliness, and a feeling of wonderful, yet dubious promise, up a hill between dark buildings, past the YMCA and into the city, where evening lights were scattered, "Helena Street" and *The Razor's Edge* bulky in the pockets of his brown sport jacket, his whipcord trousers wrinkled, his throat dry, his eyelids heavy.

He was in Pack Square, in the middle of *Look Homeward, Angel.* Across the square was a restaurant that he was certain was the one Wolfe used to go to late at night and drink pots of black coffee. He crossed and entered the restaurant reverently. Having pissed out Cherokee, he ordered apple cider and chili. On the way out, he bought a cigarillo, and when the waitress left the cash register immediately after taking his money and he saw her fat check pad on the counter, he swiped it, as a souvenir of the place where Wolfe used to hang out.

Sitting on a bench in front of the courthouse, Lucius felt an urge to commemorate the experience he was having. He took a pencil from his coat pocket and wrote on the first green page of the waitress's check tablet:

"The sharp edge of a razor is difficult to pass over: thus the wise say the path to Salvation is hard. Katha-Upanishad."

He checked the wording with the epigraph of *The Razor's Edge.* It was exactly the same. Then he wrote:

"Well here I am. The act, the very old act of adolesence has been fully committed now. Apple cider and cold chili in my belly, blowing Robert Burns cigar smoke into Pack Square. On the way Nature's offsprings were in a tranquill mood. Stark, blunt, powerful rawness of magestic and common terrible beauty. Purple blossoms tipping tiny black twigs. Pink blooms blurring by. Often the things I saw—ragged rock cliffs with drippings of cool water from out of the mountains: Rock quarrys like a mountains mouth coughed out its rocky guts, machinery motionless at the base of the brown spillings: a lime mill by the tracks, smoke and white dust, rough buildings solid white: Slim trees shooting into the cold blue sky: made me think of the definitions of beauty as expressed by Thomas Wolfe, to whose hometown destiny has railroaded me."

On the third page, he wrote:

"To mother: 'You earn the food, I will earn the fame.' "

Lucius began walking away from the square, drawn into a search for Wolfe's house. In a dark alley, he felt Wolfe's presence, walking behind him, protecting him from the Wolfman. He saw, beyond a fence, three barred windows lit up dimly. He looked at the windows of the houses across the street, expecting to see a girl gazing out across the open space into a cell where her sweetheart paced. But the windows were dark, shaded, heavily curtained. The smell of coal smoke from the chimneys of the old houses made him homesick.

The image of the cell windows haunted him as he walked down a road. He'd sleep on Thomas Wolfe's porch tonight.

Lucius prowled the streets of Asheville. Though they resembled Cherokee's, they looked strange. His feet stung and ached and his brace chafed his leg, and a cool wind made him flip the collar of his jacket up around his neck. When he passed a cop, Lucius the runaway felt like Maddog Earl in *High Sierra*. Maybe Momma had the cops out on a three-state alarm, like the time he stayed gone when he was three in his pink sunsuit and brown tam, playing in a rich boy's enormous toy room, riding his three rocking horses until dark and the police car was parked in front of the house when he sauntered home, its radio crackling. Maybe Momma told the FBI to check the borders into India. Aw, shit, that's silly. He felt compelled to keep moving, exploring. He passed a cheap hotel called the North Carolina, and then he was in the residential district.

Lucius finds out from the Merchant Marine office in London that Larry Darrell was a sailor on the *Queen Mary*. The Captain tells him that Larry went only as far as India.

After going through much hell, Lucius finds the place where the Saint lives, but the servants tell him that Larry is in the mountains. Lucius sends a servant up to the hut with a letter in which he tells.

Larry that Isabel still loves him and that she's on the verge of suicide. Larry comes down. He doesn't know what to do. He'd lost all hope. Finally, he tells Lucius to let Isabel know where he is.

Before Lucius goes, he gives him some advice: "Whatever you do in life, Lucius, do it just for the hell of it, instead of because you're *supposed* to. That makes the difference. You do a thing for the love of it. Not because you have to, not to make money, but just for its own sake. Take any situation in life, good or bad, and you can transform it into something else, something better. Something about the presence of real human beings turns something loose in you and you can't stand to see an occasion collapse just because it's geared that way. Turn what looks like a failure into a moment of triumph." He gives Lucius the special coin for remembrance.

Lucius goes back down to the town and sends Isabel a telegram. When he learns that she'd started up the mountain, he is happy. Because of the riots in India, the Saint can't get back home. Until the Saint has shared some of his wisdom with him, he isn't allowed up in the mountains. He sets out for France.

In Florida, Raine works in a mill. At Palm Beach, she meets Somerset Maugham, who tells her about Lucius. He gives Raine money to get to India.

In Calcutta, Raine sees fighting and lives in squalor and is hungry most of the time. In a small town near the Saint's home, she meets Isabel, who buys her breakfast. Then they go to meet Larry, who cannot believe that she is the very girl Lucius had described to him. Larry tells Raine that Lucius went to France.

Walking through quiet, neat neighborhoods, feeling safer now but homesick as he looked at the lighted windows, the warm living rooms, Lucius inspected porches from the sidewalk, doubled back several times to get up courage. Gliders especially tempted him. Swings were possible but creaking rusty chains might wake the people inside. But he couldn't get up nerve to try it. One house looked so promising, he got halfway up the broad front steps before his knees turned weak and wobbly. Finally, he headed back toward the lights of uptown, remembering the ratty little North Carolina hotel, but hoping he'd suddenly see Wolfe's front porch.

In France, Lucius gets mixed up in a killing that he didn't do. Ernie Garber, a French detective, tracks him down. Ernie likes Lucius and believes he's innocent so he finds him a meek home in a Catholic monastery. The priest can't understand Lucius, but thinks he has a rare gift from God. After a few weeks, Lucius, who has helped many people in the monastery, escapes and goes to Paris. In the Rudalap, some apaches beat him up.

Ellie MacFarland, daughter of the Australian ambassador, finds Lucius on the beach. He tells her many things about life. She loves him and wants to understand him, but can't. Lucius and the ambassador dislike each other. Ellie nurses Lucius back to health.

Lucius gets a gang together and tears the Rudalap open, taking revenge on the apaches. Danger of retaliation from the apaches makes Lucius leave Ellie's mansion. He has changed her life for the worse. She can't eat or sleep and becomes very sick. Lucius signs on a cargo ship to America to see Raine.

Raine and Larry and Isabel become good friends but she gets off the ship in France and they go on to America.

In Paris, Raine goes hungry and is picked up by police. She prays for her release. When they let her go, she sleeps in the monastery where Lucius had stayed. The priest tells her of Lucius. She meets a sailor who stows her away in a ship to America. When Bill Easterday, the captain, discovers her, he lets her go on to New York, never knowing that she is the great love of his old friend, Lucius.

Finally, Lucius reached uptown Asheville again at about eleven o'clock, dragging his feet, hurting worse than after a Saturday night On the Spot at the Bijou. Every few steps, he hammered his foot on the pavement to tighten the metatarsal bar, and nightwalkers turned to stare at him. Looking in his pockets, he found two dollars and ten cents. Maybe he could find a flop joint for a quarter, but he'd need most of his money for cans of beans until his first payday. He'd work in Asheville awhile, maybe even carry papers on Tom's old route, and get enough money to make it on down to New Orleans and get a ship and sail to India. Or maybe be an usher.

Passing a newsstand that was just closing, Lucius, eyes bleary, saw the front page of the Cherokee *Messenger,* impressed to find it all the way down here. A picture showed a number 3 Clinch View streetcar going down Sevier Street, flanked by drum majorettes, American flags draped across the top of the front window, a banner drooping over the large head lamp: LAST RUN. He'd forgotten the rumor. Staring at the fact, he stood there on the sidewalk, rocking and reeling, utterly exhausted. Loraine had vowed to love him forever and he'd thought that her love was the most enduring thing around him and so he'd taken the everlastingness of other things for granted, and now he was standing on a street corner in Asheville reading about the last run on the last streetcar in Cherokee.

Lucius stepped in a gutter full of water. When he walked, his shoes made a sucking sound.

A small square sign hung on rusty hinges. The hotel was brick, two windows open in the front above the sign, and a faint wind blew a fine rain into dirty white curtains and peppered it against the dusty window-panes. Lucius climbed the stairs and nervously waited at the desk for somebody to come. His heart beat fast and his breath came hard. His clothes were damp from the prickly rain and stuck to his skin. He stood in the dim hallway, leaning on the small, shaky desk, letting a little puddle of water form around his shoes.

Along the narrow, dim hallway toward the small high desk at the head of the stairs walked a white-haired fat Negro carrying a bucket, humped over, limping.

"What you want?" He went behind the desk and spreading his hands out, leaned over it toward Lucius.

"Got a place I can sleep tonight?"

"One dollar in advance."

Lucius gave him a dollar in change and followed him back down the hall.

The large room vibrated with the stink of filth, sour bedclothes, and pissed-on mattresses. The old Negro pulled a chain on a light that hung on a long cord from the ceiling in the center of the room. Lucius's stomach lurched when he saw a man on an iron bed, his sharp rump under the thin, dirty cover, his bushy head sticking out, for he'd ex-pected a room to himself. The light showed yellow peeling wallpaper, a chest of drawers that slanted, minus one leg. He blinked against the glare of the light and looked at a narrow cot against the wall. "Ain't you got a room for one?"

"What you want for seventy-five cents?" The Negro in the doorway handed Lucius back a quarter. "This is all we got, take it or leave it."

"Okay."

"Twelve o'clock is checking out time."

"I'll be out soon's I open my eyes."

The old Negro pulled the light chain, then closed the door, and Lucius standing beside the bed, aware of the furious tempo of his heart, listened to his footsteps fade.

Sitting on the hard edge of the cot, Lucius took off his sports jacket and laid it neatly across the seat of a chair by the bed. Staring hard through the dark at the bed in which the man slept, he pulled off his whipcord trousers, and quietly removed the silver from his pockets and set it in stacks on the inside ledge of the cot. Bedsprings sang—in the dark, the man was turning in his sleep. Tense, Lucius lay back on the cot, looked up nervously at the ceiling, unable to stop the trembling of his body.

As he slipped off his watch, the band snagged the hairs on his wrist. Quietly, he ripped the rotten cover of the mattress and embedded his watch in the cotton, remembering the scene in *The Killers*, Dumdum tearing Ole Anderson's mattress into a cloud of lint. He felt a little better.

Rats ripped sharp nails along the innards of the walls. Lucius dared not turn toward the wall at his back. The snoring throbbed in the dark, stopped abruptly. Sagging rusty bedsprings yawned, then the light clinked on.

In yellow long underwear, the wrinkle-faced man stood tall, his long arm dropping from the bright bulb. Behind his arm, a yellow grin spread the sun-browned wrinkles beneath the tangled hair on his head. The dropped trapdoor in the rear of his long underwear exhibited his skinny rump.

"Hidi. Say, you mind ifin' I turn on the light? Jest a minute?"

"Naw. Tha's okay."

"Welp."

Lucius strained his neck slightly to watch, his fear slowly ebbing. Comic. Good ol' guy. I hope. Coming in from the mountains to visit the city. Yeah. Overalls. Dirty, mud on the cuffs. Brogans. A shapeless hat. Sure, he's comic.

His big bare feet slapped softly over the floor to the green chest of drawers where a bucket set against the wall. His lanky frame leaned against the wall to brace his head against the faded dahlias of the wallpaper, standing back so that his legs spread, his bare rump hiked slightly, he let piss fly into the empty bucket in static rhythm, one arm dangling at his side, the other obscured by his body.

Burying his face in the stinking mattress, Lucius smothered giggles until his ears burned. It was okay. He could sleep now. The ol' briar jumper wouldn't murder him in his sleep.

But for two hours, Lucius turned and breathed heavily and sighed and couldn't sleep.

Lucius finds nobody home at Raine's house. His own house on Bluff Street is empty, both apartments. He goes to Mammy's. She tells Lucius that Momma has moved to South Cherokee, into the old house on the bluff where Daddy was raised. Mammy tells him that Raine has run off from home and that Mrs. Clayboe is in the hospital almost dead of grief. Lucius visits Mrs. Clayboe. She hates him, calls him names, blames him for Raine's leaving. She loved Raine deeply, and once liked Lucius. He promises to bring Raine back to her.

Lucius goes to see Momma and they are happy, but she can't understand him. Bucky and Earl have reformed and are doing well in school. Bucky plans to be a doctor, Earl a lawyer. The next morning, Lucius slips out early.

About to catch a bus to Frisco, he sees Daddy in the bus terminal and takes him home to an old half-sunken houseboat on the river. Lucius gets him sober, then criticizes him for ruining his life. Lucius stays in town about a week, and one night Daddy comes to see him. He has been to church and has prayed. Lucius gives him ten bucks, then follows him. Daddy is hunting a job.

Lucius goes to Frisco, where he meets Bill Easterday in a bar on the waterfront. Bill tells Lucius that he now realizes he has met Raine.

Raine comes home to find that her mother has died and that her family has moved to Florida. She can't bear to see them now. Mammy tells her that Lucius has just left town, going she knows not where.

Raine goes to New York. She meets Harry on Forty-second Street. He is a banker now. They talk about the past. Harry loans Raine some money to get to Paris, where she hopes to find Lucius.

When Lucius woke, he realized that for the first time since he could remember, he'd not reviewed his life and gone to sleep talking with God.

On the waitress's check pad: Got up at 8:30 the farmer was gone. Bought a comb. Ate breakfast. And hung around the courthouse where a man was shot before I woke up trying to escape from jail. "Lock a man in there, by time *you* be home, he'd be home," says this one-legged old man. Looked in paper for a job.

* * *

Three old negros on a bench. "Who?" "Thomas Wolfe." "No. Not me. You, Jim?" "Who?" "Thomas Wolfe." "No. Why? What's wrong with him?"

* * *

Keep thinking of that old farmer in the hotel. Like Jeeter Lester in *Tobacco Road*.

* * *

Talked with newspaper editor who knew Wolfe. But mostly he wanted to talk about Ben, Tom's brother.

Past a hedge, then suddenly, two-storey white house, the long porch sweeping across the front, thrusting back along the side to the sun porch of many windows. Above the front steps, the sleeping porch. Three close-together tall windows down, three upstairs, thrusting upward to a gabled roof—sense of a tower. Room upstairs, stained-glass windows, where Ben died? Curtains hung at most of the windows, but the sprawling house looked empty, neglected, the rosebushes and shrubs growing wild and ragged along the porch and about the yard. No swing, but on the side porch, a lone rocking chair. Lucius was excited, walking in the hot sun in nervous anticipation.

Lucius looked around. He'd expected something momentous to happen when he found the house. A crowd of admirers perhaps, among whom he'd walk with greater authority since his love was greater than all others. But now he felt privately possessive. Didn't those people driving by and walking on streets a block away know that this was the place made famous by Thomas Wolfe's books? Were their lives as real and rich and important as this house that they could just go on about their business as usual? Lucius didn't go on up the walk, expecting somehow to be arrested for going near this house, which even now he didn't feel was quite real. It wouldn't be, until he'd actually gone inside and walked around.

He walked up and down Spruce several times on both sides of the street. A bowlegged old woman wearing an apron came to her screen door across the street and watched him. Then she went in. From where Lucius stood, he saw a hotel, and he couldn't understand how there could be an ordinary warehouse behind Tom's house, and an ordinary house on one side and a ruined house on the other. Tom's house was Lucius's alone, for his affections had seized it, but he would be happy to share it with others. OLD KENTUCKY HOME. Tom had changed it to DIXIELAND. The old woman sat in her swing on her front porch. Maybe she was Helen, Tom's sister, keeping watch.

Spruce was a one-block street, a monument set aside within the city's swarm of winding streets. The house seemed enclosed within a magic zone of timelessness, while the ongoing world around it threatened with a cruel aura of transience.

The house where Tom was born on Woodfin is of an old English type. The orchards are weed choked, and a very dumb family lives there haunted by people wanting more of Wolfe. In one of the windows as I passed along the drive at the side I saw a woman remove her slip. It was strange. I didn't watch her. Another woman let me look at the old fire place where old man Gant made roaring fires in the morning.

"Excuse me, sir, could you tell me where I can find W. O. Gant's monument shop?"

"Gant? Monument shop? Never heard of any Gant with a monument shop in Asheville. Now, they used to be a Wolfe."

"Yeah, that's who I mean."

"Well, why didn't you say so? They pulled it down and put up that skyscraper in its place."

When Lucius looked up, the sun hurt his eyes.

In a drugstore, on Patton Avenue, Lucius flipped through *Screen Romances*, Ingrid Bergman in *Arch of Triumph* on the front. In another magazine, he saw an ad for *Calcutta* with Alan Ladd, William Bendix, and Gail Russell, and realizing that he wasn't as thrilled as he once would have been made him feel sad.

I sat down on a bench beside a man waiting for a bus and asked him how people felt about Tom, and he said he was one of the characters in the books, and told me what page to go to, that he was a boyhood friend of Tom's. He was going to work, but he told me to get on the bus—I'm on it now, that's why the words are wiggly—and go see his sister, Aurelia, who worships Tom.

* * *

Aurelia lived in a big new house, with a lot of furniture she made herself—a couch that runs the whole length of her living room, and lampshades she colored with crayons in a special way. She's an artist. She told me a lot about Tom that I never knew. When I told her I hadn't stopped to eat anything, she fixed me up a nice lunch. She is tall, willowy, with long blonde hair turning gray and I kept hoping she'd hint that I could kiss her. She told me some people to see, then she drove me to Pack Square.

* * *

In Pack Square there is an info booth in the middle of the street. A short, grey rotund fellow with two gold front teeth and a Cockney accent is a very congiel info injector.

* * *

I am in Pack Memorial Library. There is an exhibit of photographs and books and momentos and newspaper clippings about Tom on display. A portrait of him by the poet Gene Derwood on the wall. And actual photographs of the Wolfe family and the house. Old-timey portraits of W. O. and Julia Wolfe when they got married. The house, with the father sitting in a chair on the lawn, and Tom on the stone wall out front, and Mabel (Helen) on the grass, and Julia on the porch. The trimming around the porch was more ornate back then. And a shot of the monument shop. Streetcars in Pack Square in 1900 or so. Mrs. Roberts, Tom's favorite teacher— looks a little like Shirley Redding. And the North State Fitting School on Buxton Hill where she and her husband, J. M., taught Tom. Tom as a boy—dark and very lyrical-looking. Orange Street School where Tom first went to school with Mr. Roberts. Ivy-covered, Greek-like building where Tom lived at Chapel Hill university. Tom's gravestone. Tom as famous author sitting on front porch steps at Mother's feet, she in rocking chair, OLD KENTUCKY HOME sign hanging over their heads. On a wall, a photograph of a death's head of Tom.

* * *

Walking down the streets of Asheville I see Tom walking toward me. Just as real as any of the people on the sidewalk. Right in front of Woolworth's was where I felt it and saw him most clearly.

* * *

Saw the house of Mrs. Roberts, Tom's favorite teacher, but their wasn't anybody at home.

* * *

Skinny old man at the desk in a sporty sweater at the Y said Tom used to sit around, talking to transients staying at the Y.

* * *

I am in Ashville, among people whose lives were going on before I came, and now I'm seeing them, and if I had stayed in Cherokee with Raine, I wouldn't be among these people.

* * *

Edge of town. Front of used car lot. Negro leaning against blue car, another Negro shabbily dressed standing on sidewalk. First Negro, folding his arms staring at the other Negro: "Now I'm foldin' muh ahms, see. I'm gonna let loose and hit you with bof' of 'em in a minute."

Lucius and Bill Easterday sign on a ship for England, where they part. Lucius works in a steel mill. He meets Maugham again. Then the war breaks out between Russia and America.

Lucius goes to India and finally meets the Saint, who asks God, "Who is this strange creature? How can I advise him?" The Saint wants to adopt him. Lucius's life is changed. After a long stay, he leaves.

In Calcutta, Lucius helps the British in the war against Russia. He gets shot and is sent back to England.

Raine goes to Paris, where the war rages. Her light skin is tan now and she is more beautiful. She meets Gordon Puckett, who had loved her since they were little. He is now a famous news commentator. He still loves her. Raine strings him along because she is hungry. She steals his money and continues her search for Lucius.

Lucius joins the British army again and is sent to Palestine. He meets Raine's big brother Lennis, who used to be a highway patrolman and who is now a captain in the American army. He loved Raine more than her other brothers did and has been hunting Lucius for two years. He beats Lucius up because he ruined Raine's life and caused his mother to die of grief. An old comrade finds Lucius dying beside the road and takes him to join the Jewish guerrillas. Lucius has amnesia. Harry arrives. His plane was shot down by Russians and Lucius's guerrillas capture him. He had fought with Lennis a while. He tells Lucius Raine is searching for him. They fix his plane and he flies away.

Raine becomes a nurse and is sent to Palestine. During the evacuation, she is left behind, and the Russians cut her hair off. Lucius comes with the guerrillas and frees her. Her spirit hasn't changed much, but he loves her still.

Looking out over Ashville from high on a ridge, I think of Cherokee, the Hiawassee Theatre the hub of my childhood, all the houses and theatres I lived in and the paperroutes I carried on streets spoking out from that hub. But now the Bijou is the hub of my life, and I can't see all the spokes, and don't know what they are.

A shy, young Negro, sitting in a car beside the dirt-rocky road out front of the Hidden Paradise, mountain top club for Negroes, said No, he didn't know what road it was that Tom, as a young man, had walked up into the mountains to lay in the grass and dream and brood over the Ashville that sprawled beneath him below beyond niggertown. But Tyson, a half-breed Indian and negro could tell me. Tyson, he said, has lived in Ashville for sixty years and knows everybody in town.

I wrote that at the fork of the road. The brace has rubbed a flaming sore on my leg and now the left metatarsal bar is loose, too. The Holy Man in India can heal me better with his touch than Dr. Summers with his knife.

*   *   *

Climbed to the top of the mountain to talk to Tyson. But he didn't remember anything about Tom except that he came up to the hotel sometimes. But he remembered Ben very well and told me a lot of stories about him. Tyson lives now in this rundown hotel that was a summer resort for rich people years ago, like Cold Springs where Bucky stayed. It was strange to see this hotel so high up, away from everything. His Negro wife lives with him, but she stayed back in the dark kitchen and hardly came out. Finally she sat in a chair on the back porch, behind us, while we set on some high steps, looking through the pine trees down into the valley.

He told me that down yonder lived the Madam of the whore house that tried to buy the angel Mr. Wolfe was carving for one of her whores who died of scarlet fever. He said that she married the brother of some famous band leader.

And he told about the fire. One night, the barn caught afire and he rushed out with the owner to save the horses. It was almost dark when he told it, and scarey, and he told it better than any book, and it was like I was watching a movie on the sky of something that happened years ago.

And then he told of how the business fell off and people went to Florida and other places when cars and trains were convenient to get there. And the owner shot himself at the foot of the stairs.

And Tyson heard it and came running in and the man's wife came down stairs from the two rooms they were still using. He took me inside and showed me the blood on the carpet.

Going back down the mountain that night, I fell and hurt my legs, but I made it to the edge of the Negro section at dark, and it was smokey and the smell made me feel like I was in a foreign city.

Walking down the main street, through the tough part, Lucius stopped at the Patton Avenue Bridge. Different from the Sevier Street Bridge, it had girders on top. Getting cold, he walked back uptown. Up ahead, a marquee said *Duel in the Sun,* Gregory Peck and Jennifer Jones. A big fancy theatre like the Tivoli, the entrance up six stone steps off the sidewalk, the door right there on the corner. Its shape, its location was very different from any of Cherokee's twenty-eight theatres. Coming: Alan Ladd and Gail Russell and William Bendix in *Calcutta.* More than anything else, this odd theatre made him feel he was in a strange town. He was jealous that people had gone to this theatre in Asheville and that he hadn't even known it existed. But he wanted to know which one Tom went to most.

Met a man in the old timey drugstore that used to know Tom. They don't seem to hate him any more for putting them in his book. Most of them brag about it. He told me which movie theatre Tom used to go to. "I think he might have been an usher there at one time."

Kids standing around out front and people going in and coming out of the brightly lighted theatre had been going here all the time Lucius had been going to theatres in Cherokee and now here he was standing in front of theirs. The still displays and decorations were more like the Hollywood than the Bijou. Roy Rogers, his old hero before Alan Ladd, with Dale Evans in *Apache Rose.* He'd rather see *Duel in the Sun* again at the other theatre, but he wanted to sit where Tom used to sit, and maybe he could usher here himself.

Self-conscious, afraid somebody, the pretty ticket girl maybe, would think he was trying to slip in, as he'd slipped many times into the Hiawassee and the Venice and the Hollywood three years ago, still feeling guilty for those times now, even when he had approached them with passes from Hood, Lucius opened the lobby doors. Somebody tapped sharply on glass. He turned. The pretty young ticket girl was hitting the glass with the telephone, and motioning for Lucius to come to her. He went up to the ticket booth.

"I need to see the manager."

" 'Bout what?"

"Do they need any ushers?"

"Maybe. But you're too little."

"I used to work at the Bijou in Cherokee, Tennessee."

"Carl ain't gonna believe it, but you can go on in and ask him. Tell the ticket taker." She smiled and Lucius felt her eyes following him. Was she making fun of him, or delighted by his sweet personality?

"Where's the manager at?" Lucius asked the ticket taker, an old man with a face like Popeye's, no teeth.

"Upstairs. What's you want with him?"

"See 'bout a job." Lucius walked on up the carpeted stairs, seeing himself stepping across the lobby to Hood's office to ask for a job, stroking a still as he passed a stand on the landing, comparing everything here with the Bijou layout, the differences exciting, scaring him slightly. He was in a strange theatre, hearing Roy Rogers sing to Dale Evans. Ratty place, like the Hollywood, where Luke was an usher when the Hollywood baby-sat Lucius, Earl, and Bucky.

In the long, narrow hall, the projection booth door was ajar. Aisles to the balcony on each side of the door. In the opposite wall, facing the street, MEN on the left, WOMEN on the right, OFFICE between. Lucius knocked. A woman came out of the ladies' room, picking her panties out of her crack, catching Lucius watching, giving him a dirty look. "Come in."

The manager, a scrawny little man with an eye sewed shut, sat at a desk in a dim light, a blond girl stood at the window, looking down into the street through open venetian blinds, the marquee lights turning her red and yellow in bars.

"Sir, you need anybody to usher for you?"

"Yeah. You know anybody old enough?"

"I'm fifteen myself."

"Hey, Loretta, he look fifteen to you?"

The girl was turning, and for a moment, Lucius thought she might be Loraine, her name changed to Loretta, but the face looked more like Cora, without the red sparks of hair. "They, hell, no, he looks like my little brother."

"Come back when you grow up, Lightnin'." The man's hair was very greasy and wavy, like a country music singer.

"I sure need a job, sir."

"If we need you, we'll call you."

Shutting the door, Lucius heard the man ask Loretta: "You ever seen that kid on the streets of Asheville?"

"They, hell, no. Probably run off from the reform school. Acted kinda funny to *me*."

The pretty ticket girl asked, "Child or adult, honey?"

"Child," he said, and got back sixteen cents for his quarter.

Hugging a bag of warm popcorn, unpeeling a 5th Avenue crunch bar, feeling secure with six penny Tootsie Rolls in his shirt pocket. Lucius sat down in the middle of *Apache Rose.* Thomas Wolfe sat beside him. By the time the news came on, with the rolling, ominous tones of a familiar voice narrating a disaster, the rhythms of the voice synchronized with the movement of smoke roiling up over acres of oil drums, Lucius imagined Bruce Tillotson On the Spot, the only Bijou Boy left, telling people the news as they came in out of the main lobby. Then came Bugs Bunny in *Hare Grows in Manhattan,* then *Flicker Flashbacks # 6,* then *Movietone Adventures in Zululand.* In the first part of *Apache Rose,* Lucius kept waiting for Gabby Hayes to show up, but he never did. He was eager to get back to Pack Memorial Library in the morning and thumb through *Look Homeward, Angel* to see if Tom really did usher here.

Pausing under the marquee, Lucius felt reverence for this theatre, as if it were a shrine, as he'd feel, he knew, when he stood, perhaps as long as a year hence, in the temple of the Saint in India, his destination. The ticket booth was shut up, the marquee lights were out.

The air was cold, but Lucius walked up to Spruce Street and gazed at Tom's house awhile in the dark, and then he had to piss so bad he could hardly walk and his legs were stiff and sore and weak and one foot was asleep in the brace as if full of tiny needles. He went to the Trailways bus station.

The smell of the busses excited him. A tiny popcorn stand off to the side, some taxis parked around a small orange-and-black-painted stand, telephone booths nearby. The station was smaller than Cherokee's, and the gates were on the same level as the waiting room area, not down steep stairs as in Cherokee. From the platform, Lucius stepped through the wide glass doors into the cool, clammy, modern, brightly lighted waiting room.

The terminal was full of soldiers and sailors and bums and tough kids and old ladies and women with babies and crippled men and bus drivers and young girls painted up, clutching red wallets, wearing high heels and paint-on stockings, and some had feather bobs, but most had long, long hair down their backs, and looked tough and sexy. Like the same bunch he might find any night at the Greyhound Terminal in Cherokee, but different enough to be fascinating. Feeling shy as hell in this atmosphere, Lucius swaggered to the stairs that led up to the men's room.

Outside a black door with a steel handle, a soldier, his tie droopy, was getting a shoeshine. He heard two men shuffling around inside a pay booth at the back. "Watch it, motherfucker," one said. Lucius heard a bottle crash on the floor, glass skittered over to his feet, and he kicked it on into the urinal. "Goddamn you, you fuckfacedmotherfucker!" screamed the man. Afraid of getting caught in a cross flash of knives, Lucius got out of there.

Awkwardly, uncertainly, Lucius walked between brown benches out the front entrance, into the cold mountain night air again.

He tried to find a room for a quarter or fifty cents but none charged less than seventy-five. The YMCA was closed. He was shocked that the three church doors he tried were locked. Then remembering seeing so many people asleep in the Cherokee bus terminal and a few in this one, Lucius went back to the station.

Three police cars were parked out front. Lucius hid in a doorway. The police coming through the glass doors that opened right on the sidewalk held one man by the back of his pants and another man's arm twisted behind his back.

Lucius went over to see what was going on. The lower part of the doors was busted and glass lay on the sidewalk. Inside, a sailor sat on one of the benches, facing the door, blood all over the front of his suit, holding a long rip of a woman's slip over his face, and a Negro man held his sailor's cap. Hearing a siren in the distance, Lucius went inside behind a cop. The police cars out front struck up their sirens and faded away and the other siren came closer. Lucius stood beside the instant photo machine and watched.

The sailor looked up at the cop who stood in front of him and said, "Ain't nobody callin' me no motherfucker and live, by God. I just got home from Japan and I'm sick of people walkin' all over me."

"Take it easy, boy," said the cop, a brawny man with an athlete's stance. He shifted his cods. "Okay, sailor, let's get it," said the cop, lifting him by his elbows.

Lucius saw the open doors of an ambulance at the curb. He went out the side door where the gates were and came around in time to hear the sailor say, "I want somebody to go with me. I'm bleeding too much. This is too much blood to bleed. I might die on the way. I wasn't really at Iwo Jima. I just got *out* of the hospital." Two men in white guided him up into the ambulance. "Ask the lady to come with me."

After the ambulance left the curb, Lucius went back in and ambled around, looking at the people who were all talking about the incident, and each person looked very vivid, as though he'd known each a long time. A lady sat on a bench, sipping something from a paper cup, threads of her torn petticoat clinging to her nylons. A man sitting next to her had flung his trenchcoat around her shoulders. Had he met her here after years of separation—lovers since childhood?

Lucius sat on a long, empty bench. The 7 Up clock on the wall between the two stairs leading to the restrooms said midnight. He was amazed to figure that thirty-four hours ago, he was standing under a wind-blown oak in front of Peggy's house on Clayboe Ridge talking to Raine.

Stretching out on the bench, he tried to sleep. But every time a taxi driver or soldier or cop or bus driver or newspaper hawker opened the doors, a cold blast came in on the back of his neck. He moved his seat seven times.

I am in the bus terminal. It's cold in the mountains even in June. The light shines glossily in places on the smooth brown seats and the gray metal lockers. Travelers are checking their bags for a dime, sleeping in odd positions, some nooked in the corners of the long brown benches, their luggage at their feet, some, their children squirming around their legs and upon the benches; the travelers busy about, rushing in and rushing out, and for a few moments I absorb it all with the intriqing intrest of the artist, a strange excitement prowling in my youthful bosom. A swaggering, tall, skinny sailor behaves quite comically in front of his two comrades in blue.

Then the thought strikes me like a bright light, that I am alone, near penniless, far from home, and that those who scurry and shuffle about me are total strangers, and I, Lucius Hutchfield, have run off from home in serch of new meaning in life. I do not know whether I will find it in Ashville but nevertheless here I am, and the situation is a very disturbing one.

*   *   *

The old days are gone. Will we ever see them again? Has God all these years been taking movies of us? I would like to sit through my personal movie. Bull!

Lucius and Raine help evacuate the rest of the Jewish refugees. Karla, the leader of the guerrillas who lives only for murder and takes pity on no one, hits Raine when she refuses to get out of his way. Lucius attacks him and he shoots Lucius. The men come that night to pick up the dead. Raine wakes up in a train full of corpses. She hunts among them for Lucius, finds him, and nurses his wound. Lucius tells Raine that he has always loved her. The train stops, the door is opened, and some guerrillas help them. In the city, they make out as best they can. Lucius goes hunting for food.

Russian soldiers capture Raine, but turn her loose on a country road. She helps the wounded who are fleeing the city. Returning from hunting for food, Lucius finds Raine gone. He looks for her. The Russians attack again and Palestine is ruined.

The Russians put Lucius in the concentration camp where he meets Richard E. Stackton, a talented man who cares for nothing. An American doctor, using primitive instruments, amputates Richard's leg. He curses the general for letting it be done. He is transferred to another camp and Lucius is sent to work in the mines.

Raine finds Palestine ruined when she returns. The Russians put her in the concentration camp where she hears about Lucius.

Lucius tries to escape from the mines to help the Americans win the war, but he is caught and beaten and put on harder labor. Then the Americans win the war and Lucius is liberated.

In Paris, Lucius meets Richard Stackton begging in the street, almost insane. By talking to him, Lucius helps him restore his faith. Then Lucius meets Della Snow who is now a famous author. She says she always loved Lucius. They have fun and she takes him to a party to meet Constillini, the great violinist.

Lucius goes to see Constillini the next day and they walk through Lucius's favorite parts of Paris. Constillini is overwhelmed by the beauty Lucius points out and deeply moved by the way Lucius talks about life and music. Constillini plays for Lucius alone several times, and, inspired by him, becomes a better and more famous violinist.

Momma and Daddy and Mammy and Gran'paw Charlie and Bucky and Earl and Luke and Raine were there when the nurse gave him a shot, and as they wheeled him away. He lay on a table outside the operating room, cold, terrified of the ether. A nurse came with a needle.

"But they already gave me a shot."

"This is to put you to sleep." She shot him. "Now start counting backwards to a million and one."

Lucius slept fitfully, waking again and again, to daylight the last time, and people were eating breakfast at the counter in one part of the terminal. His head ached, his joints were sore, he had a crick in his neck, and he felt sad, knowing he was fired from the Bijou, that he'd not see Raine, nor Momma, nor Mammy for years. He ate breakfast, spending most of his money. Groggy, he went out into the bright sunlight.

Slept in bus terminal. Still tired. Tried to sleep some more in a church up town. Nun woke me up. I asked her if the preacher would loan me some money. She was the same as anybody and nice. I hunted for a church to loan me money. A woman gave me advice to go to the Traveler's Aid.

* * *

I am sitting in Riverside Cemetery, where rabbits bounce thier cottony buts upon the graves. When I saw O. Henry's grave, there was no mention of that name. A stone for William Sydney Porter—

Gravestones like grey ticks on the belly of a brown dog. I'm sitting on top of Tom's monument. Beside me is the grave of his mother and father and nearby are his brothers, Ben and Grover. Wilted Iris on long stems on Tom's monument. The plots are very long in contrast with the others here among many trees. Next ot Wolfe's plot is the Westalls and a monument to Julia's father and mother made by W. O. Wolfe. I looked all over the cemetery for the Angel statue he made but it was nowhere in sight. The sun glows through the trees and a covey of birds just went over above, sounding like sudden raining in the trees. It is a wonderful feeling to know I am near Tom. In the distance dogs bark and children yell. Nearby squireels rustling leaves, birds chirping, cones dropping.

Tom
Son of
W. O. and Julia E. Wolfe
A Beloved American Author
Oct. 3, 1900–Sept. 15, 1938
"The Last Voyage, the Longest, the Best"
—Look Homeward, Angel
"Death bent to touch his chosen son with mercy,
love and pity, and put the seal of honor on him
when he died."
—The Web and the Rock

He has his train going nearby, "the lone, forgotten whail," below this hill, across the river, where I came in from Cherokee. I laid upon his giant body just now and smoked a Robert Burns for him and picked grass out of his eyes, and to show him I understand and share his love of raw life and strange actions, I spit a loving spit, and pissed a loving piss upon his grave.

* * *

A beautiful blonde girl, about ten, came with her father to see her mother's grave.
Story of a girl evangelist
Father a trumpet player, fanatic.
Girl is collasal. "Slogan" is "A Child Shall Lead Them."
Heals sick. Father buys fancy new car.
After all that talk. He explains to her.
She sees real evil. Puts ear on floor to hear woman untrue to husband. Bed springs, etc.
Get glimpse at railroad station of boy evangelist.

He had come to the end of the waitress's pad.

Lucius meets Somerset Maugham in England and teaches him a great many things. He tells Lucius about Larry who has been missing in action. Della Snow is grieved when Lucius says he must go.

A title occurred to Lucius for his epic saga of the future. On the last remaining line of the waitress's green check pad, he wrote NAKED DESTINY by Lucius Hutchfield. "*Naked Destiny*, starring Alan Ladd as Lucius Hutchfield." Remembering Maugham's symbol, he wondered whether Wolfe ever had one, and what it looked like. He *should* have had one. In the dust on the ledge of Tom's monument, Lucius improvised his own mark: Through the middle of H in Hutchfield, Lucius drew an eye. It looked good. He curled the first leg of the H outward and stuck a dot in the curve, and curled the second leg of the H at the top, and poked a dot. ⊱⊰ It looked like India. Maybe the eye in his improvised symbol was the evil eye Maugham's Moorish symbol was supposed to ward off. Perhaps the Hutchfield eye was as evil as it was good, for it looked upon both. It was his symbol. From now on.

Lucius goes to India to hunt for Larry. The Saint is glad to see him, but he knows nothing of Larry. The way to the mountain is barred by an avalanche. But Lucius has an intuition that Larry is there. Lucius goes up into the mountain and finds Larry in the hut. He has found happiness and great wisdom and gives Lucius advice, and tells him he's seen Raine.

Lucius leaves Larry and meets Mahatma Gandhi who is worried over conflicts between British and Indians. Lucius advises him but won't work for him. Theirs is a great friendship.

The Russian-American war over, Raine returns to America where she works as a nurse. Then she goes to Cherokee, the only city not ruined by the war in America. With the help of Richard Stackton, who comes to Cherokee to see Lucius, she restores the city into beauty. When the work is completed, she becomes a nun.

Lucius returns to America. He meets Raine in the nunnery. She has found a deeper vision of God and is the same as Lucius is. Raine wants to show him something. They go to Cherokee and she shows him beauty unsurpassed. She had wanted him to share it. They marry and the Sisters say good-bye.

Lucius restores the old Bijou Theatre, and shows many of the old movies again.

Raine is going to have a baby. She notices that Lucius is restless. He walks in storms. He stays gone for three days. She finds out he went up into the Smokies. She gets up a search party. They find him in the mountains, reading, with his dog, in a hut. Lucius is not beside her when she awakes next morning. Raine runs outside and finds him admiring the sunrise. He talks to her of the beauty of life and she understands. Both were once cruel and hated people, but God has changed them and they have found *their* world. The End.

Sitting beside the road below the cemetery, his shoes off, pounding the metatarsal bar into the sole of the shoe to which the brace was attached, Lucius heard the train whistle coming out of the hills, and as he watched the train cross the river trestle, he realized that today was the last day of school at Bonny Kate, and that he was missing Errol Flynn in the classic of the week, *The Sea Hawk*.

The bars were still loose on both shoes. He threw the bars into the river and wished he could rip the brace off without tearing up the shoe.

Passing a newspaper splashed along an empty bench, Lucius picked it up to see what it was like—the paper Tom delivered when he was a kid, through "niggertown," maybe a ridge route. But it was the Cherokee *Messenger* and a man was getting off a Delta plane. The caption said Kermit Hood was arrested getting off the plane in Atlanta, and that he had $10,000 with him, which he'd "extorted" from the Bijou as manager over the past two years. Lucius yelped, laughed, tossing the paper into the air. A cop looked at him across the terminal. Lucius sat sedately and read the story that started beneath the picture.

Regina had reported Hood to the police after she discovered he'd not returned from his routine trip to the bank, and she became suspicious when he left his office door locked, having asked her that morning for her own key to the door. Miss Atchley said she'd overheard him making reservations for a flight to Atlanta. Also arrested at the airport was Minetta Samins who'd come to meet the plane. She'd run away to Atlanta the day before, pregnant by Hood, who admitted that they were on their way to Mexico when he was arrested. His wife, Bonita Hood, manageress of the Tivoli, was resigning her post to return to her home in Yolanda, Mississippi. Mr. Hood had been a major in the Air Force, having initially tried to stay out of the armed forces as a conscientious objector. He shot down eleven Jap Zeros in the Pacific Theatre of Operations and was decorated as a hero by MacArthur. He is a native of Portsmouth, Ohio. Mr. Hood stated that he didn't care what happened to him. He had lost interest in life since the end of the war. "I thought a new life in Mexico would change things. But even as I got off the plane in Atlanta to transfer to the flight to Mexico City, I felt nothing. I'm not sorry for what I did. I'm not glad either. I am guilty. Lock me up, and let it go at that."

The first time Lucius read the article, he sneered. The second time, he felt awe and bewilderment, trying to imagine this new Mr. Hood, who never really existed for him except as a figure of authority, and whose vested authority was more forceful than the way he carried it out, for the authority of a battery of more hateful men and women in Lucius's life seemed back of Hood's. The third time Lucius read it, forcing himself not to cry made tears sting his eyes. He felt the connection between Hood's paleness, his thin hair falling over his brow, his nervous, shell-shocked look—there in the flash-flooded picture on the front page, too—and his flight to Atlanta.

Lucius lay back on the pewlike bench. The evening sunlight was red on his eyelids. He opened the Cherokee *Messenger* like a tent over his eyes and thought back on Hood, but could not see his face now, and he didn't want to look at the picture again. His tears made the pages of the paper stick to his cheeks.

> O lazy, remote, baffled, heavy, spirit,
>   That doth to the last ring of hell cling!
>   Cast off thy cancerous burden: soar!
>   (LH)

he wrote on the back of "Helena Street," lightly.

Hungry, a quarter and a nickel in his pocket, Lucius started out to find a grocery store. But curtains drawn back at a booth by the door attracted him. He walked over, went inside, drew the curtains. He had an impulse to preserve the way he looked at this moment in the history of the world. He adjusted the seat so that his eyes were level with the white line, put his quarter in the slot, sat back, very still, and when the red light in the middle came on, smiled, then turned his head profile, looking for the red light out of the corner of his eye, smiled, faced front, smiled, turned and looked over his shoulder, frowned.

Out on the street in Pack Square, heading for Woolworth's to buy a nickel bag of maple chews that would sustain him until he could find a church that would loan him some money or a mission that would feed him, hunger pains stabbing his stomach, he was walking behind an old woman who was holding out a tin cup in one hand, a fist full of yellow pencils in the other. He wondered if they were good ol' number two pencils. Nobody was dropping anything in. She paused on the curb, waiting for someone to lead her across. People were giving her the eye. Lucius, too, walked past her. In the middle of the broad street under the light, guilt stopped him in his tracks and he turned to go back, but a man in a business suit was taking her by the arm. Lucius paused on the other side, staring, feeling sorry for her. She was worse off than the blind lady who sat by the brass fire hydrant that stuck out of the white marble wall of the Cherokee National Bank. At least she had a husband to keep her blindness company. They even had a sort of aristocratic, snobbish air. Lucius skipped to catch up and dropped his last nickel into the old woman's cup. It struck loud.

"Thank you, son," the blind woman said, in a sweet voice that made Lucius feel good until he saw the meaning of her words.

The air was chilly again. Lucius thought that the farther south you went, the warmer it got. Wasn't Asheville the deep South? And in June, what was it doing so chilly? Shivering, he tried to put his hands in the pockets of his sport jacket, but they were packed with "Helena Street" and *The Razor's Edge*. Between a garage and a house, Lucius saw the many windows of the back of Tom's house.

Having looked around, he ducked through the hedge. There stood the brick pillars that held up the back of the house and that Tom in a rage tried, impotently, to pull down. Lucius leaned against one hard, his heart pounding blood in his ears. One brick was loose. He pulled it out. Afraid it might be the lair of a snake or the nest of a black widow spider, Lucius stuck *The Razor's Edge* inside and wiggled it around. It was hollow. Two other bricks were loose. Lucius balanced *The Razor's Edge* and "Helena Street" on the double brick shelf, then carefully put one brick instead of two back in the opening. Once he found a job and a place to stay, he'd retrieve them. His hands felt snug in his pockets now.

In the damp seclusion under the long back porch, Lucius feared spiders and snakes, but he looked around anyway. A flight of steps rose from the earthen floor between the pillars to the porch.

The back door was unlocked. Lucius resented the negligence of whoever was responsible for watching over the house. Some hoodlums might break in and rogue everything in the house—stuff that belonged to Thomas Wolfe, immortal writer.

Lucius stuck his head in the door, feeling as he had felt many times going into a vacant old house—a sense of nostalgia for someone else's past as if it were his own, and fear that it might be haunted.

"Anybody here?" he whispered, as if afraid to rouse the ghosts or to alert some killer, ignorant of Wolfe, hiding out in the house.

Lucius stepped over the threshold into the kitchen, seeing himself objectively: lightnin' blond, blue-eyed, sawed-off little fucker.

Under a layer of dust, an iron on an ironing board, a skillet, a green spoon. He felt the presence of the real people he'd imagined in scenes in the novel—heard fragments of their words. Bare windows let in cold sunlight on the wide creaky boards. The two huge iron stoves where Tom's mother and sisters and helpers had cooked the great feasts, the long wooden table, the chairs, the stool, its straw seat sunken, looked as if abandoned when the people became characters in the book. Tiptoeing in absolute awe, Lucius felt he, too, moved in a book.

In the large dining room, sideboards, lace curtains on the windows, tables, set for dinner, awaiting the boarders Tom hated and feared.

Lucius imagined the aroma of corn bread and felt a pang of hunger.

Evening light poured into the parlor through a floor-length window, mellowed the keys of the upright piano, the worn stool, the heavy-framed family portraits on the wall, the flowered rug, the table, the chairs, and the sofa.

On the many-paned sun porch, cane easy chairs, casual tables, a lamp with a colored glass shade.

Slowly, climbing the steps, imagining following young Tom, who knew Laura James slept on the sleeping porch. Standing at the door, wanting to go out onto the sleeping porch, stand, look out over Asheville as Tom often did, but afraid the old lady across Spruce Street stood at her window, watching the house.

A back bedroom, full of shadows. Tom's room. Or Laura's. A stark V of light on the bed. Dim, the high carved headboard and old-timey ornate dresser, with a mirror and two little drawers mounted on the marble top on each side.

In the room next door, a stout table, two hard chairs, an enormous two-armed brass lamp, with kerosene-lamp chimneys, holding light bulbs. Tom visiting his mother, writing here. In the wastebasket, some wadded yellow, buff paper. Lucius unwadded a sheet. Blank. Stuffed it in his pocket anyway.

In the hall, he stopped, afraid he'd heard someone walking. He listened. No sound.

Large bedroom, the three floor-length front windows, towerlike. Shades drawn, behind delicate curtains, to keep the sun from fading the room like an old photograph and strangers' eyes from violating it. Stained glass rimming windows, like a church, large middle squares clear. The wide bed low, thin brass spokes at head and foot. A washstand, a large porcelain bowl, dust, dottle of dead flies in it. The room where Ben died. Lucius stood on the sill, unwilling to desecrate the room by entering it.

Wanting to avoid dissipating the intensity of his emotions by prolonging his prowling, Lucius turned to leave, but noticed one room in back that he'd not looked into. All the other doors had stood open.

Lucius turned the white porcelain knob very slowly, wincing at the rusty creak. Cold pale light filled the room, cool as a cave, windows all around like his own sanctuary except the sills were almost level with the low, sunken bed. Someone had slept in the bed, kicked the patchwork quilt to the foot, laid the sheets bare. As Lucius stares, the mattress slowly puffs upward, making the wrinkles in the sheet wriggle, a prickle crawl over Lucius's scalp.

More than books, the folktales his grand-mother tells him and the movies he sees influence Lucius. To him, Vivien Leigh, Clark Gable, Cary Grant, Laurel and Hardy, Lana Turner, and Zorro are the gods and goddesses to admire and emulate, and *Notorious, The Postman Always Rings Twice, Sister Kenny, Humoresque,* and *Night and Day* are the stuff that real life is made of. From the movies he derives his attitudes about people and sex, and after seeing Tyrone Power in *The Razor's Edge,* Lucius makes a heroic attempt to run away to India but gets only as far as Asheville, North Carolina, the hometown of his new hero, Thomas Wolfe.

BIJOU is a superb episodic novel whose unifying force is Lucius's unwavering response to the world he experiences both on screen and off, a world which he transforms in awe and egotism. Madden creates a sense of the way life, literature, and the movies interact with illusion and reality to shape the imagination of an adventurous adolescent. Lucius is one of the most memorable characters in recent fiction, a boy on the threshold of being rich and famous . . . and fourteen.